Inspirational Romance Reader

A Collection of Four Complete, Unabridged Inspirational Romances in One Volume

• Historical Collection No. 4 •

Hope That Sings
JoAnn A. Grote

The Promise of Rain
Sally Krueger

Escape on the Wind
Jane LaMunyon

Lost Creek Mission
Cheryl Tenbrook

© 2000 by Barbour Publishing, Inc.

ISBN 1-55748-736-2

Hope That Sings
ISBN 1-55748-870-3
© MCMXCVI by JoAnn A. Grote

The Promise of Rain
ISBN 1-57748-253-0
© MCMXCVII by Barbour Publishing, Inc.

Escape on the Wind
ISBN 1-57748-248-4
© MCMXCVII by Barbour Publishing, Inc.

Lost Creek Mission
ISBN 1-55748-693-X
© MCMXCV by Cheryl Tenbrook

All Scripture has been taken from the King James Version of the Bible.

All rights reserved. Except for use in any review, the reproduction or utilization of this work in whole or in part in any form by any electronic, mechanical, or other means, now known or hereafter invented, is forbidden without the permission of the publisher.

Published by Barbour Publishing, Inc., P.O. Box 719, Uhrichsville, Ohio 44683

All of the characters and events in this book are fictitious. Any resemblance to actual persons, living or dead, or to actual events is purely coincidental.

Printed in the United States of America.

Hope That Sings

JoAnn A. Grote

For Myles, a gift from God.

Chapter One

St. Louis, Missouri—1882

"I must be addlepated, Grant Chambers, accompanying you to a match game of Base Ball!" Carrie clutched her brother's arm to keep her footing in the jostling crowd. "I've always heard spectators at these matches are uncouth, and now I know it for truth."

Excitement sparkled in the eyes laughing down at her, their rich brown color so different from the blue of her own. "You won't be sorry you've come, I promise. One day you'll tell your grandchildren you saw the great Dexter Riley play for the St. Louis Browns' first American Association match. You'll love the match, you'll see, and you'll love Dexter, too. Everyone does."

She pressed closer against Grant's side, lifting her chin until it barely reached his shoulder in order to make herself better heard above the crowd. "It would be rather inappropriate for me to entertain such strong emotions toward a young man on first acquaintance. Especially a base ballist, whom everyone knows tend to be. . .ungentlemanly. I expect Emmet might object to such a reaction on my part, also."

Grant's hand cut through the air in careless dismissal. "Emmet Wilson is a good man, but he's not to be compared to the likes of Riley. Even if you are half-engaged to Wilson." His chuckle rang out. "Though I have to admit, Wilson's likely better marriage material than a base ballist."

Grant had been singing the base ballist's praises since the men became friends at Washington University two years ago. Each time Grant wrote a letter home or visited her and their parents in Ridgeville, their small hometown one hundred miles to the west, Mr. Riley's name and virtues had been lavishly sprinkled throughout his conversation. The man's primary virtue was apparently his Base Ball abilities.

Grant might think a man a king simply because he could catch and strike a ball, but a man had to accomplish far more than that to win her respect, she thought. Most importantly, he had to love the Lord, as Emmet did.

The crowd of smoking, hurrying men pushed the two along toward Sportsman's Park, where the match game would take place between St. Louis and Louisville.

"Oof!" A large masculine elbow barely covered by a shabby jacket sleeve caught her in the chest, and she lost her hold on Grant's arm. She stopped short, one hand pressed against the front of her garnet basque jacket, and stared at the man's back in disbelief. He hadn't even bothered to apologize!

"Hey, sister, git movin' or git out of the way." A heavily whiskered face scowled at her beneath a derby three sizes too small.

The man moved on before she could turn her sputtering protest into words, but out of sheer fear of being trampled, she took his advice.

Grant's slim hand closed about one of her elbows. "Turned around and couldn't see you for a minute. Best stick close to me."

She'd "stick" all right! Why had she ever agreed to join him?

"The Louisville club is coming!"

"Out of the way for the Eclipse club!"

Carrie looked sharply about at the crowd's calls, careful not to stop in order to do so this time. A colorful horse-drawn trolley, its warning bell clanging loudly and ineffectually, made its way through the pedestrian-filled road.

Catcalls and derisive comments concerning the Louisville club's playing ability and integrity came from every side. The base ballists returned the insults with good humor, but Carrie's face heated in shame at the crowd's rude manners.

She smiled at a wide-eyed, jaw-dropping group of boys watching the slow-moving conveyance enter Sportsman's Park. They should be involved in more edifying pursuits than Base Ball, she thought, but their misdirected hero-worship was rather amusing.

Grant grabbed her upper arm and pointed to the back of a man nearing the boys. The man wasn't overly tall, maybe five feet and eight inches; taller than her own five foot one but not as tall as Grant. The stranger was compactly built, with wide, powerful shoulders beneath his well-cut jacket. The typical black bowler covered all but a couple inches of russet brown hair that appeared neatly trimmed above the back of his collar. In one hand he carried a long, thin leather bag.

"That's him!" One of Grant's arms pierced the air. "Dexter! Over here! Over here, Riley!"

He shouldered his way through the crowd, dragging Carrie unceremoniously along behind him. When they finally reached his hero, the player was speaking to a raggedly dressed lad of about twelve. Dexter flashed Grant a smile of recognition before continuing his conversation, and Carrie had a glimpse of a pleasant wide face with smiling green eyes above a large mustache that completely hid his top lip.

His attention returned to the boy. "You here with a friend?"

The boy nodded his dirt-covered face, eyes wide in awe. He pointed to a lanky boy beside him dressed as shabbily as himself.

"What's your name?"

"J–Jack."

"Here to see the match?"

Jack swallowed audibly. "Can't. Costs a quarter."

"Maybe we can strike a business deal. Could use a lad to watch over my willow while I change into my uniform and when our club is in the field. Be worth twenty-five cents to me."

"Wow, Mr. Riley! Truly?"

Riley nodded sharply. "Willing to take the job?"

"Yes sir, Mr. Riley, sir!"

Grant leaned close to Carrie's ear. "Dexter always does that. Boy carrying the bat gets into the grounds free, and the quarter lets the boy's friend join him."

A sliver of admiration slipped reluctantly into her estimation of Grant's friend.

Riley handed the bat bag and a quarter to the boy and turned to Grant, reaching to shake hands, a grin topping the wide jaw beneath the thick mustache. "Glad you could make it to the match. Did your family arrive safely?"

"Yes, thanks. Father's being interviewed this afternoon for the position with the local church I told you about, and Mother's with him. Have to be introduced to the people in charge, you know, and see whether they can pass muster. But my sister, Carrie, is with me." Grant's hand drew her forward. "This is her first match, do you believe it? Nineteen years old and never seen a Base Ball match!"

Dexter touched thick, crooked fingers to the brim of his bowler and nodded at her respectfully. Unexpectedly long lashes rayed above green eyes that kindled with sudden interest. His eyes were the color of new leaves in spring, alive with the glow of sunshine. His gaze touched the thick black hair swirled sedately beneath her bonnet, dropped to the nose—was he noticing the smattering of freckles?—before meeting her eyes again.

Carrie's gloved hand clutched the embroidered revers of her garnet basque. It felt as if her heart had simply fallen out and tumbled at his feet, right in front of his dirt-covered shoes. She barely stopped herself from glancing down to see whether she could sight it there. A laugh gurgled up within her at the fanciful thought.

And she'd believed friendship with Emmet and her high ideals made her immune to such schoolgirl emotions! Well, surely this inane reaction would pass, like a bad case of croup. The admiration she saw reflected in his eyes didn't help her self-control, though she noticed her heart was back where it belonged, beating wildly against her ribs. She knew her own eyes reflected a similar admiration for him to see, but she didn't know how to hide it.

His look lingered. "I'm delighted to make your acquaintance. I hope you'll enjoy the match."

She gave him a tremulous smile. There was a pleasant hint of controlled Irish accent beneath his words. "I wish you and your club well this afternoon. I understand it's a special match game."

His smile shot into a boyish grin. His glance darted away and back again, making him appear as embarrassed as a schoolboy being teased over a girl. "Yes, well, at least to us in the clubs it's special."

She liked his modesty, liked his evident enjoyment of his work. . .if one could call playing Base Ball work.

He turned his attention back to Grant. "I'd best be getting along. I'm not even in uniform yet, and the Louisville club has already arrived."

Grant gave Dexter's shoulder a hail-fellow slap. "See you show them how Base

Ball is meant to be played, old man."

Dexter's gaze darted back to her. "Why don't we join your parents at their hotel for dinner after the match, Grant?"

"They're dining with the present pastor, but Carrie and I will be available. But, say, won't you be dining with the rest of the Browns?"

His wide shoulders lifted his jacket in a nonchalant shrug. "I'll have to put in an appearance, but if it's like any normal after-match dinner, it will be primarily a liquid feast. I'll be glad for a legitimate excuse to leave early."

"We'll expect you at the Planter's Hotel, then. Say, you plan to bring your sister, don't you?"

Carrie glanced at Grant out of the corner of her eye. His question had a transparently casual tone.

Dexter's teasing grin added to her suspicion. "Expect she might be persuaded to endure your company for an evening."

His glance slipped to her face for a long moment before he turned away, making her suddenly feel it was very important to him that she be at the dinner.

"Ready, Jack?"

The boy and his friend hurried along beside him, swelling visibly at their obvious association with the man being greeted by spectators on every side as they made their way across the grounds.

She liked the way Dexter Riley carried himself, his back straight but not stiff, his wide shoulders loose, his head high, his step easy with almost a bounce to it.

She recalled the crooked fingers he had touched to his hat. "What happened to his hands, Grant? His fingers looked as if they might have been broken."

"Most of them have been broken, some more than once. Man can't play ball for years without some broken fingers. After all, nothing between their hands and a flying ball but a thin piece of leather, if that."

Ten minutes later Carrie looked down at the unpainted, backless wooden bench in distaste, holding her gray skirt away in case of dirt or snags. Was this where she was expected to spend the afternoon, on a hard piece of wood amidst a crowd of uncouth men? And these were the better seats, in the grandstand, with at least the pretense of cover in the wooden canopy overhead.

"Hey, lady, sit yerself down. Think yer made of glass? A man's gotta see the field, ya know."

Carrie sat down abruptly and felt the wood smartly through the layers of cloth beneath her wire bustle. She couldn't remember when she'd been spoken to so rudely by so many men in one day! Were all the men in St. Louis except Grant and Mr. Riley ignorant of proper etiquette?

A man inched down the aisle six feet away, a white apron covering his trousers, one arm balancing a tray of large, amber-filled steins over his brown-and-white-striped hat, which fit his fat head closely and had a brim only in the front. She wondered how he managed to keep from spilling the steins' contents with the crowd shoving him about and the tray tipping one direction and then another, like a boat on the nearby Mississippi River on a choppy day. She indicated the man to Grant. "What has he on his tray?"

Hot red color surged over Grant's narrow face. He shifted his gaze quickly to the parklike field before them. "Beer."

Carrie closed her mouth, all too aware her bottom lip had fallen in a most unbecoming manner. She touched one hand gloved in thin garnet cotton to her high-standing jacket collar. "Oh, my!"

One could as well be in a drinking establishment! And they had each paid fifty cents for the "privilege" of a hard, backless seat in the grandstand amidst a sweaty crowd of rude men on a warm May day with beer being served all about in the most open, careless manner! What would members of the congregation for which their father was being considered even this minute think if they knew? Thank the good Lord no one here would recognize her and Grant as his children!

Not that the Lord could possibly approve of their attendance, whether they were recognized or not. Her glance swept the crowded seats. There weren't more than half a dozen other women in the grandstand, though there were more in the cheaper, uncovered seats. Why had she ever allowed Grant to talk her into attending?

No matter why. There could be no excuse for remaining. She shot determinedly to her feet.

Grant frowned up at her. "What's wrong?"

"I'm departing."

"But the match is about to begin."

A loud roar from the stands swallowed her reply. The crowd surged to its feet. Carrie looked about, bewildered.

Grant, on his feet beside her now, grasped her arm. "The clubs are entering the grounds."

"But I mustn't stay. It's worse than I imagined."

The crowd noisily returned to its seats, and the large man behind her poked her shoulder with a blunt finger. "Look, lady, either sit yerself down or move."

She turned to leave, but a dozen large, masculine knees were between her and the aisle. She saw at least as many obstacles in the other direction. Defeated, she took her seat, her back even stiffer than her corset demanded. Surely there would be an opportunity to depart later; she'd watch for it.

The men from the Louisville club spread out across the parklike field. "They certainly present a colorful view, I shall admit that much."

Grant grunted. "Look plain silly if you ask me. American Association decided instead of the traditional club uniforms, the players would dress according to their position. For instance, the Louisville hurler is wearing that sky blue shirt."

Carrie saw the man he meant standing in the middle of the diamond-shaped ground. His belt and cap matched the silk top, which laced up the front. "Hurler?"

"He tosses the ball to the batsman."

"What color does Mr. Riley wear?"

"Red and black striped. He's a center fielder. He says these uniforms won't last long. The players are already protesting them and insisting on returning to regular uniforms."

Carrie was at a loss to understand the rules of the sport. Grant spent an inordinate amount of time explaining what was happening and why, much to the fury of the man behind her. Carrie was amazed the man could hear Grant speak, for she had difficulty hearing him herself. Hollers and jeers from spectators filled the air until she thought she could see as well as hear the sound. Men hawked beer up and down the aisles. A local band played music when the clubs switched positions on the field.

She was inordinately pleased when Mr. Riley, at his first attempt as batsman, managed to run all the way around the field. His clubmates pounded him on the back, wide grins beneath their mustaches. When the clubs changed positions and Mr. Riley was playing in center field, he caught one of the flying balls, rendering the opposing batsman "out," according to Grant, and the clubs changed positions once again.

The next time Mr. Riley was batsman, the man behind her and a number of men around him rose in a roar of venomous taunts. Horrified, Carrie grasped Grant's arm and demanded an explanation. Grant's smile was wide. His brown eyes danced with unbridled excitement. "They must be from Louisville. Riley's such a good player that they're trying to upset his concentration."

"Where is their sense of justice and fair play?"

His smile only widened. "No such thing in Base Ball. Any player worth his salt can take this kind of abuse from the kranks without it affecting his play."

"Kranks?"

Grant's hand waved casually while he turned his attention back to the field, where Riley stood beside the white rubber square. "Male spectators are called kranks. Ladies are kranklets."

A high-pitched "thunk" sounded when Riley's bat struck the ball. It flew straight above him and came down between him and a man Grant called the catcher. The catcher tossed the ball back to the hurler, and Riley took up the batsman's normal stance.

The crowd surged to their feet again, their roar increasing.

Disgusted, Carrie rose, too, weaving her head back and forth, attempting to view the field through the people.

Beside her, Grant cupped freckled hands about his lips. "Murder the ball, Riley!"

The man behind them shoved a huge hand against Grant's shoulder. "Hey, what's the big idea, rootin' fer the Browns?"

Imagine this loud, uncouth man upbraiding them for supporting their friend! Just as though this wasn't America, where one might speak one's own mind. Or yell one's own sentiments at a ball park. Her fists settled momentarily where her tailored basque covered her hips. She glared into the ruddy, bewhiskered face towering above her. "We shall call for whomever we please, sir!"

Turning about, she cupped her gloved hands delicately about her own mouth and rather timidly repeated Grant's call.

Grant burst out in pure laughter. Carrie flushed.

A loud crack sounded through the park, and she saw the ball whiz across the field. Riley hurtled toward the first sandbag, his powerful legs in their knee-high brown socks pumping madly.

All decorum fell away. "Run, Mr. Riley, run!" she screamed.

By the time Dexter Riley was back at the Home Base, Carrie's throat was sore from the strain of its unaccustomed use, Dexter's clubmates were leaping about him like a group of uniformed frogs, and the kranks behind her were using language more colorful than the clubs' uniforms. She felt an immense satisfaction at Dexter's accomplishment and her own choice to cheer him on.

Chapter Two

It was considerate of Dexter to choose the hotel at which she and her parents were staying to have dinner, Carrie thought later in her hotel room, looking through the few outfits she'd brought for the week they expected to be in the city. Dexter's choice gave her the opportunity to refresh herself and change into a proper gown for the evening, and she did need the opportunity after a day at the ball grounds!

What would her mother and father say when they discovered her afternoon outfit smelling like beer from the stein the man behind them had spilled upon her? Most likely he had poured it upon her by choice rather than accident, she thought angrily, pulling the stained, tailored skirt over the small wire bustle with difficulty.

She hesitated only slightly before selecting a favorite gown of ice blue satin for the evening, its basquelike top trimmed with deep white lace, which met in a point beneath the large satin bow attached just over the understated bustle. The double rows of matching lace trimming the wrists were set off with tiny satin bows of deepest sapphire, as was the high collar. The ivory-colored slippers with raised embroidery of the same shade felt wonderfully light after the sensible, high-topped, brown leather shoes she'd worn that afternoon.

Using the large mirror topping the low, two-drawer bureau to place faux-pearl studded combs in her swirl of black hair, she had to admit the gown was a decided improvement over the functional garnet basque and gray skirt she'd worn to Sportsman's Park. She well knew the ice blue was one of her most flattering dresses, setting off both her coloring and figure to advantage, yet demure enough to be considered proper for a lady, and a reverend's daughter at that. What would Dexter Riley think of her in the gown?

Mr. Riley's thoughts were no concern of hers, she reminded herself for the dozenth time while closing the door to the room and entering the spacious, carpeted hallway. *I am simply dining with my brother and his friends. It's not as though Mr. Riley is calling upon me. I'd never betray Emmet in such a manner.*

Still, she was looking forward to spending the evening with one of the city's most popular young men of the day. She was sure the afternoon's match had been much more exciting because she'd met one of the men involved. It thrilled her that Dexter's St. Louis Browns won the match nine runs to seven. She couldn't wait to congratulate him for his excellent play.

Not that her heart was threatened by this lively young man with the wonderful smile and laughing eyes, she hastened to assure herself, discounting her initial reaction to him.

But when Dexter and his sister met them in the lobby minutes later, her heart performed the same dropping act it had performed upon meeting him earlier in the day. Dismay swept through her at its betrayal of her commitment to Emmet.

As though she had any reason to be concerned that she might have an opportunity to be unfaithful! If the rumors she'd heard about base ballists were true, women fell all over themselves for the privilege of their company. Not the type of women a gentleman would court, of course. Still, it was unlikely Mr. Riley would single her out for attention, in spite of the respectful admiration that glowed so plainly in his eyes.

He was devastatingly handsome in a silver-gray dress coat and crisp white linen shirt front with gray silk jabot. The formal attire couldn't hide the wide shoulders that had filled the red-and-black-striped base ballist's shirt that afternoon, nor the power that lay beneath the civilized linen shirt. Yet he didn't act like a man aware of the attention he drew, and she found him all the more appealing for his attitude.

His hair was no longer hidden by the bowler he'd worn when they met or the brown-and-white-striped hat he'd worn while playing. *It's wonderful hair*, she thought, *thick and shiny, its brown color richly steeped in wine red.*

She liked his sister immediately and wasn't surprised to find they were twins. Amanda had her brother's coloring, her eyes as clear as peridot green. Her thick hair, the same wonderful shade as Dexter's, glowed in the light of the chandeliers and was wound in a smooth figure eight covering the back of her head. Jade-tipped tortoiseshell hairpins studded the waves. The emerald swirled silk she wore added to her beauty. Like Dexter, she was quick to smile and laugh and had a pleasant manner that casually shunned compliments directed toward herself and pursued only the kindest of topics involving others. Carrie hoped they would become friends if her father accepted the position with the church in this city.

If Grant's devoted attention to Amanda was any indication, she would have every opportunity to meet the girl again!

But Carrie couldn't avoid paying attention to Dexter by observing his sister too long. Dexter gave her his arm on which to enter the dining room, and his warm smile started a curling tingle in her stomach. She fervently hoped the lighting flattered her as well as it did Amanda.

Not that anyone else would notice. A number of patrons stopped the couple on their way to the table, but she received only brief glances. Everyone's attention was focused upon Dexter, one of the nine young men who had made the city proud that day.

Only moments after they were seated, Dexter asked if she'd enjoyed the match game that afternoon.

"Did she enjoy it? I'll tell the world she enjoyed it!" Grant answered for her. "It was a sight to make a brother proud. She may have been a novice this afternoon, but this evening she's the Browns' most ardent kranklet."

Carrie's cheeks warmed at Grant's comments and she lowered her gaze. "I would hardly call myself a—"

"You should have seen her, Dexter," he continued on as though she hadn't spoken. "Man behind us was so large he looked like he wore a barrel beneath his vest. His hands could meet about a ripe watermelon. Had a face like a storm cloud. Tried to make me stop cheering you on, but he didn't frighten Carrie a bit. She told him in no uncertain terms that this was America, and a person could support whomever they chose. And then she yelled so loud for you to whack that ball that she drowned out all the kranks sitting about us."

Carrie busily brushed an imaginary speck of dirt from the lace at her wrist. "You are exaggerating, much to the detriment of my reputation. I admit supporting Mr. Riley's efforts, but I certainly did not suggest that he 'whack' the ball, nor could I possibly have called louder than those monstrous, coarse men sitting about us, even if I had wished to do so." Shooting him an indignant look, she caught him winking at Dexter, his grin wide, and her mortification increased.

Dexter's large, firm fingers touched her wrist briefly, drawing her averted gaze to his. "I'm honored you championed me and my club, Miss Carrie. I've no doubt you did in a proper manner."

She expected to see a sarcastic grin on his handsome face in spite of the respectful tone in his voice. There was none. Still, she was convinced he was silently laughing at her along with Grant. "Is your brother a man to be trusted, Amanda? For I give you fair warning, Grant is not!"

Amanda laughingly ignored Grant's sputtering protest. "You'll know when to distrust Dexter, for when he starts peddling the blarney, an Irish accent fills his speech." She tipped her head slightly, observing her brother with sparkling eyes. "The same thing happens when he's angry. He never raises his voice or his fists, but he slips into our grandparents' manner of speaking."

Carrie shared a blatantly conspiratorial look with Amanda, then glanced teasingly at Dexter. "I'll remember that. An Irish accent means his words are blarney."

His green eyes twinkled. "No fair! How am I to know when you are kissing the blarney stone?"

"Why, I'm surprised at you, sir. A true gentleman never finds a woman's behavior deceiving, only charmingly mysterious."

Dexter's laugh rang out at her nonsense.

But moments later when two young couples stopped to congratulate him on the day's ball match and she turned her attention back to Grant and Amanda, she was surprised to see her brother watching her with a puzzled frown. Did he think her too flirtatious with his friend?

When the base ballist's admirers left them, she was quieter and more reserved at first, but it wasn't long before Dexter had her laughing again with the rest of the party with tales of antics pulled on trips with ball clubs throughout the midwestern and eastern states. She'd never known anyone who traveled so extensively and often, and it made his acquaintance even more exciting.

Grant apparently forgot his concern for her, also. He laughed and joked along with the rest of them, but he had eyes only for Amanda. Carrie soon realized the two had the comfortable atmosphere between them that spoke of many past hours together.

Well, Amanda seemed a lovely woman, intelligent and charming. If she could bring that devoted look to her brother's eyes—and hopefully devotion to his heart as well—Carrie could only hope Amanda returned his affections.

"I've rented a carriage," Dexter announced casually while they were finishing bowls of lemon-flavored ice cream. "Since Carrie hasn't seen the city, I thought we might show her how it looks at night from the bridge."

Carrie lectured herself sternly while retrieving her elbow-length cape from her room, telling herself she must maneuver it so she sat with Amanda in the carriage. But when the four reached the rented conveyance, Grant handed Amanda carefully into the rear seat and stepped immediately up beside her, for all the world as though he hadn't felt Carrie's restraining hand on his forearm or heard her offer to join Amanda. There was nothing left for Carrie but to sit beside Dexter.

She lifted her skirt with one hand in preparing to enter, giving Dexter a slight smile. She hoped he hadn't heard her intention to sit beside his sister and been insulted by it. Of course, there had been nothing said by any party indicating the two of them were to consider themselves coupled for the evening, but even so. . .

She was uncomfortably aware of him sitting beside her, their bodies swaying slightly with the motion of the carriage, and she held herself quite rigid at first. It wasn't long before Dexter's casual manner in pointing out St. Louis's attractions relaxed her, though it was difficult to appreciate the architecture in the gaslit night. She knew that Fourth Street, where the hotel was located, catered to the wealthy elite, and a number of buildings were quite magnificent. It was all very different from the small town of Ridgeville.

Dexter sprinkled bits of history into his tour, telling how the French settled the area and named it over one hundred years earlier, to be followed by the Spanish, and, in the middle to late part of the current century, by large contingents of German and Irish immigrants.

"That last is how Amanda and I arrived here." He laughed at himself. "Or more accurately, how our grandparents arrived. We made our appearances much later."

"Did your grandparents come over during the potato famine?"

"Yes. My mother's and father's parents were friends. They came over on the same boat, eventually settling here. My mother was ten at the time, my father fourteen."

"I've heard stories of the famine, awful tales of what people endured both in Ireland and on the emigration boats. I'm sorry your parents and grandparents experienced it."

"Their life improved after they settled here."

She unconsciously smoothed the gloves over the back of her hands. "When I consider what some people suffer, I think I've not been tried at all by life."

Though most of his face was shadowed by the night and the brim of his formal high hat, she saw his smile blaze down, throwing her heart into that uncomfortable, wonderful frenzy. "You're not so ancient. Take heart! Life's hurler might throw a couple trying experiences your direction yet."

She laughed with him. "You are quite correct. Anything might happen!"

He turned the conversation away from problems and continued his comments on the buildings they passed. She found his enthusiasm for his home contagious; she'd like to be part of this city and hoped her father would take the position if offered him. Of course, her life wouldn't be cast with her parents for long. When she married Emmet, her place would be beside him, wherever he chose to live.

Her mind skittered away from the suddenly uncomfortable thought.

They entered one end of the bridge and Carrie gasped. "I didn't realize it was so large! I believe three or four carriages could meet easily."

"This bridge is considered one of the engineering wonders of the world."

Lights along each side stretched the entire length of the bridge, above high wrought iron railings, creating a shining corridor beneath the sky's black dome. Carrie found the effect breathtaking.

Dexter halted the carriage where the bridge formed a baylike outcropping. A bench waited patiently in the mellow rays from a large gas lamp for someone to settle himself down and enjoy the view. The Mississippi River lay in a long, wide black ribbon, but Carrie could hear the water lapping against the great pillar beneath them. Rippling gold reflected the lights of passing ferries, barges, and steamboats. Along the banks of the river and the rolling lands behind, lights from the city burned through a foggy haze. Dexter explained the haze was the city's constant companion from the riverside industries that depended upon the water-road for their survival.

Her gaze locked with Dexter's when he helped her from the carriage, sending her heart on another wild gallop. When her delicate evening slippers stood securely upon the bridge, he tucked her gloved hand beneath his arm in as natural a manner as if they'd been promenading together for years. She tried to act as casual as he did, not wishing him to know his effect on her.

Grant and Amanda joined them after a moment. The four of them crowded companionably on the wrought iron bench, making the usual comments about the weather and the view. Yet it seemed wildly romantic to Carrie, seated snugly between Dexter and Amanda, Dexter's hand still resting intimately upon hers.

Others were out enjoying the warm evening air, and Amanda told her the bridge was a popular place for young couples. The identification of the bridge as a trysting spot awakened again the disturbing feeling that she was betraying Emmet's trust, and Carrie gently removed her hand from Dexter's arm.

A breeze from the river played with her cape, and she was glad she'd taken time to put on her best bonnet. The wide ribbon of ivory satin was tied in a huge, soft bow at one side of her chin, framing her face in addition to securing the bonnet against the wind. The admiration she saw in Dexter's eyes let her know he found the picture appealing.

She exclaimed in delight when the unexpected music of an exquisite Viennese waltz filled the night. The four of them rushed to stand along the railing. The steamboat from which the music came slid from beneath the span near them, people promenading and dancing along the gaily illuminated decks.

Dexter swept off his high top hat with a flourish and bowed deeply. "May I have the honor of this dance?"

Before she thought to decline, she was in his arms, his strength whirling her about with unexpected grace. He didn't hold her tightly, but the intimacy of their contact momentarily erased the rest of the world for her, and there was nothing but the exquisite freedom of moving with him to the music, the compelling wonder of the smiling green eyes whose gaze never left her own. His cologne wafted in and out of the wild smell of the river and the stringent lingering of smoke from the boats below, forming an invisible, fragrant fence around the little world that included only the two of them. She enjoyed the energy Dexter generated as much as the dance itself. Emmet would never act in such an impromptu manner; he always weighed any possible consequences before acting.

It was the sight of Grant taking Amanda in his arms to join them in the dance that brought her to her senses. She'd only danced twice in her life, both times at wedding receptions, and couldn't recall ever seeing Grant dance. Obviously the entertainment was not new to him, she thought, watching the way he expertly turned Amanda. She wondered where he had become so skilled. Their parents discouraged dancing. Her father believed it encouraged young men to take inappropriate liberties with their partners and to believe their partners would welcome such liberties.

Laughter and applause of approval from a passing carriage brought Carrie's feet to a halt, almost tripping Dexter in her suddenness. He released her without comment when she stepped back from his arms, but she had more difficulty releasing her gaze from his. "The music is ending," she explained breathlessly.

The music was indeed fading down the river. Carrie leaned against the cool metal railing, watching the boat with its gay passengers move into the night, the paddlewheel at its rear as busy as the bustle on a large-hipped woman.

Grant and Amanda had drifted a few yards up the bridge. Carrie saw that they, too, had stopped dancing, but Amanda remained in his arms. As she watched, he bent his head and kissed her.

Carrie jerked her gaze away. She hadn't intended to spy on them. It wasn't as though Grant was toying with Amanda, she argued with the part of her conscience that accused him. He couldn't so much as look at the vivacious young woman without revealing his love for her. Yet she wished he would show more discretion than to kiss her in such a public place, even though darkness covered them from all but the nearest passing carriages.

Beside her at the railing, Dexter shifted his weight, and his arm came to rest lightly against hers. She went completely still, her heart pounding wildly, staring out at the midnight blackness of the river. Had he seen Grant and Amanda's embrace? She didn't dare look at him. What if he tried to kiss her? Should she have taken Amanda's laughing reference to the bridge as a local lovers' lane seriously? Did a man consider it an invitation to improper advances if a girl allowed herself to be escorted here?

Surely not! Grant would never have allowed her to come, would never have left her to Dexter's escort, if such a thing were true. The realization gave her a sense of relief, though she was still overly conscious of Dexter's presence.

Yet she couldn't help wondering what Dexter's kiss would be like.

She was relieved when Amanda and Grant rejoined them.

Moments later, an unusually loud, raucous, unladylike laugh jolted her thoughts toward two couples making their way unsteadily toward them. There was nothing improper about the women's attire, but their manner was entirely unseemly. Each leaned against one of the men for support, and the men leaned back upon the women. For every step forward, they took three weaving stumbles back.

The women's obviously drunken state so horrified Carrie that she barely noticed the men until Dexter said quietly, "It's Browning and Mullane, Grant."

Carrie recoiled from his words. Surely her brother and Mr. Riley could not be on familiar terms with these intoxicated people!

Her brother muttered something beneath his breath. Dexter walked around the bench to intercept the staggering foursome.

Chapter Three

The drunken men greeted Dexter exuberantly. Carrie flinched when the tallest one stumbled against him, leaning heavily on his shoulder. He burped loudly in Dexter's face. "Riley, old man, good ta see ya! Want ta join us in a liddle li. . .liba. . .in a drink?" He held an open bottle toward him.

"Think you've had enough, Mullane. If you plan to beat us on the grounds tomorrow, you'd best be hitting the sack instead of the bottle."

"Huh! Think just 'cause your ol' Browns skinned by us today we can't whip ya tomorra!"

Dexter grinned. " 'Skinned' by you? We walked away with the match! Why, Browning here didn't manage a single hit in the four times he came to the plate!"

The man named Browning leaned forward, wagging a finger beneath Dexter's nose. "Jest didn't have the right encouragement." He kissed the girl beside him with a loud smack that sent the blood rushing to Carrie's cheeks. "Now thet's encouragement."

Disappointment drained the joy from Carrie at the realization Dexter counted these men among his friends.

Mullane peered over Dexter's shoulder at the bench, and Carrie wished she could simply step over the edge of the bridge and disappear beneath the wide expanse of black water. "Thet Amanda over there? Why, sure is! Browning, it's Amanda! How ya doin', sweet thing?"

She was amazed to hear Amanda's bubbling laughter as he brushed past Dexter, stumbling heavily against the bench. Grant reached out quickly to keep him from falling. The man was remarkably good looking, Carrie noted, or would have been if he'd been sober. His jacket, on the other hand, was outdated and looked as if it would fall apart at the seams at the slightest provocation.

A watery grin appeared beneath Mullane's thin black mustache. "Why, it's Chambers! Didn't recognize you at first. 'Course, I had my eye on the ladies, ya understand." Carrie was sure his exaggerated wink was meant to be conspiratorial. "Who's this lovely creature aside ya?"

"No one you need to know," Dexter said, grasping the man's shoulders from behind and pulling him back. "Where's your buggy?"

Mullane squinted toward one end of the bridge, then pointed. "Thataway. Somewhere." The hand with the bottle went up to his forehead in an impossible attempt to scratch his head. His derby flew over the wrought iron railing and drifted from sight, revealing the thickest black wavy hair Carrie had ever seen on a man. He leaned against the top of the railing, raised his thick brows, and peered over. "Oops."

The woman with him laughed hysterically. Browning, his own derby resting safely on top of his large ears, looked down at the river. "It's gone, old man."

Dexter slipped one of Mullane's arms over his shoulders. "You two need to get back to your hotel. Wouldn't want your owner or the press to see you in this condition, what with a match tomorrow."

Grant stood up with a sigh. "Don't care to leave Amanda and Carrie alone while we escort these two yahoos to their buggy, so I guess I'd better retrieve their buggy while you wait with the ladies."

"I'll have to see them back to their hotel."

"Aw, Dex, you don't have to do any such thing," Grant protested. "Don't let them spoil our evening. It's not your responsibility these two are painting the town."

"They're my friends." His voice was low, but brooked no argument. "Besides, it isn't good for Base Ball for players to be found in this kind of shape."

"The public knows good and well the way most base ballers live, but since you're bound and determined to be honorable about it, I'll see them back to their lodgings. Suspicious as base ballers are about each others' clubs, it wouldn't surprise me if you were accused of getting these two drunk to better the Browns' chances tomorrow, should you be seen with them."

"Hadn't thought of that. I suppose you're right."

" 'Course I'm right."

"Hate to leave the job to ye, though."

"Don't see anyone else here to do it. Those two ladies hanging on their arms sure aren't going to be an asset in the situation. Since you're one of the few base ballers who doesn't drink, falls to you all too often to look after your mates. Besides, someone has to see Carrie and Amanda back safely." His gaze lingered on Amanda before he turned toward Mullane and Browning, taking a deep breath as he did so, as if fortifying himself against an unpleasant task, which Carrie could well imagine he thought it.

At least she was glad to hear Dexter apparently took no part in his friends' manner of recreation.

When Grant had retrieved the men's conveyance and he and Dexter had loaded the four wobbly passengers into it, he drove off.

Amanda patted gloved fingertips lightly against her lips to hide a yawn. "I hate to admit to being a social disaster, Carrie, but I'm afraid I won't be able to stay awake on the drive back. Would you mind awfully keeping my brother company?"

What choice had she but to defer to Amanda's wishes and join Dexter once again in the front seat of the open carriage? She tried to deny the ribbon of joy that floated inside her at spending more time intimately at his side.

They hadn't gone far before he cleared his throat. "I'm sorry your evening had to end this way. I wish your first evening with. . .in St. Louis could have been perfect."

"It's been a lovely evening. But. . .will Grant be safe with those men?"

"Of course, he will." She wondered whether he was trying to convince himself as well as her. "Mullane and Browning aren't so bad when they've not been drinking. I played with Browning on the Louisville club before Von der Ahe signed me up for the Browns. I'd probably have stayed with Louisville if St. Louis wasn't my hometown. Anyway, Browning and I joined Louisville the same time, five years ago now, when we were fifteen."

She knew a number of young men who supported themselves at that age, but not as base ballers!

"Mullane, now," Dexter was continuing, "he's some terrific hurler. Helped me improve my throw."

"You plan to abandon center field to become a hurler?" She couldn't help the bit of pride she felt in recalling his position.

He laughed good-naturedly. "No. I'll never be good enough at it to be a hurler."

"Is Browning a hurler?"

"No, but he's got the stuff to make one of the top hitters of our day, if he'll just stay off the liquor. It was Browning told me it's nearly worth a player's career what willow he chooses."

"Willow?"

"Bat. Most clubs keep a supply of willows, and the players choose from among them when it's their turn as batsman. But Browning says if a man uses the same willow long enough, he gets used to the feel of it, knows exactly what he can do with it, ups the percentage that he'll hit any hurler's ball. That's why I carry my own willow to each match game, though most players think I'm a fool for going to the trouble and expense of it." He shrugged slightly. "I tried Mullane's suggestions and tried Browning's advice, and sure enough if my playing didn't improve. I'll never be as good as either of them, but I'm consistent, and for many ball club owners, that's worth a lot."

They turned onto a narrower street, and Dexter gave his attention to keeping the horses in line when they met a carriage coming from the opposite direction. Picking up where he'd left off, he said, "Suppose Base Ball is like any business. Only room for so many men to make a living at it, so players are pretty stingy with advice. Figure I owe a lot to Mullane and Browning."

"Are you always so loyal to your friends?"

He shifted his shoulders, keeping his gaze on the street. Was he uncomfortable at her mention of his virtue? Did he think her amused by it? "It is an admirable quality," she assured him quietly.

A moment later they turned another corner. "We're almost to the Planter's." A few paces further he opened his mouth, shut it, then tried again. "I was wondering, would ye. . .that is, is there for being any reason I couldn't. . .or ye wouldn't. . . I mean, would ye be for allowing me to call on ye while ye be in the city?" he finished with a rush.

She was touched by his uncharacteristic stumbling and the broadening of his

Irish accent, which she recalled Amanda insisting happened only when he was speaking blarney or was upset. She didn't think he was teasing now, and he wasn't angry, so he must be nervous. Imagine a well-known base ballist nervous at asking to call on a small-town preacher's daughter!

Her sympathetic amusement fled at the memory of Emmet. "I. . .I am being courted by a young man back home."

He said nothing, only stared ahead. She wished it were day so she could see his expression. It would help if he would even remove his stovepipe, as its brim deepened the shadows over his face.

"I. . .his name is Emmet. Emmet Wilson."

She heard him swallow. "Ye say he is courting ye, but haven't said that ye've promised yourself to him."

The simple statement sent her thoughts into confusion. Had she not said so because her heart refused to acknowledge such a thing in his presence? She could say it now and never see Dexter Riley again. It was the honorable thing to do. She would say it to any other man; she had said it to a number of them.

She felt as much as saw him turn toward her. "Carrie?"

The word was spoken softly. Only one word, but she heard the hope expressed in it, and it was that hope to which she responded. "I've made no promise to him in words, nor has he asked me to do so."

"Then, may I call?"

"I don't wish to mislead you. Emmet is. . .I'm very fond of him. We've been close since we were children. I never thought of. . ." She broke off, embarrassed. Dexter had simply asked whether he might call on her. How could she, in reply, say she'd never considered marriage to anyone but Emmet? That in spite of her desire to see Dexter again—and she wished to do so desperately—she was sure she would still marry Emmet?

They stopped in front of the hotel entrance. A uniformed hotel employee held their horses while Dexter assisted her down. His hands remained lightly at her waist, his rich brown eyes still asking the question, though he didn't repeat it.

"I don't know how long we'll be in the city."

He must have recognized her comment for the permission to call on her that it was meant, for his smile blazed across his face and shone from his eyes in a joy that humbled her.

"We play Louisville again tomorrow afternoon. I won't be able to call until the match is over. Perhaps you will be among the spectators?"

Did the eagerness in his question mean he wanted her there? "I don't know. Grant may have classes, and I doubt my father would escort me." It wouldn't be proper to go unescorted, of course, nor would she dare to do so, considering the manner of people to which she'd been exposed among the spectators today.

"Then, if at all possible, I'll be here by seven tomorrow evening."

His look was so ardent, she had to glance away, but she thrilled to it nonetheless.

She nodded and hurried toward the door.

Three paces from the entrance she whirled back around. "Oh, Mr. Riley!"

Her words weren't spoken loudly, nor did they need to be, for she saw with pleasant confusion that he was still standing beside the carriage, watching her. He stepped toward her eagerly. "Yes?"

One hand clutched the top of her cape, where the black velvet frog secured it. "I forgot to wish you well in the match game tomorrow."

His smile brought a trembling one from her before she went inside. She resisted the urge to turn about once more for a last look at his dear face.

Tomorrow. Tomorrow she'd see him again. Less than twenty-four hours.

Anticipation put wings on her ivory satin slippers as she crossed the thickly carpeted foyer to the ornate elevator that would take her to her floor.

❧

Best day of his life.

Since attending his first match game of Base Ball at the age of five, Dexter had had only one goal: to be a base baller, and a good one. When he signed the contract with the Louisville club five years ago, he'd thought he'd never again feel so heady over anything.

But today left that accomplishment in the dust. Today, for the first time, he'd played in a season game for a major league club, played well, and his club had won. One couldn't expect life to get better than this.

But it had. Better than a shutout against your ball club's worst rival.

He'd met Carrie.

There wasn't a doubt in his mind that she was the woman for him, for the rest of his life and then some. He clasped his hands behind his head and stared out the window beside his bed at the stars trying to shine through the constant factory-smoke haze camouflaging the St. Louis skies. The grin that had barely left his face all day stretched wider.

She was a beauty, Carrie was. Known Grant for two years, and not once had the fellow told him how beautiful she was. 'Course, being her brother, he wouldn't be likely to notice.

Though it was beyond him how even a brother could be blind to skin that glowed like a dogwood blossom in moonlight, framed by hair that shimmered as sleekly black as the Mississippi River at night.

He lifted his hands, their twenty-year-old knuckles already permanently swollen from injuries received catching base balls, and examined their lumpy silhouettes against the light of night coming through the window, imagining the softness of her hair against his tough, callused skin.

He let his hands fall back to his sides, picturing her face as he'd first seen it. He loved the way the unexpected cocker-brown freckles sprinkled across the tiny bridge of her nose and beneath her blue eyes. Couldn't be more than a dozen of the things. He'd count those freckles the next time he saw her, indeed he would.

His laugh rang out bright and clear at the thought, and his boardingmate, who played first base, snorted and rolled over at the sound. Dexter closed his grinning lips hard together. He and his boardingmate had made a good play that day, a perfect play, smart, sharp, efficient, putting a Louisville player out at third. His hands stung yet at the remembrance of catching that fly, for the player was a slugger of the first degree, though not normally as good as Browning.

The joy in his chest tempered somewhat at the thought of Browning. One of the best base ballers he'd ever seen play, but the man would drink as many nickel pails of beer as a person could line up in front of him. Only thing that kept this day from being perfect was Browning and Mullane putting on that disgusting display in front of Carrie. Didn't take much to see she wasn't accustomed to men in such condition.

Of course, one would expect a preacher's daughter to be protected from the world. Likely she felt as strongly about God as Grant, who often urged him to try trusting Christ. Dexter didn't know many other men who felt so strongly about their religion.

Well, he liked an attitude of reverence toward God in a woman. The women who followed the base ballers didn't mind a man who drank, or used coarse language, or told unseemly stories in their presence, or stole a few kisses—or made more improper advances. He enjoyed the heady feeling a woman's attention gave any man, but he refused to take advantage of the silly creatures, even if they didn't appear to mind being compromised.

Least of all did such women consider God important. Not that he could condemn them for that. He hadn't much use for God himself. He didn't even know whether he believed in Him or not. God, if He did exist, didn't appear to take much interest in men, not that he could notice, anyway. And he'd seen men who professed faith who were as base as those who openly shunned religion. Of course, there were a few men of faith who seemed sincere—men like Grant. He supposed Carrie would prefer such a man.

Carrie. He folded his hands behind his head and grinned. Guess he might as well get used to her keeping him company in his mind. Only thing that came near to being as pleasant to think on was a perfect play like he and his roommate had made today, or an uncatchable hit with three of your clubmates on base.

Those delicate black eyebrows of hers were as pretty as a base ball in flight, and just as deceiving. A wrapped ball flying through the air didn't look like it could pack a powerful wallop, any more than a man would suspect the things an innocent raising of those eyebrows could do to his stomach.

And she'd granted him permission to see her tomorrow evening.

Yes sir, it had been a pert'-near perfect day. Best day of his life.

Chapter Four

Carrie didn't attend the match the next day. Dexter's team lost, but he didn't appear disconcerted. He was as entertaining as he'd been the previous evening. Her parents and Grant joined them for dinner, and she was delighted to see her parents liked the young man as well as she and Grant did.

With ruddy cheeks, he'd presented both Carrie and Mrs. Chambers flowers he'd purchased from the raggedy flower girls who filled the street to earn a few pennies in front of the hotel from dawn to sunset.

"They aren't the city's finest flowers, but—" He'd shrugged and left the explanation unfinished.

But she knew he meant no slight to her and her mother. Rather his kind heart went out to the children in their poverty as it had to the boys he allowed into the ball grounds without damaging their pride. She liked him the more for it but didn't diminish his kind act by saying so or by telling him she purchased a bouquet for her room daily. Instead, she pinned the most delicate blossom to her gown and sent a maid to her room with the rest. She was pleased when her mother did the same.

She and Dexter didn't go riding or promenading after dinner, but spent the evening in the elegant lobby. The hours went by too quickly as they grew better acquainted, liking each other more with each bit of knowledge, eagerly drinking in the way the other looked, the unique timbre of their voices, seeing their growing admiration and affection for each other reflected in each other's eyes.

Her mother protested slightly the next day when Carrie told her Dexter would be joining her for the third evening in a row, but Carrie assured her there could be nothing amiss in spending time with Grant and his friend, and the older woman was appeased for the moment.

That evening Dexter, Carrie, and Grant attended a play together at Washington University. Amanda had a small role in the play, and she performed her part admirably with an appealing energy that won the audience's wholehearted approval. Carrie enjoyed spending the hours beside Dexter, sharing glances during the performance, and discovering with delight that they laughed at the same things. Often their gazes would catch and mingle in the dim light, and they would forget the play until the laughter of those around them rang out and brought their gazes back to the stage.

Toward the middle of the last act, Dexter rested his hand over hers. She darted a surprised look at his face, her heart pattering explosively in her chest and ears. When she didn't pull her hand away, he smiled at her; not the usual, easy-going smile that seldom seemed to leave his face, or the friendly smile he gave admirers who approached him, but a smile warmed with something akin to devotion. She turned her gaze back to the stage, but her attention remained with the large, rather disfigured, callused hand that claimed her own and the eyes that held the suggestion of a whole new world.

As usual, a number of people in the audience recognized Dexter, and Carrie waited patiently while they stopped to speak with him after the play. A few asked him to autograph their programs, which he did, laughingly commenting that it was the performers who should be signing. In their eagerness to get close to the popular base ballist, some of the crowd pushed their way between Carrie and Dexter. Carrie stepped back to give them way, but Dexter, smilingly excusing himself to the responsible parties, drew her back to his side.

The action caught the attention of the onlookers, who eyed her curiously. Some of the young women gazed at her boldly, their looks accusing her of being where she had no right. One of the female admirers rested a glove on Dexter's other arm, leaning against him and smiling alluringly into his face. He responded respectfully to her gushing compliments and moved discreetly in such a manner that her hand was forced to slip away.

Carrie, accustomed to life in a small community, found it a heady experience to be escorted by someone so readily recognized and admired, to say nothing of a man whose company was sought after by women in such a forward manner. Still, though the experience was exhilarating, it wasn't his perhaps temporary fame that caused her to enjoy his company so much. It was the man himself she enjoyed, she thought, watching him discreetly while they drove together later through Lafayette Park in the one-seat open carriage.

She had been dismayed when Grant informed them he and Amanda had made their own plans after the play, but she agreed eagerly to Dexter's offer of a drive.

It was a beautiful spring evening, with clear skies that appeared almost bright from the light of the surrounding city. The upper-class community was far enough from the river that it escaped the city's industrial haze, and a handful of scattered stars dotted the sky. The slight breeze carried the scent of new leaves, which blended with the mixture of leather from the carriage and reins, the horses, and her own violet scent.

Dexter pulled the horse to a gentle stop alongside a small lake, across which the emerging moon cast a wavering path, catching the shimmering veil of water from a man-made fountain in its midst. Carrie caught her breath at the sight, leaning forward slightly. "How lovely!"

"Sometime I'll bring you here during the day, when you can see it well. We'll take a small skiff out and row to the island."

He wanted to continue seeing her! The wonder of it made her speechless.

He lifted his eyebrows and grinned. "Difficult to find time to spend with you during daylight hours, though. The afternoons we don't have a match game scheduled, we have practice."

She wanted to ask whether they couldn't come to the park on Sunday afternoon, but the suggestion was too bold, so she said instead, "I'd like to attend another of your matches before we leave for Ridgeville."

He dropped his gaze to his fingers, which played idly with the reins. "Your father probably doesn't approve of Base Ball or of base ballers."

She replied to the true question she suspected buried in his statement. "He has expressed no disapproval of you. On the contrary, he told Grant what a fine young man he believed you to be and that he was glad Grant had found such a friend here."

He turned his face to her. "And has your father commented on my escorting you?"

She hoped he couldn't see her flush in the darkness. "My parents have no objection to my assisting Grant in entertaining his friends."

He didn't respond immediately. Only the stirring of the horse in its harness broke the silence until he said, "Some people are embarrassed to associate with base ballers. I know a player who changed his name when he joined a professional ball club so as not to bring disgrace on his family." He hesitated, and when he spoke again, his voice was low. "Are you ashamed to be escorted by me, Carrie?"

The pain in his voice resonated through her. "Never!" She leaned toward him in a spontaneous gesture, resting her hand on his forearm and looking up into his face. "I'm proud to be escorted by you. Not because of your profession, but because of the type of man you are: kind and compassionate and loyal and fine and—"

"Carrie!" Her name barely left his lips before he'd drawn her close and covered her mouth with his. The kiss was warm and lingering, and she thought only of how wonderful it was, how different from Emmet's brotherly kisses.

And even the memory of Emmet didn't cause her to draw away from Dexter's embrace.

"I was afraid ye could never care for me." His breath fanned her cheek with his cracked whisper.

Tumultuous joy bubbled through her. She pulled her head away from his to meet his gaze and laugh softly. "The great base ballist, Dexter Riley, afraid?"

"Terrified. You, Miss Chambers, are far more frightening than any flying ball or tossed willow."

His arms encircled her, and she rested against his chest with a contentment that was new to her. His embrace was a haven, enclosing the two of them from time and reality.

"There's something I must tell ye."

Unease slipped into her peace at the cautious note in his voice and the tell-tale Irish accent. Was there some reason he shouldn't care for her? Had he promised himself to another?

"I don't usually tell people much about my past, but I want ye to know the truth about me, right from the beginning."

Truth? *Beginning*? Which word made her nerve endings tinkle like icicles in the wind?

"My grandparents hadn't much money when they arrived from Ireland during the famine, but Da's parents had a mite more than most. Enough to establish a business." She heard him swallow, felt his chest rise with a ragged breath. "A saloon."

Her heart stopped for the space of a beat, then continued on. "Your *grandfather* started this saloon?"

He nodded.

A little wave of relief trickled over her. Two generations had passed since then. It wasn't as though Dexter was a saloon keeper.

He cleared his voice and continued. "They had ten children. Da was oldest, fourteen when they came to America. Da intended to leave the saloon when he married Mother. He wanted to farm land in the northwest. But Grandfather died almost immediately after they married, and Da took over the saloon. He needed the money to raise his brothers and sisters.

"Mother always hated the saloon. She had to help in it. All of us children were brought up in it. Some of my brothers and sisters—there's six of us—are barely younger than my youngest uncle."

"Your parents were essentially raising two families."

"Yes. My older brothers and sisters helped out when they were old enough. Mother used to tell of Amanda and me crawling about underfoot in the kitchen where she could keep an eye on us. She never allowed us to work in the bar area, but we saw and heard plenty, just the same."

His fingers tightened over hers. The gaslight standing sentry nearby gained a halo from the mist in her eyes. How different his childhood had been from hers, where serenity filled their modest parsonage.

"Mother was determined at least two of her children wouldna grow up to work in a saloon. She constantly reminded Amanda and me that we must get all the education possible and do something respectable with our lives.

"She made sure we went to church, too. We weren't too old before we discovered why she wanted us away from the saloon. Many parents, especially the church members, wouldna let their kids play with us.

"I like Base Ball. Most of the people in the part of the city where we grew up liked the sport. I was not knowing the wealthier classes disapproved of it. So when I had the chance to sign with the Louisville Eclipse, a minor league team, for more money than I thought a fifteen-year-old boy would ever see, I grabbed it, glad to be getting away from the saloon like Mother wanted.

"Then Da and Mother were killed in a train accident."

She touched her lips to the back of one huge hand. She hadn't known he and Amanda had lost their parents.

"My oldest brother, Frank, took over the saloon, The Irish Stars. I moved into an apartment with another base baller."

"After joining the Eclipse, did you continue your education as your mother wished?"

"Yes. Had time in the winter, when the ball clubs dinna play. And attended night school. Slow going, but eventually I was accepted at Washington University, where I met your brother. 'Course, it's slow going there, too, since I can't take classes year 'round. Hope to be a counselor at law one day. Can't play Base Ball all my life. A man's body won't take the strain."

"Your mother would be proud of you."

His lips pressed against her temple, tipping her hat.

"I wanted ye to know, lass. If ye find it disconcerting to be escorted by a base baller whose family owns a saloon, then it would be a kindness if ye'd tell me now, before I lose my heart to ye further."

The huskiness in his voice brought out her protective instincts. "*You* don't own the saloon, and you are not a drinking man. I think you are. . .wonderful."

"Oh, Carrie, girleen. . ."

She lifted her lips eagerly to meet his kiss.

A long while later, his chest lifted beneath her cheek in a deep sigh. "I wish I could see you tomorrow, but the club is traveling to Louisville. We meet the Eclipse there again the following day."

"But you've played them three times already this week."

"We meet them five times in this series, and the last two match games will be at their ball grounds."

She did some quick calculating. This was Thursday. If the next game was Saturday. . .

She pushed away from him, trying to curb her panic. "But that means you won't be back until we've gone home."

"We'll arrive back Monday morning."

Disappointment was too swamping for her to hide. "I was hoping you would attend church with us Sunday. Father has been asked to give the sermon at the church that is considering calling him." Then it dawned on her, and she sat up straighter, unconsciously adjusting the hat that had slipped over one ear. "If you have two match games left with Louisville, and you're returning Sunday night, you will be playing on Sunday."

"We have no choice. It's one of the tenants of the American Association league, that the clubs play on Sundays in the cities where it's legal."

She tried to search his eyes, but it was too dark to see them clearly, though she heard the wariness in his reply. "You agree to play on the Lord's Day?" she asked slowly.

"I must. All the players must. If we don't, Von der Ahe could let us go."

"Let you go?"

"Release us from our contracts."

"Couldn't you sign with a club that doesn't require you to play on Sundays?"

He gave a slight laugh that was almost a snort. "A player can't simply choose the club he'll play on, he has to be asked. And no clubs in the National League, which doesn't play on Sundays, have asked me. Besides, I want to play in St. Louis, for my hometown, and I want to play in a major league."

"Did you *know* when you agreed to play for the Browns that you would be required to play on Sundays?"

"Yes." The single syllable was crisp.

"I see."

He pulled his hat off and ran a hand distractedly through his thick hair. "It isn't easy to start a new major league. The club owners invest a lot of money. They want to be sure they draw enough spectators so they won't be losing their investment. Most ordinary laborers work six days a week. The only day they have free to attend a match is Sunday."

"But it's the Lord's Day."

They were both quiet for a long time, over five minutes by the clock in the leather reins' holder attached to the carriage's dashboard, Carrie noticed.

His hand caressed her shoulder. When he finally spoke, his voice vibrated with misery. "I can't be changing the fact that for most people Sunday is a holy day, nor can I be changing the fact that I'm obligated by my contract to play any day Der Boss orders it. But I'm not wanting to leave ye tonight with this between us."

"I don't want that either," she whispered. "We won't allow it to stand between us."

With a ragged sigh, he wrapped his arms tightly about her.

Pain twisted in the middle of her chest. He would be gone until Monday. She didn't know when she might see him again, and the uncertainty was unbearable.

"When the train gets in Monday, I'll come straight to the hotel. If ye are still in town, will ye wait for me there?"

Relief eased the pain, but the tears spilled over. She nodded, unable to speak. Unclasping her handbag, she removed a delicate lace handkerchief never meant for serious use and dabbed at her cheeks.

With an exclamation of concern, he leaned over her, one hand closing over hers with the handkerchief. "You're crying!"

Pride abandoned her. "I shall miss you." He couldn't have heard the wobbly words if his face wasn't so near hers.

He crushed her to himself, and she thought in embarrassment that his cheek would be wet from her tears. "I'll think of you every moment we're apart. I'll not be worth anything to Der Boss in Louisville!"

A church bell rang the midnight hour, and she could feel the reluctance with which he pulled away. "I'd best be for getting you back, or your father will be having me hide, and properly so."

But before he took the reins again, he gently pulled her hand through his arm, and her shoulder rested intimately against his until they reached the hotel. She felt a desperate need to cherish every moment granted her with this man who had such a hold on her heart.

Dexter couldn't wait to get back to St. Louis—to Carrie, he corrected himself—and they'd barely left the St. Louis depot.

He'd wanted to tell her last night that he was in love with her, but how could he expect her to believe it on such short acquaintance? Still, it seemed ungentlemanly to ask for and accept her embrace without declaring his intentions. Her kisses were innocent and sweet. The eagerness with which she'd welcomed his arms humbled him, for he knew it meant she cared. She wasn't the type of woman who gave her kisses lightly, expecting no promises.

Not that he'd ever exchanged more than a couple kisses with any woman. He wanted more than an evening with a woman. He wanted a lifetime—with the *right* woman.

With Carrie.

Would she be willing to share life with a base baller?

He'd thought Base Ball would release him from the reputation of being raised in a saloon. He'd been wrong. Base Ball wasn't respected by his "social betters." They liked meeting base ballers and watching them play, but didn't consider them equals. More like toys or baubles to dangle in front of their friends. Some of the base ballers, maybe most of them, responded by using the people who tried to use them. Fair exchange, the players thought. They only hurt themselves and the silly hangers-on. Couldn't see beyond the moment.

That was why it was so important he continue with his law courses. One day he'd be a counselor, a man whose profession wouldn't shame Carrie. If she'd have him.

The thought of losing her twisted his stomach with an unfamiliar fear.

Chapter Five

Carrie stared out between the hotel room's velvet window dressings into the busy street below. The incessant clang-clang of rushing cable cars in the next thoroughfare appeared to set the pace for pedestrians and horse-drawn vehicles. Eight o'clock, and the city was already bustling with businessmen rushing to their day.

She'd seen hundreds—it seemed like thousands to someone with her small-town background—of workers dashing along the city's streets during the past week. Bankers, lawyers, architects, office boys, draymen, hackmen: Vocation and age were of no matter, they all presented the same demeanor. They scurried about at an impatient clip, each trying to exceed the speed of the person ahead. Tension shouted from the set of their shoulders, whether below finely hand-tailored suits or poorly fitting jackets purchased from a cheap emporium. Strain-chiseled furrows marked their faces.

They were so unlike Dexter at his work, or away from it for that matter. Some of his clubmates scowled while they played, heaped abuses on members of the opposing club, and even resorted to kicking and fisticuffs, but not Dexter. Beneath his mustache, his smile never left his face, only changed in degree. Tiny lines rayed from his wide-set eyes despite his youth, but the lines were a badge earned squinting against the summer suns during years of Base Ball, not carved from business worries.

She was glad he was content in his vocation, though his choice of profession did cause her a niggling worry. She preferred he not work on the Lord's Day and in an atmosphere that did not include spectators drinking beer and other spirits.

At least Dexter wasn't a drinking man, she thought with relief. Of course, she wouldn't have been attracted to him if he were one. She had never allowed a drinking man to escort her. What was the sense of becoming involved with a man who had habits she knew she would not want in a husband?

Husband. She'd always thought Emmet would be her husband. Now she knew that in spite of her fondness for him, something was missing.

Dear Emmet, who had been her close friend through the years, then her first escort, and who waited patiently and trustingly for the day they would marry. They didn't share great passion—even the word heated her cheeks, remembering the way she responded to Dexter. But she and Emmet had an honest enjoyment of each other's company, a respect for each other's ideals, and a shared joy in their faith in Christ. With his quiet, almost gentle nature and plain face beneath straight, dishwater blond hair, he would never compare well to a man like Dexter Riley, at least in most women's minds. But she knew Emmet was finer than most men. She'd known when he was a boy that he'd grow up to be that kind of man: one who would always do the honorable thing, with no fanfare and no excuses and no hesitation. The kind of man who would gain the respect and trust of men, women, and children.

After all these years and all the warm moments and special dreams they'd shared, she couldn't bring his face clearly to mind. The only face she could picture was Dexter Riley's, with its confident, laughing green eyes beneath straight, thick brows and the mustache that covered his top lip, framing his smiling mouth. Her heart had never quivered uncomfortably at Emmet's smile, though it did at Dexter's.

It was unthinkable to be attracted to a man on such short acquaintance, and a base ballist at that! Shame fought with the attraction in her breast. How could she for a moment be interested in him when she had the love of a man like Emmet?

Well, doubtless the attraction would pass. Dexter would tire of her, and in a few weeks, she would forget she was reacting so foolishly.

Arms crossed over her tailored promenade polonaise of sapphire blue, she leaned her forehead lightly against the window glass and rubbed her upper arms in their narrow sleeves. The city had lost its glow of excitement for her since Dexter left for Louisville. It wasn't that the past three days had been unpleasant, but that she had merely been but passing time until Dexter returned.

Now Monday morning had arrived, and her parents had the day planned for them: the last day before they returned to their hometown to await the decision of the local congregation. She glanced at the marcasite-set watch pinned to her polonaise; *ten past eight*. With a sigh, she picked up the ivory-vellum envelope containing the note she'd written telling Dexter where she'd be for the day. She retrieved the bonnet that matched her promenade outfit and, swinging it carelessly by its satin ties, went down to the lobby to await her parents.

She had just left the note at the desk when she felt a touch on her arm and heard her name spoken by the voice that had already grown dear to her. Joy washed everything else from her senses.

She whirled to face him and he captured her hands in his own, his eyes roaming over her face as though he was starved for the sight of her. His obvious pleasure in once again being in her company filled her with wonder.

"I didn't think you would. . . ," she started.

"I was afraid I wouldn't. . . ," he began at the same time.

They laughed together at their stumbling start.

"I was afraid you would be gone," he said, and the thankfulness in his tone spread warmth through her. "I came directly from the depot."

"We leave tomorrow morning. Grant is showing us Washington University today. He's eager for us to become familiar with his school."

He rubbed the palm of one knotty-knuckled hand over his face and grinned. "I need to freshen up and shave again. I tried to shave on the train, but I'm afraid I wasn't too successful." Half a dozen brown-red nicks along his chin and neck attested to the fact. "Do you think your parents might allow me to steal you away this afternoon? I could show you Lafayette Park in daylight."

It was on the tip of her tongue to say that the afternoon was much too far in the future, but she caught back the unladylike statement and nodded eagerly.

It was a lovely afternoon for rowing, Carrie thought later, leaning back against the cushions Dexter had thoughtfully provided. The day was warm for early May, so the breeze off the water wasn't chilling. A canvas top over the swan-shaped boat protected them from the sun's rays. She trailed the fingers of one hand in the barely ruffled waters and watched Dexter row.

"What are you thinking?"

She cast him a frankly flirtatious grin. "That you remind me of a Venetian gondolier."

He rolled his eyes and shook his head. "Faith, and I've given my heart to a romantic!"

Her breath caught in her chest at his words. Had he truly given her his heart, or was he simply speaking the blarney that falls easily from the lips of a man who is sought after by women?

For the moment, at least, she resolved to believe it. She didn't want anything to mar these last hours with him before leaving the city.

He rested his chest against the hands gripping the oars. "Happy?"

"Oh, yes! It's perfect."

"The lake, or the company?"

"Both are perfect. Everything is perfect. Or. . ."

"Or?"

"It would be perfect if you didn't have to play Sunday ball."

He bent to the oars once more, their dipping motion making a pleasant splash. "Nothing has changed since we last discussed this. I don't know what else I can say."

She leaned forward earnestly, her elbows on the knees draped by her tailored, sapphire blue skirt. "But if you told Mr. Von der Ahe it was against your religious beliefs to work on Sunday, surely he would release you from the need to do so."

Frowning, he looked away quickly, then back to her. "More likely he would release me from the need to play on any day."

She looked out over the water. She shouldn't have broached the topic. It only added a depressing note to the otherwise lovely afternoon.

"Besides—" he started, then he broke off.

She turned back to him when he didn't continue.

Looking directly into her eyes, he spoke gently. "Besides, it isn't against my religious beliefs to play on Sundays."

She tilted her head, frowning. "Surely the church you attend teaches the third commandment, 'Remember the Sabbath Day, to keep it holy.' "

"I don't attend church."

Her blood turned to ice. He *couldn't* be an unbeliever, he couldn't, her mind argued. She could never have fallen in love with a man who didn't love the Lord. "Why?" The one word croaked from her tight throat.

"When Mother was alive, I attended regularly. Church was important to her, so I and the rest of the family went every Sunday. But we went to please her, not because it was important to us. Only me da never went. He didn't believe in God and said on the chance he was mistaken about His existence, he wasn't about to dishonor Him by pretending to worship Him when he didn't believe."

Her chest trembled at his words. "You. . .don't believe in God?"

"I don't believe in Him or not believe in Him. If He exists, He doesn't appear to pay attention to the people He made, so I can't be seeing that it will disturb Him if I'm not paying Him much mind."

"How can you say God doesn't take notice of us when He sent His own Son to take the punishment for our sins?"

"I know Jesus walked this earth, but I don't know that He was the Son of God. How can I believe Jesus is God's Son, when I don't even know whether I believe God exists?"

She had no answer to that. "Does Amanda believe?"

"She feels as I do."

Carrie looked across the water, wondering that it could be so calm when she felt she was in the midst of a hurricane. Five minutes ago her world was almost perfect, and now—now everything wonderful had been ripped from her.

Nothing was what it seemed. She'd always thought believers were Good People, in spite of their imperfections, and that unbelievers were Bad People, with imperfections impossible to miss. But Amanda wasn't a horrible person, and Dexter. . . Her gaze slid back to him, and she studied the handsome, pleasant face, now without its usual charming smile. Dexter certainly wasn't an awful person. It was all so confusing.

The Bible's command wasn't confusing, however. It clearly warned that believers and unbelievers weren't to wed. How could a person who loved God be truly one with a person who did not believe in Him, let alone love Him and choose to follow His ways?

Over the last few days, she had started pushing Emmet from thoughts of her future and replaced him with the dream of a life with Dexter. The dream would have to die, and the knowledge tore through her, leaving a gaping wound in place of her heart.

She was quiet during the few minutes it took to land the boat and return it to the docksman, responding only with a nod or a single word when Dexter addressed her.

Dexter drew her from the public shoreline to a bench, obscured by a large clump of lilac bushes, their buds flooding the air with their distinctive, cloying scent.

When they were seated, Dexter rested a rough palm against her cheek with a gentleness that made her ache anew. "I can't be bearing to think of your leaving tomorrow, girleen. I'd follow, but I can't. I can't even be promising to visit ye in your hometown often. We have ninety-six matches scheduled this season and will be traveling all over the central and eastern states to play in addition to the matches we play here and the exhibition matches. I'm not wanting to be apart from ye. I know this is sudden, Carrie, but—I'm loving ye so! Will ye marry me as soon as possible?"

Marry him! Such a short time ago it would have been the sweetest request in the world. Now she recognized the cruelty in it.

"I can't. I can't marry you."

Chapter Six

"Why won't ye marry me, Carrie? Because of that Emmet Wilson? Ye can't be loving him. Ye love *me*. Surely ye can't be denying it."

"No." Carrie rested an unsteady hand on his crisp linen shirt front. "No, I can't deny it." The words were barely a whisper. She wondered that he even heard them, but he must have, because his strong, huge arms surrounded her, hauling her against his chest until she could smell the fresh-ironed scent of his shirt mixed with the popular scent of bay rum cologne.

"Tell me, Carrie. Tell me ye love me."

His Irish accent was urgent against her hair. She could feel his need to hear her declaration in the stiffness of his limbs, in the way his broad chest stilled with his baited breath.

She couldn't possibly marry him when he didn't love the Lord. She'd never allow herself to see him again after today. But her heart and mind had been battering to speak her love of him for days. Perhaps it was unwise, but she wanted to say the words to him. *Just today, and never again, forever.*

Her arms crept around his neck. She tightened her hold on him, leaned her cheek against his own recently shaved one, and whispered the words she'd waited a lifetime to say. "I love you. I love you, Dexter!"

His breath whooshed out in relief. He stood, pulling her with him, and nearly squeezed the breath out of her in the next instant when he lifted her off her feet with his hug. "I knew it!"

She laughed through the tears in her throat. Her hands pushed ineffectually against his shoulders. "Put me down. What if someone should see us?"

"I'll not put you down until you promise to marry me."

Her laughter stilled into a small, closed smile, and she averted her gaze from his.

His arms froze once more, and she wished she never had to hear him ask the words she knew were coming. If only time could stop at this moment, could stay filled always with his first joyous knowledge of their shared love.

"Say ye'll marry me, Carrie." His voice was tight, urgent, wary.

She couldn't bear to look at him, so she hugged him closer, his hair against her cheek.

He lowered her slowly until her feet touched the ground. "Look at me."

She knew her eyes were filled with sadness, that he'd see it and know her answer to his proposal, but she met his gaze. The pain there crashed through her, washing over her with the ferocity of a tidal wave.

"If ye love me, why be ye hurting us both this way?"

His voice was thick with torment. It filled her with aching regret. She shouldn't have let it go this far. She should have done as her conscience demanded, stayed faithful to Emmet and refused to see Dexter apart from the family. Instead she'd told herself she couldn't possibly lose her heart to him.

She swallowed, her throat almost closed from pain. "We don't share a faith in the Lord. We can't marry without that."

He stared at her stupidly. "Ye aren't refusing me to marry another man, but refusing me because I'm not knowing what I believe about God?"

"I decided years ago that the Lord was the most important thing—Person—in my life, and I promised Him I would always put Him first."

"But I dinna object to your attending church. I'm not objecting to your faith. I wouldn't be asking ye to forsake it."

"I know, but the Bible says believers aren't to marry unbelievers."

He stepped back from her, looking as if he'd been slapped, and she was suddenly cold, standing there without his arms about her. His face was colder, chilling her through with its anger and hurt.

She reached for him impulsively, longing to draw him back into her embrace, to comfort him and make him understand that she wanted nothing more in the world than to be his wife, but the choice wasn't hers.

He stepped back, just beyond her reach. She felt stranded, as if she were on an island near a populated shoreline with no rescue in sight.

His jaw tightened. She knew he was struggling to keep his temper at bay. "I won't pretend that I'll change for ye. I won't be a hypocrite and pretend to serve a God I'm not certain exists."

"I don't wish you to become a hypocrite." She took a step toward him, eager to get closer, where it would be easier to talk.

He stepped back again, bringing himself abruptly against the trunk of a huge elm.

She could take advantage of that elm, she thought, but what was the point when he so obviously did not want her touch?

"I can't be promising to become a believer, either, or even that I will try to become one."

She nodded. Of course he couldn't promise to become a believer. How could anyone promise such a thing?

They stared at each other. Was misery as heavy in her face as it was in his? The minutes grew long, and the air filled with the sounds of others enjoying the lake beyond the screen of fragrant lilac bushes, oblivious to two lives that would never be the same after this afternoon.

"I love ye. Ye say ye love me. That's all that's important. Don't let this silly thing keep us apart." His voice was husky with pain. He reached for her.

But this time it was she who retreated. If she allowed herself to be held in those arms for even a moment more, she just might forget that "silly thing" and turn her back on her Lord—who never turned His back on her—and stay forever in Dexter's embrace.

She shook her head slightly. "I love you, but I can't marry you."

She stumbled slightly over an unexpected rise in the path, caught herself, turned, and fled.

One can't flee the pain of spending life without the one you love, she thought four months later, staring out the parlor window at her mother's garden in back of the St. Louis parsonage.

If only her father hadn't accepted the call to the St. Louis church! Now she couldn't leave the house without watching for Dexter, hoping their paths would cross, knowing they mustn't or her heart would play her traitor.

The days on which match games were played at Sportsman's Park were the worst. She forced herself to stay away, but couldn't concentrate on work or conversations. Knowing where he was, knowing it was within her power to see him, made it impossible to think of anything else.

It didn't help that the citizens were so taken with the St. Louis Browns. The twenty-five-cent entrance fee, serving of beer at the ball grounds, and Sunday match games garnered a loyal following for the American Association—or the "Beer and Whiskey League" as it was so appropriately and popularly called.

She heard the names of the clubs and members spoken often by boys and men who followed the sport as though their livelihoods depended upon the scores. The best players' names were becoming as well known as the names of politicians, especially the local players. Mullane and Browning were often mentioned as rising stars, and she couldn't hear their names without remembering Dexter and their first evening together at the bridge.

Dexter wasn't gaining the fame of his two friends, but he had garnered quite a following just the same. He was, as he had said, considered a consistently good player, though not one of the sports' shining stars, good both at hitting and in the outfield, which apparently could not be said for most players. His reputation was that of a player who would not drink, or fight, or play unfairly.

He hadn't played unfairly with her, either. He hadn't pretended he would serve God when he learned she would not marry a man who was not committed to the Lord. She was the one who had been unfair; unfair to herself, and Dexter, and Emmet. She'd had no right to spend time with Dexter when she'd allowed Emmet to think she would marry him.

Her attention was caught by the red roses swaying in the gentle breeze. Most of the pink and red flowers that had dotted the garden when the family moved in two months ago were being replaced by cheerful yellow, orange, and russet blooms.

She wished she could believe her heart would also be cheerful soon. She'd believed it at first. Believed she would be able to forget Dexter. Believed one morning she'd wake up and no longer hurt when she remembered he was gone from her life forever. Believed she'd see a child without wondering what it would have been like to raise a family with Dexter, wondering what his children would look like, imagining him grin watching them play. Believed one day she would smile without pretense, happy with life.

Believed she'd truly come to love Emmet Wilson as deeply as she loved Dexter. After all, Emmet was everything she wanted in a man. He was a Christian, moral, intelligent, and kind. He would make a good husband and father. They'd share the joy of serving the Lord and raise their children to love Him.

Except she couldn't marry Emmet. It wasn't right to marry someone as good as Emmet with a heart that was filled with another. Emmet deserved a better love and marriage than that. She'd shied away from telling him so for a week now. He would be calling Saturday; she'd tell him then.

The thumping of brass against brass sounded dully from the hallway, and a moment later she heard her mother's steps hurry toward the door. Her mother hadn't mentioned guests were expected today, she thought idly.

Filled with an overwhelming weariness, she leaned her forehead against the cool pane. Disgust at herself for the manner in which she was treating Emmet engulfed her. She'd always despised women who treated a man's love like a worthless toy, discardable when it no longer suited. Now she was treating Emmet's love in that despicable way.

"Lord, if it is the only thing I learn in life, teach me to love as Thou dost love," she whispered.

"You have a visitor, Carrie."

At her mother's soft voice, she turned from the window, startled. Her heart zoomed to the floor faster than one of the fancy wrought iron elevators in the Palace Hotel where she'd dined with Dexter, for there he stood, his gaze anxiously searching her face over her mother's head.

Mrs. Chambers looked uncertainly from one to the other, tightened her thin lips, and quietly left the room.

Carrie loosened her grip on the rich tapestry drapery. She hadn't realized she'd crushed the fabric in her fist when she saw Dexter in the doorway. She should stop staring at him, greet him, welcome him into the parlor in proper manner, but she couldn't gather her wits. He looked so good, standing in the doorway in his gray suit, his matching bowler in one hand at his side, his wine red hair slightly mussed from pulling off his hat.

He slid one hand into his trouser pocket, letting his weight rest mostly on one leg. His eyes looked quickly off to one side, then returned to her before he raised his eyebrows and quirked one corner of his mouth into a smile. The gesture was over in a moment, but its sweet familiarity sent a cool, jelly-like curl through her stomach. He was as frightened and uncomfortable as herself and as glad to see her as she was to see him.

"Hello, Carrie." In spite of his smile, his eyes were bright with uncertainty.

She started to grip the drapery again, caught herself just in time, and clutched her hands behind her. "Hello, Dexter."

He shrugged his shoulders and eyebrows at the same time. "May I come in?"

"I. . .I'm not certain that would be wise."

"Don't ask me to leave. Please."

The huskiness in his plea made the muscles in her legs melt. She reached behind her, gripping the window sash through the filmy lace undercurtain with both hands to steady herself.

The mustache above his smile was trembling just like her legs, she realized, astonished. Her gaze darted to his eyes, and the pain standing there stark and bare seared her.

"Why—" The word came out of her dry throat like a croak. She swallowed and tried again. "Why are you here?"

He shifted his weight, one hand remaining in his pocket, the other rhythmically bouncing the bowler off his thigh. "I hoped ye might reconsider."

"Reconsider?"

His gaze darted away and back again. "Reconsider marrying me."

Hope set her heart soaring. "You've changed your mind? You believe in the Lord?"

His lips pressed together until the furrows bracketing them whitened. "No."

Disappointment chased away the hope in her chest. "Then—"

He crossed the room swiftly, his steps thudding dully in the thick Brussels carpet. He tossed the bowler to one side, not watching whether it landed on the round table he passed.

He stopped directly in front of her, so close she would bump his chest if she swayed ever so slightly. His gaze burned into hers, longing mingled with pain. "I was not knowing it was possible for a man to hurt as much as I've been hurting over ye." He gave her his silly, crooked grin. It didn't erase the glaze in his eyes. The knowledge only hurt her more. "Hurt more than the time a hurler hit me arm with the ball when I was batsman. Broke it. The arm, not the bat." The grin slipped slowly away. "Don't be turning me away again, girleen."

His low-spoken words trembled in the small space between them. He opened his arms slowly, but didn't move to take her into them. She realized he was waiting for her to choose. The fresh smell of soap and manly cologne and starched shirt wrapped around her. Her gaze caught tight in his.

She swayed slightly toward him. In a moment his arms were around her, her cheek pressed against the weave of his linen jacket. She'd fought the desire to be in his embrace for months, and his arms felt incredibly good.

One of his hands slid to the back of her neck. "I love you, Carrie!"

Tears burned her eyes, and she pressed her cheek tighter against his chest. How was she going to make herself walk away from him again? Last time had been difficult enough. Now that she'd allowed him to hold her. . .now that she'd allowed herself to be held, she corrected silently, how was she going to walk away from this man who made her feel more wonderful than anyone else?

She took a shaky breath. "I love you, too, but, the Lord. . ."

His arms tightened. Was he afraid she would push herself away from him?

"My beliefs haven't changed. I'd do most anything to please ye, but not lie to God, or about believing in Him. But I'll go to church with ye, and I'll never stop ye from doing what ye think is right."

If he goes to church, surely Thou canst speak to him, Lord. If I don't marry him, he might continue to stay away from church, and Thou might never reach him. Am I to be Thy way of bringing him to Thee? A sliver of unease slipped through her at her argument. It didn't stand up well against the Bible's admonition to believers not to marry unbelievers.

His hands closed lightly but firmly about her shoulders, and he pushed her slightly away until their gazes could meet. She smiled and touched his cheek with trembling fingertips. "In my heart, I am already your wife, my love."

Joy followed unbelief in his eyes. The grin she loved spread wide beneath the red-tinged mustache. She longed for him to kiss her, but he glanced away again, then back. "Is it certain ye are?"

She nodded eagerly.

One arm held her close, the rough, blunt fingertips of the other tracing her cheek with a gentleness that awed her. "I can hardly be waiting to marry ye, girleen." The words were a whisper against her lips, and she thanked him with a kiss.

Doubt rumbled like distant thunder in her mind and chest, but she pushed it away, rejoicing in the wonder and beauty of Dexter's love.

Chapter Seven

"You're going to marry that. . .that. . .*base ballist?*" Reverend Chambers bolted from the cavernous comfort of the upholstered chair in his study, his black coat trembling on his sparse frame. Thin black brows broken with a spattering of gray hairs arched above the eyes so like Carrie's, eyes which glowered at her, almost shaking her determination.

Lifting her chin, Carrie attempted to return his gaze evenly. She must make him see there was no chance he could sway her; he mustn't suspect the way she quailed inside at his displeasure. She forced her lips into a smile, hoping her father wouldn't notice their propensity to quiver. "Yes, aren't you fortunate? Think how popular you'll be with the men in the congregation as the father-in-law of one of the country's best base ballists."

The expression on his narrow face was anything but pleased. "Players of Base Ball are hardly considered men of high moral or *spiritual* character."

Carrie moved to the mantle, forcing a bounce into her step, and unnecessarily rearranged the silver candle holders to keep from facing him for a moment. "Isn't it wonderful Dexter is the exception?"

His snort of disgust would have done a horse justice.

Carrie squeezed her eyes tightly together. This discussion was going worse than she'd anticipated. With a quick prayer, she turned about to face him again, her fingers linked loosely behind her. She kept her voice light with an effort. "You can't deceive me, Father. I know you like Dexter. I've heard you tell Grant what a fine man he is."

"Not fine enough to marry my daughter." Anger increased the craggy effect of his features, making him look cruel, belying the kind nature she knew lay in his heart.

She tipped the corners of her lips with the teasing smile she'd used to win her way from him innumerable times in the past. "You would think that of any man I wished to marry."

His glower didn't weaken. "What about Emmet Wilson?"

Her gaze dropped to the floor. *Emmet*. She hated the way this would hurt him. She hated the shame and disgrace that wormed its way through her chest whenever her conscience reminded her of her disloyalty to him. Still, even if she didn't marry Dexter, she couldn't marry Emmet. Not now.

She swallowed the painful lump in her throat that had traitorously absorbed her voice. "Would it be a kindness to marry Emmet when I lo. . .when I love Dexter?" Silly how difficult it was to express her love for a man to her father.

His frown deepened, the thin brows meeting above the long, narrow nose. The anger in his eyes faded into confusion and sorrow while his gaze searched her face. He rested slender hands on her shoulders. "There can be no lasting happiness for you with a man who doesn't share your love for God."

His voice was rough with concern for her, and she f
"Until Dexter, I never thought it possible I could love a m
beliefs. Now, I can't imagine spending the rest of my life

The hands slipped from her shoulders, and he wipe
though attempting to wipe the last few minutes from
given us laws and commandments only to show us how i
guides to a life of joy, peace, and contentment. He warn
who don't share our faith because He knows the sorrows
How can there be joy ahead for you if you try to follow
lowing his own desires? How can you be one?"

"I tried refusing him, Father. When Dexter asked me
I insisted I couldn't because he doesn't trust in Christ. I
marry Emmet. I thought if I tried to do as God wished
love for Dexter and increase my love for Emmet. Bu
every waking moment since walking away from Dex
returned yesterday and asked me again to be his wife."

His lips thinned into a determined line. "You'll kn
marry him."

Slowly she reached for his hands. He allowed her to ho
ing the pressure of her fingers. "You've always told me G
you mean He can do anything but change Dexter's he
Dexter a believer?"

"You know God allows each person to decide for him
follow Him."

She started to argue, but he cut in quickly.

"If a man is drowning, it is easier for the drowning m
rescuer down with him than it is for the would-be rescu
man. It is the same when we share our lives with those
It is easier to be enticed from the Lord's way than to c
low Him."

She dropped his hands, took a deep breath, and threw
don't intend to allow Dexter to drown, whatever the ri
your blessing, but I expect you will not allow yourself to

Sadness carved itself deeply into his face, buried itse
eyes. "I cannot."

Her chest burned with frustration, fury, despair. "I sha
your blessing, then. I shall love him into God's kingdom
I'll not spend the rest of my days without him."

❧

Her father wasn't nearly as formidable to face as Emmet

Carrie hadn't seen much of him since her family m

Chapter Seven

"You're going to marry that. . .that. . .*base ballist?*" Reverend Chambers bolted from the cavernous comfort of the upholstered chair in his study, his black coat trembling on his sparse frame. Thin black brows broken with a spattering of gray hairs arched above the eyes so like Carrie's, eyes which glowered at her, almost shaking her determination.

Lifting her chin, Carrie attempted to return his gaze evenly. She must make him see there was no chance he could sway her; he mustn't suspect the way she quailed inside at his displeasure. She forced her lips into a smile, hoping her father wouldn't notice their propensity to quiver. "Yes, aren't you fortunate? Think how popular you'll be with the men in the congregation as the father-in-law of one of the country's best base ballists."

The expression on his narrow face was anything but pleased. "Players of Base Ball are hardly considered men of high moral or *spiritual* character."

Carrie moved to the mantle, forcing a bounce into her step, and unnecessarily rearranged the silver candle holders to keep from facing him for a moment. "Isn't it wonderful Dexter is the exception?"

His snort of disgust would have done a horse justice.

Carrie squeezed her eyes tightly together. This discussion was going worse than she'd anticipated. With a quick prayer, she turned about to face him again, her fingers linked loosely behind her. She kept her voice light with an effort. "You can't deceive me, Father. I know you like Dexter. I've heard you tell Grant what a fine man he is."

"Not fine enough to marry my daughter." Anger increased the craggy effect of his features, making him look cruel, belying the kind nature she knew lay in his heart.

She tipped the corners of her lips with the teasing smile she'd used to win her way from him innumerable times in the past. "You would think that of any man I wished to marry."

His glower didn't weaken. "What about Emmet Wilson?"

Her gaze dropped to the floor. *Emmet.* She hated the way this would hurt him. She hated the shame and disgrace that wormed its way through her chest whenever her conscience reminded her of her disloyalty to him. Still, even if she didn't marry Dexter, she couldn't marry Emmet. Not now.

She swallowed the painful lump in her throat that had traitorously absorbed her voice. "Would it be a kindness to marry Emmet when I lo. . .when I love Dexter?" Silly how difficult it was to express her love for a man to her father.

His frown deepened, the thin brows meeting above the long, narrow nose. The anger in his eyes faded into confusion and sorrow while his gaze searched her face. He rested slender hands on her shoulders. "There can be no lasting happiness for you with a man who doesn't share your love for God."

His voice was rough with concern for her, and she fought against its effect. "Until Dexter, I never thought it possible I could love a man who didn't share my beliefs. Now, I can't imagine spending the rest of my life without him."

The hands slipped from her shoulders, and he wiped them over his face as though attempting to wipe the last few minutes from existence. "God hasn't given us laws and commandments only to show us how imperfect we are, but as guides to a life of joy, peace, and contentment. He warns us not to marry those who don't share our faith because He knows the sorrows that lie along that path. How can there be joy ahead for you if you try to follow God and Dexter is following his own desires? How can you be one?"

"I tried refusing him, Father. When Dexter asked me to marry him last May, I insisted I couldn't because he doesn't trust in Christ. I told him I was going to marry Emmet. I thought if I tried to do as God wished, He would remove my love for Dexter and increase my love for Emmet. But He didn't. I've hurt every waking moment since walking away from Dexter last May, until he returned yesterday and asked me again to be his wife."

His lips thinned into a determined line. "You'll know greater pain if you marry him."

Slowly she reached for his hands. He allowed her to hold them without returning the pressure of her fingers. "You've always told me God can do anything. Did you mean He can do anything but change Dexter's heart, anything but make Dexter a believer?"

"You know God allows each person to decide for himself whether to love and follow Him."

She started to argue, but he cut in quickly.

"If a man is drowning, it is easier for the drowning man to pull his would-be rescuer down with him than it is for the would-be rescuer to save the drowning man. It is the same when we share our lives with those who don't follow God. It is easier to be enticed from the Lord's way than to convince another to follow Him."

She dropped his hands, took a deep breath, and threw her shoulders back. "I don't intend to allow Dexter to drown, whatever the risk to me. I'd hoped for your blessing, but I expect you will not allow yourself to give it."

Sadness carved itself deeply into his face, buried itself in the caverns of his eyes. "I cannot."

Her chest burned with frustration, fury, despair. "I shall marry Dexter without your blessing, then. I shall love him into God's kingdom myself, if I must. But I'll not spend the rest of my days without him."

Her father wasn't nearly as formidable to face as Emmet.

Carrie hadn't seen much of him since her family moved to St. Louis. He'd spent the summer in Ridgeville, their hometown, working in his father's store. They'd corresponded regularly, however, and Emmet had occasionally visited.

He'd arrive in St. Louis this afternoon and would be staying with Carrie's family and leaving on the train Monday morning for his last year at the university. He and Carrie had planned this evening for a long time: dinner at the magnificent Lindell Hotel. Emmet had suggested the Planter's, where she had eaten with Dexter, but Carrie couldn't bear the thought of the memories it would raise. Not that she told Emmet her reason for wishing to eat elsewhere, of course. And easy-going Emmet never suspected a thing.

She found the evening most trying. If she told him of Dexter at the beginning of the evening, the entire night would be ruined for him. But she could think of nothing but the truth she must eventually reveal, and she was unaccustomedly quiet.

The parsonage was a lovely home, built of stone, with a wide porch along the front and sides. A number of cushion-filled wicker chairs were scattered about the porch, with a large wicker swing at one end of the front portion. It was to the swing Emmet led her when they arrived back from dinner.

Light from the silk-shaded parlor lamp shone mellow through the huge window, which was topped with colorful leaded glass. There was enough light for her to see his face clearly in spite of the late hour. A few houses down the street, a family was on their own porch, enjoying the mild evening, singing softly to the accompaniment of a guitar.

Emmet kept her hand in his when they sat down in the swing.

He shifted to face her, pushed the swing into rhythmic movement with his foot, and briefly touched his lips to her gloved fingers. His eyes smiled at her over their joined hands. "The music makes a nice background for a man to say good-bye to his favorite girl."

She noted his narrow lips, so different from Dexter's. Emmet had kissed her numerous times through the years, but never with the passion in Dexter's kisses. Of course, one couldn't marry a man because of the way he kissed!

She tucked her chin against the lacy breast of her dress, avoiding his gaze. "I. . . there's something I must tell you."

"Must be pretty serious. The last time you avoided looking at me, you told me you'd freed my pet frog."

The memory brought a welcome, releasing laugh, and she met his gaze with merry accusation. "Frogs aren't meant to live in boxes, even to keep ten-year-old boys happy."

He shook his head. "Ten years old. Seems like we've known each other forever."

The laughter died. She looked sharply away. "Yes."

She suddenly realized that she would miss his comfortable company. There would be no more evenings of talking and laughing together. No more discussions of the Bible or friendly arguments over the meaning of certain passages. No more times of prayer together for each other's needs or those of friends or family. She had been acutely aware that her marriage to Dexter would hurt Emmet; she hadn't realized until this moment that she would miss him, the same as she would miss Grant if he disappeared suddenly from her world.

His soft, tapered fingers touched her cheek, urging her to face him. "Darling, what's wrong?"

She looked into the face as familiar to her as her own and batted away the tears in her eyes. "I don't want to hurt you." The words were barely a whisper.

His eyebrows met in a puzzled frown, and his hand slipped from her cheek.

She took a deep breath, wringing the dainty handkerchief in her lap with both hands. "Do you remember Dexter Riley?"

He nodded. "Of course. Grant's friend, the one who plays on the St. Louis Browns."

"I. . .I've promised to marry him."

The music down the street filled the silence. The ache in her chest and throat grew to mammoth proportions. Wouldn't he ever respond?

Finally he rubbed a free hand over his chin. "When you give a man news, it's a headliner."

"I'm sorry." Never had an apology seemed less adequate.

"What about us? What of all the times we talked about our plans for the future?"

"You. . .never actually *asked* me to marry you."

"I presumed from the way we talked, the way we kept company, that you knew my intentions and wanted the same thing."

She stared at her hands, miserable in her guilt. She had wanted the same thing until she met Dexter. Emmet likely wouldn't find the knowledge comforting.

He took a deep breath. "I don't suppose it would do any good to ask you to marry me now?"

She caught her bottom lip between her teeth and shook her head.

"I was afraid of that." He leaned back, studying her face as though he'd never seen her before. . .or was he memorizing it from fear of never seeing her again? Guilt squirmed through her at the confusion in his amber eyes.

"I wish there were a way I could marry Dexter without hurting you."

His narrow lips twisted in the first sarcastic smile she'd seen on his face since he was fourteen. "It doesn't work that way, darl. . .it doesn't work that way."

The music stopped. Voices drifted down to them. A door squeaked open and slammed shut. Then only the swing's creak filled the awful chasm between them.

Her chest felt as though it must burst. If she hurt this bad, what must Emmet be experiencing?

"I can't imagine not having you in my life, Carrie."

"I feel the same."

A wry, harsh laugh broke from his lips and tore through her. "I doubt you feel *exactly* the same."

The swing continued its back and forth journey, going nowhere. But their lives had changed course, Carrie thought.

"This Riley, is he a Christian?"

She shook her head, not daring to meet his gaze.

The swing stopped.

"Surely you aren't going to marry a man who doesn't follow the Lord?"

"I love him. I believe God will use me to show him the truth."

He grabbed her shoulders, turning her to face him. "You know you can't count on that."

"I must."

"Don't do this. Don't marry me if you don't wish to, but don't marry a man who doesn't share your faith."

The desperation in his voice touched her more than anything had all evening. In spite of his own pain, he was concerned for her happiness. "It will work out, I promise you."

He picked up his wide-brimmed bowler from the seat beside him. "That's something you *can't* promise, and you know it."

Chapter Eight

1884

Carrie slipped out of bed and opened the pale blue velvet draperies to allow July's morning sunshine to spill into the room through the lace undercurtain.

Dexter groaned and squeezed his closed eyes tighter to shut out all trace of day.

She grinned down at him, trailing the deep lace ruffle at her wrist lightly along his cheek. He tried to dodge it, his eyes still closed, then brushed feebly at it. Finally he opened his eyes, staring at her with an unfocused gaze.

"Good morning, sleepyhead."

A slow smile spread over his face. "You even look good in the morning, Mrs. Riley."

"Irish blarney! You can't even see yet; your eyes are still glazed over with sleep!" But his flattery made her feel special, just the same, she admitted to herself. She could hardly believe they'd been married almost two years!

"That's not sleep, me love. It's your beauty blinding me."

She laughed softly and stood. "More of your blarney; but I like it."

He grasped her hand. "Where are you going?"

"To dress, start breakfast, then wake our son and dress him for church."

He pulled her back down beside him, running his hands over her night robe's torchon lace sleeves. "Couldn't all that wait awhile?"

She allowed him one sweet, lazy kiss before pulling away. "If it waits, we'll be late to church. Nine-month-old boys don't dress themselves, you know. Now don't you dare go back to sleep. You need to prepare for church, too."

She was almost at the door before he said, "I don't think I'll be going to church today."

Dismay swept through her. She turned to look at him, not speaking.

"I'm tired, Carrie. Train didn't get in until four this morning. Couldn't sleep a lick on it last night, with the wheels clacking and the box rocking. The clubmates were noisy, too, celebrating yesterday's win. And we have to play this afternoon."

She wanted to beg him to come, but she knew what he said was true. He'd be too exhausted for today's match if he didn't get more sleep. Besides, when the Browns were in town, he'd been true to his promise to attend church with her since they married. Missing services this one time wouldn't change anything.

"All right, dear." She tried to swallow her disappointment, but couldn't.

Two hours later Carrie and Benjamin slipped into the pew beside her mother and Grant. She smiled and whispered hellos to them, uncomfortably aware of Dexter's absence. She knew her family and others in the congregation were accustomed to seeing her and Benjamin attend services without Dexter when the

St. Louis Browns had matches out of town. But she knew, too, that people were aware of the club's schedule and knew he was playing in town today. It left her feeling vulnerable.

The plain, plumpish, gray-haired woman across the aisle gave her a pleasant nod in greeting, and Carrie returned it self-consciously. She'd always pitied devoted Mrs. Hannah Kratz, who attended every service alone. She couldn't recall ever seeing Hannah's husband attend, and her children seldom accompanied her now that they were grown.

After the service, she explained quickly to her parents and Grant why Dexter wasn't with her. She smiled and tried to act nonchalant, as though it were perfectly reasonable that he'd stayed away, and it didn't bother her a whit.

She almost convinced herself until Hannah stopped to greet her. Sweet Hannah, with her soft smile and gentle manner, only increased Carrie's discomfort today.

The older woman rested a wrinkled, worn hand on the soft yellow silk covering Carrie's forearm. "Good morning, Mrs. Riley. How is that handsome husband of yours?"

Carrie forced a smile. "Fine, Mrs. Kratz. He didn't arrive in town until early this morning, and he needed sleep before playing this afternoon." Why had she felt compelled to offer an excuse for him?

Tiny Hannah nodded and patted Carrie's arm. *I wish she'd stop smiling that sugary sweet smile*, Carrie thought, irritated. Guilt immediately flooded her.

"I'll be praying for him. One of these days the Lord will get hold of him, you'll see."

Carrie adjusted Benjy in her arms so Hannah had to remove her hand. "Dexter will be back in church in two weeks," she assured the diminutive, wrinkled woman.

Hannah only nodded and kept smiling. "Come see me sometime, my dear. We church widows must stick together."

Carrie couldn't control the shiver of distaste that ran through her. "Church widows" was the congregation's term for the women whose husbands didn't often accompany them to services. *To think when I was single I pitied such women. I never thought I'd be among them. Of course,* she hastened to reassure herself, *I'm not truly one of them. Dexter attends when possible.*

At least, he attended in body. He didn't believe in God yet, but that would come eventually.

She tried to ignore the fear that wriggled through her. The other "church widows" were younger than Hannah; their attendance without their husbands wasn't as disturbing. Like Dexter, the men likely had many years ahead of them to come to the Lord.

But Mr. Kratz was in his late sixties. Carrie didn't like to think about how long Hannah had been praying for his salvation.

Benjy stirred impatiently in her arms, and she gave him her attention, relieved to have her thoughts drawn in a more pleasant direction.

But a minute later Hannah was at her side once more. "I almost forgot, dear. A group of us are beginning a quilt for the missionary. We hoped you'd join us. We'll be meeting Tuesday evenings at my home. You're welcome to bring your son."

Why not? With Dexter out of town so often, the evenings were lonely, even with Benjy for company. "I'll be glad to join you."

Maybe if she became more involved in church projects, Dexter would realize the importance of church, she thought, watching Hannah hurry down the aisle with her bouncy waddle. She already spent Wednesday evenings at choir practice, Thursday afternoons at the women's Bible study, and she taught the children's Sunday school. But evidently that wasn't enough, because Dexter hadn't seen yet how wonderful it was to be involved in the church.

Maybe this fall, when Base Ball was over for the year, things would be different. He would be home every Sunday from November through March. Surely five months of Sundays would be enough to show him the joy of being an active church member. Dexter was not going to be another Mr. Kratz. Not if her example could change him.

Dexter leaned against the door frame, one hand stuffed in a pocket of his brown flannel trousers, the other holding a cup of coffee. A warm sense of family settled inside him as he looked over the men filling their parlor: Louisville base ballers Tony Mullane and Pete Browning, and the St. Louis Browns' Charlie Comiskey, Pat Deasley, Hugh Nicol, Arlie Latham, Jumbo McGinnis, and Bob Caruthers. Except Comiskey, he was closer to these men than he was to his own brothers, and that was saying something.

He crossed his arms over his tan shirt and brown vest, chuckling at the picture they made: a group of large, rather rowdy men in casual clothes seated on his wife's dainty furniture with its curves and narrow cushions. Their chins all but rested on their knees.

Grant was the only man in the room who wasn't a base baller, and he was apparently enjoying himself just fine. That is, when he wasn't glaring at Amanda, who was flirting outrageously with Pete Browning. What was going on with those two, anyway? Amanda knew Browning was as insincere as a man could get when it came to females.

Had Amanda and Grant had a falling out? Was she just trying to make Carrie's brother jealous? If so, it was his guess she was succeeding better than the National League succeeded in the championship game against the Association this year, which they'd won with a hurrah. He shook his head slightly. He'd thought she had better sense.

Carrie hurried past him with a china plate piled high with slices of buttered pumpkin bread. The spicy odor blended with her flowery perfume in a tempting combination. The loud laughs and buzz of conversation continued among the men while she placed the plate on a round, marble-topped table in the middle of the room. Men grabbed for the food, but the conversation didn't falter for a moment.

He wondered how any man could see Carrie enter a room without giving her his full attention, even if, as now, she was only a month away from having a child. If there was a more beautiful woman on the planet, he'd not met her.

He stopped Carrie on her way past him, smiling down at her. "Stay with me."

He thought for a moment she would refuse, insisting she must be doing something in the kitchen, in the manner women have when there's company about. He was glad when after a moment's hesitation she nodded.

He slipped his arm about her enlarged waist, drawing her close to his side. She rested her weight against him in the familiar manner that always made him feel he hadn't been quite whole without her.

A small sigh slipped from her soft pink lips, and her head touched his shoulder. He pressed a discreet kiss to her temple. "Tired, me love?"

She gave him a little smile, but didn't answer. He supposed she was always tired these days.

"Look!" He nodded toward a pile of blue and red beneath a small table at the end of the rosewood couch. Benjy was sound asleep, his blue-clad bottom up in the air. "How can he sleep with all this noise?"

"I expect he's inherited your hearing abilities. After all, his father thinks the sound of an overflowing ball ground is as soothing as the sound of the river to most people."

He chuckled at her comparison, contentment flowing over him. He had more than any man should expect out of life. A wonderful wife, a strapping son, a vocation that was nearer his heart than anything but his family, and friends enough to fill a parlor. What more could a man want?

"Riley, old man," Browning called over the din to get his attention. "Hear you went east to see Providence play the Mets for the World's Series."

"That's right. Mullane and I went together."

"Is Hoss Radbourne's hurling everything it's talked up to be?"

"And then some. He walked away with the series; his club barely had to help. The hurlers in this room are going to be hard put to keep up with those clubs who use Radbourne's overhand pitch when it's legalized in the Association next season."

Hoots from the Browns' hurlers greeted his statement.

"Riley's right," Mullane agreed. "I plan to spend the winter learning Radbourne's throw. Has a lot more power and speed to it than the underhand toss, as you might guess from his sixty-win season and the way National League batting averages tumbled last year. Suggest you men spend the winter practicing up, too." He grinned. "Unless you don't mind losing to my club, that is."

"And what club might that be by this time next year?" Dexter asked with a laugh. "You were with Louisville two years ago, played with us last year, then turned traitor and moved on to the Toledo Blue Stockings. Never know where you'll show up."

"What's a man to do but move on when he's sampled all the women the town has to offer?" Mullane winked broadly at Amanda, who laughed at him.

"Heard you aren't too popular in Toledo," Charlie offered, his gaze on the slice of pumpkin bread in his big hands. "Heard you stole one of your clubmate's women."

Jeers filled the room.

Mullane's exaggerated shrug lifted his out-of-fashion, threadbare, once-brown shirt. His broad hands spread in a gesture of defeat. "How does a gentleman turn down a lady's attentions? I was tryin' ta avoid hurtin' her feelings."

Guffaws met his claim of innocence.

The others obviously didn't believe Mullane any more than he did, Dexter thought. The scene turned Dexter's stomach as effectually as a drink of sour milk. Tony played as dirty in love as Comiskey played on the ball grounds. In spite of the unwritten code that no player poached on a woman a clubmate was courting, the men here treated the matter as a joke. Most likely the other player and woman involved didn't feel that way.

He liked Mullane as a player and usually enjoyed his company, but not when he was like this. Never did like seeing a man treat women as though they were toys made for men. A number of the players were womanizers, but Mullane and Browning were two of the worst. His glance rested on Amanda's laughing face, flushed with excitement, and uneasiness snaked through him. Was she scheduled to be Mullane's next victim?

"Planning to use the flat-sided bat next season?" Grant asked.

Was Grant trying to change the conversation because he was as uncomfortable as he was himself with the nasty scene that had just played out before them?

Tall, slender club manager Charlie Comiskey shook his head. "With all the changes the leagues are hurling at us this season, sport won't be the same."

Looking at him, Dexter wondered what was ahead for their club with Comiskey leading it. He'd rather liked their last manager, but couldn't blame him for leaving after all the brawling between club members. The former manager had told him he'd "rather tackle a hundred angry water works customers than a solitary St. Louis base baller—especially when the slugger is drunk and in possession of the idea that it is his solemn duty to slug the manager of the nine."

His glance moved among the Browns seated in his parlor: frail-looking Bob Caruthers, the best base-running hurler in the profession, but a ladies' man, to put it delicately; Scottish, fleet-footed Hugh Nicol, with a strength that belied his five-foot-four-inch frame, who thought nothing of incurring his clubmate's wrath by passing them on the basepaths when they'd batted before him; Arlie Latham, a quick, talented player, but with a mouth so foul some of the kranks came to the ball park only to hear him abuse the members of the opposing club; Pat Deasley, talented catcher, but a heavy drinker and envied by his clubmates for his club-high salary; Jumbo McGinnis, a good pitcher and possibly his favorite of the Browns group, a huge boy of twenty with a heart of gold, a family man like himself with a year-old daughter. No angels in the group, but on the field they put aside everything else and pulled together for the glory of the Browns.

He liked each of them, when they weren't drunk or just generally acting like fools, which they did far too often. If they would put their immature tempers and jealousies behind them, the Browns just might make a decent club next year.

"I figure hitting and kicking's as much a part of the sport as pitching, striking, and catching," Comiskey said slowly. "You might all want to keep that in mind, especially with the changes in hurling and other rules. Me, I don't aim to be party to a losing ball club."

Discomfort walked through the room, leaving silence behind. *So that's what it will be like with Comiskey in charge*, Dexter thought. His words were a warning to the Browns, he knew. Those here would be expected to pass the advice to their clubmates: Win at any price. Well, here was one player who wouldn't play by that motto, even if it cost him his position.

His glance shifted to Carrie. She was staring at Charlie with her lovely lips open slightly, too stunned for once to comment. An uncomfortable thought startled him. He had a wife and child to support and another child on the way; he couldn't be careless with his position. He'd have to perform better than ever to avoid being forced into cheap plays to keep his berth on the club.

"Say." Browning pitched his voice loud enough to drown out all the kranks in Sportsman's Park, as usual, and the entire room gave him their attention.

"What do you think about those Sabbatarians? They've been out strong this year. Think they might get Sunday ball canceled?"

"Eastern teams would like that," Dexter replied, "since most of their hometowns have laws against playing on Sundays. They end up in matches away from home on Sundays." The topic of Sunday ball made him a little uneasy. He hadn't been to church with Carrie much in the last few months, and he didn't like the guilt he felt when the topic was broached.

"Von der Ahe calls kranks 'fans' for their fanatical devotion to Base Ball. Appears to me the term more aptly applies to the Sabbatarians," someone volunteered.

Mullane chuckled. "Did you hear about the Columbus-Indianapolis match the Sabbatarians pushed the police to break up? Police arrived at the grounds, all right, but waited to watch the Columbus Buckeyes win over the Brooklyn Grays before arresting both clubs."

Dexter felt Carrie stiffen and a weary dread rolled over him. Couldn't she keep her religious battles out of sight for one night? No sense riling up the company. Not that he expected for a moment she would consider that.

She didn't. As soon as the guffaws over Mullane's story died down enough for her to be heard, she said, "It's against the law to play Sunday ball in Columbus, and the club members and their owners well knew it. Besides, a little more church and a little less Base Ball wouldn't hurt any of you or the spectators who spend their Sundays drinking beer and watching you play."

Comiskey gave her a saucy grin. "No law against Sunday ball in this town, but sounds like you're planning to organize a division of the Sabbatarians here anyway."

Eyes flashing, she crossed her arms over the top of her baby-large stomach. "Perhaps I shall."

The room screamed with silence. The men stared first at her, then at their hands. Dexter swallowed a groan. Sunday ball was one of the Association's biggest draws. The Sabbatarians threatened the livelihood of every player in this room, but she'd never understand that.

Grant tossed a crumpled bit of newspaper at Comiskey, grinning when the man looked up at him. "Guess nobody warned you our father is a minister."

Comiskey gave him an uncharacteristically sheepish smile. "No, no one did."

The others gave nervous laughs and began conversing again.

Dexter let out a sigh of relief. All he needed was to have volatile Von der Ahe hear a rumor about Carrie organizing a chapter of the Sabbatarians in Der Boss's backyard! Carrie wouldn't need to worry then about Sunday matches keeping him from church. He'd be tossed out on his ear and not be playing any day of the week. Not be paid either. W*onder whether her religious fervor would disappear when there wasn't any food for us or the little ones!*

The atmosphere never regained its former comfort, and half an hour later Mullane convinced the others to adjourn to Von der Ahe's saloon near the Sportsman's Park for the remainder of the evening "since Grandmother Riley doesn't believe in servin' men's drinks in his house and refuses to pay the bill at his brother's saloon."

The comment was accompanied by a friendly grin, as references to his refusal to drink always were. The other base ballers seldom called him Grandmother, Parson, or Deacon, as they did other nondrinking players. He never preached at them to give up the bottle. He knew they were glad enough for his sober state when their legs wouldn't support them any longer and they needed assistance getting to their beds. He'd played the role of caretaker for each man in this room except Grant. It wasn't a role he relished, but a man had to be loyal to his clubmates.

Alarm rang in his brain when Browning tucked Amanda's hand in the crook of his arm. Surely he wasn't planning to take her along on a drinking party!

Anger rolled over him. He could hear it in his tight voice. "We'll see Amanda home." He drew her away from Browning's side.

Pete looked from him to Amanda in surprise. "Isn't that for her to decide?"

Dexter usually didn't allow himself to show anger toward his player friends, but he deliberately made an exception this time and knew his eyes were speaking more plainly than his low-pitched words. "She's my sister, and it's my home."

Browning stared at him for a moment, then shrugged. Turning to the sputtering Amanda, he took her hand and touched his lips to her fingers. "May I take you for a buggy ride tomorrow?"

"You may take me with you now." She tugged at her arm, trying to loose it from Dexter's grasp.

He only gripped it harder and whispered against her hair, "Don't act the fool. These men have their choice of women. It's those whose behavior demands they be treated like ladies that impress them."

He was relieved to see from her expression that his warning had the desired effect, although she was obviously still angry at his interference.

When the others had filed out, Grant said to her, "I'll take you home."

Her anger rippled out once more. "Ye'll do no sech thing! Dexter can see me home."

Dexter looked from one to the other, puzzled. The two of them had been wildly in love from the day they met. He knew his sister's temper well, but he'd never seen her turn it toward Grant. What had happened to set the two of them at odds?

Grant's usually easy-going face was stiff with repressed fury. "There's no need to take Dex from his family just because you're too proud to put up with my presence for a few minutes. He has little enough time with Carrie and Benjy, what with being out of town so often."

His argument apparently convinced her, for Amanda agreed, with obvious reluctance, to ride with him.

Watching them depart, Dexter braced a shoulder against the tall porch pillar. "Wonder what that's about?"

She shook her head. "I don't know, but surely they'll resolve it. They are so much in love."

Dexter shifted his weight and slipped his arms about her waist from behind, smiling against her hair when his hands would barely touch. He adjusted them slightly until they rested above her own hands, above the exciting lump where her stomach usually existed. He nuzzled her neck, then whispered in her ear, "Grant is no more in love with her than I am with you. Not even close."

Her hand rested on his cheek. The softness of her skin against his sun-roughened face amazed him as it always did and sent a thrill running along his nerves.

She sighed sweetly. "I needed to hear that tonight. I don't feel very lovable when I'm this big with the child."

"Our baby only makes you more lovable." He touched his lips to the palm of her hand at his cheek.

"Tell me how much you love me, Dexter."

He could hear the smile in her voice. "My love is too. . .too immense to be expressed in mere words."

Her laugh was filled with relaxed, carefree joy. "That is pure blarney, Mr. Riley. Don't think you can escape answering so easily."

"My love for you is no blarney, me love." Blarney came easy. Important things were difficult to express.

Besides, women asked the silliest things. How could a person explain how much he loved someone? Didn't promising to spend his life with her show her the depth of his love? What could he possibly say to expand on that?

"Look!" She pointed at the sky. "A shooting star!"

They watched in silence while it flared and faded.

"I'm still waiting."

He'd thought she'd forgotten. Wished she had. He could no more explain his love than explain the stars.

The stars. "Can you count the stars, girleen?"

"Of course not." She laughed. "And stop trying to change the subject."

"I'm not. That sky full of stars is how much I love you, but that one shooting star is all the love I'm able to express."

She brushed her cheek against his shoulder, and he liked the softness of her hair moving against his chin. "What a beautiful thing to say, Dexter! But. . ."

"But what?"

"If you love me so much. . ."

"Yes, me love?"

"Why do you no longer attend church when you know how important it is to me?"

The sweetness of the moment fled. "One thing has nothing to do with the other."

"Doesn't it?" She turned to face him, pulling out of his arms. "Before we married, you promised to attend church with me whenever you were home on Sundays, but since last July, you've attended only twice."

He stuffed his hands in his trouser pockets. "I feel like a hypocrite when I go. I can't sing those songs and repeat all those phrases everyone is supposed to say about what they believe. Makes me uncomfortable, like I'm lying."

"I'm uncomfortable, too, attending without my husband. Some members have told me they are praying for you! They think you are backslidden."

"What does that mean?"

"That you aren't following the Lord anymore."

"Well, I'm not. What's so embarrassing about them thinking the truth? Is that why you're upset? You're worried about what people will think?"

"No! I'm upset because the most important thing in the world to me is for you to love the Lord."

He dragged a sigh from deep inside himself. He was so tired of arguing about his faith, or more accurately, his lack of it. "Ye've known from the beginning that I'm not even knowing whether I believe in Him. Nothing has changed."

Her eyes were large, pooled with tears that made him feel as though someone had carved up his insides.

"Everything has changed, Dexter. Maybe you don't understand that yet, but it's true. At least when you were attending church, you were hearing God's Word. Now you're refusing to allow God even that little opportunity to convince you He exists and loves you." Tears rolled over her bottom lashes to dribble down her cheeks in accusing little droplets. "Everything has changed," she whispered again.

Benjy's cry startled them. The wail stopped a second, then resumed. He recognized the cry. The boy had awakened and was waiting for someone to come to him.

Carrie brushed past him and hurried into the house.

He dropped down on the top step, disturbing a few crisp leaves that had drifted to the porch, and ran both hands down his face. She was right. Everything had changed. He'd decided he couldn't continue acting like a hypocrite, going to church and talking and laughing with the members of the congregation when he didn't share their faith.

He hadn't expected his marriage to change because of his decision.

Carrie had tried to tell him. Way back when he'd first asked her to marry him. She'd told him the difference in their beliefs would become a wedge between them, driving them apart.

He hadn't believed it. He hadn't thought anything was powerful enough to come between them when he loved her so much. Of all things, how could her faith in a God who was supposed to be Love itself be the thing that came between them?

Of course, she'd say it wasn't her faith, but his lack of it that was the dividing force.

Either way, he didn't like what it was doing to their life together. But what could he do about it? He could hardly order her not to believe in God and wouldn't want to if he could. Her faith meant too much to her. But he couldn't make himself believe, either. He snorted and looked up through autumn-bare branches. How did a man force himself to have faith?

The question left him feeling more hopeless and alone than a rookie hurler facing the league's top club for the first time.

Chapter Nine

Carrie broached the subject of Amanda with Grant a number of times over the next few months. He refused to discuss it.

She was surprised to find Amanda was almost as reticent, since she felt they'd become close friends. "I love him, Carrie," she said in a trembling voice, her green eyes tear-studded, "but he doesn't believe we are right for each other."

When Carrie pressed her, she said she didn't think it proper to say more. "Grant is your brother, and Dexter is mine. I don't wish either of you to feel you must stand for or against me or Grant."

Carrie and Dexter reluctantly respected her stand, hurting for the couple and wishing there was a way to help them find each other again.

Nearly a year passed before Carrie discovered the reason for the couple's division. She'd been telling Grant about the celebration planned in honor of the Browns' winning the pennant.

"Amanda said everyone in the old neighborhood is as excited for Dexter as if he was a member of their own families. She's helping their oldest brother, Frank, plan a special party for him at the Irish Stars tomorrow night."

She hated Dexter's family's events, especially hated when they were held at the Irish Stars saloon, even when Frank arranged for a special streetside restaurant to be set up in front of the establishment, lit with mellow glowing gaslights below a star-sprinkled blue awning in imitation of the city's finest cafes.

She tossed off her preoccupation and glanced at Grant, surprised he hadn't commented. She recognized the guarded look that always came to Grant's eyes at the mention of Dexter's sister and said cautiously, "You never told me why you stopped courting Amanda."

"Didn't I?" He stared straight ahead. His hard voice didn't invite her to continue.

She did so anyway. "I thought the two of you so much in love."

It was a minute before he responded. "You're just a romantic, like most women."

She laid a hand on his forearm, staring silently at him until he looked at her. "I'm not trying to be a busybody. I care about your happiness. It's easy to see she still loves you. You loved her, too. What happened between you?"

She watched his gaze search hers, saw the tick at the corner of his mouth when he decided to answer.

"You and Dexter happened."

Shock bolted through her. She couldn't even get out the question she knew must be showing in every inch of her face.

He rubbed his hand over hers. "I could see things weren't everything they could be between you, in spite of your love for each other. I mean, he hardly ever comes to church. You avoid talking about religious topics when he's around so you won't make him uncomfortable. All our lives it's been normal to talk about spiritual things, remember?"

She nodded slowly.

"Sometimes I. . .I feel guilty for introducing you to Dexter. Remember how you and Emmet and I would get into friendly arguments about Scripture passages or pray together for each other? We don't do that with Dex."

She stared at the black-and-white, four-in-hand necktie above his black, three-button cutaway coat. She didn't want him to see her eyes. She longed desperately for the intimacy of sharing her spiritual life with Dexter, but hadn't realized anyone but Hannah knew how she felt, least of all Grant.

"Amanda and I couldn't share that either." His voice had softened. Cautiously, she raised her lashes to search his gaze. A sad little smile sat on his lips. "I tried to talk with her about the Lord, but she didn't want to hear about my faith. She doesn't believe in God any more than Dexter does."

"I'm sorry."

"I'm sorry, too. I don't believe Amanda and I could have much of a life together without sharing our faith. But mostly, I wish she knew the peace that comes from trusting God, and I'm afraid for her that she might never let herself experience it."

His eyes looked ancient, and the acceptance of continual pain she saw there caused her chest to burn with empathy. She knew that particular pain; the same pain she'd lived with through three years of marriage waiting for Dexter to choose to believe in God.

"I've been courting Phoebe Wilson since opening my law practice in Riverton last spring."

"Phoebe Wilson?"

He nodded.

"Why haven't you told me before?"

"Wanted to wait until I was certain I'd continue seeing her, what with her being Emmet's sister and all."

"And are you certain?"

He nodded again, smartly. "I've decided to ask her to marry me."

"M–marry you?" Quiet Phoebe with the pale brown hair and reserved nature? She was as different from sparkling Amanda as the moon from the sun. Not that she wasn't pleasant, but Carrie couldn't imagine her brother looking at her with love glowing in his eyes the way it did when he looked at Amanda.

He grinned. "Cheer up. She may not have me."

"As if any woman with sense would turn you down," she championed him. "But. . .are you certain. . . ?"

"I care deeply for her, if that's what you're asking."

"As much as you love Amanda?"

It was a moment before he replied. "Not in precisely the same manner, but then, does anyone care for two people in exactly the same way? Besides, love is more than. . .emotions. Phoebe and I can have a good life together. I'll devote myself to her."

But would he spend his life with her missing Amanda? Her chest and throat burned with the thought of a future for him without the woman he truly loved.

However, it was painful, too, living with Dexter when they didn't share the bond of faith. Grant apparently was looking at the possibility of both pains and choosing the one least difficult for him.

Fear and despair twisted together, joined cruel strength, and constricted her heart. Things had changed between her and Dexter in the last year or so. The joy had been replaced with tension. Sometimes she even wondered whether Dexter still loved her.

Perhaps Grant had made the wiser choice.

"Quite a day! St. Louis is batty about you Browns!"

Dexter grinned his agreement of Tony Mullane's comment as they followed Carrie, Benjy, and the neighbor boy, Joey, into the house. Hadn't stopped grinning all day, he admitted to himself. Same way yesterday, when they arrived back in the city on the special train decorated with flags and the huge banner emblazoned "St. Louis Browns, Champions 1885." Half the population had been waiting at the depot to congratulate them.

"They deserve the attention, after the way they've played their hearts out for Mr. Von der Ahe this year."

Carrie's fierce statement surprised him and warmed him all the way through. He'd been afraid they were growing apart this last year, and he hadn't known how to stop it. Sometimes he'd even wondered whether she still cared for him.

He'd thought for a while she was simply worn out from the baby, but Margaret was almost ten months old now.

Perhaps it was his fault, this distancing. He knew he'd put up some barriers against her constant pestering to get him to believe.

When he'd asked before they married whether she was embarrassed by his vocation as a base baller, she'd insisted she wasn't. Something had changed. He was certain she was embarrassed by him now. Maybe when he completed his degree, put Base Ball behind him, and became a counselor at law, she'd not find their marriage distasteful.

He'd been celebrating with the club and the kranks for two days and two nights, but she was the only one with whom he truly wanted to celebrate—at least, he wanted to celebrate with the woman she'd been when they married.

He watched her attempting without much success to collect the lads' jackets and hats. The little tikes were still excited about the exhibition game and Buffalo Bill's Wild West Show they'd seen at Statesman's Park that afternoon. Von der Ahe had gone all out to celebrate their pennant win. All the way home, the boys had been going back and forth between playing cowboys and base ballers. At that, he reflected, cowboys were probably the only men who led a life as independent and free of restrictions as base ballers.

In spite of the boys' chatter, the house felt empty without little Margaret. He'd be glad when she was home from Carrie's parents' tomorrow.

"Mr. Riley."

Dexter looked down to see frail-looking, six-year-old Joey staring up at him solemnly. *If he were a puppy, he'd be the runt of the litter*, he thought irrelevantly. "Have a good time today?"

A smile filled the skinny face. "Oh, yes, Mr. Riley! It was the best day of my entire life!"

"Mine, too." He glanced across the room at Carrie, still trying to relieve Benjy of his jacket. "Well, almost." Nothing compared to the day he met Carrie, except maybe the day she first said she loved him.

"Mr. Riley, could you teach me ta be a base baller?"

Mullane shouted with laughter. "Have a mighty bit of growin' ta do before ya can be a base baller!"

Dexter shoved an elbow in Mullane's side. "Don't mind him. He's just jealous of you 'cause he's so tall he has to look down at almost everyone else on the planet. You don't have to be tall to start learning how to play. I started playing right about your age."

"Really?"

"Just with the neighbor kids, of course."

Joey's thin eyebrows met. "Oh. The other kids won't let me play. They say I'm too small."

"Tell you what. You come over every day I'm in town, and I'll practice with you. After I've taught you a few things, I bet the others will be fighting over which club you join."

"Wow! Thanks, Mr. Riley!"

The men sat in the parlor chatting companionably while Carrie settled the boys into bed. She'd been wise to tell Joey's mother he could stay overnight with them, considering what a long day it turned out to be.

She joined them in the parlor later, and he got a sinking feeling in his stomach when he saw her frown at the fat cigar clenched in Mullane's lips. He knew she didn't care for the odor, but he was so glad Mullane wasn't drinking today that he wasn't about to complain about the cigar.

He was relieved when she didn't mention it, either, but simply offered them coffee and cookies. His Base Ball friends and even his brother, Frank, seldom visited at their home anymore. He couldn't blame them. He'd observed their discomfort at his wife's caustic remarks concerning Sunday ball and drinking among kranks and players. Carrie had stopped suggesting dinner parties involving his friends and family, other than Amanda, whom she still welcomed. Besides, her afternoons and evenings were so full of church activities, there wasn't much time available to entertain friends.

He'd come to dread the pinched, prim look about her lips, the martyr-attitude she wore like a funeral dress when around his favorite acquaintances.

He studied Mullane, who was reliving an especially difficult play made during the match that day. Drinking was beginning to take its toll. Tony's stomach was a little too large and round for his tall frame. Puffy bags of flesh beneath his eyes and a florid complexion marred the famed good looks.

Why did so many men refuse to recognize the cost they paid for what they considered enjoyment? He counted too many of his friends among that group. Grant was one of the few who didn't drink or womanize. Of course, his strong faith kept him from such things.

His attention was distracted finally at Mullane's mention of a wager he'd made. When Carrie returned with refreshments, they were laughing so hard they were holding their sides.

"What is so humorous?"

"Fresh Arlie," Dexter managed to choke out.

She wrinkled her nose in distaste. "That awful third baseman who is always in trouble for his foul language?"

"The same," Mullane confirmed cheerfully.

"Did you see the race before the exhibition game?" Dexter asked. "Arlie was sure no one in either major league could run faster than himself, that he put up a challenge to pay any player who could outrun him."

Mullane pulled the cigar from his lips. "It was a beautiful sight ta see, Billy Sunday whippin' past him that way. Can that man move!"

"Sunday. What an inappropriate name for a ball player."

The laughter inside Dexter died at her sarcastic tone.

He noticed Mullane's grin didn't decrease the length of a fairy's footstep, as his grandmother used to say. "You joined those Sabbatarians yet?" Tony challenged her.

"Only in spirit, unfortunately."

About the only religious-related organization she hadn't joined yet, Dexter thought.

"Does Cincinnati allow Sunday ball? That is the club on which you play, is it not?"

Mullane's guffaw indicated he hadn't noticed the barb in her question. "Guess you weren't payin' much mind ta the match today, Mrs. Riley. I was hurlin' for the Cincinnati Reds against the Browns."

"Well, do they play Sunday ball in Cincinnati?"

"Yep. Draw the best crowds of the week on Sunday."

Better try to change the subject before she gets up on her soapbox, Dexter thought. "Surprised you were allowed to pitch today, Mullane, since you were suspended the entire season."

Tony shrugged with his usual good nature. "It was just an exhibition match.

Season is officially over." He crushed the cigar stub onto the edge of one of Carrie's best china plates. Dexter watched her cringe, relieved she didn't upbraid their guest. Mullane rested his arm along the ornately carved walnut sofa frame. "Be nice ta make a salary again. Can't thank you enough for the help over the last few months."

Dexter waved his thanks away. It made him decidedly uneasy having Tony bring it up. "You'd lend me funds if I needed them."

He caught Carrie's surprised look. He hoped she wouldn't say anything and embarrass all of them. He supposed he should have told her about the loan, but. . .

"I never understood why you were suspended," she said, and Dexter felt his relief escape in a sigh. When had he become so uncomfortable about her actions around his friends? "You didn't break any of the rules, did you?"

Mullane grinned his usual self-confident grin. "Only one: I wanted more money. That's the worst thing a player can do, accordin' ta the owners."

Dexter shook his head. "Owners just don't want players moving from one club to another every year. Weakens the clubs."

"The owners don't give a hill of beans for the clubs' health. All they care about is their pocketbooks. I've played with four clubs in as many years and made more money each time I changed. That's what scares the owners."

"You're only bitter," Dexter argued.

"Mark my words, there's rumors of a salary cap comin'."

They argued the issue until all three of them were too tired to continue and Mullane left for his hotel.

Alone in their room, Dexter's exhaustion fled when he slid his arms around Carrie's waist and drew her into his arms, lowering his lips to hers. She didn't resist his kiss. She never did, but he couldn't honestly say she responded to his kiss either. He couldn't recall the last time she'd kissed him back.

Loneliness swelled through him, filling him until he thought he couldn't bear it. How could a man feel lonely with the woman he loved in his arms?

"I've missed you."

The words didn't say half of it. He'd missed her company and her arms while away on the last trip. But more, he missed the part of her she'd deliberately pulled further and further away from him over the last year. He missed the way she used to lean into his arms with complete abandonment, lifting her lips eagerly to his. He missed the way she'd delighted in his presence, laughed easily with him, shared the smallest parts of her days and her deepest dreams.

"I've missed you, too."

She could as well be saying, "I made dinner this evening," for all the passion in the words, he thought, frustrated.

Desire to have her respond to his arms as she used to made him prolong his kisses. He teased at her lips with tiny, tender pecks, lifted a hand to the back of her neck, then higher to play his fingers through her thick hair. He kept his kisses gentle, whispering his love between each touch, longing for her to return his passion.

Her lips remained stiff, her arms cool.

He closed his eyes and rubbed his chin over the top of her head, swallowing his disappointment. "Only one trip left this year. We go to Chicago next week to play the National League champs. Come with me."

She shook her head against his shoulder. The waves of her hair brushed against his hands seductively. "I can't. What would I do with Benjy and Margaret?"

The tone of her voice told him she hadn't for a moment considered the question serious, but he continued to press her. "Your mother or Amanda would watch them." He wanted to keep his face hidden from her so she couldn't see how important this was to him, but for that very reason, he forced himself to look directly into her eyes. "It's the first match I'll ever play in between the two major Base Ball leagues. I want you there."

He knew the moment she realized he was serious. She pulled back from his arms, straightened her dress, and crossed to her vanity to reach for her hairbrush. "It's out of the question." Her voice was crisp and efficient. "There's not only the children to consider. You know I'm in charge of the Ladies' Needlework Society at church. We've a special entertainment scheduled for next week to raise funds. I missed an important planning session to attend the festivities for the Browns today. I cannot possibly miss the event, also."

And when are we to be scheduled? he wondered, watching her pull the pearl-handled brush through the hair that fell like a glossy black cape about her shoulders.

At least in Base Ball there was always another opportunity, he thought, if not this year, then next. But when that special fire between a man and a woman went out, it couldn't always be rekindled. Maybe it was already too late; maybe Carrie no longer cared.

At the thought, he recognized the sinking feeling he always got in his gut when the Browns were behind and the umpire called the match game's final out.

Chapter Ten

1887

Why did she have this sinking feeling in her stomach, Carrie wondered, watching the shiny, flower-bedecked coach carry away Grant and his new bride, Phoebe. A wedding ought to be a happy occasion. Certainly the bride and groom appeared overjoyed. So why wasn't she?

Two years had passed since Grant asked Phoebe to marry him. She should have been accustomed to the idea of them together by now.

"Faith, and it be strange to think of Grant married to someone other than Amanda. I kept hoping they'd patch things up."

She nodded at Dexter's comment. He must be more upset than he appeared outwardly over the wedding. His Irish accent was stronger than usual today.

"Ye look mighty handsome in your black suit with the yellow rose and streamers, Mr. Riley. 'Tis a fine lookin' groomsman ye be."

He laughed, as she'd hoped he would, at her poor attempt to imitate the Irish. A ribbon of regret wound through her. They so seldom laughed together anymore.

Yet her compliment was true. As usual, women's gazes had followed him about during the reception. Ladies had eagerly hung on their escorts' arms when the men had stopped to speak of Base Ball to the now-famous player.

Margaret leaned against his leg, patting the black material with a chubby almost three-year-old palm. "Han'some."

Dexter lifted the girl into his arms and smiled into Carrie's eyes. "All the Riley women are full of Irish blarney today." The smile gentled. "You look tired. Why don't I take these two youngsters home? I know you want to help your mother with a few things before coming home yourself."

She nodded, grateful for his thoughtfulness. "That would be nice. Things will go quicker without the children to watch."

She saw him glance over her shoulder briefly, but paid it no mind. She kissed the children good-bye. When she straightened, she was surprised at Dexter's peck on her cheek.

"I love you," he whispered, his warm breath fanning the tiny curls in front of her ear. Her heart gave an unusual little jolt. He seldom spoke those words in public anymore. Or in private, for that matter. When they were first married, he'd whispered them everywhere they went.

She watched him go down the wide steps to the street with the children, then turned to re-enter through the huge oak doors the church her father served. She stopped short. Emmet stood there, watching her over the shoulders of departing guests.

Had Emmet been the reason for Dexter's small show of affection? Was it possible her husband was jealous of her former suitor?

Emmet nodded at an elderly couple directly in front of him and approached her. She felt suddenly lightheaded, wanting to speak with him, wondering what she could say, wondering what he felt toward her.

His face was as wide and plain as ever beneath the mouse-brown hair that had receded slightly in the five years since she'd married Dexter. He stopped two feet away from her, smiling down with friendly eyes. "Hello, Carrie. You look lovely. I always did like you in blue."

He greeted me as casually as though we'd seen each other only yesterday. "You look well, also."

He couldn't know—no one must know—the way her heartbeat had quickened earlier that day when she'd looked in her mirror after dressing. She knew he would be at his sister's wedding and couldn't help but wonder what he would think of the way she looked in her new gown with its fitted waist and huge, fashionable bustle that made her more shapely than she was in truth.

"Are you happy, Carrie?"

"I. . .as much as I have any right to be, I expect." Especially considering she was wondering whether she had married the wrong man! She missed Emmet's friendship, the easy way they had together, the way she'd been able to share anything with him, and especially the many long, exciting conversations about the Lord and the Bible. Her relationship with Dexter seemed shallow by comparison.

Had she confused passion for love in marrying Dexter?

"You have a fine-looking family. Only the two children?"

She nodded. There weren't likely to be any more if things didn't improve between her and Dexter. Dexter's chaste kiss a few minutes earlier was his only intimate touch in months. They took pains to avoid romantic gestures of late.

"I understand Mr. Von der Ahe named some apartment buildings for the Browns' players after they outplayed Chicago, the National League Champs, last year. You must be proud of your husband."

"Of course." She searched for another topic of conversation, almost afraid she'd blurt out the truth about her miserable marriage. "Phoebe said you've not married yet."

He shook his head slightly, his smile not changing. "No. Haven't found a woman who will have me."

It was on the tip of her tongue to say she had made a foolish mistake in not marrying him. Her chest ached with the effort to keep the words inside. She knew he wouldn't want to hear them, and she wouldn't much like herself for saying them, either. To put the thought into words would demean them both. She'd vowed to be faithful to Dexter for life.

"I've been offered a pastorate. Did Phoebe tell you?"

"No. Where?"

"A small church in North Carolina." His gaze dropped to his feet. When it met hers again a moment later, it was slightly less open than before, though he continued to smile. "It will be quite a new experience, in the mountains and all." He shrugged one shoulder. "I thought it would be good for me to move away from this area. The congregation preferred a married man, but evidently none of the married men they asked accepted the call."

She studied the pearl buttons running up her elbow-length gloves and fought down the feeling of loss flooding through her. She could have been the wife of a pastor—how she would have loved that! Instead she was married to a base baller who did not even believe in God.

"Perhaps the Lord has a woman waiting there for you—the future Mrs. Emmet Wilson."

He didn't respond.

When she looked up, she caught the longing in his gaze, and it brought tears to her eyes.

"Perhaps." His whisper cracked.

She should leave now, but she couldn't seem to pull herself away.

He licked his lips. Was he as nervous as she?

"I pray for you and your husband every day."

"You do?"

He nodded. "That the Lord will bless both of you in your marriage. And for your husband's salvation. Has he found the Lord yet?"

She looked away, ashamed. "No."

He touched her elbow, then immediately removed his hand, and she knew he was uncomfortable with his impulsive act.

"Don't give up on him, Carrie. God won't." One corner of his straight, thin lips lifted in a smile, but his eyes remained sad. "Look with whom God has allowed him to share life. He must love Dexter a great deal."

Guilt poured through her, burning like hot cooking oil. Emmet was such a fine man. She was glad she hadn't given voice to her baser emotions.

"There you are!"

Carrie jerked in surprise at her mother's voice. The middle-aged woman bustled toward them, her elegant mauve gown of watered silk rustling, pointed shiny black toes flashing out from beneath the skirt. Her hand enveloped Carrie's. "I know you'll excuse us, Emmet. There's so much to be done."

Carrie murmured a hasty good-bye over her shoulder and followed her mother inside.

Glad there was no remonstrance forthcoming for her unseemly behavior in speaking alone with a man who once courted her, she immediately went to work helping her mother collect the flowers and satin bows decorating the sanctuary. The large room was thick with the smell of yellow and white roses.

Twenty minutes later she and her parents stood before the altar and surveyed the sanctuary.

"Do we have everything?" Carrie asked.

"Yes." Her mother's double chin plumped when she nodded her head. "Maybe I'd best check the reception hall downstairs one more time."

While they waited for her, Carrie ran her fingers along the smooth altar rail, staring up at the huge painting of Jesus praying in the garden. She'd always loved that picture; it had such a serene quality. But she knew from the Bible story it depicted that Christ hadn't felt serene that night. Had He felt as tired as she did now? "Don't give up on him," Emmet had said of Dexter. She almost had given up, she realized. She was too fatigued to keep fighting for Dexter and their marriage.

Her father leaned back against the rail beside her.

She took a long, shaky breath. "You were right, you know, about Dexter and me."

"What are you talking about?" She could hear the frown in his voice.

"Remember telling me that believers couldn't be happy married to nonbelievers? You were right."

Her father swallowed hard. She supposed she was making him uncomfortable with her confession, but now that she'd started, she wanted to continue.

"I made the wrong choice when I married Dexter. I thought if I had enough faith, God would find a way to reach Dexter's heart. If anything, he's further from God than on our wedding day."

She turned to her father and saw tears in his gray eyes before her own vision blurred. "He hasn't gone to church in three years except at Easter and Christmas, as you well know. He avoids even saying grace at meals, asking the children to say it instead. And you've heard of the Browns' awful exploits this year. It's horrid to think about the kind of people with whom he associates and to whom he exposes the children." She sniffed loudly. "So you see, you were right. I should have married a Christian. I should have married Emmet."

She surrendered to the sobs that welled up inside her. Her father rubbed one hand on her back, and she wondered whether he who gave guidance to so many felt at a loss to comfort his daughter.

"You're probably right," her father agreed when her sobs had finally slowed to jerky breaths and unladylike sniffles. "Since the Bible warns us not to marry unbelievers, it probably *was* God's will that you marry a man like Emmet who shares your faith."

Carrie dabbed a woefully inadequate square of heather-scented linen at her nose and sniffed. "What can I do? I can't divorce him."

"No, I don't believe that would be God's will, either. When we purposely choose to act in defiance of God's Word, we have to live with the consequences. I have no way of knowing what the consequences will be during the years you spend with Dexter. But I know that if you ask God's forgiveness for acting against His Word and ask Him to guide you from this point on, He will do so. Shall we pray together?"

Her father put a comforting arm about her when they knelt at the altar rail.

"Dear Father God," her father began in the deep voice that could rumble through the sanctuary like thunder on a Sunday morning, "thank Thee for this daughter Thou hast given us to love, and for Dexter, whom Thou hast allowed to love her, and be loved by her. We long for the day when he shall know Thee, and thank Thee that Thou wilt not quit asking for his heart. We ask Thee to teach Carrie how to love this man she has vowed to Thee to cherish forever. Show her where she must change, and assist her in so doing. In Thy Son's name, Amen."

Fury routed self-pity from her veins. "Change me?" she demanded.

Her father stood up calmly and offered her a hand to help her rise. "Well, it's obvious you can't do anything to change Dexter. Isn't that what you've been trying to do for the last five years?"

Her hands balled into fists. "But I'm the Christian! Why should I be the one to change? If he becomes a believer, everything will be fine."

Her father bent his head, lifted shaggy black-and-gray brows, and peered at her over the top of his wire-rimmed spectacles. "A common misconception, that becoming a Christian solves all life's problems. Believe me, I've spoken with enough unhappily married Christians to know. Every one of us still has a lot of changing to do after we accept Christ's salvation."

"But there is nothing wrong with me that needs changing! I tell you, the problem is Dexter. I've tried everything I know to make him a believer."

Her father nodded. "Except changing yourself."

Speechless with rage, she rushed down the aisle and out of the church to await her parents in her father's buggy.

She had humbled herself before him, allowing him to see what a mess she'd made in defying him and God to marry Dexter. And what was his response? Loving sympathy for her plight? No! Instead he advised her—*her*, a woman who had followed the Christian faith all her life—he advised *her* to change!

Chapter Eleven

Why had she invited her parents over to help celebrate her and Dexter's fifth anniversary? Carrie asked herself for the tenth time that day. She had a throbbing headache. It had started before she got out of bed that morning and grown worse every hour. It made it difficult to act civil toward anyone.

No, that wasn't true. It wasn't just the headache.

She'd been irritable ever since Grant's wedding last week. Discussing and praying over the situation with her parents had made everything worse. Now it wasn't only she and Dexter who didn't get along, but she was so angry with her parents that her teeth clenched just thinking of them which only made her head pound all the more.

So did the boys screaming out behind the house. Dexter's offer two years ago to teach Joey to play ball had grown into a neighborhood effort since the other boys discovered one of the St. Louis Browns would take time to teach them, and her yard was their favorite ball ground. After all, one of the older boys had explained to her, Mr. Riley was out of town with the club so often, that the boys had to be around in hopes of catching him when he was home.

They caught him all too often. At first she'd been pleased to see him show an interest in the boys. She'd actually thought it an endearing trait! But she'd had no intention of all but adopting a dozen loud boys.

A "thunk" was quickly followed by the sound of the back wall reverberating from a solid hit by a base ball. She threw shut the kitchen window as cheers and jeers were raised in the yard.

She hadn't expected the broken windows, chipped paint, or destroyed flowers and vegetables that came with the small base ballers, either. She grabbed her head. The pounding had definitely worsened.

The grandfather clock in the front hall sent its booming message through the house. She groaned. Did everything have to thunk or pound or boom today? Five o'clock. Her parents would be here any minute, and the new cook had only begun the meal.

Dexter came in from the yard, slamming the back door behind him. "Hello!"

She gritted her teeth and went to the pantry for a blue spatterware pan. When she returned, Dexter was staring out the window with a freshly pumped glass of water in one hand.

He must have heard her crossing the floor, for he said without turning around, "I'm worried about Joey. He's too skinny for eight. His veins show blue through his skin. Think he could be sickly?"

"When he's about eighteen he'll suddenly turn muscular like all the rest of you men."

He did turn from the window at that, with the laugh she so seldom saw anymore twinkling in his green eyes. He set the glass on the counter and slipped his arms about her waist, nuzzling her neck. "All the better to take care of our womenfolk."

She pushed him away impatiently. "My parents will be here soon." After hardly touching her in months, why had he started again during the last week?

Drawing water from the pump beside the iron sink into the spatterware pan, she cringed at the high-pitched creak the pump handle gave. She dropped the pan into the sink with a clatter and grabbed her head. "Can't you oil that?"

She hated her petulant whine, but hated, too, that he'd been too busy playing Base Ball with the boys to maintain the pump.

He was at her side instantly. "Does your head hurt?"

"It's been throbbing all day. That noisy pump doesn't help it."

"Where's the cook? She should be doing this, not you. That's what we hired her for."

"She's helping the new maid, Jane, prepare the dining room. I told her I'd start the potatoes."

He kissed her temple, and she closed her eyes, struggling not to shove him away.

"Why don't you lie down for a few minutes? I'll bring you a cold cloth for your head, and—"

"How can I lie down when my parents are coming, and the children aren't even cleaned up yet? Benjy is bound to be a mess after playing Base Ball in the muddy yard."

"Your parents will understand if dinner is a few minutes late." He grinned. "If anyone is starved, we can always start with the cake while the rest of the meal cooks. Your mother is bringing us a cake for our anniversary, isn't she?"

She just glared at him.

He took her arm and urged her toward the door. "You're laying down and that's that. I'll clean up Benjy and Margaret." He glanced down at his sweaty brown shirt. "And me."

"But—"

"No buts. If you lie down without complaining, I'll wake you in half an hour."

She was glad she finally gave in. The cold cloth he brought for her forehead felt wonderful, and after the short rest, she did feel better.

Her parents didn't murmur a whit at dinner being served later than normal—and they didn't begin with the cake. They'd completed the rest of the meal and were eating the lemon pound cake piled high with whipped cream when there was a knock on the front door.

Carrie wasn't surprised that their visitor was Joey; their house was his second home. He was unusually patient with Benjy. The two of them spent most of their hours together with willow bats over their shoulders and at least one of their pockets bulging from a big ball.

Curiosity tickled at her over the tall, narrow item he carried, which was covered with a pretty blue cloth. Mischief and pride mingled in his slender face beneath pale blond hair.

Dexter grinned from ear to ear and asked Joey to set the item on the floor beside her. When the boy had done so, he said, "Happy Anniversary, Carrie."

She slowly lifted the cloth cover. A beautiful trill greeted her. "A canary! Oh, Dexter, I've always wanted one!" Tears sprang to her eyes.

Joey's excited laugh showed how thrilled he was to be in on such a successful surprise. Beside him, Benjy jumped up and down, clapping his hands. Margaret grasped Carrie's knees and tried to push past the energetic boys to see what had excited them.

Carrie barely noticed the din the children caused. She truly had wanted a canary since she was a child and had seen one in a parishioner's home. Now, when their marriage was an absolute shambles, her husband gave her this precious gift.

It brightened the rest of the evening for her and for the children, who couldn't be budged from its cage. But it didn't keep the interest of the other adults for long. While admonishing the children not to open the cage under any circumstances, Carrie overheard Dexter telling her parents about some work he was planning on the house.

Her father gave him a friendly pat on the shoulder. "Won't embarrass you by saying this more than once, but I thank God for giving our daughter such a good husband. Not all men take such care of their wives and children. Built her this fine home. Never degrade the name you gave her by dragging it through the mud the way so many base ballers have done themselves and their families. It's a blessing to have a son-in-law like you, and that's a fact."

Was her father saying that to remind her that he thought she was the one who needed to change? Well, Dexter certainly seemed to be eating it up. He was ruddy from the unusual praise and looked embarrassedly modest, but knowing him as she did, she could see he was pleased. No wonder. He hadn't often received such compliments from her parents. Likely he still recalled the way her father had argued against their marriage.

If only I had listened to his warning! Both she and Dexter were miserable because she'd been so stubborn.

"Appreciate the money you gave toward repairing the church roof last month, too," her father continued. "Thanks to you, that's one bill that's paid off."

Carrie stared at Dexter in surprise. He hadn't told her he'd given money for the roof. He hadn't even been underneath that roof since Easter services last spring. She'd mentioned the need to him, but she'd never expected him to contribute to it.

The conversation drifted onto other topics, and eventually she remembered Emmet's news. She told her parents of his plans to shepherd a church in North Carolina. "Doesn't that sound exciting?"

Her parents agreed enthusiastically and asked a storm of questions she couldn't answer. "You'll have to wait until Grant and Phoebe return from their honeymoon trip and ask her about her brother's plans," she said with a laugh.

Dexter's gaze snagged hers. He no longer looked pleased, but contemplated her with a darkly curious stare, as though frightened by something he saw in her. But that was silly. What could possibly frighten him?

The look was still there when her parents had left, the children in bed, and the canary's cage covered for the evening. She had just pulled the pins from her hair and begun to brush it when he came up behind her, and their gazes met in the long narrow vanity mirror.

His hands gently pulled her hair back over her shoulders. The unexpected move, so reminiscent of the early days of their marriage, made her throat ache in longing for happier times. "I like it when you wear your hair down."

He'd said that often. Still, she seldom wore it down. It was less work to wear it up; it didn't get in the way of her work, and it stayed cleaner. Besides, it wasn't considered proper for a woman her age to wear her hair down in public.

He searched her gaze in the mirror with that same quizzical look he'd been watching her with all evening. "What is it?"

He didn't pretend to misunderstand. "Do ye ever wish ye'd married Emmet Wilson?"

Her heart stopped. Plunged on faster than ever. She tugged her hair back over one shoulder and brushed furiously. "What a silly question."

"Is it?"

She concentrated on her hair, refusing to meet his gaze again.

His hands at her shoulders gently but firmly turned her about. He took the brush from her and set it on the vanity. "Ye think I'm not a good enough man for ye, don't ye?"

"Of course not!" But it was true, and she hated the truth of it, despised herself for feeling superior to her own husband because he wasn't a Christian.

One of his crooked, callused hands cupped her cheek. She avoided his eyes as long as she could. When she finally made herself look into them, she knew he saw the truth in her face and was ashamed it was there for him to see.

"I'm sorry I haven't made ye happy these five years." His voice was so uncharacteristically and incredibly gentle that she could feel the pain in it. "I only wish. . .that ye could love me just as I am."

"I do!" She pressed her hand to the hand against her cheek, eager for him to understand. "I don't want you to change at all, except. . ."

"Except?"

"Except I want you to love Jesus."

He shook his head slowly. "Can't be seeing that becoming a Christian *would* change me?"

"But only in—"

He continued as though she hadn't spoken. "I used to be thinkin' I was too honest to pretend to believe in God, even to be winning your heart. But not anymore." A rough-tipped thumb traced her cheekbone. "I love ye so much, Carrie. If I thought pretending to believe would make things right between us, I'd pretend. But pretending won't help, will it?"

"If you'd just *try*—"

He tugged firmly at the hand she still clutched. She released it reluctantly, for it was as if he was pulling away his will for their marriage to work, and it terrified her to think he might be giving up on them. Strange, when *she'd* thought she had given up on them lately.

He turned back at the door. "If it was a Christian husband ye wanted, ye should have married Emmet Wilson. He wouldn't have had to change to win your love."

In stunned disbelief, she watched him leave. Moments later, she heard the front door open and close. She sank down onto the thick blue comforter and drew her legs up under her skirt, hugging her knees in a vain attempt to chase away the chill in her bones.

How could she have been such a fool these last weeks, allowing her thoughts to revolve around Emmet and what their life together might have been like? Living in a world that could never exist.

She'd dwelt so long on her dissatisfaction with her marriage that she'd lost sight of what life would be like without Dexter.

Maybe she would have been happier with Emmet if she'd married him instead of Dexter five years ago, but now everything was changed. Even if Dexter wasn't a Christian, they shared so many memories. And the children. To truly go back in time and marry Emmet would mean Benjy and Margaret wouldn't exist. Oh, likely there'd be other children—hers and Emmet's. But she couldn't imagine life without feisty Benjy and sweet Margaret.

Or Dexter. In spite of the spiritual life she wished they shared, he *had* been good to her and the children, as her father said earlier. She well knew many men did not treat their wives and families with the love that Dexter showered on them. She didn't truly want to give up life with him.

It was all terribly confusing. She couldn't go back. She wouldn't leave her marriage. Her beliefs demanded commitment, even if her heart wavered. But she wasn't happy, and neither was Dexter.

Her father's comments and prayer last week had infuriated her, but he was right, much as she hated to admit it. She had been trying to force God to do things her way.

Exhaustion overwhelmed her, body and spirit. The thought of beginning again was numbing. Five years of living to redo. It was too much. It was impossible.

It was the only way.

She took a deep breath. Before her resolve could melt away, she rested her forehead against the arms crossed over her knees, and with halting words, asked forgiveness and thanked God for Dexter's faithfulness as a husband and father.

What had happened through the years to destroy her belief that God would win Dexter's heart? She recalled the conviction with which she'd faced her father before they married: "I shall love him into God's kingdom myself, if I must."

How childish! She'd spoken from no experience at all.

Tears heated her eyes. "I only wanted him to love Thee, Lord," she whispered. "Can that be wrong?"

Nothing spoke to her mind or spirit.

Wearily, she changed into her new flannel nightgown with sprigs of violets against a snow white background. The softness was luxurious and comforting, and she crawled between cool, heather-scented sheets eager to sleep and escape the emotions that had racked her throughout the day and evening.

She couldn't escape. Images of the day's events swam through her mind like a play she was forced to watch. Worst was the memory of Dexter's sorrow-filled eyes when he said in a pain-tightened voice, "I only wish that ye could love me just as I am."

She, who had boasted she would love him into God's kingdom, instead made him feel he wasn't loved at all. She shoved her hands into her hair. How had everything gone so wrong?

She sat bolt upright, staring into the darkness. "Just as I am." Her heart beat wildly in her ears.

That was it!

God loved her just as she was, and no amount of faith or good works would make Him love her more. He just loved her. The same as He loved Dexter.

The same as she must love Dexter.

She'd loved him that way in the beginning. When had she put requirements on her love? In her marriage vows she'd promised to love him always, no "if's" or "but's" attached. Somewhere through the years, she'd changed her commitment.

Excitement danced along her nerves. Her mind exploded with the wonder of new possibilities. She laid back on her pillow, drawing the comforter under her chin, barely noticing how cold the satin felt against her skin.

She laughed, feeling suddenly free. When she learned to love Dexter as God loved him, surely God would answer her prayers and draw Dexter to Him! And save their marriage along the way. Not the fact of their marriage, but the essence, the life of it.

Her father had been right about everything. She was the one who had to change.

Frustration shoved at her excitement. She didn't even know how to begin to change!

"Father God," she whispered into the darkness, "I beg of Thee, teach me how to love my husband."

Chapter Twelve

Carrie awoke the next morning eager to face the day. The excitement of her "discovery" the night before still danced within her. What would the Lord show her about love?

She was relieved to find Dexter beside her. She couldn't recall him coming to bed. Had he stayed up most of the night? At least he'd come home. Of course, he always did. He'd never stayed away all night because he was angry with her.

She began to put up her hair. Hesitated. Pulled out the hairpins, caught the sides above her ears with tortoiseshell combs, and allowed the black waves to fall down the back of her red-plaid flannel day gown. Her fingers rested a moment where her hair waved on her shoulders, and she remembered the way Dexter liked to caress it. Would he notice she was wearing it down today?

As it turned out, they barely spoke that morning. The children had been about during breakfast, and then he left to meet the Browns for the day, as usual, at Von der Ahe's saloon and ball grounds.

First Corinthians thirteen. The words ran like a refrain to a tune through her head most of the day. From the first she'd realized their significance, of course. First Corinthians thirteen, the love chapter. She went about her duties—aired the house, prepared the day's menus and examined the larder in order to make up a marketing list for the hired girl, checked the water vessels about the house and determined which lamp chimneys needed washing—and played with the children, all the while eagerly awaiting the brief afternoon moments when her children collapsed into their naps and she would have time alone to read the precious chapter.

Surely this was an answer to her prayer last night, she thought more than once as the day wore on. What could be more reasonable than to start with the love chapter of the Bible when learning how to love her husband?

Seated in her favorite tapestry-upholstered rocker, her shoes on the low, curving maroon footrest, she turned the thin pages eagerly, then read the words aloud.

"Though I speak with the tongues of men and of angels, and have not charity, I am become as sounding brass, or a tinkling cymbal.

"And though I have the gift of prophecy, and understand all mysteries, and all knowledge; and though I have all faith, so that I could remove mountains, and have not charity, I am nothing.

"And though I bestow all my goods to feed the poor, and though I give my body to be burned, and have not charity, it profiteth me nothing.

"Charity suffereth long, and is kind; charity envieth not; charity vaunteth not itself, is not puffed up,

"Doth not behave itself unseemly, seeketh not her own, is not easily provoked, thinketh no evil;

"Rejoiceth not in iniquity, but rejoiceth in the truth;

"Beareth all things, believeth all things, hopeth all things, endureth all things.

"Charity never faileth."

She frowned down at the page. She'd been sure the chapter was going to show her how to put love into practice in actions she could begin immediately, but the wording was woefully lacking in specifics.

One thing for certain, she had "suffered long" during the last five years, but not with kindness! She had badgered Dexter with the knowledge of her suffering, blamed him for causing her suffering by his lack of faith.

She scanned the words again. Strange, not one mention of the passionate emotions that tumbled through a person when one fell in love. Of course, the verses applied to love beyond the relationship between a man and a woman. Still. . .

She wanted to get the *feeling* of love for Dexter back. Wasn't it the passion, the desire for the loved one, that made it possible to act in a loving manner? But the words didn't refer to the emotions she wanted to recapture. Instead it spoke of suffering and enduring.

She rested her head against the chair's high back and sighed. Apparently God's idea of love and her idea of love were far apart. Learning how to love in God's manner wasn't going to be easy.

One of the day's rare rays of sunlight slipped into the room, and the canary burst forth in a gay trill. Smiling, she walked to the tall cage, her heart warming at Dexter's gift.

Canaries always reminded her of Emily Dickinson's poem. "Hope is the thing with feathers that perches in the soul. And sings the tune without the words, and never stops—at all."

Like *love*, she thought, *which never fails.*

Well, she wasn't going to stop hoping either, not at all.

She stuck a finger through the bars of the cage, pulled it back out when the canary ignored it. "I think you've just received your name. From now on, you shall be called Hope."

The front door opened and closed sharply. She knew it was Dexter arriving home, and her hand froze on the cage.

She ran the palms of her suddenly sweaty hands over her flannel-covered hips and swallowed nervously, her gaze on the betasseled entry between the parlor and hall. What would he say after last night?

He stopped in the doorway, his hands smoothing his wine red hair, and she realized he'd removed his coat and hat. His gaze tangled with hers and neither of them moved.

There was a cautious look in his eyes. She tried to give him a radiant smile that would put any doubts he had to rest, but she felt her lips tremble and knew her attempt a failure.

"I. . .I hate when we fight." Her voice quivered just above a whisper.

"Me, too."

She watched his gaze searching hers. There was no trace of his usual smile. Weariness lined his face. But it was the hint of fear in his spring green eyes that caught her heart in a painful grip. Was he truly afraid he'd lost her love, that she wished she'd married Emmet?

One of them had to remove the fence they'd built these last few years, risk the possibility of being hurt by the other. He'd begun, she realized, when he asked last night about Emmet. It was only right she take the next risk.

She crossed the room slowly, barely noticing the canary's song filling the room. By the time she reached Dexter, her heart was pounding as quickly as a trotting pony's hooves during a race. She laid a hand on each side of his face, stood on tip-toe to kiss him lightly. "All day I've wanted to tell you that I'm glad it is you I married, Dexter Riley."

He didn't respond, didn't return her touch, only continued to search her eyes until she wanted to cry out with the fear writhing within her. Was she mistaken? Did he no longer want her love? Would he tell her instead that he wanted one of those ghastly marriages that were nothing but form?

"Are you for bein' sure, girleen?"

It was all she could do to nod in response. Why had she thought for a moment that risking her heart to tear down the fence between them was noble? It was terrifying.

"I'm not likely to change my stripes at my advanced age."

A smile pulled at her lips. He didn't know the power of God's love! But she only said, "Nor I, so you'll not expect me to stop praying for us."

His mustache twitched, and his hands closed about her wrists lightly. "You wouldn't be my own dear colleen if you gave up practicing your faith."

He took a deep breath and squared his shoulders. Regret shimmered through her when he released her wrists.

"Der Boss has arranged for us to do a post-season tour with the National League pennant winners, the Detroit Wolverines; a seventeen-day tour of the eastern states with a special train of parlor cars. A fifteen match game World's Series, beginning here in St. Louis. What do you think of that?"

Seventeen days! Carrie tried to match Dexter's smile, but knew she was failing miserably. "Quite an honor."

"Have to admit, I'm excited about it. Just hope we play well enough that Der Boss doesn't make us pay our own way home after the last match, like the Chicago's National League owner did to his club last year."

"I doubt Mr. Von der Ahe will be tempted to do that, considering how well the Browns are playing this season."

He started to reach for her, hesitated, then circled her waist with his arms. Something in her chest that had been frozen for a long time came to life with a sudden throbbing ache, like fingers frozen by winter wind responding to the warmth of a parlor stove. How long had it been since they'd reached for each other with that precious lack of self-consciousness they'd once known, reached for each other expecting their touch to be welcomed?

"Will you come on the tour?" His voice was rough, his eyes questioning. "There's never been anything like it in Base Ball. I'd like ye with me."

"There's so much going on at church, I'm not sure I can be spared."

The light in his eyes died.

"Perhaps I could get away for a couple days." She didn't want to disappoint him, not now when she believed God wished to give them a new beginning. She'd refused to go the last time he asked her to accompany him on a Base Ball trip, two years ago. "But seventeen days is a long time. Besides, you know Mr. Von der Ahe doesn't approve of the wives traveling with the club."

He nuzzled her neck, his mustache and warm lips sending delightful shivers through her. "Well, I approve, and if Der Boss thinks about it, he will, too. After all, why shouldn't a man play better when his wife is watching?"

"Why, indeed?" she murmured, slipping her arms about his neck to welcome the lips he lowered to her own.

Carrie's glance swept the opulent restaurant, taking in the three enormous crystal chandeliers beneath the domed, pale blue ceiling edged in gold leaf. Light glittered off silver and fine etched crystal on tables throughout the lower level of the huge room. Opposite her and Dexter was a balcony with half a dozen secluded dining areas, each with a table set between sapphire blue velvet draperies tied back with gold braid from which hung foot-long tassels.

Their own table was in just such a spot on a matching balcony. The orchestra at one end of the room provided a lovely undercurrent of music to the guests' conversations.

"It's beautiful, Dexter."

He beamed at her across the small table. "Best place in Detroit."

"Will Mr. Von der Ahe be upset that you're out tonight? You do play tomorrow."

"I expect Der Boss will save his fury for the base ballers hitting the city's saloons, not those enjoying quiet dinners with their wives."

"I hope you are right. He is awfully unpredictable."

"You said something there!"

"Hey, Riley!"

Guests gasped, then twittered at the loud call. She saw impatience flicker over Dexter's face before following his glance to the lower level to discern the source of the yell. A tall man in an ill-fitting cutaway jacket with a top hat sliding off his thick, wavy hair stood grinning up at them.

"Why, it's Tony Mullane!"

"Why did he have to show up here?"

She giggled at Dexter's growl. "I can't believe he'd enter this restaurant, as closely as he holds onto his money." *Except what he spends on drinking*, she amended silently.

Tony was already hurrying up the wide marble stairway at one end of the room, his hand tucked beneath the elbow of a lovely young woman in a low-cut red gown. Without asking whether they were welcome, he seated the woman and himself at their table, his well-cut but threadbare jacket looking grotesquely out of place against the elegance of white-on-white satin and velvet upholstery.

Uneasiness rippled through her. Even though it was early, the yeasty smell of beer overpowered Tony's cologne.

He didn't bother to introduce his friend. Carrie gave her a friendly smile, while the men greeted each other.

"Who's goin' ta see the rest of the Browns get ta their beds instead of the local jail, with you out bein' respectable with yer wife?"

"They'll have to look out for themselves for once. What are you doing in this part of the country, Mullane?"

Tony leaned back and stuck one of his fat cigars in the corner of his mouth. "Came ta see ya play in the World's Series." He leaned forward, his elbow knocking over an empty crystal wine glass. "Say, I hear Der Boss is gettin' stingy as usual, threatenin' ta give each of you players only a hundred-dollar bonus and keep the club's share of the Series' pot. Pot will probably be 'bout twelve thousand dollars. Any truth ta the rumor?"

"Who knows? Anything is possible when it comes to a club owner and money."

"Heard some other things, too. Like, Comiskey is so mad he's tryin' ta talk some of the other club members into helpin' him throw the Series so's Der Boss won't make as much money."

"You've been around the game a long time, Mullane. Think a base baller's apt to go about talking of throwing a match? Same as cutting off your career."

"Maybe. Have ta be proved first, though. Think you're goin' ta take the Wolverines?"

Dexter shrugged. "We'll try. Your club might have had a chance at this series if you hadn't been suspended again this year."

"Aw, it was only a month or so this time."

"But a bit more serious than usual."

Carrie was surprised to see color steal up from Tony's black-and-gray-striped four-in-hand and creep over his face. Could this be Tony Mullane, embarrassed?

"Guess I had a bit too much ta drink."

"I guess," Dexter repeated dryly. "You threatened to shoot a man, Tony. You need to get yourself in hand and quit rushing the growler."

"Yeah, maybe I will one of these days."

"Do it soon, friend."

She glanced at Tony. He was staring at Dexter, shock written clearly from his famous wavy hairline to his cleft chin, and no wonder. Dexter seldom reprimanded his friends.

Tony shifted his gaze, and his attention quickened. "Hey, look! There's Der Boss!"

He was right. Von der Ahe's distinctive portly shape was indeed in the process of being seated on the balcony across the way. Accompanying him was a woman with an hourglass figure, her elegant gown weighed down with pearls, her shoulders bare. The purple plume on her hat wrapped almost all the way around the crown above a flattering wide brim.

Carrie's fingers flew to her throat. "Why, that's not Mrs. Von der Ahe!"

Mullane chuckled. "Fortunately for him!"

She'd never seen Dexter's eyes so dark with fury, his full mouth so rigid beneath his mustache. "Mullane, I hate to sound like I'm giving a friend the brush-off, but I promised me wife this would be our special night. Ye understand, I'm sure."

Tony weaved a little as he stood. "Sure, I understand." But Carrie noted his thick black brows scrunched together when he looked at his friend. "C'mon, toots, let's leave the man with his wife."

"Does Mr. Von der Ahe often escort women other than his wife when you're out of town with the club?" she asked when Tony and his companion had departed.

He rubbed a large knuckle over his chin and looked out at the crowded room. "I should never have asked you to come on this trip."

"Because I might see him with this. . .this woman?"

He nodded.

"And the other players? Do they—"

"Some of them. They aren't angels. You know that. You've reminded me of it often enough."

"But. . .adultery!"

She should have suspected, of course. She was well aware that women eagerly sought the base ballists' attentions. But to think the club owner, a man well respected across the country, would be so immoral as to brazenly appear with another woman in one of Detroit's finest restaurants! Why, he didn't even attempt to keep his affair hidden.

And her husband worked for this immoral man!

Grant had warned her before their marriage of the temptations surrounding a base ballist. She remembered thinking Dexter too fine and strong to give into them. Her gaze studied Dexter now with new eyes. Could any man resist temptation when it surrounded him continually?

His touch, covering her hand with his, brought her from her jumbled thoughts. "I've never been unfaithful to ye."

"I know." Could he hear her whispered answer to his fierce declaration?

She believed him—but had she been unfaithful to him?

She'd prayed so stalwartly through the years for him to believe in Christ. She'd hardly thought to ask God to help him stand against temptation in his work each day. *Lord, show me how to pray for him. Show me his needs.*

Waiting in their hotel room the following evening for Dexter to return from the match, she recalled Mullane's accusation of match throwing. She wouldn't have considered it possible the Browns had done such a thing, if it weren't for his suggestion. But what else could she think when the clubs were tied today one-all in the bottom of the thirteenth inning, and then Comiskey—who never failed the club at a critical moment—muffed a throw, allowing the Wolverines to score the winning run?

The door opened, and Dexter entered. He dropped his bowler on a nearby table, then leaned back against the door and stared across the room at her with dull eyes.

She stood, returning his gaze. "Did they lose intentionally?"

He shook his head, weariness in every plane of his face. "I don't know. If so, they didn't ask me to join them in the attempt. They know I'd never do it. I can't believe they'd play it out to thirteen innings and then throw it all away, but. . ."

But Mullane had said it was Comiskey who was instigating the idea, and it was Comiskey who had dropped the ball and lost the match, putting the Browns behind in the Series two games to one.

All last night and today, anger had burned inside her. How could Dexter stand to be a part of this Base Ball world, with its lack of values and morals? How could he work and laugh and play with men who cheated their employer of his money, who cheated themselves of their reputations, who were known even within the base ball community for their unsportsmanlike play, who went so far as to commit adultery, flaunt it, and not be shamed by the fact?

It took all her self-control to keep her tongue and not rail at him as she wished to do, challenging him with the very questions that plagued her. Despair wove through her, shoving away the anger. How could she expect him to walk away from it all when he didn't follow the Lord?

His values were high compared to his fellow base ballers. She knew it, his clubmates knew it, and the kranks knew it. It was hard for him to see his friends throwing away their lives on excessive drinking and unfair play and. . .adultery.

Charity "beareth all things, believeth all things, hopeth all things, endureth all things."

She crossed the room and put her arms around him. "*You* played well today, anyway. I'm proud of you."

He rubbed his chin against her hair and sighed with a weariness that caught her in its wave. "Every one of those men has talent and abilities for which other men would exchange fortunes. Why do they continue to live as though life demanded no payment for such foolishness?"

When would he learn, she wondered, *that they would continue to live in that manner until they turned to God?*

Chapter Thirteen

Delicate, rose-bedecked teacups clattered cheerfully against matching saucers in the Riley parlor a few weeks later. Carrie's women's Bible study group filled the room with their chatter and laughter. Now that the day's discussion was behind them, the women were enjoying the petite frosted cakes decorated with sugar-created pansies that Cook had prepared.

A young woman across the room caught her gaze and smiled engagingly. "I'm so glad you suggested a study on First Corinthians thirteen. It's the most wonderful study we've done."

A number of other women nodded or agreed audibly.

"I'm glad you're finding it enlightening."

A chorus of "Oh, my yes!" and "Definitely so!" greeted her.

She darted a look to the other end of the room, where Hannah Kratz sat quietly on the long velvet-covered sofa, and the older woman sent back a sweet, understanding smile. Mrs. Kratz was the only woman here to whom she had confided her reason for wishing to study the chapter.

It was hard to imagine she'd ever been uncomfortable around Hannah, her fellow "church widow." They'd become close friends the last couple years, praying together for their husbands, children, and marriages.

A door slammed, and boys' voices, high pitched with excitement, came from the kitchen. *Dexter must have allowed them in for water once again*, Carrie thought.

Another door slammed, louder this time, and she stood hastily, ready to face the culprit. She'd only taken a step before Dexter burst into the room.

Dread shot through her at the strained look in his eyes. "There's a fire at Sportsman's Park! I'll catch a trolley there. I'm not knowing when I'll be back!"

He was out of the parlor before he finished speaking.

His interruption had stopped the women's chatter. Only the canary's quivering song broke the silence. Then everyone began speaking at once: How bad was the fire? How had Dexter found out about it?

Their questions went unanswered that evening. It was three in the morning before he returned. Carrie hugged him tightly, heedless of whether her blue satin wrapper was ruined by his soot-covered, water-soaked clothes. The acrid smell of smoke was thick about him and filled her lungs. Her throat hurt with aching gratitude that he'd not been injured.

"I was so worried!" she whispered into his neck, clinging to him.

When she'd satisfied herself that he was truly unhurt, she drew him into the kitchen, where his filthy clothing wouldn't harm the furnishings. He sank wearily onto a hard oak chair beside the rectangular worktable while she poured a cup of coffee she'd kept heated for him.

He wrapped his hands around the cup and took a large swallow. "Tastes good."

"Was anyone injured?"

He shook his head. His face looked heavy with fatigue. Light from the plain electric ceiling fixture cast eerie shadows over his blackened skin. "No one was hurt, but the players' dressing room was destroyed and the handball court and gymnasium damaged. So were the clubhouse and Der Boss's Golden Lion Saloon."

"The bleachers?"

"Saved." He set the cup on the table, closed his eyes and slid down, stretching out his legs and resting his head against the hard chair back. "Reporters were there, asking disgusting questions, making slanderous accusations."

"About what?"

"Some of them suggested Der Boss might have started the fire to collect insurance money."

"He wouldn't!" She frowned. "Would he?"

"He's not the city's most honorable man, but I doubt he'd commit arson and robbery."

"My first reaction was the same as yours. But wouldn't a man be capable of almost anything if he practices a. . .adultery?" She found the nasty word difficult to pronounce.

"Because a man condones one sin doesn't mean he condones another," Dexter said impatiently.

"You needn't snap at me! I'm not accused of either sin!"

He caught her hands. "Sorry. I'm just tired."

So was she. She'd been up for hours, worrying about him, praying for him.

"Caruthers was there," he commented.

"Bob Caruthers, the Browns' hurler?"

"Yep. Says Der Boss sold him to Brooklyn for eighty-five hundred dollars."

"But he's the best hurler in the country! Well, one of the best."

He grinned at her, raising his eyebrows in the playful way of old. "So you've been keeping up with Base Ball news, girleen! You'll be a true fanatic yet." The laughter in his eyes slowly died. "Der Boss told Caruthers he's selling other players off, too; four more of our best. If he goes through with it, he'll gut the club."

"Why would Mr. Von der Ahe do that?"

"Says it's because he thinks we lost the World's Series to spite him." He snorted. "The sell-off idea seemed a lot more amusing last year when it was the Chicago owner selling off his base ballers because our team beat them in the World's Series."

"You don't believe that's Mr. Von der Ahe's real reason?"

"Well, rumor is, he needs money."

"Does he?"

His shoulders lifted wearily. "Who knows? Reporters are saying so."

"You mean, they're saying he's selling the base ballers and burning the buildings because he's broke."

"That's the general idea."

"If that's so, why didn't he keep the gate receipts from the World's Series?"

"Guess people have forgotten about that." He sighed, and the depth of it tore at her heart. She lowered herself to his lap and snuggled her cheek against his shoulder, wrinkling her nose at the smell of smoke. His arms slipped around her.

"Didn't think life in Base Ball could get much better than last year and this," he continued. "We won ninety-three matches last year and then won the Series. This year we won ninety-five match games. We were on top of the world until the World's Series. Every man and boy in the country wanted to be one of the St. Louis Browns nines—except those other base ballers who wanted to knock us down a notch," he admitted with a grin. His grin faded. "So why has everything gone so wrong the last few weeks?"

"Everything always goes wrong when people worship themselves and money instead of God."

"God! He's your answer for everything."

She felt him tense and tried to keep her voice reasonable. "Look at the way most of the base ballers on your club live. They flaunt their sin as if it were a reward instead of something shameful. For instance, that new young hurler, Silver King. Why, you told me yourself that Mr. Von der Ahe kept a woman from prosecuting Mr. King over two illegitimate children, and Mr. King is only nineteen years old! Almost all of the men drink to excess and make complete fools of themselves in public. Your own good friend, Mr. Browning, is publicly known as Red Light District Distillery Browning. Some of the other base ballers' wives have told me of a number of players who have contracted diseases from. . .loose women. You see, I asked some questions after our Detroit trip. And—"

"I'm not wanting to discuss it."

"Look at your own good friend, Tony Mullane, and all the trouble he's been in over the last few years. It's only by God's grace he hasn't been arrested for attempted murder! And Mr. Browning—"

He jerked to his feet, his eyes like black caves as he stared down at her, his voice tight with fury. "Base ballers don't pretend to be angels. But if I remember correctly from me church goin' days, Christians aren't to be judgin', they're to be lovin'. And more to the issue, bad things happen to people who say they serve God, too. Or aren't ye knowing any Christians who lose their jobs or have fires destroy their business places?"

The truth of his words lanced to her very soul, shaming her. "I'm sorry, I—"

He waved his hands at her in disgust, his lips twisted with contempt. "I'm goin' to bed."

When he had left the room, his back stiff, she dropped into the chair he'd vacated and pressed the palms of her hands over her eyes, which felt gritty and swollen from lack of sleep.

Things had been so wonderful between her and Dexter lately. Had she ruined everything with her accusations?

He must hurt unbearably tonight at the thought of his friends being sold to other clubs, Mr. Von der Ahe pushing their lives in directions they might not wish. Dexter would miss them, regardless of their weaknesses. He'd tried to tell her before of the joy he felt when they played together, working as one—some of the best men in the world at what they did—combining their efforts to give memories that lived for years to the crowds that thrilled to the matches.

He hadn't needed to be reminded of his friends' faults, she knew. He had too often rescued them from the consequences of those faults. He'd bailed some of them out of jail when drunk, lent them money to pay fines, brought them home to keep them from winding up in the "paddy wagon," nursed them, cleaned up after them.

No, he hadn't needed her self-righteous listing of their faults. He'd needed her comfort. She'd failed him again, even after weeks of studying and praying over the love chapter. "I obviously haven't yet developed that part of love that 'is not puffed up,' Lord!" Indeed, all she'd learned was her inability to love like Christ.

Would she ever discover how to love her husband the way she should? "For Dexter's sake, help me, Lord."

Dexter undressed by the light of the moonbeams shining between the ice blue draperies, which looked black silhouetted against the windows. He tossed his smoke-clogged clothes in the general direction of a chair with a needleworked pad and slid between the heather-scented sheets, shivering at their unwarmed smoothness.

Every muscle in his body screamed for sleep, but the anger in his brain wouldn't let rest's healing power come.

God again! Carrie's reverence for God was once one of the things he'd loved about her. Now it was like a weapon she used against him, against their marriage.

Guilt immediately took a punch at his conscience. She didn't mean to use her faith that way, but that was how it affected him. He was tired of getting angry at her and God—all over Someone he didn't believe existed.

He snorted and flopped over on his stomach, punching his pillow into a tight little wad. How dumb could a man be, getting angry at Someone he didn't believe was real?

Was she right about God punishing the Browns for their blatantly immoral acts? But everyone had faults, didn't they? The base ballers just didn't try to hide theirs behind smug, church-going manners.

He wished he could believe in God. Not that he saw any benefit in being a believer, except that he wouldn't be fighting with Carrie as much. He didn't expect God would bother to repair Von der Ahe's Sportsman's Park or buy back Bob Caruthers's contract and let the Browns stay one big happy family. Never did see God going out of His way for any of the people He was supposed to love so much.

'Course, if all faith in God did was make Carrie love him more, it would be well worth any bother it caused. He had promised before they married that he'd attend church and give God a try. A bit of guilt wriggled through him. He hadn't given Him much of a try, but then, God being God, He shouldn't need too much time to prove Himself, should He?

He rolled onto his back again, pressing the heels of his hands to his eyes. He had to get some sleep. First day of his off-season law clerk position started tomorrow. Today, that is, in just a couple hours.

He hated arguing with Carrie. He could count on not sleeping well after a quarrel, at least until they resolved things. Trouble was, the arguments about God were never resolved.

He threw his hands in the air and let them drop with a soft "thud" on the thick bed covers. "I give up! If Ye're there, God—and I'm not sayin' Ye are, mind Ye—but if Ye are, would Ye be findin' a way to show me? For Carrie's sake."

He turned onto his side. *Thought people were supposed to feel better when they prayed.* He didn't. He *sure* didn't.

"If Ye happen to be answerin' prayers tonight, I could be usin' some sleep."

Well, it couldn't hurt to ask.

Chapter Fourteen

1888

Carrie glanced up from the pile of silver she was polishing when Dexter entered the kitchen. Early summer sunlight streamed through the windows between sheer yellow curtains. She noticed with a sudden realization of passing time how the cheerful rays intensified the green of his eyes and highlighted the grooves bracketing his mouth, which had deepened in the six years since they'd met.

He leaned a hip against the wooden table beside the sink, tossing a base ball casually with one hand in the habit Benjy and Joey had adopted. "The lads play their first match against the West Side club tomorrow afternoon. Will you come?"

"Child base ballers have kranks and kranklets now, too?" Carrie wiped her hands down her practical, oversized navy-and-green-striped apron, stalling for time. She hated always disappointing him when he asked her to do things, but her commitments at the church filled most of her afternoons and evenings. And with the spring cleaning so far behind due to the rain that fell almost the entire month of May—

"Say you'll come, Carrie. The lads want you to see their new ball grounds."

"I don't know whether I can spare the time." She waved a hand toward the sink filled with recently polished silver. "There's the spring cleaning to be completed, and it's already June, and—"

"Isn't that what we're paying Hannah's girl, Millie, to do so you and Jane can keep up with your own duties?"

"Now if that isn't just like a man! You have no idea how much is involved in keeping a house respectably clean. Millie cannot possibly do the entire spring cleaning for a home this size herself."

"Well, it won't hurt for the two of you to fall one afternoon behind."

"We're already a month behind! All the woolen garments, rugs, and blankets must be snapped, brushed, and packed in moth protectors and wrappers. The wicker and wooden porch furniture has still not been painted for summer—and you know we'll need that for the next meeting of the Ladies' Needlework Society if it doesn't rain. Every wall in the house must be dusted, all the chimneys and shades from the chandeliers and gas jets cleaned, the windows washed, the door handles polished, the dining room and parlor cleaned, and—"

She stopped for a breath and he took advantage to interrupt. "My apologies for misunderstanding the gravity of the situation. Perhaps I shouldn't have had this house built for us and caused you all this trouble."

"I love this house!" she responded to his teasing words, "but it does require much upkeep. Without Cook, Jane, and Millie, I couldn't possibly run it." She leaned toward him and shared in a conspiratorial whisper, "To be honest, when the help was first hired, I was almost afraid to speak to you for fear something personal in nature might be overheard."

His whoop of laughter lightened her spirits. It had been a long time since they'd truly laughed together. "I felt the same way."

She spread her hands. "As you can see, there is much to be done. And I've Bible study tomorrow."

"Is it to be held here again?"

Was he upset over the meetings she held in their home? If so, neither his voice or manner revealed it. "No, it will be at Mother's. Hannah was supposed to hostess it, but her husband isn't feeling well."

"Touch of the grippe, I suppose. With the cold rains we've had lately, it's pretty common."

"I'm surprised Joey and Benjy haven't come down with it. The rain hasn't kept them from practicing Base Ball, in spite of my protests. The other day during that bad storm I had to resort to hiding the new bat you had made for Benjy to keep him from going out to play."

Dexter braced a hip against the iron sink, tossed the ball, and grinned. "He's just a base baller, born and bred."

"If he's born to it, why does he have to practice so much?"

"I did the same thing when I was a lad. Never could stand to let a day go by without seeing whether I'd improved from the day before."

She leaned against the counter beside him, loving the thought of him at Benjy's age. "I wish I'd known you as a boy."

"No you don't. Girls and boys are mortal enemies at that age." He wiggled his eyebrows. "I think we like each other much better now than we would have then."

"Oh, pooh!" She turned away from him and went back to work on the silver. "Joey's been awfully good with Benjy, hasn't he? He plays so patiently with him, instead of teasing him unmercifully the way boys can do with one a couple years younger."

"Teaching him great things, too. Like where to find the fattest nightcrawlers for fishing."

"Wonderful knowledge, I must admit."

He chuckled at her sarcasm.

"I have been concerned for the boy lately, Dexter. Remember saying last year that Joey seemed spindly for his age? Benjy is much rounder and healthier."

"Joey's not holding his own against the rest of the lads on the club, either. Maybe he's just one of those natural beanpoles."

"Maybe." She could see by his frown he didn't believe it.

"Enough of this stalling, woman. Will you come tomorrow or not?"

It must be especially important to him; he doesn't usually press me like this, even couching it in that pretend gruff voice. She made a saucy face. "Since you want me so awfully, I suppose I've no choice but to join you."

He dropped a quick kiss on the bridge of her nose. "Good! It will make the lads' day."

Maybe, she thought, watching him leave the room, *but I already feel guilty for missing Bible study.* Perhaps she should ask her father at the midweek service tonight whether she'd done the right thing.

"Of course you did the right thing," Reverend Chambers declared unequivocally while she helped him straighten up the pews after the service, putting hymnals and Bibles in their proper places. "Don't know why God wouldn't want you to join your husband and children in a bit of pleasure."

"I know He wouldn't deny me their company. It's just. . .well, I want so desperately for Dexter to become a believer. . .and you know what it says in First Peter about a wife winning her husband to the Lord by her example."

He stroked his trim black and gray beard with long fingers. "First Peter. Hmmm. Are you referring to the third chapter, where it says 'Likewise, ye wives, be in subjection to your own husbands; that, if any obey not the word, they also may without the word be won by the conversation of the wives; While they behold your chaste conversation coupled with fear'?"

"Yes, that's it. I haven't succeeded in winning him with my nagging, so I hoped my example would do so."

"By attending church functions?"

"Partly, yes."

"Have you forgotten the first part of the verse?"

"What do you mean?"

"The part that says, 'be in subjection to your own husbands.' "

"Oh." She shifted uncomfortably. She didn't like to think about that part.

"A few verses further along Peter reminds the reader of Sarah. Do you recall how she obeyed her husband, Abraham, when they were in Egypt?"

Uncomfortable warmth spread up her neck and over her face. "Yes. Abraham told her to let Pharaoh think she was his unmarried sister, and allow him to take her into his home, so his own life wouldn't be endangered."

"That's right, and God protected her there. I doubt Dexter will expect anything of you like Abraham asked of Sarah. I can hardly see why the Lord will be upset with either of you for watching some boys play Base Ball." He peered at her over the top of his spectacles. "It's not the most respectable pastime, but the boys won't be playing Sunday ball or serving beer, I presume, like the Browns do at Statesman's Park."

She smiled briefly, then sobered. "But, what if Dexter expects me to give up more of my church activities?"

"Has he asked you to do so?"

"No, never."

"What if he does? Think you'll lose your faith?"

"Of course not, but—"

"Think the church can't get along without your hand in every organization?"

"No! And I'm not in every organization!"

He stroked his beard again, pursed his lips. "Nope. Haven't seen you at the men's Bible studies. Not yet, anyway."

"Father!"

He patted her shoulder. "Now don't be getting into a tizzy over nothing. You've been a faithful member of this congregation. I've appreciated your efforts, and I'm certain the rest of the members have, too. But as the Good Book says, there's a time for every season under heaven, and this just might be your season to be a Sarah. Besides, won't hurt some of the other women in the church to fill in where you've been working so hard."

"But, Mother was always helping at the church or assisting one of the members when we were growing up. She still does so."

"Your mother married a minister. You married a base ballist. He has different needs from his wife than a minister."

She'd have to reflect on that. Surely he couldn't mean the Lord meant for her to assist Dexter playing ball! "What if you can't find anyone to replace me?"

"People are always replaceable. One of the facts of life."

He makes it sound as if I won't even be missed. He'll change his mind if I do give up some of my commitments and he finds how difficult it can be to convince people to help. "Well, if you're certain it's what I should do—"

At his impatient nod, she walked toward the back of the church. *My chin is probably dragging worse than the train on my dress.* She loved her church work and being with others who loved the Lord. She wasn't looking forward a bit to the possibility of a "Sarah's Season."

"Oh, Carrie!"

She spun around. "Yes?"

"You'll not give up the children's Sunday school, I hope?"

"Not if you'd rather I didn't, unless Dexter specifically asks it of me." Joy bubbled up inside. There was nothing she enjoyed more than working with the children, and she couldn't imagine Dexter asking her to relinquish it.

The sun blazed from a cloudless sky late the next afternoon when they arrived at the lot two blocks from their home where the match game was to be held. Joey and Benjy, who had accompanied them, rushed to join the boys already busy "warming up," as they called their practice. Millie and Jane were watching over Margaret.

Carrie tucked a hand in Dexter's elbow. "Benjy must have asked fifty times today whether it wasn't time for the match to begin. He's been on pins and needles! I must admit, I've caught a bit of his excitement."

He smiled down into her face, creating a world with just the two of them, in spite of the two dozen boys hollering only a few yards away. The smile warmed the green of his eyes, wrapped around her heart, and put to rest the guilt that had been festering in her conscience like a splinter over the time she'd stolen to join them.

She unfolded the brown wool blanket she'd brought to sit upon. Before it touched the ground, Benjy was running toward her. "Hey, what do you think you're doing, Mom? You have to sit on the bleachers, you know!"

"Bleachers?"

He grabbed her hand and tugged. "Yes, over there." He nodded to the other side of the lot, where a warped, weathered board lay across two overturned fruit boxes in the midst of calf-high weeds. "We built it 'specially for you."

She shared an amused glance with Dexter, who was losing a valiant struggle not to laugh. He grabbed the unfurled blanket and started across the lot behind them. She smiled her thanks when he laid the blanket across the dirty old board.

Benjy held her hand in a most gentlemanly manner, his five-year-old chest puffed out with importance, when she lowered herself with as much grace as possible to her wobbly seat of honor. In a flash, he rejoined his friends.

Trying not to think of the bugs and wood ticks in the weeds about her long skirt and high-topped shoes, she looked out at the field and was surprised to find the boys had stopped practicing to watch her be seated.

Dexter set down a large tin pail with a dipper hooked over the edge. "The lads will be glad you thought to bring this water along."

From the bench beside her she lifted a large linen dishtowel tied in a knot. "I expect they'll enjoy the sugar cookies, too."

He rested a foot on the board, leaned an elbow on his knee, glanced at the boys, then back at her. "Feel like a queen?"

"Indeed I do."

"Consider me your servant, also, m'lady."

She laughed at his nonsense. It had been the right thing to do, sharing this day with him. This time, anyway.

"I understand why Der Boss calls the Browns 'mein poys' after working with these youngsters. The lads out there may be just a bunch of ragtag kids who won't even remember me in a few years, but to me they're 'me boys.' "

His husky declaration brought a lump to her throat. She wanted to hug him for his uncharacteristically sweet admission, but restrained herself. She was sure 'his laddies' wouldn't approve of such female behavior bestowed upon their "Cap," as they called him, short for "captain."

The last couple days of sunny weather had begun to dry the water-soaked ground, but there were still puddles here and there on the weedy, unleveled lot. She noticed with dismay that a number of the boys' trousers were already mud-covered and was grateful she had someone to help with the wash. Many of the boys' mothers hadn't that luxury, and a couple, she knew, took in other people's wash.

At least all those flying little feet wouldn't be tracking mud across her kitchen floor today! She turned to Dexter. "Did I remember to thank you for purchasing this lot for the boys? Millie and Jane thank you, too!"

"So do our neighbors and my pocketbook, after the glass I've replaced over the last couple years."

He called the boys over and opened the leather valise he'd brought, pulling out a dozen black-and-white-striped jockey hats. "Thought you lads should look like a ball club."

Cries of pleasure rewarded "Cap."

"Maybe we can all wear black socks in the next match, too, like real base ballers," Joey offered eagerly. The other boys jumped on the idea.

When the game began, Carrie was joined by a number of the players' sisters and brothers, but no other mothers. Guilt slipped its wedge into her conscience again at the thought that the other mothers were working, not watching boys play.

With an effort, she pictured herself shoving the guilt out the door of her mind and hanging out a plaque emblazoned with the words Sarah's Season. Silly, perhaps, but it helped.

She enjoyed cheering the boys on, along with the help of the young kranks and kranklets.

As Dexter had said, it was rather a ragtag group. The boys ranged in age roughly from seven to ten, with only a couple as young as Benjy. She was surprised to see how well he performed in comparison to the older boys. But then, she reminded herself, he was Dexter's son.

It was Joey's play that signaled alarm within her. He was the worst player on the field. He hadn't the strength or the dexterity of the other boys. Even Benjy was more coordinated in his efforts. No wonder Dexter had expressed concern.

Her heart went out to the gangly boy in the third inning when there were three boys on base and it was Joey's turn as batsman. Some of the older boys pleaded with Dexter to let someone else bat.

Joey lowered the willow until the large end rested on the weed-covered ground and turned large eyes on Dexter, awaiting his verdict.

Dexter, arms crossed over his wide chest, nodded at him calmly. "Go ahead, Joey. Do your best."

As Joey stepped up to the dirt-filled flour sack that served as home base, Dexter turned to the rest of the club. Carrie couldn't recall ever seeing his face set so sternly. "A club *always* supports its mates."

The words were spoken low and quietly, but the effect was instantaneous. There were no more groans or comments, although glaring eyes and pouting lips filled the young faces.

Everyone was surprised when Joey's third wobbly strike at the ball connected with just enough force to knock it halfway to the hurler. The runner on third made it to home base only inches before the ball. The Rangers went wild.

Joey's next turn as batsman wasn't as successful. Or his next. He struck out both times. His clubmates forgot their earlier cheers for the run he'd batted in, though Dexter's sharp looks reminded them to hold their ridicule in check.

She'd been so jealous of the time Dexter spent with the Rangers that she hadn't realized how much he loved the boys. Did he lavish so much attention on them because he wanted them to know the approval he hadn't known as a child? Was that why it was so important to him that the boys learn to be loyal to their clubmates, so that at least within the Rangers, they would always know they were accepted?

The thought brought her up short, forcing her attention from the boys in front of her to the boy her husband had been. Her gaze rested on him, trying to imagine him a self-conscious boy with wavy dark hair and shining green eyes and skinned knees. Did part of him still need that respect he'd been denied by the church members he'd known as a child? Was it that insecure little boy he'd once been who was behind the statement on their fifth anniversary last fall, his statement that he wished she could love him just as he was?

A ball whizzing past her head jolted her back to the present. A moment later she was cheering the Ranger running around the bases as fast as his short legs would carry him, weeds whipping as he raced past.

She was as thrilled when the Rangers won as she'd been the first time she watched Dexter's club win on a day in May six years ago. From the sparkle in Dexter's eyes and the bounce in his walk, she suspected he felt the same.

He caught her hand in his while walking home. For over a year he had stopped reaching for her in those simple, almost unconscious ways that show a man cares for a woman and is glad to have her beside him. At his touch, her eyes heated with threatening tears and her throat constricted.

Perhaps this Sarah's Season wouldn't be so intolerable after all.

Chapter Fifteen

September, 1889

Sun-drenched color from the tall stained-glass windows set in gray limestone walls dappled the chapel. The air was thick with the scent of delicate white, yellow, and pink rosebuds on the edge of opening to life—like Rose Marie, the little girl in Grant's arms.

Carrie watched Phoebe straighten a fold of Rose Marie's French nainsook gown, which fell at least two feet beyond the six-week-old child's toes. Tiny embroidery covered the last six inches of the robe.

Grant's gaze met Phoebe's above the child's head, and Carrie's throat constricted at the love that passed between them. What a special day for them!

A couple she didn't know—friends of Phoebe's—stood before the altar and her father with Grant and Phoebe. Strange to think her brother and his wife had chosen someone other than her and Dexter to raise Rose Marie should anything happen to them.

Perhaps it wasn't strange. Why would they want her and Dexter to raise their child? She had chosen to marry a man who didn't serve the Lord. Amazing, the consequences one never realizes will result from one's actions. She never thought before that her brother wouldn't trust her with his children.

If she'd married Emmet, her brother and Phoebe would be willing to entrust Rose Marie to her.

It was a short but heart-tugging ceremony dedicating Rose Marie to the Lord. Prayers were offered by not only her father, but also Grant and Phoebe.

What would it be like to pray together with Dexter over their children, she wondered, listening to Grant's simple prayer. The thought left an aching void of loneliness in her chest. If she had married Emmet—

I didn't. I won't allow myself to dwell on what might have been. Besides, it's not Emmet I miss, but the spiritual closeness he and I would have had that Dexter and I don't share.

Will our children be the worse for our inability to pray for them together, Lord? When they are older, will they choose not to walk with Thee, the way Hannah's children have done, because their father doesn't know Thee? Fear slithered into her heart at the thought. Another consequence she hadn't considered when she agreed to marry Dexter. When she insisted upon marrying him, she corrected herself.

Margaret leaned against her, and she looked down to see her daughter stretching her slender neck above the pew in front of them, her eyes alight with excitement at what was happening with her new little cousin.

Beside her, Benjy tried hard not to be impressed, his bottom lip jutting out in a pout, and his arms crossed hard over his two-piece suit of checked cassimere, but the green eyes so like his father's showed a glimmer of interest, just the same.

She reached behind Margaret and pulled the black and white Rangers hat from Benjy's head. When and how had he managed to slip that on without her or Dexter seeing it?

His hand whipped to his suddenly bare head. He caught sight of the hat in her hand, and his eyes widened before he deepened his scowl.

On the other side of her, Dexter looked down at the hat, raised his eyebrows, glanced at his son, and grinned. He tucked her gloved hand beneath his elbow. A moment later he nodded toward Grant and Rose Marie, then leaned down with mischief dancing in his eyes to whisper, "Why don't we have another one of those?"

She knew she was blushing all the way from the high ivory lace neck of her new pink chiffon gown to her hairline, though no one else heard him. Even so, she couldn't keep from smiling at his query. He did so love children. It was one of the dear things about the man.

But she wished they could pray together for the children. Or anything else, for that matter.

The thought returned to her later that day while watching Dexter hold little Rose Marie. After the service, the family had come to her and Dexter's home for dinner and visiting. They didn't see nearly enough of Grant and Phoebe, since the couple lived in Ridgeville, where she and Grant had grown up.

When Rose Marie made it obvious she'd had quite enough visiting for the afternoon, Carrie accompanied Grant to Margaret's room. The reluctance with which he gently laid the child in the bonneted cradle from Margaret's baby days caused a sweet twinge in her breast. She blinked back a mist of tears.

"What do you think of your new niece?"

"I think she is far lovelier than a girl should expect to be with you for a father."

He grinned from ear to ear. "I agree completely."

He lightly ran a blunt fingertip over Rose Marie's round cheek. "I wonder what her life will be like, what kind of man she will marry? I hope he's the best man on the face of the earth."

The fierceness in his voice choked her, and it was a moment before she could say, "Dexter said the same thing when Margaret was born. The two of you might give the girls a chance to grow up before you worry over their marriage partners."

"But it makes so much difference in life, who you choose to spend it with." He looked up, pinning her gaze. "Doesn't it?"

What does he want me to say? That I should have married Emmet instead of Dexter? Or was part of him sorry he hadn't married Amanda? The memory of him and Phoebe at the dedication service flashed in her mind. They appeared devoted to each other, but were they? "It seems almost. . .indecent. . .to ask this, but do you ever," she caught her bottom lip in her teeth, grabbed her courage, and rushed boldly on. "Do you ever miss Amanda? Are you sorry—" She couldn't complete the sentence.

Dusky color flooding his face didn't reassure her. His lips tightened.

"Forgive me for asking." She turned her back to him, unnecessarily rearranging Rose Marie's soft, tiny blanket.

"It's all right, Carrie. Amanda and I, we weren't at the right places in our lives to be together." She pivoted slowly to face him, her gaze searching his eyes, wondering if they hid a private pain. "I finally realized I was trying to push Amanda into becoming a Christian before she was ready."

"But the Bible clearly tells us we're to tell people about Him."

He nodded. "I tried to convince myself that was all I was doing. I wanted her to know Him, but I wasn't willing to wait for Him to water the seeds you and I and others planted in her life. I wanted her to believe when I thought she should, not when God had her heart fully prepared for Him. I didn't help God's efforts. I only hope I didn't hinder them.

"Fond as I was of her, I had no right courting her. I knew how she felt about the Lord from the beginning. It wasn't right, allowing her to think we might have a future together. If I'd cared for her as much as I thought I did, I wouldn't have hurt her."

Was that what she'd been doing with Dexter? Pushing him, expecting him to accept beliefs before God finished the necessary work in his life? It would be like expecting a person barely introduced to the fundamentals of Base Ball to be a hurler for a major league club.

Grant rested a slender hand on her shoulder. A smile tipped his lips. "Don't worry about me, little sister. I love my wife. If I had to make the choice again, I'd choose Phoebe."

"I'm glad. Amanda's beliefs haven't changed."

He grimaced. "I'm sorry to hear that."

"She hasn't married, either." She didn't think he'd wish to be burdened with the knowledge that Amanda still loved him.

"Does she still see Browning?"

"Yes."

"Browning is a confirmed bachelor and a drunkard. He's no good for her." His mouth tightened. "Beats me why some people fight God so hard."

She wondered whether he was referring to Amanda, Mr. Browning, or both.

She sighed deeply, swallowed her pride, and confided, "Last year I actually hoped Dexter might be changing. He was upset over the way things were going with his friends, their drinking and cheating and such, and with Mr. Von der Ahe selling so many members of the Browns the year before. He and the others were so sure the club's future was destroyed when the five best players were sold. But then—"

"Then the Browns took a group of untested rookies and won the '88 pennant anyway, to the surprise of everyone."

"Yes. I'd hoped he would see that people couldn't turn their backs on God and expect Him to bless them in return, but then everything worked out so well for the Browns. Why did God do that?" Was that her voice, scaling an octave in frustration?

His laugh broke through the strain in the room. "Are you asking why God didn't punish your husband and Von der Ahe?"

"I guess that does sound silly." Her smile felt sheepish.

"A mite. Must have pleased you when the major leagues slapped a $2,500 salary cap on the players and reduced your husband's earnings."

He chuckled when she wrinkled her nose at him, but then sobered. "Dexter is a fine man. Finer than most. He just doesn't believe in God."

"Yes, but that is a large 'just.' "

How much longer would she have to wait for Dexter to open his heart to the Lord, she wondered, walking beside Grant back to the parlor.

Charity suffereth long. . .endureth all things. She had been looking for things to do, actions she could take, when she first read the love chapter two years ago. Was she being told, instead of doing, to wait and allow God time to work? Was that one of the things God meant for her to do during her Sarah's Season, to cease struggling and wait for Him to act? Could He ask anything more difficult?

Is anything too difficult to endure for Dexter's soul?

The words were spoken only in her heart, but she heard them as clearly as though they'd been spoken aloud. Of course nothing was too difficult! Did the Bible not say that we can do all things through Christ, who strengtheneth us?

Charity suffereth long. . .beareth all things, believeth all things, hopeth all things, endureth all things. She hadn't realized what a large part of love involved waiting!

"Base Ball is even gaining a bit of respectability now that President Harrison's wife has admitted to enjoying the matches," Dexter was saying when they entered the parlor.

"And how is that boy doing, that Joey you speak of so often?" her father asked when the laughter died down.

Her glance collided with Dexter's. They didn't care to discuss Joey too candidly in front of Benjy. "He's weaker," Dexter replied cautiously. "Can't play with the lads much anymore; it tires him out. But he comes to most of the matches and gives advice to the little guys, keeps up with the willows, things like that."

Joey had begun getting weaker about six months ago. His spirits were still cheerful—most of the time, anyway, when he wasn't thinking about the Base Ball he was missing.

"He still tags about Dexter every available minute," she shared.

He smiled across the room at her. "That's not entirely accurate. I have to share him with you, like I do most of the lads now." He turned to Grant. "The lads have taken to coming over after every game for her cake and lemonade. She's the Rangers' private nurse; bandages the blackened eyes, split lips, and bunged fingers that happen to base ballers of all ages. They call her Mrs. Cap."

The pride in his voice and eyes filled her with gratitude for the closeness God was slowly working between them. "They ask Dexter's advice on every topic under the sun. You'd think not one of them had parents with whom to consult."

How could she have considered for a moment that she might not love this man? What if she hadn't decided to hang on tight to her vows and work to make their marriage good? Would they still be at each others' throats, living under one roof but a world apart in their hearts?

"Speaking of the Rangers, I've something to show you."

She hurried from the room, returning with a hat box. Opening it, she handed a bib of white flannel to Dexter and another to Benjy. "I've made one for each member of the club."

Dexter's grin couldn't have grown wider. "Shields for the lads' shirts, with a fancy black "R" for Rangers. Well done, girleen o' mine!"

Her parents, Grant and Phoebe, and Phoebe's parents and friends crowded about to see, while Benjy immediately tied his shield over his suit jacket with its wide white collar.

A pounding at the front door broke into the group's admiring comments. A moment later, the maid appeared at Carrie's side, and Carrie hurried into the hall to greet Hannah's daughter, a pale Millie Kratz.

"Oh, Mrs. Riley, come quick! Ma needs you!"

"Has your father taken worse?"

"He's. . .he's dead!"

Was the early September wind unusually chilly? Carrie wondered three days later, shivering on the bleachers close behind the Browns' bench in Brooklyn's Washington Park. The roar of the fifteen thousand spectators and the ever-present smell of cigars and beer on nearby kranks barely touched her awareness today.

The Browns were ahead three to two in the sixth inning, and Comiskey, with one of the sneaky tactics Dexter so deplored, was arguing fiercely with the umpire that it was too dark to continue—much to the kranks' dismay.

She couldn't care less whether the match continued. Dexter had thought it would do her good to get away for a few days following Mr. Kratz's death, and she'd finally agreed to accompany him for the three-match series with the Brooklyn Bridegrooms. It wasn't possible to leave behind her burden for Hannah, however.

Hannah's husband is dead, Lord. How could Thee have allowed him to die before he came to believe in Thee? Didn't Hannah's years of prayers and faithfulness count for anything in Thy sight? Forty-five years she trusted Thee to save him!

Her heart had been frozen since Millie told of her father's death. Helping Hannah through the last few days was the most difficult thing she'd ever been called upon to do. She could assist her with decisions, with the children, with refreshments for the guests who came to express their sympathy—but she had nothing to share to help her grieving spirit. What could she say when they both knew her husband hadn't believed in God?

She knew well her father's explanation of why people like Mr. Kratz—people with every chance to know the Lord—never came to Him. God won't force Himself on those who don't want Him, he would say. He's given each of us the power to choose whether we will love Him or not. He won't take that away from us. He wouldn't take it away from Mr. Kratz. He wouldn't take it away from Dexter.

And that was the most frightening thought of all.

But I believed if I loved Dexter the way Thou dost love him, he would come to Thee!

The way God loved him. Unconditionally. Expecting nothing in return. Even Dexter's salvation.

Her heart stumbled.

She'd known, at least in her mind, that it was possible to go through the rest of their lives together loving Dexter and praying for him and still to never see him come to the Lord, but she hadn't truly grasped the possibility. Loving him as she did, she couldn't imagine such a thing. She'd believed Dexter would accept Christ's gift of salvation eventually, even if they were both bent and gray at the time.

But that was what God had meant by loving him the way God loved him. Expect *nothing* back. Only give love.

The spectators about her rose to their feet in a body, their bellow all but lifting the roof that covered the grandstand. It jerked her out of her absorption.

Mr. Von der Ahe was setting candles about the Browns' bench, supporting Charlie Comiskey's contention it was too dark to continue the match.

It wasn't too dark to see a form hurtle through the air and bounce off the ground near the candles. And then another, and another, and then a drove. Some made crashing sounds, and she realized with a coiling of fear in her stomach that outraged kranks were tossing beer steins, attempting to put out the candles, succeeding in knocking some over.

The Browns ducked, attempting to protect themselves with upraised arms from the missiles, stumbling away from the flickering flames that were inciting the crowd.

Her heart pounding in her throat, Carrie's gaze searched for Dexter, but she couldn't see over the wild throng. She stepped up on the bleacher and stretched her neck. Catching sight of him about ten feet from the bench lessened her fear slightly.

"Fire!"

The people almost trampled each other in their attempt to flee the flames that suddenly leaped only a few feet away, licking at the grandstand. Had the overturned candles started the conflagration?

She caught sight of Browns team members darting toward the flames, Dexter among them. They were joined by spectators and players from the Bridegrooms, and the flames were soon thoroughly doused—not so the clubs' or kranks' anger.

Grumbling loudly, the crowd returned to their places. They stood rather than sat, not wanting to miss a moment of passionate disagreement. The clubs' captains and the umpire gave them a show in ungentlemanly behavior, continuing to argue over whether it was too dark to play. The umpire sided with the Bridegrooms, in spite of the overcast skies, and play continued.

Carrie's attention was fully on the match now, her hands clenched together in her lap until the knuckles ached. Police had arrived and stood along the edge of the grounds. Would Dexter and the others need their protection?

She breathed a prayer of thanksgiving when the ninth inning was reached with the Browns ahead four to two. The match would soon be over and she and Dexter safely back at their hotel.

Her relief was short-lived. The Bridegrooms were about to come up to bat when the Browns' outfielder was caught dunking the ball in a bucket of water. She thought the crowd would stampede the field in their fury, but with the encouragement of the police, they eventually settled down to watch the finish—although amidst complaints as loud as rumbling thunder.

The rumble grew to a cheer from excited Brooklyn kranks when one of the Bridegrooms attempted to steal second base and arrived at almost the same time as the ball thrown by the Browns' catcher. The runner was declared safe.

The cheer changed back to dangerous thunder when Comiskey insisted the throw beat the man to the base, but the umpire was unable to tell due to darkness.

Carrie hugged her arms to her chest and looked at the furious faces about her—it wasn't too dark to see the kranks' angry expressions. Couldn't Charlie tell by now that the umpire wasn't going to be convinced by his argument of darkness? The Browns were ahead by two runs. Hadn't he enough faith in his clubmates to play the match to the finish? It was that competitive nature that drove him. Win at any price.

Competition. It was built into each of the players so fiercely it was as much a part of them as their fingers or noses or hearts.

She was in a competition, too—a competition for Dexter's soul.

Forgetting the crowd about her, she lifted her face. "Help me, Lord."

Her whisper was lost in the crowd's roar. She realized suddenly that Comiskey had pulled the club off the grounds and forfeited the match. She glanced at the marquisite watch pinned to her jacket. It was just past six-thirty.

Beer steins hurtled through the air once more, pelting the Browns. The police attempts to protect the players were woefully inadequate.

She pushed through the crowd, her fear for Dexter's soul temporarily routed in the immediate, all-consuming fear for his physical safety.

Chapter Sixteen

Dexter received only minor bruises and cuts from the rain of beer steins, to Carrie's relief. The player who was caught drenching the ball received the worst of the attack. Still, there were two matches yet to be played against the Brooklyn Bridegrooms, and the attitude of the kranks was frightening.

She felt much better the next day when the Browns forfeited the Sunday match, furious they'd been denied their share of the Saturday gate receipts for withdrawing from the Candlelight Match, as it was being called.

The withholding of the money convinced the club manager, Charlie Comiskey, and Mr. Von der Ahe to play the final match on Tuesday, however. Dexter assured her extra police protection had been arranged for the Browns, but rather than calming her fears, the information established their validity to her.

She was even more upset when Dexter insisted she return by train to St. Louis on Monday, knowing he was trying to keep her from a possibly dangerous situation. The lurid newspaper reports about the Candlelight Match and consequent Browns-Bridegrooms feud that she devoured on the long trip back did nothing to comfort her. She lifted numerous prayers for Dexter's safety and the club's, and she slept little.

Tuesday afternoon she took a covered cab to Frank's Irish Stars Saloon. Since Frank had a telegraph service there in order to draw customers interested in the latest sports news from across the country—as did many other saloons—she knew he would hear immediately if a serious situation developed during the match.

She was so relieved to find the Tuesday game had been postponed due to rain and no attack made upon the police-protected Browns by the kranks, that she threw her arms around the bulky Frank and thanked him as though he was personally responsible for the good news.

The deep chuckle so unlike Dexter's laugh shook his large chest when she hastily stepped back. His hands grasped her waist, steadying them both.

"Dexter will be comin' back to ye safe and sound, don't ye be worrying."

"I hope so." The friendly twinkle in his eyes made her feel welcome in spite of their past animosity.

He waved a large hand at a man behind the counter. "Bring the colleen a cup of coffee."

"Oh, I couldn't! I must be getting home." Now that she knew the situation in Brooklyn, she was eager to leave the saloon with its rough-looking characters and yeasty odor.

He brushed away her protest, pulling out a chair at a nearby table. "I want to hear from your own lips what happened at Brooklyn. Did any of those Bridegrooms' kranks' beer steins hit me baby brother?"

She hesitated for a moment, then relented and took the seat he offered her. After all, he loved Dexter, too. Of course he'd want to know what had happened.

In the end, she surprised herself by inviting him, his wife, and Amanda to dinner when Dexter arrived back. It had been years since any of Dexter's family other than Amanda dined with them. She hadn't cared for his brothers' company, and Dexter hadn't insisted, choosing instead to visit his family alone.

It would be good for him to have friendly faces around when he returned from this trip, she told herself, waving good-bye to Frank while he watched the cab he'd paid for pull away from the saloon to take her home.

She put extra care into her toilette the next day. There would be no cheering crowds at the depot today as there had been during the Browns' glory years. Those close to the base ballers would be the only welcoming faces.

Fancy combs with faux pearls held the sides of her hair back from her face in flattering rolls, allowing the back to hang in loose waves the way Dexter liked. The combs would go well with the new gown of swirled rose silk she planned to wear for dinner that evening.

The children grew tired of watching for the horse-drawn cab and were out playing with neighbor children when he arrived at the house.

Carrie was at the door when he reached it. He dropped his valise on the doorstep and wrapped his arms around her, burying his face in her hair. His breath was warm against her neck, and she welcomed the touch of his lips there.

"I missed you," he murmured against her skin.

"I should have been with you. I've been wishing I'd stayed ever since entering the railroad car in Brooklyn."

His lips claimed hers with a hunger that first surprised her, then drew a similar response.

She tipped back her head to smile into his face and froze. Her heart constricted at the purple and garnet bruise on his cheekbone. She started to touch it, caught herself just in time, a moan working its way out of her throat. To think those awful kranks had hurt him!

She clutched his narrow, scratchy lapels and sought the truth to her question in his eyes. "Was it perfectly dreadful?"

One corner of his mustache moved up in a half-hearted smile. "Yes, it was, actually. The entire city of Brooklyn seemed to be against us. We took buggies to Washington Park Tuesday, dressed in uniform and ready to play, but the match was postponed on account of rain."

"I know. Frank told me."

He held her off, staring at her, astonishment written large across his face. "You asked Frank about the match?"

She played with a button on his coat, keeping her eyes carefully from his, embarrassed to admit the truth after her objections to Frank and the Irish Stars for so many years.

"I was worried about you and knew he'd have early news over the telegraph service."

He chuckled, and she looked up at him, sticking out her chin belligerently. "I may wish that he'd become a teetotaler and give up the Irish Stars, and he may wish I would become a not-so-secret tippler, but we both love you. He understood that I wanted to know what was happening."

"Why you old fraud! After all these years, you've gone and become a true kranklet!"

"Don't be absurd." She shoved against his chest without effect. "It's not Base Ball that interests me, but a certain base baller by the name of Riley."

His eyes twinkling with laughter, he bent until his lips all but touched hers. "This Riley only *interests* you?" He kissed one edge of her mouth lightly, then the other.

"Well. . . " Her arms slipped around his neck. She began to return his kisses, but he pulled his head back slightly.

"Well, what?" he teased.

"I love you, Dexter Riley."

"That's what I've needed to hear," he whispered, and kissed her tenderly, thoroughly.

Minutes later she reluctantly pulled away. "We're having guests for dinner; Frank and his wife, and Amanda, and Mr. Browning."

He looked at her in surprise, and she was grateful he didn't comment on her unusual guest list.

"I hope you aren't too tired for company after your trip. Your family and friends don't see you often enough, and they were eager to come by."

He shook his head slowly. "No, I'm not too tired."

The gentle, joy-filled look in his eyes was ample reward for the evening ahead.

Hours later, Dexter closed the large oak door with its etched bevel glass behind their guests, the pleasure of their company still warm inside him. It had been good to visit with his brother and sister-in-law in his home again.

He slipped his arm around Carrie and looked down at her black curls as she tucked her cheek against his shoulder. What had persuaded her to invite Frank and his wife after all these years? She'd been comfortable with them, too, not stiff and prim the way she used to be around his family. Whatever the reason for her change of heart, he was all for it.

"I'm glad you invited them," he said, starting toward the parlor with his arm still around her. He liked the secure, comfortable feeling it gave him to have her at his side like this.

She stepped away from his arm when they reached the parlor and began to gather cups and saucers. He took the stack from her hands, setting them on the carved rosewood table in the middle of the room. "Leave them. I want to visit with my wife. Haven't seen her for a few days, you know, and she looks mighty pretty in that rose-colored dress."

He caught her hand, pulling her down beside him on the sofa, enjoying the color and sweet laughter his comment caused. He dropped a light kiss on the tip of her nose. "You were a wonderful hostess tonight, me love. I think you even charmed Browning. He was certainly on his best behaviour."

"I'm sure that's due to Amanda's charms, not mine."

He slid his arm around her shoulders and leaned his head against hers, her fragrant hair soft against his cheek. "Maybe. I never thought he'd still be escorting her after all these years."

"They don't see each other exclusively."

"No. Don't expect Browning will ever settle down to one woman." The fact Browning escorted Amanda at all made his stomach decidedly queasy. But she was a grown woman. There wasn't much he could do, except warn her. He'd tried that, but it had only made Amanda angry. He wished for the hundredth time that Grant had married her. "Did you hear about his fishing escapade?"

"No."

"Got so drunk, he went fishing in a rainstorm, in the gutter in front of his hotel." He snorted, frustration pouring through him. "I want someone better than that for Amanda."

She shifted in his arms and cupped his cheek with one hand. "I know, my love. But perhaps she feels the good she sees in him outweighs the bad. Don't forget that Mr. Browning saved a boy's life a few years ago, when he pulled the child from beneath a moving streetcar." She dropped a quick kiss on his lips and stood. "Now, I must be getting those dirty dishes to the kitchen."

He watched as she went quickly about her business, the swish of her rose silk gentle beneath the clatter of china.

It wasn't like Carrie to champion his friends. He was accustomed to hearing her list their faults, not their virtues. He knew she still believed in people holding themselves to high standards. So what had changed her attitude?

Chapter Seventeen

1891

"Now I lay me down to sleep. . ."

Dexter leaned against the door frame, hands in his pockets, and smiled at the homey scene. Carrie knelt between Benjy and Margaret beside the bed scattered with dolls and toys. The children were in their nightclothes, their hair still damp from their Saturday night baths.

Their backs were to him, but he could hear the children just fine, reciting their evening prayer in unison—though Benjy spoke with a slight lisp due to the tooth he'd lost earlier that day.

The scene struck a familiar chord. He remembered his own mother kneeling beside him, listening to his childhood prayers.

Was that why he'd fallen in love with Carrie, because she reminded him of his mother? She was lovely, sweet, and a sincere Christian, just like his mother had been.

A sense of loneliness settled across his chest like a fog, a loneliness he hadn't been consciously aware of in years. He missed his parents. He wished he'd had the chance to know them as an adult.

What would his mother think of the man her son had grown into, the man whose little-boy prayers she'd listened to every night before bed? A discomfort akin to shame wormed through him. Carrie had told him often that his mother would have been proud of the man he'd become, but he expected his mother would be mightily disappointed to know he'd not only abandoned the church, but the loving Christ about Whom she'd taught him.

Only the church people hadn't loved the saloon-keeper's family. He tried to push away the thought. Wouldn't he ever get over that pain? He was a grown man with a family of his own. Time to put away childhood's hurts.

With a sigh, he crossed his arms over his chest and concentrated on his own children while Margaret finished her "bless you's" and Benjy started on his, tripping a bit over his new lisp.

"God bless Mother and Father, Margaret, and Grandpa and Grandma Chambers, and Joey, and the Browns and the Rangers."

Dexter grinned. Trust Benjy to stick in both their ball clubs.

"And please make Daddy come to church and be a good man. Amen."

Dexter felt his face grow stiff as he watched Benjy jump to his feet and start to climb up on the bed.

"Benjy." Carrie stopped the boy with a gentle hand on his back. "Why did you pray that just now, about your father?"

"Our Sunday school teacher said people are supposed to go to church." He looked into her face with a sober, old man expression and batted his ridiculously long eyelashes once. "I don't want God to be mad at Daddy."

Dexter swallowed the lump that had suddenly appeared in his throat and shivered. His son thought he was a sinner. Well, he was, of course, but he wasn't quite ready for Benjy to give up his hero worship of him yet.

Margaret still knelt on the braided rug, elbows against the side of the quilt-covered mattress, resting her pointed little chin on her chubby hands, watching Benjy and Carrie intently. Carrie remained beside her, one hand rubbing Benjy's back. Dexter wished he could see her face. What was she thinking?

"Benjy, your father is a wonderful man."

"But our Sunday school teacher said it's a sin when people don't go to church."

"Yes, but we all have faults, Benjy. You must always remember that your father loves us and takes very good care of us. He sees that we have lots of good food to eat, and nice clothes to wear, and a beautiful house to live in." She paused and brushed a damp lock of dark hair back from his forehead. "You have one of the best fathers on earth."

"But I can still pray for him to go to church, can't I?"

"Yes, Benjy."

Dexter heard her sigh just before he turned and headed down the stairs toward the parlor. Wave after wave of fury and despair swept over him. His jaw ached from his clenched teeth. He wasn't ready to lose his son's respect. He *wouldn't* lose it, even if it meant eating his words and attending church.

❧

Dexter chanced a sideways glance at Benjy, seated beside him in the pew, looking uncharacteristically angelic in his light blue suit, the huge white collar of his shirt lying about his shoulders like a mantle. The grin was still there, that huge grin that hadn't left the boy's face once since he'd seen his father arrive at the breakfast table dressed for church.

Likely the urchin thought his prayer was solely responsible for his father's presence. Well, it was, he admitted to himself, but not in the way the boy thought.

He stared at the picture above the altar. He couldn't help but feel like the entire congregation was watching him instead of listening to Reverend Chambers's sermon. Likely just his stupid pride. Why should anyone but Benjy, Carrie, and Reverend Chambers care whether he was here or notice the many times he hadn't been over the last few years?

Was Carrie as uncomfortable around his Base Ball friends as he was at church? He always felt the church members were weighing him and finding him wanting, though they never actually said anything to make him feel that way. Did she feel the same about his friends, knowing they didn't share her values? She used to complain bitterly over his friendships. He'd only thought she was being uppity. It had never occurred to him before that he was asking anything difficult of her in expecting her to spend time with his friends.

Or had it? Had he wanted to see whether she could follow the Golden Rule with people who weren't like her?

He shrugged away the disconcerting thought and ran a finger beneath his starched collar, keeping his eyes carefully trained on the painting. Wasn't hearing a word of the sermon. He'd given himself a good talking-to last night and this morning; figured that was about as much of a sermon as he could take in one week.

It was hard to make regular conversation at the dinner table later. He and Carrie were both trying too hard to avoid mention of his church attendance, he realized. They were smiling too brightly and laughing too long at small comments across the table set with the best china and crystal she always used for Sunday dinner.

When Benjy and Margaret were given permission to leave the table, they dashed toward the hall. Benjy stopped in the doorway and turned back, that huge smile still in place. "I'm glad you came to church today, Daddy."

A moment later he was racing out the front door after Margaret. The children's voices and laughter drifted through the open windows along with the spicy scents of early autumn.

Dexter took a deep breath and finally met Carrie's gaze. "And I was beginning to believe I was going to make it through the entire day without any of you commenting on it."

"I'm glad you came to church today, too." Her eyes were filled with joy, just as he'd known they would be, and guilt flooded through him, just as he'd known it would.

He crumpled his linen napkin into a ball with one hand and dropped it beside his plate. He tried to speak softly, even though his trampled pride was trying to send up angry signals. "I haven't had a change of heart. I went to church because I heard Benjy's prayer last night."

Was it pain that shot across her eyes? He felt the soft touch of her hand on his. "I'm sorry, Dexter. I wish you hadn't heard."

She was sorry? She'd defended him gallantly.

"A lad shouldn't have any cause to be ashamed of his da. If it will keep Benjy from being embarrassed of me, I'll even go to church gladly." He jerked his gaze from her, expecting that like his voice, his eyes showed anger, not gladness.

"Your son has no reason to be ashamed of you." Her fingers caressed the back of his hand as lightly as a feather, as soothing as her soft voice. "I'm sorry some church members were cruel to you when you were a boy."

Surprise locked his gaze on their hands. She knew him so well. He hadn't realized she understood how deeply he'd been hurt as a lad.

"Church isn't a place people go because they are better than others," she was continuing. "At least, it shouldn't be. I think it's a place people go because they realize they aren't good enough or strong enough to get through this life alone.

It's a place for people to reach out to God and each other, not shun each other. Benjy has to learn that."

He stood, still reeling from the knowledge that she knew his deepest secret, too deep and still too painful to discuss, even with Carrie.

Turning to the window near the table, he looked through the lace undercurtains into the yard, where Margaret and Benjy were already playing with the neighbor children. It was time he apologized to Carrie. *Past* time. He'd never have the courage to if he had to look into her eyes when he did so, not after all these years.

"It shouldn't have taken Benjy's prayer to get me to church. I promised ye years ago that I'd always attend with ye." Wouldn't ye know that Irish would slip in again? Could never make a comment sound offhand with that accent betraying him. "My behavior must have embarrassed ye with your own da, him being a reverend."

The silence grew long. Wasn't she going to respond? He glanced over his shoulder. She was still seated at the table, staring at him. Tears shimmered in her eyes. How could such fragile things as teardrops have the power to stab through him?

He turned toward her, guilt filling him, and held out one hand. She came to him without hesitation, and he pulled her back against his chest, where he could continue hiding from her eyes. Not that those beautiful, tear-filled eyes accused him. It was the lack of accusation there that cut through him, making him feel more of a cad than ever.

He leaned his cheek against her hair, the light, sweet fragrance of her lily-of-the-valley cologne filling his senses. "I've resented your church-going, Carrie. And resented the time ye've spent with your church friends. Don't be thinkin' I've not been noticing ye've given up time ye'd rather be spending with them to help with the boys' Base Ball club, and watch me play, and entertain my friends."

Her hands squeezed his where they lay at her waist. "It's no sacrifice to spend time with you, me love."

He kissed her temple. "I'm not so sure. I know how uncomfortable I feel around church goers. Ye're probably just as uncomfortable around my Base Ball friends."

"Perhaps I was at one time. But you're careful to insist they act like gentlemen around me and the children."

Dexter grimaced. He wasn't as noble as she believed. True, he'd told his friends that drinking, swearing, and off-color jokes weren't allowed in his home, but he'd let them believe he was simply honoring his wife's wishes. He hadn't stood up to the men and admitted that he didn't want such behavior around his wife and children.

"I broke my promise to ye. I'll not be breakin' it again."

"Dexter!"

He winced at the joy in her cry and hugged her closer, preventing her from turning to face him. "Mind ye, I'll not be attending every church event, but when Der Boss allows, I'll be in the pew beside ye on Sunday mornings."

"Thank you, my love."

A new peace filled him. It was such a little thing to make her so happy. Why had he resisted it so long?

Working on a needlepoint wallhanging of the love chapter four months later with Hope's cheerful canary song a background for her thoughts, she still couldn't believe it. Dexter had accompanied them to services every Sunday since that day in November. She hadn't dared comment on his attendance for fear he would become embarrassed and quit coming.

He didn't attend any of the other church activities, but at least he was once again hearing God's Word on a regular basis. Did he allow himself to open his heart and mind to it, or did he continue to rebel against God inside while faithfully joining them in the pews each Sunday?

Footsteps hurried across the wide wooden floor of the porch that swept around the front and sides of the house. The front door flew open. A cold March wind breezed into the parlor to greet her along with Dexter's eager voice.

"Carrie, look who I've brought home!"

She'd barely left the tapestry-covered, armless oak rocker before he arrived in the room with another man in tow, both in popular, finely checked brown sack suits. Dexter tossed his derby to a small inlaid table, while the guest removed his, revealing neat, short-cropped brown hair above a wide forehead. The man, who couldn't be more than thirty, did look vaguely familiar.

Dexter's mustache rode his wide grin. "Remember the man who beat our fresh third baseman out of a pile of money in a foot race a few years back?"

"Of course! Billy Sunday! Welcome to our home. Have you joined the Browns?"

"Browns aren't so fortunate as that, lass. He's here to speak at the Young Men's Christian Association."

"That's right, Mrs. Riley. We're organizing Base Ball clubs for boys at Y's across the country. Many of the larger cities already have clubs. In spite of the way professional Base Ball has become a cesspool of greed, the sport itself is clean and lends itself to producing a healthy body. I believe if boys have Base Ball to occupy themselves, they won't become involved in occupations more conducive to temptations."

She glanced at Dexter. "Dexter has advised a group of boys in the neighborhood with their Base Ball club for years. I must admit, they use every spare moment for the sport and not one boy has yet developed into a troublesome youngster. However, I do fear for when they are older, attend matches regularly, and are exposed to beer sold on every side."

His straight mouth widened in a smile, and his eyes flashed with friendliness toward a recognized sympathizer. "I agree. One of the next fights must be against liquor at the ball grounds. And along with that, the outlawing of Sunday ball."

"You'll have a tough time with those fights. Men like Der Boss consider beer and Sunday ball the edges that add the profit to their pockets." Dexter waved a broad hand toward his favorite overstuffed chair. "Sit down, man. Make yourself comfortable."

Billy took the chair offered, and Dexter dropped onto the green velvet sofa opposite. Carrie lowered herself to the rocker once again.

"What do you think about beer and Sunday ball?" Billy's direct gaze beneath straight dark brows challenged Dexter, though his tone was conversational.

"I wouldn't mind spending Sunday afternoons with my wife and family." He smiled at her, and their gazes tangled. Somehow he'd made the simple statement an intimate, sentimental admission that wrapped her in love. He glanced back at Sunday. "And as to beer, I'm a bit tired of kranks throwing steins at the players when they don't like what's happening on the grounds."

Billy's laugh filled the room. It was a pleasant laugh, Carrie thought, full and rich.

"In case you hadn't noticed," Dexter informed her, "Billy has gotten a little religion."

Billy shrugged good-naturedly. "More like a lot of religion."

"And, it doesn't disturb you?" she asked hesitantly. "Your involvement in a profession which promotes beer and Sunday ball?"

"I play in the National League. They don't allow beer served in their ball grounds, you may remember. As for Sunday ball, after committing my life to the Lord, I insist my contracts stipulate I won't be required to play on Sundays."

Dexter, who had been listening with his chin resting on one hand, leaned forward. "Your owner actually signed such a contract?"

Billy smiled. "I have a more powerful Owner than the owner of the Cubs."

"I'm serious."

"So am I. But yes, the Cubs' owner signed it, and he sticks by it."

Dexter rubbed one of his thick knuckles back and forth beneath his chin, his eyes thoughtful. "Of course, no owner would want to lose a talented player like yourself." He shoved a thumb in Billy's direction and glanced at Carrie. "He stole eighty-four bases this year."

"I'm planning to leave Base Ball. I've been asked to work with the Young Mens' Christian Association full-time. I've enjoyed the sport, but helping to shape boys' lives is more important to me. Because of my Base Ball fame, the kids listen to what I say."

"The boys in our neighborhood are the same with Dexter. They actually seek him out for advice." Carrie couldn't keep the pride from her voice.

Sunday snapped his fingers. "Say, why don't you join forces with me at the program this evening, Dex? Sounds like the Lord already has you working with St. Louis's boys."

"I'm not much of one for talking about God. Wouldn't know what to say."

"Well, come along with me, anyway."

"Sure, if you'll stay with us tonight instead of at a hotel. Give us a chance to visit some more before your train leaves tomorrow. How about if Carrie and the kids come along with us tonight?"

"The more the merrier."

"There's someone I'd like you to meet before we leave for the meeting. A neighbor boy, Joey. Loves Base Ball. Doctor says he'll never play it again, though."

Billy agreed immediately, and the two set off together with a copy of the new dime novel *Muldoon's Base Ball Club in Philadelphia*, which Dexter had picked up for the boy. It was a humorous book, but she knew Dexter found particularly amusing the fact that Muldoon's Base Ball club was Irish.

Carrie couldn't quell the hope that rose inside her, sending an excited buzz along her nerves while she prepared herself and the children for the evening. Listening to Billy tell the audience how his faith in God had changed his life, would her husband finally open his mind and heart to God, also? She could barely pray that he would, for the hope was so strong. After eight years of praying and hoping and waiting and loving, was tonight the night Dexter would accept God's gifts of love and salvation?

The room hummed with excitement that evening. Boys from five through twenty-five came to hear Billy speak. They howled with appreciation when he entered the stage, sliding across the polished oak floor in a stimulating rendition of his famous base-stealing play. They laughed when he told of praying he would make a pennant-winning catch while running over benches and through spectators.

There wasn't a single deriding hoot from the audience when he told how his faith in Christ had changed his life and how He could change their lives. When he asked anyone who wanted to make a decision to live for God to come forward, Carrie held her breath until she thought her chest would burst, hoping Dexter would join those walking up the aisles.

He didn't.

When they sat up until the early morning hours talking, they didn't discuss the Lord, either. At least not while she was with them. Instead they talked Base Ball: the new Players League formed in opposition to the $2,500 salary cap set by both National League and American Association owners, the many players deserting the National League for the Players League, rumors of gambling on Base Ball matches, Von der Ahe's suspicions of match throwing and subsequent player fines, mass desertion by most of the Browns for the new Players League and the Browns' surprisingly good third-place showing in spite of it. And their shared disappointment at the way things were deteriorating within the game they both loved.

Knowing Billy, she was sure he would confront Dexter about her husband's faith when she left them and went to bed. She arose in the morning hoping to hear Dexter had discovered the joy of Christ's salvation. But neither man mentioned that Dexter had had a change of heart.

"I had such high hopes over Billy's visit," she whispered, watching between parlor draperies as the two men left together for Union Depot.

The canary's song gaily spilled through the parlor. Carrie walked to the tall brass cage. The bird's yellow feathers were a cheerful note in the otherwise darkly decorated room. Hope tipped its head, eyeing her curiously, then continued its song.

"Are you reprimanding me for being such a poor sport? The St. Louis Browns would never have won so many pennants if they gave up as easily as me, would they? 'Love never faileth.' Hope 'never stops—at all.' Thank you kindly for the reminder."

Chapter Eighteen

1892

Carrie slipped her arms into the loose-fitting top of soft, dove gray merino that buttoned discreetly up the front beneath boxy pleats that hung over the top of her skirt. She loved the freedom pregnancy gave her from her binding corsets, which seemed to grow tighter each year.

She rested her hands lightly on her stomach. *A baby*. There had been a time when she'd doubted she and Dexter would ever have another child.

That was almost five years ago, when Emmet had said, "Don't give up on him."

She hadn't given up. She hadn't won yet, either.

Of course she hadn't, she corrected herself. There is no winning or losing in love. There is only loving.

She patted the top where it hung loosely over her bulging middle. "I hope you marry someone as nice as your daddy, but someone who loves Jesus."

She laughed at herself. She'd teased Grant and Dexter about worrying over their daughters' future husbands while the girls were newborns, and here she was doing the same thing, only this child wasn't even born.

The bedroom door opened, and she turned toward it in surprise. Her heart lurched. Dexter stood staring at her, one hand gripping the brass knob. His usually sun-warmed skin was gray. His eyes burned with shock and confusion.

Fear shot through her. She wanted to shut the moment out of time. She didn't want to know the terrible thing he knew.

"What is it?"

"Joey. The nurse who's been staying with the lad just stopped. The doctor said. . .he's in a bad way. His only chance is surgery, and that's for bein' dangerous at best."

Joey! It didn't seem possible.

"His parents sent a message. Joey wants us to come."

They brought the children along. In case the worst happened, Benjy must have the opportunity to see his friend one last time.

He's stronger about this than we are, she thought later, watching the boys together.

Joey's skin was almost as pale as the pillows against which he was propped in his narrow bed. He was so slender that his body barely made a dent in the bedding. His breathing was shallow and shaky, and she wondered whether they should tax his strength when he needed every ounce of it so badly.

Benjy sat on the stool that allowed him to visit on an equal height with Joey. She knew his frequent visits had taught him that it was painful for Joey to be jostled about, so he didn't attempt to sit on the bed.

"You can have that book we finished reading yesterday if you want to, Ben."

"The one about Double Curve Dan, the Base Ball detective?"

"Yeah."

"That was a good story. The other guys on the club will prob'ly like it, too."

Carrie heard Dexter, standing beside her with Margaret in his arms, swallow hard. "Going to tell Joey the news about the club, Benjy?"

"Oh, yeah!" He leaned forward eagerly, his green eyes sparkling beneath his long lashes, a healthy flush on his cheeks that made her feel guilty to have a son who was so alive. "The nine voted yesterday. We're not going to be the Rangers anymore. We're going to be Joey's Rangers."

The tiniest hint of color touched Joey's drawn cheeks. "Honest?"

Benjy gave a sharp nod. "Honest. You're the one who got us started, remember?"

The pale lips quivered in a smile. "I like Base Ball. Say, you be sure ta practice that throw Tony Mullane taught you. Maybe one day you'll be a champion hurler like he is."

"Think I might?"

"Sure. If ya practice every day like I always tell ya."

"Benjy," Dexter's voice was low, but Benjy heard and understood.

He slid down from the oak stool and stood as close to the bed as possible without leaning against it. "Guess I better go." He took one of Joey's hands carefully in his own and gave it a gentle, solemn shake. " 'Bye."

" 'Bye."

Dexter touched Benjy's shoulder. "Will you and Margaret wait in the hall, Benjy? Your mother and I will be out soon."

When the door closed behind the children, she and Dexter moved from the foot of the bed to the side.

"He likes ta be called Ben now."

She smiled at Joey's gentle reprimand. So like him to be watching out for Benjy—Ben—even now.

"We'll try to remember." Dexter's voice sounded thick.

Joey nodded slightly. Closed his eyes.

The simple motion sent fear darting through her. The few words he'd spoken with Benjy had cost him dearly in strength.

His eyes opened again, and distress washed over her when she noticed that his skin was almost as blue as his eyes. "He's a good kid."

Still speaking of Benjy. Ben.

Dexter nodded. One of his large hands massaged his neck. She wondered whether his throat was as tight as hers, whether he was having difficulty getting words through it. "Yeah." The word wasn't much more than a hoarse whisper.

He cleared his throat and laid a hand gently on Joey's shoulder. "Ye're one of the reasons he's a good kid, and a good base baller, too. Ye look out for him just like a big brother would. Means a lot to me, knowing ye're watching out for him, 'specially since I have to be away at match games so often."

The edge of a smile touched the thin lips. Pride shone in the tired eyes.

Her own eyes burned from trying to hold back tears. Were they as red as Dexter's? His had an unusual sheen to them.

He dug one hand deep into his trousers pocket and took Joey's hand with the other. The boy's fingers looked tiny, white, and helpless beside his.

A tear rolled over Dexter's lashes and down his dark cheek. At the sight of it, her own tears escaped. Not once in all the years they'd been together had she seen him cry!

"Don't worry, Cap. Doc's pretty good, and if he can't fix me, I'm not afraid ta die. I trust in Jesus, just like ya said I should. I know He'll take care of me."

She swallowed hard, trying not to sob. Joey was being so brave. She didn't want to make it harder for him.

Suddenly his words penetrated her mind, and she gasped. Dexter had told him to trust in Jesus?

"Ya think there's Base Ball in heaven, Cap?"

A shaky laugh burst from Dexter. "I'm not for knowing much about what heaven's like. All I know is that 'tis a good place, where people aren't for hurting each other, and we never have to say good-bye. But I expect since Jesus was a little boy on earth once Himself, He'll not be objectin' too strenuously to a Base Ball match now and then."

"Clouds will be pretty soft for sliding into base on, don't ya think?"

Joey's words came back to her that evening after they'd tucked the children in bed. She hoped it would be a long time before Joey discovered whether the clouds were soft to slide upon.

She followed Dexter into the parlor, where a fat, rose-shaded lamp shed deceptively mellow light through the properly stiff room. He stopped in the middle of the colorful Persian carpet, his hands clenching and unclenching, again and again, at his sides.

She slid her arms around his waist, wishing she could draw his pain away, into herself.

He reacted instantly to her touch, burying his face in her neck, crushing her shoulders in his embrace. Warm tears dampened her skin and the collar of the gray merino top she'd donned with such joy that morning.

The desperation in his manner spoke louder than the words she knew he would say if he could: "I love him." "I've never felt so helpless." "What if it were Benjy?"

She drew him down on the couch. They held each other all the night through.

Not once did she consider moving, even when her arms fell asleep from cradling him.

Not once did she ask about the faith in Jesus to which he and Joey had alluded, though her spirit cried out to know when he had accepted the freeing belief for which she had prayed so many years.

Not once did she get up to cover Hope's cage, the canary Joey had brought to their home, a symbol of their love and commitment; the canary who sang them gentle songs of comfort throughout the night, and never stopped—at all.

Joey didn't discover that year whether clouds were soft to slide upon, but his recovery was slow.

In the days after learning he would live, Dexter seemed filled with unbounded joy. Carrie waited eagerly for him to mention the faith she'd learned of at Joey's bedside.

He didn't.

The longer she waited, the more difficult it was to broach the subject. She was on the well-known pins and needles, watching for signs he was becoming more like Grant and her father and Emmet.

She hesitated before saying grace at meals, hoping he would eagerly step in to express their thanks.

He didn't.

She read her Bible while sitting beside him in the parlor evenings, hoping he would offer to read with her.

He didn't.

After two months, she could stand it no longer and asked him straight out when he had changed his mind and heart about the Lord.

One edge of his mouth beneath the closely trimmed, wine red mustache lifted in the self-conscious smile so different from his usual grin. He turned his sparkling gaze away for a moment, then returned it to her in the familiar manner that spoke of his unease.

"One day I found myself talking to Him." He snorted and shook his head. "Talking to Someone I didn't believe existed. Suppose that was the start of it."

He pulled her closer, until her head rested against his chest. She knew he was hiding from her his eyes and face with their revealing natures.

"I asked Him that night to show me if He was real. It was a long time before I realized He was showing me Himself through your love, girleen. I thought I wanted something bold to happen, like when God appeared to the apostle Paul." He pulled back slightly, allowing her to look into his face for a moment, and grinned. "Ye see, I have been listening to your da's sermons."

His fingers slid through her hair, cupping the back of her head, and urged her cheek back against the cool linen of his shirt.

"God had a better way in mind for me. He showed me what it's like to be truly loved."

She blinked at the tears that suddenly filled her lashes and hugged him tighter while he cleared the huskiness from his throat.

"When ye first told me ye loved me, I was. . .overwhelmed. In spite of the saloon, even though I was a base ballist, ye loved me. And then ye told me ye wouldn't be marrying me because I didn't share your faith, and all the old hurts I'd known as a lad came rushing back."

She caught back a cry, distress pouring through her.

"Shhh, lass." His breath was warm against her hair. "It's all right now."

"But I never meant to hurt you so!"

"I know, love. Ye were only being true to your beliefs. And then ye agreed to marry me anyway." His fingers played with the hair at the back of her head, and he rested his cheek against her hair. "I knew it went against your beliefs to marry me, and because of that, I always felt ye were ashamed of me, that I wasn't quite good enough for ye."

"It was never that you weren't good enough!"

"I know that now. But I. . .I'm ashamed to be sayin' I was testing your love. I wanted ye to love me in spite of my faults. I think that's one of the reasons I stopped going to church and why I fought God for so long. I knew your faith was the most important thing in your life. If you could love me even if I didn't share your faith, then I'd know your love was real. But I didn't truly believe it was that strong."

She strangled the protestation that rose to her throat.

"By our fifth anniversary, I figured I was right, that ye didn't love me, that ye wished ye'd married Emmet." His arms squeezed her tighter. "I'm sorry, me love. I wasn't fair to ye or to God. Ye went against your father and your beliefs to marry me. Ye've stuck beside me even when I went against my word to you. Ye've befriended my friends when I shunned yours. Ye loved me and believed in me even when I rejected your faith for all these years."

"But it's different now."

"Yes. One day I realized He'd shown me through ye how faithful His love is. Mother always told me not to judge church goers by the worst of the lot, but by the best. I never listened to that advice. Until you. So I asked God to forgive me, the way your da is always saying people have to do, and thanked Him for sending Christ to bring me to Him."

"I'm so glad. But why haven't you told me before?"

Hands at her shoulders pushed her firmly away until he could meet her curious gaze. "I'm not good at talking about such things. Some things are too personal and. . .too difficult to explain." His eyes warmed, and he drew her back into his embrace. "Like my love for you," he whispered against her lips before claiming them.

Surrendering to his arms, she remembered the stars.

Lafayette Park was as beautiful in fall as in May, Carrie thought, looking about at the lovely blend of muted bronzes, golds, and crimsons surrounding them in the trees and among the fallen leaves. The colors reflected in the pond, where leaves drifted lazily along on the top of water barely rippled by the slight breeze, which carried the spicy, moldering scent of autumn on its wings.

It had been May, with the air thick with the scent of lilacs and everything newly green, the first time she'd been here with Dexter. It would always be lovely to her. The first time he'd told her he loved her had been in this place.

That was ten years ago. It hardly seemed possible. So many things had changed, not the least of which was the existence of their children, who were merely hazy dreams when the two of them fell in love. Now nine-year-old Ben and almost eight-year-old Margaret played along the water's edge with Dexter, while Joey sat watching them, still weak six months after his surgery. Three-month-old Joseph slept beside her, peacefully wrapped in a pale green blanket of softest merino wool.

She brushed a crisp brown leaf from her skirt and smiled. Fashions had changed, too, for which she gave bountiful thanks. The tightly bodiced gown with bindingly close sleeves and the uncomfortable bustle that she'd worn the day she met Dexter had been replaced by a far more feminine suit. She removed her gloves and smoothed her hands over the lavender and deep green figures on the cream background of her challis skirt. How nice that Dexter had insisted she treat herself to a new outfit now that Joseph had arrived and her figure was returning to something resembling her original size!

Dexter had changed, too. His mustache wasn't as large, and he was even suggesting the possibility of removing it completely. She hoped he wouldn't. She liked its softness against her skin when he kissed her. His hair wasn't as thick as it was ten years ago or the color as wine-shaded. The lines at the outer edges of his eyes were deeply etched from years of playing Base Ball in the sun.

He had all but retired his black derby for the popular dark gray Boston with its creased crown and a black band above the wide brim. She had to admit, he looked handsome in it. The sight of him still set her heart tripping like a trotting carriage pony, the same as when they'd met.

The largest change was inside Dexter. She knew it was there. Knew it in the relaxed manner he had when they were in church. Knew it in the joyous comments he would occasionally make concerning the discovery of faith in another. But he still wasn't like most of the Christian men with whom she'd grown up.

He dropped down on the quilt beside her, surprising her from her thoughts and her gazing upon Joseph. He grinned, noting the direction her gaze had taken. "Still can't get enough of looking at him, even after three months of changing and feeding and staying up nights, can you?"

"No." She laughed.

"Neither can I."

She loved his sweet admission, loved the way his voice was thick with love for their child.

He ran a knuckle lightly along her cheek, his eyes shining into hers. "I like watching you watch him. Like being a mother, don't you?"

"Love it." She looked down at Joseph. She didn't dare look at Dexter when she made her request, for fear he'd be offended by her disappointment if he denied it. "I've been thinking of the service Grant and Phoebe had for Rose Marie. Would you mind if we had one for Joseph?"

"No, that sounds like a fine idea. We should have had them for Ben and Margaret, too."

His quick agreement was a pleasant surprise.

"It would bring me comfort to know that together we've entrusted our children to the Lord."

He was watching Joseph, running the twig of a red maple leaf lightly over the blanket, and she knew he was somewhat embarrassed by the topic.

"Would. . .would you pray with me, Dexter?"

He glanced at her then, giving her a tight smile. "Sure."

He slipped an arm about her shoulders, and she leaned against him, resting her cheek on his afternoon frock coat. After a minute, he squeezed her shoulder and dropped his arm. "I love you," he said quietly with a self-conscious smile.

She gave him back a smile with trembling lips. It was always the same. She'd asked him to pray with her a handful of times since discovering his faith, and always it was just like this. He held her close, prayed silently, and afterward looked like he'd been caught pilfering the neighbors' apples.

At first it had disturbed her. Now, she was grateful he prayed with her, even if it wasn't in the manner to which she'd grown accustomed in her parents' home and in her friendship with Emmet. She would have preferred they pray aloud together, but the Lord had said that wherever two or more were gathered together in His name, He was there; that was all that was truly important.

"I think it's time I left Base Ball, Carrie."

She stared at him, stunned.

He slid a sideways glance at her and wiggled his eyebrows in his dear, funny way. "Think you can bear having your husband in town every night of the year?"

In spite of his smile, his eyes revealed her answer was important to him. "I should love having my husband home every night. But why. . ."

"I told Der Boss I wanted a clause in my contract saying I needn't play Sunday ball. He said I wasn't important enough to the club to agree to such a concession."

"I'm sorry." Her heart thundered above her quiet words. To think he'd actually asked to be released from playing on the Sabbath! Surely the Lord was working in his life. But she hated that Mr. Von der Ahe would hurt him this way. "He was wrong about your importance, of course."

He smiled, his eyes warm with gratitude for her support, but shook his head. "I'm getting to be an old man in this sport. I've been playing Base Ball for sixteen years now. Those first years with the Browns, they were the best. But most of my friends have been sold to other clubs. Now that the American Association has merged with the National League, nothing is the same. Grant's offered me a position with his law firm, now that I have my degree. Like to move back to your hometown, Carrie?"

"Sounds wonderful!" It was the only place she would want to live other than St. Louis. How good of the Lord to arrange it for the next step of their life together!

Dexter drew up his knees, leaned his elbows on them, and gave his attention to the children, who were busy pulling two small wooden tugboats about by strings through the shallows at the edge of the pond. "Remember your father's sermon this morning? Where Solomon asked God for wisdom and God made him the wisest man to ever live?"

"Yes." *How unusual for him to discuss a sermon!*

"What would you ask for from God, if you could have only one thing?"

Your salvation. The words leaped to her mind. She had been praying for him to come to the Lord for so many years! But now the prayer had been answered.

There was another she'd almost forgotten. Ten years ago, before she'd known Dexter was returning to ask her to reconsider his marriage proposal, she'd made a request of God. She recalled the moment vividly: Standing in the parlor at the St. Louis parsonage, looking out on the cheerful fall garden, she'd begged, "Lord, if it is the only thing I learn in life, teach me to love as Thou dost love."

In the years since she'd begun studying the love chapter and seeking to be taught how to love, she'd not once remembered that prayer.

Her heart stood still. Beat on, as quickly as a hummingbird flutters its wings. Had God used her marriage to Dexter to answer her request? Would she have gone to the effort to love Dexter that she had these last years if she hadn't promised God to stay with Dexter for life?

He was still awaiting her answer, watching her with curiosity behind an unusual veil of reserve. She looked directly into his beautiful peridot green eyes and put all the warmth she could into her gaze. "I'd ask Him to teach me to love you as much as He does, Dexter."

The veil of reserve dissolved. His eyes glistened suspiciously in the moment before he caught her to himself. "And I'd ask Him to make me worthy of your love, girleen." The admission was a husky whisper against her hair, a whisper that filled her chest with an aching desire to be able to express the tender love she felt.

She pulled back slightly, resting her head on his shoulder, looking up into his face, adoring him. Her hand touched his cheek. "You are worthy, just as you are."

The look that leaped to his eyes humbled her with its joy.

Contentment such as she'd never before experienced filled her. Perhaps Dexter would never be like other Christian men she knew. A small sigh escaped her at the thought of the sharing of the Word and in prayer that she might never know with him. But he was a child of God and took wonderful care of her and the children, and in his own quiet, unobtrusive way, he touched people for Christ who weren't being touched by people like her.

Perhaps their marriage hadn't been God's perfect will. Perhaps she had made the wrong choice when she married him instead of Emmet. But God had helped her to honor the vows she'd taken, had helped her to learn to love the man she'd married.

Why had it taken so *long* to learn to love him?

She'd thought she loved him when they married, that the passion, the overwhelming desire for his presence and his arms was love. She hadn't known anything about love then. It had taken ten years of struggling, choosing to act in a loving manner, to begin to know what love was all about. Doubtless the Lord had a great deal left to teach her on the subject.

A warm rush of tenderness flowed through her. The rewards of learning to love were well worth the lessons.

"It will be our tenth anniversary next Sunday, Dexter. I'm so lucky to be married to you."

A chuckle broke out above her ear. "I don't think you're lucky."

She pushed away from him, miffed.

He reached to pull her back but stopped when a middle-aged woman appeared on the walkway with a skinny little white dog on a lead. Dropping his arm casually about his knee, he leaned over to whisper, "I don't think we were lucky. I think it was planned."

Planned? Perhaps. Perhaps not. But it wasn't long ago he hadn't even believed in God, and now he believed God planned their love. Wasn't that a miracle?

Sweet joy snuggled down inside her and curled up around her heart.

The Promise of Rain

Sally Krueger

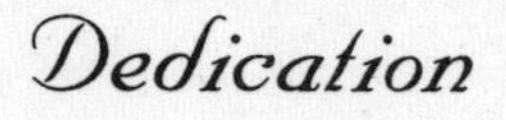

For Myles, a gift from God.

Chapter One

Kenya, Africa—1923

Each day as Ruth fruitlessly scanned the horizon for some sign of rain, she let her eyes drift longingly downward to the jewel-green line of trees that filled the gorge as it cut down the hillside toward the valley just below the farm. Then, exhausted and hot after working all day in the sun's heat, she would make her lonely way through the dust and the long, dry grasses, squinting into the sun's relentless glare until she slipped into the cool, green light of the little valley. She had been coming often these days.

She made her way along the narrow pathway she had worn through the trees to the small, cold pool of water. Ruth slipped off her boots and began dangling her toes in the cool water when she felt her skin prickle with fear. Even before she saw them, she knew she was no longer alone. The weight of an ancient, primeval presence had silently settled on the valley, and the hair on the back of her neck stood on end. She was afraid to look up.

An agonizing moment later, she finally forced herself to face them. Ruth beheld an enormous cow elephant, with her calf proudly standing beside her. Their immense leather ears twitched and scanned for the slightest sound. Their trunks, one long and weatherbeaten, one small and supple, tasted and sniffed the cool air. A scent of danger spread itself like a mist throughout the little glade.

The elephants had emerged silently from the bush on the opposite side of the pool. Ruth was paralyzed with fear, but they hadn't seen her yet, and she was downwind. She felt herself dwindle and shrink in their presence. The mother elephant took a step toward the water. Ruth knew she must get away.

There was an old thorn tree directly behind her, but the lowest branch was at least eight feet off the ground. As the cow turned to encourage her calf, Ruth saw her opportunity. She must not hesitate. Desperately, silently, Ruth jumped and reached for the branch, clawing painfully with her fingers until she was able to scramble up the trunk with her bare feet. She could hear the two elephants wading into the water behind her. Breathless with fear, she climbed as high as she could. At last she clung tightly to a thin branch, while they filled their trunks with water from the pool directly underneath her.

She had never seen elephants in this valley before. They usually stuck to the plains below. But it was late in the dry season, and the streams down on the plain had become small, dirty trickles lost in the bottom of the wide, mud-cracked riverbeds. While precariously clinging to the tree, Ruth peered down through the branches at the two elephants.

The mother's great, gray legs stood like tree trunks growing out of the earth up toward Ruth's sanctuary above. Her ears, huge and delicate, flared outward, sensitive to each insect and every sound. Her trunk, as tenderly as any mother's arm, caressed her baby.

The mother elephant sucked up a trunkful of muddy, churning water and squirted a fountain at her baby. The baby, gleefully catching onto the game, shot a little fountain back at his mother. Soon the trees all along the edge of the pond were awash with spray. Bright, dancing drops fluttered between the sunlit leaves and through a hundred little rainbows, drenching Ruth to the skin as she clung like a terrified monkey to the huge old thorn tree.

If elephants could laugh, the whole of the small valley would be ringing with the sound, Ruth thought, in spite of her fear. *Their laughter would rumble and peal, echoing all the way up into the hills above, filling all the earth with the awesome sound.* And here, so close to the source, Ruth ached with joy to hear it. Her own heart was so small and hard in comparison to the huge, free-living hearts of these great creatures, she was afraid it would shatter like glass just to be in their presence.

The fountain sprays washed the red plains' earth off their backs, and they changed color before Ruth's very eyes until they were the brown of the earth up here in the hills. They frolicked together, as joyful and fresh as the morning sunshine, yet as ancient and as timeless as Africa itself.

Ruth's heart had stopped beating wildly, and she felt safer now as she watched them playing in the water. As she watched, she was entranced by the love between the mother and the child. An immense longing came over her—to be loved and to love with the same intimate joy. She longed to have it wash over her, immersing her with joy and life. But she shook the feeling away the instant it began to overwhelm her, and she focused her attention on the two creatures below her.

The baby elephant noticed Ruth's boots on the edge of the water. He reached out with his trunk, picked one up, and tossed it high up into the air. Ruth watched it sail up past her head and crash down through some branches into the pond below. The little elephant bellowed with delight. He picked up Ruth's other boot and tossed it, too. Forgetting herself, Ruth laughed out loud, giving herself away. Suddenly everything became perfectly still. The mother sniffed the air with her trunk. Then as quickly and silently as they had come, the elephants withdrew, melting softly into the trees on the other side of the stream.

For a moment, the whole of the little valley was absolutely silent. Ruth held her breath. She was still afraid, yet she savored the sensation, like a mouthful of bittersweet liquid to quench an old thirst. For a few minutes, she had actually been alive with the terror and the joy. Quietly, she waited along with the rest of the valley to see if they returned; but there was only silence.

Then cautiously and slowly, the stream and valley began to stir again. After one or two tentative chirps, the chorus of birds resumed their musical banter. The muddy water swirled slowly around, settling the mud back into place until it ran clear and clean once more.

Ruth climbed stiffly down from her tree, noting all the scratches and bruises she had sustained in her flight upward. She stood barefoot on the rock overhang, peering into the middle of the pool to see if she could see her boots.

The presence of the elephant still lingered down here. It still flowed in the tumbling stream and hovered over the waters of the still, clear pool, a memory of joy. Ruth waded into the water to retrieve her soggy, mud-laden boots. The water was clear and shockingly cold. She felt the gentle current moving under the surface of the pond. Her boots were already covered in the settling silt. She picked them up, held them against her khaki shirt, and waded out of the water on the far side of the pool—the side from which the elephants had come and gone. Ruth looked both ways, and then she slowly made her way up the other side of the valley, her bare feet tender and bruised on the forest floor, her eyes watching for snakes that lurked in the undergrowth.

At the top of the valley, Ruth came out onto the dirt cart track that followed the little valley up the hillside to the lone farmhouse where Ruth was headed. Although the sun was low on the distant hills in the west, heat waves still radiated upward, stirred up by a scavenger wind, blowing hot over the arid landscape and devouring every green and living thing in its path. Ruth pulled out a crumpled khaki hat from her pocket and put it on. She plastered it low over her short, curly red hair and covered her green eyes and freckled cheeks, hiding them as best she could from the relentless sun and wind. She walked with long, lanky strides, picking her way over the burning dust of the road. Her wet khaki trousers and shirt whipped against her tall, lean body. She cut a lonely figure.

The farmhouse looked down on her from the hillside above. Its corrugated iron roof glinted a hard welcome in the sun. She didn't look up, but she knew her father was sitting on the veranda by now, waiting for the day to end. It was he who had forged this farm out of the stone heart of Africa forty years before. There were no other settlers in the area, and he was alone on the hillside, except for the Africans who belonged to the landscape and blended in with it the way he never would. Yet, over the decades, Africa had weathered and worn away at him, even as he had tried to shape it. Now he sat watching, like an old and gnarled anthill, long since abandoned, but not yet ground back to dust. Except for Ruth, he was still alone.

Her mother had come to Africa from Scotland along with her family, the Campbells, a fierce, resolute clan that had founded the town of Campbellburgh on the plains below Jack Jones's farm.

Morag Campbell was a delicate, gentle woman, and no one knew what she had seen in Jack Jones. In any case, she didn't last very long up here on the farm. She had died of typhoid fever when Ruth was only five years old. People said it was Africa that had killed her. Ruth treasured the few gentle, faded memories of her mother that she had hidden in her heart. What a difference it would have made to her life had Morag lived. Life with Jack had been hard and tough.

Even at this distance, she could feel his eyes on her as she made her way up the hillside. He was always watching, always squinting into the sun. She still didn't look up, but she knew where he was, sitting on the veranda under the bougainvillaea.

Jack had withdrawn into himself after Morag had died. It had made him harder and surlier than he already was. Ruth had been left to fend for herself. But he had taught her to farm, and these days she ran the farm almost single-handedly while her father watched from the veranda. It was hard work, and they would never be rich, the farm being so far into the hills as it was. It was too high and too remote, but Jack had intended it that way. He saw freedom in the isolation. And as he had predicted, the valley below had become riddled with settlers as well as with trophy hunters and tourists.

For Ruth, the isolation of the farm was her bondage. As she drew closer to the little house, the joy and lightness that had filled her while she watched the elephants seeped out into the dusty road and the parched grass. She trudged slowly up the hill, feeling as tired and empty as the cloudless afternoon sky hanging heavily above her. Her eyes were tired of searching, but still she scanned the distant horizon for the boiling thunderheads that signaled the beginning of the rains.

She climbed a wooden fence and made her way through the boma, its dry, scorched grass scratching at her ankles. The sun was starting to sink toward the hills on the far side of the valley now. Ruth could tell from the way it shone onto her back. It had weakened suddenly, the way the sun does in the tropics; and the wind, without its fierce accomplice, was beginning to hesitate and falter.

Ruth vaulted the fence on the other side of the boma and made her way across some patchy, scrubby grass that served as a front lawn. She had never much bothered with the finer points of gardening, except for the huge bougainvillaea vine that grew along the veranda. Her mother had planted it before Ruth was born, and Ruth always took great care to see that it was properly watered and trained. It was her one beautiful possession, the only thing she had ever had simply because it was beautiful, left to her by her mother, and she treasured it. Ruth glanced protectively over it as she walked gingerly over the spiky grass. It arched, blooming profusely with red-tissue petals all across the mantel of the veranda, and Ruth looked past it for her father. His chair was empty. He must have gone inside to refill his glass.

She hurried up to the veranda and put her boots to dry on the steps in the evening sun. She heard the front door open just as she scurried around the side of the house and slipped through the kitchen door. A burst of steam escaped as she went in, and she closed the door carefully behind her while her eyes adjusted to the muted indoor light.

"Jambo, Memsahib!" came the warm greeting from Milka, the cook. She and Ruth spoke in Swahili. "How are you? Here is your cup of tea." Milka pushed a tray with a teapot and cup across the table that stood in the middle of the kitchen, and Ruth pulled up a chair and sat down.

She poured out her tea and watched Milka bustling about the kitchen. Her white apron, always perfectly ironed and clean, and her crisp blue cotton dress underneath stood in stark contrast to her gently wrinkled, broadly cheerful face. Pots sputtered busily on the huge wood stove that stood in one corner. In the other corner sat a little toto, dutifully peeling potatoes. Milka chattered busily to him, scolding him and hurrying him along. Ruth sipped her tea quietly, as she did every evening, watching Milka get supper ready.

For Milka, the preparation of the evening meal was a task fraught with excitement and energy far in excess of its everyday regularity. Ruth always wondered how she made everything, no matter how ordinary, into a thrilling adventure. She had such untiring enthusiasm for living. Drained and empty, Ruth slouched her elbows on the table, watching Milka whip up some eggs for the Yorkshire pudding. Fat sizzled fiercely in the oven and water for the potatoes boiled rapidly on the stove. The very air crackled with energy as it swirled and eddied around Milka as she worked.

Milka brought a religious fervor to her work. Having been at the mission school for one year when she was a girl, Milka had proudly embraced the Christian faith and considered her place in the Joneses' home to be God's personal calling to her. It was Milka's deepest sorrow, she'd told Ruth, that Jack had never allowed his daughter to attend church. Milka, with true Christian zeal, had tried unsuccessfully to instill something of her faith in Ruth's life. Over the years, Ruth had grown accustomed to hearing Milka's constant assurance of her prayers. If Milka had ever become discouraged, Ruth would have had to admit that she would genuinely miss them. In a strange, disbelieving way, Ruth had grown dependent on Milka's prayers for her.

She had been their cook since Ruth was born. In fact, she had been trained by Morag, which was quite unusual because most cooks were men. Milka had never ceased to take her unique position as cook, as well as her unofficial position as mother to the lonely little girl who grew up here on the farm, with the utmost seriousness.

Milka whisked a mug out of the cupboard and poured herself some tea. The Yorkshire pudding was in the oven, the potatoes were peeled, and the long-suffering toto was washing bowls and pots. "How was your day, Memsahib?" she asked, sitting down opposite Ruth with one eye on the toto and the other on the potatoes. When Ruth told her about the elephants, Milka's eyes grew wide with horror.

"Memsahib, you must be more careful! They could have trampled you to death. Lord have mercy! He must have had His angels watching for you today, 'Sahib!"

Ruth laughed at Milka's concern for her, but then she grew more thoughtful.

"You know, Milka, when I saw such magnificent, gentle, fearsome beasts as I hung up there in that tree this afternoon, I couldn't help thinking that they must indeed be a work of God. So much power, and yet what loving-kindness perfectly blended into one creature."

"Well, praise be to God above!" said Milka, lifting her eyes dramatically to the ceiling, where the steam from the boiling pots was collecting like a pillar of cloud. "He has given you a sign at last. My prayers will soon be answered. I am certain of it."

Now it was Ruth's turn to roll her eyes heavenward, and she laughed. This was not the first time Milka had received signs from God; and Ruth, as always, responded with good-natured skepticism. She even found herself wishing for a trusting faith like Milka's now and then. Wouldn't life be so easy? she patronized. Out loud she laughed and said, "Well, Milka, if the elephants are a sign from God, I for one certainly have no idea what He could possibly mean by them. He will have to be more explicit, thank you very much."

"Ah, but God moves most mysteriously," countered Milka, her eyes twinkling with the challenge. This was her favorite type of discussion. "You can never tell what He is going to do, but He is up to something, you mark my words." She spoke in solemn and dramatic tones.

Ruth shook her head and put her empty teacup down on the table. Usually she would tease Milka about a God who would give people signs from heaven whose meanings were impossible to understand. Surely, if He were truly God, she would say, He would be capable of making Himself clear. And Milka would exclaim passionately that He did indeed make Himself clear for those who had eyes to see and ears to hear. But today Ruth didn't argue or tease, she just pushed her chair away from the table.

"I'd better go and wash for supper," she said. Ruth had an odd flicker of feeling that God might, indeed, be stooping to touch her life after all these years. But the flame was too tiny and uncertain to talk about to anyone just yet, even Milka. She went out through the door that led down the hall to her bedroom. The house was quiet and cold. Night was moving in quickly.

Dinner was served formally in the dining room, a ritual left over from Morag's time and kept in perfect obedience by Milka. Even Jack dared not usurp Milka's authority on this issue. Ruth sat in her usual place at the long mahogany table, under the glare of the huge lion's head that hung on the opposite wall. Its glassy eyes, flickering sinisterly in the light of the hurricane lamp, glowered down at her as they had every night since she could remember. All along the other walls were the heads of antelope of all kinds, leering hungrily, yet unable to eat, like guests at a macabre banquet. Ruth shuddered and glanced quickly up into the rafters above, where, contrary to the natural laws, darkness seemed to overcome light, and the hurricane lamp shivered with fear even in the stillness. Supper was always served just after sundown. Ruth cringed, awaiting her father's entrance.

She heard him coming. He slammed the veranda door behind him. His footsteps echoed emptily across the hardwood floor of the lounge. The door burst open and Jack's presence filled the room. He was still a powerful man. He prowled unsteadily to the head of the table, sat under the mounted head of the lion, and glowered menacingly at the joint of beef in front of him. You could still see the vestiges of his youth, although his full head of once-black hair was now gray. He had a huge mustache, still as black as it ever was. Jack was a big man, although a lifetime of hard work had left him stooped and tired.

Milka came in from the kitchen and bustled about, serving the supper dishes. Ruth waited until she was finished.

"There were elephants down at the valley today," she ventured. "Only two, a cow and her calf. It was a close call, but I managed to get up a thorn tree before they saw me."

"Well, I'll have to go and shoot them if they come any closer or they'll get into the coffee." Jack dug into the roast beef and the boiled potatoes. "Which way were they headed?"

"I didn't see," Ruth answered shortly. Jack didn't reply.

"Are you going to Angus Campbell's funeral tomorrow?" She tried another tack.

"Humph!" came the reply. "I'd sooner stick my head in the jaws of a crocodile than go anywhere near that Campbell woman." He stuck another forkful of meat into his mouth.

"Besides, she's called some sort of landowners' meeting for the day after her own husband's funeral, and she can't expect me to go scurrying back and forth into town every day of the week. I have better things to do. Go yourself."

It was Ruth's turn not to reply. She wondered what kind of meeting Florence would be calling so quickly after her husband's funeral. But it was the funeral that concerned Ruth most. She loathed social occasions of every kind. She hated being stared at because of her old-fashioned, badly fitting clothes that once belonged to her mother. She hated being too timid to talk to anyone. On the rare occasions when someone did speak to her, she usually managed to say something completely inappropriate in reply. But Florence would be expecting her, and Ruth was too afraid of Florence to risk her wrath.

Angus Campbell was her mother's brother and the son of old Hamish Campbell, the founder of Campbellburgh. Angus had finally died after a long, drawn-out illness whose actual nature had never been diagnosed. Upon hearing the news, Jack had growled that Florence had hounded him to death. Any man would have died after thirty years of marriage to her—it was a miracle he had survived that long!

Ruth couldn't help but think Jack was probably partly right. Florence was indeed a fearsome woman, and everyone in Campbellburgh lived in terror of her tongue and her temper. Everyone except Jack Jones. Unfortunately for Ruth, Florence had developed a special interest in her upon the death of her sister-in-law and had taken it upon herself to see to her niece's proper Christian upbringing. Every month or so, she arrived in her surrey and descended upon the little farmhouse like a battleship putting into a humble fishing village. Ruth, who had been notified by toto of her impending visit, would stand on the veranda to receive her, while Jack rumbled and grumbled in the background.

Florence would sail up the veranda steps armed with a large, folded sunshade held lancelike under one arm and an incongruously dainty handbag in the other. Her fiercely feathered hat set off her flashing eyes and the determined set of her chin. She was still a very handsome woman, but only, in Ruth's opinion, if one were able to look past the warlike character that radiated around her. Her ample bosom was swathed in silk, and her skirts rustled richly as she bore down on Ruth for the kiss. Ruth braced herself and endured the onslaught of perfume that stung her eyes like gun smoke.

When it was over, Florence would turn on Milka, who had been standing by unobtrusively, and demand tea. Milka would shoot her a sullen glare and angrily scuttle off while Jack emerged from the lounge. The two old generals would glare at each other for a moment, confirming the tense truce between them. Then Florence would sail into the lounge with Ruth meekly in tow. This scene was as familiar as old curtains to Ruth.

Sometimes Florence brought along Annie, her pretty daughter, as an example to Ruth of proper, ladylike refinement. Over the years, Annie and Ruth had developed a genuine friendship through these visits. Annie possessed a bubbling joy that Ruth envied with all her heart. It was the joy that made her as beautiful as she was. She actually looked very much like her cousin Ruth; but where Ruth was tall, Annie was willowy; and where Ruth moved clumsily, Annie was graceful; and where Ruth had carrot-red hair, Annie's hair was a delicate strawberry blond.

Ruth wondered how Annie was now that her father had died. She had idolized him, and she must be suffering deeply. Ruth wished there were something she could do for Annie. As she looked over at her own father finishing his plate of supper under the protective glare of his lion's head, she knew she, in her powerless and helpless state, would never have anything to offer her cousin. She knew that even in her grief, Annie would be drawing on reserves of her secret store of joy to see her through. The silence at the table was becoming oppressive.

Ruth pushed her plate away. "Excuse me, Father. I need to get to bed early tonight since I will be going into town for the funeral tomorrow."

Jack grunted as he disposed of another forkful of supper.

Ruth slipped off to her bedroom. She put on the cotton men's pajamas that she wore to bed and went to sit in her chair by the window as she always did in the evening before going to sleep. The loneliness crept through her like the dangerous darkness of the African night. The window was open, and she looked desperately outside to the night; but there was no help for her there.

The big thorn tree rustled mysteriously, and insects noisily went about their night's work in its leaves. The air outside wafted gently inside, carrying the scent of distant smoke and evening flowers all mingled. Silver-lined shadows flickered on the grass. There was a carpet of softly glowing stars miles and miles above the dark rafters of the house where freedom roamed, alive and vibrant, all across the

African night. Far down in the valley, the sound of an elephant trumpeting rolled up into the hills above. An old, old memory somewhere inside Ruth stirred again, the way it had this afternoon as she watched the elephants playing.

She thought for an instant that someone was calling her name; only whoever it was, was still too far away to hear clearly. She strained her eyes to make out the dark shapes of the hills far across the plain, and the echo of the elephant trumpeting faded far away into them. The African night wrapped around her in unfathomable mystery as she got up and went to bed.

Chapter Two

Ruth bumped along the cart track in the morning heat. She sweltered and seethed in the black cotton dress that had once been her mother's. Her mother had been a smaller woman than she was, and Ruth had to sit tall and rigid on account of the tight dress. She hung her head, despite the straightness of her posture, as though the weight of the wide-brimmed straw hat were too much for her to bear. In reality, it was the worry of her impending encounter with her aunt that bore down on her in the relentless sunshine.

The road to town wound down the hill to the little stream valley, joining it just below the pond where Ruth had seen the elephants yesterday. At the bottom of the hill, the road straightened out, stretching businesslike across the flat plain of the Rift Valley and making a beeline for Campbellburgh, whose red tile roofs sparkled proudly in the distance. The town was situated on a lake, just at the mouth of a lazy, winding river. Ruth looked over to where a cool, green belt of trees meandered along to the left of the road as the river headed slowly for town.

It was hot out in the open. Even the little clusters of African women walking alongside the dusty road with huge baskets of vegetables on their heads seemed cooler and more comfortable than she was. They wore long, loose clothes that captured every hint of a breeze. Their beads jangled from their ears and around their necks in gay, carefree colors. Ruth stared at them enviously, feeling hotter and more miserable with each look.

She passed a massive baobab tree standing alone in the middle of the plain. Its enormous trunk bulged and bubbled like a giant carbuncle on the face of the earth. Ruth had always hated the old baobab. It was so out of place among the stately thorn trees whose graceful flat-topped branches so beautifully echoed the straight lines of the plains around them. But she could never bring herself not to stare at the baobab as she passed by. It always reminded her how little she fit into the life of the town of Campbellburgh.

Lately, a flock of slate-gray guinea fowl had taken up residence in the grass near the old tree. When Ruth passed by, they scurried off, cackling indignantly into the protection of the bulging trunk, and she was forced into a smile in spite of her bitter mood.

Ruth approached the town slowly. Dust from the wide streets rose into the air, and the whitewashed walls looked as though heat were dripping and rolling off them. The streets were full of people of all shades and hues. White settlers marched stiffly along the covered boardwalks in front of the shops. The men wore light suits and pith helmets, while the women floated gently alongside in soft, filmy dresses and wide, whimsical hats. Out on the dusty street, stately African ladies strolled along with huge baskets on their heads; while men lurked against posts, catching up on the latest news. Totos scurried in and out, darting past buggies and carriages that were heading, like Ruth, toward the church whose spire rose right up from the dead center of town.

Ruth was, indeed, a strange sight as she arrived at the church with the other mourners. Many of the townspeople of Campbellburgh were related to Angus and were arriving in droves, flocking into the gray stone church from all directions. As they passed by Ruth hitching her horse to the post, they smiled politely, if they noticed her at all, and went inside in muted little groups. Ruth stood by and watched them for a moment. She knew almost all of them by sight, as she was related in one way or another through her mother to many. They were a dour, sober lot, and they wasted no words on miscellaneous chatter. Watching them pass by her, she felt more acutely alone than she ever did up on the farm.

She looked furtively about for Florence, then realized she would be inside already. She breathed a sigh of relief and headed up the steps to the huge wooden church doors along with the rest of the townsfolk.

Ruth slipped into an empty pew near the back. She tried to make herself as small and inconspicuous as possible.

The church was filling fast, and Ruth's pew was becoming crowded. John Cooper, the town lawyer, and his wife, Mabel, squeezed down to Ruth's end of the pew. They nodded politely to her. Ruth nodded timidly back. John was a very large man, and Ruth found herself tightly pinned in the corner of the pew, pressed up against the wall. *At least no one can see me here,* she thought. She set her face like flint, grimly determined to endure the service and leave as quickly as she could.

The organist had been playing softly as the people entered. Suddenly the music roared loudly to begin the funeral. Florence sat regally in the front pew; but Annie, who sat beside her, looked shaken. Her heart went out to her friend, and she tried to send her a sympathetic smile, but she was too tightly jammed against the wall to be seen. The organ music suddenly ceased, and the reverend took up where it left off with his own funereal tone. Angus Campbell was the wealthiest, most influential person in town, and he would therefore need to be buried accordingly.

The church was hot and full, and it was not long before Ruth began to feel distinctly uncomfortable. John Cooper seemed to have inexplicably expanded, and Ruth's tight corner between him and the wall was shrinking considerably. The air inside the little church thickened and congealed like bland gravy so that Ruth found herself gasping and gagging, trying to get enough of it into her lungs. Still the Reverend Montgomery droned on and on. Women began to pull out fans and flutter them in front of their faces. Children were fidgeting, and the smaller ones began to whine. The men began to sink and slump into their starched shirts, coughing ominously like lions in the night. And still the air thickened and still the reverend droned.

Ruth was convinced Mr. Cooper was now twice his original size and sweating like a bull. Her stomach began to rise in protest, and the once orderly, straight rows of pews in front of her waved sickeningly before her eyes. Her ugly dress grew tighter and more uncomfortable with each breath she took. She knew she would never be able to stand to negotiate a path around Mr. Cooper in the state she was in, yet it would be dangerous to stay put. Panic gripped her like a cold claw. She was trapped. But it was the cold panic that saved her. She straightened up and faced the front. Only the most intense effort of will kept her from being ill. Mercifully, the Reverend Montgomery finally wound down like an off-speed gramophone, and there was a palpable sigh of relief from the entire congregation.

Florence and Annie Campbell sailed past as the coffin was borne out, and then everyone slowly oozed out into the aisle. Ruth stood up unsteadily. The wait for her pew to empty seemed interminable. But at last it was their turn, and Mr. Cooper shrank back to size and moved away. Ruth could hardly wait to breathe fresh air again.

Slowly the crowd rolled forward. But Ruth's relief was short-lived. Even in the aisle, she couldn't see anything past Mr. Cooper. The wait became unbearable, and Ruth began to gasp for air again. It was turning out to be much more difficult to stand than it had been to sit. She felt the blood drain from her face, and Mr. Cooper's black coat took on a strange movement of its own, as if he had suddenly taken to doing some new kind of dance.

By the time Ruth and the last of the crowd reached the churchyard, the Reverend Montgomery was already speaking. The afternoon sun was beating down on her black dress. There was not a breath of wind.

Ruth could feel the sweat gathering under her dress and along her brow. The churchyard began to spin dangerously, and she knew she had better find some shade. The slow, stately river that had traveled beside her into town ran along below the church. Ruth slipped out of the churchyard gate and made for the line of trees along the riverbank. She leaned for a moment against the trunk of the nearest one. She was hot and sick, and she must somehow cool down. Spying the river glinting through the undergrowth, she found a little path and followed it down to cool her face in the water.

Standing precariously on a rock, she hiked up her skirts and reached down for a handful of water. There was a sickening rip and a sudden loosening of the dress around her waist. She stood up quickly and found a gaping tear all the way from under her arm to the small of her back.

"Oh, no!" she groaned out loud. Quickly she pulled the dress together and held her arm firmly over the ripped black material. Just then the branches behind her rustled, and out of them onto the bank stepped a stranger. He was tall, with wind-blown sandy hair. Ruth stared at him in horror. As he smiled kindly at her, she was struck by the brilliant blueness of his eyes.

"Are you alright, ma'am?" he asked.

Ruth opened her mouth, but there were no words. She wanted to get away before he noticed her dress. Her right arm was clamped firmly to her side, holding her dress together. She stared past him to the path she must take to get back to the churchyard.

"Yes, I'm fine, thank you," she stammered at last, and she fled past him and up the path through the bush. Heat from embarrassment burned up inside her. Palm leaves whipped across her face like razors as she rushed through the undergrowth.

Finally she pushed her way onto the grassy lawn of the churchyard. Townspeople were just beginning to mill about, so the service was over at last. She furtively looked about for Florence and Annie among the mourners. She still had to offer them her condolences before she could escape.

She caught sight of Annie standing near her mother and chatting quietly with a group of her friends. Even in her grief, she was the image of perfect beauty, with her wavy blond hair, her fair skin, and sky blue eyes. Her navy blue dress swept gracefully down to her ankles. She looked cool and crisp, and Ruth stared enviously at her as she fearfully clutched her own dress.

One or two of the more eligible young men in town were standing watchfully near Annie. Ruth smiled ruefully. Annie had always led a train of captive hearts in her wake, but the man who managed to pass the muster of Aunt Florence and actually marry Annie would be a lucky man indeed.

She caught sight of Jimmy MacRae standing just outside the circle watching Annie. Poor Jimmy, Ruth thought, he must have fallen for Annie as well. Surely he knew that he didn't stand a chance. Florence would skin him alive if she even so much as caught a hint of those feelings. Ruth felt sorry for him. She liked him, even the little of what she knew of him. He had always spoken kindly to her when they met delivering milk at the train. But he was poor and he came from a poor family. The MacRaes had not settled on a very good piece of land, and they had always had trouble with one thing and another not going their way. It was just bad luck for the most part. But the wealthier farmers in the area had always looked down on the MacRaes, and Florence had been the leading figure in the campaign. Poor Jimmy MacRae.

She saw Annie smile over at him. She was always such a sweet person, Ruth thought. Just then Annie caught sight of Ruth watching her. She waved and called her over. Ruth smiled and hesitated, her right arm pressed stiffly against her torn dress. Soon everyone would see. She was sure Annie's friends were smiling condescendingly at her, and she hated it. She smiled tightly as she met their gazes. Annie stepped away from them.

"Oh, Ruthie, my dear, it's so nice to see you!" She put her arms around Ruth and hugged her. Ruth stiffly hugged back with her free arm, but she was grateful for Annie's greeting.

"Annie, I'm so sorry about Uncle Angus," Ruth whispered in her ear.

"Thank you. It was kind of you to come. I will miss him terribly." A shadow of sorrow fell across Annie's face, but Ruth thought that strangely it suited her. She looked more womanly, and there was a depth of feeling to her voice that Ruth hadn't heard before. "I don't honestly know how I will manage without him." She spoke the last in a whisper. Ruth thought Annie was about to cry, but suddenly she pulled herself together. "Anyway, it was awfully good of you to come, Ruthie." She smiled bravely.

"Aha, Ruth! I see you did come." The shrill voice of Florence Campbell pierced their conversation and they turned to face her. She strode toward Ruth, who had the sudden sensation of a cornered animal.

"I. . .I'm. . ." Ruth tried to spit out the proper sentiment. But Florence, as always, interrupted.

"Out with it, girl! There are people waiting. Do you think you're the only one at the funeral? Good Lord, you look ghastly. What have you done to your dress?" She reached over and tugged at Ruth's stiff arm, but Ruth held firm.

"I tore my dress," she whispered, hoping against hope that Florence would leave her alone.

"My word! How could you possibly tear your dress at a funeral, girl?" she shrilled. "What were you doing? Dancing?" Ruth's burning embarrassment flared into white-hot shame. She hung her head as tears of rage and helplessness scorched her eyes.

Florence smiled. It was a condescending smile, her interpretation of kindness.

"Well," she announced. "It's a hideous dress anyway. I wouldn't even give it to my house girls. But, as it was your mother's, no one can fault you for not being thrifty. And since you have no looks to speak of, at least you have that to your credit. Now run along, and do try not to look so miserable. It's bad enough to be burying Angus without having to put up with ill-looking mourners.

"By the way," she added as Ruth turned to go, "make sure you remind your father that I expect to see him at the meeting tomorrow, especially as he didn't have the courtesy to attend Angus's funeral. And tell him not to be late."

"Yes, Aunt Florence," whispered Ruth. How her aunt could possibly mention a business meeting at a time like this was beyond her.

"Please accept my condolences, Aunt Florence." She lowered her head and made for her buggy. She could feel the eyes of Annie's friends burning into her back. Florence turned triumphantly from Ruth and bore down on the girl standing closest to Annie.

"Why, Mary, how good of you to come."

Ruth hurried over to Chui, her horse, and unhitched him; then she turned to climb up into her buggy. Her head felt light and she was still unsteady on her feet. She stumbled and landed in the dust.

"Here, let me help you up, miss. You seem to be having a rather difficult day." Ruth scrambled awkwardly to her feet just as someone took her by the elbow. "Are you all right? You look really ill."

It was the tall stranger again. She turned and looked up into his face. Again, it was his eyes that drew her attention. He looked kindly down at, or rather right through, Ruth. She had the distinct impression she was being diagnosed.

"Are you feeling faint, miss? Perhaps you should lie down in the shade for a few minutes before you get on your way." He spoke with an American accent, one disconnected part of her mind noticed.

"Oh no, thank you," she sputtered, wiping dust out of her eyes. "I am just a little overcome by the funeral. He was my uncle. I'll be fine once I'm on my way." Ruth turned quickly to climb back up into the cart. She stopped. She couldn't do it without exposing her gaping tear. She turned and faced him.

"I've torn my dress," she explained helplessly.

To her surprise, he reached forward, picked her up by the waist, and placed her on the seat.

"Thank you," she said.

He lifted his hat. "Don't mention it. It's always my pleasure to help a lady in distress. Do you have far to go now?"

"Oh, no," she lied, and flicked her reins. The stranger tipped his hat again, but Ruth was too overcome to look at him. She just wanted to get away and be alone again as quickly as she could.

As she drove across the dry plain toward the blue hills shimmering tantalizingly in the distant heat, she relived over and over the humiliating encounter with Aunt Florence. Hot flushes of shame repeatedly washed over her skin, and now and then searing, angry tears scorched her cheeks. Automatically she scanned the sky, looking for rain clouds. Perhaps they might relieve some of her pain, washing it away with a storm and a flood of raging water. But it was too early for the rains, and there wasn't even the faintest scent of rain in the air. She drove past the baobab tree, squatting like an ugly blot on the otherwise lovely landscape. Even the guinea fowl scuttling out of her way only irritated her this afternoon.

The sun was dropping low over the hills on the other side of the plains behind her as she reached the bottom of the hillside. She was worn out with the memory of the afternoon and finally too tired to think through the pain again.

Her thoughts shifted to her meeting with the American stranger. She wondered who he was. She remembered how his blue eyes sparkled warmly when he spoke to her, and she smiled into the cool, green forest. *Yes,* she thought, *if I were pretty like Annie, that is the kind of man I would set my cap for.* And then, without warning, her whole being filled with an ache, a powerful, longing, yearning ache, and she wished with all her heart she wasn't driving alone up into the hills. *If it were possible for a woman like me to fall in love, that would be the man I would fall in love with. And if I did fall in love,* she thought to herself, flicking the reins, *I would chase him and follow him and relentlessly pursue him until he succumbed and fell in love with me. I would do whatever it took to capture him, and he wouldn't have a hope of escape.*

The songs of the birds in the trees were heart-wrenchingly lovely, Ruth thought as she drove through the dappled golden evening sunlight. They were singing only for her. The very air in the forest overflowed with their bittersweet melodies. She drove by the little path that led down the hill to the pool where she had seen the elephants yesterday. Remembering their joy, her heart filled once more with longing and she wondered if they would return. But it was getting dark, and she must hurry home. She hadn't eaten all day, and she knew that Milka would have supper ready. Her father would be angry if he were kept waiting.

Chapter Three

Ruth saw her father off to town early the next morning with the milk wagon. He was dressed uncomfortably in a suit and tie, bought many years earlier when he was younger and leaner. His raw, freshly shaved face stuck out the top of his shirt. *He looks like a plucked, gooseflesh chicken, trussed and dressed, ready to roast,* Ruth noted, *and about as cheerful.*

"What do you think Florence wants?" she had asked him while they sat silently eating their steaming bowls of oatmeal under the watchful glare of the lion and the antelope.

"Humph," he grunted, shrugging his shoulders without looking up as he gulped down the dregs of his porridge. It seemed to Ruth that he had grown a crust or a shell around him. He had become hard and lifeless, someone that no longer had the capacity to communicate or love, just like one of his trophies on his wall.

Ruth stared at him, and the thought crossed her mind that perhaps there was only one thing that made him different from his trophies—the hopeless tragedy of his condition. After all, he was human, not an animal, a man who had been loved by his wife, her mother. A familiar wave of heart-sinking horror rose into her throat, and Ruth pushed away the thought that she was looking at herself thirty years on.

"It's clinic day," she'd announced suddenly, pushing her chair loudly away from her untouched porridge. Jack stood up, too, and strode out of the door. A weight of loneliness settled on Ruth's shoulders. Another day of hot, dry, hard work lay ahead. Mechanically Ruth set out to do it—but first there was her clinic to take care of.

She went out through the kitchen door to make sure Milka had all the household jobs under control, though it was more just to see a friendly, welcoming face. It had been years since Milka had questions about how to run the household.

Already there was a cluster of women and children from the compound waiting in the yard behind the house and in need of medical help. Despite their ailments, the women cheerfully chattered, and the children squealed as they chased loose chickens and a couple of the farm dogs.

Ruth always looked forward to days when she held her clinic. For many years, as she was growing up, she had dreamed of becoming a nurse; but as it was, there had never really been any choice. Her father always needed her; and anyway, there would never have been enough money to send her off to school. She still looked back to her dream now and then, but it was just a fleeting fantasy now, sweet and impossible. She had her clinic, and she was rewarded by the trust and gratitude of all the people on the farm. Memsahib Daktari they called her and sent their friends from the countryside all around to her clinic. Ruth managed to eke a little bit of pride out of that fact.

Today, however, as she surveyed the sea of turned-up faces in the front and the pleading eyes of mothers holding their babies in the background, she sensed that there was a little flurry of unusual interest somewhere in the crowd. Sure enough, a toto rushed up to Ruth with an envelope in his hand.

"Memsahib Daktari, for you alone." He spoke with the utmost solemnity and handed her the envelope. His dark brown eyes, wide and serious with the importance of his task, looked up at her. Ruth felt she should make a little bow in accepting such an important missive.

She opened the note and read.

Dear Ruthie,

Would you join me for lunch at one o'clock? I need to talk to you.

Love, Annie

Ruth quickly scribbled an acceptance and returned it to the toto with a sixpence.

"For Memsahib Annie alone." She spoke in the same solemn tones and even returned his formal bow. The little boy scooted off in great glee with her note.

Ruth stood for a moment, thinking. She was puzzled about Annie. Annie was not in the habit of sending her notes or invitations to lunch. For a moment she wondered if there was any connection between this invitation and her father's errand in town this morning, but the totos were clamoring for her attention. Each one wanted to be the first to be treated by her. They pulled on her trousers and held up various parts of their bodies, wounded or swollen, and she was forced to pay attention to her task at hand.

After she had finished the clinic and given orders for the day's work, she went to her room to wash up. She stood stripped down to her underclothes in front of the closet. There were only two things hanging in there, her black funeral dress and a tweed skirt that her mother had brought with her as a young woman from Scotland. She had never dared to ask her father for money for anything else to wear because she knew exactly what his response would be. Her mother's clothes were good enough for her mother and should be good enough for her as well. End of discussion. Besides, Ruth went out in public so rarely that she had forced herself not to give the issue any thought. As she stood staring at the ugly, brown, scratchy, shapeless old skirt, she thought of how Annie would be dressed. She would probably wear a light cotton print that would make her look cool and as fresh as a dawn-lit forest, even in the middle of a dry spell like this. Ruth detested her old skirt with all her heart. The humiliation she had endured from Aunt Florence yesterday flared back into her mind, and she didn't think she could ever bear to go to town in her mother's old clothes again.

She reached for the skirt anyway. As she felt the warm tweed scratching against her fingers, a small seed of rebellion sprouted from the bed of bitterness in the bottom of her heart. She walked over to her dresser drawer, opened it, and pulled out a tiny pair of sewing scissors. Sitting deliberately on her bed, she took the scissors to the skirt, snipping and clipping at it with tiny, deadly snips. She cut right up the front from the hem to the waist, then she ripped off the waistband. She took the rest of the skirt and snipped and ripped until there was nothing left of it but little triangles and squares of tweed scattered on the bed and the floor all around her.

Well, she thought, *surveying her work, that feels fine.* She strode over to the chest of drawers and pulled out a pair of clean khaki trousers and a crisp white shirt.

When she was dressed, she picked up her hat to leave the room. If she had had a mirror in her room, she would have seen a surprisingly fresh and attractive young woman. But guilt for what she had done to her mother's skirt was already beginning to settle like cold, gray silt in her mind. She swept up the remains of the dress and stuffed them in the back of her bottom drawer. She had wantonly destroyed a piece of her mother's sacred memory. Shame swirled through her mind and heart. She pulled her old hat low over her eyes and slunk outside to saddle her horse.

It was a long, hot, midday ride down the valley to town. She hoped she wouldn't see her father on his way back home, and she was relieved when she reached the driveway of the Campbell estate, just before the outskirts of town. She turned into a wide, tree-lined boulevard and into the soft, cool shade that rained down onto her like the tiny purple petals falling from the flowers when the breeze whispered through the jacaranda trees above. Ruth breathed the scented air greedily.

She could see the red tile roof of the house on the hill at the end of the driveway. The jacarandas led up to lush gardens with spacious, green lawns and huge, shady trees placed strategically here and there. The house itself stood in a pool of color. Blooms and buds of every sort of flower rippled in the wind. Off in the distance, the shining river wound past the town of Campbellburgh.

Ruth pulled the buggy up at the veranda steps and got down awkwardly. She stood for a moment, looking at the elegant furniture on the veranda, regretting what she had done to her tweed skirt. *How could I have come to lunch in trousers?* she thought, as a red-hot rush of embarrassment flooded her cheeks. *Perhaps I could turn around and go home. I could send some excuse with a toto.* But just then, the door flew open and Annie rushed out to greet her.

"Ruthie! Thank you so much for coming!" As Ruth had predicted, Annie was a vision of loveliness. Her long, golden mane was swept softly back into a large roll behind, and she wore a beautiful, pale blue dress with soft, flowing sleeves and a wide skirt that rustled crisply as she walked, or rather ran. She threw her arms around Ruth and gave her a welcoming hug.

"Ruthie! I'm so glad you could come. It's been ages and ages since we've had a chance for a chat. How are you? You look wonderful!" She surveyed Ruth from head to toe. "I wish I could bring off wearing trousers the way you do. You're so lucky to be tall and slim!" Ruth smiled. *I should have known.* Annie could always make her feel better.

"Come in, have some squash, and cool off. Lunch is almost ready. You're probably starving." Annie took Ruth by the arm and led her inside. The cool air of the house rushed out the open door to meet them. Ruth adjusted her eyes to the dark room. Silk-covered settees were scattered tastefully here and there, more to be admired than sat upon, Ruth thought. There were little round tables of dark wood polished so thoroughly that they perfectly reflected the elegant china figurines or bouquets of flowers that sat daintily upon them. Annie negotiated her way around the furniture and led Ruth through the French doors at the far end of the room and out onto the patio.

Two places were set out for lunch, with yet another vase of flowers on a wicker and glass table under a large, fragrant frangipani tree. Annie and Ruth sat on wicker chairs with pretty chintz cushions. The lawn spread out before them as smooth as a lake on a calm day, right down to a little arbor covered with flowery vines, a rather inadequate foil against the powerfully green, lush jungle behind. Ruth couldn't see the river, but the jungle was watered by it as it wound its way around to Campbellburgh. Every time the air stirred, she caught the damp, heavy river scent rolling up the lawn toward them.

Annie was already chattering away a mile a minute. She asked Ruth all the usual questions about her father and the farm and the weather this year, but Ruth noticed a hollowness to her voice. Annie paused only long enough to register Ruth's answer before quickly flitting onto the next question. Ruth sipped on her orange squash and wondered what was the matter with Annie.

She was relieved when lunch was served and Annie paused long enough to let Ruth help herself to the cold cuts and jellied salads that were being brought in one after the other. Ruth piled her plate high. Each dish seemed so fresh and enticing after Milka's heavy Scottish cooking, which was more suited to cold, dark winters than tropical afternoons. Each time a new platter was offered, Ruth felt she just couldn't resist. Annie looked on smiling and helped herself to some fruit and cheese. When the platters finally stopped coming, Ruth looked down at her plate and blushed, but Annie put her hand across the table onto Ruth's arm.

"Ruth, you work out on the farm all day long; you have to eat properly to keep up your strength, and you don't have an ounce of fat on you. And look at me. I eat like a bird, do nothing all day, and the mere sight of food adds inches onto my waistline."

Ruth looked wryly down at her plate. "Well, don't look in this direction, then." Annie laughed her old bubbly contagious laugh, and Ruth realized it was the first time she had heard Annie laugh since she arrived. She was ashamed that she hadn't even asked her how things were now with her father gone.

"Annie, how are you? It must be an awfully difficult time for you." Ruth spoke seriously and Annie stopped laughing. A shadow passed across her face.

Annie's voice was suddenly low and unhappy. "I think I am all right, Ruthie, but I'm quite worried about Mother. She is not herself at all; but I suppose with all she's been through, it's very understandable. All the same, you know how difficult she can be?"

Ruth nodded, restraining herself from commenting on Florence's behavior. Annie went on.

"She has become very strange the last few days, and I am frankly worried about her sanity. That is what I wanted to talk to you about." Annie leaned forward. "Do you know that I am not allowed to leave the house?" she whispered.

Ruth let her fork clatter down onto her plate. "What do you mean, Annie?" *Annie must be exaggerating* was the first thought that came to Ruth's mind. Aunt Florence couldn't be that bad, not to Annie, who was always given anything she ever wanted or needed. But Annie continued.

"You know Jimmy MacRae, don't you? He and I have been friends for a long time. We got to know each other at church, mostly. Jimmy takes his Christian faith very seriously, and I have come to admire him a great deal because of it. We spend a lot of time together discussing the meaning of life and what it means to love and serve God. We began to discover that we had a lot in common. Ruthie, I wish you could know him as I do. He is such a fine Christian and such a wonderful person." Ruth smiled. Was there anybody about whom Annie had anything bad to say?

"Anyway," Annie went on, "a few weeks ago he asked me to marry him. I was so surprised, Ruthie! I didn't know what to say. I had never thought of him in that way before. But as I got over my surprise, I began to realize that I really was in love with him, and I couldn't possibly ask for a finer Christian man to be my husband. Oh, I was so happy!"

Ruth was astonished to hear how sad Annie's voice was as she spoke the last words.

Annie paused and composed herself before she went on. "I accepted Jimmy's proposal, and he came to ask Father for my hand. Father gave him permission. He always had a secret soft spot for Jimmy, and he would never have denied me anything to make me happy. But when Mother was told what Father had done, she was livid. She has never had even the time of day for the MacRaes, what with their bad luck and never being quite well-off enough to suit her.

"It was the day after that when Father took his turn for the worse. Mother insisted that it was the effect of Jimmy's visit on him. And now that Father has died, she is blaming Jimmy and me for it. She actually says that Jimmy only wants to marry me for the money he thinks I will inherit!"

Annie pulled out a lace handkerchief and buried her face in it. Ruth looked away. She felt desperately sorry for Annie, but she didn't know what to do when Annie started to cry. What could she do to make Annie feel better? Her thoughts rushed around in a panic. She didn't know where to look when people cried, no matter how much she cared, and Annie's problem was so far out of her depth! But she must do something. Annie was sobbing, and with each breath she took, Ruth felt her own heart slowly breaking painfully open. She took a deep breath; she couldn't stand it any longer.

"Annie, Annie, don't cry." Ruth reached forward awkwardly and put her hand on Annie's arm. Why, oh why, hadn't Annie chosen to unburden herself on someone more helpful?

"Oh, Ruthie!" Annie looked up out of her handkerchief into Ruth's panic-stricken face. "Mother has forbidden me to see Jimmy or even leave the house. And she won't let me see my friends from church alone because she says she doesn't trust them. Ruthie, I am afraid the strain of losing Father has made my mother a little mad! I can't understand why she is behaving like this.

"And the worst of it is that Jimmy came over to see Mother the day after Father passed away. He wanted to see if he could do anything to help her or to make things better." To Ruth's horror, Annie put her face back into her handkerchief and sobbed as if her heart had broken all over again. Ruth could only sit and watch her, paralyzed with embarrassment and pity. But, suddenly to her immense relief, Annie took a deep shuddering breath and stopped sobbing.

"Mother was awful to him! She shouted at him to leave and accused him to his face of marrying me for my money and of killing my father. But Jimmy was wonderful in the face of it all. He explained to Mother that he only ever wanted to make me happy and that we loved each other and that if I had changed my mind since my father's death, he would never again bring up the subject of our marriage.

"Mother told him that he had better never bring it up again if he knew what was good for him. And she ordered Juma to throw Jimmy out of the house. And that is when I came in. I had been standing outside the door listening. I couldn't help it. I came in and told Mother that I loved Jimmy and he loved me and that I intended to marry him no matter what she said. I have never stood up to Mother like that before.

"Oh, Ruthie, I was just as shocked as she was! She just stood there with her mouth open. But before my very eyes, she gathered herself together and she turned cold. I don't know how else to describe it, but I saw it happen. She turned to ice, and I was afraid, Ruthie.

"That was when I wavered. I just became afraid of her and I wanted to stop her from being so cold and cruel—I just wanted it to end! I told her I didn't want to disobey her, and I would never want to hurt her, and I really didn't want to lose my family by marrying Jimmy. But she didn't let me finish. She turned to Jimmy and ordered him to leave the house. Jimmy looked at me before he went, and I wanted to tell him I loved him, but I was paralyzed. She had turned me to ice, too." Tears were running down Annie's cheeks again.

"I just stood there, and Jimmy looked at me and he said, 'I love you, Annie,' and he left. And I just stood there like a stone watching him go." Annie stopped and regained her control over the tears. Ruth waited for her in silence.

"Then Mother turned to me and said that until I renounced him, I would not leave the house except to go to the funeral. That was three days ago, and since then, it has been a nightmare, Ruthie. I have told her again and again that I won't disobey her and marry Jimmy without her consent, but she refuses to believe a word I say! She is sure I am plotting against her." Annie put her face into her hands and cried, "I just had to tell someone, Ruthie. I don't understand what has happened to her."

Ruth wanted to get up and put her arms around Annie and hug her, but she couldn't make herself move. She tried to speak.

"Annie," she began, but she had to clear her throat. "Annie," she tried again, "have you written to Jimmy and told him how things are?"

Annie burst into a renewed outbreak of sobs, and Ruth waited, mute with embarrassment at seeing the effect of her question on her cousin.

"She's instructed all the servants that I am not to be allowed to get or to send any letters, and I know Jimmy has sent me something because I saw her receive a letter from the houseboy at the MacRae place. She tore it up." Annie paused; then in a low, calm voice, she went on, "Ruthie, I think Mother has actually gone mad. She is holding me a prisoner in my own home, and she won't believe me or trust me. I am frightened, Ruthie. I am frightened for her even more than I am for myself. She seems to have crossed over into some mad sort of place since Father has gone, and no one knows it but me.

"That's why I wanted to tell you, Ruthie. You are family. I couldn't let anyone else in town know what is happening. It is too shameful. She is too proud for that kind of information to ever get about. Really, I don't want to hurt her." Annie sat back in her chair. She suddenly looked exhausted, but she was no longer crying.

Ruth felt as though she were reeling backward. How could she possibly help Annie? What could she say?

"Perhaps if you just give her a little time, she will get over it," Ruth ventured timidly.

"I had thought at first that would help," replied Annie tiredly, "but somehow I have the feeling that there is more to it than that. She's getting worse, not better. As soon as Father died she became so strange. Dr. Mowatt came over, but he wasn't terribly sober, you know what he is, and he really wasn't much help at all. He just gave her some more sleeping pills and told me that 'Time heals all.'

"And then there is this odd business with Douglas MacPherson. She seems to have taken a very strange dislike to the poor man. I know him quite well because he comes to church. He is a friend of Jimmy's and mine. Anyway, just because he doesn't want to marry the first woman he meets in Campbellburgh is no reason to dislike him with such passion. Besides, he is a confirmed bachelor. He doesn't want to marry anyone. A man has a right to live as he chooses.

"But Dr. MacPherson is wealthy, and Mother started scheming from the first moment she laid eyes on him. When he refused to go along with her plans, she flew into a temper. She vowed to run him out of town before she would allow him to build that hospital of his. I shudder to think what she is up to at that meeting today."

Ruth was puzzled. "Who is Douglas MacPherson?" She had never heard his name before.

Annie looked at her in surprise. "My goodness, Ruthie, you really are too isolated up there on that farm of yours! Douglas came to town a month ago! He is a Canadian missionary doctor and very rich. Mother tried her best to marry me off to him; but as I said, I don't think he intends to marry anyone. All he wants to do is buy the land down by the river, next to the railway station. When Mother and Father discovered what he intended to do with it, they absolutely refused to sell the land to him."

"What does he want to do with it?" asked Ruth, still confused.

"He wants to build a hospital for the African people since they suffer so terribly with European diseases and yet have almost no access to proper medicine. It is a noble and Christian enterprise, and I hope he succeeds in it! But Mother says it will ruin the entire town to have a filthy hospital for Africans right in the center of it. They have cured their own diseases with witch doctors since creation and they should continue to do it that way. It would only confuse them to make them submit to modern medical practices. Besides, she says a hospital would attract them from all over the countryside. They'll clog up the railway and pollute the river. The tourist business will be completely ruined! No one will want to come and stay at Daddy's hotel or arrange safaris from Campbellburgh, and we will become destitute! Everything that the family has worked so long and hard for will go right down the drain.

"And don't for a minute doubt that Mother can't stop him. After all, we Campbells do have first refusal rights on all the land inside the town limits, and I can't imagine any of the farmers outside town daring to stand up against Mother. After all, can you imagine how difficult she would make it for them to do any business in town?"

"So that's what she called the meeting in town for today, then." Ruth spoke more to herself. "She probably wanted my father there because of Mother's land." As an original Campbell, her mother had been given a lot within the town limits. It was an undeveloped piece on the river next to the church. Upon her mother's death, her father had, of course, inherited it, even though he was not actually a Campbell by blood. No doubt he was still bound by the Campbell rights for first refusal.

Annie was now surprised. "Your father owns land in Campbellburgh?"

Just then there was a loud clattering of wheels, and they heard Florence shouting orders at her servants.

"Good gracious, look at the time!" Annie jumped up, panic stricken. "We've been chatting far too long. Mother will have my hide! I am forbidden to have visitors."

Ruth stood up as well. "Don't worry, Annie," she said, sounding braver than she felt. "I'll just tell her that I was passing through and I dropped in for lunch. It's only me. I'm not really a visitor, as you said before, I'm just family." But the thought of a confrontation with her aunt, especially after what Annie had just told her about her state of mind, sent a chill of fear into the pit of Ruth's stomach. She silently stood next to Annie as the two of them listened to Florence sweep into the drawing room. A moment later the doors to the patio flew open.

Turning immediately on Ruth, she swept her eyes from the top of her short, unruly, red hair, down past her white shirt and khaki trousers, to her dusty old boots, and snorted with disdain.

"What, may I ask, are you doing here? Annie is to receive no visitors!" She spoke as though Ruth were deliberately disobeying her.

"I was just passing by on my way home," stammered Ruth.

"Well, I suppose as it is only you, I'll make an exception. Only see to it that you don't come back. If you intend to meddle in Annie's affairs, let me warn you, young lady, you'll pay for it!"

"I must go now, Aunt Florence," said Ruth quickly. She flashed a helpless smile at Annie. "Thank you for inviting me for lunch."

Annie smiled back weakly, but Florence boomed at Ruth, "You were in town today? I never saw you arrive with your father. I trust you are not conniving behind his back. It is impossible to trust any young people these days, not even one's own children." She glared significantly at Annie, her face as hard and rigid as a mask.

Ruth wanted to get as far away as quickly as she could. "Good-bye," she whispered and slunk past her aunt like a dog with its tail between its legs. As she scuttled through the drawing room, she could hear Florence. Her voice was different. Annie was right. It was colder than ice. A splinter off her voice sliced right through the cool air of the drawing room and struck Ruth between the shoulder blades as she ran to the door. She felt suddenly wounded and sick. She hurried Chui at a trot down the soft lane of jacarandas.

She trotted briskly over the grassy plains. When she at last came to the bottom of the hill and the road wound alongside the river again, Ruth allowed herself to think over what Annie had told her. She found she could hardly contain her anger at Aunt Florence for treating Annie so shamefully. *If only I were stronger and more courageous.* Ruth bit her lip and kicked Chui to hurry up. She was angry and frustrated at her own helplessness. And Annie's. Silly, trusting Annie. She should have chosen a better person to confide her plight to—someone who actually had the courage and the power to do something about it. *What could I do to help her? Absolutely and completely nothing. Nothing at all.*

The air was scented and cooler up here on the hillside in the shade of the trees, and Chui, knowing that they were getting close to home, walked a little faster. The wide, slow river had shrunk into Ruth's own stream again, and it bubbled cheerily beside the road and over the smooth, slippery stones. Slowly, Ruth began to realize there might be something she could do for Annie. She could at least go and see Jimmy MacRae and explain to him what Annie had told her. Perhaps between the two of them they could come up with a way to help Annie, even a little bit. Yes, she decided, as Chui emerged from the forest and the farmhouse came into view, I will go over to the MacRae place and see Jimmy tomorrow.

Chapter Four

Ruth was mildly surprised that evening when her father wasn't home in time for supper. Rather than eating in the dining room alone under the glowering glares of the animal heads, she took her supper in the steamy, noisy kitchen with Milka and her toto. The plain boiled meat and vegetables seemed dull and bland compared with lunch at the Campbells', but Ruth relived every dish and each mouthful of lunch for Milka's benefit. She told Milka of Annie's predicament and Florence's invitation to Douglas MacPherson. Milka rolled her eyes in disgust.

"Jimmy MacRae is a fine Christian. Memsahib Campbell should be glad that her daughter wants to marry a man like that. It doesn't matter what his father was like, he will do well, I know. He is a very hard worker. I have a cousin who works for young Bwana MacRae, and he admires him very much.

"But Memsahib Campbell never learned to look at anyone else but herself. She will make very many mistakes that way, especially now that her *bwana* is gone." Milka stood up and took away Ruth's empty plate.

"Bwana said he would be home for supper. I wonder what he is doing."

"It is strange," Ruth replied with a small twinge of uneasiness. "Perhaps he stopped at the hotel for a drink. He may have lost track of the time." Ruth noticed lately that her father's drinking had begun to control his life and his word had become rather unreliable.

"Yes, I am afraid that is what has happened." Milka looked pityingly at Ruth, but Ruth stood up to go.

"I am going to town tomorrow," she said. "I am going to see Bwana Jimmy about Annie."

Milka clucked her lips and shook her head with disapproval. "You know Memsahib Campbell," she said ominously. "She finds out everything sooner or later. And when she learns you have been speaking to Bwana MacRae about Miss Annie, she will be very angry and she will make your life a miserable thing. She is almost as bad as a witch doctor, even worse perhaps. You watch out, 'Sabu! I will have to stay up all night in prayer if you are not careful!"

"Florence Campbell couldn't really do too much to make my life more miserable than it is already, so don't you worry about me, Milka," Ruth laughed. Suddenly it felt surprisingly pleasant to be risking the ire of Florence Campbell in order to help Annie. She marched boldly out of the kitchen and tossed a look of scorn at the glare of the lion in the dining room.

The door burst open and Kamau rushed in. "Bwana's been hurt! Come quickly, 'Sabu!"

Ruth crashed back to reality and rushed after Kamau into the lounge, where her father was stumbling toward the couch. He must be very drunk, she judged by the way he staggered and the stream of foul language coming from his mouth. His face was covered in mud and blood. He'd gotten drunk and fallen off his horse.

With more disgust than pity, Ruth hurried over and helped him to the couch. It was then that she saw his leg. His torn trouser leg was soaked in blood, and he was dragging it on the ground like a lifeless thing.

"What on earth happened to you, Father? How did you get hurt?" She turned to Kamau. "Quickly get hot water, clean cloths, and bring me the dawa from the cupboard."

Jack groaned as he lay on the couch, and Ruth realized he was in great pain. His skin, what she could see of it, was unnaturally white. A stab of fear tore through her heart. Jack most reluctantly submitted to Ruth's ministrations, cursing and spluttering every time she touched the cuts on his face. They turned out to be fairly superficial. It was the mud that made it all look worse.

"What about your leg, Father?" she asked. "What happened?" He was losing blood fast, and the couch was already soaked and red.

"Leave my leg alone." Jack emitted a vicious growl. "And pass me a whiskey!" Ruth fetched him a glass of whiskey to relieve some of his pain. She carefully cut the leg off his trousers. Not only was his thigh torn open, but she guessed that the bone was broken badly and would need to be set.

"Cursed motorcars," he began, speaking, or rather growling, more to himself than to Ruth. She listened. "They should be run off the road. I was just riding along, minding my own business, down by the Campbells' place, when I hear this great roaring noise behind me. It didn't sound like any animal I'd ever heard, so I assumed it was one of those automobile contraptions. It was a long way off, or so I thought, when suddenly around the bend, right behind me, here it comes, like he owned the road! Simba reared and I came off, more from shock than anything else."

Ruth thought uncharitably that if he hadn't been drunk, he would have kept his mount.

"I certainly couldn't blame Simba," he was saying. "It was that maniac driving that motorcar." Jack paused to take a couple more swigs from his glass and compose himself.

"Oh, my leg hurts! Don't you dare touch it!" He snapped at Ruth as she stood up to look at it again. She stopped in her tracks.

"I had better send for Dr. Mowatt, Father. I am pretty sure it is broken."

"What! That old coot? I might as well just lay myself down and die, for all he can do for me. He kills more people than he saves. Look how much he did for old Angus Campbell!" Jack snorted with derision.

"But, Father, no one could have saved Uncle Angus, and Dr. Mowatt did all he could." Ruth tried to speak in her most reasonable tone of voice, but it had the opposite effect from what she had intended.

"So, you're trying to kill me, are you? You can't wait to see your inheritance, is that it? Or maybe you just want to be rid of your old man? After all, I'm just a chain around your neck these days, don't think I can't tell. Perhaps you're right. It would save a fortune in doctor fees if I died now, wouldn't it? Ask Florence Campbell, if you don't believe me!"

"Father!" Ruth was horrified. "How could you say such things? I only wanted to have your leg looked at because it is broken. I didn't know what else to suggest."

She watched silently as her father finished his drink; and without being asked, she got up and refilled his glass. He took it absentmindedly and continued with the story of his accident as if the subject had never changed.

"Simba bolted, right over me and back down the road, and the car came to a stop just inches, inches from my head! A fine sight, I tell you.

"Well, lo and behold." Jack's voice prickled up with sarcasm like the spikes on a hedgehog. "Who should step out of it but our Dr. Douglas MacPherson, all dressed up to the nines like he was going to meet the queen. He was all apologies and 'may I help you, sirs,' but I wouldn't have any of it. Not from him, after what he's been up to, and then throwing me off my horse like that."

Ruth snapped to attention. "What's he been up to, Father?" she asked quietly.

"He's trying to buy up the entire town and turn it into some sort of haven for blacks. He's probably connected with some secret organization to try to incite the natives into rebellion against the British. Building hospitals and schools and what have you, so he says. Campbellburgh is right at the center of everything with the railway and the river. Why, if he got our blacks armed and going, we could have a full-scale rebellion on our hands before we knew where we were. We'd all be murdered in our beds!"

Jack held out his glass for more whiskey, and Ruth got up to fetch it for him. "Who on earth told you this, Father?" She handed him another full glass.

"It's all over town; everyone knows. That's why Florence called the meeting today. She's going to stop him. And a good thing, too. He'll have a fight on his fancy American hands if he tries to take us on." Jack chuckled happily. He was beginning to feel no pain. It was the drink.

"The man is a monster, and both he and that monstrous car should be run out of town. I'd be the one to do it, too, but for what he's done to my leg. I think Simba stepped on it. But I don't blame her. It was that motorcar that frightened her."

"Father, you must let me look at it again," Ruth pleaded. "If Simba stepped on it, it is certainly broken. We must fetch Dr. Mowatt." Jack knocked back the last half of his glass and lay back on the couch. Ruth took it as a sign that he was ready to be examined.

Jack was drenched with blood. His entire thigh was swollen, and the gash ran down almost the whole length of it and was full of dirt.

"Father, we must get you to the hospital at once. You will have an infection in that gash by morning. You need some stitching, and the bone must be set by a doctor."

"Hah, you'll never get me to that hospital. If it's my time to go, I'll go alone.

Just get me another drink, will you?" Ruth ignored him.

"Well, we at least need to get Dr. Mowatt," she pleaded. "This is extremely serious. Your leg will be infected soon. I don't know how you even managed to ride home. How did you catch Simba?" Ruth stood amazed at the strength of character that could make a man ride so far in such pain. Reconsidering, she handed him another drink. Maybe, she rationalized, it would not only keep the pain down, but it might fight infection that would surely set in quickly. She would send Kamau for Dr. Mowatt at first light, no matter what her father said.

"MacPherson caught him for me. A fine sight he was, too, all covered with sweat and dust. I don't know where he was off to all dressed up like that, but he won't be making much of an impression when he gets there." Jack chuckled wickedly to himself at the memory.

"He tried to make me go with him. Said he was a doctor and he could make sure I was all right, but he was probably waiting for the chance to do me in completely, having failed the first time."

Ruth washed and patched the wound as well as she could. He must have lost a lot of blood. She settled him on the couch for the night. The whiskey had done the trick, and within a very short time, he was sleeping fitfully.

Before dawn Ruth woke with a sense of foreboding, which had settled into the pit of her stomach through the night. It weighed her down like a stone as she heaved herself wearily out of bed. She had been awake often through the night and had checked her father several times.

She made her way down the hall in the gray morning light. The grayness made everything look ugly and grim. She slipped quietly into the lounge and stood motionless behind the sofa. She had the horrible fear that her father would be lying dead. After a few minutes, she could see the blanket rising and falling steadily and rhythmically. Letting out a long breath of relief, she tiptoed back to her bedroom. She was surprised at herself for being so nerve-racked. *I'm turning into a fussy old spinster,* she thought, irritated.

Kamau was already waiting faithfully for her in the kitchen when she arrived a little while later. She sent him off to town to fetch Dr. Mowatt as quickly as he could. The sense of foreboding in the pit of her stomach turned into a fear-burdened loneliness in the silent, empty kitchen. She sat down heavily at the kitchen table and waited for Milka to arrive.

Suddenly the loneliness rose in her throat, and tears filled her eyes. She put her head down on the table and sobbed. She couldn't bear it if anything should happen to her father. She would be all alone. It's true, he wasn't much company these days; but the thought of living up here on the farm alone, day in and day out, year in and year out, was frightening beyond belief. She stared with horror down the road stretching out before her straight and narrow, arid and endless.

There was a scuffling of feet in the hall, then the kitchen door burst open and in bustled Milka. Ruth jumped with surprise. "Milka, you startled me!"

"Lord have mercy! 'Sabu Ruth!" Milka exclaimed in surprise. "What are you doing here frightening the living daylights out of me like that?" But when she saw the look on Ruth's face, she instantly became worried. "Your father, is he all right?"

"He's still sleeping. I don't know, but I'm worried about that gash on his leg. It's pretty deep, I'm afraid. And the bone is broken. I hope Dr. Mowatt gets here soon. I told Kamau to make him hurry."

Milka came over to Ruth and put her arm around her shoulders. "Don't worry, 'Sabu Ruth. Everything will turn out just fine, you'll see. I have been praying for you."

"Ah, Milka." Ruth smiled up into the kind, loving eyes of her friend. "If I thought God cared about me as much as you do, I wouldn't worry. But even you don't have the power of God over life and death."

Milka laughed. "I wouldn't be so sure that God doesn't love you, 'Sabu Ruth. You'd be surprised what He will do for us when we ask. Just you watch." Milka's laugh, loud and sure, filled the whole kitchen, and the heaviness that had been gripping Ruth all morning loosed its hold a little. She straightened her shoulders and sat at her usual place at the table. Life had regained some perspective with Milka's words. Even if she didn't believe in God, she believed in Milka's loving-kindness.

It was only halfway through the morning when Ruth heard the sound of a motorcar in the distance. Her father hadn't been awake very long, and Ruth was trying to get him to eat some of Milka's porridge. He was in considerable pain. His leg looked worse and was very swollen. Ruth knew she would somehow have to persuade him not only to let the doctor see it, but also to go to the hospital in Nairobi.

The motorcar was almost there. Dr. Mowatt traveled by buggy, and she wondered who would be coming up to the farm in a car. Perhaps Dr. Mowatt had understood the urgency of the situation and persuaded this Douglas MacPherson to bring him here, she thought as she ran outside onto the veranda. She could hear the wheels churning up the soft dirt on the cart track. A plume of reddish-brown dust billowed up from below the brow of the hill.

Slowly, a sleek, black car appeared in the distance, and Ruth watched fascinated as it drove up to the front of the house with Kamau sitting proudly in the front seat next to the driver. Where was Dr. Mowatt? Surely Kamau hadn't returned without Dr. Mowatt? The car pulled up to a halt in front of the steps, and Kamau jumped out.

"*Jambo,* Memsahib!" he called excitedly, but Ruth was furious.

"Kamau, where is Dr. Mowatt? Why didn't you come back with Dr. Mowatt?"

"Excuse me, ma'am." It was the driver. Ruth glared at him as he walked around the car toward them. She was angry to be interrupted at such a desperate moment. He put out his hand to shake hers. "Dr. Mowatt is delivering a baby on one of the outlying farms. You'll just have to make do with me, I'm afraid. I'm Dr.

Douglas MacPherson." Ruth didn't move.

"I believe we've met before, but I didn't have the pleasure of learning your name." Ruth stood stupefied, recognizing the stranger who had helped her onto the buggy at Angus Campbell's funeral. Surely there was a mistake. This couldn't be Dr. MacPherson. But he was standing there in front of her holding out his hand.

"Ruth," she replied quietly. "Are you really a doctor?" she asked.

"As I live and breathe" came the quick reply. "Now lead me to the patient. I understand there is some urgency."

"Yes, come with me," said Ruth, turning back into the house. This was not what she was expecting. She'd never known any other doctor but Dr. Mowatt. She had no idea what her father would do when he laid eyes on Douglas MacPherson again, but she really had no choice.

"I am terribly sorry about your father," he said, following her inside. "The whole thing was entirely my fault, and I am sick at the pain I have caused you and your father." Ruth stood in front of the couch where her father lay. She breathed a sigh of relief—he had fallen back asleep. While Dr. MacPherson bent over to look at her father's leg, she forced herself to look at him. He was a big man with broad shoulders and a head of thick, sandy hair, blown straight backwards from the wind of the motorcar. But he had gentle hands and a genuinely kind face as he carefully looked over Jack.

"I had no idea he was hurt this badly!" He straightened up looking shocked. "How could he have possibly gotten back up to the farm with a broken leg? If he had only let me take a look at it, I would never have let him do it. I'm terribly sorry about it all. I took the corner too fast, not really expecting that there would be anyone out riding such a lonely road. Please accept my apologies, Miss Jones."

"It's not too badly broken, I hope," Ruth replied politely, without any conviction.

"I'm afraid your dad isn't in very good shape," he replied seriously.

My dad! Ruth had never dreamed of being so familiar with him. She always called him "Father." Dr. MacPherson bent over again and touched the wound ever so carefully. Jack woke up, and Ruth braced herself for the worst. It wasn't long in coming.

"What do you think you're doing here?" Jack's eyes flew open, and he spat the words out like venom. But, as he was unable to lift himself off the couch, they lost some of their potency. Dr. MacPherson ignored his greeting and calmly replied that Dr. Mowatt was busy and, since he was the only other doctor in town, he had come.

"Perhaps, in some small way I can make amends for what I did to you yesterday."

He may as well save his breath, Ruth thought to herself. *Father never listens to apologies.* But to Ruth's utter amazement, her father slowly laid back down, closed his eyes, and cursed quietly under his breath.

Not realizing the enormity of what had just occurred, Dr. MacPherson continued examining her father's leg. Ruth stood staring. Either this Douglas MacPherson had cast some sort of a spell over him, or her father was much sicker than she had realized.

After a short while, Dr. MacPherson looked up at her. "Miss Jones, your dad is in serious need of medical care, much more than I am able to give him here. He will be okay, but we must take him to a hospital right away."

He was speaking to her quietly and firmly. "He's broken his thigh, and the gash is getting infected already. We had better get him to the hospital in Nairobi today. I'll take him in my car. Get some blankets and some water. We should leave at once."

Ruth looked at her father's face. It was so white that his freckles stood out individually like patches of mold on pale cheese. She had never seen him look so ill. In fact, until now, she would never have believed it was possible to bring him so low. He had always been in charge and, even in the depth of his drink, he still had a menacing sense of control. It was frightening to see him so helpless, and a fresh wave of fear surged up from the depths of Ruth's stomach. But they would get him to Nairobi. Dr. MacPherson would get him there and everything would be fine.

Dr. MacPherson looked up to see that she was still standing, staring at her father's leg.

"Miss Jones." He stood up slowly and touched her on the shoulder. "Please don't worry. We'll take him to the hospital and they will fix him up just like new. Come along, now." He spoke to her slowly and compassionately, and she was enveloped with an overwhelming sense of gratitude to him for helping her father. She wanted to reach out and hug him and thank him for being so hopeful. Instead, she rushed off to fetch the blankets.

She quickly pulled blankets from the chest in her father's bedroom. Her heart was flooded with strange feelings. Oh, how right she had been about Douglas MacPherson at Angus's funeral! She did like him! Thoughts swirled about her head. It must be the sleepless night that is making me feel so odd. Somehow, she had to control herself. *How can I be thinking this way when Father is so ill?*

She came back into the lounge with an armload of blankets. Dr. MacPherson and Kamau were already carrying her father to the backseat of the car. He looked so small and fragile in their arms. They eased him inside the back of the car, and Ruth covered him gently with a blanket. It was horrifying to see how quickly he could diminish into this poor, old, sick man. He just closed his eyes when she covered him. Not even a whine or a murmur passed his lips. *Please, Milka's God, help us to get him to the hospital safely,* Ruth prayed silently.

Dr. MacPherson was standing at the open front door of the car waiting for her. She slipped quickly inside. The leather seats crinkled softly as she stiffly settled back into their luxurious embrace. The pungent aroma of hot leather swirled about her. All the dials and meters gleamed importantly in the polished wooden dashboard before her. Dr. MacPherson got in beside her. He pushed down on one of the pedals on the floor, and the car purred and moved slowly forward.

There was a moan from the backseat.

"Are you all right, Father?" asked Ruth, turning around to look at him.

A low, angry growl was the only reply, and Ruth sighed with relief and hope.

"We'll get him there as quickly as we can." Dr. MacPherson spoke soothingly to her, and she was ashamed of the sudden urge she felt to reach out and hold onto him. She looked down at her large, sunburned hands clutched nervously in her lap.

They were flying down the road faster than Ruth had ever been in her life. All the familiar turns and trees and bumps in the road were rushing swiftly past. A huge cloud of dust churned behind them, and the engine roared and whined as they negotiated the curves in the road. Ruth held tightly to a small handle on the door beside her.

It was a breathtaking ride. Ruth felt that she was in a world by herself, cut off from everyone and everything around her by a wall of noise and speed. At the bottom of the hillside, before they reached the Nairobi road turnoff, a stand of Masai stood at attention, watching them pass. Their red blankets and feathered headgear blew suddenly in the breeze of the passing car. Then as Ruth looked over her shoulder, they were swallowed by dust and disappeared from sight. A few guinea fowl scuttled into the dry bush beside the road. Ruth could hear their indignant squawks over the roar of the engine, but only for a moment as they, too, were lost to the dust behind them.

At last they slowed and turned onto the long, straight Nairobi road, and Ruth noticed that the countryside became bigger. A purple hill, with the typical cone shape of a volcano, appeared far away on the plain to the right. Off in the distance ahead of her loomed the blue-green ridge of the escarpment where they were headed. Their big black motorcar shrank in comparison to this vast landscape. It seemed to Ruth that they were only a tiny beetle inching its way slowly across the wide, dry plain, never noticeably getting closer to the wall of the escarpment or any farther past the volcano in the dusty distance.

The thorn trees on the plain slowly stalked past, holding up the sky with their tabletop branches. Now and then they passed a giraffe or two nibbling on the lower leaves. As the motorcar approached the giraffes, they loped away, their huge necks and legs moving in slow motion. They drove past herds of antelope, which bounded quickly out of sight and into the grasses. And still they flew on.

The rolling plain and the roar of the engine were having a calming effect on Ruth's nerves. She felt soothed and peaceful. She drifted farther and farther into her own world, still isolated by the sound and the speed. Nothing touched her. The warm sun shone down through the windshield, and the breeze blew into her face. She closed her eyes. Everything was going to be fine. *How different life looks in the heat of the day,* she thought to herself as she remembered the sense of fear and panic with which she had awakened in the cold, gray predawn.

"Reminds me of Alberta." Dr. MacPherson broke the silence.

Ruth jumped. Quickly gathering herself together, she quelled the sudden surge of panic she felt at the prospect of a conversation and timidly asked, "Alberta? Which part of America is that?" Pleased with herself for her efforts, she smiled at the doctor.

"It's Canada, not America!" replied Dr. MacPherson laughing. "Alberta's one of the western Canadian provinces, but I'm usually considered an American here in Africa. I'll never get used to it, though." He shook his head.

"I have heard Canada is a very beautiful place, but it must be awfully cold," ventured Ruth, more bravely this time.

"Only in the winter," he explained. "I can't tell you how many people I've met who think there is ice and snow all year-round. In summer it can get just as hot as it is here. And it even looks the same. That's why it reminds me of Alberta. Alberta has grassland like this; and with the wind blowing through the grass and the wide, blue sky shimmering with the heat, we could be in Alberta just as easily as Africa."

Ruth was amazed. "Surely you must be exaggerating!" For a moment she had the unpleasant feeling he must be teasing her as he laughed at her surprise.

"No, it's true," he said, sweeping his eyes around the landscape. "But I will admit there are some differences. For one thing, we don't have acacia trees in Alberta, nor do we have huge herds of animals grazing on the plains. There were enormous herds of buffalo in years gone by, but they are gone now.

"Maybe it's the vastness of Africa that reminds me of Alberta," he went on. "The wind roaming over the wide-open plains and the immensity of the sky. Even in the deep of winter, there is the same feeling of immensity and vastness that you get here."

"I can't imagine what winter must be like," Ruth said, almost to herself, but Dr. MacPherson answered her quickly. He seemed pleased to talk about his faraway home in Alberta.

"The thing I miss most about winter is how beautiful it is. Of course it can get cold—so cold you can't even take a breath without your lungs hurting. But, on those mornings when everything is frozen solid, there is a deep, deep silence that chills you as much as the air does. Every now and then you hear a crack from the trees, or down at the lake at the bottom of our field you can hear the ice creaking and shifting. The stream that runs into the lake sometimes freezes into the shape of rapids and waterfalls making icy castles, whole cities of them, wherever the stream splashes over the rocks."

Ruth stared out to the horizon rolling heavily in the noonday heat and tried to imagine the ice castles crackling in the quiet, cold air. But her horizons hemmed her in. She couldn't see beyond this walled African garden.

He went on, "I miss the beauty of winter, even though Africa is so wild and so much more exciting than even I imagined. But there is nothing quite like winter."

"I would like to see winter for myself one day," she ventured timidly, "but I don't suppose I ever will. My life is here on the farm with Father." She glanced worriedly over her shoulder. He was dozing uncomfortably, wincing with each bump of the car.

"I'm sorry we can't get there any faster," Dr. MacPherson said. "Your poor father is having a pretty difficult time of it."

Ruth looked at him in surprise. "Why, we are going faster than I have ever been in my whole life!" she exclaimed.

Dr. MacPherson threw back his head and laughed. "Well, it is certainly a rare privilege to take a girl out for her first ride in a motorcar. I must confess that I have been very remiss in my manners. "Miss Jones, I'd like to introduce you to Wild Rose, Rosie, to her friends." He tapped the dashboard in front of Ruth and grinned proudly. "Rosie is named after the wild roses that grow everywhere in Alberta. Even though Rosie and I made each other's acquaintance in Nairobi, I figured she needed a good Canadian name if we were going to be partners."

Ruth was beginning to relax in Dr. MacPherson's company. Perhaps it was the American familiarity with which he spoke to her. It was as if he just assumed they were friends. She liked it and it made her bolder. "I hear you are trying to build your hospital in Campbellburgh," she said. "What brought you to Africa all the way from Canada?"

He shot a quick glance over to her. "So you have heard about my difficulties with the local aristocracy, have you?"

"Oh no, not really." Ruth was suddenly afraid to offend him. "Florence Campbell is my aunt, that's all. Her daughter Annie is my friend and she just mentioned it briefly, but I really don't know anything about it."

Dr. MacPherson chuckled mischievously. "So you are a blood relation of the formidable Lady Campbell, are you? I'd better be on my guard, then. She has her spies everywhere!"

"Oh no, not me!" Ruth spoke quickly. "Aunt Florence doesn't approve of me at all. She would never discuss business with me." She had a sudden urge to make it quite clear to Dr. MacPherson that she was not on Florence's side. She wanted him to like her. She rattled on, "I think a hospital in Campbellburgh is a wonderful idea. I just hope you are successful, because we do need a hospital here. I run a clinic up on the farm, and there are so many times I would send someone to a hospital if there were one close by. But to send them all the way to Nairobi is very difficult. I only do it if it is a matter of life and death." She stopped, embarrassed by her outpouring of opinion. But Dr. MacPherson smiled broadly.

"Well, thank you for your vote of support. I was beginning to think there was not one person in the entire town who had anything good to say about a hospital. They have all closed ranks against me."

Ruth looked ahead at the escarpment in the distance. It was looming larger now, and she could make out the road winding up the side. How quickly they were coming to the other side of the plains. Her father was still sleeping in the backseat. Ruth was grateful at least for that. She turned to Dr. MacPherson. "Whatever made you come to Campbellburgh to build a hospital? Surely it's not the only place in the world that needs one."

He smiled. "That's a long story, but I guess we have the time, if you really want to hear it." Ruth nodded.

"I grew up on a farm out in the middle of nowhere, like you. My mother is a very faithful Christian woman, and one day when I was about twelve or thirteen, she took me and my brothers to hear a missionary speaker who was passing through the area. A huge tent was set up in a field, and people came from all over the countryside to hear the man speak. I was so excited by the novelty of it all that I could hardly sit still, and I still remember my mother threatening to sell me to the zoo if I didn't stop behaving like a monkey!

"Well, after a few restless minutes and a well-placed swat from my mother, I settled down and started to listen. The missionary spoke about how he had worked with Albert Schweitzer in his mission hospital in West Africa. He had a real sense of adventure and excitement in his spirit, and he told story after story of what Africa was really like. I was spellbound. Then he spoke about the need for people to hear the Gospel—people whose lives were burdened with superstition and fear of dark, unpredictable gods. And he also told of their suffering with sickness and disease and how we in more 'civilized' countries had much of the help they needed. But there was no one to go to them. They needed doctors, hospitals, and above all, Christian men and women to tell them about the Gospel so they could be set free from the dark powers that ruled their lives." He took a deep breath.

"It was then and there that I decided to be a missionary, though I confess that back then it was more likely the lure of adventure in darkest Africa, fighting against evil, not to mention lions and snakes and other fearsome creatures, that spoke to my soul rather than the pure Christian love that should have been my first motive.

"But the Lord works in mysterious ways, and my mother had always prayed that one of her children would become a missionary. So, as time went on, my motives changed and I felt the true call of God to the mission field. And remembering the old missionary at the tent meeting, I felt that medical training would be the most useful way to prepare myself to serve in a practical way as well."

Dr. MacPherson slowed the car down, and Ruth noticed that the escarpment had loomed up before them quite suddenly. The dry grasses had given way to green bushes, and they in turn were becoming trees as the road began the steep, winding climb ahead. As they started to climb upward, Ruth could feel Rosie's engine working harder. She glanced back at her father, who had awakened with the change in the sound of the motor. "Are you all right, Father?" Ruth asked.

"How much longer do I have to stay in this bouncing monkey cage?" Ruth was startled to hear him speak so clearly; but before she could reply, he had already closed his eyes and lapsed back to sleep. She turned to Dr. MacPherson with a worried look.

He smiled at her reassuringly. "It won't be long now and we'll be at the hospital. Why don't you tell me about yourself? I've been doing all the talking."

"Oh no," answered Ruth quickly, "I was so interested in your story. There's nothing to say about me. Besides, you still haven't explained why you came to Campbellburgh."

"Well, are you certain I'm not boring you?" Ruth shook her head, and he continued. "After I had finished my training, my father died and left me a small inheritance since the farm was going to my younger brothers. I spent many hours in prayer deciding what to do with the money. By this point I had made up my mind not to marry, so I felt that as I wouldn't have to support a family, I would like to invest it in the furthering of God's kingdom. Gradually I concluded that God was telling me to build a hospital in East Africa as Dr. Schweitzer had done in West Africa. Since East Africa has opened up to the European settlers with the railway, the African natives are being decimated by disease.

"I studied maps and spoke to as many people as I could find and concluded that Campbellburgh was an ideal location. First, there is no hospital facility in the area. Second, it is served by both a railroad and a river, making it accessible to Africans from a large surrounding area. Therefore, I set my sights on Campbellburgh."

"That is the very reason you are having such trouble building a hospital there then," Ruth replied. "It is also an ideal location for tourists. My uncle's hotel does a brisk business with big game hunters starting out on safari and fishermen because they can come in by rail and get just about anywhere easily from Campbellburgh. Aunt Florence thinks that too many sick Africans hanging about will ruin the quality of tourism in the town."

"Well, even if that were true, which it isn't, I don't understand why she won't let me build my hospital farther up the river. But she's got the settlers up in arms all up and down the line. And I don't want to be too far away from the railroad because I'll need supplies and all sorts of things." He paused. Ruth didn't say anything. She was too intimidated by his passionate frustration with Aunt Florence. But he spoke again a few moments later in a more composed voice. "I must just remember that it is the Lord's work I am doing, not my own. He will open the doors I need when He is ready. I tend to forget that sometimes!"

He smiled at Ruth, and she found herself smiling warmly back for an instant before she suddenly blushed and lowered her eyes to look at her rough, work-worn hands in her lap. There was a new ache in her heart suddenly, and again she remembered what she had thought driving home in the buggy after Uncle Angus's funeral. *If I were at all pretty or feminine, or even if I knew the first thing about men, like Annie does, this is the man I would choose. If there were a God like the one he and Milka seem to know so well, why, oh why, has He forgotten so completely about me?*

Rosie was laboring up the steep hillside, switching back and forth as the road wound a little higher with each turn. Then without warning, there was a screech of brakes and Ruth was thrown forward against the dashboard. Dust billowed all around, and there was the sound of bellowing. Her father cursed loudly in the backseat.

"Elephant!" said Dr. MacPherson, already leaning over the back of his seat to help her father and make him comfortable again. Ruth pushed herself painfully away from the dashboard and turned to help him. "Came out of nowhere," he said. "Are you okay, Ruth?"

"Yes, I think so. What about you, Father, are you all right?"

But Jack only swore quietly under his breath again. He appeared to be only a weak and pale imitation of his former vigorous and intimidating self. Ruth's heart sank.

"It's all right, Ruth, he's about as well as you can expect under the circumstances." Dr. MacPherson was speaking reassuringly to her. "But we need to get him there as soon as we can." Ruth noticed a shadow of worry cross the doctor's handsome face as he looked at Jack. She knew he was doing his best. She wished they were there already. As she turned around to look ahead, she gasped with fear.

They had been silently surrounded by a herd of elephants, a river of them flowing and passing around the car as though it was nothing but a boulder tossed carelessly into their midst.

They sat quietly and waited, watching the massive shapes of elephants swaying majestically past. A familiar tingle shivered up Ruth's spine. These creatures carried a presence with them far more ancient and awesome than her small and fettered mind could conceive. The huge legs swayed like tree trunks as they went by Ruth's window, yet at the same time they were quiet and graceful. An old bull lifted his trunk and trumpeted. The earth shook with the wild, mournful noise echoing right down from the beginning of time.

"Look at the behemoth, which I made along with you." Dr. MacPherson spoke the words aloud. A thrill of awe washed over Ruth, and her heart reached out to worship, in fear and trembling, the creator of such magnificent creatures. But the moment passed almost as suddenly as it had begun. And the elephants were still streaming past.

It was a large herd, and it took a long time passing.When the last gray shape faded silently into the bush, the world lay hushed and awed. Even the birds waited in silence. With a quick glance at Jack in the backseat, Dr. MacPherson slipped out of the car and turned the crank to start Rosie's engine. The brash, rude roar instantly made the world a smaller, tamer place again. Ruth's burden of worry about her father descended again, and they drove on, quickly and urgently climbing and climbing.

She tried to fill her mind with the memory of the elephant, as she had done after she had seen the mother and baby in the pool at the farm; but it didn't work.

Fears for her father continued to intrude. She looked over at Dr. MacPherson. He was concentrating on steering Rosie around the hairpin curves and along the steep-sided roads. She wondered if he would tell her more of Canada. It was an interesting diversion.

"Please tell me more. About Canada, I mean," she asked.

As he spoke, Ruth listened, more to the sound of his voice than his actual words. She thought about him coming all the way here from Canada to build a hospital because of God. The fleeting thought crossed her mind that it would be so pleasant to be able to believe in God when people got sick and when they died. But she dismissed it quickly. She couldn't just pretend to believe something that she didn't know in her heart of hearts to be absolutely true.

They were nearing the top of the escarpment now. There were more Africans walking alongside the road, many of them women carrying huge kikapus, or baskets, filled with fruit and vegetables on their heads. There was a village of huts and chickens and children off to one side where the road flattened out. They had finally reached the high plain. Nairobi was not far off now. Ruth was very glad.

"When will we get there?" growled her father from the backseat. Ruth was startled by the tone of his voice. His old fierceness had disappeared completely, and there was something lifeless and empty about his voice without its passion. "If you don't get me out of this dreadful contraption soon," he complained, "you might just as well take me straight to the undertaker."

"We're just at the top of the escarpment now, Father, so it won't be long." Ruth didn't like the gray pallor of his complexion. He lapsed into silence.

Nairobi was a bigger version of Campbellburgh. The roadside quickly became crowded with people walking to and from town. The late afternoon sun reflected off the red and silver rooftops, and dust filled the air. The rows of shops had long, covered walkways in front of them Everywhere people were selling every type of food, or shape of basket, or color of cloth you could think of. They had to push Rosie through thick flocks of totos that continually surrounded them. By the time they reached the hospital, her father was in a lot of pain. They parked Rosie at the main entrance, and Dr. MacPherson went inside to fetch a stretcher, leaving Ruth and her father to wait. He came back in a few minutes accompanied by a nurse and two stretcher bearers.

Ruth stood helplessly watching her father disappear inside the wooden green door. She tried to swallow the lump in her throat and blink away the tears in her eyes. Dr. MacPherson stepped up to her and took her by the elbow.

"Come along now, Miss Jones." He spoke soothingly and steered her up the steps. "I know the doctor who will be looking after your father, and you'll like him. Let's go inside and meet him. After you." He opened the green door, and Ruth stepped inside to be greeted by the strong smell of disinfectant.

She had been here before, but it had been many years ago and there had been a few changes since then. She wasn't sure which way to turn. Dr. MacPherson took her by the elbow again and steered her down a hall to a small green and white office. "Stephen?" he called, tapping lightly on the open door.

A young doctor looked up from the desk and stood up to greet them. He was very tall and stooped slightly as he leaned forward to shake their hands. He had pale blond, thinning hair and wore wire-rimmed glasses. His smile was warm and welcoming.

"Miss Jones, I'd like you to meet Dr. Stephen Burgess, a friend of mine. Steve, Ruth Jones. We just brought her father in from Campbellburgh with a broken thigh. His horse bolted over him. Would you look in on him for us? Miss Jones is very worried."

Dr. Burgess shook Ruth's hand. "I'm sorry about your father. But please don't worry. We'll take good care of him. My colleague, Dr. Mancini, is in the emergency room at the moment, so your father is in good hands. Come with me and we will go and see how he is doing." The three of them set off down a long corridor.

Leaving them to wait outside a large swinging door, Dr. Burgess went in to check on Jack for them. He emerged only a few minutes later with a serious expression on his face.

"I'm afraid your father must have had quite a serious fall," he said. "They are working on his leg just now. Infection has already set in, so it may be a little while before we can stabilize him and tell you exactly the extent of his injuries. Would you like to wait here? It will be a rather long wait, I'm afraid."

Dr. MacPherson spoke up. "We haven't had anything to eat since breakfast this morning, so I think I'll just take Miss Jones to the Lord Stanley, if that is all right by her?" He looked inquiringly at Ruth and she blushed crimson.

"Oh, you can't possibly. . .I've never been in a. . .I mean, I haven't brought any money with me," she stammered helplessly.

"Oh nonsense!" breezed Dr. MacPherson, leading her back down the hall followed by Dr. Burgess. "Supper's on me! Come along!" Ruth was swept along to the front doors. Dr. MacPherson turned and thanked Dr. Burgess, and Ruth shook his hand and thanked him again. In a moment they were back in Rosie and heading off to the Lord Stanley.

"I can't possibly go to supper in a. . .a. . . ," Ruth spluttered nervously. "It's just that I'm not dressed and I've never. . ."

"Oh, don't be silly," said Dr. MacPherson firmly. "We haven't had a bite since we left the farm this morning. Surely you must at least be thirsty?"

When they arrived at the hotel, a group of cool, crisply dressed women stepped smartly up the steps in high heels and silk stockings. They were chattering and laughing like the birds in the trees back home, and Ruth wished she had never left her farm. She looked down at her wrinkled khaki trousers.

"I can't possibly go in there dressed like this. I'm dressed for work."

Dr. MacPherson turned to look at Ruth as if it were the first time he had seen her. "Well, as far as I'm concerned, being dressed for work is nothing to be ashamed of. You are clean and tidy, and I for one am proud to be dining with a woman who is dressed to work. Come along, I'm starving, and I'll bet you are, too." He jumped out of the car and escorted Ruth proudly up the steps.

They were seated at a table in the corner and Ruth had her back to the rest of the patrons. She was glad. The room was dark and cool and quiet, but Ruth couldn't shake the feeling that everyone in the restaurant was looking and laughing at her, a country bumpkin who came to the Lord Stanley Hotel in work clothes. Dr. MacPherson chatted so easily she longed for self-confidence to match his.

Gradually, she began to relax a little as Dr. MacPherson explained what was good to eat and what wasn't. She asked him to order for her, embarrassed again, in case she chose something too expensive. He cheerfully ordered some chicken for both of them and leaned forward to speak to Ruth. She felt herself enveloped in his warmth and enthusiasm. His eyes caught hers, and he lowered his normally loud voice to suit the quietness of the place.

"Tell me about your life, Ruth, if I may call you that. I don't stand much on formality, so please call me Douglas." Ruth blushed hotly again at the very idea of actually being familiar enough to call him by his first name, but he pretended not to notice. "We've spent all morning talking about me, now I think it only fair that you get a turn, too. So go ahead, tell me about yourself." He sat comfortably back in the large mahogany and zebra-hide chair and waited expectantly for her to begin.

It was the first time in Ruth's entire life that anyone had ever asked her about herself. But what could she possibly tell him? When she thought about herself, there was really nothing there. "There's nothing to tell you," she stammered. "I have a pretty quiet life, just running the farm with my father."

"Ha!" Douglas let out a loud guffaw and banged his fist on the table, utterly forgetting his restaurant voice. "Ruth! Don't tell me that I have come all the way from Alberta, Canada, to have lunch with a lady who, people say, pretty much single-handedly runs a farm in the middle of Africa, and she tells me she has a quiet, boring life, like some sort of spinster aunt living with her cats and knitting woolen booties all day long! Tell me another one!" He laughed his loud, merry laugh, and Ruth felt the eyes of everyone in the restaurant searing into her back. Just to keep him quiet, she thought she'd better come up with something.

"Well," she began slowly, hoping the darkness of the room would hide the redness of her face, "my mother died when I was little, and as soon as my father felt I had had enough schooling, he taught me how to farm. It is really the only life I know. We grow quite a bit of coffee, and we also have a herd of dairy cows." She told him about the intricacies of growing coffee and of the weather and the cows and the difficulties of finding good help. Finally, the waiter brought the chicken, and Ruth stopped talking, grateful for the interruption.

Ruth was indeed starving, and she tucked into the chicken with relish. It tasted delicious; and when she was nearly finished, she stopped eating so quickly and made a conscious effort to savor the rest of the meal. Douglas laughed when he saw her pause.

"You really were hungry, weren't you?"

Ruth nodded, her mouth full. "It's delicious," she mumbled gratefully. "Our cook doesn't make chicken like this!"

"I'm glad you're enjoying it so much. I don't imagine you get much chance to get out, living way up where you do."

Ruth took another bite and shook her head.

"It must be quite lonely for you, with just your father to talk to," he continued.

Ruth swallowed her mouthful. He was sounding suspiciously like he was becoming sorry for her. Not a genuine sorrow, but a sort of patronizing pity that she had come to recognize in people's voices when they spoke to her, as though she couldn't be treated quite as an equal. She loathed it. Once Douglas succumbed to it, he would never come out of it. Of course, it was bound to happen sooner or later. There was, after all, no one who didn't come to that conclusion about her eventually. But not today, not yet.

"I actually am not a bit lonely," she protested. "I'm far too busy. And Milka, the cook, has been a mother to me. I couldn't have asked for anyone nicer, really." Ruth realized she was talking too quickly. She took a deep breath. "I also have a very good friend, Annie Campbell. I think you know her. So really my life is not the slightest bit lonely."

Douglas quickly responded, "I'm sorry, Ruth. I didn't mean to offend you. I guess I just thought that running a farm so far away from town with only your father, it must be a little isolating. Of course you have friends. I did meet Annie. She is a very nice person, though to be absolutely honest, I can't say the same for her mother!" He chuckled ruefully.

"By the way, I was wondering whether you are planning to stay here in Nairobi. I would be very happy to lend you a little cash if you want to stay at the hotel." Douglas had resumed a more businesslike voice. "I have to stay myself, so I will be able to drive you over to the hospital in the morning."

"Oh, my goodness," Ruth panicked. "I can't possibly stay. I haven't told Milka or Kamau. I can't leave Father alone here, either. Oh dear, but I ought to be at home."

"Well, we can go back and see how your father is. Then, if you want to go home tonight, you can catch the overnight train and you will be in Campbellburgh in the morning. I would be able to look in on your father tomorrow for you. I shouldn't think there is much you'll be able to do for him until he is feeling a little better. You may as well go home and straighten out things and then come back when you can stay a few days.

"My cousin Alex arrives by train tomorrow night, so I won't be back in Campbellburgh for a couple of days. I can keep an eye on your father for you while I'm here, and I'll bring you news when I get back."

"Thank you!" Ruth sighed gratefully. The thought of spending an entire night here in Nairobi sent her into a flat spin. Douglas could look after Father now and she would return later. "Would you give me a lift to the station after we go to the hospital then?" She still hadn't found the courage to use his first name, but she managed to bite her tongue before she called him Dr. MacPherson again.

Douglas reached for the check. "Of course."

Back at the hospital, Ruth found Jack newly installed in a ward, his leg in a huge cast that effectively pinned him to the bed.

"Hello, Father," she whispered, pulling aside the curtain just enough to let herself in. He greeted her with an angry growl, like a cornered animal facing its attacker. She felt hot tears rushing to her eyes. He didn't belong here. *What have I done to him?* He looked so out of place wearing a green hospital gown that revealed a strip of white exposed flesh on his neck where his collar always covered the sun. It was indecent. She had an overwhelming urge to get him out of bed and take him home as fast as she could. She suddenly wanted everything to go back to the way it always was. It was too painful to see him like this.

With a shaking voice, she asked, "Have they been treating you well, Father?"

"They might as well just take me out back and shoot me. It would save everyone a lot of trouble."

Ruth tried another tack. "Is your leg feeling better with the cast on?"

Jack snorted with derision, and otherwise deigned not to reply. Footsteps sounded in the hall, and Dr. Burgess walked in.

"Hello, Miss Jones." Dr. Burgess stood on the other side of the bed. "I have a couple of things to discuss with you."

"I have already spoken to Mr. Jones about this, Miss Jones. I would like him to stay here for at least a month. Despite the pain killers we have given him, he will still be in considerable pain with the fracture in his leg and the infection. But what I am more concerned about is his high blood pressure. I would like to do a few tests to see if we can discover the cause of it." He patted Jack consolingly on his arm. "I know it is an inconvenience, but I wouldn't want you returning home unless you were well enough for your daughter to look after, and I am afraid that is just not the case at the moment." He smiled at Ruth, ignoring Jack's angry snort. He put out his hand and Ruth shook it, then he vanished quickly out of the curtain. Ruth was left looking desperately at Jack, who deliberately closed his eyes.

"I am sorry, Father," she whispered sadly. There was no response. "I will come back and visit as soon as I can, and don't worry about the farm. I will take good care of everything, just the way you would."

Jack opened his eyes, and Ruth was shocked to see a cold, calm fury glaring out at her. There was a sickening pain filling her stomach as she looked at him.

"You will go home now and stay there." He was speaking with deliberate, controlled rage at her. "You will not come back here. I don't want to see you. Now get out." Ruth stared, paralyzed with horror and disbelief.

"Father. . .," she whispered at last.

"You've had your way. You brought me here, now get out!" he hissed.

She turned and fled through the curtain. She wouldn't see him again at the hospital. She may as well take the train home tonight. She began to shake as she walked down the echoing corridor.

Douglas was waiting for her at the end of the hall. "How is he?" he asked, looking at Ruth with careful concern.

He must know that my father hates me, thought Ruth irrationally. "Not very well, I'm afraid," she replied in a shaken voice.

Douglas put his arm around her shoulders and helped her into the car. They drove quickly to the station and bought Ruth a ticket for the train. People were busily milling about. Everyone seemed to know just where they were going. Ruth felt lost. She was confused. The rage in her father's face blocked out all rational thought. She just wanted to be alone. Douglas steered her to a train car. She turned to say good-bye at the steps, but to her horror, when she tried to speak, tears filled her eyes and she stood speechless.

Impulsively, Douglas reached forward and gave her a quick hug. "Good-bye, Ruth. I'll be seeing you."

"Good-bye, Douglas," she whispered back before she turned and fled up the steps.

Chapter Five

Early in the morning two days later, Ruth nervously mounted Chui and set out on the dusty road down the hillside, making for Jimmy MacRae's farm. She hated the thought of leaving home in case Douglas brought her news of her father, but she had to help Annie. The last days had been intensely long and horribly lonely. She hadn't wanted to tell anyone that her father refused to see her. It was shameful.

She had caught herself in the depths of her loneliness, longing to see Douglas MacPherson's face again. She wanted to talk to him once more and feel the same warm familiarity that his presence brought to her. She remembered over and over again the sound of his voice, the shape of his mouth, and the sparkle of his blue eyes. For two days now she had been riding through the hot, dusty fields checking on the bibis toiling in the dry soil. But her eyes were really seeing lovely, intricate castles made of sparkling ice, set in shimmering lacy forests where she and Douglas walked and talked and laughed together. The memory of her father lying sick and broken in the hospital in Nairobi, which always brought a sick stone of pain crashing into the pit of her stomach, faded as she thought of Douglas. Oh, how she didn't want to leave the farm in case he came. But Annie's pleading face also intruded into her mind, so Ruth decided to get up early and visit Jimmy MacRae. She had to do something to help. She couldn't let Annie down—not Annie, of all people.

As Ruth rode out onto the plain, the silver roofs of Campbellburgh were glinting in the rapidly warming sunshine. She was hot. She hoped Jimmy was at the farm and wished the MacRae farm were on the same side of town as hers. The ride across the plain seemed to have become longer and harder than she ever remembered it before. Even the ugly old baobab didn't capture Ruth's imagination the way it usually did, and she passed it by with barely a glance. Just before reaching Campbellburgh, she turned south.

The MacRae farm was much smaller than theirs. As she rode up the driveway, chickens and ducks scurried out from under Chui's feet with indignant cackles as if to demand why a mere horse should have right-of-way. A couple of goats contentedly munched on dry grass inside a small boma off to one side, and some totos sat on the fence in front of them, waving cheerfully at Ruth as if they were playing a game of trying to make her wave back. She did.

The house was small and old and had a thatched roof and no lawn or flowers in the front. Ruth was ashamed to find herself feeling a degree of understanding for Florence's dislike of having Jimmy MacRae for a son-in-law. It would certainly be a terrific blow to the Campbell pride to have one of their daughters marry into such lowly situation. But when Jimmy himself came striding purposefully from around the back of the house, his hands dirty and his black hair plastered down with sweat and a broad, welcoming smile on his face, Ruth smiled back rather sheepishly. Annie was right, he was a good man.

"Good morning to you, Ruth Jones," he shouted cheerily. "What can I do for you this morning?"

Ruth jumped lightly down from Chui. Jimmy was not terribly tall, and he had a wiry build. Ruth could look him directly in the eyes. She realized with surprise that it had been a very long time since she had actually seen him, let alone spoken to him. He was friendlier than she remembered. She came straight to the point.

"I'm here to bring you a message from Annie." She was touched to see his face immediately light up from the inside. "But it's not very good news."

"Is she all right?" Jimmy's light faded as suddenly as it had appeared.

"I think so. I had lunch with her a couple of days ago. She is quite depressed. She is worried that you may feel that she too easily gave in to her mother's wishes not to marry you. At the same time she is afraid of disobeying her mother. And her mother will allow her no visitors or correspondence in case she is secretly getting in touch with you."

"I must do something!" Jimmy's voice was quiet with worry. He shielded his hand across his eyes. "I'm sorry I couldn't come sooner," Ruth said. "My father had an accident and I had to take him to the hospital in Nairobi."

"I am so sorry to hear that! I hope it was not too serious." Jimmy remembered his manners quickly, but Ruth could tell his mind was only on Annie, so she merely nodded and went on.

"I will call on my aunt to tell her about my father's accident. I will try to pass a message to Annie from you if you would like."

Jimmy brightened again. "Oh, thank you very much, Miss Jones. I would be very grateful to you. Please excuse my terrible manners and come inside for a glass of orange or lemon squash!" He led the way onto the little, bare veranda and opened the front door for Ruth. "Perhaps we can even have an early lunch. I so rarely have visitors, but I'll go and see what the cook has. Excuse me for just a moment."

While Ruth's eyes were still adjusting from the glaring midday sun, he slipped away through a door on the far side of the room. Ruth stood awkwardly by the door and looked around. There was one large, well-worn, burgundy brocade armchair next to a rough stone fireplace. The table next to the chair contained a huge, equally worn, open Bible. Over the fireplace mantle, Jimmy had placed a wooden cross instead of the usual hunting trophies. The two pieces of wood were bound with string and unpolished.

Otherwise, there was very little else in the room. A real bachelor's home, Ruth thought. Annie would have the place cozy and inviting in no time. Jimmy returned carrying a tray of glasses and a jug of squash, which he set on top of the Bible.

"Sorry to keep you waiting." He pulled out a couple of chairs that Ruth hadn't noticed behind the door and carried them outside onto the veranda. Ruth picked up the tray and followed him outside. He took it from her and balanced it on the veranda railing. They sat down.

"You know, Florence Campbell is right," Jimmy began. "Annie does deserve a husband who can provide all the finer things in life for her. I know I don't have very much at the moment, but I work hard; and if I could just have a bit of time, I'll be able to provide Annie with the kind of life she deserves. And Annie says she'll wait for me." *Poor Jimmy. He sounds so hopeful.* Ruth wanted to say something comforting.

"I'm sure that Florence will relent soon. After all, Uncle Angus's death is so recent. After she recovers a little more, she will begin to see that you and Annie are truly in love, and then she will give her consent."

"Thank you, Ruth. I hope you are right." Ruth felt Jimmy's eyes looking gratefully toward her, and she blushed.

There was a small silence, and Ruth heard the soft padding of footsteps in the house behind her. The door opened, and a very tall man came out, carrying a tray of cold roast beef and a jellied salad.

"Thank you, Karioke," said Jimmy as Karioke set the tray down on the veranda railing next to the drinks. "You will join me for lunch, Miss Jones? I'm afraid it isn't much, but we can eat on our laps, if you don't mind."

"No, not at all," Ruth replied as Karioke passed her a clean, but chipped plate and a tin knife and fork.

While they ate, Jimmy politely questioned Ruth about her farm, and they discussed the price of milk and coffee. Afterward, Karioke came and took away their plates and brought them each a cup of coffee.

Jimmy turned to Ruth. "Would you mind if I left you for a moment while I just write a note for you to give to Annie?" She nodded and he went inside, returning a short while later with an envelope.

"Thank you, again, Miss Jones. This means so much to us both." He smiled at her with deep gratitude.

"It is a pleasure," replied Ruth, wishing he wouldn't call her Miss Jones. She held out her hand. Jimmy shook it. She ran down the steps, untied Chui, and waved good-bye as she cantered down the road. She turned back once to see Jimmy standing forlornly, watching her go. Poor Jimmy.

Just on the outskirts of town, Ruth pulled Chui up for a minute on a little knoll that overlooked the river and the town of Campbellburgh on the far side. She looked right across the river from the church where Angus Campbell's funeral had been. And there, next to it, lay the empty plot of land that had belonged to her mother, spreading down toward the river. She wondered if her father would ever use it for anything. Her parents had once thought of building a house and retiring there, at least her mother had; but her father would never be content so surrounded by civilization.

Ruth let Chui graze half-heartedly in the dry grass by the road. She jumped down, threw the reins over a little bush, and walked down to the banks of the river. Her mother's land was mostly dry scrub, but there was a green bank of lush bush along the riverbank. It was a lovely, serene spot. Ruth wondered what Florence had told her father about the possibility of selling it to Douglas MacPherson for his hospital. She would no doubt exercise her right of first refusal if he tried.

She made a quick stop at the Campbells', and in the shock at the news of her father, she managed to slip Jimmy's note to Annie without being seen. Then she rode back up to the farm on the hill in the heat of the afternoon. She had so much to think over that she didn't really notice how hot it had been until she reached the little river valley.

The cool air welcomed her home like an old, beloved friend, refreshing and relaxing her with just its very presence. The winding track led her along the still waters of the pools and the musical rapids bubbling between them. A feeling came over Ruth that the foundations of her life were imperceptibly, but irrevocably beginning to shift. *Perhaps it's just the worry of Father in the hospital,* she thought, shrugging the feeling away. A cool wind blew past her face and rustled the trees behind her on its way down through the valley. *There is freedom in the wind,* Ruth thought.

As she walked up the path from the stable, the low growl of a motor gradually began to imprint itself onto Ruth's consciousness. She looked up quickly. Sure enough, a smudge of dust was rising up from the side of the hill. Ruth pushed her hat back on her head and walked faster to reach the house before the motorcar arrived. She noticed rather sheepishly that her cheeks were flushed with excitement. Soon she would see Douglas again. But she also felt a flutter of apprehension as she wondered what news he was bringing of her father. She pulled her hat back down over her eyes to hide the telltale signs of her excitement and worry.

Rosie emerged from the valley just as Ruth hurried onto the veranda to look for her. She squinted into the glare of the afternoon sun behind the car. She suddenly realized that she was hot and perspiring. Her face was likely streaked with dust, and her shirt was damp and dirty. Quickly, she turned and fled inside. Running lightly down the hall to her bedroom, she found the washbasin in her room already filled for her. Splashing her face quickly, she pulled off her old shirt and threw a clean white one over her head. She was just tucking it into her trousers when she heard voices in the lounge and Milka's footsteps padding down the hall to find her. She reached for her brush, pulled it two or three times through her hair, and opened her door to tell Milka she was coming.

The flutter of excitement that had carried her through the last few moments, suddenly dropped like a stone down into the pit of her stomach. What news was Douglas bringing her of her father? Surely she wasn't so callous as to be worrying about the impression she was trying to make on a man, rather than considering her father's health. Feeling guilty, she ducked past the glaring animal eyes above her and went quickly down the hall. Nervously, she burst into the lounge and stopped short.

"Good afternoon, Ruth," came Douglas's cheerful voice as he stepped forward to shake her hand. "I just thought I'd run up to bring you news of your father." But Ruth stared past him. There was another man standing behind him. Noticing her look, Douglas turned to the man. "I'd like you to meet my cousin Alex. Ruth, Alex Kendall. Alex, Ruth Jones."

The man stepped up to Ruth and they exchanged polite greetings. Alex Kendall was a thin, dark-haired man, elegantly dressed, complete with a silk shirt and a red ascot around his neck. He had a pencil-thin mustache and a quick flash of a smile. Ruth thought he was rather formally dressed for a visit to a farm.

"Alex arrived in Nairobi last evening," Douglas said, and Ruth turned her attention back to him.

I'd forgotten how warm his smile is and how kind his eyes are, she thought as she looked up into his face, trying to remember every nuance of his presence to savor later.

"Miss Jones," Alex interrupted her thought. His voice was smooth and confident. "This is certainly a lovely location you have here for your farm. Douglas tells me you run the place single-handedly."

Ruth quickly glanced at him. His eyes were the same piercing blue as Douglas's, but they weren't brimming with merriment like his cousin's. They seemed almost expressionless, with maybe a hint of calculation underneath. Douglas was already starting to tell Ruth how her father was.

"I dropped in at the hospital this morning before we left Nairobi. I didn't actually see your father, since I didn't want to upset him, but I spoke with Dr. Burgess. His thigh is pretty badly broken, but given time it will heal, even at his age." Ruth smiled hopefully at this news, but Douglas's face became more serious.

"Unfortunately, there seems to be something wrong with his liver, and Dr. Burgess is running some tests to try to determine exactly what it is. He thinks it will be quite a while before your dad will be able to leave the hospital. But he wanted me to assure you that Mr. Jones is doing as well as can be expected under the circumstances. He is, of course, a little angry at being confined to bed and, as a result, is not always the most cooperative of patients. But the nurses are used to handling all sorts of people, so not to worry. Dr. Burgess says you need not rush back to Nairobi until you are quite ready. Your father is in very capable hands."

"Something's wrong with his liver?" Ruth echoed, remembering the weight of worry that she had felt earlier. Her shoulders slumped and she felt blood draining out of her face. Douglas quickly stepped up and put his arm around her shoulder.

"Here, Ruth, sit down." He helped her to the nearest chair. "Now you really mustn't worry about your father. Dr. Burgess is an excellent physician, and he won't let anything happen to him. Perhaps it is providential that he had this accident, although I don't want to make any excuses for my driving. But if there is something the matter, we will be able to nip it in the bud. I'm sure your father will be up and about just as soon as humanly possible. Come now, I'll go and find us all a cup of tea. Look after her, Alex, will you?" Douglas went out through the door into the hall, and she could hear him calling *"Jambo, jambo!"* as he looked for the kitchen.

Alex Kendall sat on a chair near Ruth's. "I'm most terribly sorry about your father," he said politely.

"Thank you," Ruth replied, wishing he would go away. She couldn't think of a single thing to say to him. They sat for a few minutes in uncomfortable silence until the sound of Douglas's footsteps could be heard coming down the hall.

"I found Milka in the kitchen," he said coming in and sitting beside Ruth. "She'll be here with a cup of tea for us in a moment." Ruth smiled up at him gratefully. She was even more grateful when he chatted with Alex about the kind of farming that they did in this part of Africa and the type of hunting and fishing in the area.

Milka came in with the tea and cake and scones and bustled about, serving everyone. Ruth sipped hers thankfully and listened as Douglas teased Milka about luring her away from her job as Ruth's cook to come and work for him. Milka giggled and demurred, half embarrassed and half pleased. It was unusual to have a visitor pay any attention to her. Ruth glanced over at Alex. He was looking on rather disapprovingly, she thought, his long fingers curling around his teacup like tentacles.

Milka set the teapot down on the table next to Ruth. "Will the bwanas be staying for dinner?" she asked Ruth pointedly.

"Oh, I don't know," Ruth stammered, panicking at the thought of entertaining two gentlemen alone. At least she wouldn't have minded if it were only Douglas, but his cousin was rather haughty. Well, there was no polite way out of it. Milka was standing in front of her waiting for an answer.

"Please, won't you join me for dinner," Ruth said quickly turning to Douglas. "I usually have quite a plain one, but I would be so glad to have you both stay."

"Thank you most kindly, but we really must be getting back to town. Alex is still tired from his journey and he needs an early night. Perhaps another time when we have more time we'll take you up on your offer." Douglas spoke quickly and firmly. Ruth felt relieved. It had been a long day for her, too, and she just wanted to crawl into bed and worry about her father. Maybe if it had been Douglas alone. . .

But Alex was speaking to her. "While I am here, I would very much like to take a safari and do some big game hunting. Do you know anyone who does that sort of thing in Campbellburgh?"

"Oh, yes," Ruth replied. "That is easy to find in Campbellburgh. There is a white hunter named Terry Matthews, who works for Angus Campbell. He regularly takes tourists out on safari. You just need to inquire at the Campbell Arms Hotel."

"Oh good, I'll do that. We are staying at the Campbell Arms."

They chatted easily now about big game and the various hunting grounds in the area. Ruth asked Douglas if he was going on safari also, but before he could reply, a snort of laughter came from Alex. Ruth turned to him in surprise.

"Our Douglas doesn't hunt, Miss Jones," Alex said condescendingly. "He saves lives, not destroys them! Have you not heard he is planning to build a hospital in Campbellburgh?"

"Yes, I have," Ruth answered, feeling brave with annoyance at his tone of voice. "I am very glad of it. The Africans in the area are in serious need of a hospital they can reach quickly and easily."

"Well, they've survived nicely for centuries," Alex replied. "It hardly seems worthwhile to go to such trouble and expense when they have their own methods of dealing with sickness. Probably they're just as effective as ours when all's said and done."

"Alex, one day's sojourn here in Campbellburgh hardly qualifies you to judge whether or not the native population would benefit from a hospital." There was a distinct note of irritation in Douglas's voice as he responded to his cousin.

Alex laughed cheerily. "Well, well, Doug, my boy, there is no need to be so serious about it all. After all, we didn't come here for Miss Jones to hear us argue about the merits of medical missionaries. Besides, it doesn't look as though anything will come of your plans if you can't even get these Campbells to sell you one small plot." Alex sat back smugly, having had the last word, so he thought.

"I'm not done with the Campbells yet, Alex." Then he turned to Ruth. "Thank you so much for the tea, Ruth, but we really must be on our way." He shot a significant glare at Alex as he spoke.

Then smiling kindly, he went on, "Your father will be as right as rain when Dr. Burgess has finished with him, so please don't allow yourself to worry needlessly over him."

"Thank you for your kindness," answered Ruth, wishing with all her heart there was some small way she could tell him how much his kindness had meant to her over the last few days.

Ruth saw them off at the veranda and stood watching as Rosie headed down the hillside, her cloud of dust trailing gaily behind her. She was not sorry to see the last of Alex, but she wished that she had been able to have Douglas to herself again. Their trip to Nairobi together already seemed like an old, old dream. She slowly turned to go inside the quiet, empty house.

Milka was in the lounge collecting the tea tray.

"I have heard about the *bwana*." Milka's voice sounded hushed with impending tragedy as she turned to speak to Ruth. "I fear he will not return to us. That hospital cannot cure what it is that is making him ill."

"Oh, Milka, you are speaking nonsense again." Ruth spoke harshly despite the pang of fear that Milka's words sent into her heart. "How can you possibly know anything about the *bwana*? He is in the hospital in Nairobi under the care of a very good *daktari*. Daktari MacPherson said so himself!"

Milka ignored her speech and continued in a portentous tone, "I pray that God will perform a miracle for him, just as He is doing for you." She walked out the door into the hallway.

Ruth followed her, despite herself. What was Milka going on about now? Miracles and such nonsense. Humph.

Milka set the tea tray in the kitchen and demanded her hapless toto wash them up instantly. Ruth sat down at the table.

"Now, the new American, Daktari MacPherson, he is a fine man. I can see it just by looking at him. He likes you very much, too." Milka smiled conspiratorially to Ruth.

"Milka!" Ruth retorted. "What are you getting at? Dr. MacPherson is not interested in me. He is not interested in anybody. He told me so himself!" Milka just raised her eyebrows and looked down her nose at Ruth with a knowing smile.

"Just stop it, Milka!" Ruth felt her cheeks getting redder by the second, and she simmered with frustration at herself, at Milka, at her life. "Douglas MacPherson is not going to marry anybody. Even if he were, I'm sure I would be the last person he would choose. He is a kind person; that is all there is to it!"

How did Milka know everything about me and Douglas and about Father, too? Really, she was getting far too big for her boots, Ruth fumed. She could tell that Milka was smiling, even though she had her back turned and was reaching up to put away some of the china that the toto had finished washing. Ruth stood up.

"Well, I'm tired!" She picked up her hat and stalked out of the door.

Ruth went straight to her bedroom and threw herself onto her bed.

How could Milka be so frustrating? But it was true. Milka was right; she wanted Douglas MacPherson. She wanted to be with him and knew it now. Absolutely, without a shadow of a doubt. And without a shadow of a doubt, she also knew that she would never have him. Her dreams of joy shattered like glass the moment she dreamed them.

She glared out of her window into the quickly darkening evening. The colors of the treetops were gray and cold. The sky itself was neither blue nor black, but some empty, colorless vacuum. Ruth felt gray and dead inside. How could Milka be so unkind as to talk that way about Douglas when there wasn't a hope in heaven of anything coming of it?

And what about Father? What would I do here forever and ever without him? It is too soon for him to die. He couldn't go just yet, I'm not ready. Surely Douglas was right, he would be right as rain soon. Douglas had to be right. He had to be.

A heart-shattering sob exploded out of her breast and hot tears burst out onto her cheeks. She buried her head in her pillow and sobbed like a baby. No, she thought, no baby ever had a heart hard enough to break like this. She wept for fear of being alone. She wept because of her father. She wept because of Douglas.

And when Ruth finally became quiet, everything was the same as it had ever been. Everything except her. She wanted life, a life of her own. She smiled grimly. She had no idea how to even begin to live her own life. She was poor, plain, tall, and utterly alone. Standing over by her window now, she looked out into the vast, empty sky. Even the stars were still few and far between. For the first time since the old, old days of her childhood, she uttered a prayer out loud, sending it soaring out of the darkness of her bedroom, soaring out beyond the darkness of the night outside.

"Please, God," she begged, "I want to live. I want to marry Douglas MacPherson and live. You made me a living woman, and I want, somehow, no matter how hopeless it is, to at least try to be alive before I die."

And just for a moment, she was acutely aware that she had now done everything she could, and the rest would have to be up to God, if He was there, if He cared. She was helpless.

Chapter Six

Early in the morning, a week later, Ruth received word that her aunt Florence would be making a visit to Ruth to comfort her in the time of her father's illness. The news set Milka into a flurry of baking and cleaning, and Ruth went to her bedroom to change into her tweed skirt. Only after she opened her closet did she remember what she had done to it. She stood staring into the empty darkness with mingled relief and guilt. She could wear the only other dress she owned, her black funeral one, but that would mean fixing the tear on the side. Besides, the black dress was even hotter and more uncomfortable than the tweed skirt. Florence would be expecting her to be in a dress, like a well-brought-up Christian girl. She sat on her bed to think the matter out.

This was absolutely ridiculous, she decided. Here she was, a thirty-two-year-old woman, and she didn't even own a proper dress in which to receive visitors. Surely she and her father weren't that poor! But her father always handled all their money, and she was only given a very small allowance to buy certain necessities. The only clothes her father approved for her were men's trousers and shirts.

She had gradually become aware this week that she would have to go into town to see the bank about the money. Each morning she collected the milk money and put it in the cash box in her father's office. He took it into the bank once a month and deposited it, complaining bitterly about what a pitiful amount it was and how difficult it was for an honest farmer to eke out a living these days. It had been the same ever since Ruth could remember.

But for now, as she sat staring into her empty closet, she decided at last that she would face Aunt Florence in her cleanest trousers and white shirt. Then, before her father came back from the hospital, she would go to town and have Mrs. Singh, the dressmaker, sew her a dress. When her father saw it, she would just explain that her old clothes didn't fit anymore. There would be nothing he could do then. She shuddered in fear at making her father angry, but she resolved in her mind that it was time she had at least one plain dress.

Florence's buggy sailed up to the farmhouse at precisely three o'clock. As usual, Ruth awaited her arrival on the veranda. Today, much to her astonishment, not only were Aunt Florence and Annie in the carriage, so was Alex Kendall! Ruth stood and stared as Alex jumped out and handed first Aunt Florence down and then Annie. *Annie looks tired and thin,* Ruth thought, as she saw Annie quickly let go of Alex's hand after she reached the ground.

Aunt Florence had surged up the steps to Ruth, then stopped short in front of her. "Good Lord, Ruth Jones, your poor father goes into the hospital and not two weeks later you are receiving visitors in khaki trousers, like some sort of bush farmer who knows no better! Your mother will be turning over in her grave at the very thought. How could you do such a thing! And we have Mr. Kendall here, too. I was so hoping you would make a favorable impression on him, you know, for the sake of the family! We don't want him thinking we are utterly uncivilized out here, even if we have to reside in darkest Africa!"

She turned toward Alex and Annie, who had followed her up the steps, and laughed a high-pitched, apologetic little giggle for Alex's benefit and continued her monologue. "As I told you, my dear Mr. Kendall, Ruth is one of the less accomplished of the Campbell girls, but her dear mother was a saint. It is because of her mother that I have taken it upon myself to see to it that her father brings her up in a proper Christian manner!" She swept a withering look at her niece and stepped majestically aside.

"Miss Ruth Jones, may I present Mr. Alex Kendall. Mr. Kendall, Miss Jones."

Alex stepped forward and bowed slightly in Ruth's direction. Turning to Florence he said, "Mrs. Campbell, Miss Jones and I have already had the pleasure of being introduced."

Complete shock actually struck Florence dumb for a moment. Alex seized his opportunity. "I came to see Miss Jones with my cousin, Dr. MacPherson, on the first day that I arrived in Campbellburgh in order to bring her news of her father's condition."

Florence recovered quickly. "I see," she said coldly, eyeing Ruth. "You do not waste much time in meeting the eligible young men in town, do you? I hear you even persuaded our Dr. MacPherson into driving you and your father all the way to Nairobi."

Ruth turned crimson with shame and embarrassment. "I. . .he just. . .I mean it's not like that at all," she stammered and stumbled over her words. Annie rushed to her rescue.

"Mother! How could you say such a terrible thing about Ruth? When has she ever behaved like that in her entire life? Honestly, Mother, how could you!"

Florence was slightly taken aback at the strange outburst from her usually obedient daughter, but she wasn't going to be put in the wrong. "You are very young, my dear, and obviously you know very little about the ways of the world. Women of a certain age can become desperate in affairs of the heart. One can never be too careful, you know."

Ruth was utterly appalled at the turn the conversation was taking, and they hadn't even gone inside the house yet. Aunt Florence must have read her mind because she suddenly set sail for the door and swept through it.

Milka was just setting out a tray of tea things on the table. Florence descended on the table with relish, poured herself a cup of tea, and loaded her plate with the cakes and scones that Milka had baked for the occasion. Taking a huge helping of whipping cream to cover everything, she then chose the largest of the chairs in the room and sank heavily into it. Alex steered Annie over to the tea table and supervised her birdlike helpings before he, too, covered his plate in cake and whipped cream. He followed Annie over to the other side of the room and sat in the chair next to hers. Annie looked unhappier than Ruth had ever seen her, and her heart went out to her.

"Oh, my dears," Aunt Florence was now expounding thickly through a mouthful of scone, "you've no idea at your young and carefree ages how it is for such as me. Not, mind you, that I am that far advanced in years." She glanced coyly at Alex. "I do have a grown daughter, I admit, but I married very young. Angus was in a dreadful hurry, and I gave in to him. But now here I am, far before my time, a widow. It is a dreadful thing, a dreadful thing." She reached down into the depths of her quivering bosom and produced a large, lacy hankie with which she dabbed her eyes.

Alex leaped up and offered her his handkerchief as well.

"There, there now, Mrs. Campbell, please don't upset yourself. I'm sure everything will turn out fine. Just remember to have faith in the One above. I once trained for a minister, and I know how much comfort one's religion can give at a time like this."

Florence took his handkerchief and placed it tenderly into her bosom. "Thank you so much, Alex." She looked up tearfully at him. "You must call me Florence. I feel so close to you already."

Ruth had the uncomfortable feeling she was intruding on an intimate family discussion. She looked over at Annie for support. Annie was staring with undisguised disgust at Alex and her mother. Ruth was shocked at the frankness of her expression, but Alex turned around to return to his chair, and Annie's expression was quickly replaced with a smile of polite approval. Ruth wondered if she had imagined Annie's disgust, but Florence had recovered her composure and was already addressing her.

"Alex is not at all like his cousin, Douglas MacPherson, you know, Ruth, my dear. Alex is truly a gentleman. In fact, he has been kind enough to come all the way out here to check up on his cousin, merely out of the goodness of his own heart. It seems that because of his religious convictions, Dr. MacPherson is always getting himself into scrapes of one sort or another. Not that religious convictions are altogether a bad thing, mind you. We all must be true to our religion, but everything in moderation, I say. It just doesn't do to become fanatical about these things."

Ruth, who was the main target of this address, smiled weakly. She wasn't quite sure how to answer, but she needn't have bothered, because Florence was not looking for Ruth's opinion, she was informing her of it. She continued.

"Now, Ruth, I insist that you do not become too chummy with this cousin of Alex's. I know he is concerned for your welfare what with taking your father into the hospital, but after all, it was his fault that your father was hurt in the first place. Don't forget that, Ruth. You really must put a proper distance between yourself and him. I insist upon it!

"By the way," she continued regally, "I will take charge of your father's care from now on, and I will make sure he is properly looked after. I came here to tell you that I went up to Nairobi for a couple of days this week. Your father is not at all well, but it is really no wonder with the nursing care they provide in that hospital. It's a wonder anyone comes out alive! And the hygiene! Appalling!" She sniffed with disgust. "It is far beyond your capabilities to deal with those things. I have instructed that long drink of water, Dr. Burgess, that he be under continual care. I will have nothing but the best for him, my dear, don't you worry about that!"

"Aunt Florence!" Ruth was taken completely by surprise. "You never mentioned that you saw my father! Will he be able to come home soon? What did Dr. Burgess tell you? Is he getting better?" It was humiliating to have to glean any news of her father from Aunt Florence, but Ruth was desperate. She didn't even care that her aunt was taking control of his care.

"Well, as far as I am concerned, he is in terrible hands. He should really be nursed at home, the way I nursed my dear Angus. But one can't really do a thing once those doctors get hold of them. Of course, since he won't have anything to do with you for having put him in there and with the help of that dreadful MacPherson man, Alex, here, will keep you abreast of your father's condition for me, so you may feel free to drop Dr. MacPherson altogether. Again, I insist on it." She looked over at Alex and smiled triumphantly.

Ruth felt tears of fury and shame flooding into her eyes. She desperately blinked and swallowed them back. She glanced over at Annie, but Annie just sat and looked helplessly back at her. She looked at Florence. Florence took a sip of her tea and continued, taking Ruth's silence for consent.

"Of course, I have taken all the necessary steps to prevent a native hospital from being established by Dr. MacPherson. Tourism is such an important industry in this town, I would insist that nothing jeopardizes it. Least of all, a hospital that would draw in hundreds of undesirables from all over the country."

Ruth could hardly believe Aunt Florence was talking about this hospital when her father was so ill. But recklessly, she threw out a defense. She just couldn't let Aunt Florence off this particular hook. "But, Aunt Florence, don't you think that it would be good for the hotel to have people coming into Campbellburgh? They will need a place to stay."

Ruth instantly realized her mistake.

"Good heavens! How can you possibly suggest such a thing? To have my hotel filled with riffraff and goodness knows what! I would rather sell it and move to Timbuktu! Ruth, I am surprised at you!" Ruth reached for her hat but, of course, she wasn't wearing it. She clasped her hands in her lap and stared at them nervously. Stupid mistake, she thought to herself.

"Well, Miss Jones," Alex was condescendingly addressing her. She really couldn't stand this man, and she wondered what on earth Douglas tolerated him for. Maybe there was something wrong with Douglas after all. "I really feel it is my duty to warn you not to get too involved with my cousin. I have known him all my life, and while I love him as a dear relative, it is important to keep things in perspective. He is rather fanatical in his beliefs. He has been that way from childhood. He gets it from his mother, God bless her soul, poor woman. If it hadn't been for the good sense of her husband, she would have given away everything she had. People were constantly taking advantage of her generous nature and, unfortunately, she had a great effect on Douglas. Although he has many commendable ideas about helping the disadvantaged and destitute, we must try to keep our good deeds on a reasonable level so that they don't interfere with people who are just trying to make an honest living.

"So, Miss Jones," he concluded, "I suggest you not get yourself involved in something that your family would find most regrettable. And, regrettably, this is a time when they desperately need all you can give them. May I add that you do have my heartfelt prayer for your father's quick and complete recovery." He smiled charmingly, but Ruth was suddenly left with the most unreasonable impression she had been spat at.

Ruth forced herself to sit quietly. She wanted to run away, but if she did anything, she should stand up and defend Douglas. She was frozen with the fear of making another mistake. She felt like a complete coward. She sat in shameful silence.

Milka returned with a fresh pot of tea and some more cake. For a few golden moments, there was silence while they waited for Milka to finish passing the food around.

As Milka left, Florence decided to change the subject to something more pleasant. She turned toward Annie, who sat with Alex at her side. "Of course, we are so fortunate to have the pleasure of Mr. Kendall's company in our town. I have invited him to stay with us during his sojourn in Campbellburgh, and I feel he has, even in this short time, become the son to me that I never had." She paused and looked significantly at Annie, who blushed and avoided her gaze. Alex Kendall smiled and basked openly in her approval of him.

Florence, pleased with his response, continued, "After all I have been through with the death of my dear husband, it has been a great consolation to me that the good Lord above has at last seen fit to send someone to be a solution to the desperate straights I so unhappily find myself in."

She lapsed into a woeful recounting of her tribulations. "No one knows," she began tearfully, "how hard it is for me these days. I have deeper sorrow than I ever thought I would have in this life. I can't even bring myself to mention the most painful part of it to anyone. The burden is entirely my own." And she broke down into a flurry of sobs. Annie jumped up and rushed over to comfort her mother.

"There, there, Mother, everything will be all right, you'll see. I know it will. You are just rather overwrought with Uncle Jack being ill. Come along, you'll be yourself again soon."

"Yes, perhaps you're right," replied Florence, blowing her nose, "but I do feel a little weak." She stood up and took Annie's arm. "I must go home now. Alex, please come here, my dear." Alex rushed over and took her other arm, and together they led her outside to the waiting surrey. They settled her into her seat with much fuss and bother, while Ruth stood watching the scene incredulously.

Poor, poor, Annie, she thought. *Aunt Florence is scheming to marry her off again.*

"Now, remember, Ruth," Florence launched her parting shot, "you will no longer have anything more to do with Douglas MacPherson. I simply won't have it!" The buggy started with a sudden jerk, and Annie turned over her shoulder and waved sadly to Ruth.

Ruth spent a fitful night thinking about Annie and her new predicament with Alex Kendall. Every now and then she relived the shame and embarrassment of Aunt Florence's attack on her and her relationship with Douglas. And over and over again, she cringed shamefully at the memory of her father's furious face glaring at her in helpless hatred from his hospital bed. Tendrils of bitterness and anger wound themselves around and around her broken heart, binding it painfully together again in an unnatural wholeness.

In the morning Ruth woke with a sense of cold resolve. She would take the milk money out of the cash box and head into town with the milk cart. She would visit Mrs. Singh's and order the most beautiful dress Mrs. Singh could make for her. She didn't care how ugly she was. If Aunt Florence thought she had designs on Douglas MacPherson, let her think the worst! She would never again be without at least one dress in which to receive visitors. And she resolved not to care what her father thought. She didn't regret cutting up that ugly, old tweed skirt.

Later that morning, when she rode angrily into town behind the milk cart, the milk money burning a hole in her pocket, she noticed that Rosie was parked outside the Campbell Arms Hotel. Impulsively, she turned Chui down the drive, calling to the milk cart driver to go ahead without her.

As she rode into the circular driveway past the large, white Campbell Arms sign, she realized it had been years since she had actually set foot on the grounds. This was the heart and hub of the Campbell empire. This was the source of their money and their power.

She was surprised at how old the place looked now that she was up close. The white paint on the outside of the big main building was worn and dull, and the thatched roof was ragged around the edges and paled by too many years in the glaring heat. Even the gardens looked rather dry and faded. But there was still an air of stately elegance about the old place that was in no way diminished by its slight slip into shabbiness.

There were wide, curved steps leading up to a veranda covered by a massive old bougainvillaea. To the left of the main building were the rondavels, little thatched circular huts where the guests stayed, stretching out in a curved line that circled the lawns. On the right side, the veranda opened out into a wide patio, where tables were set among potted palms and flowering bushes.

Ruth pulled Chui to a halt in front of the steps where Rosie was parked and realized that she had no idea what she was doing here beyond the ever-present hope in her heart to see Douglas MacPherson again. Angry with herself, she kicked Chui harder than she meant to, and Chui gave a surprised whinny of pain before setting off at a trot around the far side of the driveway. Hurrying away, embarrassed at herself, she heard someone shout from behind her.

"Ruth! Miss Jones!"

The thought flashed through her mind that she could get away quickly by pretending she hadn't heard.

"Ruth!" It was Douglas. Blushing with embarrassment and trying to come up with a reason for her presence here, Ruth pulled Chui to a halt and turned him around slowly.

Douglas was standing on the veranda by the tables waving Ruth over to him. "Hey, Ruth!" She waved back self-consciously. "Come and join me for lunch. You're not doing anything urgent, are you?"

Douglas stood smiling a cheerful welcome at her, looking for all the world as if he were waving to a long-lost friend. She dismounted and tied Chui's reins on the rail of the veranda. She could feel the eyes of the patrons in the restaurant staring curiously at her. Glancing quickly over them, she thought she recognized several townsfolk. Looking shamefully down at her boots and trousers, she slipped up the steps. Douglas was holding out his hand to shake hers.

"It's great to see a friendly face, here. I'm tired of eating alone all the time. Come and join me. Lunch is on me!"

"Oh, no, really I couldn't. I'm not properly dressed, and the milk. . ."

"Oh, nonsense, we've been through all this before!" He steered Ruth to his table and pulled out her chair. Ruth sat down obediently, aware of the eyes of several of the townspeople openly staring at this interesting little rendezvous.

"Waiter, another coffee," called Douglas, "and how about some of that delicious mango salad you were serving this morning?" He turned to Ruth. "I don't know what they do to it, but it's really worth trying." Ruth smiled. She felt ridiculous, but it was worth it to be here just to have him smile at her like that.

"Have you heard from your father? How is he?" Ruth snapped to attention.

"Aunt Florence came to see me yesterday. I couldn't really get a clear answer from her, but I'm afraid he is rather ill." Douglas's face fell.

"Ruth, I am sorry. It is all my fault. Is there anything I can possibly do? I feel simply awful about the whole thing."

"No, no," Ruth protested quickly, shocked to see the remorse on his face. "No, it's not your fault at all. Dr. Burgess told me so himself. In fact, it is a good thing he hurt his leg, otherwise he would never have received the treatment he needs. It's his liver. It's because he. . ." Suddenly she stopped. Douglas was such a good person. She felt embarrassed to explain her father's drinking.

"Have you made any progress with building your hospital?" she asked suddenly, pleased to have thought of a new subject.

Douglas sighed. "I think I have been completely stonewalled here. I'm going to try somewhere else, perhaps all the way into Uganda. It's funny. I was so certain this was the spot for the hospital. I even thought I had God's guidance to find the very place." He shook his head and spoke very quietly, "I guess I must have made a mistake."

"Don't give up just yet," Ruth blurted out. "There must be a way. You said that God wanted the hospital here. He will surely find a way then. You can't give up so easily." Douglas looked up at her in surprise. Ruth was surprised herself. *What an outburst,* she thought, looking down at her lap. *What on earth has come over me these days?*

Douglas was speaking. "Thanks for your vote of confidence, Ruth. I appreciate it. But I think you're the only person in this entire town who feels that way. I must have misinterpreted God's leading me here. I was mistaken." He looked defeated and discouraged.

"I'm sure something will come up," she said, still anxious to find him a solution. "Well, surely she can't tie up every place that's for sale in town?"

"Maybe she can. And in any case, she has a lot of influence."

"I'm sorry your cousin Alex has not been able to help you with my aunt," Ruth said, wondering how he fit in.

Douglas sighed deeply again. "It was a terrible mistake for him to come here, worse than you'll ever know. I fear my cousin has designs on Annie. I really must leave Campbellburgh, and I am trying to persuade him to come with me. The trouble is that he is staying with the Campbells. Florence has taken a liking to him, and I can't get him to agree to come with me."

Just then, the concierge of the hotel appeared beside their table. Ruth looked up in surprise. When she saw his face, a chill went down her spine.

"Miss Jones." He leaned over confidentially. "Dr. Burgess from the Nairobi hospital is on the emergency radio. He would like to speak with you." The color drained from her face, and she stood up weakly. Douglas came and took her arm.

"How did he know I was here?"

"He didn't," explained the concierge. "He just called with a message, but I explained you were dining here, so he asked if he might speak to you himself."

"It's all right, Ruth, steady now." Douglas was walking her into the darkness of the lobby. "It may only be a small thing." Ruth was glad for his comforting presence, but she knew people didn't use the emergency radio for small things.

When she heard Dr. Burgess's voice on the radio, the familiar sickness in the pit of her stomach reappeared and began to rise into her throat. "Miss Jones, I am so glad to find you at the hotel." He paused and took a deep breath. "I'm afraid I have very bad news about your father. He suffered a massive heart attack early this morning, and there was nothing we could do to save him. I'm terribly sorry, Miss Jones." Ruth was silent. Her nightmares had come to take over her waking hours.

Douglas reached for the radio. "Stephen, this is Douglas. We'll be in touch with you later. I'll let you know what to do with Mr. Jones. Over and out." He turned to Ruth. "Come along, Ruth, come to my room for a few minutes. Then, I'll drive you home; but first you probably need a couple of minutes of privacy to compose yourself."

Ruth was grateful for his thoughtfulness and his calm control of her situation. She couldn't think. She couldn't even see anything. Tears were smoldering like hot coals in her eyes. She allowed Douglas to take her by the arm and lead her outside. She could smell the damp, sweet riverside scents as they walked along the walkway in front of the hotel. When they came to Douglas's rondavel, he opened the door; and leaving it open, he had Ruth lie down on the bed.

She curled into a ball and started to cry. The loneliness was unbearable, already. No one in the world had ever been alone like she was alone now. She felt that everything and everyone in the world had been wrenched away from her and were now far, far away on the other side of an immense abyss. She was all alone forever and ever.

Douglas sat on the bed next to her with his hand on her shoulder, but he may as well have been on the far side of the moon. After a while, her sobs ran dry and she lay silent. She began to feel grateful for Douglas's touch on her shoulder. It was kind of him, she thought, and the chaos that her life had become suddenly receded a bit.

"If you will be all right for a minute, Ruth, I'll just go and start Rosie and bring her round to pick you up." Ruth didn't move. She wouldn't be all right for a minute and she didn't want him to go, but she couldn't tell him so. He waited for her reply, and when none came, he left. Ruth heard the door close behind him and she started to cry again.

When Douglas came back, she was sobbing deep, agonizing sobs that shook the whole bed.

"Ruth, Ruth!" He rushed over and took her in his arms and hugged her. "Ruth, don't cry so. I know it's a terrible blow, but don't worry, I'll help you out. Whatever you need. Come along now. Wash your face and we'll be on our way. I'll take you home. Milka will be there, won't she?"

Ruth stopped crying and looked up into his face. "It's just that I have no one else left now. He wasn't always the easiest person to live with, but we did have each other. I will miss him terribly."

"I know you will." Douglas took her by the hand and helped her to her feet. He filled the washbasin in the corner for her and she washed her face.

"There, feel a little better now?" he asked with a kind and gentle smile.

"A little." Ruth actually found herself returning his smile.

"Good. Come along now, I'll take you home."

A few minutes later, Ruth found herself speeding along the road to the farm in Rosie. The wind blew into her face, and she let her head fall back against the seat.

Letting it blow her sorrow away gave her a temporary respite.

When they arrived at the foothills, Douglas slowed down. Ruth felt strangely exhilarated from the speed, so when Douglas asked her how she was feeling, she was able to smile bravely.

"Tell me," he asked, "how long has your family been farming in up on the hill?"

"My father came here from England forty years ago. He started off by himself, but the Campbells were already settled in the valley, and that's where he met Mother. She died when I was only five." Ruth stopped, and Douglas asked another question.

"Do you think you'll continue to farm the place alone?"

"Yes. Father taught me everything he knew about farming, and I've done it all."

Ruth suddenly had an urge to tell Douglas everything she could about her father and what he had done with his life and what he had done for her. So she talked and talked as they drove the long, winding road up the hill; and Douglas listened and nodded and asked the odd question. By the time they pulled up at the farmhouse, Ruth was actually smiling now and then.

The sound of the approaching motorcar had brought Milka running out onto the veranda to see who it was. Ruth opened the door and ran up the veranda steps to her.

"Oh, Milka," she said. "It's the *bwana*, he's. . .he's. . ." She couldn't get the words out of her mouth before the reality of the pain and the loneliness surged forward again and she started sobbing. Milka rushed forward and put her arms around her.

"Memsahib, '*Sahib,* come inside, come with me." She steered Ruth into the house, whispering comfort from her faith in God. "The Lord will care for you. He comforts those who mourn. He will always be with you. You just let me look after you now." She sat Ruth on a chair and looked over at Douglas, who had followed them inside. "I will get the tea."

Douglas pulled a chair up beside Ruth. "Are you going to be all right alone here tonight? Perhaps I could call on your aunt and she could send someone up to stay with you for the night."

Ruth shook her head. "No thank you, I'll be fine. Really. But I suppose I had better tell my aunt what has happened. She should be the first to know, and Annie, too."

"Don't worry, I'll stop at their place on my way back to town and tell them about your father. Is there anyone else you would like me to tell?" Ruth shook her head again.

"Ruth," Douglas spoke with some hesitation now, "I know you are still overwrought and shocked, but we need to think about making arrangements for the funeral. Would you like me to suggest to your aunt that she help you with that? It may take a load off your mind just now."

The thought of Aunt Florence arranging Father's funeral hit Ruth like a slap in the face. He would never have allowed it if he were alive. "No," she said loudly. "No, not Aunt Florence. I must do it myself. It is the last thing I can do for him. I wasn't even with him when he died. I must at least do this for him. I will speak to the Reverend Montgomery. Father never went to church, but Mother is buried in the churchyard and Father would want to be next to her."

Douglas looked relieved to hear Ruth speak so passionately. Milka brought the tea in and set the tray on the table. She poured Ruth and Douglas each a cup and offered them some scones. Ruth felt she couldn't touch a thing, but Douglas took one gratefully. Milka bustled about making Ruth feel comfortable and making sure she drank her tea.

When Douglas finished his scone, he stood up. "Well, I should go and call on your aunt before it gets too late," he said. "I will also send word to Dr. Burgess to send your father's body down on the train as soon as can be arranged so that we can have the funeral."

"Thank you, Douglas," Ruth said gratefully, using his name for only the second time. "I appreciate everything you are doing. Thank you."

Douglas looked a little embarrassed at her gratitude. "Not at all. I am just glad to be of service. Please let me know at once if there is anything else I can do to help." He looked at Milka. "Look after her tonight."

"Of course I will, Bwana. She is like my own child," Milka responded, standing protectively beside Ruth.

"Yes, I know," said Douglas, and then without warning, he leaned down and kissed Ruth on the cheek. "God bless you, Ruth," he whispered in her ear. A moment later he was gone, and Rosie's engine roared and faded away down the road.

Chapter Seven

The syce from the hotel had brought Chui back that night. In the morning a surrey arrived from Florence with the message that Ruth was to come down to see her now. Ruth sent the surrey back empty, saying that she would call later. She felt too weak to face her aunt just yet. After breakfast, Ruth headed into town. She was numb with the shock of her father's death and she rode absentmindedly.

At the turnoff to the Campbell place, she stopped Chui on the side of the road. She stood looking up the driveway for a long time. She really couldn't face Aunt Florence even yet, so giving Chui a gentle spur, she headed into town. She decided she would make the funeral arrangements, and perhaps she would feel a little stronger once that was behind her; then she would face Aunt Florence.

The whole town already knew of Jack's death. As Ruth rode to the church, several people stopped to offer her their condolences. They spoke to her with quiet respect as they looked up into her tired, unsmiling face. Ruth could tell by their reaction that her grief and loneliness must seem, even to them, like an open wound.

She rode past her mother's land and wondered for a moment what she would do with it now.

Mrs. Montgomery greeted Ruth at her door, and with many kind offers of condolence, she ushered Ruth into her husband's dark, hushed study. The Reverend Montgomery stood up to greet her with an appropriately dignified, yet sorrowful smile on his lips. He offered her a chair in front of his desk.

"I am so glad you have taken the trouble to call on me, my dear Miss Jones. Mrs. Florence Campbell just left here this morning with the news of your poor father's passing." The Reverend Montgomery offered a bland, polite version of Milka's faith, Ruth thought to herself as she sat stiffly in front of his desk. He explained all the correct protocol of a proper Christian burial, even for such an inveterate sinner as Jack Jones.

"You are so deeply fortunate to have such a fine Christian woman as Mrs. Campbell for your aunt. I'm sure you will derive a great deal of comfort from her presence," he droned. Ruth tried to smile politely and agree. Apparently, he and Aunt Florence had decided that the funeral would be held on the following afternoon. The casket would arrive on tonight's train.

Ruth's polite boredom evaporated with this comment. "Excuse me, Reverend, but I would very much like to make my father's funeral arrangements myself, if you don't mind." She tried to speak firmly, with authority.

"Oh, of course, my dear Miss Jones, of course. But you must be careful not to overdo things in your fragile state, and your aunt Campbell is so concerned about you. You simply must allow yourself to rely on her help, my dear."

Ruth pulled her chair closer to the reverend's desk and forced herself to go over every detail for the funeral that she could possibly think of. Several times she was interrupted by the reverend. "Miss Jones, please don't let yourself be bothered with such small details. I know that Mrs. Campbell would be most happy to see to such things as the cards and the flowers. I am going to call on her this afternoon, and she has already explained that she is intending to help us."

Ruth sighed and sat back in the chair. In a flat, empty voice she said she would like her father buried next to his wife. The Reverend Montgomery and Aunt Florence had already arranged for that, but the reverend was careful to give Ruth the impression that he agreed to it more for her sainted mother's sake than for her father's.

Ruth was exceedingly irritated at the end of the interview and very glad to get out of the stuffy office into the heat and the sunshine of the African afternoon.

A few minutes later, Ruth climbed the narrow stairs to Mrs. Singh's little shop, which was in a room over her husband's duka. Mrs. Singh warmly welcomed Ruth into her cluttered room. Ruth noticed the large black and gold sewing machine under the single window that looked out over the street. There were long tables and mannequins taking up most of the rest of the room and tape measures, scissors, and pincushions scattered on every available surface. Over in one corner was a mannequin wearing an exquisite white silk wedding gown. Ruth looked at it quickly and thought that it would look lovely on Annie.

Mrs. Singh herself was an elegant woman, wrapped neatly in a yellow sari. The material was delicately interwoven with silver thread, which shimmered as she moved.

"Good morning, Miss Jones," she said, her lilting voice strongly tinged with an Indian accent. "It is my pleasure to see you here. Please accept my deepest condolences on the death of your father. You will no doubt miss him terribly."

"Thank you, I will," mumbled Ruth, still embarrassed at the sorrow that people felt for her loss. But Mrs. Singh floated toward her and led her to a richly brocaded gold armchair, the only chair in the room besides the one at the sewing machine. She motioned for Ruth to sit.

"How may I be of service to you?" She bowed slightly and smiled warmly, pulling her chair away from the sewing machine and sitting opposite Ruth.

"It will be my father's funeral tomorrow," Ruth began, "and I would like to have a new dress for the occasion. Would it be possible to have one readied that quickly?"

Mrs. Singh smiled. "For such an important occasion, I would be happy to be of service to you. It would be helpful, of course, if we could choose a dress with quite a simple pattern. Did you have something particular in mind?"

Ruth felt embarrassed at her lack of knowledge of the intricacies of dressmaking. "No, I don't really know much about dresses," she confessed, "but something simple would suit me, too. And perhaps not in black, either. Maybe a blue," she added impulsively. She couldn't face another black dress like her mother's.

Mrs. Singh stood up and pulled a bolt of fabric from behind a curtain. "With your very beautiful red hair and fair complexion, perhaps this green would be nice. It is quite dark, but lightweight, and would not look too out of place in the church."

She held the fabric out for Ruth to touch. It was silky and had a delicate leaf pattern woven right into the material. Ruth thought she had never seen anything so lovely in her life.

Ruth was still fingering the fabric. She could hardly believe that she could actually wear something so pretty, and to a funeral, too. "It's lovely," she said.

"Let me measure you," said Mrs. Singh, pulling a tape measure that was hanging around her neck. Ruth stood up and Mrs. Singh wrapped the tape around her.

Suddenly Ruth had a worrying thought. "Will it cost very much money?" she asked quickly. "The material, I mean."

"No, no, not too much. I will keep the price down by making your dress very simple. Let's see, we will need about three and a half yards." Mrs. Singh's voice trailed off as she calculated the cost of the dress.

When she finally came up with a figure, Ruth was pleasantly surprised to discover that her milk money more than covered it. As she left, she felt she was ready at last to face Aunt Florence. She hoped the Reverend Montgomery wouldn't be there.

Juma, the Campbells' houseboy, ushered Ruth into the dark, scented lounge where Florence was sitting drinking tea with Annie and Alex.

"Miss Jones is here, Memsahib," Juma announced. Florence stood up and turned around in surprise.

"Oh, my goodness," she declared, "I was expecting the reverend." She descended on Ruth and kissed her brusquely on the cheek. "I am so sorry about your father, my dear child, but just because you are upset must not cause you to forget your manners. I especially sent my best surrey up to fetch you this morning. I had to go into town in the old buggy, you know. I was really quite a sight to be seen driving around in that old thing, and then you never even came. We were expecting you at luncheon!"

"I'm sorry, Aunt, but I wanted to see the Reverend Montgomery about Father's funeral."

"Ruthie, it is so good you are here at last," interjected Annie, who came over to hug Ruth. "How are you? Are you all right? Dr. MacPherson came by yesterday and told us you were doing quite well and that Milka was taking wonderful care of you."

"I'm fine, thanks, Annie," said Ruth. Alex had reached forward to shake Ruth's hand.

"Please accept my sincere sympathy, Miss Jones," he said in his smooth American accent.

"Thank you," mumbled Ruth in reply, while they all took their seats again.

"Juma, bring a teacup for Memsahib Jones," commanded Florence before turning on Ruth.

"My dear child, you have no need to be bothering the Reverend Montgomery about the funeral arrangements. I will look after that. After all, what would a child like you know about holding a funeral?" It was not really a question she intended Ruth to answer because she launched straight into the subject that interested her more. "I am absolutely shocked that you would allow that Dr. MacPherson to drive you home again, after I so explicitly warned you against having anything to do with the man!

"On top of that, I could hardly believe my eyes when he marched up here yesterday, as bold as brass, to inform me of a death in my own family! Informed by a perfect stranger about your own brother-in-law's death because my own niece can't be bothered to come herself!" Florence was working herself up into one of her tirades already.

Ruth sat and listened in near disbelief. She had actually assumed that because her father had just died her aunt may have deigned to show her some sympathy. But here she was, listening to her nearest relative ranting over her poor behavior yet again.

"What do you have to say for yourself, young lady?" demanded Aunt Florence for the second time. And in the moment of silence that followed it occurred to Ruth that she could say whatever she chose. She had nothing to lose anymore. Her father would never know again whether or not she had been polite to her aunt.

"Aunt Florence," she said standing up, "I have had enough of you trying to run my life. In the first place, I have a right at my age to associate with whomever I please, and I please to associate with Dr. MacPherson. I would appreciate it if you would no longer tell me stories of his evil intentions." She glared over at Alex. "He is a friend of mine.

"And secondly, I didn't come to see you this morning because I want to arrange my own father's funeral. You do not need to arrange it for me—I will do it myself, thank you. If you would, please tell the Reverend Montgomery when he comes that I would like the funeral to be the way he and I discussed earlier."

By now, Florence had risen and stretched to her full height, a good six inches below Ruth's. "I will do no such thing," she spluttered, her face turning a dangerous shade of purple. "Now, you listen to me. . ."

For the first time in her life, Ruth lost her temper. She leaned over Florence and glared down into her eyes. "Yes, you will, and I will not listen to you," Ruth hissed slowly through clenched teeth. To her utter astonishment, Florence was taken aback. She sat back in her chair.

"Oh dear," she began in a mournful tone, "I suppose there is nothing I can do. After all I've done for you, you no longer even listen to me. I see, poor woman that I am, I am utterly powerless to prevent you from doing whatever you want.

"I am to see my own brother-in-law buried without even so much as a thank-you-very-much from his daughter for the help I try to give her in her time of need. Then, I am mortified in front of my entire family." She paused and blew her nose.

"Dear, would you fetch me another hankie? This one is completely used up. Oh, dear, what am I to do?" Alex jumped up, and she wailed pitifully. Ruth was transfixed with anger.

How dare she criticize the funeral arrangements she had made for her own father, as if Florence had ever given him more than the time of day when he was alive. Ruth sat simmering with fury, speechless, impotent, and angrier than she had ever been before. The bonds that had kept her tied up and submissive all her life had strained to their breaking point.

The minute Alex was out of earshot, Florence turned on Ruth. The whimpering widow had vanished. "I know all about your Dr. MacPherson," she snarled, "trying to lure sheltered young women into his web of intrigue so that he can use them for his own ends. You aren't the first, and you won't be the last." Alex returned with the handkerchief, and Florence suddenly burst into renewed tears.

"I'm sorry that is your opinion of Dr. MacPherson, Aunt Florence, but it isn't true," said Ruth furiously. "How dare you call yourself a Christian and yet spread evil lies about a fine Christian missionary!"

Florence uttered a pitiful little scream and threw herself onto Alex's shoulder. "Oh, dear, what have I ever done to deserve this?" wailed Florence. Annie and Alex were both hovering over her. Annie was flapping a hankie over her face to give her air. "I am going to be ill. Quickly fetch some smelling salts and some brandy. Oh, lay me down on the couch. Oh, dear, what will become of me, and Angus so recently departed, too. Oh, oh, oh, oh."

Ruth watched the performance in cynical rage, turned heel, and went outside. But as she closed the door behind her, she glanced over her shoulder. Annie was standing up by her mother staring at Ruth in surprise and awe. Ruth smiled. Annie smiled back. The world seemed far away and very calm.

As Ruth rode back into town the next morning for her father's funeral, her heart was filled with apprehension for what her aunt would do to repay her for her behavior the day before. But with newfound courage, she no longer gave in to the fear. She wrestled it off. It was hard sometimes, when the fear circled its long cold claws around her chest and nearly squeezed her breath away; but she broke out of its grip time after time and told herself she was no longer afraid of Florence. She could do no more to hurt her.

The big old baobab tree on the way into town stood welcoming her onto the plains like an old friend. The huge boils of wood no longer seemed grotesque to Ruth, but were now the familiar blemishes and scars on the face of one you have loved for a long time. The guinea fowl squawked and scattered, and she smiled as she rode by.

The little church where her father would be buried looked as lonely and empty as Ruth's own future, but Ruth rode right past and went straight into town to Mrs. Singh's shop. She had the money for the dress stuffed into the pocket of her trousers, and she fingered it once more as she tied Chui to the hitching post outside the duka.

Mrs. Singh greeted her with her warm welcoming smile. "Come in, come in, Miss Jones. Your dress is all ready. I just finished hemming it this morning. I think you'll be very pleased, very pleased indeed!"

She floated over to a mannequin standing by the wedding dress that Ruth had noticed the day before, and there was the loveliest dress Ruth had ever seen. A simple bodice with short, capped sleeves and a full skirt with a thin white belt at the waist. Ruth gasped with pleasure.

"Are you sure it will look as nice on me as it does on the mannequin?" asked Ruth shyly.

Mrs. Singh laughed delightedly. "Well, try it on and we'll see!" Carefully, she pulled the dress off and brought it over to Ruth.

One hour later, Ruth walked out of Mr. Singh's duka in her green dress, new silk stockings, and brown boots with buttons up the side. "Oh Chui, I can't possibly ride you to the church in this getup. We'll have to walk," she said, untying the horse. "But we still have lots of time."

Ruth was half embarrassed and half proud of all the attention she attracted as she walked through town. Men politely tipped their hat to her, and women nodded with undisguised curiosity. Being an object of admiration was strange and exhilarating. Ruth nodded back at each one of them until she reached the church. It was early and no one was there yet. The thought of paying a call on the Montgomerys again sent a shudder down her spine. She walked past the church and out to her mother's land.

As she walked along the side of the dusty road, she heard the roar of a motorcar approaching. It was heading toward town. Ruth stopped, expecting to see Rosie round the curve ahead. But the car that appeared wasn't Rosie. It drew up alongside Ruth, and a man Ruth had never seen before leaned out of the window and pulled a cigarette out of his mouth, blowing the smoke toward Ruth. Another man leaned forward and eyed Ruth lecherously. "Would you be so kind as to tell me where I might find Mr. Kendall?" he asked.

Ruth had an irrational feeling that she shouldn't tell them where to find him. But, she thought, Campbellburgh is a small place, and if I don't tell them where to find him, I don't suppose they will have much trouble finding someone who will. Ruth pointed in the direction of Florence Campbell's house up on the hill behind them. "He stays there," she said. The man put the cigarette back into his mouth, tipped his hat, and turned the car around with a squeal of the tires. Ruth shuddered, glad they were gone, and wondered what Aunt Florence would make of them.

She turned Chui into her mother's land and led him down to the river. On the way down, she stopped to pick flowers from some of the bushes growing nearby. She would lay them on her father's casket. Flowers from her mother's land, picked by her hand for her father's burial. Tears flooded into her eyes. A warm breeze blew along the water across the river and rustled the bushes and reeds nearby. Ruth was glad of it. It cooled her damp face and evaporated her tears. She was glad she had taken the trouble to dress for the occasion, the occasion of saying good-bye to her parents. Now she would be completely alone.

After letting Chui drink from the river, Ruth walked back to the church. Other people were beginning to trickle toward it, Ruth noticed. She tied up Chui and walked back to the stone steps of the church, holding tightly to her bouquet. Only a few people were coming compared with Angus Campbell's funeral.

She nodded to Mr. Cooper, the lawyer that she had sat next to at Angus's funeral. Some of the farmers from the surrounding countryside had ridden in, and Ruth tried shyly to acknowledge them, too. She went up the steps and into the dark, stone building. No one else had gone in yet, but the Reverend Montgomery was inside supervising the lighting of the altar candles. Her father's casket was already placed on a table at the front. Slowly Ruth walked up the aisle, clutching her wild bouquet. She carefully placed the flowers on the coffin and sat down in the front pew behind the discreet sign that announced "reserved for family." Hearing her movement, the Reverend Montgomery turned and nodded to her, but his look was stern and unwelcoming. A pang of fear clutched at Ruth again as she realized that he had been told of her behavior by Aunt Florence. She bowed her head and prayed to Milka's God. "Please help me, God, to be strong enough to be alone," she whispered out loud.

Someone slipped into the pew behind her. She froze but didn't dare to look behind her. A few more people came into the church, but Ruth stared ahead. She focused on the flowers she had placed on the coffin and willed herself to think only of the old, old days, when she and her mother and father were all together.

Suddenly there was a loud rustling at the door of the church and Ruth knew that Florence had arrived. She steeled herself. She could see, even without looking, Florence sailing majestically down the aisle in her black silk funeral dress with her black hat swathed in yards and yards of tulle. There was a blast of eau de cologne as Florence bore down on Ruth's pew far enough to allow Annie and Alex enough room to sit beside her. She shot Ruth a veiled, but hostile glare, and Ruth glued her eyes to the flowers in front of her.

The Reverend Montgomery had a short funeral, as befitting a non-church-going member of the clan by marriage. He kept it simple, the way Ruth had requested, and in a thankfully short space of time, the casket was carried out to the burial plot. Ruth stood up, but Aunt Florence pointedly refused to allow her room, with Annie and Alex escorting her to follow directly behind the casket. Ruth stood to walk behind Florence, humiliated yet again at being outmaneuvered. Annie looked over her shoulder; she had been crying and smiled tearfully at Ruth. It was too much for Ruth. She put her hands to her face and tried to stop her tears. How could I have forgotten to bring a handkerchief to a funeral!

Suddenly an arm went around her waist, and a large man's handkerchief was offered. She looked up into the familiar blue eyes of Douglas MacPherson, who had slipped out of the pew behind her just in time to escort her out to the churchyard. Ruth leaned gratefully against him.

"It's all right, Ruth, come along," whispered Douglas, who had noticed Ruth's dismay. "Just concentrate on saying good-bye to your father. It is for him that we are here, not for them." Then he slipped away quickly before Florence saw him.

Ruth looked straight ahead. The coffin was already in place, and the Reverend Montgomery spoke a few words of comfort to Florence as she approached.

After they had laid Jack to rest, Florence came up to Ruth. She knew Florence wasn't finished with her yet.

"I felt I should come today out of respect for your father, the husband of my dear husband's sister." Florence tossed the words out like a fighter throwing punches to begin the round. "Although I will tell you that I have never in all my life been treated so rudely as yesterday. And just because you are upset about your father's death is no excuse for such unconscionable behavior." Ruth opened her mouth to protest, but Florence cut her off. "Don't even try to apologize to me, young lady."

Ruth responded in honest surprise. "But, I didn't intend to apologize. And I didn't say those things because I was upset about my father. I said them because I was upset about you."

Florence opened her eyes wide and turned purple. "Well!" she exploded. "Let me tell you, young lady, I know what you are up to, looking like the cat who just ate the cream, even at her own father's funeral. I tell you I am utterly appalled, and the only thing I can be thankful for is that Jack and your dear mother are not here to see it. They are both likely turning over in their graves at this very moment."

Ruth felt this was a rather macabre comment, considering how newly buried her father was and that they were still standing in the cemetery.

"I will thank you not to comment on my parents' attitudes, Aunt Florence," Ruth announced icily, surprising even herself at her boldness.

"Good heavens!" Florence turned to Alex. "Take me home. This is all too much for a poor woman who has just lost her own husband, to be treated this way by someone who I have tried so hard to be charitable to for so many years. And this is all the thanks I get!" Alex handed her a handkerchief as if on cue and led her away.

Ruth turned her attention to Annie, who was coming forward to give her a hug. "I am so sorry about Uncle Jack, Ruth," Annie said. Ruth was surprised to see her looking so shaken. She hadn't even seemed as upset at her own father's funeral, Ruth thought. Annie began to cry as she hugged Ruth, then she whispered quickly. "Mother wants me to marry Alex, and Alex has agreed to marry me, and she says if I don't she will cut me out of her will and disown me. She says it is my duty to marry well. I owe it to her. She has spent all her money on trying to cure father. She can do nothing else now, and she says it is my duty to look after her by marrying Alex."

Ruth listened in horror. She held tight to Annie for a moment. This was ghastly. She had no idea Florence would go to such desperate extremes. Poor, poor Annie.

"In order to prevent me running off, I have to marry Alex on Saturday. This Saturday! Ruth, tell Jimmy for me. And please help me. I have no one else to turn to," she whispered desperately, letting Ruth go.

Florence had, with Alex's obsequious help, recovered her composure. "Let's go, Annie, that's enough!" she bellowed from her surrey.

Ruth sighed and turned toward Chui, who was waiting patiently by the church for her. It was time to start the rest of her life now. She wondered how long she would be able to cope with the loneliness before it drove her mad. But before she had untied Chui, Douglas drove up.

"Come, Ruth, I'll drive you home. You must be very tired."

Ruth thanked him gratefully.

They took Chui to the hotel stables, and then Ruth found herself bouncing along the plains in Rosie yet again. But this time, she felt that she was being led to prison, to a lifetime of solitary confinement. The key had already been thrown away.

She looked down at her hands, conspicuously red and rough against the beautiful green dress she was wearing. But she was still glad she had bought it. It was just a small act of rebellion, and nothing would change; but she wouldn't have missed walking proudly through town this afternoon for all the gold in Sheba. She wondered how much money her father had left her to work with. Even if it was nothing, she was glad she had bought the dress. She put her face into her hands and cried quietly.

The sun was setting behind them as Ruth and Douglas drove into the hills. Golden light flowed like a river from the sun, pouring itself out into the earth until it sank down into the darkness below the horizon. Ruth could feel Rosie's engine pulling against the steep hill. Douglas said nothing, but let Ruth cry quietly as he drove up into the green-gold jewel valley where the brook babbled alongside the road. She was grateful for the silence.

When she looked up at last, they were climbing out of the valley away from the brook. She looked for the spot where the little path that led down to her secret pool joined the road. She remembered the mother and the baby elephant she had seen there; it seemed like eons ago now. All that was left of the joy she had felt watching them play together was only a faded, half-remembered dream.

"Stop. Please," she announced suddenly. She surprised even herself. Douglas looked at her quizzically and brought Rosie to a halt. For a moment there was only the gentle purr of Rosie's engine at rest.

"Come, I want to see something before I go home," said Ruth, pushing the door open beside her. She realized she still had her new dress on, and she paused, wondering if she should just get back into the car. But the thought of driving up to the lonely house with all those dead animals staring down at her from the walls sent a shudder up her spine. Douglas was standing beside Rosie, waiting to see what she would do next. Ruth walked over to the tiny slit in the bush by the road and carefully picked her way past the branches so she wouldn't tear her dress along the path down to the pool where she had seen the elephant. Douglas followed her.

"Where on earth are you going?" he asked, peering through the branches into the little ravine.

Ruth turned to look at him. "Come with me," she said. "There's a pool down here I want to see before we go home." She went slowly and carefully down the little trail, clutching her dress to her legs. The bubbling of the little stream got louder, and the air became cool and dark as they descended. Already the frogs were croaking and the birds were becoming quieter as night fell.

Ruth stepped into the little glade beside the pool. The big thorn tree she had climbed to escape the elephant loomed mysteriously out of the shadows on the far side. Douglas stepped out of the bush beside her.

"Oh, this is beautiful," he whispered, trying not to disturb the peaceful scene before them.

"Yes," Ruth breathed a quiet reply. "I just wanted to come here before I went back to the house." She paused, then added, almost under her breath, "I don't think I can face the loneliness just yet."

"You know," whispered Douglas, "that Jesus can take care of that for you—the loneliness, I mean."

"I don't think He cares too much for me; look what has happened to my life!" Ruth spoke in a normal tone of voice, shattering the peace and beauty of the moment.

"Have you asked Him to care for you?" Douglas responded in a matter of fact tone, as though it was like going to the doctor and asking him to take care of your bunions.

"Oh, Milka does that all the time, but I haven't noticed that it has made any difference to my life."

"But you have to ask Him yourself!" Douglas said. "He won't just waltz in and take over your life because someone else asks Him. He wants your consent. It's you He wants to deal with, not Milka."

Ruth was silent. She had never thought of it that way before. Had He really not helped her simply because she hadn't asked Him to? The peacefulness of the darkening night quietly crept back into the clearing again. Ruth remembered the elephants, and she felt that perhaps God had been trying to tell her to talk to

Jesus then, too. The presence of God reached inside her and touched her. She felt His voice in her mind, immense and loving.

I am here now, Ruth, will you love Me?

No, came Ruth's answer in her heart. *I'm not ready yet.* She still wanted something she could touch and see. She couldn't trust that Jesus would actually stay with her through the long lonely days and years ahead. Ruth looked over at Douglas standing solid and sure beside her.

I love him.

There was silence.

After a little while, Douglas spoke to her of Jesus and what He had done by dying for her on the cross and how He rose again and how it was He who had come to find Ruth and come to live with her. He told her of the Bible and the Church, His own body.

The night was warm and vibrant with life now. Stars thronged across the sky like the numberless herds of game that roamed the plains below. Cicadas thrummed relentlessly, beating out their own rhythm and making the very air seem alive with sound. Ruth looked up into the great African night, immense and free, the antithesis of her own heart. She listened to Douglas carefully, but she didn't tell him what she had already told God.

"I will think it all through," she said quietly when he had finished.

"I will pray for you, then," he replied, and they stood together in the night for a few moments.

Finally, Douglas said, "Are you ready to go home now?"

"Yes," Ruth replied. The moon had begun to appear behind the branches of the thorn tree across the pond. By its light, Ruth could see Douglas looking down at her. *He has an odd expression on his face,* she thought.

"Ruth, you are beautiful tonight. Your dress shines in the moonlight like your eyes."

Ruth felt her heart skip a beat, and quickly she looked down to hide her thoughts from Douglas. But he stepped toward her and lifted her chin gently up to his face. He bent down and kissed her lips. She closed her eyes and thought she would melt with the warmth that spread all over her body. But as soon as it began, it was over. He took her by the hand and led her back up the dark path. Afterwards Ruth didn't remember anything about how she got home.

The next thing she knew, he was coming around to open the car door for her. They had driven to the house in silence. Ruth could see the lights flickering inside the windows. Milka was waiting for her.

"Thank you for bringing me home, Douglas," she said, getting out of the car.

"Ruth, I'm sorry about what I did at the pool just now. I shouldn't have."

"Don't mention it," mumbled Ruth, turning to run up the steps, but he caught her hand.

"Ruth, wait. I just want to say, I have to leave. I am going to look at some land in Uganda tomorrow. I didn't mean to give you another impression, only you just looked so lovely. I'm sorry, Ruth."

Ruth snatched her arm away from him and ran inside. She ran straight to her bedroom and wept. She wept for her broken heart. She remembered Annie this afternoon, and she wept for Annie's broken heart, too. Milka came in with a cup of tea and tried to comfort her, but she wept until finally she fell asleep, still in her green dress and silk stockings.

Chapter Eight

It was almost noon when Ruth awoke the next day. She lay in bed and relived the day before. Over and over she thought about Annie and she thought about Douglas, and she remembered how his kiss felt on her lips. After a long time, she got up and wandered into the kitchen. Milka had some meat pies warming in the oven and the kettle simmering on the stove.

"Ah, Memsahib!" she jumped up and rushed over to Ruth. "How are you this afternoon, 'Sabu?"

Ruth sat down heavily on the kitchen chair and put her head in her hands. "Oh, Milka," she groaned, "I don't think I'll ever be all right again."

" 'Sabu, 'Sabu, of course you will. It takes time to heal, you know. I pray for you all the time and the Lord Jesus, He will comfort you."

"Oh, Milka, I wish with all my heart that I could believe you, but there is so much wrong, and it is not just because Father is gone now. It is Annie and Aunt Florence, and I don't know what can possibly be done now."

Milka put a meat pie and a cup of tea in front of Ruth and sat down across the table. "Come, come, 'Sabu, you tell me what the matter is and we will see what can be done."

Ruth talked and ate and drank her tea, and she told Milka all that had happened at the funeral and afterwards. She told Milka about Annie and Jimmy and Alex, and about Douglas, everything she could think of except the little detour they took down to the pool before they came home. Milka listened and nodded sympathetically.

"Well," said Ruth firmly at last when she was finished, "we have to do something for Annie." She felt better for having told Milka everything—almost everything. "All Annie needs is a way to get out of her house and away with Jimmy, just long enough to get married. Once they are married, Florence can do her worst." She thought for a moment. "The first thing we have to do is to tell Jimmy, and we must do it soon. Today is Tuesday and Annie is to be married on Saturday. Tomorrow I should go into town and see Mr. Cooper about Father's estate. First I'll stop at Jimmy MacRae's and tell him what is happening to Annie." Ruth was glad to have something to fill her mind. She could avoid thinking of the years that lay ahead for her, at least for a little while.

When she reached Jimmy's place the next morning, he had seen her coming and was outside waiting to greet her.

"Good morning, Ruth. You're here bright and early. I heard about your father and I am very sorry."

"Thank you," she responded, and dispensing with the preliminaries, she got straight to the point. "Jimmy, I have some more bad news about Annie. We need to talk."

Jimmy's face fell. "Come in. We'll talk inside." He motioned to a chair. Ruth sat down and looked into his anxious face. Her heart went out to him.

"Jimmy, I'm sorry, Florence Campbell really has outdone herself this time. But if we act quickly, we still have time to stop it. She intends to marry Annie off to Alex Kendall this Saturday."

"Good Lord have mercy!" Jimmy leapt up out of his chair and began pacing around the room in desperation. "Surely Annie couldn't have consented to such a plan." Suddenly the color drained from his face, and he sank back down into his chair like a shot antelope. "She hasn't consented, has she?" His voice was small and scared. "Perhaps she has fallen in love with Alex Kendall. After all, he probably has a lot more to offer her than I ever will. I wouldn't blame her."

"Good gracious, Jimmy," exclaimed Ruth. "How could you have so little faith in her? She wanted me to tell you so that you could come and fetch her. She loves you, and she asked me to come to you to tell you to help her. She is desperate. I am really worried about her."

"But, surely, she won't disobey her mother. She clearly told me that she would never do that."

"Jimmy!" Ruth was becoming impatient. "Jimmy, she can't marry a man she doesn't love just to obey her mother. It wouldn't be right. Her mother can't possibly expect her to be unhappily married for the rest of her life. And what about Alex Kendall? It wouldn't be fair to him, either!"

"Well, what can I possibly do to help her?" he asked in his small, confused voice.

Ruth was surprised by her own strength. "Jimmy, we must get word to her that she should leave her house, perhaps in the night. You will meet her and marry her as quickly as you can, then Florence won't be able to do anything about it. Of course, Annie is being watched like a hawk, so it won't be easy. But the important thing, once we get Annie, is to get you two married as soon as possible. Do you know anyone who would be able to do it for you? The Reverend Montgomery would be hopeless. He would never dare do anything to upset Aunt Florence."

"I know a priest up at the French mission. He would probably do it if I asked. But he would have to come over the hills from away out beyond your place. I could send word to him. But how on earth would we be able to get Annie out? Florence has that place guarded like the crown jewels."

The two of them sat in silence pondering their dilemma. Ruth finally spoke up. "If we could get Annie as far as my place, you could meet the priest there and he could marry you. Annie might be able to find a way to slip out just before dawn, while everyone is still sleeping. You could meet her on the road and bring her up to the farm. Florence would likely expect you to run off to Nairobi, so she would probably look there first. Maybe you could go to Uganda? Perhaps you could even throw Aunt Florence off your trail by buying train tickets for you and Annie to Nairobi, even though you don't intend to use them."

Jimmy let Ruth's plan sink in for a few minutes. "How can we let Annie know which night to meet me?"

"Yes, that will be rather a problem, I'm afraid. I've burnt my bridges with Aunt Florence, I fear," answered Ruth. Jimmy sat with his head in his hands. He looked as though he were praying. Ruth sighed. That would be a difficult problem. But all at once she remembered the wedding dress in Mrs. Singh's shop. "That's it!" she burst out. "It is Annie's wedding dress!"

Jimmy nearly jumped out of his skin at Ruth's outburst. "What are you talking about?"

"I was at Mrs. Singh's dressmaking shop," said Ruth excitedly. "She had a wedding dress there. I'm sure it must be for Annie! Who else would be getting married? Annie will be having her fittings there. Mrs. Singh would pass a message to Annie for us! I'm sure she would!"

"Well, I can go and ask her."

"I'll do that for you, Jimmy," laughed Ruth. "I can't imagine Mrs. Singh giving you the details of Annie's dress fittings."

"Thanks, Ruth."

"Don't mention it. You have enough to do anyway. Now, just let me know which night your priest will be coming, and I'll get the message to Annie."

Ruth got up and headed for the door. "Well, Jimmy, all the best of luck to you." She put out her hand, and he shook it gratefully.

"Thanks, Ruth, you've been a real friend to us both." She flashed him a quick smile and stepped out into the hot midday sun. Pulling her hat low, she rode back into town.

She walked quickly up to Mrs. Singh's shop. Mrs. Singh greeted her with her usual friendly smile. "Come in, come in, Miss Jones. What can I do for you today?"

"Well, I actually only came to ask you a question, Mrs. Singh."

"That is fine, my dear, what question do you have?"

"It is a rather delicate matter," began Ruth, "and it has to do with my friend Annie Campbell. I believe she is to be married shortly, and I wondered if you were making the dress for her."

"Yes, yes." Mrs. Singh smiled broadly. "I have the honor of doing so. It is a rather rushed job, though, so I have been working on it day and night. But it will be very beautiful. Pure white silk with embroidered pearls." She ran over to the mannequin and fetched the dress for Ruth to see.

"It is lovely," smiled Ruth. "Could you tell me if Annie is coming in for a fitting before it is finished?"

"Oh, but of course! I must make certain everything is just so. I am expecting her here tomorrow afternoon."

"Does she always come with her mother?"

Mrs. Singh was becoming a little puzzled at Ruth's line of questioning and rather cautiously affirmed that she did.

"You see," Ruth said because she felt she owed her some explanation, "Annie is not marrying of her own free will. Her mother is keeping all messages from reaching her from her friends. As a result, I wonder if you might give her a message from me and do it without her mother seeing it."

Mrs. Singh's eyes lit up, and Ruth knew she had found herself a coconspirator. "Ah, I wondered why everything was to be so rushed, and with poor Mr. Campbell so recently passed away, too. Poor Miss Campbell, I thought she looked rather distraught. I like her very much and would be most happy to pass a message on from you."

"Thank you, Mrs. Singh. I am very grateful to you, and I know Annie will be, too, and so will the man she wants to marry, Jimmy MacRae."

"Ah, yes, I know him."

"Mrs. Singh, either Jimmy or I will return tonight or tomorrow morning with a message for Annie. Please make sure Mrs. Campbell doesn't see it."

"You can trust me, Miss Jones. I will give it to her inside my fitting room while her mother is waiting outside for her to change. It will be very simple." She bowed slightly and showed Ruth to the door. "Good-bye, Miss Jones, and good luck!"

Ruth went down the narrow stairs and stepped onto the walkway next to the street.

She walked across the street to the little door with Mr. Cooper's sign on it and went shyly in. Her father had dealt with Mr. Cooper from the time when her mother had died. He was a large, methodical, but pleasantly fatherly man, as she remembered. And it was at least an hour later when she came out, her head crammed to the hilt with legal terminology and spinning with new information. Ruth stood outside Mr. Cooper's, blinking into the afternoon sunshine for a few minutes, assimilating the information and adjusting to the glare of the day.

Her mother had been given land in Campbellburgh when she was a child, as all the Campbell progeny had, and her piece consisted of the entire undeveloped plot next to the river. It was a huge piece, much larger than what Jack had led Ruth to believe, and now that Campbellburgh was a growing concern, it was quite a valuable piece of property.

However, as Mr. Cooper so carefully pointed out to her, if Ruth sold the property, the Campbells all had first refusal rights. In reality that meant Florence, as the other Campbells had not flourished to nearly the same extent as Angus had. Most of the rest were simply poor cousins like she was. Her father had left some money in the bank. Not a lot, as Ruth had suspected, but enough for her to continue to run the farm.

She went back to Jimmy's farm to tell him that Mrs. Singh would pass his message to Annie. Jimmy had a look of grim determination on his face when she got there. He had sent a message to his friend at the French mission and expected an answer back tonight. He was counting on Friday night, which was two nights away, to elope. Since the mission was up in the hills beyond the Jones farm, he and Ruth decided that they would all meet at her farm, where the wedding ceremony would take place. If they bought tickets for the train to Nairobi, Florence would most likely search for them there, which would give them some breathing room to escape. Ruth and Jimmy parted company, but not before Jimmy clasped her hand and looked hard at her.

"You're a good friend, Ruth. A real Godsend." Ruth impulsively put her arms around him and gave him a quick hug.

"Good luck, Jimmy. I'll expect you and Annie before dawn on Saturday, unless I hear otherwise." She mounted Chui and shook the reins.

Before going home, she stopped at the pool again. The little valley was as cool and green and refreshing as it always was. Ruth, as always, felt the weight of the world lift off her shoulders as she descended into it. The little river sparkled easily over the mossy rocks and plunged fearlessly into the deep dark pools. Ruth found her grassy glade and pulled off her boots and her hat. She slipped her bare feet into the silky water and leaned back against the smooth trunk of the old tree. It seemed so different in the daytime than at night. She thought about Douglas's kiss. Remembering it made her glad she was doing something to help Annie and Jimmy find the joy and happiness they so deserved.

And she remembered the elephant and its child that were here that time and how she had ached with longing for a life of her own. Everything had changed so much since that day. Soon Annie and Jimmy would be gone, and Douglas was already gone. Her father was gone, and, as far as she was concerned, so was Aunt Florence. The elephants had come and gone. And she was still here, still farming, and still alone. Only now it felt more lonely and painful than it ever had before.

As she sat in the quietness, Ruth made a plan. It was a bold and unusual one, but it was her only hope. She would try it. She herself would ask Jesus to help her to carry it out. She would speak to Him and tell Him of her plan. She would pray for success and leave the results up to Him. If He chose to give her success, then she would know He had listened to her, but if her plan failed. . . She didn't want to face it until the time came, if it came.

She would write Douglas a letter as soon as she found out where to send it. There was very little time left, so she had to act quickly. Otherwise time would slip away from her as inevitably as the water slipped away down the hill. She had no second chance. Ruth reached down and scooped a handful of water onto her face, letting it soak her hair and shirt, and she prayed with all her heart for God to give her success. And when she stood up to put on her boots, she was fixed on her course as steadfastly and surely as the rivers run down to the sea.

Chapter Nine

At last it was Friday. Ruth spent a long night in her room waiting for morning. She prayed for Annie and wished she could be with her to help her and to comfort her. Poor, poor Annie. What a terrible price to pay for happiness. Ruth looked outside. The stars twinkled peacefully in the infinite night sky as if this were only a night like any other since time began. The insects clicked and chirped into the scented night air as they had done every night since creation. This night was no different. Far away Ruth caught the distant laugh of a hyena, and a cold shiver of fear ran down her spine. She listened for the trumpet of the elephant. The ancient and echoing sound would comfort her, and surely then she would know that everything would be fine in the morning. But there was nothing. The night stretched out interminably into the deep, dark distance.

The minutes, by sheer determination, at last became hours; and the hours inched ever so uncooperatively by until at last most of the night was done. Milka brought in the morning tea long before dawn. Only the faintest shade of gray was discernable on the hills. Ruth dressed in her new green satin dress. The priest had said he would come at six.

And when at last six grudgingly arrived, she went out onto the veranda to look for him. There he was, striding across the eastern meadow, in the slanting morning sun, as though he had only just been created out of the earth itself.

Ruth was surprised at how young he was. He must only be in his midtwenties, she thought, and with his fair hair and fair skin, the long cossack he wore was oddly incongruous. But his eyes were alive with the conviction of his faith, and when Ruth reached out to shake his hand, he grasped it firmly and warmly. He spoke with a heavy French accent.

"*Bonjour,* Miss Jones. I am Brother Jean. My friend Jimmy MacRae has spoken very well of you. It is very kind of you to assist him like this."

"I am glad that you were able to come," said Ruth, ushering him into the lounge. The curtains were open and the morning light poured inside like liquid gold, reflecting on the dark wooden floor and the dark tables.

He had walked a long way from the mission in the hills, and he was hungry. They had breakfast together in the dining room. Milka bustled about enthusiastically. She considered it a great honor to serve such a man of God. Ruth, however, had no appetite.

"How do you know Jimmy MacRae?" Ruth asked, making conversation, a new skill she was learning.

"He came to our Christmas Eve mass two or three years ago. We have a very beautiful service. It is truly a time of worship. Jimmy and I got talking and we have remained friends ever since. He regularly comes to the mission to worship with us. He is a fine man. Your friend will be fortunate, indeed, to have him for a husband."

"Yes, I know. I only hope that Annie was able to escape last night. I am so worried."

"Yes, it is a very unfortunate situation. Mrs. Florence Campbell is well known in our area for her views on native education and hospitals. I think she is indeed a very difficult woman. Her daughter has my deepest sympathy. We French, you know, even in the priesthood, never like to stand in the way of true love." He smiled warmly and continued, "But I do not think Jesus stands in the way of true love, either, so I have prayed for Jimmy and Annie, and I am sure the Lord will hold them in the palm of His hand."

Ruth liked this man. She decided to risk her idea of having the wedding in the little valley.

"Since it will be such a rushed wedding for Annie," she began tentatively, "I thought that I might try to make it a little bit special for her. There is a little river valley on the farm, and in the valley is one of the most beautiful spots I have ever seen. The road from town, the one on which Annie and Jimmy will arrive this morning, goes very close to it. I wondered if it might not be a rather lovely spot to hold the ceremony." Ruth felt a little insecure suggesting such an unusual location. She was relieved when she saw him smile with delight at the thought of it.

"Why, yes, I think that would be most romantic to have an outdoor wedding. After all, there is nothing to make the day beautiful but God's own creation. It is a lovely idea."

"I hoped you would agree," said Ruth. "If we start to walk there, we could intercept Annie and Jimmy on the road, and I could take you all to the spot."

As soon as Brother Jean was finished eating, they set off. The dew was thick and wet on the dust of the road, so they left dry footprints and lifted thick clods of mud up with their shoes. Brother Jean carried his Bible and looked refreshed and filled with cheerful anticipation. Ruth, on the other hand, was a bundle of jagged nerves. She wished she could know if Annie was safely in Jimmy's buggy, wending her way up the hillside.

As the road slipped into the little ravine, they thought they could just make out the sound of an engine rising from the valley below. And within a few minutes, they saw Rosie roaring up the road toward them. Annie was in the front seat and saw them first.

"Ruthie," she shrieked, waving wildly. Ruth waved back and ran down the road to meet her. In her excitement, it didn't occur to Ruth that she wasn't expecting them to come with Douglas. Annie jumped out of the car and threw her arms around Ruth. "Oh Ruth, I am so glad to see you. Jimmy told me what you did. Thank you! Thank you from the bottom of my heart!"

"Annie, I'm so glad to see you. I haven't slept a wink all night worrying about you. How did everything go? Did you get out without being detected? It must have been a dreadful ordeal!"

Annie laughed. "I'd like to say it was and that I was very daring and brave, but all I did was walk out of the house. Mother will be beside herself with fury when she discovers I've gone. I was shaking in my shoes as I left, but not one of the dogs barked at me. In fact, they followed me all the way down the road, and I sent them back just before I met Jimmy and Douglas."

"Douglas?" Ruth looked up, and sure enough there standing by the door of the car stood Douglas. He was watching her.

"Hello, Ruth, how are you doing?" He put out his hand and shook hers warmly. Ruth suddenly felt overwhelmed with shyness, and she could hardly raise her eyes to meet his. He was still looking down at her. "You look beautiful in green, especially in the morning light like this." He spoke almost longingly, but suddenly catching hold of himself, he said more loudly, "I returned for what I thought was Alex's wedding, but instead Jimmy asked me to come out and stand up for him." But Ruth was looking down. She had never heard a longing note in his voice before, and she was too shy to let him see how it made her feel.

"I'm going to drive them to Uganda tonight," he went on. Ruth wondered if she had been given a chance to carry out the plan she had devised. Would she have the courage?

"Oh, I'm so glad," she managed to say. "That will be so much safer for them."

Jimmy and Brother Jean were talking together. Brother Jean had told Jimmy about Ruth's idea for a wedding down by the river and Jimmy was pleased.

"Come along, I'll show it to you," Ruth said. They all got into the car.

When they reached the little path, Ruth led the way down. The sunshine came slanting in horizontally through the leaves, which were aflutter with birds who burst into the most joyful repertoire of music she could imagine for a wedding. The pool shone like a mirror, doubling the beauty of the trees above it. The stream whispered its way over the rocks as though it was in awe of the beauty of the new day.

"Oh, Ruthie, this is the perfect place," whispered Annie.

"It is indeed," agreed Jimmy quietly. They stepped over the stones to cross the river.

"Well," Brother Jean spoke when they were all across, "I suppose we shall begin." He stood under the canopy of an acacia tree, the grass spread out at his feet like a carpet.

"Just hold on a minute!" Douglas had stepped out of sight in the undergrowth just beyond the stream. "I'm just fetching something for the bride."

Annie laughed nervously, and Jimmy reached out to hold her hand. Ruth watched them standing together in her special place, which would now be forever theirs. They looked so beautiful, with the golden sun making a bridal wreath of light on Annie's blond hair. Her simple, soft yellow dress was a perfect color for the green bower that would be her wedding chapel. Jimmy was looking at her as though he would burst with pride.

"Here we are!" Douglas burst out of the bush, his arms full of flowers. "You can't have a wedding without flowers for the bride." He held out a cascade of red and yellow forest flowers that Ruth had seen a thousand times in the bushes and trees. They made a beautiful bouquet. Annie carefully picked a yellow and white frangipani flower out of the bouquet and put it in her hair. Douglas was right; now she looked like a real bride.

"There," he said, "that's better!" And he turned to Ruth and gave her another bouquet. Ruth took it and looked up to thank him. As he smiled down at her, her heart missed a beat. Surely there was more to his look than his usual kindness. How could she know for certain? And yet it seemed to Ruth that the sun shone more brilliantly through the leaves and her flowers exuded a deeper, more passionate scent than they had the moment before. Annie's smile was even more joyful than she could have imagined it ever would be. She went over to Annie. Douglas was sticking a huge bird of paradise flower in Jimmy's buttonhole. She drew Annie away from them.

"Come, Annie, you must have an aisle to walk down." They went to the far end of the clearing and waited for Douglas to organize the men. Ruth whispered, "If you listen to the music of the river and the birds, it will be the loveliest wedding march ever heard—God's own music."

"I know it will be, Ruthie. I can't believe I'm going to be married." She looked at Ruth, suddenly panic stricken. "Even after all that I've been through, I'm terrified."

Ruth suddenly felt the same way. "You know," she answered solemnly, "I would be, too, if I were getting married."

Annie laughed nervously. "Thanks very much, Ruthie. You certainly know how to make someone feel better!" Ruth laughed, too.

"Come along, you two!" Douglas called. "This is no time to start giggling. We have a wedding to attend. Let's go!"

The men were arranged in a row under the tree. Brother Jean had his Bible open, and Jimmy and Douglas were standing at attention to the side. Ruth and Annie looked at each other, and Ruth gave Annie a quick hug. "God bless you, Annie," she said, and like a bridesmaid, Ruth turned and walked slowly toward Jimmy and Douglas. She could see Jimmy proudly watching Annie behind her.

As she reached the front, she caught Douglas's eye. He smiled at her, and it was as though they were alone. The birds were singing for them and the sun was shining on only the two of them. And Ruth knew what she must do.

Annie was next to her now, and Brother Jean began the wedding. As Annie and Jimmy repeated their vows to each other, Ruth's eyes filled with tears. She always thought people who cried at weddings were a little soft in the head, yet here she was doing it herself. But her heart was truly moved to see two such fine people standing here before God, promising to love each other for the rest of their lives. It was the first time she had ever understood how much that meant, and her heart overflowed with joy for them.

When Jimmy had kissed his bride and they were well and truly married, the five of them stood in the little glade in silence. It was as though Jesus Himself were pronouncing a benediction for them. A breath of wind passed through the trees above them and as it went, it parted the leaves and a shaft of sunlight shone down on them. A moment later it was gone and everything was still.

"May I be the first to wish you all of God's blessings on your marriage." Douglas spoke while he reached out to shake Jimmy's hand and leaned forward to kiss the bride.

"Oh, Annie, I'm so happy for you both. God bless you." Ruth hugged Annie and kissed Jimmy.

Back at the house, Milka had set out a brunch on the veranda. She had taken out Ruth's mother's best linen and crystal. There were vases of flowers and bowls of fruit. Ruth gasped. She hadn't seen the linen since she was a very little girl, and the crystal had only sat quietly in the cupboard year in and year out. Milka was standing shyly to the side, smiling with pleasure.

"I hope you don't mind me using your mother's things, 'Sabu Ruth, but I thought that Miss Annie deserved the very best for her wedding."

"Milka, thank you. You have outdone yourself this time."

"Milka, you shouldn't have!" Annie added.

" 'Sabu Annie, may I congratulate you on your marriage. May it be filled with God's blessings and be fruitful and long. And congratulations to you, too, Bwana." She spoke to Jimmy and beamed with pleasure. Then she turned to Douglas. "Welcome again, Daktari MacPherson." She turned and smiled slyly at Ruth before leaving to fetch the first course.

After the meal, Brother Jean took his leave and headed back through the hills. The four of them stood on the veranda watching Brother Jean disappear across the fields.

Jimmy turned to his bride. "Would you like to accompany me for a walk?" Annie smiled up at him. Jimmy looked at Douglas. "It's going to be a long drive to Uganda, and Annie and I haven't had a chance to talk for so long. A few minutes' delay won't hurt anything, will it?"

Douglas smiled at the newlyweds. "We should leave here in an hour." Jimmy took Annie's hand, and they started off down the hill, back to the valley.

Ruth watched them go. Jimmy had put his arm around Annie's shoulders and she leaned her head on his. *They are made for each other,* Ruth thought. *They have a lifetime of joy. No matter what happens, they will be together to love and help each other.* And watching them, she felt immensely alone. The loneliness reached around her like the touch of ice-cold fingers. She felt herself grow breathless in fear. One hour and she would be all alone. All alone forever and ever. She must carry out her plan or she would never have another chance.

She glanced sideways at Douglas. He was standing with his hands in his pockets watching them go, smiling to himself. Noticing her looking at him, he turned to face her.

"Well, I'm sure Milka has some more of that delicious coffee!" he said, cheerfully. "Shall I get you some, too?"

"Thank you, that would be very nice," replied Ruth. She sat on the veranda while he went inside, calling out for Milka.

Ruth looked out across the jewel green treetops and past them to the blue hills. Automatically her eyes scanned for clouds, but there was nothing but dry, blue sky. It was relentlessly hot. She wondered if the rains would fall this year. *Please, God, bring the rain,* she found herself praying. *Please, God, let Douglas say yes when I ask.* She knew she didn't have the kind of faith in God that Douglas spoke about; nor did she have the relationship with Jesus that he said was so important. But she felt that in the last few weeks she had at least come to believe in God's existence, and surely that allowed her to pray to Him. Surely God must listen. She couldn't face the rest of her life alone; surely He understood that.

Douglas came with two steaming cups of coffee and set one down beside her.

"Well," he said, sitting down in the chair next to hers, "I think that was the most beautiful wedding I have ever attended in my life."

"It is the only wedding I have attended," Ruth said quietly, "but I know it was the most beautiful I'll ever see."

Douglas looked over at her and smiled his twinkling blue smile and melted Ruth's heart once again.

"I hope it won't take them long to settle in Uganda. There's some fine farming country there. I expect there will be a lot that I can do there, too. It must have been God's plan for me all along, if only I had listened to Him more carefully."

Douglas chatted on about where he was going to try to establish his hospital in Uganda. He already had plans to look along the shores of Lake Victoria. He was very enthusiastic. Ruth nodded politely whenever he paused, but she hardly heard a word he said.

At last, he looked at her and said, "I'm awfully sorry. I must be boring you to death with all my plans."

"No, no, not at all," Ruth replied, but they sat in silence for a moment. It was not their usual comfortable silence, and Douglas noticed.

"What's on your mind, Ruth? You look as though you're a million miles away. Is it Annie and Jimmy?"

This was her moment and she had to take it now. She took a long breath and closed her eyes for a silent, desperate prayer.

"Douglas, I have a proposition to make you," she began slowly and deliberately.

Douglas laughed. "Well, when a woman tells me she has a proposition, I usually make for the hills, but since it's you, I won't."

Ruth didn't laugh. This was not an auspicious start. She decided to take the bull by the horns. "Douglas, you have made it quite clear that you are a confirmed bachelor." She noticed a shake in her voice, and she took another deep breath. She could see Douglas's face become concentrated and serious.

"Yes, I am," he said firmly and quietly. Ruth's stomach sank like a stone. But she had begun now, and there was only one way to go on.

"As you may have noticed, I am not the marrying kind, either." Douglas's face relaxed slightly. "Nevertheless," she went on bravely, "I have an idea that may be of benefit to both of us. I am hoping we might come to an arrangement." She began to talk faster. Douglas was ominously quiet.

"I have something you need, and you have something I would very much like to have. Since my father's death I have discovered that I own the piece of land next to the railway station. I cannot sell it to you because of the first refusal rights that the Campbells have over it. This brings me to my proposal. We could form a partnership, but in order for it to work, you and I would need to be married." Douglas still said nothing, so she rushed on.

"Of course, I understand that you would not like to limit your freedom with the responsibilities of marriage, and I am not proposing the kind of marriage where you will be limited in any way to your home base. I have been alone all my life, and I know how to look after myself." Ruth hardly paused for breath. "It would actually be to your advantage, since you do not intend to marry anyone anyway, to have this kind of arrangement with me because I would be willing to provide the bookkeeping and accounting for you as a partner, and you would therefore be free to practice medicine without all the administrative worry that you would otherwise be burdened with." She stopped talking at last, suddenly, and sat breathing hard, looking into her empty mug, afraid to look at Douglas.

Mercifully, Milka chose this moment to arrive with fresh coffee. They sat in silence until she went away. But Ruth glanced quickly at Douglas's face and knew she was lost.

"And what would the advantage of this arrangement be to you?" Douglas asked. His voice was quiet, and Ruth thought she detected a note of anger. Icy fingers gripped her heart, but she had to plunge ahead.

"You have something that I cannot seem to get hold of myself." She coughed. Her throat was constricting. She cleared it again. Douglas waited. "You have a life, and that is all I want. A life to call my own. Away from this farm."

"But you have a life. I don't know many women who would be able to run a farm in the middle of Africa single-handedly."

"Not many women would be able to stand being alone like I am. I have no one but me. I have nowhere to go and nothing else I can do. I am alone up here, and if I don't marry you, I will be alone up here for the rest of my life. I am good at farming, but I would never have chosen it myself. I would have been a nurse if I had a choice. It is too late for that now, but I can do bookkeeping and help with the nursing. In return for my land, you would give me the chance to do something I have chosen for myself. I think it is a fair bargain." She spoke with every last ounce of conviction she could muster. But Douglas's face was hard and inscrutable.

She looked down at her empty coffee mug again. She had done all she could. She spoke to God silently. The rest was now up to Him.

"Ruth." Ruth looked up in surprise. Douglas's voice was gentle and kind. "Ruth, I am sorry but I could never enter into that kind of a marriage. It is more of a business arrangement than a marriage. It wouldn't be fair to you, and it would be utterly despicable of me to marry you for your land." Ruth's throat tightened like it had a noose around it.

She cleared it again. "Douglas." She forced herself to be firm, but she knew it was a lost cause. "I need your hospital. I need it so I won't be tied forever to this farm. You say that God told you that Campbellburgh was the place for your hospital, and now I am offering you a way of letting it happen. Why are you not taking me up on it? There are no disadvantages for either of us. You are not planning to marry anyway, and no one will marry me. We could make a good partnership out of this."

"Ruth," Douglas leaned forward and looked intently into her face, "would you intend for us to be truly married? The way Annie and Jimmy are, for instance?"

Ruth blushed down to the tips of her toes. She had not intended to have to answer this kind of a question. She tried to open her mouth to speak, but she found it was impossible. She wanted with all her heart to say yes, but she couldn't possibly bring herself to actually utter the word. She riveted her eyes on the gold pattern on the edge of her cup. She could feel Douglas's eyes on her.

There was a long silence, and Douglas didn't move, and she couldn't look at him. Finally she found a last vestige of courage. "I always wanted to have children." She said it quietly and without looking up. Douglas leaned back in his chair and let out a long sigh. Ruth knew the worst was coming. She steeled herself.

"Ruth, I could never marry you. You deserve more than a business arrangement. You are right, you do deserve a life of your own, and you need someone who will truly be able to share it with you. I would be a poor excuse for a husband. I know you are upset with me for turning you down, but believe me, you will be happy one day. You will find someone much better than me, and you will be happier than you ever would have been with me.

"If you devote your life to loving God, as I have explained to you, He won't let you down. He came so that we could have life and have it abundantly. I am so sorry, Ruth, but it's for the best. It truly is."

Ruth looked up at him at last. Her eyes were dry and she found herself surprisingly calm. It was over now. She had done all she could and she had failed. She wished Douglas wouldn't bring God into it. God had done nothing to help her. But she smiled and his face betrayed a glimmer of relief.

"Well," she forced her voice to be strong and clear, "I hope I haven't embarrassed you. I felt I had to at least try all I could do. Let's put it behind us, shall we?" She smiled bravely into his face, expecting more of the relief she had just seen there, but his eyes were filled with pain.

"Believe me, Ruth, it's for the best." He looked almost desperate that she understand. But Ruth was not in the mood to help him with his pain. She was just starting out on a lifetime on her own, and she needed to preserve her strength.

There was another half hour before Annie and Jimmy would be back, and Ruth now decided it was going to be the longest half hour she had ever lived through. They sat together in silence, both grimly staring out onto the dry, dry valley.

"I hope the rains don't fail this year," said Ruth at last.

"Yes," Douglas replied, his voice quiet and almost sad. "Perhaps the wind will change soon."

"Oh, I hope it will." Ruth's voice had an unexpected note of desperation in it, and she fell silent.

A long silence later, she made out the figures of Annie and Jimmy returning up the dusty road. As they got closer, Ruth could feel their happiness radiating around them like a bright halo. In its center they moved and talked, blissfully unaware of the strained, unnatural silence between Ruth and Douglas.

It was time to go. Ruth looked at her friend and wondered when she would ever see her again. Annie reached out to Ruth and hugged her.

"Oh, Ruth, I'll miss you with all my heart. You've been the best friend I've ever, ever had. I wish you could be as happy as I am now. I will pray for you, Ruth."

"Good-bye, Annie." Her tears were falling. "Please write and tell me where you are. I'll miss you."

"Good-bye, my dearest friend." Annie hugged her more tightly. She was crying, too.

"Thank you for everything, Ruth." Jimmy came over and Annie turned away from Ruth while he helped her into the car. "You have been a true friend." Jimmy put his hand out to Ruth and she shook it. Then, overcome with emotion, he drew her to him and hugged her good-bye.

Ruth was too filled with tears to reply.

Douglas climbed into the driver's seat and tipped his hat to Ruth. He opened his mouth to say good-bye, but suddenly he turned away from her and the engine roared. They started off with a jerk. Ruth stood waving, the tears running down her face.

"Annie, my friend," Ruth said as they drove away, "you are so lucky. I wish I were in your place, even as difficult as it is. My road leads into an endless, relentless desert, but yours will be filled with joy and love. You are so lucky." She paused, watching the plume of dust rise up behind them. "Good-bye Douglas," she said to the disappearing car and turned to go inside. An iron chain of loneliness wrapped itself around her heart.

Chapter Ten

The next few days trickled slowly by like streams at the end of the dry season, a mere shadow of the proud rivers that had bounded down the hillsides earlier. The farm life seemed dry and small. Even looking after the children who came for clinic in the mornings had shrunk to a small mechanical gesture for Ruth. She had put away her green dress in the old carved chest in the lounge, and already it smelled like mothballs, like a widow's wedding dress, the fading shell of a memory of love.

She tried not to think of Douglas or Annie and Jimmy. All that was a lifetime ago, and everyone was a million miles away now. And anyway, the rains were late, and Ruth had enough to worry about. She kept scanning the horizon for clouds, but the sky was hot and clear and as dry as the cracked riverbeds. Ruth felt her life trickling away into the dust.

Milka fussed over her, making her cups of tea at every opportunity and speaking cheerfully and enthusiastically about every little piece of news. She hadn't heard any news of Annie and Jimmy, and that was a good sign; they must have escaped. Ruth found herself saying a prayer for them now and then, before reminding herself that she didn't believe anymore. She could sense bitterness trying to grow in her heart like some unnatural thing that didn't need water or sunshine.

One day, she had to go into town to see Mr. Cooper to sign some papers to transfer the deed of ownership of the farm from her father's name into hers. Riding down into the valley, she realized that today she would be the sole owner of a farm in Africa. She, Ruth Morag Jones, a landowner and farmer in her own right. It was not the life she would have chosen, but nevertheless it was her own life now, and she had the power of control over it. She could retreat into a shell and subsist, or she could throw herself into it and at least lose herself in the work. And there would be some compensation. After all, while she would be alone, she would also be independent. Just like her father. She smiled ruefully to herself.

Riding out from under the canopy of the trees and into the searing heat of the hot, flat valley floor, she headed for the lone baobab tree in the distance, standing gnarled and proud out on the empty plain. Ruth smiled as she drew closer. The ancient tree greeted her like an old friend. The little flock of guinea fowl that lived in the shady grass nearby cackled and scuttled away as her horse approached, scolding and teasing her the way only those who know each other well can. And looking up into the branches of the tree, she thought she sensed a change in the wind. A breeze, like the forerunner of something new, slipped by overhead, rustling quickly through the dry leaves, and then it was gone.

Ruth sat straighter in her saddle. She would celebrate her new status by going to the hotel for lunch after she had seen Mr. Cooper. She would be dining alone, but she would hold her head high. The bitterness in her heart shrank a little.

A new thought moved into her mind: *I now know the feeling of life.* Just asking Douglas to marry her had made her feel alive if only for a few moments. And pain and tears were part of being alive. Even if God wouldn't listen to her prayers, even if she only barely believed in Him, she decided that she would at least be thankful for the little life she had. It was her own—she hadn't realized that until now. At that moment her bitterness shrank and shriveled away.

It seemed oddly quiet in town as she rode in. Without Douglas and Jimmy and Annie, the life had gone out of the place. Even the people on the streets looked quiet and subdued. Jimmy and Annie and Douglas will be bringing life and love and adventure to the people at their new towns, just as they had brought it here to her. But she would remember the lesson she had learned from them and thank God. Ruth smiled a friendly greeting to the people she recognized on the street, and they greeted her in return, a little surprised, she thought.

She conducted her business with Mr. Cooper efficiently and quickly. *It's funny,* she thought to herself, *he doesn't seem quite such an enormous man anymore. Maybe Mabel has put him on a diet. On the other hand, perhaps it's just that I'm not so afraid anymore.*

"Have you spoken to your Aunt Florence, lately?" he asked as he stood up to usher her to the door.

Ruth laughed a little sheepishly. "I'm afraid my aunt doesn't speak to me anymore."

"Oh, I'm sorry to hear that. I don't mean to intrude, but frankly, I'm a bit concerned about her. You have heard that Miss Campbell has eloped with young Jimmy MacRae?" Ruth nodded. "Well, naturally she is quite upset, but I'm afraid she hasn't seemed to be quite well, and I fear she is very much under the influence of Alex Kendall. I only hope everything will turn out for the best."

"I hope so, too," agreed Ruth. She put out her hand. "Thank you for your concern, Mr. Cooper. Perhaps it's time I tried to mend some fences with my aunt. I'll see what I can do."

Ruth left his office and headed for the hotel. She really did feel sorry for Aunt Florence, despite her unkind behavior. I'll call in to see her on my way out of town, she decided; but she would fortify herself with a good lunch before facing up to her.

It was a little sad riding up the driveway of the hotel, knowing that Douglas wasn't there anymore. The little thrill of joy with the hope of seeing him was gone, and there was a lonely, empty place in Ruth's heart now. But she set her face like flint. She was alone, and she was going to get used to it. She tied Chui up next to a large black car that looked suspiciously like Alex Kendall's friends' car, which she had seen before her father's funeral. Looking up into the dining room window, Ruth saw them sitting at a table where they could see all the comings and goings from the hotel. She wondered what they wanted. She hoped that Aunt Florence hadn't somehow gotten involved with them.

Like the town, the dining room seemed empty and quiet. But the food was still delicious.

It was just after her main course that Ruth noticed Alex Kendall's two friends stand up and look out of the window. There was a flurry of activity in the lobby, and the other diners stopped eating to watch. Suddenly, waiters began to rush about here and there, moving tables and chairs. Ruth put her knife and fork down and tried to figure out what was happening.

There was a flutter and a flurry of pink gauze and into the dining room burst Florence Campbell, dressed from head to toe in pink and carrying a huge bouquet of pink roses. Ruth stared in blank confusion. Alex Kendall appeared behind her. A small throng of admirers, including the Reverend and Mrs. Montgomery, were following them closely. Florence and Alex swept over to the tables that had been rearranged just moments before.

The waiters settled them at their table and the entourage at the tables around them. Ruth noticed that the two men were now standing at the doors, almost like sentries. She could tell Alex was aware of them. He kept glancing in their direction, but they gave no indication that they noticed him.

A few minutes later, Florence rose majestically from her seat and cleared her throat. There was immediate silence.

"Ladies and gentlemen," she began in a regal tone, "as you all know, I have suffered a great deal in the last several months, what with losing my dear husband Angus, after having nursed him myself through a long and difficult illness. And now I find that I am suffering another deep and painful loss as my daughter, Annie, has, despite all my desperate attempts to help her make a good match, run away with a local farmer and married him. It has been a terrible trial to me, almost more than I can bear, but in the last few weeks I have been sustained by the care and, yes, even the love of this good and kind man, Alex Kendall." She turned to Alex and he stood up beside her.

"I am happy to announce to you all, my friends and relations, who know how much I have suffered and have tried to do your part to give me hope throughout it all, that I have found true happiness at last!

"Alex Kendall and I were married this morning in a quiet ceremony at the church, and we now ask all of you to join with me in celebrating our joyful union."

There was a ghastly hush from the entire crowd. Ruth gasped out loud.

Gradually, as the news sank in, the crowd from the dining room began to buzz. Dutifully, people began to step forward to offer the bride and groom their congratulations. Alex was busy keeping one eye on the two sentries at the door, and Florence was wrapped up in a flurry of hugs and kisses and pink gauze and roses.

People filed back to their seats, and the waiters brought out bottles of champagne and glasses and distributed them to all the tables. A gentleman seated next to Florence, one of the poorer Campbells and a neighbor of Florence's, stood up.

"Ladies and gentlemen, I would like to propose a toast to the bride." There was a scraping of chairs and glasses everywhere clinked as the stunned diners all murmured, "To the bride."

Ruth stayed seated and left her glass of champagne untouched. The crowd, now over their initial surprise, buzzed with the excitement. Florence beamed brightly and Alex watched his two guards cautiously, as the waiters rushed around serving the wedding party lunch.

At last, as the diners began to filter out, returning to work and their daily lives, the room grew quieter. Florence began to gather her bouquet and got ready to leave. Alex grew visibly nervous. He glanced up at the sentries by the door. They were watching him. Ruth saw Alex look over at Florence. She was talking to the head waiter and had her back to him. Ruth could almost see him physically gathering his courage. He marched determinedly over to the two men and engaged them in intense conversation. At least Alex was intense, gesturing angrily and frowning, but the men simply shook their heads.

Alex turned and marched back to Florence. He drew her aside and whispered something in her ear. She went and talked with her new husband behind a stand of potted palms. Ruth saw her turn white and glance at the men by the door. They smiled thin, evil smiles at her. She looked pale and stunned, but nevertheless she took Alex by the arm and led him over to the far side of the dining room. He was cowering like a bad puppy.

Florence marched over to the two men. The sentries appeared grimly glad to see the effect they were having on the happy couple. They nodded as she approached them, but they didn't smile at her. She spoke to them sharply. The four of them sat together, and there was another intense discussion. Ruth watched fascinated. After a short while, Florence stood up and Alex and the two men followed suit. Florence grabbed Alex by the elbow and marched him out of the dining room. The two men sat, ordered more coffee, and turned their chairs to watch the lobby. Alex and Florence burst into the manager's office, and a moment later he came scurrying out like a scalded cat. The door slammed behind him.

A warm breeze blew through the potted palms, and everyone looked a little calmer with Florence and Alex gone. Ruth paid her bill and slipped quietly down the flagstone steps into the garden. She wanted to think about this new development. She was stunned. How could Florence have married Alex Kendall, of all people? He must be at least ten, if not twenty years younger than she was. What on earth could have possessed her to do such a thing?

The sun burned itself into the hills behind her, as it had often been doing these days on her drives back to the farm. The old baobab stood glowing goldly with its shadow stretched out thinly behind it. It looked so much more lonely in the afternoon shadows than it did at midday.

Yes, thought Ruth, *maybe that's why Florence had married Alex. Like me, Florence couldn't face being alone, and Alex had agreed to her proposal.* She sighed. *A woman like Florence knew how to attract a man, while I couldn't even buy one to save my life.*

I'll go and make my peace with Florence after she's settled, Ruth thought. It seemed so strange to think about Alex Kendall taking the place of Angus Campbell. Ruth shuddered. But who could put oneself in another's shoes? Florence had her own pain. And her own way of coping with it.

She started up the hill and thought, *I look up to the hills from whence my help cometh. It must be a quote from the Bible,* Ruth thought. *Milka must have mentioned it to me once. Well, if there is any help for me in the hills, that is where I am going to be for most of my life,* she thought wryly.

Ruth rode home. Remembering her new resolve, she thanked God for her farm and for her livelihood. Thinking of God reminded her of Annie and Jimmy and Douglas, and she missed them all more than she could have ever imagined was possible. For the first time since they had left, her eyes filled with tears. She dismounted in front of the veranda steps with tears pouring down her cheeks. Through her tears, Ruth, as she did every day, scanned the horizon for clouds. "Oh, God, please bring the rain," she spoke out loud. The words felt as though they had been wrenched out of the center of her heart. In the silence that remained, someone answered.

It's coming. Soon. She felt, rather than heard, the reply. God answered her prayer. She was no longer alone. He was here, too. And there in the dust and the darkness in front of the veranda, she opened her heart and prayed to Jesus.

"Lord Jesus, I believe." She knew she was no longer alone, and the tears streamed down her face once more. Tears of relief and tears of joy. She was home at last.

Chapter Eleven

The week went by in a blur of activity for Ruth. Milka was overjoyed at her decision to believe. "I have prayed all your life for you, and the Good Lord has at last answered my prayers. May His name be praised!" Milka lifted her hands to the sky as she said this and Ruth laughed with joy. For the first time in her life, she understood the joy that Milka always told her about when she spoke of her faith. Ruth had a million questions for Milka. Every afternoon while they drank tea together, she poured over the Bible at the kitchen table with her. It was a golden time.

Still the rains hadn't appeared, and the whole farm seemed to be holding its breath, waiting and waiting. But Ruth and Milka were busy in the house. Ruth pulled all her father's trophies off the walls. She covered the empty walls where the animal heads had been with her mother's pictures that she had brought with her from Scotland. Curtains were taken down and washed, floors were polished, and furniture was rearranged. Ruth took all the whiskey her father had kept in the sideboard and poured it out. She put china figurines and vases of wildflowers in place of the bottles and glasses. Light poured into the little farmhouse, and it was filled with the scent of flowers and fresh air. Ruth looked around her and again she thanked God.

There was only one discordant note that week. Kamau brought back news from town that Florence and Alex's marriage didn't appear to be going very well at all. Alex was living by himself at the hotel while Florence remained at home. There were rumors among the staff that the hotel was up for sale. Florence was at home and refused to see or speak to anyone. The whole town was buzzing with wild stories about what had made Florence marry Alex. In Kamau's opinion, she had run out of money on expensive nursing and cures, trying to save Angus's life.

Ruth felt deeply sorry for her aunt. She must have been suffering with fear and pain for a long, long time. She and Milka sat at the kitchen table the evening Kamau brought this news and prayed for Florence with all their hearts. Ruth thought she would try to go and see her aunt and apologize for her rude behavior toward her. She felt deep remorse for what she had said to her and prayed often that Florence would forgive her for being so unkind. But, even if she didn't, Ruth knew it would be good to show her that she had tried.

The next Sunday morning, Ruth left the farm in the buggy just at dawn. Ruth was on her way to church. Even the thought of the Reverend Montgomery's dull voice couldn't quench her enthusiasm for worshiping God. She was wearing her new green dress, and she felt as fresh and light as the leaves on the trees in the valley below.

Already the day promised to be hot. She strained her eyes looking into the distance for a sign of the rains. She remembered the promise of rain that she had been given and wondered when it would be fulfilled. Her faith was so new to her, she wondered if perhaps she had made a mistake. But Milka assured her that waiting on God was something all Christians must learn, and she was already in the middle of her first lesson. She drove on through the forest, jiggling the horse's reins. She didn't want to be late for her first morning in church.

As Ruth passed by the elephant pool, the birds sang as sweetly in the slanting morning light that rippled through the leaves as they had the day the elephants had come to play. She remembered how far away and elusive joy and love had seemed to her then, as she clung to the tree watching the two elephants frolic together in the pool below her. And here she now possessed both love and joy. Truly God had already begun to speak to her then. He had spoken first. She bowed her head and whispered a prayer of thanksgiving to Him as she went by. The birds set it to music for her and sent it winging up to heaven.

Later, as she neared town and saw the roofs twinkling in the distance, she wondered how Florence was. She had half decided to stop in at the Campbell farm on the way back from church. Perhaps Florence would be at the service and she could get some sort of idea of what her condition was. Ruth had spent too many years suffering pain with Florence's sharp tongue to think about paying her a visit without a serious amount of trepidation. And she didn't yet really understand how Jesus could help her, but she had made up her mind that she would visit Florence soon.

Ruth arrived at church early, and there were only a few people trickling up the steps. The last time she had been here was at her father's funeral. So much had changed since then. She smiled warmly at the people going up the steps and received friendly greetings in response, although she could sense their surprise at seeing her here. She walked in the big wooden doors and stood for a moment, adjusting to the darkness inside. She wasn't sure where she should sit. Perhaps people had their own particular pews. She began to walk timidly up the aisle.

"Hello, Ruth!" Ruth recognized Constance Bishop, a friend of Annie's who was standing in front of the altar making last-minute touches to the flower arrangements. She smiled. "Come and sit here at the front with me," Constance said, walking up to meet Ruth and taking her by the arm. "Jimmy told me all about what you did for Annie before he left. We are all so grateful to you. We have been praying for you and for Annie and Jimmy. Have you heard from them yet?"

"No, I haven't heard anything." She gratefully sat next to Constance.

Ruth and Constance's pew began to fill up, and Constance described Ruth's role in Annie's marriage to her friends. Ruth quickly found herself in the center of an admiring circle. "But, don't worry," whispered Constance to Ruth, "no one will tell Florence Campbell. She has enough troubles of her own these days anyway, poor, poor woman."

Ruth was worried. "What do you mean? What has happened?" But it was too late. The organ launched into the first hymn and the choir came walking down the aisle. As Ruth turned to look at them, someone caught her eye as he slipped quietly into the back pew. Surely it couldn't be Douglas MacPherson? She tried to catch another glimpse of the man, but he was directly behind her and hidden by several rows of people. It would be too impolite to turn around and crane her neck. It didn't matter anyway. She had probably just imagined someone else was Douglas, because she still thought of him so much. She quickly squashed the little flutter of anticipation that flared up whenever she thought she might see him.

She had a life of her own now, and she had Jesus to share it with her. She concentrated on the words of the hymn.

"Be Thou my vision. . . ," the congregation sang, and with all her heart she sang, too.

After the service was over, she was again included in the conversation of her new friends. It was a strange feeling to be welcomed and spoken to by people she had hardly known, but it filled her heart with a peace and warmth that she truly had never thought possible. When Constance suddenly looked right past Ruth and waved to someone standing behind her, Ruth was completely taken by surprise to discover Douglas MacPherson standing there watching her. She had forgotten that she thought she had seen him earlier. The memory of their last meeting made her blush to the roots of her hair with embarrassment. She lowered her eyes and tried to avoid his gaze. Constance and the others were already crowding around him and asking for news of Annie and Jimmy.

Douglas explained that they had found some land and were in the process of putting up a house. Already Jimmy had decided that the crop he was going to try would be cotton. Annie was very happy, though she was anxious for news of her mother. As soon as he mentioned Florence, there was a sudden uncomfortable silence.

"What about your hospital?" someone asked. "Have you found the right location yet?"

Douglas paused and shot a quick glance at Ruth. She looked down to her shoes again and decided that she would slip out and fly away home. She only wanted to know that Annie was all right. Douglas's plans were too painful a subject for her to discuss objectively just yet.

"I haven't quite decided on anywhere just yet," she heard him explaining as she tiptoed down the church path, hoping no one would notice. "But I was called back to town on some urgent business."

Ruth didn't want to hear another word. She hoped his business wouldn't keep him long. She unhitched Chui and was just about to jump up into the buggy when someone took her by the waist and lifted her up. She caught her breath.

"Douglas!" She knew who it was before she looked.

"Lucky I caught you trying to sneak away!" He spoke with a tease in his tone of voice, but the softer look in his eyes betrayed that he understood why Ruth was running quickly away.

"Listen, Ruth," he said when she didn't smile, "I need to talk to you about something. Please come and have lunch with me at the hotel."

"Oh no, Douglas, I couldn't possibly do that. Really, I made a terrible fool of myself the other day. I can't imagine what came over me, but everything is different now." Ruth spoke as quickly as she could, trying to get away before he could persuade her otherwise. "Please do me the favor of completely forgetting we ever had that conversation. That would truly be the nicest thing you could do for me. I must go now. It was very nice to see you again, good-bye!" Ruth spoke desperately.

She couldn't face listening to his plans after the way she had tried to change them. She would have liked to tell him about her new faith in Jesus. After all, he had a lot to do with it, but the whole conversation would be too difficult. However, he had already thought of that angle and was using it to his advantage.

"All right then." He had a sly twinkle in his eyes. "If you won't listen to what I have to say, at least come with me and tell me what you are doing here in church this Sunday. I think you owe me an explanation of that, since I have told you all about my faith, not to mention encouraging you to have your own." He smiled up into her face, and Ruth's resolve evaporated. The only person to whom she had told the story of her faith in Jesus was Milka, and the need to tell someone, especially Douglas, was too much to resist. She slid over on the seat, and he hopped up onto the buggy beside her.

Ruth was surprised when they reached the hotel. All the staff greeted Douglas by name, and he and Ruth were immediately seated at the nicest table in the dining room. Douglas asked her to tell him the story of what brought her to church, and all through lunch they chatted about Ruth's new faith. Ruth was touched because Douglas seemed particularly excited about it.

"From the day I set eyes on you at Angus Campbell's funeral, I have been praying for you," he said. "I sensed that the Lord had His hand on you and was searching for you."

"Searching for me!" Ruth said in surprise. "It was me who was searching for Him!" But they both laughed together. "No, you're right, it was He who made the first move," she said, remembering the elephants at the pool. As she looked at Douglas laughing with her across the table, she knew that everything was the same again between them. They were friends. Just for a moment, she felt a pang of regret, wishing there was more than friendship, but instead, she remembered to thank God for restoring her friendship with Douglas. No one could want a nicer friend than he.

As they finished their lunch and the waiter brought coffee, Douglas became serious. "Ruth," he said, "there is something I want to tell you about me."

Ruth had a sudden fear that he was going to bring up the subject of her proposal. "No," she said firmly, "let's just be friends as we are. You don't need to discuss anything else with me!"

"Ruth, stop!" Douglas interrupted. "Stop and listen to me. I need to explain something to you if we are to be friends. It is important to me."

Ruth sat silently. She steeled herself against the thought of being embarrassed by the mention of her proposal. But she needn't have worried.

"A long time ago," Douglas began, "when I was just starting my medical studies, I was in love with a young girl from my hometown in Alberta. Her name was Jane. We were engaged to be married, but we had to wait until I had finished my studies in Toronto.

"Jane and I wrote back and forth to each other regularly. She was looking forward to my return that summer. But in the spring, my cousin Alex returned from the Klondike, where he had been looking for gold. He hadn't found much, or if he had, he had already spent it on gambling.

"Anyway, the long and the short of it is that when I returned to Alberta that summer, it didn't take me long to figure out that Alex was trying to steal Jane away from me. I was terribly upset, and I lost my temper with Alex, said terrible things to him, and we got into a fistfight. I am ashamed to say it was in front of Jane. Jane was horrified at my behavior, and I can't say I blamed her. I behaved very badly. She dropped me like a hot potato and began to see Alex. She seemed very happy, and by the end of the summer, when I went back to Toronto, she and Alex were engaged to be married.

"I threw myself into my studies and tried not to think about what had happened that summer. At Christmastime I received a letter from my mother explaining that Jane was expecting a baby and that Alex had left town. If I was angry with Alex before, I was beside myself with anger now!" Douglas paused and took a deep breath.

"Anyway, I wrote to Jane and offered to come home and marry her. Now that I look back on it, I must have seemed awfully arrogant to Jane. Although I wrote several letters, I never heard back from her.

"The following summer, when I went back to work on the farm, I discovered that Jane had married a local boy, and she had had her baby. Her new husband was a poor farm worker and they didn't have much. But her baby had a name. She wouldn't speak to me and avoided me whenever she could.

"Each summer that I came home, Jane had another baby, and she was poorer than ever. There were rumors that her husband drank and beat her. But still, she wouldn't even look at me if I passed her in the street.

"Finally, when I was studying in seminary to prepare for the mission field, I heard from Mother that Jane had died. The story was that her husband had come home one night, having had too much to drink, and beaten her. She was expecting another baby, and with the beating, the baby came too soon and there were complications. Both Jane and the child died. The other children were put up for adoption, and I heard no more.

"But I thought about it all the time. I vowed to never allow myself to go through that kind of pain again. I decided that I was called to be single, and anyway, taking a wife and family into the mission field would be too difficult. I had made a decision and I put the matter of marriage behind me. But I had never put the matter of Alex behind me. I was furious with him. Of course, a good missionary doesn't go around being angry with people, so gradually after several years my anger grew cold and hard. It didn't go anywhere, it just took on a different, more manageable shape.

"When I was home and saw Alex at family gatherings, I was polite and formal, just the way a good Christian ought to behave, so I thought. Alex began to take an interest in my goal of going to Africa. He had heard that there was money to be made in Africa, and Alex always had an ear for money-making schemes, although he never stuck with any of them long enough to actually get rich.

"Last year, when my father died and I inherited my share of the estate, Alex tried to persuade me to go into the safari business with him. He said it was the new age of tourist travel and we would double our money in five years. Of course, I ignored him and came here to build my hospital. But, as you know, he followed me. He tried to talk me into his schemes when we were staying at the lodge. What I didn't know at the time was that he had racked up huge gambling debts, and he needed a way to pay them back. When I wasn't helpful to him, he decided to marry Annie and at least use some of her money to pay off his debts. But there wasn't a lot of time because, as you know, the people he owed money to tracked him here and were demanding it soon.

"So when Annie eloped with Jimmy, it put him in a very difficult position. He turned to Florence, not realizing that Florence had also been counting on his marriage to Annie for entirely different reasons. Florence had spent all her money and mortgaged the hotel to the roof trying to find a cure for her husband's illness. She thought that, like me, Alex had family money, and she would be able to use it to get herself out of debt once he was her son-in-law.

"You know the rest of the story. Alex sent me a telegram last week asking for help. I was about to give him my usual response when I realized that God forgave me my sins, but I refused to forgive Alex his. I was overcome with remorse for all the years I had played the holier-than-thou Christian with Alex, and I wired him the money he needed. We are also going into the tourism business together. I paid the back payments on the hotel's mortgage, and Alex will run the hotel and try to make some honest money. I have enough left to start my hospital in Uganda, and with God's help, we will make a little from the hotel to finish off the hospital."

Ruth and Douglas sat together in silence for a few minutes while Ruth absorbed all this news.

"What about Florence?" she asked at last. "Are she and Alex going to make a go of their marriage?"

"That's one thing I can't tell you," Douglas replied. "I don't honestly know how a marriage can work when it began under such a cloud of deception. But, I suppose we'll just have to wait and see."

Ruth sighed. "Why did you tell me all this?"

"I wanted you to know. I know our last meeting was difficult, but I hope with all my heart that we can still be friends. I would like it very much if we could."

Ruth couldn't bring herself to look at him. She put her elbows on the table and put her face in her hands. Perhaps they had gone too far together, and now they couldn't go back to just being friends after all. "Douglas, I don't know," she heard herself say. "I thought we could, but now I feel perhaps I was wrong."

Douglas scraped his chair backward and stood up. He walked around and took Ruth's arm as she stood up, too. "Look, Ruth," he said quietly, "I'm sure it has been a long day for you, and it's getting late. Why don't you think about it? Would it be all right if I came to see you the day after tomorrow, before I go back to Uganda? If you think we can no longer be friends, just send me word here at the hotel and I won't come."

"Okay," Ruth replied, glad to have a way out for a day or two. "Bye, Douglas." She turned and fled from the dining room, aware that his eyes were on her all the way.

It was with a full heart that she drove back out of town and up the hillside to her farm. The old baobab tree standing alone on the plain with its little flock of guinea fowl nodded a friendly greeting in the wind, and Ruth was sure she sensed a change in the air. Surely it wouldn't be long now before the rains came.

Chapter Twelve

Ruth spent the next day immersed in prayer and thought. She knew that somehow she would have to find a way of controlling her powerful feelings for Douglas. She simply couldn't let him go without being his friend. She would regret it for the rest of her life, so she didn't send him word not to come. On the day she expected him, she dressed in her green dress and carefully brushed her hair, but her hands were shaking with nervous anticipation. She prayed for strength and peace. She wanted with all her strength to be bright and happy and friendly when he came, but it was nearly impossible. She had no peace. Perhaps it was a mistake, she thought as she saw Rosie's cloud of dust rising above the brow of the hill, but it was too late now.

Douglas pulled Rosie up to the veranda steps and jumped out. Ruth was surprised to see him wearing a suit and tie, with his hair firmly brushed down. But instead of his usual breezy hello, he took Ruth by the hand. "You look beautiful today," he said.

"Hello, Douglas," replied Ruth carefully. There was a moment of awkward silence as they stood at the top of the veranda. Ruth turned to lead the way inside.

"Listen, Ruth," Douglas spoke quickly, "how about a walk before we have tea? I thought it might be nice to walk back down to that spot where Annie and Jimmy were married. It is so beautiful down there, I'd really like to see it again."

"Well, don't you think we're a bit overdressed to go tramping through the bush?" It was now Ruth's turn to speak nervously. That place meant so much to her, and all her memories and feelings would be so close to the surface there. But she had been taken off her guard and she couldn't come up with a way to say no.

"Come on," he said, opening Rosie's door for her, "let's drive down the hill."

Why would Douglas get himself all dressed in a tie and leather shoes just to traipse down into the bottom of a jungle path with me? He is really a very baffling man, she thought as they drove together in silence.

When they reached the little glade by the pool, Douglas stood beside her as she stopped and looked into the water. The pool itself seemed to be holding its breath, waiting for the rain. The water that fell into it from the stream was a faint trickle, and the ring of dried mud that surrounded the pond looked thirsty and parched. There was complete silence. Not even a bird twittered in the trees above them. The whole place seemed to be waiting nervously. Ruth could feel Douglas's presence beside her in the quiet more intensely than she had ever felt him before. She held her breath.

"Ruth," Douglas broke the silence. His voice was low and quiet, as though he were afraid of his own words. "Ruth, I need to apologize to you for something."

"No, I'm sure you don't." Ruth spoke quickly, suddenly embarrassed.

"Please listen to me, Ruth. I must speak to you about this." Douglas was firm and Ruth listened. "Remember our conversation on Annie and Jimmy's wedding day? I haven't been able to get it out of my mind." He paused to see that Ruth understood what he was referring to.

She was horrified. She could hardly believe Douglas would actually bring up such a painful subject.

"Douglas, it was nothing," she said desperately. "Please forget about it. And you owe me no apology. If that is all you came to discuss, please don't. I would rather we left now." She turned to go.

"Ruth!" He took hold of her arm to stop her from walking away from him, and she looked up into his eyes. "Ruth, I have made a terrible mistake. When I told you that I never planned to marry, it was not because that was God's will for my life, rather it was out of bitterness and unforgiveness. It was wrong of me." He paused and took a deep breath.

"Ruth, I want to ask you to marry me. I love you."

Ruth felt a warm breeze blow around her. She felt there was nothing else in all the world but Douglas and she and the soft, warm wind blowing around them. She closed her eyes, and his words continued to flood over her.

"Ruth," he said, "I've been a fool. I have loved you since the day I met you, and I should never have let you have to ask me to marry you. I should have asked you long before it came to that. And to think you felt you had to offer me your land. How could I let the woman I love think I married her for her land? I am so sorry." He reached forward and took her two hands in his. His voice was a whisper now. "Ruth, I love you. Please marry me."

Ruth couldn't answer. All she could do was smile up into his face through the tears that were falling like rain down her cheeks. She felt his hands let go of hers, and he put his arms around her and drew her to him and kissed her. He kissed her mouth and her cheeks and her eyes and her neck, until she was completely immersed in his love for her. And she kissed him back.

A long time later, the wind began to blow strongly and insistently. Douglas and Ruth held each other closer, and then rain began to fall. As the drops splashed down on them and around them, they drew apart. The rumbling in the distance that they had been only dimly aware of a few minutes before was suddenly shaking the earth under them and rattling the trees around them. Flashes of lightning tore through the sky.

"I think we'd better go up to the car quickly," Douglas said in a hoarse, intimate voice Ruth had never heard before. He put his arm around her waist and led her up the hillside.

Lightning flashed around them, and Ruth was terrified. Douglas pulled her closer to him, and they scrambled quickly up the path. Finally, they came to Rosie. Douglas lunged for the door and threw Ruth inside and himself after her. They sat for a few moments listening to the rain drumming onto the roof and streaming down the windows around them. Then Douglas got out and turned the crank, starting Rosie up with a welcoming roar. Slowly, they made their way up the hill. When they came to the house, they made a dash for the door and stood dripping and laughing together on the threshold.

Milka came running in to greet them and gave a shriek of delight when she saw Douglas. "Bwana Douglas, I knew you would be back! I knew it. Praise be to our Lord! Let me get you some tea."

She bustled off in a flurry of excitement, and Ruth found Douglas some dry clothes. She looked ruefully at his mud-coated leather shoes and his soaked white shirt and shook her head.

"Well," he spoke sheepishly, as he took the dry clothes, "I wanted to make a good impression on you."

"You did that a long time ago." She looked down shyly at the floor.

And a few minutes later, they were dry and cozy, sitting together in the dining room sipping tea, with Milka peeping around the corner every two minutes to make sure Douglas hadn't left.

Douglas looked around at the light, cheerful room. "My, you've changed things since I was here last!"

Ruth laughed. "Yes, everything has changed since you were here last! I have changed."

"I'm not so sure of that," Douglas replied. "It's more like you have become yourself now." He reached for her hand and kissed it.

Ruth reveled in her happiness. She could smell the damp earth outside, and she could almost feel the grass and the land drinking in the rain and filling up and growing green again. The storm was passing over now, and the sun was setting behind it. A shaft of red-gold light flashed into the room, and everything was as golden and glowing as Ruth felt in her heart.

Escape on the Wind

Jane LaMunyon

Dedication

This book is dedicated to my husband, Jim,
an aviation expert, who never tired of answering my
many questions about planes and flying techniques.
It is also dedicated to three of my relatives whose names
I found in Jersalem's Yad Vashem's records of those
taken to Nazi concentration camps:
Elias Van der Noot, 8/4/17 to 8/27/43, Auschwitz;
Hans Jack Van der Noot, 9/28/42 to 8/27/43, Auschwitz:
and Louis Van der Noot, 5/16/10 to 3/26/43, Sobibor.

Chapter One

September 2, 1934

After Amanda's birthday dinner, Stanley, the servant, cleared away the crystal water goblets, then pushed a linen-covered cart to the table, between Amanda and her father. Stanley removed the white linen to reveal a pile of brightly wrapped presents, then moved back to stand beside the door.

"Thank you, Stanley," said Amanda's mother. Her blue eyes sparkled in her round face as she cast a satisfied look at the dinner guests. The double circle of braids crowning her head glowed softly in the light from the chandelier.

With a dimpled grin, Amanda's sister, Victoria, said, "Open them! I can't bear the waiting!" Her two aunts nodded fondly in agreement.

Amanda opened her presents, thanking her family for the lovely items, some of which were clearly meant for her hope chest. The French linen tablecloth with Battenburg lace edging from Aunt Edith brought admiring sighs from the guests, but Amanda wondered if she'd ever have a use for it as she quietly folded it back into its box. Aunt Emma's gift was a dozen matching napkins.

Her father presented her with a leather-bound first edition of Stendhal's works. She gasped in pleasure, running her hands over the gilt letters of the top book, *Lucien Leuven*. "Oh, Father, you remembered. Thank you!"

Her father nodded brusquely. "Hm. Yes. You always did favor those French writers."

Soon there was a pile of wrapping paper on the floor beside her chair, the boxes stacked neatly on the tray. "Thank you, all," said Amanda. "I am—"

"Wait!" Delbert pushed his chair back and stood. He flashed a smile at the seated guests, then took Amanda's hand, drawing her to her feet. "I haven't presented my gift yet."

Amanda looked at him with some confusion. She glanced at her father, leaning back in his chair, looking smugly satisfied, and then her mother, who clasped her hands with anticipation.

"Amanda, we've grown up together," Delbert began. "Everyone here knows how I feel about you."

Amanda could feel her face coloring.

Delbert's brilliant dark eyes glittered as he continued. "On this auspicious occasion, and before these beloved guests, I offer this, a token of my love and esteem." He pulled a small box from his jacket pocket and presented it to her.

She almost recoiled from it, a premonition shouting warnings in her head, but she held out her hand and he laid the box in her palm. *Let it be a locket,* she prayed silently as she slowly lifted the lid.

But it wasn't. A large marquise diamond, flanked by two smaller ones in a graceful setting, winked up at her. She stared at it in shock.

"Will you marry me, Amanda Chase? Say yes, and make me the happiest man in the world."

Taking a deep breath, her cheeks burning, she looked away. Her father didn't seem surprised. The image of him and Delbert in deep discussion last week filled her mind. Now her family eagerly watched for her reply.

Delbert flashed a bright, confident smile.

She pushed back a flush of anger with a small laugh. Her aunt Emma smiled and wiped her eyes with a lace handkerchief. With iron control, Amanda said, "I'm speechless! Delbert, this is such a surprise; I don't know what to say."

She could almost hear the silent group saying, *Say yes, say yes.*

She closed the lid over the sparkling diamond. "I'm too overwhelmed to answer right now." She set the box on the table. "Thank you all, and please excuse me." With her head held high, she walked out of the room.

Her heels clicked on the parquet floor of the hallway as she fled. Mrs. Heathman, the cook, pushed the swinging kitchen door open. "Happy birthday, miss!" she said.

Amanda glanced back, a tight smile hurting her face. "Thank you." Continuing on through the parlor, she made a quick decision not to go upstairs to her room and went out the front door.

The cool night air did little to dampen her hot anger. She stomped her way past the two cars parked out front, through the posts lighting the driveway, over the grass to the knoll. She took a few deep breaths to calm herself. Holding onto a low branch, she looked out over the lights of Boston below.

How could Delbert humiliate her? Sure, they'd been friends for the last two years, but that's all it was—friendship. They'd talked about marriage and she'd explained that marriage and family weren't in her plans right now. He contended that *settling down* was what a woman must do—take care of home, family, and her man.

That's fine for Mother, Amanda thought. *But not for me. Not yet.* She sighed with regret, thinking of her mother's and aunts' looks of bright anticipation. To them there was no higher call than that of wife and mother. *But there must be something more,* thought Amanda. Some warm, even passionate feelings. And there should be spiritual agreement. Delbert always shrugged when she brought up God, as though the topic wasn't important to him.

As she tiptoed through the wet grass to the stone bench, she heard the front door close and Delbert calling her. She glanced back to see him walking down the driveway behind the post lights. She felt her indignation rise in response to his approach.

It's time to take care of this, she thought. "I'm here!" she called.

Peering through the darkness, he loped across the grass toward her.

Knees pushed into the stone bench, hands gripping its back, she watched him approach. His long legs took the distance quickly. He looked perfect in his three-piece suit and tie, his dark hair neatly combed back.

"Sweet girl, are you all right?" He came around the bench to her side. She looked away.

"What?" he asked, his eyes clouding with concern.

"I'm fine, Delbert." She sat and slipped off her shoes, setting them beside her. He sat, too, the shoes between them.

He reached into his pocket and brought out the ring box again. "I may have made a mistake, darling. Maybe you'd rather I asked you privately to marry me."

Leaning forward, he presented the box again. Putting his right arm along the bench back, he stroked her neck slowly. "Will you, Amanda? You know how much I care for you."

She stared into the bright luster of his eyes. "Delbert, you and I are too different to ever become one." She folded her hands in her lap, ignoring the box.

"I know your job is important to you, but my company is doing well, and I make more than enough money to support us." He continued to hold the box toward her. "You can go to church, but you'll be so busy with other things, you won't have time for much else."

"It's not going to church or my job, Delbert." She paused for a second, then asked, "What 'other things' would keep me busy?"

"Oh, the running of our home, our social engagements, and—you know—being my wife."

"You're asking me to give up everything to take on the job of making your life easy?"

"It's a big responsibility," he said.

"And what I do now isn't?"

He looked baffled. "Sure it is. I'm proud of your little newspaper stories. But someday you'll have to stop examining other people's lives and settle down to a real life of your own, you know—your own home and family."

She froze, her words coming out in icy chips. "I have a real life. And my work is more than 'little newspaper stories about other people's lives.' "

He lowered the box, resting it in his lap. "You want that more than a loving husband and home of your own?"

"Delbert, you're a good person, and you're doing well in your profession. But I don't feel any more for you than I would a good friend. I do know that I couldn't love anyone enough to give up my beliefs and my life's work."

An expression of pained tolerance swept over his face. "I'll go to church with you, sweetheart."

She expelled her breath in aggravated surprise. "You don't understand! Going to church isn't the same thing as being a Christian."

With a confused expression, he stared at her. "What do you mean?"

"I mean, it's more than walking in the church door, more than just *saying* you're a Christian. It's a whole new life; it's being born again."

"You're talking in riddles, my dear."

"No. I've told you before, and you've heard it when you went to church with me. It's believing that Jesus is the Son of God, that He was born of a virgin and died on the cross for your sin, that He ascended to heaven and sits at God's side. It means that you look for Him to come again as He said He would."

"Well, that's a lot to think about." He thrust the ring box back toward her. "Keep this, and think about our engagement."

She jumped up and slipped her shoes on. "We've never really communicated, have we, Delbert?" She walked away. There was nothing more to say.

He followed her back into the house. Her aunt, uncle, and two cousins were leaving. "Here are the lovebirds!" said Aunt Joan, reaching for her left hand. "Let me see the ring!"

Amanda pulled her hand back. "I'm not wearing it."

"Yet." Uncle Mark put his arm around her shoulder and winked at her. "He's a prize, girl. Don't let him get away."

Amanda slipped her arm around her uncle's waist and held out her hand to her aunt. "Thanks for coming, all of you."

After all the guests had gone home, Amanda's father took her arm and said, "Come with me. I want to talk to you." He led her to the study. Victoria followed them, eyes wide and curious.

"Maybe Victoria should go on up to her room now," said her mother, with an appeal in her glance to her husband.

"No. Victoria is part of the family, and she'll learn something."

Still strong with the resolve to hang onto her career and the feeling that she'd been right to refuse Delbert's proposal, Amanda closed the study door and turned to face her father.

She'd always liked this room, with its wall of books, the smell of leather, and the solidarity of the huge mahogany desk where her father worked with his gallery accounts. He stood beside it now, resting one hand on the edge. Her mother sat with her back erect in the leather chair beside the fireplace and folded her hands in her lap, waiting. Victoria leaned against the bookshelf, her slim legs crossed.

Her father stared at Amanda beneath heavy eyebrows. "I'm not going to beat around the bush with small talk. Tonight we celebrated your twenty-fourth birthday, and I want to know why you didn't accept the proposal from that decent young man."

Before Amanda could answer, her mother spoke, her words coming rapidly as if she could no longer hold them back. "I can't imagine what you're thinking! You're twenty-four years old! Twenty-four! And you're still a spinster. When I was your age, I'd been married for five years and had a child. Delbert's a good man with a successful business, which, as you know, in these times is a miracle. I know you like him. How could you turn him down? And in front of everyone!"

Amanda carefully took a deep breath to stay calm.

Victoria chuckled. "Spinster?" She wrapped a blond curl around her fingers, smiling at the odd idea.

"What your mother is trying to say," her father said, "is that we gave you the best education money could buy—how many girls study at the Sorbonne in Paris these days? You've traveled the world, had all the right social connections, and for what? Here you are, still single at an age when most young women are taking care of their own households and husbands."

Her mother nodded her head. "You don't visit your friends lately. They *are* married, and you don't have much in common with them anymore."

"My career. . ."

"Your what?" Her father glared at her. "Is that why you're so often late for dinner? Were you out making headlines for that rag? Were you scooping Walter Winchell on the Boston Ladies' Sewing Guild luncheon? You call that a career?"

Amanda answered with quiet firmness. "The *Boston Chronicle* isn't a 'rag.' It's a reputable newspaper."

Victoria's hands flew to her mouth to cover a smile, and Amanda hastily added, "Beating Walter Winchell to a story has never been my goal." Today she had covered the South Boston Women's Croquet tournament. That morning in the seedy part of town she took notes and talked to people for a feature story on the plight of the depression's abandoned children. But she wouldn't give her father the satisfaction of either laughing at her trivial croquet story or berating her for the danger of consorting with "undesirables."

"All right. So you don't want to be a better reporter than Winchell. That puts us back to my original question. Just what *do* you plan to do with your life?"

Her mother leaned forward in the chair, her blue eyes pleading with Amanda to agree with her. "Her goal is the same as any normal young woman. A home and family—eventually. Am I right?" To punctuate her point, she added, "After all, you're not getting any younger."

Amanda gazed down at the familiar scrolled pattern on the Turkish rug and girded her resolve. She looked up at them. "Mother, Dad, I've always done my best in what you've asked me to do. I went through school earning honors, and I was valedictorian at college graduation. Should all that knowledge go to waste while I plan menus and entertain the hoi polloi for the benefit of some man?" She cast an affectionate look to her mother. "You're a wonderful wife and mother, but I'm not you. I'm just starting my career, and it's important to me. I'm sorry if I'm a disappointment to you, but I can't give up my life to some man and never know what I could have done or been."

She looked her father right in his eyes and struggled to keep from trembling. "I must devote my life to improving this world in the best way I know how, by documenting and exposing society's goodness and evils. If I can make someone understand this world a little better and change a life because of it, then I will have been successful. That's my goal."

"Poppycock! Most people glance over headlines, find the comics and crossword puzzles, then wrap their garbage in the papers. The poor wretches sleeping on park benches cover themselves with it, and I hear that they even slip them inside their shoes to cover the holes. We're in a depression right now, and I don't know how that rag stays in business."

Amanda bit her lips together. This was as frustrating as the scene she'd had with Delbert. She hadn't communicated the inner flame, her passion for her career. They didn't understand.

"What you're going to do is wake up and do what's right. I won't support this hobby you're glorifying into a career. You resign and either marry Delbert or start seeing other men, with the intention of being a real woman and settling down."

Stunned, she stared at him. "I am a real woman, Father!"

His gaze never wavered. "We'll do all we can to help you. But if you don't take your responsibilities seriously, I'll be forced to take steps to persuade you to comply."

Her mother leaned forward, her elbows resting on the chair arm. Her face lighted up with joy. "Think about it, Amanda. We can have a gala engagement affair; we'll invite everyone who is anyone, it'll be the event of the season, and—"

"Oh, I do so adore parties," said Victoria, looking into a scene only she could see. "I can see the Chase sisters turn this town on its ear!" She frowned as Amanda moved her head slightly from side to side. "Oh, don't be so dreary. It'd be such fun."

Amanda kept her eyes locked with her father's. "What steps?"

"Face it, girl. Your job is taking you nowhere. If you persist you'll never find a man to take care of you and you'll grow old, living at home. That would be detrimental to you and an embarrassment to us. I'd be a poor father to allow that to happen. There is no option. You must give up this notion of saving the world and face reality."

"Or?" Amanda's voice was so low, she wasn't sure her father heard her.

"Or I'll have to curtail your allowance and speak to your editor and resign for you. Then you'll take the proper responsibilities of a young woman."

She tried to read regret or hesitation in his eyes, but she could detect neither. His gaze hid any emotions he might be feeling.

She was no longer a child he could order to take a certain class in school or dictate who she could and couldn't visit. But she knew him well enough to know that approaching her editor was no idle threat. Cold fear clenched her stomach, but she resisted it with every ounce of energy she could muster, lifted her chin, and said, "I've planned my career, my life. I told Delbert I can't give up my plans for him or anybody." She broke her gaze with her father to look at her mother, who was staring at her with stunned disbelief. "I'm sorry," she said to both of them.

"I know this is hard for you to understand," said her father, "but I am doing what's best for you. I'll give you a week before I take action. Do you understand?" She nodded. "Good. You're a smart girl. I fully expect by next week you'll be back on course toward a full and happy life."

Later, she paced restlessly in her room. Although her father still didn't believe her, for the first time in her life she had defied him. It was scary, but she had to do it. She planned on being independent eventually, before the shadowy idea of marriage and family became a reality. In these modern times, lots of women had careers. She mentally tallied up her material assets: her savings account, her annuity, which she'd received from Grandpa Morganstern when she turned twenty-one, and her meager pay from the *Chronicle.*

She pushed the balcony window open and stepped out into the cool night air. Hugging her shoulders, she looked up. "Oh, God, what am I going to do? I feel a restless urge toward something; I don't know what." A breeze trembled through the oak tree, and after another minute she went back inside. They thought she couldn't take care of herself. Well, she vowed to prove them wrong.

Chapter Two

September 2, 1934, 5:36 A.M.

Curley Cameron's eyes snapped open. The rain had quit. A drop of water snaked down the closed window as the predawn light glowed feebly into the barracks room. Curley pushed off the heavy cover, shivering as he crossed the room to the window. He slid it up and leaned out into the coolness with his hands braced on the sill.

Wildflowers bloomed nearby, and their fragrance surrounded him. The clouds were mostly gone, the wind was light, and he knew if he got high enough he could see for miles. "Hot dog!" he said to the new day and quickly dressed.

He stuffed his few belongings into his duffel bag and took a last look around before quietly closing the door behind him and tiptoeing past closed doors; most of the airmen were still asleep. In the latrine, he splashed icy water on his face, shaved quickly, and left for the mess hall and a cup of coffee.

He saluted to the officer of the day, who was also up early for his duties. Avoiding puddles of leftover rain, he scanned the horizon over the airstrip, and with long happy strides, walked faster. Flying weather at last! The reveille bugle pierced the air as he went inside the warm mess hall. Chow wasn't ready, but the cook gave him toast and jam with his coffee.

Back outside, he slipped the catch from the hangar door and pushed it sideways. It was still dark inside, but dawn light glowing behind him touched the propeller with a gentle gleam. "Hello, sweetheart," he said, patting his DeHaviland Moth. "We're going up today!" A Harley-Davidson crunched through the gravel toward him, its lights still on, as he pushed all the hangar doors to the side, opening it up.

He circled the plane, checking for loose bolts, feeling for uneven wing surfaces, and anything else that could cause an in-flight problem. When he finished, the sky was fully light, and he could hear guys moving around on the other side of the wall. He stuck his head outside to see two men pushing a P-26A out of a hangar down the line.

By 6:30 A.M. all but one of the hangar doors were open, four planes had already taken off, and Curley had gotten assistance in pulling his Moth out onto the tarmac. He stowed his duffel bag in the back and fueled up, then pulled his clipboard out from under his seat and stood beside the struts, studying it.

He'd mapped out his route to California three days ago, before the rains slowed him down, and he had studied it every day, marking airfields he'd touch down in. Nevertheless, he checked the flight plan once more, memorizing the route.

His concentration was interrupted by the warmth of a soft body pressed to his back and smooth white arms circling his chest.

He lowered the clipboard to his side and turned. She held on so tightly, he had to lift his left arm over her head. He grinned down at her. "Ah, Jenny! What brings you out so early?"

Her lips puckered into a lovely pout. "I think you're leaving without saying good-bye."

"Honey, you know I have business to take care of."

Her chocolate-colored eyes gazed at him wistfully. Then she stood on tiptoe and put her head on his shoulder and nuzzled his neck. "Stay one more day," she murmured.

He stepped back and took her face in his large hand. "It's time. I have to go."

Her eyes narrowed with sudden anger. "You think you can just toss me aside like an old shop rag?" She looked down her nose at him under half-closed eyes. "I have other fellas calling on me, you know."

"I know that, sweet one. You're much too fine a girl for the likes of me." He rubbed her chin gently with his thumb.

She stared over his shoulder at the airplane. Not meeting his eyes, she said, almost to herself, "You won't be back." She turned her compelling eyes on him, and he had to force himself to pull his hand away from her soft cheek and step back.

He shook his head slowly. "Don't think about it. Turn around, walk away, and forget about me."

"But we. . .I. . ." She looked around in desperation as if searching for the answer to a confusing puzzle. "You can't just leave!"

He shook his head. "I go where the Army Air Corps sends me. That's the fact of it."

"But—"

He put his finger on her lips, not wanting to prolong their good-byes. Holding the clipboard at his chest between them, he gave her a light kiss on her cheek and said, "Good-bye, Jenny."

She stared at him for a moment, then raised her chin and defiantly informed him, "In two weeks—in two minutes, I'll have forgotten you, like this!" She snapped her fingers and walked away without a backward glance.

Curley watched her walk away, feeling admiration for the way she turned the situation around to seem as if she were leaving him instead. *Women!* he thought. They craved rose-covered cottages and forever-afters. He never met one who didn't either hint or downright talk openly about it. Why were they always in such a hurry to get themselves tied down?

He glanced at his flight map, then walked back to the hangar, thinking of how dependent women were, needing a man to complete their lives. *Bless them, though, they sure make life a lot more interesting,* he thought, smiling.

His thoughts were interrupted by a summons to the base commander's office.

He entered the colonel's office, saluted, and said, "Reporting as ordered, sir." He stood at attention until the commanding officer said, "At ease, Captain." The colonel tapped the papers on his desk with his pencil. "Captain Cameron, I have orders here that you are to depart immediately and report to General Franklin in Washington."

"Sir?" Curley eyed the official envelope under the colonel's fingers. "I'm geared up and ready to report to Muroc Air Base."

The colonel handed him the sealed orders. "Report to the general at 1100."

"Yes, sir." Curley took the envelope, saluted, and left the CO's office, wondering what this was all about. He'd been looking forward to going back to California, where the only family he knew waited for him.

He pushed his plane back into the hangar. Approaching the CB-5 he'd fly to D.C., the mechanics and pilots he'd worked with wished him well.

The minute the wheels left the runway, as always he felt as though a weight holding him to the ground snapped free, leaving him to float on the air, climb the currents, and ride the sky. This was where he belonged. Everything below seemed unreal. This was reality. He soared into the heavens, his plane merely an extension of himself, and then dipped the left wing, heading in a northerly direction toward Washington, D.C.

❧

Amanda drove herself to work Monday morning, with Delbert following. He'd come by to pick her up, but keeping her goal in mind, she had insisted on driving herself.

Her father's threat worried her. Would Mr. Mitchell fire her at her father's request? He certainly wouldn't want trouble from one of the most prestigious families in Boston. And her stories hadn't exactly been banner headlines. But she didn't get the plum assignments, either, and there was only so much she could do with the topics she covered.

Her hands gripped the steering wheel as she drove through neighborhoods that had once housed families filled with dreams and hopes. With the Great Depression they faced the terrible loss of work, and few managed to keep their homes. Grass and weeds stood tall in the small yards in front of the row of forlorn-looking houses. Downtown the employment office was besieged by a crowd, waiting for the doors to open. For every rare job offer, a hundred hungry people applied. She didn't notice until she arrived at the *Chronicle* building that Delbert was no longer following her.

Inside, the smell of paper, ink, and pencils settled over her like a familiar cloak. Noise filled the room: the clatter of typewriters, ringing phones, and the hum of the fan, which didn't efficiently rid the room of cigarette smoke. Her coworkers glanced up from their work and smiled as she passed.

She stood over her desk, checking for messages. She was relieved to see a note from Mr. Mitchell, asking her to come to his office as soon as she arrived. She wanted to see him right away, too.

She tucked her croquet tournament and abandoned children's stories under her arm and made her way through the desks to the glassed-in corner office. Behind his desk, Titus Mitchell leaned forward, clutching the telephone in one hand. With the phone's earpiece in his other hand, he gestured her to come inside.

She paused inside the door, but he motioned her to sit, and she perched on the edge of the chair, her stories on her lap. Mitchell paced behind his desk with restless energy, the phone stand in one hand and the earpiece in the other. In his dynamic presence, Amanda felt her resolve shrinking.

He finally hung up the phone and smiled at her. Glancing at the papers in her lap, he said, "Croquet story?"

"Yes. And a feature on the plight of homeless waifs."

He grimaced. "Too depressing. I don't—"

"There's a group of people trying to help. This is an upbeat story, with hope."

"Well, lemme see it, and I'll let you know." He held out his hand, and she placed her stories in it. He'd barely glanced at the top page when Eileen, his secretary, opened the door.

"The battle between hired goons filling strikers' jobs in Pittsburgh is getting bloody. Details are starting to come through on the ticker tape," she said.

"I'll be right out." He looked at Amanda and said, "I want you to interview Edith Barnett about the Women's Works Program."

"Yes, sir."

"And see what you can find out about the Boston Relief Committee's plan to distribute food to the poor."

"We did a story on BRC last week."

He shrugged. "Then find a new angle."

"Mr. Mitchell, I. . ." Amanda's fingers tensed in her lap, and she chided herself for tending to stammer.

Mitchell, now standing at the door, glanced at the activity in the newsroom, then turned his gray eyes on her. "Yes?"

She sat straighter in her chair, gathering her courage. "I'd like to do a big story. Something that will be different from anything the *Chronicle* has ever done."

"And I assume you have that big story figured out?"

"As a matter of fact, yes," she said. "Many papers, even ours, have run stories about Germany's prosperity and growth since they elected Adolf Hitler. Clean streets, happy people, all with jobs, and order from the chaos they used to have."

"Yes, so? That's not news."

She leaned forward. "It's not true." She saw that he was going to argue, so she quickly added, "Not all of it."

He hardened his mouth around the word, "Propaganda?" He stepped closer to her. "We don't print propaganda!"

"No, of course not," she agreed. "I think we just don't have the complete story."

"And you, I suppose, can get this complete story?" He looked at her as one would at a child who'd just said she'd had breakfast with President Roosevelt.

With quiet but firm resolution, she said, "My mother's sister and family live in a small town near Berlin. They're Jewish, and from their letters I know it's not all peaches and cream there. I intend to bring back the real story."

"Girlie, you're good at what you do. Stick to fashion and society news. If there are sinister happenings in Germany, it'll get back to us. Besides, if what you say is true, it could be risky."

"I know there's a story there, and I can cover it because I have sources the correspondents there don't have. I'll write a story that will touch our readers' hearts."

He craned his neck to see if the Teletype story had started coming. "No Germany trip. You don't even have an expense account. You think I'd send you on a wild goose chase halfway across the world?" He turned and shook his head in disbelief.

"I'll cover the expenses myself, and when I bring you my story, I want a byline, and better assignments."

He laughed. "Amanda, girl, you just want a vacation." She stood as a crowd gathered around the ticker-tape machine. He left to get the tape as it came ticking out and didn't look back at her.

Amanda stomped back to her desk. He'd laughed at her! This was the last straw. She found a paper sack in the supply closet and began dumping her personal belongings from her desk. After several phone attempts, she found a boat going to Europe in two days. She'd have to share a cabin, but that was fine with her. She typed a letter to her aunt Esther to tell her she was coming and a note to Mr. Mitchell.

She went home to pack, vowing to bring back a story that would knock the socks off Mr. Titus Mitchell, make people think, and earn her a headline and a place on his reporting staff. There were respected women journalists in this world. It was time for the *Boston Chronicle* to enter the twentieth century.

As she drove up the curving driveway at home, she braced herself for the scene that would follow when she told her mother and father of her plans.

Curley touched down at the airfield near Washington at 10:15 A.M. and taxied to a parking area as directed by the ground crew. He shut down the engine, grabbed his duffel bag, and climbed out onto the tarmac. The flight-line sergeant asked, "Any problems with this ship we need to look after?"

"No. No problems. She's a good little plane."

A soldier drove up in a pickup truck, leaped out, and saluted. Curley tossed his duffel bag in the back and they drove to the flight operations building, where Curley logged in, then to the headquarters building.

In the latrine, he took off his flight suit, put on his uniform, and combed his hair. A quick look in the mirror told him he was presentable.

In the general's anteroom he waited on a stiff wooden chair. Finally, the secretary announced that General Franklin would see him. Curley took a deep breath and marched into the general's office. He saluted and said, "James Lee Cameron reporting as ordered, sir."

In his early forties, General Franklin had close-cropped hair with a touch of gray at the temples, and a thick mustache covered his upper lip. Curley stood, legs spaced apart, hands behind his back, watching the general scrutinize him with the eye of a man sizing up a new team player. "Captain," he said, "drag up a chair and make yourself comfortable. How about a cup of coffee?"

"Thank you, sir."

General Franklin touched a button and before Curley got the chair pulled toward the large desk, his secretary rushed in, then out again to fetch the coffee.

The general settled back in his chair. "Captain, I have a mission that requires a special man. You're one of our best pilots, you know as much about the planes as the mechanics, and you've shown yourself to be, shall we say, adventuresome. I've followed your career and feel you're the man for the job. Are you interested? Before you answer, you should know that if you decline, it won't be held against you."

Curley took a quick breath, curious about the assignment, then answered, "Yes, sir, I'm interested."

"Good. Now here's the plan: Our English friends tell us the Germans are starting to rearm in violation of the Treaty of Versailles and are building their air force back up." The general leaned forward and said, "I've made arrangements with the RAF. Your mission, in an unofficial capacity, will be to travel into Germany and find out what you can. Bring back facts and figures. Report to no one but me when you return.

"While in England you will study German terrain and politics. Also, an instructor will teach you phrases and as much German language as you can absorb in ten days. Your unofficial duties will be as a civilian delivering a Vega to Holland. You've been checked out on the 247. It's been equipped with extra gas tanks and fuel diverters. You'll be on the crew taking it to England tomorrow afternoon. Any questions?"

Besides the thrill of flying the big new 247, Curley had lots of questions. For one thing, he knew that a military man out of uniform and in civilian clothes sent into another country could be shot as a spy. But then, Germany was not an enemy. He asked, "What's my time period for this surveillance?"

"Take as long as you need, within reason. I expect you to use some of that ingenuity you displayed while you were a cadet."

By the glint of amusement in the general's eyes, Curley knew he meant the weekend air shows he participated in every chance he got. He nodded. "Yes, sir."

That afternoon he visited the Post Exchange and bought slacks, a shirt, a jacket, and a suitcase to put them in. The next afternoon he stowed his duffel bag full of military clothes in the base locker. Wearing his flight suit, he carried his new suitcase filled with civilian clothes onto the big 247.

Chapter Three

Perched on the edge of her bed, Amanda frowned over her open suitcase, stuffed with so many clothes the lid wouldn't close. Victoria sat cross-legged, resting her back against the headboard, her white batiste nightgown stretched over her knees. The turmoil that had followed Amanda's announcement of her trip to Germany hadn't fazed Victoria; she was elated over Amanda's adventure.

Amanda, however, swallowed hard, bravely choosing clothes for the trip, while her heart was in chaos. She grieved at the rift between her and her father, but she felt a strong need to prove she was a person in her own right.

Victoria picked up a peach-colored sweater from a pile beside the suitcase. "I can see you strolling the deck, looking out over the ocean. A handsome man comes up." She caressed the soft wool with a faraway, dreamy look. "You shiver slightly, he whips off his jacket and puts it across your shoulders. You. . ."

Amanda rolled her eyes. "There's a full moon, a zillion stars, and the man looks like Clark Gable. Which movie did you see that in?"

Victoria dropped the sweater on the bed "No, silly, it's Delbert! He's as handsome as Gable!" She leaned forward and looked into Amanda's face. "Just think of it—this could be your honeymoon trip!" She sat back, grinning.

Amanda solemnly studied the clothes stacked in the suitcase. She slipped her hand between two skirts and carefully pulled one out. "The only men paying any attention to me will be the porter carrying these suitcases and the dining room waiter," she said, balancing the skirt on the discard pile.

Victoria expelled a long sigh and clasped her hands behind her head, lifting her hair. Blond curls bounced beside her sparkling eyes. "Delbert can put his arm around me anytime!"

"Victoria!"

"What? I'm sixteen, and I've been kissed. Lots of times."

Amanda paused with her hand on the suitcase. "Oh? When?"

Victoria looked at the ceiling and pursed her lips as if trying to remember all of them. Amanda eyed her suspiciously as the door opened and their mother came in, a worried expression chiseling a vertical line between her eyebrows.

Amanda's throat tightened at her mother's pained expression. Holding in her churning emotions, she turned and shut the suitcase with a click of finality.

"Amanda," her mother began, "please. . ."

"Mom, it's all right." Leaning over the closed suitcase, she bit her upper lip to keep control. If she explained once more, would her mother understand? She touched her mother's shoulder and said, "Please believe me, Mom. This is something I have to do."

Her mother's eyes misted over. "But it's so sudden, and your father. . ."

"I know," Amanda said softly, "Dad doesn't understand; but I'll be fine. Really.

I'll be with Aunt Esther and Uncle Jacob, and I'll write as soon as the ship docks in London."

Her mother still looked worried, but Amanda knew that she was looking forward to hearing firsthand news of her family.

Although her mother had left the Jewish faith when she married Amanda's father, the ties between the two families had remained strong down through the years, and they had visited back and forth, the children spending summers together with one family or another. In fact, it was during one of those summers that Amanda's nanny, Miss Whitney, had taken Amanda and her cousin Martha with her to church, and both girls had accepted Christ as their Savior. Amanda smiled, remembering, and the tiny lines that puckered her mother's forehead disappeared. "Well," her mother said, "so long as you're with your aunt and uncle, I suppose you'll be all right."

The next morning Amanda, her mother, and sister rode to the pier in a taxi. Her father, unwilling to condone any part of her crazy notion, had said his good-byes at the front door. He'd given Amanda a stiff hug and slipped two fifty-dollar bills into her hand.

On board the ship, Victoria eyed each of the passengers, looking for celebrities; and quite a few male heads turned toward her youthful attractiveness.

At Amanda's cabin, they found suitcases on one bed and a cosmetic bag open with a turquoise scarf lying beside it on the dresser. Her mother agreed the cabin was "nice," but insisted that Amanda should have it to herself. "And you didn't bring enough clothes," she added.

"Mother, I have to carry both suitcases. What would I do with a trunk?"

"There are ways. Porters are everywhere."

Amanda put her arm across her mother's shoulders. "Look at it this way. At least Uncle Jacob won't think I'm moving in."

Her mother's eyes grew teary. Amanda hugged her and said, "I'll be all right, Mom. Really."

"I hope so," her mother said, dabbing at her eyes as she looked at Amanda sadly.

Victoria took Amanda's hand. "It's not too late for me to come along." Before Amanda could say anything, she continued, "I know I don't have clothes, but we could go shopping in London. Wouldn't that be a lark?"

Her mother smiled weakly and took Victoria's hand. "You're coming home with me. I'm not letting both my girls go away at once."

Amanda walked them to the ramp, and they said their last good-byes. A few minutes later the ship moved away from the shore. She'd been on many departing ships, but this time it seemed as though the ship sliding away from the shore was like fate, pulling her away from her family toward a new destiny. The shouts of the crowd faded away as they receded with the harbor, until her mother and sister were no longer distinguishable.

Swept along in the swarm of exhilarated passengers leaving the rail, she left them at the hallway to her cabin, while they headed for a party in the ballroom. The hallway was deserted except for a young mother holding the hand of a toddling little boy. They nodded and Amanda continued on.

Inside her cabin, the feeling of unreality was underscored by the ship's gentle swaying. Amanda sat on her bed, absorbing the almost monastic solitude. After a moment she reached inside her carryall bag for her notebook and pen. She'd really done it; she had asserted her independence and was bound for Germany.

She slowly rotated the top of the pen between her teeth, lost in thought. Her bravado had carried her through the past two days, strengthening her to stand up to her father's disapproval, disarm her mother's worry, and laugh off her sister's fantasies. Thoughts bombarded her in a crazy mixture of excitement and nervousness. She had to succeed. She couldn't go back without her "big story."

She had no intention of failing. This was her most important assignment, even if she had delegated herself; and she'd write the best story of her career.

She opened her notebook and wrote in bold letters at the top of the page: "GERMANY, THE REAL STORY," then underneath, "by Amanda Chase."

A few lines lower she wrote: "HITLER—LIBERATOR OR TYRANT?" Too strong. She had no proof of the vague rumors she'd heard. Besides, reports touted him for miraculously bringing order and justice to the chaotic German politics and economy.

She crossed that headline out and wrote "GERMANY, A MODERN-DAY UTOPIA" and a subtitle, "Or Does a Secret Shame Mar the Image?" She smiled. For now, that would do. She imagined a front-page headline, with inches and inches of story and a photograph beneath her byline.

She hung up her clothes in the small closet and folded her underwear in the dresser. Her Bible went on the nightstand. Slipping her book, *Guide to Germany,* in her purse, she left. It was time to meet people and find her roommate. There must be Germans on board, and she intended to meet and interview them.

After seeing his wife and two daughters off, Amanda's father sat in his drawing room, drumming his fingers on the desk, thinking. Amanda had always been a dutiful, obedient daughter. Perhaps the philosophers were right—it wasn't a good idea to educate a girl too much. But she was bright, and he would have been wasteful to restrain her curious mind from exploring all the knowledge she craved.

He moved the inkwell a fraction of an inch, wondering if he should have introduced her to more young men; but he'd been proud when she devoured the business details of the galleries. If she'd been a son, she'd have followed in his footsteps and be running one of them now.

But she was a girl and therefore had led a sheltered life. She'd always traveled with the family and had no idea how dangerous traveling alone could be for a woman. He paced the room, grinding his teeth. *Should have forbidden the impetuous girl to go,* he thought. But he'd tried that, and she lifted her chin in defiance, stating she was free, grown up, and was going.

He stared out the French doors. Reaching a decision, he strode back to his desk and picked up the phone.

Curley and the crew relaxed as the powerful Boeing 247 flew high over the Atlantic Ocean toward England. After the sun set behind them, the blackness was punctuated by stars above and a few weak lights from an occasional boat below.

Motioning to Jim Blake, his copilot, to take over, Curley pulled off his headphones and worked his way to the rear of the plane. He pulled a Coke from the ice cooler, popped off the cap, and took a long swallow. He glanced at his watch: 6:40 P.M. East Coast time. Smith, the other crew member, was stretched out across two of the airplane's seats, asleep.

Curley had been in the cockpit for hours and had no desire for more sitting, so he braced his arm above one of the windows and looked out. These same stars shone over California, where he'd be right now if his orders hadn't taken him east instead.

It had been almost two years since he'd been back west. He'd looked forward to surprising Johnny and Meredith when he flew his Moth onto their airstrip. But he'd have to wait.

A wispy cloud passed the window, disappearing like smoke. He dropped the empty Coke bottle into the box beside the ice chest and went to the other side to look out. Another gauzy cloud flew past, and he had to catch hold of the seat back to maintain his balance as the plane began to climb.

He made his way forward and got into his seat. Blake glanced at him. They were climbing through clouds and the turbulence jabbed at the plane, rocking them in their seats. Curley motioned to Blake to continue taking her up over the problem, while he grabbed the swaying flight chart off its peg and checked the instruments. They were 522 miles east of St. John's in Newfoundland.

The big plane bounced its way up, as if ascending stairs. For ten minutes both pilots fought to hold it steady. Suddenly a vicious blast of wind shoved them sideways, and the right wing dipped, dangerously threatening to send them into a stall.

"We can't climb out! Clouds too high," Curley yelled. "Let's take her down and see if it's better underneath."

They pushed the controls slowly forward, carefully maneuvering the plane down through the turbulence.

"Trouble on engine one," called Blake. Curley looked to his left. Through ice particles flying past, he saw small flames flickering behind the propellers.

"Hold on, baby," he murmured, and eased up on the throttles enough to let the plane glide slightly, yet enough to maintain control. Smith had entered the cockpit and stood, bracing his hands on the ceiling, watching the struggle against the buffeting winds.

According to the altimeter, they were six hundred feet above water. "We'd better bottom out under this storm soon or we'll be in the drink," shouted Smith. With one last jolt as if they'd been spit out, they emerged from the cloud.

They turned southward, staying beneath the cloud, until they found its edge and rose again to higher altitude. Following their radio beacon, they were soon back on course.

They all three sighed in relief and began checking the damage, especially to engine number one. Smith went to the rear, while Blake and Curley checked electrical and pressure gauges.

"Manifold pressure is down," said Curley. Blake nodded. "We can't land and fix her," he added, "so we'd better start lightening our load."

"There's not much cargo back there, sir," said Blake, "but we can toss out seats and fixtures."

"You and Smith get on it, and I'll keep her steady."

"Yes, sir." Jim Blake disengaged himself from his seat and left the cockpit.

Curley shut the traitorous engine down and feathered the propeller to keep the plane on a steady course with the one remaining engine. With over a thousand miles to go, even if they lightened the load, the chances of setting down in England were small. He considered turning back, but the chances of running into the storm behind them checked him.

He felt the surge of lightness as the crewmen reduced the load. When Blake and Smith returned, he said, "One engine is damaged. The plane won't make it unless we lighten her load even more. Only two people are necessary to fly this baby, so as soon as we see a ship, one of us is going to book passage."

"I'm the heaviest," said Smith. "I volunteer."

Curley shook his head. "We're all checked out to fly her, so what we're going to do is draw straws to see who takes a cruise."

Blake pulled out three matches, broke one, and turned aside, arranging them in his fist. Smith pulled the first, a whole match, then Curley drew the short one. "But, sir. . ."

"That's the deal, and there's nothing to say," said Curley. "Now, when you get to Sedley Field, report what happened, and tell them I'll report in as soon as possible. Now let's hope the first ship we come across is a seaworthy vessel heading east."

Handing the controls to Smith, he went aft to secure his suitcase near the cargo door and strapped on a parachute. He scanned the black water below, suddenly engulfed in the horrible image of water closing around him, crushing him. These disturbing anxieties surfaced occasionally, since the day his father's foreman had broken the news of his father's death in a collapsed Arizona cave. Curley was nine at the time. He shook off the gruesome vision, renewing his vow to avoid caves and dark underground chambers. Compared to that, jumping into the darkness below would be a breeze.

On deck, Amanda clutched the railing and hunched her shoulders against the cold wind. Ilsa, her redheaded Norwegian roommate, stood beside her. Ilsa had been curious about Amanda's ubiquitous notebook and pencil, and when she found out Amanda was a reporter, she appointed herself as her assistant. The same age as Victoria, Ilsa proved to be a cheerful companion.

"If my uncle Eric were here, he'd say the wind is charged with the feel of a coming storm," said Ilsa.

"It's whipping up the water." The slap of waves against the side of the boat almost drowned out Amanda's reply. In the four days they'd been collaborating, they had investigated the ship, its operation and crew, and some passengers.

"I followed those two big fellas to the lounge this morning. They spent a lot of time in there. I think they're gangsters."

Amanda moved her hands away from the warm spot they'd made on the railing, then moved them back. "We could interview them and ask them."

"But, they wouldn't tell us! I think we should. . ."

". . .give those two wide berth," said Amanda. "I'm more interested in interviewing the Mexican acrobats who are going to entertain us tonight."

"Remember, you said I could come with you."

"Right. Now let's get back to our room and go over our list of questions."

That night, after the acrobats finished their show and two encores, Amanda and Ilsa interviewed them with the handsome purser there to translate. But the father of the talented family spoke some English, giving Amanda good quotes for a story.

While she was asking the age of the youngest girl, an ensign rushed in and urgently tapped the purser on the shoulder, telling him the captain wanted him right away.

Sniffing a story, Amanda quickly thanked the Escobar family and followed the purser to the bridge. Captain McNally and several of his crew held receivers to their ears, listening with great concentration. Amanda's eyes darted from one to the other, trying to figure out whether another ship was in trouble or if dire world news was coming over the radio waves.

"We hear you, N-C-niner-five-five. Go ahead," the captain spoke into the ship-to-ship communications system.

Ilsa tiptoed to the purser and put a light hand on his shoulder. "What's happening?" she asked.

He shook his head and lifted his shoulders, a bewildered look on his face.

"Cut the engines," barked the captain, squinting out into the darkness. "All hands on deck. And spread out."

Amanda stepped back to let them by, then she followed. As soon as they stepped outside, they heard the drone of an approaching airplane.

Chapter Four

Curley communicated to the ship's captain that they'd be overhead shortly. When they approached the ship, Smith said, "Good luck, sir, and don't get wet."

Curley grinned and patted the suitcase tied to his parachute harness. "Hey, in my barnstorming days I could jump from a thousand feet and land on a nickel."

Smith opened the passenger door. The lights of the ship came closer, and Curley shouted, "See you at Sedley." He pushed himself into the night air and relished the brief silence.

"One thousand. . .two thousand. . .three thousand. . . PULL!" His right arm reached across his chest, found the rip cord, and yanked. He felt the jerk and then the bobbling motion of the chute opening. He looked up in satisfaction at the white canopy overhead. Below, a ring of lights glowed on a cleared area near the ship's stern, and he settled into his harness, preparing for landing.

Sensing a good story, Amanda raced down to her cabin and snatched up her camera and flashbulbs. She was back on deck in time to see four crewmen setting up a fifteen-foot circle of lights on the promenade deckhouse roof. A crowd had gathered, murmuring baffled comments as they watched the sailors.

Amanda spotted Ilsa on the roof, waving at her and tugging on the purser's sleeves. He gestured to the men at the bottom of the steps holding back the crowd, and they let Amanda by.

She snapped pictures of crewmen standing around the lighted area looking up. A large plane roared overhead and in a few seconds a chutist drifted toward them, his parachute a white dot in the dark sky. She focused on the man floating down. But he was still only a white dot in her lens.

"I hope he doesn't land in the water!" cried Ilsa.

"If he's good, and if the wind is right, he'll land right here," said the purser, quickly looking away from Ilsa's shining eyes.

Amanda hoped this man was as skilled as some of the experts she'd seen at air shows. She watched, fascinated, as the man skillfully maneuvered directly over the lighted circle. She snapped his picture. He came closer. She popped a bulb in the flash in time to snap his feet hitting the deck. She shot another as his parachute drifted down around him, and he quickly gathered it up. The crowd on the deck below applauded.

Amanda's finger froze on the shutter release. She lowered the camera to get a better look. Curley Cameron! It was really him! She pulled her gaze away, aware that she was gawking. With trembling fingers, she picked up the spent flashbulbs at her feet.

The crew had gathered around Curley, congratulating him as he loosed himself from the parachute harness. Ilsa pulled herself away from the purser and whispered to Amanda, "Oooh, would you look at him?!"

Amanda did look. She blushed, remembering back almost seven years. She had been seventeen. Her father had taken her to an air show near New York, where Curley Cameron was billed as "Curley the Kid—the young daredevil from the Wild West." He'd flown his plane in the most outrageous loops and madcap upside-down tricks, making her almost swoon with fright that he might crash, but afraid to tear her eyes away.

After the show, at a reception in her father's country club, she was introduced to him. He charmed her so thoroughly that later she haggled with a girl who'd bought his picture from a hawker and had brought it to the reception; Amanda finally persuaded her to trade the picture for Amanda's beaded purse. After that, she saved newspaper articles about him and pinned them up in her dormitory room when she returned to school in Paris a month later.

That had been so long ago, a silly schoolgirl crush. She thought she'd forgotten the appealing young man with the dimpled smile. Apparently she hadn't. She gazed at him for a moment, noticing that the years had been good to him; he looked more handsome and rugged than the eighteen-year-old she remembered.

He still had a friendly face with eyes that seemed to have a perpetual teasing light in them. His dark red hair was combed back and trimmed neatly over his ears. As if drawn by a magnet, his eyes looked directly at her. She could feel a pulse throbbing in her neck, and she raised a hand to her throat as if to still it. Then he looked away and the moment passed.

"Oh, Amanda! He looked right at me!" Ilsa grabbed Amanda's sleeve. "Come on! Let's get closer."

Amanda dropped the spent bulbs into a sack in her camera bag. He hadn't recognized her. *Of course, why should he?* she asked herself. But still, an odd twinge of disappointment nudged her. She shook it off, coming back to reality.

"Amanda!" Ilsa's urgent tugging amused Amanda, reminding her of Victoria's methods of coercion. "This is a scoop! A big story," she added. "Come on!"

Amanda snapped her camera bag shut and followed Ilsa through the shipmen surrounding Curley. He had taken off his parachute and knelt as he packed it neatly together. As there was nothing more for the crew to do, they drifted away, back to their work. The captain, purser, and an engineer remained, talking with Curley, their backs to Amanda and Ilsa.

Ilsa tapped the purser on his shoulder. "Where's he from?" she whispered.

"Looks American," he said.

". . .and I'll debark at your first port. . ." Curley's gaze slid past the captain to Ilsa, then Amanda. He stood up, the smile in his eyes revealing his delight at seeing them. "And what part of the crew are these lovely ladies?"

The captain stood back and nodded at Amanda. "This is Miss Amanda Chase, passenger and reporter," he nodded at Ilsa, "and this is Miss Ilsa Johnson, passenger and Ambassador of Cheer."

"Pleased to meet you both," he said, dipping his head slightly.

Amanda's jaw dropped in surprise for a second, before she could catch her breath. He was taller than she'd remembered, at least six-foot-three, somehow more athletic-looking, with wide shoulders looking as hard as granite beneath his flight suit.

The captain gestured with his hand to Curley. "And I'd like to introduce you to Curley Cameron, our newest passenger."

Ilsa eagerly reached out her hand, but instead of a formal handshake, Curley gave it a gentle squeeze. He glanced at Amanda for a second, then gave Ilsa a smile that made her grin and lift her shoulders in a childlike gesture of delight.

"No need to stand out here in the cold," said the captain, leading them toward the steps. Amanda clutched her sweater closer, realizing that the night wind had become chilly.

She couldn't think of a good reason to follow them, but she smelled a story too good to pass up. A few of the passengers who had lingered congratulated Curley as they walked toward the cabin-class promenade. One woman thanked the captain for the splendid show and asked why he hadn't announced it the day before so more passengers could enjoy it. Curley grinned and said he was glad she'd enjoyed it. As they walked on, he winked at Amanda and Ilsa, as though they shared a private joke.

Amanda boldly met his eyes, denying to herself the feeling that the temperature had just gone up ten degrees. She looked away, mentally concentrating on a headline: *The Man Who Dropped From the Sky.* Yes, that might do.

The ship shuddered as its great gears were engaged, moving forward again through the sea toward its first stop in France. Clutching the camera bag strap, Amanda braced her feet to steady herself. But there seemed no way to steady her mixed emotions.

Amanda and Ilsa stopped at the corridor to their cabin, and the men paused to wish them a good night.

"Mr. Cameron, I'd like to talk with you about your flying and parachuting adventures, if I may," said Amanda.

"It would be my pleasure," he answered.

They made arrangements to meet for breakfast the next morning before her ten o'clock interview with a baroness.

In the hallway back to their room, Ilsa danced in front of Amanda, skipping backward. "Let's go to the lounge. I'm too wound up to turn in!" she squeaked.

"You go on ahead. I have to plan my interview with the redoubtable Mr. Cameron."

"Plan? Don't be silly! Just ask whatever comes into your head."

"Goodness, no! I have to think of all the possible directions the interview could go and be prepared."

"Well, if you must," said Ilsa, with her hands on her hips and shaking her head, "go ahead, but at least come when you're through. I'll save a place for you."

Amanda sighed. "I might, but don't get your hopes up." Before Ilsa rounded the corner behind her, Amanda had pulled out her notepad and was scribbling: *What were you doing up there? Why did you parachute out? Did you have to? Why in the middle of the Atlantic Ocean? Was the plane in trouble?* By the time she got back to her room, she already had half a dozen questions.

She sat, looking out the porthole to the silver-lined clouds, reminding herself that she was grown up now. After all these years, the great Curley Cameron held no more appeal. Besides, he had obviously changed. That thought took her in the dangerous direction of his more manly, stronger appearance that made him infinitely more handsome and desirable than ever. *Headline, headline,* she told herself. *Airline Passenger Prefers Ocean Liner Luxury.* Too long. She couldn't concentrate.

Curley settled himself in the small cabin on a lower deck and stowed his flight suit in the bottom of his suitcase. What a day! He'd have to write to Johnny and Meredith to tell them that their prayers were working. They never failed to mention they were praying for him. *Well,* he thought, *this was one time I really needed it. If the ship hadn't been right in our path, and if the storm had covered more area than we'd thought, or if—*

He shook his head free of the negative thoughts and looked around the cabin. One room with a bunk, a desk and chair, a small closet with a dresser inside it, and a rest room just big enough to turn around in. He wouldn't spend much time in here anyway, because on the other side of the door was one great big ship to explore. The purser had given him a chart of the accommodations.

He set his suitcase inside the closet, then picked up the chart and went out to find if there was somewhere to get a bite to eat at ten o'clock. He found a small bar on B deck, where passengers in "lesser accommodations" gathered to socialize.

He ordered a roast beef sandwich and a Coke and sat on a stool watching a young couple swaying together on the small dance floor. A plaintive song tinkled from the player piano in the corner. *This is probably their honeymoon voyage,* he thought.

He took a swig of Coke and narrowed his eyes, thinking. He'd have to get out of the interview with that reporter girl. The expression in her eyes when he looked up from his parachute startled him. He'd felt the strangest glimmer of recognition, something familiar about her he couldn't place. But that couldn't be. He'd never have forgotten a girl like her. But there was something, and it bothered him.

Too bad she was a reporter. A journalist was like a dog after a bone going for an interview. If she was reporting the story for some shipboard chronicle, it would be harmless, but if the story were to somehow get into the *real* newspapers, it could mean trouble for his mission. Since he couldn't dodge her forever, maybe he could invent some boring story that wouldn't capture her interest.

The piano stopped playing, and the young husband sauntered over to start a new tune. As Curley idly watched, he overheard a man speculating with the bartender why a man would parachute onto the ship. He had to reconsider letting the girl interview him, he realized; it would be too difficult to make his story boring.

❧

Though she was tempted, Amanda decided that bringing Ilsa to her interview with Curley would be cowardly. He couldn't know that she'd idolized him, even if he did remember her. So, arriving alone at the twelve-foot-high double doors of the fashionable cabin-class dining saloon, she asked the steward to escort her to Curley's table. The aromas of coffee, freshly baked rolls, and eggs floated around Amanda, reminding her she was very hungry.

Curley held the chair for her, then sat across from her. "I'm starving. How about interviewing after we eat?"

His smile disarmed her nervousness, and she set her notebook and purse aside. "I wouldn't want to have to write the obituary of a man who starved to death giving an interview."

"Good." Curley glanced up into her eyes, entranced by the mixed shades of amber and green ringed by black lashes, and felt another strange glimmer of recognition. Something in her manner was vaguely disturbing. *Why is she looking at me like that?*

The waiter poured coffee for them and took their order. She asked him about his work, and he told her about his love of flying. She told him about newspaper reporting.

He asked her where she was going, and she told him of her aunt and uncle in Eisenburg. She glanced at the tables nearby to be sure no one was eavesdropping. "Mr. Hitler is getting so much good publicity these days, it makes one wonder how much of it is true." She lowered her voice and leaned forward. "I have sources that indicate otherwise."

He leaned forward and matched her soft voice. "Sounds like a daring adventure!"

Amanda sat up stiffly, feeling she might have revealed too much. "Oh, no. I've gone all over to get a story—even some very scary places." She sipped her coffee to capture her composure and asked, "So, what's your business in Europe?"

"Are we officially starting the interview?" he asked.

"Might as well." She pulled a pencil from her purse and picked up her tablet. Flipping the cover to her page of questions, she read the first one: "What is your full name?"

"Curley Cameron, at your service, ma'am."

She paused and looked up at him. "Is Curley the name on your birth certificate?"

"No, but I've been called Curley as long as I can remember, and it fits me better than the other, more proper names."

"Well, it'll do, I guess. So, Mr. Cameron. . ."

"Curley."

"So, Curley, where were you headed when you found yourself directly over this ocean liner?"

His eyes caught and held hers, which she found vaguely disturbing. "You're asking which direction I was going?"

"Yes."

"To Europe, same as you. How long have your aunt and uncle lived in Eisenburg?"

"I'm the one doing the interviewing."

He cocked his eyebrows and shrugged his shoulders. "Okeydokey."

His reaction amused her. "Aunt Esther and Uncle Jacob have been in Eisenburg for eight years while they've been operating my father's art gallery. Were you one of the flight crew on that plane?"

"In a manner of speaking."

"Please elaborate." She looked at him, waiting for his answer.

"Look," he said, "maybe I want to know where my story and picture are going to appear. Who do you work for?"

She nodded. "A fair question. I work for the *Boston Chronicle.* That's where I'll send the story."

"Hmm." His dark eyebrows slanted in a frown as he considered this. Suddenly, as if the sunshine overcame the darkening doubts, his lips turned up in a grin, and he nodded. "All right."

His appealing smile almost made her forget her questions. She stared at him, unable to say a word.

"How about if I just tell you what happened, and you can ask what you want when I'm through."

She nodded. "Fine. Begin."

"I was one of a crew of men bringing the new Boeing 247 to England, when we hit a storm north of here. One of our engines was damaged and we had to lighten the load. Finally one of us had to abandon the plane. This vessel was the first one we contacted, and luckily it wasn't going west. We contacted the captain, and here I am."

Amanda listened and made notes. The story seemed too smooth somehow, too convenient. He was leaving something out. "Were there passengers aboard?"

"No. How long are you going to be in Eisenburg?" He watched her with great interest, and she had to fight an impulse to lean closer toward him. *What a frustrating man!* He was distracting her from probing further into his story.

She clenched her jaw and wrote the headline, "Abandon Plane!" circling it. Keeping her tone even, she asked, "Who do you work for?"

He stood. "I wouldn't want to make any bad publicity for my bosses, now would I?" He came around the table and stood behind her chair, ready to pull it out when she stood.

Amanda made no attempt to stand. She stubbornly held her notebook up with the pencil poised over it. He leaned over her shoulder and said softly, "We can continue out on the deck." Her cheek grew warm where his breath softly fanned it. She didn't dare turn her head; his face was too close to hers. She was more tempted than offended.

Snapping her notebook shut, she grabbed her purse and stood. He held the chair out for her, and with his hand under her elbow, guided her out of the elegant dining room.

I used to dream of being with him, she thought. *But in my dreams he was mellower, more agreeable. Reality is like having a wildcat by the tail.* She fought the impulse to walk away, yet she didn't want to lose a good story.

Chapter Five

The feel of Curley's hand on her arm warmed Amanda as they walked out into the sunshine. A fresh, salt-scented breeze fanned them as they made their way across the gently rolling deck, passing other passengers who didn't recognize Curley as the man who had parachuted from the sky the night before. In his dark pants, blue shirt, and pullover sweater, Amanda thought he looked more the college man than daredevil.

He steered her around a maid walking two little prancing dogs and said, "What drew you to newspaper writing?"

She looked away from his dimpled grin. "It's my way of helping people understand what's happening in this world."

"Ah, yes. The trip to Germany." They stepped close to the rail as a group of children trooped by, herded by a buxom young woman wearing sturdy shoes. She nodded to Amanda, glanced at Curley, and dropped her gaze, then shouted to the children to keep up with her. She was the ship's junior activity organizer. Amanda had interviewed her on her first day aboard. Though she looked like a girl, the young woman was twenty-nine years old.

"So, where were we?" asked Curley.

She opened her notebook to a blank page. "We were talking about careers. So, what made you decide to fly airplanes?" Her thoughts traveled back to his wild air show escapades. It was on the tip of her tongue to tell him that she'd seen him then, but she decided not to. Maybe later, when she got to know him a little better.

He looked out over the sea, squinting at the billowy clouds on the horizon, and lifted his shoulders. "It's something I always knew I'd do." He turned and leaned back, resting his elbows on the railing. "Hung around airplanes till I was old enough to fly. I took to the air as naturally as I breathe."

She forced herself to look away from his dimpled smile and his hazel eyes that danced with life and mischief. "I know exactly what you mean," she said, jotting his statement in her notebook.

Curley watched her write, enjoying her nearness. Though he enjoyed women in general, this one intrigued him, with her hypnotic eyes the same green color as the sea. She was exquisitely beautiful, like a soft ribbon of moonlight glowing on the tops of clouds. He never forgot a face, and he knew he'd met her somewhere. It bothered him that he couldn't remember. He'd never had to resort to the old line of asking a girl if they'd met before. He was beginning to think this was the time.

They stood there for a few minutes, while he answered her questions and peppered the conversation with a few of his own.

Amanda's pulse was racing and she bit her lip to force herself to concentrate on the interview. A middle-aged man in a bad mood and a suit too large asked if they'd seen the steward. They hadn't, so he grumbled and went to look for him.

She'd asked Curley all her questions, and there was nothing more to say. But she didn't want the interview to end. She looked at her watch and gasped. It was 9:45.

"What's the matter? Coaches don't turn into pumpkins until midnight," he said, devastating her with that smile again.

She snapped her notebook shut with the pencil inside and shoved it into her purse. "I have to interview a baroness in fifteen minutes."

"Time not only passes, it flies sometimes, doesn't it?"

Amanda smiled, feeling comfortable with him. "Definitely."

Curley drew in a deep, shaky breath and guided her across the white scrubbed boards, past the linoleum stairway, down to the second-class deck, to the elevators. Each elevator had a bas-relief motif signifying its destination. The library elevator had open books over the door; a smoking cigar noted the smoking lounge. The one to the swimming pool was adorned with mermaids and shells. She entered that one, and he held the door open.

He leaned inside. "I'd like to escort you to the banquet and ball tonight. What do you say?"

He looked like a hopeful teenager asking for his first date. "You haven't finished the interview," he added.

She felt a strange tugging on her heart. "All right. That would be nice."

Curley grinned and let the filigreed door shut. He liked a decisive woman. "I'll be at your cabin at eight o'clock," he said, raising his head to follow the elevator's upward glide.

Her few words, "But you don't know my. . . ," were lost in her ascent. He stood, looking up with a happy grin on his face. "Don't worry. I'll find you." The library elevator landed with a thunk. Curley smiled and whistled a tune as he passed the opening door.

❧

Amanda hurried to the heated pool, where the baroness and her personnel occupied the stern end of the pool. The water faintly lapped against the blue and gold mosaic tiles. At the other end a waterfall cascaded over a series of lighted steps that made the water sparkle as it fell. A few swimmers were enjoying the pool, while some sat sipping champagne and showing off their French designer bathing suits.

Amanda took in the atmosphere and stored it in her memory for story background. She approached the baroness, who was as slim as a fashion model and attired in an elegant black cape over her silver bathing suit.

❧

After the interview, Amanda went back to her room and raised the blinds the maid had shut. Ilsa had been there and changed clothes. What she'd worn at breakfast was carelessly tossed on her bed. Amanda smiled, thinking of Victoria, and sat at the writing desk to compose her notes and impressions before she forgot them. She gazed out at the darkening clouds and composed headlines. *Baroness Bares All*. . . No maybe not; she giggled, thinking someone might get the wrong idea, and wrote a few more titles.

Soon it was time to meet Ilsa for tea. She folded her notes and put them in a large envelope and wrote "Baroness" on it, then freshened up in the bathroom and left.

In the Grand Lounge Ilsa sat at a table near a bank of palm fronds. With her sat a tall, very handsome blond man dressed in white pants and striped shirt. He stood and pulled Amanda's chair out for her.

Ilsa's eyes sparked with delight as she introduced Nels Thordahl. His white eyelashes fringed sapphire blue eyes. "I am so glad to meet you," he replied with a Scandinavian accent, vigorously shaking her hand.

Ilsa could barely contain her excitement. "Nels won a tennis championship, next year he might play in Wimbledon, he's from Bergen, close to my hometown, and—"

Amanda had to laugh at the expression on Nels's face. He was nodding in agreement, and he didn't take his eyes off Ilsa.

Amanda declined the turtle soup the waiter offered, choosing cucumber sandwiches and a spoonful of cashew nuts instead. She glanced across the lounge, but didn't see Curley. On the bandstand a clarinetist stood, performing his solo part as the small band played "Bye, Bye Blackbird."

Ilsa and Nels continued to describe the beauties of Norway, and Amanda promised to visit someday.

Though happy for Ilsa, who'd said she wanted a shipboard romance, Amanda felt like an old-maid aunt at their party. A short, dainty woman in a shiny pink dress passed their table, followed by a middle-aged man with dark wavy hair. The woman's strappy shoes matched her dress. This woman would be a knockout at the Grand Ball, and Amanda wondered which of her two evening dresses she should wear.

As if Ilsa had read her mind, she said, "Nels is going to be our escort to the ball tonight!"

Amanda smiled into their eager faces and said, "How gallant! But, I have an escort, thank you." A vision of Curley's boyish grin between the elevator doors brought a warm glow to her cheeks.

Ilsa sat straight up in her chair, almost knocking off the tray of hot scones, strawberry preserves, and clotted cream the waiter was placing on their table. "Who? Who? No! Let me guess!" She gazed upward and frowned thoughtfully, then beamed with delight. "The man from the sky! Right?"

"Right." Amanda glanced at her watch. "I have a lot of things to do between now and then, so I'll see you later, at the cabin." Nels quickly rose and moved her chair back for her.

Amanda chose her dusky rose satin dress with a ruffled collar that dipped low in the back. Ilsa wore black. They stood side by side before the green marble counter in their bathroom. Amanda patted loose powder on her nose, while Ilsa leaned forward to stroke pink lipstick on her pursed lips.

Pulling on her earlobe, Amanda winced. "I shouldn't have let you talk me into buying these earrings. This one pinches!"

"Here, let me fix it for you."

Amanda unclipped it, just as someone rapped on their door. She went to answer it while Ilsa concentrated on bending the earring wire to loosen it.

Amanda opened the door and gasped. Curley stood in the hallway in a black tuxedo made of some soft-looking material over a pleated white shirt with a black tie at his neck. Abruptly, she dropped her gaze, embarrassed to be caught staring, and invited him in. She caught the masculine scent of his cologne as he passed her.

Curley crossed the threshold into definitely feminine territory and held out a white gardenia corsage. He breathed deeply. "It smells nice in here." The room smelled like a rose and lavender garden, mingled now with the scent of gardenia.

Ilsa came out from the bathroom with the earring. "Hello, again," she said to Curley.

"Hello." He gulped to quell the dizzy sensation racing through him as Amanda in her shimmery floor-length gown fastened the gardenia to her dress. Most of her thick dark hair was piled high on her head, with a cascade of curls laying against her creamy skin. He was entranced by the graceful way her hands moved as she tilted her head and clipped on the earring.

She picked up her beaded bag. Another visitor knocked on the door and Ilsa started toward it. She stopped, lifted her head in dignified control, and walked slowly to answer it.

The four of them stepped off the elevator into a chattering crowd in the grand lounge. Some of the gowns were elegant, some scandalously revealing, and all very expensive. Jewels glittered everywhere. One woman had a diamond necklace so large it lay over her bosom like a sparkling bib.

A deep gong echoed through the room, announcing that the banquet was served. Curley escorted Amanda into the first-class dining saloon. The diners' entrance was like a grand procession. The orchestra played a lush Jerome Kern melody, with cymbals and trumpets punctuating the violins. The baroness entered, looking regal in a slim evening gown of gold lace. Her retinue strode behind her in the wake of her grandeur. She and one of her companions separated themselves from the group and went to the captain's table.

Ilsa and Nels found their table, then Curley guided Amanda to the captain's table, where he pulled out a chair for her. She nodded to acknowledge the baroness and sat down. The man across from her looked like an aging movie star. He dominated the conversation with a story about a recent safari in Africa.

After the appetizers were cleared away, the stewards scurried around the table with dove breasts in ginger-flavored aspic. The woman with the aging actor took up a lull in his conversation and leaned toward Curley. "I didn't catch your name," she said. Her neckline dipped dangerously low.

Amanda turned her head to avoid the view, and Curley kept his eyes riveted on the woman's face. He nodded toward Amanda and said, "Amanda Chase. And I'm James Cameron."

"Sit back, darling." The actor gently touched her bare shoulder, and she relaxed in her seat with a petulant frown on her pretty lips.

"What do you do, Mr. Cameron?" asked the man.

"Oh, a little of this and a little of that," shrugged Curley. "Nothing as exciting and courageous as your exploits."

The man leaned sideways slightly so the steward could remove one plate and place another before him. With a bored look, he answered, "It gets tiresome sometimes, and one longs for home and hearth. You know?"

"Have you ever been to Poland?" asked Curley.

This set the man off on another story that lasted through the main course, sorbet, and into dessert.

Amanda longed to ask the man if he was an actor, but decided that if he was, she should know his name; and if he was nobility or a wealthy businessman, he'd be offended. She smiled at his lovely companion, who kept glancing at Curley with a hungry look. Curley nodded at the right places in the man's story and seemed interested, but the moment Amanda glanced at him, he winked at her and reached beneath the table to grasp her hand.

She took a deep breath to maintain her poise, but a stir of something deep in her heart pushed her emotions off balance. She looked down the table, catching the eye of the baroness, who raised her eyebrows inquisitively.

At last the dinner was over and the crowd made its way to the grand ballroom. Curley put his hand on Amanda's slim waist and guided her through the moving stream of people. When the guests turned right, he steered her to the left, toward a balcony-type landing with an arched window. A cool ocean breeze drifted in from the black sky and ocean.

He put his hands on her upper arms, and in the shadowy light his features softened. He looked too good to be true. *No wonder the woman across the table from us couldn't keep her eyes off him,* thought Amanda. He was one of those rare men who could dress up and look more masculine than ever.

"Why didn't you tell that man that you're a flier?" she asked. "Especially when he told the story about flying over the Yukon snows to hunt moose?"

Curley chuckled. "He was blowing smoke. You know, telling a yarn. Why rain on the guy's parade? Especially when he's the grand marshal!"

"You skillfully evaded my detailed questions about your flying. There's some reason you don't want to talk about it. You're not shy, are you?" She grimaced, reaching up to unclip her left earring, and rubbed her sore earlobe. He looked so concerned, she smiled back at him. "New earrings," she explained.

He gazed so long at her, watching her closely, that she turned her head in embarrassment. He gently reached out, touched her chin, and turned her head toward him. "I know this may sound like a come-on, but I've met you somewhere before."

Her heart skipped a beat, and she wanted to turn her head away, but she continued to gaze back at him.

He looked past her, out to the black night. "Somewhere, I know it." His eyes focused back on her. "Or maybe it was only in my dreams."

His thumb slowly caressed her arm, and she tried to still her response to the tingling feeling racing through her. She licked her lips. "Actually, we, umm. . ."

His hand slid up to the back of her neck and he drew her toward him, murmuring, "Actually we're here right now, and. . ." His face drew nearer to hers. "And you're more beautiful than any dream I've ever had."

Amanda closed her eyes as the distance between them vanished, and he kissed her.

The warmth of his lips on hers sparked a response that surprised her. She started to raise her hands to lay them on the smooth white shirt front, then stopped herself. As much as she wanted to resist, she found herself rising on her tiptoes, eagerly responding to the delicious sensations she was feeling.

She basked in the glow for a long moment, then realized he wasn't kissing her anymore. Her eyes flew open to see him gazing at her in wonder. He was close, so close she longed to reach up and pull his head down and continue what they'd started. Somewhere inside her a voice warned against letting her feelings control her.

As if sensing her reluctance, he drew back slightly, but he didn't stop staring down at her.

"You," he breathed. "It's so. . .I mean. . ." For once, Curley was at a loss for words. He couldn't tear his gaze away from the moist gentleness of her mouth, the large, soft eyes that showed too much what she was feeling. He'd kissed enough women to know she wanted him to kiss her again, but he was disturbed by the fierce desire that rose up in him to do exactly that.

He framed her face with both of his hands and said, "Are you real, or am I dreaming?" She slowly closed her eyes, interrupting the strong force transmitted through their eyes.

Struggling for control, Amanda stood still, trying to make sense out of what had just happened. But wonderful warm waves of pleasure washing through her made it difficult to think clearly.

He grinned down at her and said, "It's pretty heady stuff out here. Would you like to go see how the other half is celebrating? There's a party on each level."

She nodded, not trusting herself to say a word.

"Come on, then." He held out his hand, and she laid hers in it, allowing him to lead her to the lower levels of the ship.

In the second-class saloon, with its dark paneling showing off floral bouquets in lighted, window-size recessed frames, the passengers were slow dancing to soft music. Curley and Amanda found a table and ordered lemon-lime fizzes. A bowl of chocolate mints and peanuts sat beside a small candle lamp set in the middle of the pink linen tablecloth.

Curley leaned forward and put his hand over hers. "At last I've got you all to myself." He raised his eyes. "Up there, too many people, too much distraction."

Amanda smiled, thinking that being on a real date with her hero, Curley Cameron, was a dream she'd given up ever coming true. But here she was, and it was happening. "I'll let you off the hook tonight," she said, removing the earrings that were still pinching. "But tomorrow we land in France, and it'll be a madhouse from then until we dock in London."

"I'll never be off your hook, Amanda Chase," said Curley. He picked up one of the chocolate mints and slowly held it up to her mouth. She laughed and called him silly, and he slipped the chocolate inside.

Amanda let the sweet dark flavor melt on her tongue for a moment, then said, "I'm going to the church service tomorrow morning. Let's finish the interview right after, all right?"

He smiled and it was as intimate as a caress. "No business tonight. Save a place for me in church. I'll meet you there, then we'll talk."

She studied him thoughtfully for a moment. "Are you a believer?"

"Yes!" he exclaimed, his face shining with glad memories. "I vaguely remember my mother praying, but then she died and my dad and I never went to church. When I was older I met up with some Christians who took me in, gave me a job, and," he shrugged, "God sort of snuck up on me." He shook his head. "No, He was always there, so trusting Him was the most natural thing in the world."

Amanda felt a warm glow settle over her.

Curley stood and grabbed her hand. She slipped her earrings into his tuxedo pocket and followed him.

They went deeper down to the third-class saloon. The air was thick with smoke, and passengers snaked through the room, stepping and swaying to some line dance. The revelers looked so silly to Amanda that she laughed, partly at the scene before her but mostly for the sheer joy of being with Curley.

They stood in the doorway, watching. Curley waved his hands before his face. "If I had a knife, I could cut a path through the smoke so we could enter." He glanced at her, enjoying the sparkle of her smile and her infectious laugh. He chuckled and, with his hand on her elbow, led her back into the hallway.

They climbed to the upper levels, passing a few people at a distance. He'd loosened his tie, and she clung to his arm while they strolled along the deck beside the rail, looking out over the water and talking. The musical hum of the engines and the gentle dip and roll of the deck cradled them in a special moment in time on the Atlantic waters. They told each other of their childhoods, their families, compared likes and dislikes, and found that they had a lot of attitudes and opinions in common.

Curley noticed that there were fewer and fewer people out on the deck, and the ship seemed to glide more quietly through the black swells. He'd never felt so comfortable with a woman, and he didn't want the moment to end. He saw her suppress small shivers, so he put his arm around her as they leaned out over the rail, watching the foam lap against the ship's wall. "Let's stay here and talk all night," he said. "I've never met anyone so easy to talk to."

Amanda watched a sliver of moon lifting from the black horizon. "Your childhood is truly fascinating. It's sad that you were orphaned at such a young age, but the way you followed your dream of flight, making a home in the hangars and eventually with a mechanic. . ." She looked at his strong profile watching the same moonrise. "It's like dime novel stories of a boy running away to join the circus."

He caught her gaze. "It wasn't all as exciting as it sounds." The corners of his mouth lifted in a slight smile. "But I did eventually perform in air circuses."

Amanda opened her mouth to tell him she'd seen him perform, but before she got the chance, he said, "I wish you could have seen my aerobatics. But since the government cracked down on daredevils, we've had to find other ways to get our thrills in the sky."

"Like parachuting onto ships at sea?" Her eyes glowed with speculation in the pale moonlight, and Curley shook his head slowly. "That's the business part, which we'll discuss later."

"Later," she agreed.

"Meanwhile, let's get you back to your cabin for a catnap so you don't fall asleep in church tomorrow."

They strolled slowly back to her cabin, neither one wanting the evening to end. Curley kept a protective arm over her shoulder. "You know," he said, "you're a courageous woman, and I admire that."

"Me? I'm merely working for what I feel is right."

"Not all women would go to such lengths to try to make sense of this crazy world. You're like a missionary."

They stopped at her cabin door. "My mission is to find the truth and reveal it to the world so people can form their own opinions."

"Well said! If you ever run for president, I'll vote for you."

She loved the amusement that flickered in his eyes and the companionship they shared. As she watched, the amusement began to disappear and a contemplative look came into his hazel eyes.

She thought for a moment he was going to kiss her, but he said, "Be careful, princess. Don't trust everything you see in Germany to be as it seems."

"But that's why I'm going!" she said with a smile.

He lifted his brows in acceptance and said, "Just remember. Be careful."

"I'm always careful." She put her hand on the door handle. "Good night, then. And thanks for a wonderful evening."

He quickly brushed his lips over hers and came away with his eyes half closed. "Thank *you,*" he said. She watched him walk away, then she slipped inside the dark cabin. She closed the door softly and leaned against it with a sigh.

Curley felt like skipping, but he settled for a fast trot back to his cabin. A note hastily stuck to his cabin door caught his attention. "Contact Captain McNally immediately." He stuck the note into his pocket and loped down the silent hallway.

A crewman ushered him into the bridge. "The captain has retired for the night, but he asked us to wake him when you arrived." He nodded to the crewman standing at the wheel. "I'll return shortly," he told him. Passing Curley on his way out, he said, "We tried to locate you, but. . ."

Curley locked his hands behind his waist and looked around. In contrast to a cockpit, the bridge seemed spacious. Rows of shiny dials lined one wall, and a gyrocompass and electric telegraph stood against the other.

The crewman at the wheel noted his interest and said, "This is the very latest equipment."

"She's a fine ship indeed," agreed Curley. He squinted at one dial. "This looks like a wind velocity indicator."

"Right. The latest in anemometers."

He was about to say more, but Captain McNally came in, followed by his crewman. The captain was in uniform and looked as if he were rested and ready to face the day. He reached into a drawer near his chair and pulled out a piece of paper. "This came over the telegraph at 0100." He handed it to Curley.

"Captain James Lee Cameron. USN dispatching ship to intercept and retrieve. ETA 0400 hrs." He stared at it for a moment, trying to make sense of it. Why? He planned to dock in France, find an airfield, then report to Sedley in England.

Captain McNally interrupted his musings. "Captain Campbell, you have exactly forty-two minutes to get your gear together and report back here."

Hurrying back to his cabin, Curley struggled to think of a way he could explain his leaving to Amanda. The retrieval ship was obviously coming at an hour that was meant to keep the rendezvous a secret from the passengers. What would she think when he didn't show up in church? He didn't have to guess. She'd think he was a playboy who was merely toying with her.

He yanked the few clothes from the hangers in the closet and stuffed them into his suitcase. What were his intentions toward Amanda? He shook his head in consternation. Maybe he'd never know. But he'd have liked to have known her better.

He glanced at his watch. He had about five minutes leeway to dash to Amanda's cabin and—and what? He couldn't tell her anything without arousing wild suspicions. And he didn't even have time to tell her he wouldn't be at church.

When he arrived back at the bridge a few minutes later, the navy ship's lights were approaching. He asked Captain McNally for a slip of paper and scribbled a short note. "Please see that Miss Amanda Chase in Cabin A-12 gets this message."

Chapter Six

Amanda awoke the next morning with the pleasant feeling of lingering, nice dreams. As she surfaced up through the sleepy fog, she realized that the images were real. She'd spent the most romantic evening of her life with the man of her young dreams.

Young dreams, she thought. A wonderful gift from her guardian angel. She inhaled deeply and opened her eyes. On the other bed Ilsa lay curled beneath her covers, clutching her extra pillow to her chest.

Amanda turned to lie on her back and gaze up at the polished wooden ceiling. "Amanda's Idyllic Evening." It would make a good headline. She blocked out a full-page photo layout complete with captions describing the lovely scenes.

She allowed herself a few minutes of fantasizing, then got herself in hand. *You've daydreamed long enough. Time for reality!* She picked up her Bible and read for a few minutes, but had difficulty concentrating. The small clock ticking away on the table between the two beds said only 9:00. She closed her eyes. *Last night was nice,* she told herself, *but a romantic moonlit evening, party-going aboard a gently rolling ship, and a charming, handsome escort are nothing to go gaga over.* Not enough to make a girl lose her objectivity.

Remember Lili, she told herself. A French girl at the Sorbonne, Lili had fallen in love aboard ship and spent the whole school term crying over a man who never contacted her again. *None of that for me,* vowed Amanda. *No man is going to tip my life into a morass of tears.*

She tossed off the covers, rejected the image of Curley's dimpled face smiling at her, threatening to unravel all her fine logic, and padded into the bathroom. She ran warm water into the bathtub, keeping busy to avoid daydreams.

At 10:30 a steward brought a silver service with coffee and flaky rolls. Amanda poured herself coffee and said, "I'm going to skip breakfast and have brunch later, after church." She didn't tell Ilsa that she was busy controlling the butterflies in her stomach and trying to quench the excitement of seeing Curley.

"Me, too," answered Ilsa, lying in bed until the last possible minute while Amanda sipped her coffee. Neither noticed the note slipped between the sugar and creamer.

They left the room, passing early morning deck strollers. The instant they turned the corner toward the Garden Lounge, Nels hurried toward them, a large toothy smile lighting up his face. He held out a hand to each of them, and Amanda couldn't help but smile in return, avoiding the urge to let her glance slide off him to search for a certain auburn-haired fellow.

"You ladies look lovely this morning," he said in his lilting Norwegian accent.

They thanked him, and Amanda allowed herself to glance around at the people arriving for church while Ilsa chattered, "It's hard to believe the voyage is almost over."

"Ya," agreed Nels. "We leave America Monday and come to France on Sunday. So fast a world!"

Two gentlemen in their gray morning coats and gray silk neckties nodded at them as they passed.

"Should we wait for Curley?" asked Ilsa.

"No, let's go on in. He'll find us," said Amanda, thinking that Curley could perhaps already be inside, saving them places.

Amanda sang the familiar hymns and tried to concentrate on the speaker without turning to look behind her to see if Curley had come in. She finally reached into her purse for her small notebook and forced herself to listen to the speaker by jotting down his main points. "Ambassadors for Christ" was the headline she gave his sermon. He reminded his listeners that no matter where they traveled, they'd always be God's ambassadors.

When she was thirteen years old, Amanda's nanny, Miss Whitney, took her regularly to church. Amanda had had the zeal of an ambassador then. But as she got busier with school and traveling, she attended less often, except when accompanying her parents to the cathedral's fashionable Christmas and Easter services. But in the last two years, she'd gone back to church, seeking fellowship and stability.

After the closing hymn, Amanda, Ilsa, and Nels followed the crowd out onto the deck.

"I wonder where Curley is," said Ilsa, frowning and looking about.

"Must have had better things to do," said Amanda, forcing a smile. A high stack of cumulus clouds had risen and was approaching like a white and gray army.

"Well! It's quite rude!" Ilsa glared at the back of a man walking by, as if he were the guilty party. "It would be so lovely to explore Cherbourg together this afternoon."

Amanda looked out over the deck rail to the dark green cliffs in the distance. "Yes, it would be. You two go on ahead. I have a million things to do before I arrive in England tomorrow." Before they could urge her to join them for brunch, she added, "I have a couple more people to interview before we dock. See you two later!"

Amanda turned and escaped to the other side of the ship, spending the next two hours on a padded wooden deck chair in an out-of-the-way corner on A deck. *I must remember that this is not a pleasure trip,* she told herself and began jotting her thoughts on paper. *I can never allow myself to forget those small stories buried in the newspapers—skeptical stories of outrageous rumors too horrible to believe. One writer of such a story was forced to leave Germany. Persecution and cruelty were never the central theme of stories of Hitler's new regime. They mostly centered around the new orderly stability.*

She couldn't think of any more to add to her notes. She simply had to get there, and assure herself that Aunt Esther, Uncle Jacob, and her cousins were all right.

Quick, confident steps approached, and her heart beat a little faster, thinking that Curley had found her. A smile locked itself on her mouth.

She blushed at her stupidity when a steward walked briskly past. *Captain Cameron means nothing to me,* she told herself. *But, what if something came up and he's looking for you right this moment? What if he's sick or if he was waylaid by. . .*

She leapt up from the chair and stomped off the deck and down a linoleum stairway. *Sure. He was kidnapped by pirates. If Captain Curley Cameron,* or CCC, as she began thinking of him, *were really interested in you, he would have been where he said he'd be. So, face it!* she told herself.

Two long, majestic blasts of the ship's whistle drowned out her footsteps as she entered the second-class lounge. She found a table near the porthole and munched on cashew nuts, watching small boats bobbing in the distance as the big liner cruised into the harbor.

After the ship docked and those passengers who were going ashore left, Amanda made her way back to her cabin.

Curley couldn't stop the easy smile that lifted the corners of his mouth as he stripped off the tuxedo in the navy ship's bunk. Miss Amanda Chase was more than he'd expected. At first she'd seemed all business; then when he'd picked her up for the dinner and ball, she had that knockout gown on that shimmered softly over her curves. Coupled with the innocence in her eyes, it was a dangerous combination.

She apparently didn't know how she affected him. Maybe she merely went about knocking guys out in her own subtle way, taking it all in stride. No, he couldn't believe that. She seemed genuinely taken aback by his kiss. Her sweet surprise wasn't faked. He found that an unusual and intriguing quality.

He began folding the tux to put into his suitcase, when Amanda's earrings tumbled out, sparkling as they bounced off his shoe and under the bunk. He picked them up, almost believing in fate. *Now I know I'll have to return these.* But the first thing on the agenda was to find Eisenburg on a map.

He wrapped the earrings in a handkerchief and put them in his trouser pocket. He closed the suitcase, thinking that he was glad he put the word "postponed" in his note to her. He'd find a way to see her again.

Amanda cabled her parents when she arrived in London. She exchanged addresses with Ilsa and said her good-byes in their cabin.

She stayed three days in London. Monday she shopped, buying a rose-colored cashmere sweater for her mother, a gold compact for Victoria, and soft kid gloves for her father, and had the store ship the gifts directly to them. Tuesday and Wednesday she visited her father's gallery and used their typewriter to type some of the ship interviews, and sent two articles to the *Chronicle*.

Helping Mr. Seton, the gallery manager, write a report for her father, she inserted her own note assuring him she was fine, hoping he'd come to terms with her plans. She telegraphed a message to Uncle Jacob that she was leaving for Eisenburg the next day.

Thursday morning Mr. and Mrs. Seton took her to the ferry to Calais. Gazing out over the water, her mind began to drift toward the idyllic evening with Curley. She quickly replaced the thoughts with story ideas. Peering past her reflection in the window, at the water sliding past, she realized she'd have to write a library full of books to cover all the story starts she'd fabricated to stop thinking of him.

Maybe, she thought, *it would be easier not to make such an issue of what was merely a nice evening.* She should simply acknowledge the pleasant thoughts when they cropped up, agree that Curley was an interesting man, shrug her shoulders, and get on with life. She knew, though, it wouldn't work: Trying to ignore an evening more fabulous than any other in her life was futile.

In Calais she boarded a short train to Paris, remembering her school years and thinking that Victoria would have loved being with her. Her Thursday night in Paris was spent quietly in her hotel room, listening to the sounds on the street. The next afternoon she was on a train to Berlin.

Finally out of the city, the lovely eastern France countryside glided by, with cows standing silently on the rolling hills. She closed her eyes, letting the swaying, clacking train gently rock her. The train ground to a stop for a few moments, and when they got rolling again, they passed a mother and her small son carrying their bags into the small depot. Amanda sighed and looked out at the darkening hills and quaint cottages dotting the landscape.

Now that she realized she couldn't stop evading memories of Curley, they came flooding in, starting with the morning they had stood on the deck talking. She pursed her lips in consternation as she remembered. She considered herself an excellent interviewer, but he had easily deflected her questions. She didn't even have enough notes to fill two column inches.

But she'd had an interesting talk on board ship with an older German gentleman who was returning home. He'd told her that he remembered the terrible times before Adolf Hitler was elected and that things were so much better now that Hitler had restored order. The wildly inflating money had stabilized, and peace and harmony were everywhere. Amanda sensed his words were too well chosen, sounding too much like they were memorized. When she tried to dig beneath their surface, he angrily cleared his throat, scoffed at exaggerated stories insinuating themselves into frivolous newspapers. He stared off into space, then informed her he had an urgent appointment.

Father, I pray that Uncle Jacob and Aunt Esther are all right. Amanda's eyes flew open as the shrill screech of brakes interrupted her prayer.

"Gelsenkirchen!" the conductor shouted, striding toward the rear of the car. They stopped briefly, then rolled on. She paged through her notebook, scanning the interview for anything of substance. The man was hiding something, but what?

Amanda made herself as comfortable as she could as the train sped through the night. Just after dawn, on the road beside the tracks, a group of children waved as they passed. This was the land of Beethoven and Goethe. It looked so peaceful. Maybe the rumors were exaggerated. She'd think positive and look for the best.

When they reached Berlin at last, Amanda picked up her two suitcases and lugged them through the crowded depot. The noise of hundreds of travelers and the shouts of trains arriving and leaving bounced off the high ceiling, mingling into a cacophonous mush. The warmth of the day lingered in the station, making her uncomfortably hot in her wool coat.

Outside the station, she set the suitcases down for a moment and took off her coat. She hired a taxi to take her to Eisenburg and settled in for the ride. She was a child when she last visited Berlin, and this visit was like seeing the city for the first time. The old, narrow streets were clean, people moved quickly, as though they had important business, and Amanda noticed there were no destitute people in front of the well-preserved baroque buildings. She was glad they didn't suffer the same plight as out-of-work Americans dealing with the depression.

The taxi pulled up by the fence in front of Uncle Jacob's house. The driver unloaded her suitcases and she gave him a large tip. The house sat quietly behind its finely manicured lawn and garden. Looking up at the windows, she hoped to see a familiar face.

She pulled her suitcases inside the gate, left her coat draped over them, and walked to the front door. The house echoed the chime of the doorbell, as though a long silence had been broken. She had the odd feeling that something wasn't quite right. The house was too quiet. . .maybe the family was out. . .maybe they were at the train station looking for her. . .maybe—

The door opened and a man frowned out at her. *"Was begehren Sie?"*

Amanda stared at him for a moment. "Who. . .I mean, *Wo ist die Familie?"*

They continued speaking in German. "Where is what family?" asked the man.

"The family who lives here." Amanda glanced around, noting that the house had changed in subtle ways. It was too perfect, like a flawless model. Not like the happy home she remembered where a family lived.

"There is no family here," the man said and closed the door a few inches, eyeing her suspiciously.

Suddenly the rumors of persecutions came into sickening focus. If they were true, even her appearance at the house was dangerous, both to herself and her family, wherever they were. She forced a slight smile. *"Danke,"* she said and stepped off the porch.

Back at the gate she put her coat on to dispel the chill she felt. She picked up her suitcases and looked back at the house, feeling that she was being watched. Though she was exhausted, she raised her chin and set off in the direction of town. Uncle Jacob would be at the gallery, and he'd tell her what was going on.

Chapter Seven

A breeze flicked Amanda's hair as she walked away from her aunt and uncle's house, wishing she'd asked the taxi to wait. The neighborhood was oddly silent for late afternoon. The houses looked deserted. It hadn't been that way years ago when she, Martha, and Tamara played tag in the front yard.

A small black car slowly approached, its tires snapping a rhythm over the brick road. The two men inside turned their heads, staring at her as they passed. The car glided into the house's driveway. *God, who are they, and what happened to my family?* she asked, turning the corner. The house had lost its friendly glow. She shivered, now thankful for her heavy coat.

Walking and lugging her suitcases made the streets back to town seem much longer. But, she reasoned, if Eisenburg was as large as Berlin, she would've had to ask the men at the house to call a taxi.

She recoiled at the thought, telling herself to be reasonable. Maybe they were very nice people and she interrupted them at a bad time. Maybe they were just naturally grouchy. That sounded most logical. Had Uncle Jacob sold the house to them? Aunt Esther's last letter hadn't mentioned they were moving.

The slanting twilight sun glinted off Eisenburg's baroque buildings. The fragrance of sausage, baked bread, and cooking vegetables wafted past her. She set her suitcases down beside a shop with a large window open to the street. She ordered apple-peel tea and a buttered roll from a thin, mahogany-haired teenage girl who smiled brightly at her.

"Bist du Eng-a-lishe?" she asked.

"Nein," answered Amanda in German. "I'm American."

The girl's eyes widened. She leaned over the wooden counter to peer at Amanda's clothes. "Ahh," she said with admiration.

They spoke of American music and fashions. Amanda told her she'd visited Eisenburg when she was very young. She sipped the last of her tea and asked for directions to Drehenstrasse. Pointing and speaking rapidly, the girl told her how to get there. Amanda thanked her and continued on her way.

She walked the three blocks down the main street and half a block down Drehenstrasse, resisting the feeling that something was wrong. An unnatural quiet breathed between the buildings. The gallery was dark, the windows boarded up, and the door had a heavy chain draped across it. A sign stuck inside the bottom of a window said, *"Geschlossen."* Closed.

Amanda stared at the dried leaves blown in and crammed against the bottom of the door. Closed! When had this happened? A slight chill wove its tendrils around her heart.

It was almost dark now. The other stores on the street were closed, and two other stores looked as abandoned as Uncle's Jacob's gallery.

Walking away, she noticed someone had scrawled on one of the boarded-up shops the words *"Kauft nicht bei Juden."* Don't buy from Jews?

Two men in uniform walked smartly past her, and she hurried to the more lighted main street. The rumors were true! To keep the fears for her family from overtaking her, she concentrated on headlines for her next story. *Jewish Businesses Boycotted in Hitler's Germany, Have Pogroms Really Been Discontinued?*

She sat down on a wooden bench under a dim streetlight and sighed. It was time to plan her next move. She would not panic or cause her father to worry until she knew more. *I'm like an actress in a foreign spy movie,* she thought. Her first duty was to find her family.

A few people, strolling after their dinner, passed her. A policeman on the corner fixed her with a bright blue-eyed gaze and approached her. He glanced at her suitcases, then asked if she needed directions.

She gripped the handles of one and started to stand. "No, thank you. I'll be on my way."

He took the suitcase from her. "Allow me, *fraulein,*" he said. "Though it's safe to walk our streets after dark, I will accompany you. Where are you staying?" He smiled, waiting for her answer.

Amanda thought quickly. "The main hotel," she said, reaching into her purse. "I have its name here. . ."

"Come," he said, picking up her other suitcase. "I know the place."

Walking beside him, she wondered briefly if he was the one who boarded up Uncle Jacob's gallery. After they'd gone one block, he turned and led her up the steps into the parlor of a three-story rooming house. He set her bags down and rang a silver bell he picked up from a small table beside the door.

A short, energetic woman appeared and warmly greeted them. She sat at the table, moved the bell, and opened a large registry book. "How long you stay?" she asked with a smile.

"A couple of days." Amanda produced her identification papers and paid the woman while the policeman stood near.

The woman, Frau Reinhardt, led them into the parlor. The policeman left them, pushing the door into the kitchen. Amanda and Frau Reinhardt climbed the stairs to the third floor and walked its carpeted length to the next-to-last room.

Frau Reinhardt adjusted a knob on the radiator beside the door and said, "The bathroom is the third door down the hall, the maid comes to clean at 11:00 A.M., and there will be no visitors, and no music or loud noises after 9:00 P.M."

Amanda nodded, glad she'd had the roll and tea, because her eyes felt heavy and her head was beginning to pound. Frau Reinhardt left, and Amanda let out the breath she hadn't realized she was holding. She sank onto the faded yellow chenille bedspread and with her toes pushed off each shoe by its heel.

On a bedside table sat a pitcher and wash basin. A closet door stood open on one wall. Curtains covered a window opposite the door. She was curious to look outside, but too tired to. *In the morning,* she thought, lying back on the cool pillow.

Thoughts of Uncle Jacob and the family dodged in and out of her tired attempts to plan how she was going to find them. She started to doze, but a loud clang startled her as the radiator began heating the room.

She lay there, her eyes closed, adjusting to the noise, letting her mind relax. Curley Cameron's face flashed across her thoughts. His eyes looked deep into hers, a dimpled smile on his handsome face.

She tried to bring her mind back to the problem at hand, but it didn't work. All she could think of was Curley, the sparks, the warm sensations she felt when he kissed her. No man had ever affected her that way. Certainly not Delbert.

The few times Delbert had kissed her, his lips felt cold, and there was no excitement, no thrill. Afterward, her heart continued its steady beating as though nothing had happened. *Delbert's a nice enough fellow,* she thought. *Handsome, rich. But even if I was attracted to him, he still wouldn't be the right man for me, not when he doesn't understand my commitment to Christ. Some girl, though, will be thrilled to be the object of his attention—but not me.*

Curley, on the other hand, had not only thrilled her heart, but he shared her faith. Or had that been just a line? His expertise at kissing was probably all part of a charming act, too. Still, he'd seemed so tender when he drew her close and kissed her. She'd never forget the lingering look of wonder he'd had on his face when she finally opened her eyes.

She sat up abruptly, fighting for control. She pursed her lips, telling herself that she was being foolish, falling for a smooth line and a handsome face. *I refuse to think about a man who plays fast and loose with the ladies. Someday I want a man who will offer true love, if there is such a thing.*

Curley must know he'd affected her, since she'd almost shamelessly begged him to kiss her again. *Maybe that's why he didn't show up the next morning,* she decided sadly. These were futile thoughts because she'd probably never see him again.

She'd certainly never be the same naive teenager who'd had a crush on him. She rolled her eyes in relief that she'd stopped short from telling him they'd met before.

Yawning, she got out her pen and paper and recorded today's events in her journal and fell asleep while trying to concentrate on planning a search for her family tomorrow.

That same night while the other guys were celebrating in town, Curley stayed in the barracks. He'd worked hard all week, hoping to finish in nine days and be on a Monday flight to Salzburg.

The next morning Amanda rose early, refreshed from her long sleep. Sometime during the night she'd changed into her nightgown. Now, she opened the window and leaned out into the cool fresh air. Below was a narrow walkway between the rooming house and the building next door. She wondered if Frau Reinhardt tended the row of rosebushes lining the walk.

She shrugged into her robe and took the pitcher to the rest room. A tall, slim woman with circles under her eyes and hair so black it could have only come from a bottle, let her in. "Ach, what a morning!" she said, peering glumly into the mirror over the sink. She pulled the belt of her pink robe tighter around her waist.

"It's going to be a nice day." Amanda smiled at her. The bathroom was as large as her room. Behind a door slightly ajar sat the bathtub.

"You are new tenant?" asked the woman as Amanda washed her hands.

"Yes, I came in last night."

"You speak German with an accent. You are English?"

"No, American," answered Amanda, filling her pitcher with warm water. "Can you tell me where I can send a wire?" she asked.

"At the post office, on the park square. But not on Sunday."

"Thank you," said Amanda. Back in her room, she took a sponge bath standing on her towel in front of the dresser. She put on her gray skirt and orchid sweater and comfortable shoes. Taking her camera and notebook, she left the room.

She followed the fragrance of breakfast to the dining room where several guests were already seated. The long table supported plates of fried potatoes, sausage, eggs, ham, and several other entrees.

Frau Reinhardt, seated at the head of the table, welcomed Amanda, motioning to an empty chair on her left. A red-haired girl carried a pitcher of cream to the table, glancing covertly at Amanda.

Amanda chose a large piece of blueberry coffee cake with streusel topping and poured herself a cup of coffee. The other tenants kept their attention on their breakfasts, hardly noticing her until Frau Reinhardt asked how she liked her room. They nodded in satisfaction when she said it was fine.

The park square was in the middle of Eisenburg, and she easily found the building with "Postamt" chiseled into its exterior. The door was tightly closed and the window shades were drawn, giving the place a forbidding look.

Church bells pealed a somber welcome, and she followed the sound to a gray, ornately baroque building with a few folks climbing the old steps and entering a door that was at least fifteen feet high. The sanctuary was cold, but the majestic organ music was like being at a concert. The service was stately and dignified, with the reading of a whole chapter from Esther, which went along with the short sermon.

Afterward, feeling a peaceful calm, Amanda walked away from the church, knowing that since it was Sunday, she'd not make much headway in finding her family. So she strolled around the quaint little town, snapping photos, then went back to the rooming house to write some letters and make notes for future articles.

Monday, Curley was a passenger on a flight into Austria, where he'd pick up a small plane hangared in a field outside of Salzburg. He'd been briefed to enter Germany from the southeast corner, delivering the plane to Holland. His flight would take him over a lot of German territory, giving him a good look at reported growing squadrons of airpower in Nuremberg, Munich, and Berlin.

Seated in the last seat of the plane, he looked out into the clear black night. The noise of the two engines changed slightly as the plane started its descent. The seven other passengers leaned toward the windows to look down. A row of landing lights glittered in the inky darkness below.

The plane touched down, bounced once, then with a roar slowed and turned around. They taxied to a stop beside a large hangar, and the passengers stood, grabbing suitcases and bundles.

He descended the steps behind the other passengers. Two crewmen stood looking up at the engines. He would have commented that she was a sweet ship, but keeping his anonymity, he didn't. He walked across the tarmac to the barnlike building. Over the door was a sign, *Flughafen von Salzburg,* between tall columns with winged cherubim sitting on them.

Curley followed his fellow passengers across the slate floor, through the terminal. The blond girl and her chaperon were met by a middle-aged man in a gray overcoat. There were no passengers waiting to board the plane he'd just left, and the only people inside were a wireless operator, a clerk, and a stoop-shouldered man pushing a loading cart out the door.

In the chilly night air Curley approached the closest of two taxis. A talkative, gray-haired driver with a large mustache assured Curley he knew the best place in Salzburg to find a room for the night. The clerk in the deserted lobby was so happy to see both him and the driver, Curley was sure they must be relatives.

He signed in, dropped his suitcase in the room, and went to find something to eat. Sitting alone at a linen-covered table waiting for his order, he suddenly wondered what Amanda was doing at that precise moment.

The thought of her made him smile, and he touched his shirt pocket, where he'd stashed her earrings. *I'll be returning these to you soon, Miss Amanda Chase.* He absently stared at the row of mugs on a shelf across the room, thinking of stories he'd heard of persecution and hardships imposed on innocent German citizens. If Amanda asked questions in the wrong places, she could get herself in trouble. He'd find Eisenburg on the map and fly in as soon as possible.

The next morning, just after dawn, Curley left the hotel, carrying his suitcase through the streets with their ornate wrought iron signs leaning out over the sidewalks. The graceful old buildings glowed in the early morning light, as he kept the sun behind him. Several signs proudly bore the picture of Mozart, their most famous son.

Curley loped past a blue-domed cathedral and crossed the bridge over a meandering river. The crisp morning air magnified the twitter of waking birds. His steps slowed as he caught sight of a grand old building perched on a hill above groves of trees. It looked as though it had been there for hundreds of years. The dawn light gave the mountain behind it a peach glow and the oval windows a golden liquid sheen.

At the end of the street a cathedral thrust its ornate spires to the sky, and a group of angels graced the arch over its door, two of them holding slim trumpets between a coat of arms. Curley made a mental note to return and explore this beautiful Salzburg, tucked in the hills of Austria. The cottages became farther apart, and soon he was in farm country, with wisps of smoke rising from their chimneys.

He found the airstrip easily by simply walking west and scanning the vista for a windsock. There it hung on a pole, limp in the quiet morning. He approached the hangar and found its doors open, the Vega's propeller shining in the sunlight.

A tall man, in his thirties, with curly dark hair and blue eyes walked toward Curley. "James Cameron?" he asked, smiling and wiping his hands on a red rag.

Curley nodded, and they shook hands. "Looks like a sweet little bird," he said.

The mechanic beamed, looking fondly at the plane as if he were a mother hen and this was his favorite chick. "You take Vega to Herr Schmidt in Amsterdam, *ja?*"

"That's right." His orders were to deliver the plane within ten days while observing all he could on the way.

Curley checked it out from tail to nose and found it to be in excellent order. He wasn't surprised, because the hangar was clean and neat. Together they rolled the Vega out onto the grass field, and Curley climbed into the cockpit. Touching his fingers to his forehead in an informal salute, he started the engines.

In the air before 7:30 A.M., he headed northwest toward Munich.

Early that same day, Amanda went to the post office in the square. Inside, a row of boxes with numbered brass plates filled one wall, near a counter with a uniformed man standing behind it. Behind him sat a wireless telegraph machine.

She sent a message home, telling them she'd arrived, was fine, and would contact them later. She mentioned that Uncle Jacob and Aunt Esther had moved from their home. Dad might know that the gallery was closed, but until she knew more, Amanda wouldn't worry them unnecessarily.

Outside, in the park, a blond boy in knee britches bounced a ball toward her and she rolled it back to him. She strolled to the other side of the park, thinking. She couldn't simply ask anyone where the family had gone. She couldn't go to the police, because she wasn't sure she could trust them yet.

First she had to see the gallery in the daylight. She turned around and headed in that direction. A young woman in a white apron and nurse's cap pushed a carriage past Amanda. Amanda looked inside the carriage fondly and smiled up at the woman, who stared straight ahead and resolutely pushed the buggy past.

Amanda slowed her steps, pondering the strange impression the town was giving. She'd met a few friendly people, but most of the others went about their business quietly, seeming to shun contact. The cold attitude was conspicuous in the midst of gracious buildings, a charming park squarely in the middle of town, and benches on the main street, made for sitting and chatting. But the people walked through this charming setting with reserved, uncommunicative faces.

The street looked different in the sunlight. On the corner the music store window displayed a gleaming trumpet surrounded by sheet music with the swastika emblazoned on their covers. Amanda walked past a tobacco shop to the Chase Gallery.

It looked even more forlorn and neglected in the daylight. One of the windows had been broken, and someone had propped a board behind the hole. Scrawled on the board, which she had not seen last night, were the words *Deutshland erwache! Juden verecke.* "Germany awake! Jews perish." A ripple of fear jolted through Amanda. Did anyone take this slogan seriously?

Where had all the artwork gone? She shook her head. Where had her family gone? Backing away, she crossed the street to take a picture of the desecrated gallery.

Further down Drehenstrasse, the other two closed businesses were boarded up, one with a hateful slogan written on its door. She snapped a photo of them also, catching sight of a shopkeeper in his doorway with his hands clasped over his massive belly, watching her. When she caught his eye, he looked away and went back inside.

Something sinister was going on in this town, and a chill crept around Amanda's heart, but she recoiled from it, determined to find the truth. *Oh, God, who can I talk to?* she prayed. *Who's behind this outrage? And where is my family?*

Chapter Eight

Amanda stared at the door behind which the shopkeeper had just escaped. Four-feet wide, painted gold wire-rimmed spectacles decorated the window, and the man's name was lettered below. She slipped her camera back into its case as she approached.

Inside, she found him concentrating on polishing a black, cylindrical device. Light from the window gilded two mahogany chairs standing before a glass-topped counter.

After a space of silence, he looked up. "May I help you?"

"I'm interested in the art gallery down the street," Amanda answered with a calmness she forced herself to show.

He shrugged and said, "I'm sure there are other art sellers in this town."

"I'd like to know what happened to the people who owned that one." She adjusted the strap over her shoulder to a more comfortable position.

"Why do you ask?"

"I know them, and I'd hoped to see them again." She chose her words carefully, avoiding the Jewish issue.

"They are gone. That's all there is to it." He set the black cylinder down and rubbed the cloth over it one more time.

"Could you tell me where they went?"

He put his hand to his forehead and looked at her reflectively. "You are very persistent about their whereabouts."

Amanda sucked in a deep breath, hoping she was right about him. He didn't seem sinister, just careful. "Mr. and Mrs. Goldstein are my aunt and uncle, and I'd really like to find them."

He stood still for an instant, as if he were frozen, then squinted at her again. He leaned on the counter that separated them and pulled a card from its depths. "You go talk to Herr Verendorf, here," he pointed to the name on the card. "He may be able to tell you something."

She took the card and slipped it into her pocket. "Thank you."

"Don't thank me. I didn't tell you anything. And don't tell anyone you talked to me." He moved sideways to look past her out the window. "Now, I think you should go."

She looked over her shoulder but saw no one outside. She thanked him again and left. Before the door closed, he said softly, "Good luck, fraulein."

Curley navigated the plane through bright blue skies, between snowcapped mountains to Munich, approximately fifty miles from Salzburg. Flying low, he scanned every possible airfield and buildings large enough to be hangars for airplanes. He circled and came back over the city again, then headed out to the countryside. Spotting a suitable road, he set up an approach and landed the airplane. He taxied off the road into a field and cut the engines. When he opened the door, the fragrance of harvested wheat rose up from yellow stubble.

He sat there for a few moments, letting time pass. Making too many passes overhead would look suspicious. He reached for his harmonica, then let it slip back inside his pocket. Making music would be redundant in this place.

He took Amanda's earrings from his other pocket. They twinkled in his palm. He pushed them with his finger, making them flash. She had looked so lovely that night on the ship, the earrings sparkling against her creamy skin.

He wasn't the kind of man to put stock in fairy-tale romances, but he'd felt a powerful pull on his soul when he kissed her.

Her green eyes, dark and fathomless, had looked up at him, begging him to kiss her again. *I should have done just that,* he thought. But something had stopped him. Maybe it was her innocent seductiveness combined with open trust. Maybe the intense emotion that hit him and rocked his world upside down just plain scared him.

Before that, when he first landed on the ship, he had felt her standing there, and his eyes were drawn to the one person in the crowd who mattered. There had been instant recognition; that was why he was sure he'd seen her before. He always remembered people he'd met, yet she eluded his memory.

He let out a deep breath and curled his fingers around the sparkling earrings. The whole event on board ship was probably due more to moonlight, ocean breezes, and a lovely woman in his arms than destiny. He slipped the earrings back into his pocket before his emotions could dispute that conclusion.

He pulled the door shut, admitting that he was looking forward to seeing Amanda again. A few minutes later he circled over Munich once more and spotted an airstrip with large hangars at one end of the field and several planes lined up near them. He waited while one took off; then when the airspace was all clear, he landed.

As soon as he taxied to a stop, two German State soldiers approached him. *"Was machen Sie hier?"*

In his simplified German, he answered that he was there to check a noise he'd heard in his engine.

Another soldier approached the two standing beside him. Curley turned to open the plane's door and retrieve his toolbox.

"Halt!"

Curley stopped and slowly turned. The three soldiers glared at him.

"Your papers," they demanded. One moved his hand to the gun holstered at his waist.

Curley grinned. "Sure." He opened the plane's door and reached inside, retrieving his passport. While the soldier studied it, Curley glanced at the facilities surrounding the airstrip.

The soldier grunted, apparently satisfied, and handed the passport back. He told Curley to work on his plane, but when finished, to be on his way. To assure that he complied, two left, leaving the third to stand near the plane, watching him.

Unruffled by their distrust, Curley couldn't help wondering if there was something they didn't want him to see. Unlatching the cowling, he glanced at the hangars and planes behind it. He memorized their number and placement.

When he was finished, he put his tools back into the toolbox and hefted it back inside the plane, anchoring it in its place behind the left seat. He grinned at the soldier guarding him and said, "Thanks for the company, sir. I need to use your facilities, then I'll be on my way."

The soldier jerked his head toward the building behind them and led Curley in that direction.

Inside the metal building, thin wooden walls separated rooms, and behind wooden-bordered glass doors was the mess hall. The civilians sitting at tables looked out at them.

"A cup of coffee would sure be nice," said Curley. "Care to join me? I'm buying."

The guard scowled, following him.

"Come now. What harm can I do in the mess hall?" He pushed the door open, and the guard followed him. Curley ordered two coffees and joined a young couple at their table. The guard didn't seem to know if he should stand or sit. Finally, he sat stiff-backed in a position where he could observe and hear everything at the table.

"Nice day, isn't it?" Curley asked the couple.

"*Ja,* a good day for flying."

"Where are you folks from?"

Their eyes glowed with joy. They glanced at the guard, then the man leaned forward. "From here, but we have just been to Nuremburg to honor our *fuhrer!*"

The woman rolled her eyes. "Such splendor! Thousands cheering, soldiers marching! Four brass bands!" She put her fist over her heart. "Herr Hitler is so wonderful! We cheered his speech for ten minutes!"

Curley nodded and took a sip of coffee. "Sounds like quite a spectacle."

The man beamed. "Our *fuhrer* has unified the people and things are going to be better. You should have seen the girls and boys marching! Germany will soon come into her glorious destiny. The future ahead is bright."

"So I've been told," said Curley, smiling. He finished his coffee and, having no further reason to delay, he stood. So did the guard and the young couple. The man said, "*Heil* Hitler!"

The guard hit his chest with his fist. "*Heil* Hitler!"

Back in the plane, Curley took off, craning his head toward the dark planes and large hangars. Two of the doors were opened, and he saw more planes inside. He banked over the buildings, counting eleven large hangars, each capable of housing six airplanes. He counted the planes tied down between the hangars and flew on, northward over the rolling hills.

He circled over Nuremberg, looking for airstrips and more planes, finally landing and inspecting an airstrip as he had in Munich.

He fueled up, left Nuremberg, arcing westward toward Frankfurt, and did the same search, eating a late lunch there. He lifted off, leaving the factories and industrial buildings of Frankfurt behind, and headed northeast toward Berlin. *What a joy to fly,* he thought as the Vega responded smoothly to his handling.

He approached Berlin from the south, looking down at the sprawling city. Three rivers converged, with dozens of bridges crossing them. He followed one river for a while, then circled and crisscrossed over the city, observing three small airstrips. *Somewhere down there,* he thought, *is their glorious leader.* From what his trained eye had seen, Curley knew the *fuhrer* was gathering the beginnings of a powerful air force.

At last he followed a narrow road due east, where the map told him Eisenburg, and Amanda, were. A few miles more and he'd be in Poland, he thought, as he saw the tiny town, seated in a shallow valley. One hill to the south sheltered the hamlet. There was no airstrip, so Curley found the flattest, most remote place he could and set the plane down. He cut the engines, got out, and pushed the plane behind a bank of bushes.

Amanda stood outside the Verendorf cottage on the hillside south of town. It had taken her two hours to find the place, and her feet were tired. No one answered the door when she lifted and dropped the knocker. She'd gone around to the side of the house, saw a greenhouse in back, but no movement, and no one answered her calls.

Her hand holding Verendorf's card dropped to her side, and she sighed. The nearest house was a quarter of a mile ahead. She slipped the card into her pocket, took her camera out of its case, and started shooting. Satisfied that at least she'd get some good shots of the countryside, she walked up the hill to the next house.

A brown-haired boy with pale blue eyes answered the door. His mother told Amanda that Herr Verendorf had gone to the Nuremburg festival and wouldn't be back for another week. Amanda thanked her, grinned at the child, and walked back to town.

She trudged up the boardinghouse steps, realizing she hadn't taken time for lunch. Tired and hungry, she looked at her watch, glad to note she had a few minutes to rest before dinner.

"Amanda! There you are."

She stopped abruptly at the parlor door and stared. It was Delbert, approaching her with outstretched arms. "Delbert! What are you doing here?"

"Why, darling girl, I've come to rescue you, if you're in trouble, or to help you if you need assistance." He flashed her his dazzling smile.

"How did you know where to find me?"

He gestured to a parlor chair. "Let's not stand here in the doorway. Come sit and we'll talk."

"I don't want to sit and chat. Please, how did you find me?"

He hesitated for a moment, then said, "Your father called me after you left. He's been unable to contact your uncle and felt you might need help. So, I dropped everything and here I am."

"I cabled my father I was all right," she said, turning her face away from him. Then, not to be unkind, she laid a hand on his shoulder and said, "Delbert, it was nice of you to come all this way, but I'm taking care of myself just fine. Go back to Boston and tell my father thank you."

"But—"

"I'm tired and I'm going upstairs." She turned from him and walked away.

In her room, she dropped her camera bag on the floor and plopped down on the bed with a long, exhausted sigh. Nothing had gone right. She pressed the heels of her hands over her eyes to soothe the burning sensation.

How would she find her family? She had no more leads. *They have to be somewhere! If they're in Eisenburg, I'll find them, even if I have to knock on every door and ask everyone in town.* The optometrist might know something more. Even though he seemed nervous about her visit, tomorrow she'd return to talk to him.

She lay back on the pillow and closed her eyes, thinking of her cousins. Were Martha and Tamara in danger? Something sinister was happening. The rumored beatings and tortures suddenly became all too possible. But how could that be in this modern day and age?

She was too tired to think of Delbert, but she appreciated her father's protectiveness. She'd have to keep her doubts and fears to herself. Delbert would approach the situation as a private eye on a federal case. She shuddered, thinking that he could endanger the family, turning their disappearance into an international incident.

At dinner, Delbert charmed Frau Reinhardt and the cook. They piled extra dollops of whipped cream on his dessert, and Amanda hoped they wouldn't credit her for his being there.

The policeman dropped in just in time for the cook to bring him a piece of apple strudel topped with whipped cream. Delbert chatted with him, praising Adolf Hitler for solving Germany's problems, claiming that Americans applauded his efforts to lead Germany into prosperity.

The policeman set down his fork and with shining eyes said, "I was in the crowds at his hotel last summer. There were thousands of us, waving our swastika flags. 'We want our *fuhrer!*' we all shouted. It was splendid." He scanned each face around the table to be sure they were listening. "He stood on the balcony for a moment. Women swooned, but men shouted '*Heil* Hitler!' "

He sat straighter in his chair and in hushed tones added, "The *fuhrer* looked down, and I knew he was looking right at me. Then he spoke." The policeman slowly shook his head. "How wonderful were his words."

The rapt expression on the man's face baffled Amanda. He viewed Hitler as some kind of god. Did Hitler really inspire such devotion? It reminded her of her studies in Roman history. The caesars, proclaimed as gods, brutally eliminated dissenters. *What happened to Hitler's dissenters?* she wondered.

Darkness had settled over the town as Curley walked the road. Behind the western hills the sliver of moon shed weak light over the road, and a chilling wind pulled dry leaves off the trees. Eisenburg was eerily quiet, until a long, black car slid up beside him and stopped. A policeman got out and blocked his way. "Who are you, and where are you going?"

"Jim Cameron. I'm headed for Eisenburg."

The policeman's eyes narrowed as his gaze darted about. "How did you get *here?*"

"What?" Curley bought a few seconds to think quickly. He didn't want to mention the plane and risk an inspection.

"Herr Cameron, you did not walk from America, *ja?*"

The other policeman got out of the car and stood, listening.

"Oh, no, I had a ride as far as a mile or so back."

"Do you have business in Eisenburg?"

Curley shrugged. "You fellows can tell by my accent that I'm an American. I've always wanted to visit your great country, and now seemed like a good time to do so, since Herr Hitler is bringing such prosperity."

The two officers glanced at each other. Curley hoped these men didn't patrol the countryside, though the plane was well hidden from the road.

The second officer opened the back door of the car. "You come with us. Eisenburg has a curfew, and you cannot be on the streets now."

Curley got into the car, setting his suitcase beside him, and they drove into town. He wondered if they were taking him to jail. But if he'd been in real trouble, they would have asked to see his passport.

He looked at his watch. 9:45. The streets were dark, and in the windows of the homes they passed, light filtered through thick curtains with a subtle glow. No one walked the streets, and corner lamps were dimmed.

"Nice town," he said, looking out the window.

He got no response, so he said no more. *God, I hope I'm not under arrest,* he thought, looking out at shops they were passing. *They can't have any idea who I am.* He'd flown over at least two hours earlier. They couldn't know the plane had landed, and even if they had, they couldn't connect him with it. Still, their militant attitude worried him.

When they stopped in front of an official-looking building and roughly pushed him inside, alarm bells began to go off in his brain.

Chapter Nine

With the disdain of a man who had seen hundreds dragged into the station, a sour-faced guard wrote down Curley's name, took his suitcase, and told him to wait. Curley sat on a high-back oak chair, trying to appear innocent of any violation they could pin on him. Knowing he wasn't didn't help.

There was a gun case full of rifles behind the guard and his desk and a large painting of Adolf Hitler on the wall beside it. A red flag with a black swastika within a white circle hung from a pole in the corner.

Curley understood that each nation had its own identity and customs, including flags and pictures of its leaders, but this was somehow different, more aggressive. After withdrawing from the League of Nations, and then in August after the death of President Hindenburg, Germany had overwhelmingly voted Hitler as its *fuhrer*. His promise to bring the people together as "one man" was probably behind the sense Curley had of a clan gathering itself for a confrontation. But with whom? They were just coming out of a depression after a long and bitter war.

Opening a door noisily, the guard who had picked him up and another officer with a bar of ribbons on his brown shirt marched into the room and ordered Curley to stand. They asked him for his passport, asked again what he was doing in Germany, and what his occupation was.

"I'm a mechanic," he said.

A flicker of suspicion glinted in the officer's eyes. "Explain."

Curley lifted one shoulder apologetically. "I do not speak German well, I fix automobiles." That was true; his Tin Lizzie kept him busy. He assured them he was in Germany as a tourist who was interested in the beauty of their land.

"Why are you walking at night into Eisenburg?"

"I explained that. I got a ride to the outskirts of town." The silence lengthened and he stood ramrod stiff, waiting for them to decide he was harmless and let him go. The ticking of a large round clock on the wall pounded like a blacksmith's hammer.

The officer glared at Curley's passport, then thrust it at the guard. "We will keep this until tomorrow. Tonight you sleep at Frau Reinhardt's." He picked up Curley's suitcase, flipped it open, and moved the clothes and shaving kit around.

He snapped it shut and told the guard who had picked up Curley, "Frau Reinhardt has two rooms left. She will not refuse. Take him and tell her nothing." He handed Curley the suitcase.

Curley glanced at his passport on the guard's desk as he walked toward the door. He wasn't sure how good their spy system was, but if it was even mediocre, he could be in hot water very soon.

At Frau Reinhardt's, he stood in his third-floor room, listening to the guard's fading footsteps. The room was at the end of the hall, with a fire escape outside the window. He climbed out and sat on the cold metal, thinking. They knew he wouldn't go anywhere without his passport. But if he didn't get it back soon, he'd have to leave anyway or face the firing squad as a spy. A light wind rustled the trees behind the building. If it continued, the wind would be a help in getting him and his plane out of here.

How was he going to find Amanda quickly? The town was small, and she was with her family. The police would be no help, but she'd told him her uncle ran one of her father's art galleries. That should narrow the search. He smiled and hunched back against the brick building, thinking of her. In his note he'd said he'd see her soon, but she'd be surprised it was this soon—and in Eisenburg.

The police could become a problem. *I should have waited until I was back in the States and contacted her then.* But he was so near, and he'd felt drawn to her, and. . .

A pebble hit a window about twelve feet away. *A lover's tryst,* he thought. He hadn't heard footsteps. Slowly leaning forward, moving barely a muscle except his eyes, he squinted down into the darkness below. Another pebble struck the window, then another. The window remained shut. Whoever was being hailed wasn't expecting it.

Then the window opened halfway, and a dark head peered out, looked down, then to both sides. Curley took a quick, sharp breath. Amanda! She looked past him, not seeing him in the darkness. From below came a soft whistle in four quick tones.

He couldn't see the person on the ground, but he heard a "Sh," and then a whispered, "Catch." Amanda held her hands out and caught something tossed up to her. She grasped it firmly, straining forward and peering down at the person below.

As Curley leaned forward to look down, the metal squeaked. He froze, but Amanda saw him.

Amanda couldn't believe what she was seeing. Curley Cameron here in Eisenburg, at this very boardinghouse? Impossible! She closed her eyes for a full three seconds, then opened them. He was still there.

He lifted a hand in silent greeting, touches of humor framing his mouth and eyes.

She grasped the rock in her hands so tightly it bit into her palm. She looked down, where her cousin Martha had stood seconds ago, and then she drew back inside her room, completely ignoring the apparition on the fire escape. She couldn't believe he was really there.

Reminding herself that after he'd not shown up at church aboard ship, she'd given up on him, taking him for a fast-talking playboy, she turned on the lamp beside the bed, adjusted the faded silk shade, and then unwrapped the note from the rock Martha had thrown to her. *"Meet me in the park tomorrow at 6:45 A.M. Tell no one, trust no one."*

She put the small piece of paper on the table, smoothing out the wrinkles, reading it again. Why all the mystery? If Martha was playing a game, it could be fun, but this was no game; the need for secrecy was real.

Amanda folded the note into a tiny square and slipped it behind the mirror in her compact. She turned off the lamp and pressed the round, gold compact between her palms, praying that God would keep her family safe.

She went to the window and looked out. The breeze felt cold against her cheeks. Weak moonlight and shadows gave the walkway below a forlorn appearance. If she hadn't heard the secret whistle she and Martha had shared as children, and had she not held the note in her hand, she'd have thought the whole thing was a dream.

She turned her head slowly to the right. Curley still sat on the fire escape, knees up, forearms resting on them.

"Hello, princess," he said softly.

"What are you doing here?" she whispered.

"Looking for you."

She stared at him incredulously.

"I told you I'd see you soon. Here I am."

"You're a little late, don't you think?" she said, instantly regretting her petulant tone.

"What?" His grin faded and his eyes probed hers.

"Never mind," she said. "Good night." She started to pull back into the room.

"Wait!" His loud whisper blended with the sound of the breeze. "We haven't finished the interview."

"Good night," she said, ducking back into the room and closing the window.

She climbed under the covers and forced her eyes closed, trying to go to sleep. She reached out and touched the sharp edges of the rock on the bedside table. She said another quick prayer for Martha, Tamara, Aunt Esther, and Uncle Jacob. She frowned. *First Delbert bursts in just when I don't need him, then Curley shows up.*

She sighed and turned to her side, hugging her pillow. She didn't really care if he was here, she told herself. Why was the first thing she said a rebuke for standing her up at church? All those years she'd daydreamed of him seemed so silly now that he was here, because the timing was all wrong. Four years ago if he'd appeared in the moonlight, she would have swooned.

She turned to her other side. *I shouldn't let him get to me.* She determined to ignore both Curley and Delbert and concentrate on finding out what was happening with her family. After all, that and the big story were her mission. *Girl Reporter Shuns Distractions to Follow Story—that's the headline for tomorrow's activities,* she thought.

Curley sat where he was for a while, perplexed. Why had she brushed him off? *You're a little late, don't you think?* What did she mean by that? He put his hands into his jacket pocket, fingering her earrings. Who had thrown the item up to her just now? Such stealth was calculated. But why? And why was Amanda here and not with her family? He turned up his collar against the cold wind, pondering these things.

The next morning after a fitful sleep, Curley awoke as the sky turned pale gray. The wind had picked up, and gusts blew the tree limbs, making them scratch against the building. He had a very short time to find answers to his questions, get his passport back, and get back to England with his report.

He was the first person in the bathroom, where he washed up and shaved. Downstairs in the kitchen the cook hadn't arrived yet, so he poured himself a glass of water and took it to the parlor. He switched on the lamp beside a rose-colored brocade couch. A magazine caught his attention. Pages of pictures showed Hitler and his officers at their headquarters with happy people gazing up with awe.

Curley sat and sipped his water, waiting for Amanda to come downstairs. The cook peeked around the doorway and offered him coffee. He eagerly traded his glass of water for it, making her smile.

Other tenants began making their way down to the dining room. Curley joined them for a huge breakfast of sausage, potatoes, rolls, and eggs. He was pouring another cup of coffee when Amanda came in.

He grinned and rose to greet her. The man across from him also stood and said, "Good morning, honey." Curley composed himself quickly and sat down.

Amanda stood in the doorway, looking from Curley to Delbert. She shook her head slowly and took a seat at the end of the table, between them. She poured herself a cup of coffee and selected a sweet roll.

Curley sipped his coffee while observing the man across from him. *A real dandy*, he thought. His dark hair was slicked back in the latest style, and he wore a striped shirt and a pale blue cardigan sweater. His hands were immaculate, the long fingers lifting the cup almost daintily. His eyes, so dark they were almost black, glittered with intelligence. They also seemed drawn like a magnet to Amanda.

She ate her breakfast, conversing in German with the older redheaded woman seated beside her. She didn't look at either Curley or the man across from him. Curley finished his coffee and left. Amanda's glance locked with his as he was on his way out. He nodded. "Miss Chase," he said, and left.

Back in the parlor, he picked up the magazine, waiting for Amanda to finish her breakfast so he could speak with her alone. He hadn't come all this way just to be brushed off. He'd find out what was going on, deliver her earrings, and get out of Germany. He'd hoped to make a date with her for when they both got back to the States, but she was acting so oddly, he wasn't sure how this meeting was going to turn out.

Suddenly Curley heard two people arguing in low tones. He recognized Amanda's voice saying, "I told you last night I don't need a baby-sitter."

"But, honey, you know I. . ."

"Don't honey me! Go back and tell my father. . ." They entered the parlor and saw Curley. She stared at him, then shrugged her shoulders and walked out. Delbert grinned and said to Curley, "Women!" He watched Amanda but didn't move.

Curley did. He walked past Delbert and up the stairs behind Amanda. He knocked on her door and waited. She didn't answer. He knocked again. "Amanda? Please. I want to talk to you."

The door opened a crack and she said, "I can't talk now. Please go away." He didn't move. She looked at her watch. "Look. I'm busy right now, but we can talk later."

"How about one o'clock in the parlor?"

"One is fine." She shut the door but he didn't hear her walk away. After a moment, he went next door to his room. In less than a minute he heard Amanda's door softly close. He opened his door a half inch and looked out. She was walking away, her camera bag hanging from one shoulder.

She moved quickly down the stairs. He followed her. Outside he saw a man fall into step behind her. The man crossed the street against the wind, still going in the same direction as Amanda.

She stopped at a corner. She looked back, and Curley sidestepped into a doorway. She crossed the street to the park. The man walking on the other side of the street crossed also and turned left. Amanda strolled into the park and seemed to be enjoying the sights. Curley stayed at the corner, knowing she'd spot him if he came any closer.

Amanda sauntered past a girl seated on a bench in the middle of the park. Then she stooped to pick up something, perhaps a rock. The man following her had circled the park and now stood on the opposite side, watching her.

Amanda sensed that she shouldn't approach Martha openly, and so she knelt, examining a pebble. "What's happened?" she asked in a low voice. "Have you moved? There were strange people at the house."

"The Nazis took our home and forced us to move into a Jewish neighborhood. They warned us that if we even came near the house we'd be killed."

A shudder coursed through Amanda, and she knew it wasn't because of the cold wind. She stood, brushing off her hand. "I can't believe it!"

"They took the gallery, too."

Amanda walked slowly past Martha. "No!"

"Don't look at me. Ignore me." Martha's pale blond hair was pulled up under a blue scarf tied beneath her chin.

Amanda stood a few feet away, her hands clenched at her side. "Tell me what this is all about." She reached for her camera and focused on a grove of trees and empty swings swaying in the wind.

"Jews are being rounded up into special neighborhoods. Father's business is gone. Tamara had a baby last week, and the circumcision ceremony is tomorrow. If we can find a *moyell* who is willing to come perform it. Everyone is afraid. We've heard awful stories of Jewish people being tortured, cut into pieces, and. . ."

Amanda whirled to face her. "Look away. You don't know me!"

"I'm an American citizen, Martha. I came to see you. Where is this. . .special neighborhood?"

"You mustn't!"

"Martha, you know we can trust God to keep us safe. Don't you remember?"

Martha looked at her at last and said, "It's all so mixed up in my mind. But you look good. I wish. . ." She sighed. "I wish God would help us."

Amanda circled the bench. "Where are you living? I want to come to the *bris.*"

"We're at the east end of Domstrasse. Number 22. Tomorrow at nine o'clock. But be careful." Martha stood. Amanda didn't dare do more than glance her way. Martha's gray coat looked like warm armor as she walked with the wind at her back. She wore wool socks and sturdy shoes.

Out of the corner of her eye, Amanda saw a figure approaching from the opposite direction. It looked like one of the men who turned her away from her aunt and uncle's home. She ignored him, focusing her camera on a drinking fountain with a dried-up vine wrapped around it.

Curley watched the man approach the girls and tensed for action. The girl on the bench got up and left. He crossed the street in case Amanda needed help. She didn't seem to notice the man, and he walked by, looking at her for a moment, then going on. His glance narrowed at Curley as he passed him.

Curley turned and gazed down the sidewalk after the girl in the gray coat. Amanda had hurried to this park, before 7:00 A.M. The only reason could be that she was meeting the girl on the bench. Why? Who was she? The girl was now two blocks ahead. He hurried after her.

Chapter Ten

Amanda trudged back, the wind pushing her toward Frau Reinhardt's. Something was terribly wrong. Martha's face was pinched and frightened and her appeal for secrecy alarming.

Inside the boardinghouse, Delbert's happy voice grated on her ears. "You're out early!"

"Yes, I have a lot to do." She smiled weakly at him, trying to be polite.

"You didn't tell how the visit with your relatives went. By the way, I've asked around and was told there's a baroque cathedral in Eisenburg. We should go see it."

"What?" Thoughts of her family's plight whirling in her brain distracted her from what he was saying.

"I said there's a cathedral we should visit. Bach may have even played there."

Amanda winced. His bright smile was a mockery to the life-and-death situation going on with her family. They weren't in jail, though; or was Domstrasse Street some kind of prison?

Delbert touched her arm. "Amanda? Are you all right?"

"I'm fine. I just have some things to do. Go see the cathedral and tell me all about it later."

"But, honey. . ."

She brought her arm close to her side, away from his touch. His endearment irritated her as much as misspelled words in a headline. "Later, Delbert," she said, heading up the stairs.

In her room she set the camera bag in the closet, beside her suitcase, and splashed water on her face. *First, I'll find a library and read some local newspapers. That may give me a clue as to what's happening here. Lord, help me.*

Curley followed the girl in the gray coat. The ends of her scarf flapped in the wind as she kept her head down against its gusts. Passing a young woman sweeping the sidewalk, she took a wide course around her. The woman shook her broom at the girl and said something Curley could not hear.

The girl hurried on, and Curley passed the young woman who freed the dead leaves from the base of the building to fly off into the wind. She smiled at him. Her light blue eyes were framed by an oval face and shiny blond hair. Nodding politely, he wondered why she showed hostility toward the girl and not to him. He shrugged. Maybe it was some neighborhood conflict.

He followed the girl past a knot of people whom she avoided by crossing the street. Several blocks later the street ended by a barricade across the last few blocks. Guards with rifles slung over their shoulders marched in front of the open gate.

The girl stopped, pulled something from her coat pocket to show the guards, and darted inside.

Curley slowed his steps at the barrier, an ugly fence of rough-hewn brown boards. Both sides of the gate were swung inside. On the fence were signs proclaiming this a Jewish holding area with a Star of David and the word *Juden-Heim* beneath. A white-painted Star of David was scrawled near the signs.

Curley approached the guards. They marched back and forth, their high black boots almost to their knees. A third guard standing beside the gate watched him. He slowed his steps, looking up at the two-story building behind the wall.

"Was machen Sie hier?" One of the marching guards stopped and gestured by lifting his head.

They keep asking me that, thought Curley. "Ich bin Amerikaner," he answered, looking up as a tourist would, and told them he was just looking. Inside the gates, people were out on the sidewalks, apparently going about their business the same as those outside the gate.

"Hmm." The guard assessed him with skeptical eyes. A third guard came and told the other one to keep moving. He saluted, clicked his heels, and continued pacing before the open gates.

Curley shoved his fists into his pockets, smiled at the blond giant, and nodded at the sign. "What is this, uh *Juden-Heim?*"

The guard took a deep breath, his chest swelling beneath his brown jacket. "This camp is protective custody for our Jewish citizens."

Curley's gaze followed the guards and scanned the fence. "Why do these citizens need protection?"

The man smiled, his blue eyes glittering fiercely. "There are those who look upon them as less than human, worthy only of extermination."

Curley's breath trembled in his throat, and he swallowed quickly. "And you protect them?" This man's feral attitude didn't seem that of a protector.

"We protect them," he snapped.

Curley ran a hand through his hair, smoothing it down in the wind. There wasn't much he could say after that. He took a deep breath and looked up at the rows of barbed wire above the fence. The two guards' boots smacked the sidewalk in front of the gates.

"Well, I guess I'll be getting back to town," he said.

"*Ja,* there are other pleasant sights to enjoy in Eisenburg." He turned and went to stand at his former post beside the in-swung gate.

Curley walked away, looking back once, with the feeling that the gate was more to confine than to protect the Jews from anything outside. What had the young girl done to sentence her to a life in this place? Was she a Jew? How was Amanda involved in this?

He had a lot of questions to answer before he met with Amanda at one o'clock. He had a lot to do in a short time.

Amanda slipped out the back door at the end of her hallway and down the back stairs of the fire escape. The wind howled between the buildings, trying to push her back as she made her way to the street. Gray, menacing clouds hung overhead.

She walked a couple of blocks before coming to the bakery where she'd had her first cup of tea. The window was closed against the strong wind, so Amanda went inside.

The mahogany-haired teenage girl smiled brightly when she saw Amanda. "Are you liking your stay in Eisenburg?" she asked.

"I certainly am," said Amanda, inhaling the fragrance of rolls, strudels, and pastries. She chose apple-peel tea and a couple of ginger cookies with thin lemon frosting.

Amanda sat on a high stool at the counter, and the girl brought her tea and cookies. "Have you seen the new movie starring Marlene Dietrich?" the girl asked with breathless eagerness.

Amanda sipped the tea and said, "No, I don't get to many movies."

"Oh! I go all the time—that is, I wish I could go more. I went to Berlin with a friend, and we stood in line for hours to see Mae West's movie." She rolled her eyes. "All I could see were the wonderful clothes she wore. I wish. . ." A clattering noise from the kitchen area startled her and she snapped her head toward the sound.

"Elisa!" A woman's voice called.

The girl raised her eyebrows and her shoulders. "That's me." She left Amanda and pushed back a gray cotton curtain in the doorway to the kitchen. "I'm coming, Grandmother."

Amanda nibbled on a cookie. She hadn't been able to get a word in edgewise. She'd have to ask somewhere else for what she needed. Thank goodness her tea wasn't boiling hot, so she could sip it quickly. She slipped one cookie into her pocket and drank the last of her tea.

She left some money on the table and was leaving when the girl returned, looking surprised and dismayed. "You're leaving? So soon?"

"I'm afraid so," answered Amanda. "I have business I have to take care of." With her hand on the doorknob, she smiled at the girl. "Would you tell me where the library is?"

"Oh, but Eisenburg doesn't have a library," the girl said.

Amanda frowned at the girl's words. "No library?"

"No, but when we need to look up something, we go to the school." With pride she added, "*They* have a library!"

Amanda's grip on the doorknob eased, and she asked, "Where is this school?"

"I have to make a delivery, and I go right by there. I'll show you!" She ran back through the curtained doorway and returned, shrugging on her coat while carrying a wicker basket.

They walked down the windswept streets, Elisa chattering away about gowns and hairstyles. They rounded the corner past a church with a steeply sloping roof and decorative ironwork adorning the eaves. "I go to church here," announced Elisa. "Do you go to church? Are you a believer? What town are you from?"

"Yes, I'm a believer, and I go to church," said Amanda. "I'm from a town called Boston."

"Do they have Jews in Boston? My best friend was a Jew, but she's gone to America now. Well, it doesn't matter, I guess." She looked about guiltily and pointed up the street. "That's the school."

"Why do you ask me if there are Jews in Boston?" Amanda looked down into the hazel eyes that looked away quickly.

Elisa shrugged. "I'm not supposed to talk about it." She stopped. A sign over the door advertised an architecture firm. "This is as far as I go," she announced. "Come back soon to the bakery, Miss Boston."

The school, a three-story building, displayed a Nazi flag flapping in the wind on the flagpole. Windows every few feet lined themselves together on each floor. Above the door a huge photo of Hitler in uniform looked down on those who entered.

Inside, her footsteps echoed on the polished wooden floors. She passed a classroom full of children, with books propped in front of them on their wooden desks. On the wall was a picture of Hitler. In the library, racks of newspapers and magazines clustered beneath a portrait of Goethe. She chose several and spread them out on a wooden table.

As she began to read, her heart pounded. She could scarcely believe the hateful words she was reading. There was nothing subtle about the venom they spewed: Germany was at the mercy of Jews; they were behind every wicked scheme to destroy the country. They were physically repulsive, said one newspaper article; another said they were a lower form of life; "parasites plundering the nation without pity," said Hitler. Joseph Goebbels summed it up: "The Jews are to blame for everything." Cartoons showed ugly, slack-jowled Jews corrupting the morals of Germany; as child molesters, enticing innocent children, seducers of Aryan young maidens, and responsible for every vile sin in the land.

Amanda's stomach knotted up and her blood ran cold. A chill black fog seemed to fill the room. She sat, stunned, for a few moments, with strange, disquieting thoughts racing through her mind. This was too bizarre to be real! Why had none of this made headlines in the States? Rumors and innuendoes were all she'd heard; and they were denied. But they were true! More than that, the rumors were mild, compared to what she was reading.

Uncle Jacob and his family were in danger. She had to get them out of the country somehow. She paged through a few more papers, hoping to find some articles disputing the shocking reports she'd just read, but there were none. She closed the last paper on a drawing describing the unappealing physical and character traits of the Jew.

Amanda looked across the room at the window. It was merely a frame for the dull gray sky. She couldn't shake the feeling of unreality, as if she'd stepped onto the stage of some nightmarish, mad drama. Her fingers moved over the papers and magazines. It was all too real.

A wave of nausea swept over her. She struggled under a heavy darkness that had settled over her mind. Suddenly the door at the end of the room opened, and a teacher led her classroom into the library. Amanda snatched up her purse and fled, willing herself to briskly walk and not run.

Outside, she took several deep breaths, but was unable to calm herself. She walked aimlessly for a long time, thinking, worrying, hoping, planning. No wonder Martha looked so frightened. *I'm an American citizen,* she told herself. *They have no power over me. Or do they?* she wondered. *I am in their country—but still I'm an American.* Having been an American student in France, she knew there were limitations on the power a foreign government had on American visitors, but from what she'd just read, this country's policy was outside all rules of decency and order.

❧

At noon, Amanda found herself back at the park where she'd met with Martha that morning. She sat on the same bench, her thoughts churning as fast as the wind shook the trees around her. *I need a plan of action. First, I must find 22 Domstrasse.*

Glad to have some direction at last, she went to the post office, looked at a map of the city, and found Domstrasse. She gasped when she saw the wall drawn on the map. Icy fear twisted around her heart and she began to shake when she thought of the hate she'd read at the library. At one o'clock she pushed the door open at Frau Reinhardt's and started dully for the stairs.

❧

Curley was anxiously waiting for Amanda. He heard the door open when she entered, and he saw her walk slowly by the parlor door. "Amanda. In here!" he called. She kept on walking. Something was wrong.

He leaped up and came into the hallway behind her. He touched her arm, and she turned. Her eyes were glazed and full of pain. "Princess! What's wrong?"

She flinched and kept on walking.

Stepping in front of her, he gripped both her arms. "What happened? You can tell me."

She shook her head. "I can't talk now, Curley. I just. . ."

He put his arm around her shoulder. "You look like a girl who could use a shoulder about now."

"I. . ." Her voice wavered and she hung her head.

"Come," he said, leading her up the stairs. He opened the door to his room and ushered her in. He sat her on the edge of the bed and pulled up a straight-backed wooden chair for himself. "Sweetheart, something happened. What was it?"

She licked her lips nervously. "My family. . .they. . ." She remembered Martha's note telling her to tell no one, trust no one. She sucked both lips between her teeth and hugged her arms to her chest. "I can't talk about it."

Curley watched her wretched sadness and understood that she couldn't talk now. In those seconds he was consumed with compassion, wishing he could take the pain and sadness from her.

He knelt before her and gently took her hand. It felt so cold. He covered it with his other hand. "Amanda, I don't want to cause you any more grief, but there are some things I think you should know."

Her eyes had a flat, faraway look in them that alarmed him. "Amanda! Tell me what happened." He looked steadily into her eyes, wishing he could discern her thoughts.

A tear rolled down her cheeks, and he melted. He moved to her side and put his arm around her. "I told you this shoulder is yours if you need it." He drew her head to his chest.

She sat quietly for a moment, then he felt her softly crying. He rubbed her back. "Shh. It's okay. I'm here." He would slay dragons or walk on fire for this woman, he realized with surprise.

He enjoyed her closeness for a few minutes more, until she drew back, sniffling. He reached into his chest pocket and drew out a handkerchief for her.

"I'm sorry," she said, patting the wet front of his shirt.

"It's fine," he assured her. "You needed someone, and I'm glad I was here for you."

"I must look a fright," she said, dabbing at her eyes.

"You look good to me," he said, lifting her chin with his curled index finger. She sniffed once more and turned her head.

"Did you have lunch?" he asked. She shook her head. "I found a quiet little place where we can talk. Let's go."

Amanda paused, as if she was going to refuse him.

"Remember, we have a one o'clock date," he reminded her.

She sighed and said, "I remember."

They sat in a booth of dark wood in a cozy restaurant. After they'd had a satisfying lunch of dumplings in a dark consomme, they talked small talk, until Amanda began to relax. He asked her what she meant when she'd first seen him on the fire escape. "You said I was a little late?"

Mentioning their date at the ship's church service, she shrugged as if it didn't matter.

"Didn't you get my note?" he asked.

"What note?"

He explained his hasty departure and apologized again. She closed her eyes, enjoying the way his words warmed her heart.

Over dessert, he leaned forward and said, "I told you earlier that I found out some things I think you should know."

Her eyes, like green polished jade, were fixed on him.

"Listen, I notice you're staying at Frau Reinhardt's and not with your relatives."

She opened her mouth to speak.

He held up his hand. "Let me finish." She nodded. "I've been around town, talking to various people, and I have heard some very disturbing things." He leaned forward and lowered his voice. "Hitler has special forces confiscating Jewish homes and businesses, sending Jews into restricted areas."

Amanda winced.

"You know about the wall?" he whispered.

She nodded. He understood now why she was so distressed. She set her spoon down and took a shaky breath.

"I took a look at it," he said. "It was horrible! Like an ugly scar stretching across the street." Curley took hold of her hand and squeezed. "Don't go near that wall. It's dangerous."

"I'll be careful."

"I'm serious. If you have family in there, have them come out to see you. But if you insist on going in, I'll go with you. Do not go there alone."

"How. . ." She clamped her mouth shut.

"How what? How did I find out about your family? That's unimportant for now. What counts is that you need to get away from here. You can work from the States to get your family out."

She shook her head. "You don't understand."

"I understand danger, and this is the real thing. Tell me, are your Jewish relatives believers in Jesus as their Messiah?"

Flexing the fingers of her hand that lay near his, she sighed. "My cousin Martha believed years ago, but I don't think she had the strength to talk openly about it at home."

"Believe me," he said, "the only way to get through something like this is to hang onto God with everything you've got."

Amanda nodded. "That's right. I must get in to see them and pray with them."

"I told you it's dangerous. We can pray together for them. I'm leaving tonight. Come with me."

"I can't do that," she answered, waving his concerns aside.

He admired her valiant determination, but the evil tide he saw building here would engulf her. "You must! There are things here that you don't understand."

"I'm a reporter, remember? I've done some fact-checking on my own, and I understand clearly what's happening here."

The waitress came to clear away their dishes, and they sat back silently, watching.

Amanda opened her purse and pulled out her compact. She flipped it open and turned her head from side to side, patting her hair. She snapped the compact shut and said, "I have to get back now." Her eyes darkened as they fastened on his. "Thanks so much for the shoulder," she said softly.

"Anytime." He stood as she slid out of the booth. He paid the waitress, and reaching into his pocket for change, his fingers brushed against Amanda's earrings.

All the way back to their rooming house he tried to think of a way to tell her of the rumors he'd heard. She may have found out about the German takeover of Jewish businesses and homes, and even of the relocations, but he didn't think she knew that plans were afoot to march Jews out of Eisenburg to some unknown place.

He had been able to glean this information from sources she'd have no access to, by putting together a word here, a gesture there, whispered hints, and fearful constraint that spoke louder than accusations.

Curley stopped outside Frau Reinhardt's. Amanda looked up at him with questions in her eyes. Reaching for her hand, he curled her fingers around the earrings he'd taken from his pocket. "You left these in my care back on board the ship."

Amanda opened her hand and looked at them, then back at Curley.

It seemed perfectly natural to him to lift her hand and kiss the inside of her wrist. "I thought it was a dream," he murmured tenderly. Again, just as on board the ship, he had trouble tearing his gaze away from the moist softness of her mouth.

The door opened, and Delbert looked out, smiling. "Are you all right, Amanda?" He peered at her as she pulled her hand away from Curley. "Did you hurt your hand?"

"I'm fine, Delbert. Just fine." She smiled at them both and swept past Delbert into the rooming house.

You will listen to me, Curley thought as soon as the door closed. *I'll not leave here without you,* he vowed. He hunched his shoulders against the wind and set out to take care of business. He was, after all, on a military mission.

Chapter Eleven

Amanda sat on her bed, with her coat on, yet she couldn't stop shivering. The soup she'd eaten hadn't warmed her at all. She slipped off her shoes and tucked her feet beneath her to warm them. But nothing could warm the icy coldness that gripped her heart.

She needed a plan. But what? Germany had become too dangerous for Uncle Jacob's family. Did they have passports, or were they confiscated? Tomorrow she'd find out at the *bris* ceremony, and she would appeal to the American embassy if necessary.

She bent the pillow and leaned back on it, pulling the blanket over her. *No one knows I'm related to anyone in Eisenburg—or at least no one except Delbert and Curley—and the optometrist.* Surely, none of them would betray her. Because Uncle Jacob was her mother's brother, their last names were not the same. The ghetto wall crouched at the edge of her thoughts. How could a country single out citizens and segregate them from society? An image of a headline she read today spooled through her memory. *Jews Open a Pandora's Box to Turn Loose Evil in the Land.*

She reached for her pad and pencil. After a moment's thought, she wrote, "Germany's Infamous Secret." Under that she wrote "Millions Suffer Persecution and Humiliation." This was the big story she'd come to find. But she felt no sense of accomplishment. Instead, she felt sick and frightened.

She flung off the cover and swung her legs over the side of the bed. With practiced speed, she wrote everything she'd seen and experienced since her arrival in Berlin, the neatly swept streets, the clean main thoroughfares where tourists walked, and the darker side of the pristine image. She described her uncle's defaced gallery, the ghetto wall. . . She quit writing at last and gazed at the gray ceiling.

The guards! How would she get in tomorrow morning? She could say she was a nurse. But they might demand identification papers. They probably wouldn't allow a tourist in. What if she told them she hated Jews and was glad to see them segregated from the decent people of Eisenburg; would they consider her a sympathizer and let her in? She grimaced at the thought of even pretending to go along with their madness.

There must be a way in, otherwise Martha wouldn't have told her to come. Maybe it was easy to get in, but difficult to get out.

Amanda began pacing the small room, from the window, past the bed, to the door and back. What if she got stuck behind that wall? *I'm an American citizen.* That carried some weight, didn't it? On the other hand, these people seemed callous enough to disregard such courtesy.

She picked up her notebook and sat on the bed again, continuing her notes. Clouds darkened the sky, and afternoon faded into dusk. A knock on the door jarred her, and she slashed the pencil across the page.

She turned on the lamp and opened the door. Delbert stood in the hallway, smiling down at her. Glancing over her shoulder, he commented, "Working hard, I see."

Amanda glanced back to see her notebook open and the pencil beside it on the bed. Delbert's handsome face beamed at her. What was he really doing here? she wondered.

She felt better for having recorded her confused thoughts and impressions. Now it was time to deal with Delbert. She sighed. "What time is it?"

He pulled his gold watch from its pocket. "Five-fifteen. May I come in?"

Amanda stepped back and let him in. He sat on the wooden chair, hands on his knees. She stood beside the bed, her hand resting on the table, near the earrings Curley had just returned. "Why are you here, Delbert?"

"I'm glad you asked." Delbert leaned forward. "Maybe I was too bold offering you an engagement ring in front of the family." He flashed her his most brilliant grin. "But I meant it. I do want you to marry me."

"But we already discussed that, and you. . ."

He put up his hand to interrupt her. "I know, I know. I didn't realize how seriously you take your newspaper career. But when you turned me down and then left the country, I had to face it. I was slightly overbearing." He rubbed his chin slowly.

"Slightly! You called my work 'little newspaper stories.' You absolutely missed the whole point." Apparently her Christianity meant so little, he didn't even think it had any bearing on their relationship. Amanda picked up the earrings and rubbed her thumb across the flat facet of one of the jewels. "Look, Delbert. We don't need to go over this again. You still haven't answered my question. Why are you here?"

"That *is* the point, honey. I see now how important your work is, and I'm here to show that I support you." He gestured toward her notebook. "Are you writing a story about the new government here? Let me help. I can talk to people and get information for you. We can work together!"

Amanda took a deep breath, trying to cover her annoyance.

"Before you say no, listen! While you were out today, I went to that cathedral and talked with some of the local people. The cathedral is magnificent. Bach didn't play there, but Brahms did. And I talked politics to the people. Adolf Hitler has unified the country. He's brought order to the chaos they were in and stabilized their money. Do you know their currency was so worthless that some housewives used it to light fires in their stoves?" He sat back with a satisfied smile. "Between the two of us we can send back interesting articles to the *Chronicle*."

"Quaint travel articles, telling how lovely it is here and how happy everyone is?" she asked.

"Exactly. What do you say, honey? Germany, from our point of view! We'd make a good team."

Amanda shook her head. "Thanks for the offer, but I need to do this by myself. And Delbert, please don't call me honey."

He hung his head sadly. "I'm sorry. You asked me before not to call you honey. But it's merely an endearment."

The silence lengthened between them. A thunderclap shook the window, startling her. She looked out, seeing nothing but darkness.

"All right. I won't call you that anymore, but it'll be hard, because you're so sweet." He stood and stepped close to her. Putting his arm around her shoulders, he said, "Please reconsider about working together. We'd make a smashing team."

Amanda moved from under his arm. "Sorry." The room was so small, she had to slip between him and the bed, taking her stance in the center of the room. "So, are you going back home soon?" If she sounded anxious to be rid of him, he seemed not to notice.

"No, I'm going to escort you back when you're ready. Meanwhile I'll be here, helping until then." He crossed his arms over his chest in a self-satisfied gesture.

Amanda clenched her jaw and maintained an even tone. "That's nice of you, but I really don't need an escort."

Delbert raised his eyebrows. "You aren't at your family's house. Why not?" Raindrops began pelting the window.

She looked away from him, unwilling to go into the story. She put her notebook and pen on the bedside table, then turned to him and said, "I'm famished! It must be dinnertime."

Delbert came forward with his hand outstretched. "I'd take you out to dinner, but it's beginning to rain. However, I'd be happy to escort you to Frau Reinhardt's table."

Amanda nodded. "All right, but I have to freshen up first. I'll see you down there later."

Delbert ran a hand over his slicked-down hair. "Good." His eyes grew serious as he stared down at her.

Amanda stepped back and said, "Later, then." She closed the door, relieved to be rid of him. A headline flew into her mind: *Gullible Delbert Benedict Approves of Nazi Tactics.*

Frau Reinhardt bustled happily around the tables, making sure her guests had plenty to eat. The aroma of meat, potatoes, and vegetables mingled with a spicy cinnamon smell. The good smell, combined with the rain pouring down and beating on the window, gave the room an aura of a cozy island in a cold, blustery world. Amanda and Delbert were seated at one of the smaller tables, set for six. The dining room was full. Most of the residents were there. Minus one. Curley was conspicuously absent.

Had he left without saying good-bye again? She sucked her lips between her teeth. He told her he was leaving, so she shouldn't be surprised or disappointed. *It's just as well,* she thought. She had no time for romantic notions. She had to concentrate on forming a plan to rescue her family from behind that awful wall.

Maybe sometime in the future she'd meet Curley again. He seemed the kind of man who attracted women, enjoyed them for a while, then moved on. A man who might be a good friend, but dangerous to become fond of. She didn't need complications right now. She bowed her head slightly and said a silent prayer of thanks for the food and also prayed for the safety of her family.

Delbert, speaking to the elderly lady with dyed red hair seated across from them, thanked her for recommending a visit to the cathedral. "A magnificent structure," he said.

"Did you also enjoy it?" the woman asked Amanda.

Amanda was on the verge of excusing herself. She had so much to plan and do before tomorrow, and this chitchat seemed irrelevant. "Enjoy? Oh, no, ma'am. I didn't get there. But Delbert told me all about it."

The woman reached out and took Amanda's hand. "There is no substitute for being there. And you can call me Winnie," she said. Wrinkles fanned out from her big brown eyes as she smiled. "Tomorrow will be sunny. I will speak to the priest, and he will open the bell tower for you. Up there you can see for miles. It is a superlative view."

"Thank you. I'll certainly think about it and let you know."

The woman withdrew her hand with a smile.

Delbert turned to Amanda. "This is a marvelous start to our partnership! Let's do it."

Amanda quickly realized she'd have to leave the house at dawn in order to avoid Delbert, his questions, and perhaps even an attempt to follow her. Too much depended on her to risk being waylaid by nosy, helpful Delbert. "We'll discuss it later," she said.

Delbert turned back to his dinner with a pleased look.

Between the main course and dessert, Frau Reinhardt checked each table to be sure all was well. She laughed delightedly when Delbert said the meal was as appealing as her sparkling eyes.

She'd just gone back into the kitchen when the front door opened and a cold blast of air whooshed inside. All eyes turned in that direction.

Curley brushed the rain out of his eyes and stripped off his soaking jacket. He wished he was wearing his leather flying jacket with the fur-lined collar instead. The warm, fragrant entryway welcomed him.

Frau Reinhardt rushed to him, taking his jacket. "Come, warm your hands in the kitchen," she said, leading him. He walked gingerly, to keep his soggy shoes from squishing. Pausing at the kitchen door, his eyes were drawn across the room to Amanda. For a long moment she looked back at him, then he forced himself to turn and enter the kitchen.

Steam enveloped him with another warm welcome. Frau Reinhardt spread his jacket over three wooden hooks near the back door and placed a towel beneath to catch the drips. The cook moved a pot from one of the burners, and Curley warmed his hands. "This is just what I needed. Thank you." He grinned at Frau Reinhardt.

"You're welcome. So much water! Good only for ducks and fish," observed Frau Reinhardt.

Curley rubbed his hands briskly. Though they were warming, his feet still felt frozen.

As if Frau Reinhardt read his mind, she said, "You have dry socks in your room, *ja?*" He nodded. "Go on, then. Warm your feet. Your dinner will be on the table when you come back down."

He touched his forehead in a mock salute. "Aye, aye, captain."

Back in his room Curley turned on the radiator and removed his shoes and wet socks. He tied his shoes together with the strings, removed the picture over the radiator, and hung them on its nail. The radiator clanked and ticked as it began heating. He draped a sock to hang from inside each shoe. A drop of water fell on the radiator with a hiss.

He removed his passport from his shirt pocket. The police had given it back with strict orders that he be gone by tomorrow noon. He'd strolled past the edge of town, then jogged out into the country to check on the plane. He found it just as he'd left it. He thanked God for the high winds and threat of rain that kept curious country folk inside.

It wouldn't be smart to take off in the storm, though this sweet little plane could do it, and Curley had the expertise to fly out, if necessary. Early would be the best time to leave, and if the storm eased up and the westerly wind continued, he'd make good time.

Back in the dining room, Frau Reinholdt directed him to sit next to the red-headed lady across from Delbert and Amanda. "You sit with your American friends. Relax."

He inclined his head to Amanda, Delbert, and the lady beside him. Giving quick thanks for the meal set before him, he felt a strange comfort at being so near Amanda.

She and Delbert had finished eating and had coffee cups at their places. Delbert laughed at something Winnie said. Amanda sipped her coffee, gazing distractedly into her cup. Long lashes lay against her cheeks. Curley flexed his fingers, longing to lift her chin and look into her clear, observant eyes.

Just as if he'd done so, she looked up with a burning, faraway look. He tilted his head and leaned forward. "Hello?" She focused her eyes, startling him with their soft emerald glow.

Delbert looked from Curley to Amanda. He laid his hand over hers, and Curley didn't miss the implication of possessiveness.

Amanda slid her hand out from under Delbert's and stood, excusing herself, and Curley and Delbert rose. Curley thought, *I have to talk to her alone and warn her of the danger out there.*

Back in her room, Amanda began her preparations. She wrote a letter to her parents, sealing it in two envelopes so that it would be difficult to hide any tampering.

She tapped her pencil on her chin, contemplating her next step, when her eyes caught sight of a small piece of paper lying on the worn burgundy linoleum just a few inches inside the door. It hadn't been there when she went down to dinner, and she must have pushed it aside when she'd come in just now.

She quickly unfolded it. Inside was a small yellow triangular patch. "Pin this, point up, on your chest, left side," was written on the paper, signed "M."

A chill zinged up her neck and her gaze darted about the room. How did Martha get this message here? All day Amanda had wondered how Martha had known she was here, and now this.

The rain beat against the window, sliding down in watery rivulets. She fingered the patch, looking toward the rain-streaked window, trying to remember details she'd read at the library. Certain citizens were given a serial number and triangle. Red for politicals, green for criminals, purple and black for something she couldn't recall, pink for homosexuals, yellow for Jews. Holding the actual symbol made it all more terribly real.

A knock at the door startled her. She crammed the note and yellow triangle into her pocket and opened it.

Knocking on Amanda's door, Curley reminded himself to be patient. As a captain in the air corps, when he issued an order, it was obeyed without question. He wasn't used to the art of persuasion. But persuade her he must.

The door opened slowly, and Amanda stood in a soft, dark pink sweater and slim skirt, with the glow of the lamp behind her. She looked feminine and vulnerable, and he relaxed. Convincing her might not be as hard as he'd thought.

"Curley! Well, this is a surprise." She glanced at his stockinged feet. "You didn't even wait for your shoes to dry." She stepped back. "Come on in."

He entered, leaving the door slightly ajar behind him. The only evidence of her occupying the room was the tablet on her bed and a wet washcloth draped over the radiator pipe.

"Did you come to say good-bye?" she asked.

He leaned his shoulder against the door and crossed his ankles. "Yes. And I'm asking you once again to come with me."

She raised an eyebrow. "And why should I do that?"

He pushed himself away from the door and stood with his legs apart. "I told you, the situation here is much more dangerous than you realize."

"Thank you for your concern, but I *am* an American citizen, and an observer, and I'm not going to do anything to draw attention to myself," she answered in a determined tone of voice.

He reached out and gripped her arms. She looked up at him with wide, surprised eyes. "American citizen or not, you'll be in danger if you stay," he said, more harshly than he intended.

She frowned, her eyes darkening. "I saw. I read the hideous lies and actions against certain citizens. But I see no danger to me."

Curley realized his hold on her was tightening. He let go of her arm. "Listen, and don't ask me how I know, but soon, maybe tomorrow, the police will take a group of its 'protected' citizens from behind the wall to some unknown place."

Amanda's mouth tightened a fraction. "Which group?" She reached for her tablet and pencil. He reached for her wrist.

"This is not to be written, yet. I don't know which group, but they will be Jews." Her raised chin of defiance irritated him. "Amanda, I'm telling you—leave now."

She looked away, not answering. Her wrist felt birdlike and fragile in his large hand. He moved his thumb and marveled at the velvet softness of her skin. He let go of her and she seemed to relax.

Gently rubbing her wrist, she said, "I can't leave right now, but I do thank you for the warning. I'll be careful."

He stared at her, wanting to shake sense into her, to tell her of the brutal look in the eyes of the guard at the wall. He couldn't explain the vicious ways of fighting men. She knew nothing of such things. "We need to pray," he said, unable to keep quiet. "Now." He reached for her hands.

She looked startled, but obediently she bowed her head.

"Father God," he began, "You have power over every evil in the world. I pray now for Amanda's safety, and for her family's, and. . ."

When he finished, he let go of her hands. "If you change your mind, you know where my room is. I'm leaving at dawn." He did have his orders to report soon.

She followed him to the door. "Thanks. And good-bye."

Curley gave in to the impulse to touch her shoulder. The lamp behind her again surrounded her in a soft glow picked up by the sweater's fine wool. "I want to see you after we both get back. Will you give me your address and phone number?" He could feel the magnetism that pulled him when he was close to her.

"All right," she said almost in a whisper. Her gaze dropped from his, and she moved away to pick up her tablet and pencil. She wrote on the bottom corner of the page and tore it out. Handing it to him, she smiled and said, "Well, then, this is it. Good-bye, and Godspeed."

This isn't a final good-bye, he thought. He'd see her again. He'd walk through hell and high water if he had to.

An overwhelming need to hold her swept over him and he drew her to him. He held her in his arms for a long moment, simply enjoying the feel of her softness against him. She brought her arms around his waist and sighed. He dipped his head and kissed her cheek, her chin, then settled his mouth on her lips.

She raised herself on tiptoes and moved her arms to his chest, then slid them up around his neck. The warmth of her lips ignited a fire that flared through him. He pulled back briefly, then reclaimed her lips again. The delicious joy that resulted almost drugged his senses. He pulled back and crushed her to his chest.

He rocked back and forth a moment, then kissed her on the forehead. "May God take care of you." He looked into her eyes, which were smoldering with embers of desire.

"You, too," she whispered. Before he gave in to his urge to stay there and kiss her all night, he reached behind him for the doorknob. She slid her hands from his neck and clasped them at her waist as he left.

Back in his room, Curley sat on his bed running his fingers through his hair. He had his orders to get that Vega to Holland. Of course, they'd given him plenty of time, but he'd already delayed his takeoff until tomorrow at dawn, hoping to take Amanda with him.

He remembered when his best friend Johnny met Meredith. Curley was only fifteen at the time, but he'd thought Johnny was foolish, even though Meredith was a special woman. Just last spring Johnny had told him that someday he'd find a woman who could inspire him to walk through fire or flood for her, just as Meredith had inspired him. Curley had scoffed then.

Now he began to see that until Amanda came into his life, he'd led a lonely, single existence. It was as though he moved all alone among people who connected with each other, never allowing himself to think there was anything missing in his own life.

He placed his elbows on his knees, hands clasped behind his neck, remembering back ten years. When Meredith came into Johnny's life, Curley was sure that such a perfect match was something that only happened once every century.

Lately, though, he was beginning to feel the stir of something in the corner of his heart that had been locked away from the time he was four years old, when his mother left. Amanda seemed to be able to reach past his defenses and touch the childlike hunger for love and acceptance.

Curley covered his face with both hands. Since Amanda came into his life, nothing was the same—that thought alarmed him more than he wanted to admit. He took a deep breath and went to the closet for his suitcase. He had a mission, and the sooner he got his mind on that, the better off he'd be.

He packed everything, closed the suitcase, then lay on the bed, fully dressed. "God, take care of her. She doesn't know the danger she's in. But You do." He closed his eyes, drifting in and out of sleep until dawn's thin light crept into the room.

Chapter Twelve

After Curley left her room, Amanda leaned against the door for support. She had dreamed of being held in his arms, but his unexpected gentleness awakened a deep feeling of peace in her heart. She took a ragged breath, surprised at her swift and passionate reaction to him. She stroked her arm, conscious of the lingering feel of his arms holding her close to his warmth.

She touched her lower lip, still warm from his kiss, inspiring an intense desire for more. She forced herself to walk across the room, away from the door, afraid of her need to go after him. She stood watching rain streak the window, and she jammed her fists into her sweater pockets.

The yellow triangle bristled against her right knuckle, as if an iceberg were thrusting itself up through her warm sensuous haze. She retrieved the note and angrily tore it to shreds. She opened the window a crack and let the storm grab the pieces.

She pushed back the closet curtain. Moving the clothes about, she finally pulled out a classic navy blue skirt, matching jacket, and white blouse. From her purse she got two safety pins and pinned the triangle to her overcoat lapel.

She longed for someone to confide in, but there was no one. Even Curley, who saw the danger, wouldn't understand her need to stay and help. She almost wished her father were here. She knew, however, that even if he were in the next room, she couldn't tell him. He'd tell her to stay in her room, then he'd take over and demand the release of his family.

But would that be the right thing to do? No. She'd done her research at the library, and she was well aware that this persecution ran deep. To face it head-on would only result in being crushed.

She stared down at her camera bag on the floor. She would take pictures of her new cousin and the rest of her family at the *bris,* but getting the camera past the guards would be tricky. She unlatched the flash attachment, took it apart, and laid the pieces, along with two new rolls of film, on the dresser. She slid her notebook inside her purse, glad now that she hadn't surrendered to the fashion rage for pert little clutches.

After washing her face and brushing her teeth, she put on her pajamas and climbed in between cold sheets. Hoping for a little sleep before dawn, she tried to push Curley and the Nazi problem from her mind. The tip-tap of the rain and the metallic noise of the radiator lulled her to sleep.

She woke with a start. The rain had eased, and the silence was heavy. She bit her lip, hoping she hadn't cried out. She'd been dreaming; she was in a large garden, fleeing from a menacing pursuer. She came to a pond and tried to go around it, but it grew to become an ocean. Waves crashed at her right, and her pursuer was closing to her left. She saw a bridge ahead and ran faster, but her legs felt as if they were running through glue.

Uncle Jacob, Aunt Esther, and the family were on the bridge, looking out to sea, unaware of her plight. She shouted a warning, but they smiled, waving at someone in the distance. She glanced over to see what the family was waving at. It was Curley, falling into the water from the sky. *No!*

Her heart was still pounding. She flicked on the lamp and looked at her watch. Three-thirty. She turned the lamp off and lay back on her pillow, wondering who was chasing her in her dream. What was her family doing there? She trembled at the vision of Curley falling from the sky. The sky was his milieu. She'd seen him perform breathtaking stunts when he was a teenager. He'd parachuted flawlessly onto the ship just two weeks ago. So why did she dream of him falling?

She understood the part about her family on a bridge, unaware of the peril; but the peril was theirs, not hers. She thanked God that He'd promised to walk with her, even through the valley of the shadow of death. *Lord, help me to speak up tomorrow, so they'll know they can trust You, no matter what the circumstances. Please provide an opportunity to show them the Gospel.*

She turned to her side, puffed the pillow, and forced herself to relax, knowing she'd need to be alert tomorrow. Actually in just a few hours.

She drifted on the edge of sleep, and when the night lightened to pewter gray, she sat up and put her feet onto the area rug beside her bed, adjusting to the semidarkness.

She wrapped her robe around her and hurried to the bathroom. Then she heard a noise. Holding a damp washcloth in one hand, she opened the bathroom door with the other, then froze. The weak light showed Curley standing beside her bedroom door. With suitcase in hand, he paused there for a moment, as though listening or making up his mind about something. Then he scowled and strode down the hall. She quietly pulled the door shut until he'd gone past and had plenty of time to get down the stairs.

Back in her room, she brushed her hair until it crackled, then gathered it in a clip at her neck. She finished dressing and slipped the flash attachment parts into her jacket pockets. Opening her blouse, she slipped in the camera, settling it uncomfortably above her waist. Over all of this she wore her overcoat.

She stole quietly through the house and slipped through the front door into the frigid morning. The sky had lightened to a silvery color. Breathing in the fresh scent of rain-washed pavement and wet bricks, she put on her scarf and gloves. The air chilled her cheeks. She checked her watch: five fifty-five.

At the corner she turned left for a few blocks, then proceeded down a street that paralleled Domstrasse, toward the barrier. As she got closer, she detoured another block, to Eisenburg's last street, in order to approach the wall as far from the guards as possible.

A block to her left was the wall's corner. She went around the corner, determined to walk all around the confine. How big was the walled-in area?

To her left were rows of fruit trees with their branches stripped by the wind. Amanda walked the path beside the wall for approximately five city blocks, tiptoeing in some places to keep her heels from sinking into the moist earth.

Wisps of smoke rose from behind the wall, and she could hear doors opening and the faraway murmur of voices. She thought she heard someone behind her and looked around quickly, but all she saw was an orange cat darting into the orchard. She folded her coat lapel with its yellow triangle to the inside and kept walking.

She followed the encircling wall to the front, which faced Domstrasse. She checked her watch again: six forty-five. She passed the only gate and walked on a few blocks down narrow streets, passing somber, unsmiling people.

How would they react if she turned her lapel out and they saw the yellow triangle? She didn't, reluctant to risk the sting of discrimination toward Jews. Was this in a small measure what her family lived with? The thought, even for a few minutes, was offensive, but how did a person live with it daily?

The aroma of coffee and sweets baking distracted and tempted her, but she didn't think her stomach could handle food. A middle-aged man seated at a table near the bakery window looked up from his newspaper and gave Amanda an appreciative glance, with a warm, friendly smile.

He looks like a nice person, she thought. Would he smile if she turned her lapel outward to show the yellow triangle? What would he say if she interviewed him about his country's policies toward Jews and other "inferior" groups? It was hard to believe that these seemingly normal, nice people would support such repulsive decrees.

The bakery door opened and someone came out. That's when she saw the sign, "No Jews Allowed." Her stomach knotted up and she turned back the way she'd come. *I've avoided this long enough,* she thought, pulling her lapel out to expose the yellow triangle. She was a fool to tell herself she was merely gathering information, learning more about the town, when the truth was that she was delaying going inside that hideous fence.

She took a deep breath, held her head high, approaching the gate where a guard stood at each side. She looked straight ahead and walked inside.

"Halt!"

Pushing back a surge of anxiety, she stopped. She took another quick breath and looked back. *"Ja bitte?"*

"Where have you been?" His eyes narrowed.

"On an errand," she answered as calmly as she could.

"I'd remember you," said the other guard with raised eyebrows. "You did not leave this morning."

Amanda looked him straight in the eye. "Maybe you were in the gatehouse."

The other guard adjusted the gun strap over his shoulder, eyeing her. At that moment a truck full of soldiers roared up to the gate, distracting him. His gray eyes hardened at Amanda and he sneered, "Move on, Jewish whore!"

Amanda felt her cheeks burn as she turned and hurried inside. Her legs weak, she steeled herself to keep going and not look back. As she gritted her teeth, trying not to reveal her anger, she began noticing details. The street and buildings didn't look so different on this side of the wall, but there was a sense of despair in the few people who shuffled past her. The light of hope gone from their eyes, they didn't speak to each other. Her footsteps echoed loudly in the quiet street.

An old man with a beard down his chest gave her a skeptical look, then he crossed the street as if to avoid her. A baby's cry from overhead pierced the silence. Amanda glanced up. The dark second-story windows all looked the same. She moved on, staying close to the building so she'd be less visible to the guard in case he was still watching her.

She turned a corner and continued walking the oddly silent but occupied streets. She encountered no guards. Apparently they didn't enter the confine; they simply guarded the gate.

She stopped at a stone wall, took out her notebook and pen, and jotted some notes. Her anger stirred as she wondered why there was no outrage, no reports of this monstrous assault on whole segments of a country's citizens.

That anger energized her as she went back to Domstrasse and found number 22. Carved figures sat upon ledges over the doors, and wrought iron railings enclosed minuscule garden spaces, most filled with yellowing grass.

By now it was almost nine o'clock, so she mounted the steps and opened the door. Her eyes took a moment to adjust to the dark foyer. She stood in the dim hallway, confused for a minute, wondering how she'd find the right door. The foyer smelled of old wood, lemon oil, and mint.

She was searching for a list of the occupants' names when the door behind her opened. Her cousin Tamara, with a blanket-wrapped bundle in her arms, entered with a man. They squinted at the darkness.

"Tamara!" Amanda touched her cousin's shoulder. "It's me, Amanda."

"Amanda! I'm so glad you've come. But it's not safe."

"So everyone keeps telling me." She nodded at the man with Tamara. "You must be Nathan. I'm glad to meet you."

A door opened behind Nathan, and Tamara nodded at the old woman who looked out. "Hello, Mrs. Mandelbaun." The woman looked uneasily toward Amanda and shut her door without a word.

"Come on." Nathan motioned, leading them behind the stairs.

The door opened into a short hallway so narrow they had to walk single file into the tiny studio apartment. The room had one small window looking out onto another building.

Uncle Jacob approached them with hands outstretched. "*Mazeltov!* Enter! Enter!" He embraced Tamara, then gave Amanda a glowing smile and hugged her, too.

Amanda, so glad to see her uncle, tried to ignore the shock at seeing the family reduced to living in such cramped and shabby quarters. She hugged him back, and he kissed her on both cheeks.

Smiling broadly, Aunt Esther entered from the kitchen with a wooden spoon in her hand and Martha right on her heels.

"Amanda!" Martha anxiously waited for Aunt Esther to step back from hugging

Amanda so she could hug her long and hard. She stepped back with a confused look. "What's this?" She felt the bulge at Amanda's waistline.

Amanda laughed. "My camera. I smuggled it in."

"It's good to see you still have your sense of humor. We're so glad to see you," said Aunt Esther, and added sadly, "but not in these circumstances."

Aunt Esther took Amanda's coat and said, "Have you seen our little David?"

Tamara had unwrapped the blanket and smoothed back the baby's dark hair so they could admire his ruddy-cheeked face. She looked up at her mother with a worried frown. "Are Rabbi Benjamin and the *moyell* coming?"

"They said they would."

Nathan shrugged. "They are afraid." The defeated words fell heavily into the silence.

Uncle Jacob waved toward the small sofa. "Sit and tell us what's happening in America. We don't get much news here."

Amanda sat close enough to the edge to leave room for Martha. "Dad and Mom are doing fine. Business is good, since most of our investments are in foreign countries. You've probably heard there's a depression in America. But President Roosevelt has everything in hand. He's instituted programs to keep people busy earning a little money."

Aunt Esther called through the kitchen arch, "Talk loudly so I can hear!"

"This place is so small you'll hear us breathing," said Martha. She squeezed Amanda's hand and whispered, "There's so much I want to tell you."

Tamara and Uncle Jacob sat on wooden chairs, while Nathan stood behind Tamara, his hand on her shoulder. Amanda glanced around while she assembled her camera, wondering where they slept. There was the room they were in, a cramped kitchen, and probably a closet behind the fringed material hanging over a shallow doorway.

She didn't want to cause her uncle sadness, but she had to ask, "What happened to the house? I went there and found some very unfriendly men."

Uncle Jacob's eyes blazed. "Those. . . ," he fumbled for a word, "those poor excuses for human beings, they ordered us out of our own home."

Amanda stared at him, dumbfounded. "By what authority. . .how could they do that?"

"Just walked in and took over." Aunt Esther stood in the kitchen doorway, fists on her hips. "We had to scramble to gather together what we could carry out." Her accusing voice grew sharp. "Those worthless curs have our family china. They better not eat off it!" The thought of that seemed to incense her more, and she added, "I'll have to disinfect everything."

Amanda liked her aunt's feisty expression, and she took her picture. She lowered her camera. "You're going back? When?"

Uncle Jacob stroked his chin thoughtfully. "I expect we'll be back home before Hanukkah." The whistling teakettle got Aunt Esther's attention, and she went back into the kitchen.

"Then you believe this displacement is temporary?" Amanda took a candid pose of Tamara, Nathan, and the baby.

"Most certainly," said Uncle Jacob. "It's a passing thing. The Nazi party wants to show its strength, that's all. This will all blow over in a month at the most."

Amanda thought of the newspapers she'd read yesterday afternoon. "The gallery. . ."

Uncle Jacob's face blanched, his fists clenched. Aunt Esther saved the tense moment by entering the room, asking Amanda if she wanted her tea with sugar and apologizing that they had no cream.

There was a light tap on the door and Martha jumped up to answer. She ushered in a stout man wearing a heavy black coat and a *yarmulke* on his head. He carried a small case in his hand and had the friendliest eyes Amanda had seen since she entered Germany.

Uncle Jacob and Nathan greeted him and clasped his hand. "Rebbe Stein. Welcome."

"Rebbe Benjamin sends his prayers for your family."

Uncle Jacob introduced him as the *moyell,* and Aunt Esther offered him a tray of scallop-shaped cookies pressed together with jam inside and powdered sugar sprinkled on top.

He took one, thanking her, and she handed him his tea. He sipped it and touched the baby in Tamara's arms, saying, "We must wake the little man and hurry with the ceremony. I am sorry, but I feel there is trouble brewing outside."

Amanda shuddered, remembering the nastiness of the guard and the soldiers arriving as she entered the gates. She shot a picture of all of them, the baby in their midst.

Tamara prepared David while Rabbi Stein opened his black case. He said the ceremonial words, then circumcised the child, who began wailing.

Tamara hugged the crying baby to her breast, while Nathan thanked the rabbi.

He washed his hands, using a special cloth he'd brought, and repacked his case. He took a quick sip of tea, picked up a cookie, and apologized for having to leave so abruptly.

Tamara handed the baby to Aunt Esther and followed Nathan as he walked Rabbi Stein to the door. "We understand. Thank you," said Nathan, seeing him out.

Aunt Esther cooed softly to the baby and he stopped sobbing. Amanda picked up her teacup and asked Martha, "How did you know I was at Frau Reinhardt's?"

Martha smiled. "It was—"

Gunshots suddenly stabbed the air, popping over and over. Panic swept through Amanda. She set down her teacup with shaky hands. Aunt Esther's eyes widened in fear. The baby wailed again, and Tamara cried, "Oh God, help us!"

The warm family gathering was shattered by a bullhorn. A roaring voice yelled, "Everyone out! Anyone left in this building in two minutes will be shot! Out! Now!"

Chapter Thirteen

Amanda gaped at the furious activity. Aunt Esther scooped something golden and twinkling from a jar on her cupboard shelf; Uncle Jacob, with knees bent, reached deep into the closet; Nathan stood clutching the bawling baby while Tamara, with tears streaming down her face, stuffed his new booties and sweater into the diaper bag. Martha had her hands in an open box, pulling out warm woolen scarves, socks, and hats. Then she reached beneath the couch to retrieve a small notebook and pen.

It all happened so fast, Amanda stood as if in a dream, watching. Martha bundled the warm woolen items into a scarf and tossed Amanda's coat to her. "Hurry!"

Amanda woke from her shocked daze. She shrugged her coat on and quickly unscrewed the flash attachment from her camera, then stuffed all the pieces into her pockets. "What can I do? Can I carry something?" She looked about helplessly.

"You're an American!" shrieked Tamara wildly, thrusting her baby into Amanda's arms. "Say he's yours. Take him to America. He has no chance here!"

Amanda shook her head, startled and shaken. "But I. . ."

Nathan reached for his son and put an arm around his distraught wife. "This is temporary. We'll all go home when—"

"Come!" Uncle Jacob held the door open while they filed out. Martha carried the bundled scarf in one hand and took Amanda's hand with the other when they got out into the dark hallway. Footsteps hurried down the steps from the upper floor. The woman in the front apartment walked unsteadily out the front door, clutching a shawl to her neck. Tamara's baby had grown quiet, and the silence was broken only by the sniffling of a young boy holding his mother's hand as they walked out into the dim sunshine of an unknown future.

On the front steps of the building, Amanda could barely believe what she saw. German soldiers stood with rifles pointed menacingly. Some used them as prods to move people huddling in the middle of the street. It reminded her of pictures she'd seen of cattle drives. People were being rounded up in the street!

Those emerging from the building behind her streamed around her. "Come on!" urged Martha, "before they use force on us."

A soldier approached, glowering, and Amanda followed Martha into the street to stand with her family. Fear and confusion threatened to erupt into hysteria as people looked from one to another for an explanation, a shred of hope or dignity, and found none.

All I have to do is show my passport, thought Amanda. She decided to wait, to endure what lay ahead with her family. Maybe the soldiers assembled the people to give new rules or to frighten them by a show of strength. Amanda put an arm around Martha. Nathan had an arm around Tamara, supporting her while she cried softly.

Uncle Jacob turned his head from side to side as though looking for a logical reason for this ousting of people from their temporary homes. Aunt Esther glared at the guard stomping through the crowd. Amanda had seen that look before, when she and Martha were children and had gotten into trouble. They always said that look could make a stone tremble. *These soldiers are harder than stone,* thought Amanda. *They won't tremble; they'll strike back.*

Amanda reached out to touch Aunt Esther, when all of a sudden they heard a wail from the building across the street. A soldier emerged from the doorway behind an old man who was clutching his hip and limping. *"Schnell!"* shouted the soldier and whacked the man across his shoulders, sending him sprawling down the steps.

Reacting quickly, Amanda dashed to the old man's side and helped him to his feet.

"Leave him!" snarled the soldier.

Amanda looked up and muttered, "He's hurt."

The icy gray eyes filled with contempt, sending a chill down her spine. "Vermin have no feelings."

She bit back an angry retort as the old man struggled to his feet.

The soldiers began pushing and urging the crowd to the gate. Faces near her looked about in panic. There were no explanations, only shouts and prodding. No one dared question the soldiers, but a raw, primitive dread shot through the group.

A suffocating tension gripped Amanda's throat. She grimly noted every nuance and action. *Outrage in Eisenburg* would be her next headline.

Curley had warned her of this. She suddenly longed for his strength. She looked up; was he up there in the skies, gone from this madness? And Delbert. What would he do? He hadn't been able to sense any trouble was brewing. Visiting tourist attractions, he might never know this atrocity was happening. *When I get out of here, everyone will know,* thought Amanda. *I'll tell them!*

"This is outrageous!" Amanda said to Martha, almost choking on her anger. She ripped the yellow triangle from her coat and threw it to the ground.

Martha squeezed her hand. "They want to humiliate us. They can do their worst, but they can't crush our hearts."

"You're right. We have to keep our faith in God."

Children, sensing their parents' fear, were crying. "Faith?" Martha cried. "You need to rethink this 'faith.' Look around you."

"Martha!" Dark blond brows drew together over Amanda's eyes. "What are you saying? Remember back when Miss Whitney took us to church and we gave our hearts to Jesus?"

Martha drew in a breath of cold air and looked up into the leaden skies.

Walking sideways, Amanda stared into Martha's face. Her light blue eyes wavered. Amanda repeated fiercely, her voice barely above a whisper, "Remember?"

Martha's face showed her pain. "I remember," she said, and looked away. "It was so long ago. I've tried to stay close to Christ since then. But where is He now?"

"He's here. He said He'd be."

A man in his thirties moved up in the crowd and put a hand on Uncle Jacob's shoulder. "Where are they taking us?" he asked, his dark eyes darting from face to face, averting his eyes from the guards hustling them through the gate.

Uncle Jacob turned a serious face to the man. "Why do you ask me? I don't know." The man shook his head, seeking answers in the faces around him, finding none.

As the Jewish group was herded through the streets of their own town, their silent fear turned to restless murmurs. Their former neighbors hung back in doorways, the younger ones watching curiously, some insolently from the sidewalks.

Amanda glanced at Tamara; she was just starting her family, but what was her future? She hadn't had time to retrieve a thing from her home. Amanda's first article would focus on this new family and what these forced moves were doing to them.

The guards made the people hurry through town. They reached the outskirts of the small town in a few minutes. A black car slid up beside them, and an officer got out. He barked an order to the guards, who nudged the people forward. Those who balked were prodded and kicked. Terror and outrage, combined with the pushing, caused a crush of people in the narrow street.

Amanda shouldered through the crowd to approach the officer, when one of the guards pushed her back. Sick with their cruelty, she glared at him and said, "Where are you taking these people?"

With a brutal stare, he pushed her back again.

"I am an American citizen! I demand to know where you're taking us."

"Pah! You are no American. You are with this trash, so you march with the rest of them."

Refusing to turn away, she pointed to the officer. "I will speak with him!" She opened her purse and reached inside.

"Get back!" he roared. The officer glanced at the disturbance.

Amanda held her passport up, waving it. "I am an American citizen! I refuse to be treated like this." She fought to keep her voice calm and authoritative.

The officer approached. "What is going on here?"

Amanda shot the guard a cold look while he saluted. Before he could speak, she said, "Yes, what *is* going on here? I am an American citizen, and I find myself rounded up, shoved about like an animal." She looked behind her. "And what have these people done? Where are you taking them?"

The officer stared from under the black brim of his hat, then he took her passport. He calmly opened it and flipped the pages, his lips thin with contempt. He gave her a measuring look, then put her passport in his pocket as if it were too filthy to look at.

Amanda took a deep breath to quell the panic welling in her throat.

"I will keep this and check your story. Now, get on the truck."

The guard grinned and gave her an extra hard shove. Amanda searched through the crowd. She spied Martha's blond head and went to her. "Where is Uncle Jacob and the rest of the family?" she asked.

Martha's eyes were bleak as she pointed through the crowd, and then they heard a cry. Everyone turned to see a pillar of smoke rise from the other side of Eisenburg. "They're burning our homes!"

Curley checked the instruments for the tenth time in as many minutes. The view outside hadn't changed. Low, flat clouds below, with glimpses of land between. All engine gauges were in the green. The airspeed indicator showed 120 mph, the engine sounded good; this sweet plane was performing beautifully.

But something was wrong. He knew it. He'd learned to trust his sixth sense when flying; it had saved his life more than once, especially on the stunt-flying circuit. Now, on his way to Holland, he felt more and more uncomfortable. Something was not right. Another check of the instrument panel and the steady drone of the engine confirmed that the problem was not in the plane. Then what?

Taking his mind off the plane's performance, he looked at the landmarks below. A bridge, a large stretch of water ahead. He'd just passed Hamburg. He stared out over the horizon. Amanda. He shook his head. She was on his mind too much. When this mission was over, he'd contact her and see where he stood. He didn't believe Delbert's statement that they were engaged.

He slipped the plane to the left to get a good view behind him and saw nothing but the sun rising. No German planes on his tail. His mission was safe, and he had an easy trip ahead. He reached behind his seat and took a candy bar from his flight bag. He peeled down the wrapper, telling himself there was no reason for this sense of uneasiness.

He bit off some chocolate and thought of Amanda again. He checked the map on his lap, putting a finger on his present location to note his progress. It didn't work. Amanda's face filled his mind. Coupled with the uneasiness he couldn't shake, he began to wonder if he should turn back.

If what he heard was true, and there was to be an uprooting of the Jews behind the wall, where would she be? Not anywhere near; not if she was smart and heeded his warning. No, she was all right. He smiled, thinking that at this minute she probably had her family with her at Frau Reinholdt's, eating strudel.

He finished his candy and flew on toward Holland. *Go back.* He turned his head sharply. He'd heard the words as surely as if someone were sitting beside him. Even the engine throbbed: *Go back. Go back. Go back.* He frowned as a vision of Amanda's face floated across his mind again.

Pressing the left rudder pedal and turning the control wheel, he made a 180-degree turn, retracing his progress. The closer he came, the more the urgency pulled at him. *Remember, God; I asked You to take care of her.*

After passing over the gray haze from Berlin's factories, he squinted at a column of smoke ahead. He hoped it was merely some farmer burning the chaff from his fields, but the smoke was billowing too high to be a burning field.

When he flew through the thin clouds low over Eisenburg, his suspicion was confirmed. The ghetto was on fire.

Curley knew he had to be careful; his mission, his very life could be in jeopardy, but he would have taxied down the main street, if it were wide enough, and rescued Amanda if she needed it. He knew now the strong urge to return was because somehow she was in trouble. And he grudgingly noted, the only trouble was in the ghetto where Amanda's family resided. He knew her—nosy reporter, stubborn champion of her family. She'd be right in the thick of things, trying to help.

He brought the plane down as close to town as he dared, making sure it was well hidden in the trees. He ran parallel to the road about fifteen feet away to avoid being seen.

Entering town from a side street, he pulled up his collar against the damp air, concealing his face, and made his way to Frau Reinhardt's. *Lord, let them be there in the parlor, away from the trouble. It will be so easy,* he thought, *to get Amanda—and her family, too, if they want—back to the plane and out of the country.*

He arrived at 11:15 A.M. Winnie, the elderly, red-haired woman, looked up as he stood at the parlor doorway. Her hand held a pen poised over a journal. Smiling brightly, she said, "Hello there! We missed you at breakfast!"

"Thank you!" She was alone in the parlor. Curley pushed back his disappointment and smiled at her. Behind him he heard low voices and the rattle of dishes as the kitchen help set out the noon meal.

He was about to ask, when Winnie volunteered that Amanda hadn't been at breakfast either. "Her friend said the two of you most likely went out to see the sun rise." She craned her head to peer behind him. "She's not with you? Ah, well, perhaps she's still in her room." She touched her chin with the top of the pen thoughtfully and said, "I hope she's feeling well."

"Thank you," said Curley and nodded to her. "Good day." He hurried up the stairs and knocked on Amanda's door.

A maid came from a room across the hall. "Miss Chase isn't in." She clutched a bundle of rolled-up sheets in her arms.

Curley looked briefly over his shoulder at her. *"Danke."* He went down the stairs two at a time, the hair at his nape prickling. *Where is she? How will I find her?* He stood at the front door, rubbing his chin, when Delbert entered.

"Hello, old man!" he said with a bright smile. "So, you're back. Did you and Amanda do some early sightseeing?" He pulled at the white muffler around his neck, unwinding it. "It's chilly out there."

"I saw smoke. What was burning?" asked Curley, ignoring Delbert's question.

Pulling off his gloves, Delbert answered. "Oh that. I heard that some apartments were burning. They wouldn't let anyone near; said it wasn't safe. The police escorted the poor folks who lived there through town, probably to a shelter."

"Which direction did they go?" asked Curley.

Delbert slapped the gloves across one hand and peered into the parlor. "What? Oh, south. Down that street by the park, the one with the shop that sells baroque figurines and paintings. Where's my dear fiancée, Amanda?"

Fiancée! He wouldn't believe Delbert's arrogant boasts. "Don't know. Excuse me." He reached past Delbert and pulled the door open. Looking both ways, he hurried away. He skirted the park, away from a policeman who stood with feet apart and hands clasped behind his back, watching the area.

He followed the street for a few blocks and, nearing the edge of town, saw nothing in the distance. If they had walked this street, it would have been over an hour ago at least. Keeping a low profile and walking quickly, but not so fast as to catch attention, he left town. As soon as he was back in the meadows, he ran to the plane.

Back in the air, he followed the winding road south of town. After a few minutes he saw them—a knot of about thirty people walking, with a black car behind them. He tipped the left wing and squinted at the group, but he wasn't close enough to pick out Amanda if she was in the crowd.

He followed the road, not daring to fly too low. The road curved its way south between low hills. He saw a bulky warehouse beside a railroad track. Three trucks and a black car were parked between the warehouse and a smaller building.

Curley flew on, scouring the area for a safe place to land and investigate. Orchards filled the hillsides, making it difficult to find a clear landing place, but the houses were few and far between, which made concealment easier.

Finally, he found a dirt road between rows of trees. Throttling back, he set the plane down, hoping the road was long enough for a takeoff later.

He tightened the wobbly tail wheel and was putting his wrench in the tool sack, when he heard the crunch of footsteps. He froze for an instant, then stood slowly and turned to face whoever was approaching.

Chapter Fourteen

Grimly, Amanda marched with the Jews, passing hills with orchards rising on both sides of the road. The guards ordered them to walk in silence. Martha's remarks echoed in her mind. Why *had* God allowed their home to be taken, and now this?

A plane flew overhead, and she thought of Curley. *If only I'd believed all of what he said and got my family away. I saw the evidence in the library; but I couldn't believe the Germans would brazenly evict the ghetto residents in broad daylight.*

Where was Curley? Probably in England by now, she figured, and wondered if she'd ever see him again. The memory of how he'd held her and kissed her last night warmly rippled through her. She glanced at Martha, attempting to divert her thoughts of Curley.

Amanda shivered in the weak sunlight as a chill wind stirred. She jammed her fists into her coat pocket, longing to get her notebook and pencil from her purse and take notes as she walked. Headlines flashed in her mind. *The Reich's Evil Side,* or *Hitler: Leader or Despot?* How she'd expose the cruelties going on here! First, she'd have to get out; and how would she do that? The ruthless officer had her passport in his pocket.

She remembered a Sunday school teacher saying God always provided a way out of trouble. *God, we need Your help now!*

Amanda and Martha were at the rear of the plodding group. Near the front, a young child suddenly stumbled. His mother, who held a toddler in her arms, stopped and encouraged him to stand. He whimpered as the guards told them to keep moving. Amanda scooped up the boy in her arms to avoid falling behind and incurring the guard's wrath. "Don't lose hope," she told the mother. "God will help us."

"Where are they taking us?" wailed the little boy.

"I don't know." Amanda hugged him close to her. "But as long as we have each other, we'll be all right."

When Amanda's steps slowed from the extra weight of the child, Martha carried him. They grew tired and thirsty, moving more laboriously as the day progressed into afternoon.

❧

Curley tensed as the man approached him. He was tall, well over six feet, thin as a prop blade, wearing a black short coat and faded black beret. The blue eyes that peered out from his wrinkled face were keen and observant.

His gaze flicked to the plane, scanning it from prop to tail wheel. *"Schones Flugzeug,"* he breathed, then narrowed his gaze back to Curley. *"Aber was machen Sie hier?"* His clear eyes held no hint of malice or suspicion, merely a bright curiosity.

What should Curley tell him? He wouldn't lie, but he didn't need to spill the details of his mission. "My girlfriend is with a group of people walking the road over there." He gestured down the hill. "And I'm here to pick her up."

The man's eyes narrowed as he studied a thin straggle of grass that he nudged with his toe. After a moment he said, "You're American, aren't you?"

"Yes, I am." Curley bent to pick up his tool sack. Putting the wrench into it, he said, "I won't be here long, sir, and I'll pay you something for the bother."

The man looked up with a troubled expression. "No. No need to pay. This is bad business," he said, shaking his head.

Curley wondered what he meant until he added, "Good and true citizens separated out, and for what? Where will it end?" He looked Curley square in the eye and said, "I will do all I can to help you." He shaded his eyes, looked down the row of trees, and whistled twice. "My grandson will help us."

Then he motioned Curley toward the plane. "Let's pull her back to a more secluded space, good for a quick takeoff."

A young man loped toward them, his eyes widening with surprised admiration when he saw the plane.The older man held out his hand to Curley. "My name is Horst Friedrich, and this is my grandson, Rutger."

Curley took his hand. "James Cameron. Thanks for the help," he said, shaking the young man's hand also.

Together they pulled the plane into a small grove, kicking aside some underbrush to make a clear path out. Walking down the hill together, Horst Friedrich told Curley he'd enlisted in 1914 as a pilot in the kaiser's war. He talked of the plane he flew, and they talked of Curley's Vega.

When they arrived at the farmhouse, Herr Friedrich offered Curley his truck. "It's a relic, like me, but reliable," he said. He waved aside Curley's protests. "Don't worry, I know you'll be back—your plane is here."

Rutger begged to go along, but his grandfather said no. Curley suspected the man wasn't sure Curley could successfully rescue his girlfriend and return the truck.

He quickly caught up with the group struggling to keep ahead of the two black cars behind them. He pushed the pad in the middle of the round steering wheel, and a baritone bark came from the truck's horn. The black cars ignored it.

Curley pulled the truck off the road and got out. He ran to one of the cars and tapped on its window, walking to keep up. The guard pretended not to see him, then finally rolled the window down a few inches and ordered him to get away.

"Stop! I need to talk with you. *Bitte.*" His German was minimal, and he hoped adding the word "please" would help.

The guard rolled the window up and stared straight ahead. The car continued moving, with Curley persistently tapping on the window again and again.

Finally the guard ordered the driver to stop and opened the door, almost knocking Curley over. "What is this? You are interrupting state business. Get out of here." The guard rested his hand on his holster to reinforce his demand.

The group huddled in the cold, their shoulders heaving with exhaustion. "One of your. . .group does not belong here. My friend, Amanda Chase. She is a visiting American citizen."

The guard's eyes narrowed. "What lies are these you tell? These criminals are none of your business."

Curley bit back his anger to keep from asking the man what crime the small children had done. Another officer, from the other car, approached and asked what caused the delay.

They commanded Curley to go, but he refused to leave unless Amanda was with him. He took a chance that they were not ready to risk exposing their present activity. They threatened to arrest him. He told them he had friends waiting for him to bring Amanda back.

Amanda approached them, and Curley smiled, calling her to join them. The other guards kept the people in the middle of the road, moving them to one side when a car passed.

"Hello, Amanda," said Curley with a smile. "What are you doing here?"

"That's what I'd like to know!" She put her hands on her hips and glared at the guard who had her passport. "I told you," she said to him, "I'm an American citizen and I want to go home."

The guard arched an eyebrow and patted his pocket. "We'll check your passport." He folded his arms across his chest. "And if you really are an American citizen, then you may go."

"Listen." Curley curbed his temper. "I sympathize with your efforts to relocate so many families devastated by fire, but I'm a businessman and don't have time for passport checking and other tedious delays." He clenched his fists. "Let the girl go."

Amanda stepped closer to Curley and touched his arm. "Thanks for coming back." To the guard she said, "Please believe me, I'm not one of these people. If you keep me you could get into great trouble with your superiors. My father is an influential man who knows President Roosevelt, and he would not rest until I was released."

"Lies!" screamed the guard. "Get back in the group."

"I will not." Amanda brought her face close to his. "Shoot me now, because I won't walk in your stupid parade anymore." She kept her voice low to keep it from wavering. She longed to demand her passport back, but feared pressing this guard too far.

After an awkward moment, the guard jerked his head toward the car, ordering the others back inside and the driver to move along. "Move, you vermin scum!" he yelled to the people huddled in the cold road.

Martha, holding the child in her arms, approached. "Amanda, what's happening?"

The guard shoved her, and she fell, clutching the child so he wouldn't be hurt.

Amanda started forward, but Curley pulled her back. "Come on. You can't help her now."

He was right. She couldn't help Martha by being arrested, but as a free person she might help. She walked away, but shouted back to Martha, "I won't leave you here!"

With tears distorting her vision, she pulled at her coat buttons. By the time they got to the old truck, she had her coat and jacket open and the lenses out of her pockets.

Curley opened the door for her. "What are you doing?"

"Documenting," she muttered. By the time he climbed in behind the steering wheel, she was fastening the lens on her camera. "Drive as close as you can," she said.

"They have guns, remember," Curley warned. "If I see one drawn, we're making a hasty exit." He turned the truck in a wide circle, almost miring it in the soft dirt on the side of the road as he jockeyed them into position for perfect photos. "Be quick. We can't make another pass."

Amanda wiped her eyes and blinked back the tears, then snapped the heartrending scene. As they sped, away she leaned out of the truck for one more shot.

When they were too far away for more pictures, she drew her head in out of the biting wind, set the camera on the seat, and rolled up the window. "Brrr. Does this truck have a heater?" With cold fingers she buttoned her jacket, then her coat.

Curley reached beneath his seat and drew out a pair of stiff gardening gloves. "I kicked these under the seat when I got in. They'll soften up once you get them on."

Amanda pulled on the cold gloves, then wrapped her coat closer around her ankles. Looking at the confident set of Curley's shoulders, the strong lines of his profile, she felt his strength as he drove them away from danger. "How. . .where did you get this truck? I thought you left this morning. How did you know where to find me?"

He used the grin that was always there on the edge of his mouth, as he said, "Hey, one at a time!" His movements were swift and graceful as he shifted the gears and steered the truck expertly down the country road.

She relaxed back against the seat, relief flooding her to be in his presence. "Right. A good reporter asks one question at a time." The gloves were beginning to warm her hands.

"I did leave this morning," he said, leaning slightly to look out the rearview mirror. "But something made me return—don't ask me what. If I had to guess, I'd say it was the Holy Spirit. All I know for certain is I just knew I had to come back. The truck belongs to a local farmer, and we're returning it as soon as I make a quick trip into town."

Amanda twisted in the seat, looking back, worry etching her brow. Doubt ate at her; had she been right to leave her family behind? Maybe she could have somehow brought them with her. Or maybe she should have stayed with them, no matter what the cost. Tears blurred her eyes. "Stop the truck!" she cried suddenly, reaching for the door handle. "I won't leave my family to those butchers!"

"Hey! Calm yourself," said Curley. The road had turned, and the group behind them was no longer visible. He pulled the truck over to the side of the road, keeping the motor idling.

Bracing his left elbow on the steering wheel, he reached over and took her hand from the handle. "Think. Alone you can't stop them. You could get yourself hurt or share whatever fate the Nazis have in store for their captives."

"But. . ." She looked back in anguish.

Curley squeezed her hand. "I know. We can't leave them there." He reached up and cupped her chin, turning her face to his. "I have a plan, which I hope will free them all from whatever those thugs have planned."

"How? What can we do?"

His fingers lingered against the softness of her cheek. The shine in her eyes that a moment ago threatened to overflow into tears now regained the intellectual curiosity he'd first noticed about her. A memory flashed through his mind from many years ago of a much younger girl with the same curiosity mixed with intelligence, looking up at him with admiration.

He slid his hand down, pulling her collar closer around her neck. "First I have to make a quick trip into town to discover for sure where they are taking them." He turned back toward the steering wheel, put the truck in gear, and started forward.

Amanda leaned toward him, peering into his face. "Who would tell you *that?*"

The truck swayed as he steered it back onto the roadway. "Trust me," he said. "We don't have much time, so I'll drop you off at Frau Reinhardt's. Gather up your things while I find out what we need to know. Then we'll make a mad dash back here to put my plan into action."

"What plan? Tell me!"

He rubbed his thumb on the steering wheel, thinking, and finally decided to tell her. "First," he said, "if I'm right, we have to wait until it's dark and very late."

He sketched the highlights of a plan and, in response to her concerns, promised to tell it in detail later.

Soon the old truck chugged up to Frau Reinhardt's rooming house. Amanda slipped off the gardening gloves and laid them on the seat. "See you in five minutes," she said.

Curley was already turning the corner as she entered the foyer. She ran up the stairs and down the hall to her room, thankful for Curley's intervention into this sordid situation.

Quickly entering the room, she breathed a quick prayer. *God, help us. We're against evil forces here that I don't understand. Without Your help we could ruin everything.* She threw one of her suitcases on the bed and snapped it open. She yanked her warmest clothes off their hangers and stuffed them in, along with her cosmetics, which were hastily thrown into their satin-lined drawstring bag. The suitcase refused to latch. She pulled her tweed jacket from the jumble of clothes. *Someone will get a lot of use from this,* she thought, laying it across the pillows.

She forced the suitcase shut and slung her purse strap over her shoulder. Reaching into the closet, she grabbed the camera case, then picked up the suitcase. At the door she took one last look before leaving. The room was as it was when she arrived, except for the jacket lying on the pillows and the clothes that still hung in the closet.

Downstairs, she was almost out the door when Delbert rose from a chair in the parlor and eyed her suitcase. With a wave of his elegant fingers, he gestured toward it. A shocked petulance crept into his voice as he asked, "Honey—oh, sorry. Amanda, my dear. What does this mean? Are you leaving?"

Amanda set the suitcase down, seeing him clearly for the first time. After all their years as friends, she felt she never really knew him. Yet, somehow he believed she would someday become his wife. He stood before her, his pretty-boy face lit from within with selfish ambition.

"Amanda?" He cleared his throat, and she realized she was still staring at him.

"I've found my family," she said, "and I'm going to them." She reached into her purse and drew out some money. "I'm paid up with Frau Reinhardt, but would you be a pal and give her this? And could you take care of the rest of my stuff that's up in my room? Have it shipped home for me?"

"Of course I will." He brought his hand back to his chest. "But I'll take care of your bill."

She pressed the money into his sweater pocket. "Really, Delbert, I insist." She pulled the door open, and he grabbed her suitcase before she could and went out with her.

"Where can I reach you?" He took her arm and turned her to face him. "After all, Amanda, I came here to be with you, to assist you however I could." When she pulled away from him, he added, "Remember, your father entrusted me with your care."

Amanda wished the old truck would appear. "So you said, and I said I was grateful for your concern. If you'll remember, I also told you I don't need a baby-sitter."

"Now see here—"

"No. *You* see here. I don't need you, Delbert. Go back to Boston." At his look of shock at her uncharacteristic outburst, she softened somewhat and added, "Please!"

As if on cue, the truck chugged around the corner and slid to a stop in front of them. Amanda opened the door before Delbert could do it for her. She slung the suitcase on the floor, put the camera case on the seat, and climbed in. Curley leaned around her and nodded to Delbert.

Pulling the door shut, she looked straight ahead and said, "Let's go!" Curley gave her a curious look, stepped on the clutch, put the truck in gear, and they sped away.

Chapter Fifteen

Curley skillfully sped down the narrow streets, braking suddenly in front of the bakery shop. "Stay here. I'll be right back." Shifting into neutral, he flung open the door and jumped out, leaving the motor running. Amanda's stomach rumbled, reminding her she hadn't eaten anything since the cup of tea and cookie at Aunt Esther's that morning. So much had happened that the morning's events seemed ages ago.

In less than a minute, Curley came out with two full gunnysacks. He slung them into the back of the truck and went back for more. Finished, he jumped back into the truck and scanned the street ahead, then checked the rearview mirror, put the truck in gear, and pulled away. Soon Eisenburg faded into the twilight behind them.

"What's in the bags?" asked Amanda.

Solemnly watching the road ahead, Curley answered, "Apples, bread, rolls, jelly, whatever the baker could assemble in a hurry."

Amanda pressed her stomach to keep it from feeling too empty and nodded. "Good idea. The soldiers certainly won't feed those poor people." She busied herself by putting the camera and pieces back into its case.

Curley's jaw muscle flexed as he clenched his teeth. "No doubt about it," he said.

Surprised by the stern tone of his voice, Amanda glanced at him. He wasn't just a pretty flyboy. Suddenly his boyishly handsome profile showed an inherent strength and power she hadn't noticed before. He gripped the steering wheel tighter and stepped hard on the gas pedal, urging the truck to move faster.

"How are you going to get this food to the people?"

He glanced at her. "Part of the plan."

She felt the shock of power blazing from his hazel eyes, and she knew that nothing would stop him from taking food to the Jews.

He switched the lights on, and in a few minutes he turned off the road, into a long dirt driveway. He stopped behind a white peak-roofed house.

A tall older gentleman and a younger similar-looking man stepped out of the porch shadows and approached the truck. The older gentleman leaned down and looked past Curley to Amanda. "I see you got her, *mein Herr.*"

The young man's eyes widened as he caught sight of Amanda. "Oohh," he breathed, then hastily rubbed his chin and turned nonchalantly as if seeing a beautiful woman was nothing new.

Curley turned off the motor and lights, plunging them into almost total darkness. He got out of the truck, and Amanda reached for her door handle, but the young man suddenly appeared and opened it for her.

She pulled her coat collar up against the biting cold as Curley introduced the older gentleman as Horst and the younger as Rutger Friedrich. They shook hands and exchanged smiles before walking into the lamp-lit kitchen. Coal embers glowed brightly in an iron stove against one wall, warming the room somewhat. Washed dishes were neatly stacked beside the sink, and a dark wood table sat against the outside wall.

"Rutger and I are alone for a few days while my wife is away at her sister's." Herr Friedrich pulled two more cups from the cupboard. "So, you will be taking off soon?" Rutger brought them each a cup of hot tea. Amanda brought in some dark bread from the truck.

Curley took a sip of the hot brew and shook his head. "No. Not while those people are captives."

Amanda curled her hands around the cup, warming them for a moment, darting him a grateful look. "How are we going to free them?"

"It's going to be dangerous. You must wait in the plane while I go."

"You don't know my uncle and aunt. I have to go with you."

Curley shook his head. "I saw you with your cousin, so that's not a problem." He leaned toward Herr Friedrich, relying on Amanda for German phrases, and laid out his plan.

After intense discussion, they determined that Rutger would go along to distract the guards while Curley did his part. Herr Friedrich nodded his assent and said, "We do nothing but we ask God to go with us. You have no objection to that?"

Curley smiled. "Not at all. He's with me everywhere I go."

"How about you, miss?" Herr Friedrich asked Amanda, looking at her keenly.

"No. It's fine." She glanced at Curley, impressed by his faith. *That must be why he has such a calm attitude about all this,* she thought, remembering with chagrin that she didn't always remember to trust in God, knowing the serene feeling that He had everything in control.

After a prayer that lifted her courage, they hugged each other. Rutger smiled and said, "God's been saving His people for generations. This isn't exactly the Red Sea, but He'll do something great tonight. Wait and see!"

They all laughed, then solemnly prepared for the night ahead.

Outside, a cold, silvery full moon hung over the bare branches of trees, silhouetted on the hillside. Horst and Rutger went to work on the truck while Amanda followed Curley along a path up the hill behind the house. He carried her suitcase and a flashlight to illuminate the path ahead, while she shouldered her purse and camera case, carefully stepping over the uneven ground.

As soon as they reached the top of the hill, she grabbed Curley's arm and he turned to face her. She steadied her camera case to stop it from swinging and glared at him. "You can't leave me behind. I need to go with you."

He set the suitcase down, taking her hand in his. He smiled. This was his feisty Amanda, ready to jump into the fray. He'd been worried by her earlier silence in the kitchen. "You can't. They'd recognize you in an instant."

"I'll stay in the shadows. They won't even see me."

"We can't risk it. You stay in the plane, I go to the rescue."

She stared at him, unable to look away. She'd never met a man like this. So gentle and loving at times, yet so hardheaded as he was now. She admired his boldness and had no doubts that he'd do exactly as he planned. But her mind was made up. "You'll have to tie me down to make me stay here."

Curley dragged his gaze away from hers to keep from faltering. "If you want to fly out of here with me, you'll go with my plan." He dropped her hand and continued walking.

She stood in the silent darkness, stunned for an instant. Then she ran after him. "Listen, mister, I'm not some dainty little woman who'll faint at the first sign of trouble."

He looked back at her, arching one brow. "No?" He shook his head, leading her through shoulder-high bushes to the plane. He opened the cargo door, placing her suitcase inside, then opened the passenger door.

Amanda slung her camera case and purse up behind the copilot seat and turned to Curley with a sigh. "Listen, I didn't mean to sound flippant. But I. . .I need to go. This is my family!" She liked his decisiveness, but there must be some way to convince him of her need to be involved.

Curley made the mistake of gazing down at her, watching the play of emotions on her face. He suppressed a sigh. She had, after all, gone right into the ghetto in search of her family. He imagined her stalking dark Boston streets, searching for a story, and knew she was right. She needed to go.

He turned away from her and ran a hand through his hair, not sure if her foray into the ghetto had been bravery or foolishness. "You heard the plan. The guards have guns. People could get hurt if something goes wrong."

She looked up at him. "I know," she said softly. "But remember, we prayed, and God will protect us."

Curley lightly touched his fingertips to her chin and then leaned down, swiftly kissing her mouth. Then he turned abruptly and went to the other side of the plane, where he opened the door and retrieved a flare, a can of gasoline, and a few small tools. He pulled the plane forward a few feet so it faced a makeshift runway for a quick, clear takeoff.

With Rutger driving, soon they were turning onto the roadway and heading south on the road she'd walked earlier. After about five miles, Rutger turned off the lights. He slowed enough to peer carefully at the moonlit stretch of road.

"It's there, on our left," he whispered, pointing. Curley and Amanda bent their heads to their knees so Rutger would seem to be driving alone.

Curley slowly opened the door a fraction of an inch. "Remember, if I don't get back right away, go on without me. I'll make my way back somehow. But don't wait!"

Rutger nodded, driving past the turnoff. He turned the truck around and came back, pulling off the road.

Rutger hopped out and reached into the truck bed, grabbing one of the sacks. Shouldering it, he walked down the gravel road toward two small buildings. Lights glowed from within one of them. The other stood dark. He grinned. The German guards would love the treats he was bringing.

Once Rutger had disappeared into the shadows, Amanda and Curley quietly pushed the open door and slipped out of the truck. Curley grabbed his flare and gasoline and a sack of bakery goods from the truck bed. Amanda took another sack, and they tiptoed toward the large warehouse straight ahead and down an incline.

They stayed close to the bushes, away from gravel that would crunch loudly with each step. They reached the warehouse and moved stealthily along the wall nearest the road, looking for windows or some kind of opening. They found steps leading down to a metal door. Curley descended to investigate. The door was rusty, looking as if it hadn't been used in years. Amanda stood straining her ears, listening for sounds of movement. It was eerily quiet. Curley ascended the stairs and they continued to the corner of the building and scrutinized the next wall. A small vent lay open a few inches off the ground.

On the other side of the building, facing the railroad tracks, they found a loading dock. The faint light from a smaller building illuminated the area.

Curley ducked back. "This is a good place to leave the sacks," he whispered to Amanda. "Stay put while I check out the other side of this building."

Amanda nodded, but after a few moments she crawled back to the spot where they'd seen the vent. She bent down, finally lying on the ground to get closer. She heard a sniffling noise and a groan. She'd found them! She picked up a pebble and tapped lightly on the wire screen. She waited, but she didn't receive an answer. Pulling her pencil out of her pocket, she stuck it inside, making contact with something.

She poked again, hoping it wasn't merely a sack of grain. The object moved. *Please don't be a rat or a cat.* She pushed her pencil in again, startled when it was drawn out of her hand.

"Hello!" she whispered as loudly as she dared. "Is someone there?"

Something or someone shifted on the other side of the wall.

"Hello. Is someone there?" A frightened child's voice came from the square hole.

Amanda breathed a sigh of relief. *Thank God.* "Shhh. Get your father or mother quickly." She heard scuffling, and then another voice came through the wires. "Who's there?"

Amanda told the person who she was and asked him to get Uncle Jacob. Soon he was there, head to the floor, talking to her. She told him of the escape plan, the bread beside the loading door, and asked him to keep the people calm and quiet.

Curley hid in the shadows, hugging the wall on the other side of the building. He found a boarded window with an open slot large enough to talk through. His message was the same as Amanda's to her uncle. When he finished, he crept silently back to where he'd left Amanda. There was a moment of pure panic when he couldn't find her. He finally spotted her; she lay unmoving in the shadows. He advanced slowly toward her, relieved to hear her faint whispers and an answering voice.

He motioned to her to be ready to run back to the truck, and he slowly made his way to the loading dock wall. There, he unlatched the loading door's bolt and slid it from its rings. Then he crawled across the loading dock and pried the bolt loose, sliding it from its rings slowly so as to minimize the noise. He glanced up at the light over the door of the guards' building, wishing he had some way to put it out. The weak light was just enough to be dangerous.

He froze as a guard opened the door and walked out of the small building. The guard turned to speak to someone inside, and Curley slipped around the corner into the shadows. A second guard came out, followed by another and Rutger.

"*Ja,* you tell the baker we liked his gift," one of the guards said as he adjusted his holster strap, preparing to make his rounds.

"I will." Rutger held the empty gunnysack in his hand, walking after them. "I could come tomorrow and bring more."

They shook their heads. "We will not be here tomorrow. You go now."

Rutger slowly walked up the road. He looked about casually, not wanting to appear nosy, but obviously wondering where Amanda and Curley were.

Curley waited until the guards walked behind the building. He closed his eyes, praying that Amanda had gotten out of the way. Then he moved around the supply shed, dripping gas down the walls and along its base. When he finished, he moved behind the warehouse and lit the flare.

A guard rounded the building. "Halt!" he shouted and started running toward Curley, who tossed the flare and dived to the ground. With a whoosh and flash of heat, the supply shed was instantly engulfed in flames. Guards shouted. More came running out of the office building. They pointed their guns into the darkness, momentarily confused. Then a voice rose above the others, giving orders.

On his belly, Curley used his elbows to ease himself forward. He worked his way along the ground beside the building, rolling into the underground doorway. Jumping to his feet, he pushed the door with all his strength. It groaned and scraped loudly, but the sounds were lost in the roar of the fire and the shouts of the scattering guards.

When Amanda heard the guards talking to Rutger, she'd slid the two gunnysacks of breadstuff toward the door, which someone inside had pushed up a few inches. The bags were slowly pulled inside. She crawled through the bushes and made her way along the road to the truck. She spotted Rutger, but didn't dare call out to him. He reached the vehicle first, spying her at the same time the supply shed went up in flames. Amanda dashed the last few feet to the truck, praying for Curley's safety. The Germans sprinted about, shouting orders, moving cars, and throwing pails of water on the fire.

Amanda and Rutger could do nothing more but wait for Curley. Minutes passed. Rutger paced impatiently. Finally he turned to her, frowning. "They know I'm here, so I'll go tell them I want to help," he said. "I'll find out what happened to Curley."

"No! Don't! What if they think you're the one who set the fire?" Her plea fell into the darkness. She was alone.

The blazing building lit up the area, and Amanda knew she had to keep down, but it was agony not to look. She caught her breath, heaving a mental sigh of relief when first one, then another car drove by the truck and sped down the road. "Come on! Come on!" she whispered, clenching her fists. "God, help them!"

She heard a light tapping and, lying across the seat, she opened the driver's door. A familiar face greeted her. "Uncle Jacob!"

Her uncle huddled beside the truck, his arm leaning on the running board. His eyes were wild and frightened. Amanda stretched the door open a few more inches. "Are you all here?" she asked.

He nodded. "In the bushes."

"Good." She glanced nervously up the road. "As soon as Curley and Rutger get here, climb in the back."

He nodded. "But we must hurry!" Then he slipped away, back into the bushes.

Less than two minutes later Rutger climbed into the truck, frowning.

"Where's Curley?"

"I couldn't find him! I'm sorry, Amanda. He has disappeared."

Amanda peeked out the window. Seeing no one, she looked frantically up and down the road. "They'll be back any minute with help."

"I know," Rutger agreed. "We have to go."

"We can't leave him!" cried Amanda.

"It's what he told us to do," Rutger insisted.

"But—"

"I don't want to leave him either, but if anyone can get himself out of this jam and back to his plane, Curley can."

Turning the trees into black skeletons, the flames leaped into the sky with a sickly orange vengeance. Amanda looked back at the bushes and saw her aunt peering out at her. "You're right. We have to trust Curley to make it." She motioned to Aunt Esther, and in a few seconds they'd all scrambled from the bushes onto the back of the truck.

Rutger started the truck, hesitated a moment, looking at the burning buildings. Now the warehouse was in flames. He didn't see Curley. He put the truck in gear. It lurched forward, and soon they were on their way back to the farmhouse.

Amanda looked back, hoping to see Curley, but there was nothing but the surging flames. She saw two people dash across the road, and she wished them well. In the truck bed all that remained visible were blankets and burlap bags covering lumps of supposed farm products.

When Curley closed the metal door, darkness engulfed him. He pointed his flashlight at the wall and pushed its button. Nothing happened. He tried again. Nothing. His fingers explored the metal cylinder and found the glass and bulb broken. The darkness grew oppressive and ominous with its silence. He struck a match, looking around, quickly assessing his surroundings. He was in a small vaultlike room, about ten feet square. Two shelves along one wall held several boxes of musty papers and a few cans that were so rusted he couldn't make out their labels.

He checked his watch. Eleven-twenty. The match died out. He stood in the darkness, waiting, knowing he couldn't go out yet. He heard muffled footsteps above, sounds of prisoners escaping. Hours seemed to pass before all he could hear was his own breathing and the slight movement of his foot on the dusty floor.

A cold, clammy feeling crept up from his belly to encompass him. He felt powerless to stop it. He stared straight ahead, straining to see something, anything, but there was nothing. Only a loathsome opacity. Fragments from old nightmares floated into his mind. The pain that started when his mother died. He was four years old. He didn't remember much about her but the aching sadness. He and his father had been close.

Then his father's death in the mine shaft, a freak accident of boulders and crushing debris. Curley's terrible dreams about it were coming true.

He had learned to hide his grief with nonchalance and an exaggerated sense of independence. Deciding never to need anyone, since no one would be there anyway, he'd gotten by, living where he could, finally ending up in Johnny Westmore's hangar. Johnny had taken him under his wing, literally, taught him to fly and to trust God to be with him always. Johnny had become the closest thing to family Curley had.

He shook himself and pulled out another match. *I'm not alone,* he thought, *I'll get through this just like I always have. By my wits and with God's help.* He forced himself to put the match back without lighting it and face the darkness. He didn't need a crutch, not even the match. This might be the worst predicament of his life, but he'd manage.

He felt the darkness closing around him, suffocating like a vise of black death. He squeezed his eyes shut, imagining the free feeling of soaring over the clouds in an open cockpit. He was an eagle, far above problems on the ground, strong, needing no one. The image faded, pushed out by the oppressive blackness, leaving him gasping and groping for the door.

He clenched his fists, fighting off the feeling of being nine years old again. Of hearing the imaginary sounds of men screaming as a mine shaft fell in on them. Of fearing he heard his father's screams. "Oh God!" he breathed. The oppression loosened a little. Curley closed his eyes and said into the darkness, "Yea, though I walk through the valley of the shadow of death I will fear no evil." His shoulders relaxed.

Johnny used to tell him there was no shame in admitting a need for God's help. *"I know I'm no lone eagle, needing no one. I know You're there, God. Thank You."*

He took a deep breath and stood for a moment, savoring the feeling of peace. Then he once more took out a match and struck it, checking the time. Eleven forty-two. Twenty-two minutes had elapsed since he'd shut himself in this musty vault. It seemed like twenty-two hours. The air was getting thicker and warmer by the minute. He wondered if Amanda, her family, and Rutger were all right. He hoped they hadn't waited for him.

He smiled. Amanda was no frail female. He couldn't think of any other girls who he'd even consider letting come with him into this situation; and she'd done it with such aplomb. A glow of determination in her eyes, courage in that thrust-forward little chin, strength to tread where angels feared, and beauty. *She's the real article,* he told himself. Suddenly he couldn't wait to get to her and get his arms around her.

The door handle felt warm. Carefully, he pulled the door open a fraction of an inch. A flame curled downward, blocking his escape. Pulling at his jacket sleeve, he wrapped it around his hand and pushed the rapidly heating metal door. The coast was clear, so he dashed out through the flames and up the steps.

He stepped right into the path of a German guard carrying an empty bucket in each hand.

Chapter Sixteen

The guard stumbled as Curley ran into him. He dropped the buckets and slapped at Curley's shoulder. Raising a fist to strike back, Curley suddenly realized the fierce burning he felt on his shoulder was his smoldering jacket. Together he and the guard put it out.

An acrid gray smoke drifted up from the burning leather. Someone dashed past them with pails of sloshing water. Before the guard could question him, Curley gestured wildly down the steps he'd just come up, then picked up the discarded pails.

His eyes darted from side to side, assessing the area. The truck had gone with Amanda, Rutger, and, he hoped, her family. Though adrenaline and tension fueled his alertness, he was relieved that Amanda was out of harm's way. He worried about her getting into another dilemma. Their safe escape depended on his getting out of here soon.

He ran with the pails to the water tower. Orange flames crept up the building where the prisoners had been kept, sending sparks flying out the narrow upper windows.

A truck skidded down the road, off the highway, the people in the back jumping out before it stopped. Curley pushed the pails under the water spout, filling them. He was relieved that others were so intent on getting water to the fire there was no conversation.

He rushed to the track side of the warehouse and sloshed water up the wall. The door was open and there was no sign of the Jews. Thank God, they'd escaped. The guards, plus volunteers, were getting the fire under control. A middle-aged man ran past him, toward the building, smothering the fire with a sack full of sand. Curley handed him the pails and ran toward the guards' small hut.

There was no fire here. No guards either. They were directing volunteers and dousing bushes and the warehouse. Their motorcycles sat next to the building. The black car was gone.

From the dark bushes behind the hut, Curley scanned the scene. Twenty or more people ran to and from the water tower. Others beat the bushes with blankets and burlap bags to choke the fire. The supply shed smoldered from its burned, blackened stubble, a pocket of water seeping from its foundation.

He heard voices near and froze. The captain came toward the guard hut, gazing from the fiery pandemonium to the bushes behind him, where Curley crouched. "*Der Amerikaner ist hier.* Bring him to me!"

Curley couldn't hear every word, but he caught the meaning. The guard was told to bring the American to his captain. As soon as the soldiers left, he sneaked toward the motorcycles and chose one without a sidecar. He guided it quietly on a well-worn footpath around the back, behind the bushfire. The flickering flames gave enough light to get the motorcycle up to the road.

He stood on the crank three times, but the machine didn't catch. He was raising it a fourth time when an oncoming motorcycle's light shined on him. Behind him, a guard ran toward him, shouting and gesturing.

Suddenly the oncoming motorcycle turned sharply and pulled up beside him. Curley shoved the kickstand down and turned, ready to fight for his life, if necessary. But it was Rutger's cheerful face smiling at him.

Rutger slapped the fender behind him. "Get on!"

Guards down the hill were wheeling their motorcycles away from the guard hut. Curley hopped on the back and held onto Rutger's seat. "Step on it, boy!"

Rutger tore off down the road as fast as the cycle would go. Curley looked back and spotted headlights behind them. At first he thought it was a car, but the lights moved independently, and he knew there were two motorcycles following him. He and Rutger leaned into the wind, keeping the accelerator wide open.

About a hundred yards before the Friedrichs' driveway, Rutger slowed and turned off the road onto an overgrown lane. A minute later he turned off the lights, but he kept a steady pace as he twisted and wound along the dirt road.

The cloudy moonlight was barely enough for him to see to steer between the bushes. The guards' motorcycles thundered past the turnoff.

Rutger rounded a bend, flicked the lights on, and gunned the engine again. They bounced through the orchard, and he cut the engine and coasted into the clearing where the plane sat.

They had only minutes before the guards doubled back, found the side road, and caught up with them. Curley vaulted off the motorcycle and grabbed the handlebars from Rutger. One of the motorcycles rumbling toward them sputtered and whined, sounding as if it had slid off the path into the dirt. The other one bore down on them.

Rutger glanced uneasily behind them toward the approaching roar. Curley took his arm and pushed him back into the shadows. "Go home. I don't want you involved in this. Get back!"

"Yes, sir." Rutger slipped silently into the shadows, saying over his shoulder, "Everyone is in the plane, waiting for you."

"Good job! Now you must go. *Go!*" The moon had gone behind a cloud and Curley stood, facing the oncoming guard, then straightened his shoulders and watched the light loom brighter. "Lord, help me," he muttered. "And keep Amanda in the plane."

❧

Amanda watched Curley face the motorcycle leaping into the clearing. In the surrounding darkness, the scene looked as if it were a stage play unfolding before her. But this was no act.

"What's happening? What is it?" Aunt Esther's voice rose to a hysterical pitch.

"It's all right," said Amanda softly, failing to keep the fear from her voice. "Mr. Cameron is here to fly us out. Sit back, and. . ."

"But I—"

"Now, now, Mother. Come, lean against me," soothed Uncle Jacob. Aunt Esther allowed him to pull her into his arms, while Tamara, Nathan, and the baby huddled together in the rear of the plane. Martha's head touched Amanda's as they peered out the small window.

"What's he going to do?" asked Martha, reaching for Amanda's hand and clutching it tightly.

"Shh!" Amanda chose her words carefully to cover her own growing alarm. "He'll be all right. Just keep our passengers quiet. Please."

She could tell by the guard's slow, deliberate motions as he stood his motorcycle on its stand that he felt he was in total control. He left the light on, pointed his pistol at Curley, and motioned toward the plane. Amanda ducked down, even though she couldn't be seen. When she looked again, Curley had edged away from the plane. He and the guard faced off, looking as motionless as chess pieces.

She touched her forehead to the cool window and said a quick prayer for all of them.

"Explain yourself! *Wer sind Sie?* Who are you? Why is this plane here?" The guard motioned to the plane with his Luger.

"Etwas langsammer, bitte," said Curley after a long tension-filled minute. "I speak very little German." He assumed a relaxed pose, but every sense was on alert.

The guard backed up to his motorcycle, all the time keeping the gun on Curley. His stare lingered as he pulled a flashlight from the saddlebag and snapped the light on. "I will inspect the plane before I escort you back to my captain."

In a voice of authority, Curley said, "That plane is RAF property and off limits."

"You are on German soil! You will do as I say." He shone his light from the propeller to the tail of the plane, stepping closer to it.

A sweat broke out on Curley's neck. Time was running out. The guard's momentary attention on the plane gave him an opening. He leaped at the man, but the guard turned, raising his gun. Curley grabbed the wrist holding the weapon.

Amanda could scarcely breathe as she watched Curley move with incredible lightning speed. He and the guard scuffled, the flashlight beam darting crazily about until Curley forced the guard to the ground. They rolled in the dirt, struggling for the gun. She watched in horror as the guard pinned Curley beneath him. The flashlight's beam shone uselessly into the trees.

Curley seemed to relax and give up for an instant, then he surged up, threw the guard off him, and knocked the gun from his hand. It skittered across the dirt under the plane's wing. The guard lunged and Curley slugged him. He staggered back, then lowered his head and charged Curley.

"I've got to help," said Amanda, reaching for the door handle.

"No!" Martha grabbed her sleeve.

Amanda gently pulled her hand away. "Keep calm! I'll be all right." She opened the door and slid into the cold darkness.

The gun glinted dully beneath the plane's wing. She picked it up. It felt like a piece of ice in her hand.

Holding it in both hands, she pointed it toward the guard. In German she said, "The only thing I know about guns is that if I pull this trigger, it shoots. So don't move, or you'll make me nervous, and you could get hurt." She breathed deeply, stilling the fear tensing her chest.

Curley moved to her side, his eyes on her face. "You surprise me, sweetheart."

The German snarled an obnoxious epithet, and Curley leveled a sudden, icy glare at him. "The lady means business. Keep quiet."

Anger faded from the guard's red face as he watched Amanda's hands shaking. She stood, arms outstretched, pointing the gun at him. To Curley she said, "I'll keep him here until the plane is ready to go. Hurry!" Curley picked up the flashlight and set it on the guard's motorcycle seat so that it spotlighted him.

The guard's eyes flickered as he watched Curley leave the circle of light.

Amanda moved the gun slightly. "Don't try anything," she warned. She moved her eyes as far to the right as she could, following Curley, but he had ducked beneath the plane. She heard the door close and fought down her fear.

The guard glared at her, tensing as if for a leap in her direction. Heavy, almost clumsy footsteps heading in their direction made him smile.

Amanda kept the gun pointed on him. The man's smile faded as Rutger walked into the light. "Who are you?" the man demanded, his voice rising to a shriek.

"I am a fellow countryman, looking for my motorcycle." Rutger looked from the guard to the plane. "Why is that here?"

"You idiot! This is not Der Fuhrer's plane!"

"Then what—"

"Both of you keep quiet," said Amanda.

Rutger peered toward Amanda. "Who's that?" A cloud drifted in front of the moon, casting unearthly shadows. The guard stood in eerie light, and Rutger, half in shadow, half in the light.

"Stop asking questions!" screeched the guard.

"You sound like the guard at the roadside. He is injured," said Rutger, glancing meaningfully toward Amanda.

She pulled in a deep, shaky breath, her arms beginning to ache. *Oh, please, Curley, start the plane!* She hadn't known there was a second guard who might come upon them at any second.

"Hey, lady," said Rutger, approaching her, "did you see who took my motorcycle?"

"Keep back!" warned Amanda.

"She has a gun, you stupid boy," snarled the guard.

"She—"

The plane's engine coughed and began to rumble. Amanda backed up carefully. As soon as she was beneath the wing, the engine was roaring. The propeller's wind whipped her coat around her ankles. Her head touched the strut, and the plane's door opened. Martha shouted, "Get in!"

Amanda threw the gun as far as she could into the darkness and scrambled up into the plane, pulling the door shut.

Curley glanced at her and grinned. "My little gun moll," he said, flipping a switch on the panel and squinting into the darkness. "Come on, moon! Come out and give us a little light."

The baby's wails combined with the engine's roar pounded into Amanda's head. They couldn't take off into the dreadful darkness outside.

Curley inched the plane forward slowly, then stopped, shaking his head. "We need more light!" The engine throbbed idly.

"God, help us!" cried Aunt Esther.

Suddenly Amanda's door was flung open, and the guard's hand reached for her. "No!" she screamed, kicking at him. He grabbed her ankle. She felt herself being pulled down.

Her terror turning to fury, she beat her fists on his head, but he held on.

Slowly, the moon slipped out from behind the cloud, and the plane edged forward. Amanda clutched her seat with all her strength. Curley wagged the plane slightly, sending the guard off balance for a second, long enough for Amanda to kick his shoulder and send him sprawling. She slammed the door shut, and the plane rumbled and bounced between the trees.

Suddenly they were aloft. Amanda closed her eyes and concentrated on calming her racing heartbeat. She was shaking like a twig in a windstorm and her ankle hurt.

Curley squeezed her hand. "You can open your eyes now."

She did so. He had a pleased, contented look on his face. One curly lock separated itself from the others. She longed to smooth it down but held her hand nervously in her lap.

She turned to check the group behind her. Aunt Esther lay against Uncle Jacob, her eyes squeezed tightly shut. Nathan looked out the window, while Tamara soothed the baby, whose wails had turned to a mewling cry. Martha's eyes glittered with excitement. "We made it!"

Uncle Jacob's face glowed as he said loud enough for them all to hear, *"Baruch atoh adnoy, elohaynu melech ho-lom shee-osoh li nays bamokm hazeh.* You are blessed, Lord our God, King of the Universe, Who performed a miracle for me in this place."

They were all quiet for a moment, their faces registering the awesome realization that God had indeed just performed a miracle for them.

"Amen," said Curley.

"I hope the others escaped, too," said Nathan.

"They were all gone by the time I got to the scene," said Curley, loud enough for them to hear over the engine's rumble. "So were the packages of bread."

"Where are we going?" asked Uncle Jacob.

"You're going to England," replied Curley, looking back at his passengers.

Nathan nodded and went back to his window view.

"Speaking of bread," said Martha, "have some." She opened the sack and handed out breadsticks. "How did you find us?" she asked.

Amanda and Curley related their stories, marveling at how the rescue had happened as if guided by an unseen hand.

"I prayed we'd get out of there somehow," said Martha, a look of wonder on her face. They talked for a while longer, until Martha sighed and relaxed in her seat, closing her eyes.

Amanda looked out at the silver-crested clouds. The vista ahead was majestic. Chewing on the crusty bread, she could think of no headline to describe it. Poetry seemed more appropriate. "It's beautiful up here!"

Curley seemed pleased that she thought so. "Look down," he said, pointing to a space between the clouds. "We're over Holland." A pleased smile curved his mouth.

As she looked down at the colorful toy-sized roofs below, Amanda wondered if he was aware of how appealing his smile was. She sighed and stretched her back. "Rutger certainly had that guard flustered."

"Rutger!" Curley glanced sideways in surprise. "I told him to keep out of it."

"He must have been watching, because he came to help me," she said. "Actually, he made himself seem like a bumbling, innocent kid only looking for his motorcycle."

"Tell me what he said and did."

When Amanda finished telling Curley exactly what happened, his expression grew still. "Hmm," he said. "He may have saved his grandparents from a lot of suspicion. Even though the plane was far from their home, there is still a chance they'll be suspect. We owe him for defusing a potential bombshell."

"I wonder what will happen to the Jews." Amanda rubbed her sore ankle, thinking of the disturbing newspaper and magazine articles she'd read in the Eisenburg school library.

Curley looked grave. "We can only pray that somehow God's presence will be with them." He shook his head. "Now, you should get some rest. We'll be in England in a couple of hours."

Chapter Seventeen

Curley flew them into the night, toward the moon that was setting below the clouds. He shuddered. Being trapped beneath the earth like his father was his most hideous nightmare. Shrugging off the feeling, he gazed out over the miles and miles of freedom before him. For him freedom was soaring anywhere he pleased. Why had he returned? What drew him back? He shook his head, knowing the truth. It had to be God.

Amanda's eyes were closed, her long dark lashes lying on her cheeks. Shifting moonlight and shadows played on her lovely face. Her hands lay open in her lap, giving her a vulnerable appearance. Gently reaching out, he brushed a soft wisp of hair that strayed toward him.

Every moment he spent with her made him want her more, and he wasn't used to that. It usually happened the other way: Women wanted him. Unlike the others, though, Amanda hadn't pursued him. She'd simply been herself, and that was enough.

When did he start caring? It hadn't come all at once, like a bolt from the blue. That sense of familiarity he'd felt from the first moment he'd seen her. . .a memory of a long-ago air show, her eyes looking up at him, burst full-blown into his mind, and at last he remembered where and when he'd seen her before. He nearly laughed aloud, for he realized his feelings had had a logical progression after all. The seed had been planted at the air show years ago, lying dormant until her eyes caught his across the ship deck. Then it was nurtured with his admiration for her zeal-like dedication to her work, and it had blossomed when he recognized the sweetness and purity radiating from within her. He loved her courage to meet her cousin in the park; he loved her loyalty when she marched beside her family through the town. He loved her tears welling in her eyes at the plight of Hitler's innocent victims.

She had broken through his barrier against commitment. He ran a hand through his hair and frowned. Somehow she'd made him want her, and her alone. All he could see was Amanda's face.

What would happen after they landed? He couldn't imagine her married to Delbert. It was wrong. Maybe it wasn't true. He'd ask her soon.

If it were true, he'd have to get over her. He'd miss her smiles, her bright eyes as the idea for the "big story" illuminated her imagination. The idea of getting over a girl was another new experience. He'd blithely gone through adolescence and adulthood enjoying the company of women, their adoration and devotion, but moving on when one began to stir his fancy. After all, like the planes he flew, he was not made to be tied down, but like an eagle, to freely soar.

Even an eagle has a nest. The thought zinged through his brain. *Where did that come from?* he wondered. *Behold, I make all things new.*

Curley knew that voice. He glanced at Amanda again. He wanted to hold and protect her. *Lord, she may be promised to someone else. Are You telling me this feeling I have for her is just to teach me what it's going to be like when I find the right woman?* Or was this retribution? Letting him know how it felt to be unlucky in love?

Love? Where did that word come from? But the idea of loving someone other than Amanda was suddenly distasteful.

He pulled out his clipboard, looked at the lights below, and studied the map. To keep his errant thoughts from straying back to Amanda, he concentrated on the terrain and the list of German airfields and number of planes he'd observed. Something was up. Who would be the target of all those planes Hitler was gathering?

Amanda awoke, realizing the sound of the engine had changed and they were descending. She hunched her shoulders and stretched her arms straight over her lap, then raked her hair back into place.

Curley lifted one eyebrow and grinned at her. "Feel better?"

"Yes. How long did I sleep?"

"About two hours. We're over the east English coast."

The first piercing rays of dawn touched the tips of trees and houses below, turning them to liquid gold. A vast amount of water on her side was changing from gray to blue even as she watched.

"They call that the Wash," said Curley, leaning over her and looking down into the bay. He banked the plane to the left, glancing at the land below and back to the map.

Amanda looked back at her family with compassion. Martha lay scrunched up around the armrests on two seats, Aunt Esther still lay against Uncle Jacob, his jacket over her, and he leaned against the wall. Nathan sprawled straight in his seat, legs thrust beneath Martha's seat, head back, sound asleep. Tamara had just finished diapering the baby on her lap. She gave Amanda a sad smile and pulled the baby's bunting down over his feet.

Amanda smiled back, then turned to look ahead. Rosy-hued, gold-tipped spires stood like sentinels among lower-roofed buildings. They loomed closer as the plane dipped lower.

By the time the wheels touched the ground, the passengers were awake. Aunt Esther straightened her clothes, Uncle Jacob pulled the sleeves of his jacket down over his wrists, Martha ran a comb through her pale hair. Nathan bent forward, tying his shoes, while Tamara held the baby to her shoulder, gently patting his back.

Four jeeps drew close the minute Curley cut the engine. "Wait here," he said and climbed out. He saluted to the approaching officer. "Captain Cameron reporting, sir. I wasn't able to complete my mission. Civilians are on board in need of assistance."

The officer looked up at faces crowded in the plane's window. "Explain."

Later, as the family sipped coffee in the barracks, Amanda cabled her parents, then she and Curley slipped outside. He tucked her hand in the crook of his elbow and they walked in the nippy morning air. Small bushes swept down the hillsides, blanketing the landscape in autumn gold and green.

"I have to leave soon," he said. The thought of her marrying Delbert haunted him. He raked his fingers through his hair. How could he ask her about it without seeming nosy or jealous?

"Where are you going?" she asked.

"Back to the States to report to my commanding officer. I was supposed to take the Vega to Holland. But my orders have been changed."

"We'll always be grateful to you," she said.

The heartrending tenderness in her gaze drew a wave of love over his heart. Confused, he shrugged. "I was glad I was there for you." They found a gate, and he pushed it open.

"Don't be modest. You're a knight in shining armor." They strolled along a path, between a line of elms, stopping at an arbor. Amanda sat on the stone bench, and Curley stood facing her with one foot on the bench beside her, bracing his right forearm on his thigh. "We have to talk," he said impatiently. "I heard you'll be marrying Delbert when you get back and—"

"Delbert?" Amanda's nose wrinkled. "I'm not marrying him!"

"But he said—"

"I don't care what he said." Amanda stood and poked Curley's chest. His foot came down, and he leaned back slightly. "Men! I'm so sick of men deciding where I'll be going, with whom, when, and how! And Delbert can go jump in a lake."

"Hold on! You're not classifying me in with the rest of those men, are you?" He gripped both of her shoulders. "I'm not trying to talk you into doing anything. I want a companion, an equal, not a slave." He hesitated, then added, "That is, if I ever decide to. . ." He dropped his hands from her shoulders, disgusted at himself for sounding like a bumbling adolescent.

"Curley?" Hearing his name on her lips almost stole his breath away.

Amanda reached up and put her hand on his cheek. Dark green specks glowed in the artless gaze she fixed on him. "If you ever want a companion, a friend, I'll be there."

That promise filled him with intense happiness. All his excuses to keep from getting tied down by some wily female were going down in flames. The cynical reckless bachelor, the lone eagle persona, suddenly no longer suited him. He had thought falling in love was being caught in a trap, but it wasn't like that at all. Instead, he felt a soaring freedom, as if a dozen invisible restraints had just been broken.

For a long moment they simply stood there, looking at each other. *She's not marrying Delbert!* A breeze moved through the trees, a finch whistled a lilting tune, and his heart sang along. She seemed to be waiting for him to say something.

"Marry me, Amanda." Another finch answered the first one.

She stared at him, her green eyes misting. Romantic cliches sprang to mind.

She took a shaky breath. "This is rather sudden, don't you think?"

"No. On the plane I suddenly remembered seeing you years ago at an air show. I knew then there was something special about you. Then from the moment I landed on that ship and took another look, I knew I loved you."

"You what?"

He looked down at her for a second, then groaned and hugged her to him. "I love you, Amanda. I didn't realize it until I almost lost you to those Germans. Or to Delbert."

"Oh, Curley," she sighed. "You were right. If I'd listened to you, I wouldn't have been captured." Then she lifted her chin. "But we wouldn't have rescued my family either. I would never have known what had happened to them if I hadn't been captured along with them."

He cupped her face in his hands, marveling at the petal softness of her skin. "God and I will always take care of you. Can you believe that?"

Amanda nodded, brushing a tear from her eye. Ever since she met him at that air show, she'd wanted him. This was one request she hadn't dared make to God, but He'd known. "I love you, too," she said. "I've loved you since I was seventeen years old."

Suddenly Curley dropped to one knee, took her hand, and brought it to his chest. She felt his warmth beneath his jacket. He looked up at her with a mixture of boyish exuberance and earnestness that made her knees weak.

"Amanda Chase, will you marry me?"

She smiled down into his eyes, blissful happiness flowing over her like a warm wave.

Before she could answer, he went on. "First, there's something you must know: I don't want you to stop doing what you love. Chasing down stories and reporting is in your blood, and it's one of your lovable charms. Of course, if you want to quit and settle down—"

"Yes."

"Yes?"

"Yes, James Cameron. I'll marry you." He rose in one fluid motion. She flung her arms around him, burying her face in his shoulder.

He talked about his duty to the army, she of her excitement for writing the truth about what was happening in Germany. He told her of the air race of the century starting that week, in Middlesex, with aces in their souped-up planes racing for Australia. "I'll pull some strings and get you a special press pass. Watch the Comet," he said. "It's the fastest thing with wings—next to my little Moth," he added, grinning modestly.

They made plans to meet and announce their engagement as soon as she arrived back in the States. Amanda felt peace, like a comforting aroma, enveloping them. She sighed. "This is a fairy tale and I'm the girl who got the prince."

He laughed and pulled her away with him. "Come on, princess. Let's go live happily ever after!"

Epilogue

Jerusalem, 1977

"God delivered Cousin Joseph's grandparents, but others were not so fortunate," said Curley to his youngest grandson, Sam. They were leaving the Yad Vashem, memorial of the Holocaust.

"Were you there?" Sam spoke softly, matching their respectful mood.

"We almost were," said Amanda, putting a hand on his slender shoulder. "But your grandpa rescued us in his airplane."

The boy looked up at them, excitement shining in his eyes. "Did you shoot 'em out of the sky?"

"No, Grandma knocked him flat on his back before we even took off." Curley caught Amanda's eye and winked.

"Wow! How did you do that, Grandma?"

"Hold still," said Amanda, removing the temporary *yarmulke* he had to wear to enter the memorial. Sunshine glinted off his curly auburn hair. "I'll tell you all about it this afternoon when we get back to Cousin Martha's house."

Sam walked ahead of them, shuffling through the postcards they'd bought. Amanda shuddered, and Curley hugged her to his side. "Are you okay?"

"Yes." She looked back at the monument. "When I think that Uncle Jacob almost went back—"

He stopped and put both hands on her waist. Their eyes on each other, he said, "Think back. No one in 1934 could have seen the horror that was coming. Many thought it was temporary and they'd get their homes and lives back. I know you feel sad; so do I, but we both had the satisfaction of helping put a stop to that madman. You with your words and me with the air corps."

She glanced back at the building again. "But so many! Millions, each one with hopes, dreams, memories, a different story for each life."

Sam tugged at her sleeve. "Please, can I have my candy now, Grandma?"

Amanda took the postcards, put them into her purse, and drew out a candy bar. Sam walked beside them, tearing the paper off.

Hand in hand they walked down the sidewalk to their car. "I can hardly bare to think of the Holocaust," said Amanda. "Thank God for this memorial."

Curley squeezed her hand. "God willing, the world won't forget—so that it will never happen again."

Lost Creek Mission

Cheryl Tenbrook

Dedication

To my dad and to my husband Gayle for always believing.
JOHN 3:30

Chapter One

The engine lurched, then chugged slowly away from the station, belching out cinders that tapped lightly on the roof. Finally, about a mile outside the city limits, the train began to pick up speed, and the staccato rhythm of wheels on tracks echoed Erin's excited heartbeat. She tucked her skirts in and tried to look dignified, but she couldn't help smiling.

Erin's friends at the orphanage hadn't been able to understand why she would want to become a missionary. Every girl at the Manchester Orphanage longed for the day when she could have a home of her own—and the only way to get a home was to find a husband. Why spend a year teaching in a backwoods school, they reasoned, when Erin was finally old enough to marry and have a real family? After all, Erin wasn't likely to find a husband out in the woods, was she?

But Erin believed she had heard God calling her to the Lost Creek Mission, and she had to obey. Besides, who could say? God just might find her a husband even out in the backwoods of Missouri. Her smile widened for a moment, and then she pushed the thought firmly to the back of her mind.

She leaned toward the window, watching as the landscape changed as they continued on south from St. Louis. Wide acres of carefully cleared farmland gave way to steep hills and dense stands of trees. The well-maintained roadways near the tracks fell behind, and now Erin could see only rough wagon trails that cut through pastures and disappeared into the woods. Above the train bed's banks, tall bluffs of orange-white rock jutted through the thin soil.

Shadows already covered the train station when they finally pulled into Mineral Point. Erin gathered her belongings and checked into the hotel next to the depot. She ate the supper she had packed for herself at the orphanage, then quickly prepared for bed, but she barely slept at all that night. Lying on the lumpy straw mattress, her mind spun in circles.

"I wonder what Douglas Teterbaugh will be like?" she thought. She knew that Reverend Teterbaugh had also been assigned to Lost Creek Mission and that he was a recent seminary graduate, but that was all the mission board had told her.

At daylight, Erin was back on the train. Rain spattered on the roof, and the sound of raindrops and the train's rhythmic motion lulled her back to sleep. Exhausted from her sleepless night, she slept while the train wound its way deeper into Missouri. Not until the car rocked from side to side, bumping her head against the window, did she open her eyes.

On the other side of the window she saw thick tree trunks an arm's length from the tracks. The underbrush was so dense she could see into the woods for only a few feet. Used to city life, Erin had never realized before how many shades of green there were. Amid the thick leaves, wildflowers bloomed, black-eyed Susans and Queen Anne's lace and little purple blossoms that grew close to the ground.

As the train pulled into the Potosi station, Erin repinned her hat and freshened up as best she could. She was certain that the other passengers could hear her heart pounding as she thought of meeting Reverend Teterbaugh on the platform. How many times had the headmistress at the orphanage told her, "A lady must always be calm of voice and confident in manner." Erin took a deep breath and started down the aisle.

The depot was a busy place for such a small town. People were milling about on the platform, greeting arrivals and unloading freight from the boxcars. Erin stepped down. At least the rain had stopped.

A slim, dark-haired man was standing near the station door. His eyes met Erin's and he hurried to her.

"You must be Miss Corbett," he said.

"Yes, and you're reverend Teterbaugh."

He smiled. "I must say I'm delighted. Not all missionaries come with such a charming face."

Erin laughed. "You're very bold for a minister, sir."

"So I've been told," the reverend admitted. "Do let me take your valise. I'll see to it that the rest of your luggage is properly handled."

"Thank you, Reverend Teterbaugh."

"Please, call me Douglas. Teterbaugh is such a long name."

"All right, Douglas, if you'll call me Erin. When did you arrive?"

"On the 5:30 from Cape Girardeau, a most ungodly time of the morning. But I suppose I'll soon have to get used to such hours."

"Yes. I imagine country people are early risers," Erin said. "Did Dr. Tichenor tell you who would meet us at the Potosi station?"

"No, his letter only said that someone from Lost Creek would be here to load our things and drive us to the Gillam farm. I would think perhaps Mr. Gillam might come himself, since we'll be staying in his home."

"I wonder what type of house it is. . .do you think it might be a log cabin?"

"Good heavens, I hope not," Douglas said. "But I suppose anything is possible."

"It's all so exciting. In a few hours we'll begin what may be the greatest adventure of our lives."

Erin ignored the amused expression that flickered across the reverend's face. She picked up her reticule and walked to the edge of the platform.

No one was there except a grizzled old man who stood holding the reins of two mules at the far end of the station. The man caught sight of them and started walking in their direction. Erin had never seen anyone quite like him. His clothes were creased and worn. Over his work shirt he wore a vest that had, at one time, been white with red pinstripes. A straw hat, curled up at the sides, rested on the back of his egg-shaped head. He walked with his toes pointed out and his knees bent as if he were used to traveling on ground that often gave way underneath him.

"Douglas, you don't suppose that he's the one. . ."

"I am afraid so. Put on your best smile. Your adventure is about to begin."

Chapter Two

When the man was a few feet in front of them, he paused to spit a thick stream of tobacco juice on the ground. Erin hoped her face did not show her revulsion. The man studied Douglas and Erin thoughtfully. He seemed in no particular hurry.

"How do," he said at last. "Would you be the folks that I was sent to fetch to the Gillam place?"

Douglas reached out his hand. "Why yes, I'm Rev. Douglas Teterbaugh, and this is Miss Erin Corbett. You must be Mr. Gillam?"

The old man laughed loudly, displaying an odd assortment of yellowed teeth. "No, my name's Jube Taylor. Pleased t'make your acquaintance."

Mr. Taylor shook Douglas's hand as if he were working a pump handle, then tipped his hat toward Erin. "Pleasure to know you, too, ma'am. My, but ain't you a looksome young thing." A mosquito landed on Mr. Taylor's neck. He gave it a sharp swat, then he continued, "Tucker Gillam, he asked me would I drive out here and carry you back to his place, it bein' a busy time out on the farm. We might ought t'git your things loaded up quick, if you don't mind. We had a gully warsher of a rain this morning and like as not the cricks and branches are rised up. I'd jist as soon make the most of the ride 'fore it gits dark."

Erin looked at Douglas and then back at Mr. Taylor. "But, it's not yet ten o'clock. Will it take that long to get to our destination?"

"Ma'am? Oh, you mean to the Gillams'. Well, we could make it a little sooner, except that I got to drop off some supplies to old man Doss at the Berryman store. But don't you fret, ole Jube'll git you there in a whipstitch. Preacher, you start haulin' your things over and I'll bring the wagon 'round where we can load it easier."

Mr. Taylor brought the team to the front of the station. To her dismay, Erin saw that he was driving an old farm wagon fitted with a single seat. If the rain started up again, it would be a long day indeed.

Douglas carried their things over to the edge of the platform and Mr. Taylor loaded them. "This is it," Douglas said at last. "Except for that bandbox and a valise."

"Great blue-nosed frog tadpoles! I ain't never seen such truck for jist two people. I sure do hope them old mules can pull all this hoo-rah." Mr. Taylor shook his head and loaded the last bag.

Erin felt guilty since most of that luggage was hers. "Mr. Taylor? I'm afraid I may have packed too many things," she said. "Perhaps we could leave some of them here and have them shipped later."

Mr. Taylor pulled the rope tight across the top of a trunk. "Name's Jube," he said gruffly. He tied off the last knot and looked up. "Aw, I reckon we can make it all right. Besides, they ain't nobody t'ship it with and heaven knows when it'd be 'fore anyone could haul it out for you."

Jube passed his hand over several days' worth of beard. "Miz Erin, you best let me heft you over to the wagon; this mud would suck in a fair-sized hog today."

"Thank you Mr. . . .uh. . .Jube, but I'm sure I can manage."

"Suit yourself, then," he said. "Let's git started."

Unfortunately, Jube was right. By the time Erin had made her way to the wagon, both her shoes and the hem of her skirt were caked with mud. Once she was seated, she looked back and saw Douglas carefully picking his way around the worst puddles. Jube turned in Douglas's direction and sent a squirt of tobacco juice to the ground.

"C'mon, Preacher," he called. "Them shoes'll clean up. We got a ways to go."

Chastened, Douglas took a determined step into mud that oozed over his shoe tops. He climbed onto the wagon seat just as Jube called to the mules and sent them on their way.

Douglas kicked at the mud on his shoes as they rattled out of town. "Tell me, Jube," he said. "Does the road improve farther along, or will it be this rough all the way?"

Jube laughed and spit on the side of the road. "Preacher, this road is smooth as a baby's behind compared to the bone rattler going into Lost Crick. That road ain't nothing but stumps and gullies. Some of it's so hilly you could stand up straight and lick a rock. It's that part of the trip that takes so turrible long." Jube looked over at Douglas. "You ain't never been 'round these parts before, have you, Preacher?"

"No, I'm afraid not. All I know is what the missionary board told me."

"Well, anything you need to know, you jist ask ole Jube. I reckon I'm acquainted with every man, woman, and coonhound from here to Steeleville."

"How many people are there in Lost Creek?" Douglas asked.

"Oh, there be ten or twelve families in hollerin' distance and a few more spread about. Course, there's some that ain't got sense enough to pound sand in a rathole, but by and large, most folks work hard and weed their own row."

"Are there many school-aged children, Jube?" Erin asked.

"Yes, ma'am, I reckon jist about every family's got a youngun or two for your school. The womenfolk birth babies real regular 'round here."

Erin could feel her cheeks warming. Jube certainly did not mince words.

"They got the old schoolhouse fixed up real pretty," Jube continued. "Tucker even went and had it painted up white as duck down."

"This Tucker, is he related to Daniel Gillam?" Douglas asked.

"Surely, Preacher. Tucker is Daniel's oldest boy." Jube looked uncomfortable. "Ain't nobody told you that Daniel passed on?"

"Mr. Gillam is dead?"

"Well, I hope so, Preacher. We sure as the world buried him. Daniel was nailin' on new roof boards up top of the schoolhouse last spring when some old wood gave way and sent him headfirst smack into the ground. He lasted on awhile, but he was so busted up there wasn't nothin' nobody could do for him. Daniel was a real good man, well thought of by everybody."

"I hope the people of Lost Creek will still be willing to support the mission despite Mr. Gillam's death," Erin said.

"Now, don't you fret about that, ma'am. Tucker has a younger brother, name of Ben, who'll be in your school. Tucker give his daddy a solemn deathbed promise to see to it that the school gits opened. If Tucker Gillam says it's right to have school again, like as not you'll have a whole bate of younguns the first day."

"Have they had a school here before?" Erin asked.

"Yes'm. We had a widower man who taught real regular till he passed on six or seven years ago. Since then it seems like none of the teachers that came along were very lasty like. Haven't had any school for near four years now. You'll be the first lady teacher ever in these parts."

"What about the church?" Douglas asked. "Have you ever had a full-time pastor before?"

"Land no! Closest every-Sunday church is out past Berryman. Last winter we had a circuit rider settle in. . .ole boy by name of Silas Butler. He preaches at the schoolhouse once a month if he don't git hung up somewheres else on his route."

"The schoolhouse? Don't you have a church building?" Douglas asked.

Jube reached in his pocket for some fresh tobacco. "Speakin' frank and actual, Preacher, most folks here don't see the need t'waste wood on a church to use once a week when we got the schoolhouse."

Douglas was obviously not pleased with this news. Erin thought perhaps she should change the subject.

"Jube, what is the Gillam place like?" she asked. "Is it a nice farm?"

Jube slapped one of the mules with the reins to get it back to the center of the road. "Oh, yes'm, it's the grandest farm around," he said. "Tucker's granddaddy homesteaded some of the best bottomland on the Cortoway River. Course, that was away long back before the war, when it was real wild country. Each generation has built on till it's a glory of a place. They got a bought lumber house with one floor piled right on top of the other. High livin' ain't gone to Tucker's head, though. He's hard workin' and honest, like his daddy. Still, ain't nobody who'll cross Tucker Gillam—he's big enough to go bear huntin' with a switch."

So far, Erin had not heard Jube mention anything about a Mrs. Gillam. Surely she wasn't being sent to a bachelor's home. "Jube, what about Mr. Gillam's wife?" she asked.

"Miz Gillam died when Ben was jist a little shaver, and Tucker ain't showed much interest in a wife lately. But if you're frettin' about staying in a house full of menfolks, you can rest easy. Mattie Cotter's been keeping house for the Gillams since before Ben was borned. She ain't never had much use for me, but she'll see you won't come to no harm."

Erin's attention was drawn away from Jube's words by the sound of rushing water. They came around the bend and Erin saw a stream flowing right across the roadbed ahead of them. She imagined it was normally a shallow stream, but the rain had caused it to rise and run fast. Jube kept talking, seemingly unconcerned about what was ahead.

"Are we going to cross that?" Erin asked.

"Oh yes'm, that water ain't even axle deep. This here's Haunted Spring. It never gits up high enough to cause any trouble. Ain't you never forded a stream before?"

"No, I guess I haven't. Isn't it dangerous?"

"On bigger cricks, in high water, surely. But not with a little one like this. You jist hang on to your hat."

The wagon splashed into the water. Erin's breath caught in her throat as the wheels rolled into the streambed, but they pulled up safely on the other side. Erin realized she was clinging to Douglas's arm and quickly folded her hands in her lap.

They stopped to eat at a place called Webb Hollow. The mules drank from a small pond and then ate grain out of the nose bags Jube buckled over their heads. After the team was fed, Jube brought out some crackers and cheese from a tow sack under the wagon seat and passed them around. They all drank from a jug of water covered with wet burlap to keep it cool. When the mules had rested, Erin followed Douglas and Jube back to the wagon, and Jube urged the animals on once again.

They had gone on just a little way when a horse and buckboard appeared up ahead. Suddenly, Jube let out a yell that would have awakened the dead.

"What's wrong?" Erin asked. "Is that man an outlaw?"

"Outlaw?" Jube laughed. "Why no, ma'am. Ain't you never heard nobody whoop howdy? Young James, you come here and show the new schoolmarm you ain't no outlaw."

The stranger pulled his rig up even with theirs, and Jube made the introductions. "James Doss, this here is Rev. Teterbaugh and Miz Corbett. James's daddy owns the store at Berryman. Why are you traipsin' about here in the shank of the day, boy? Can't your daddy keep you busy?"

"He sent me out here to find you. Asa Keller came through awhile back and said Lost Crick was rising fast. Daddy thought I'd best meet you and fetch them supplies on in so you could be sure and ford it in the daylight."

"I appreciate that," Jube said. "Jump on down and we'll switch the load. Preacher, we could use another hand, if you'd oblige us."

Douglas sighed, then he stepped down and walked to the back of the wagon. When the transfer was done, Jube and Douglas climbed back on the seat, and Jube raised his hand toward James. "Thank you till you're better paid," he said.

James waved back. "Y'all take care crossin' the crick."

They had to slow down considerably as soon as they turned onto the Lost Creek road. From what Erin could see, the road was just a narrow path of stumps and ruts cut out of the wilderness. Still, she was grateful that they were finally close to their destination.

Jube looked over at Erin. "Beauty of a road, ain't it? Gits wamperjawed like this every time we git a good rain. The water ruts up the road so bad it about shakes the hair off your head."

"Do you think we'll have any trouble crossing the creek?" Erin asked.

"We'll know soon enough. If you listen real careful, you can hear the water."

For the first time since they'd started their trip, Jube was silent, listening to the growing sound of the water. He stopped the mules at the crest of the hill.

Lost Creek churned down below them. Muddy torrents ripped through the brush on either side of the banks, then plunged and swirled angrily downstream. Even Jube had to raise his voice to be heard above the noise.

"She's runnin' high, ain't she? Here, Preacher, you best take the mules while I git down and study on this." He handed Douglas the reins and scrambled off the wagon.

"Do you think it's safe to try and cross?" Erin asked.

Douglas looked over the water. "I don't know. The current is swift, but it isn't very wide. Anyway, this Jube seems to know what he's doing."

"But, what if the mules should stumble? The wagon might overturn, mightn't it?"

"There's no need to borrow trouble," said Douglas. "Try to be calm. I'm sure Jube won't take any unnecessary risks."

Jube climbed back up into the wagon and took the reins. "Well, best I can tell, the water's three, maybe four, foot deep out in the middle. We might git our feet wet, but I reckon we can cross."

Jube started the team and they headed down the rocky bank. The water swirled around the mules' hooves and pulled through the wheels. It rose up to the axles, then finally, it poured against the bottom of the wagon box. They had made it over halfway across when the mules stopped.

Jube slapped the reins down hard. "Git up mules! Yah! Stubborn, rock-brained animals! Here, Preacher, take the lines again. I'll git down and see if I can give these ornery critters a reason to move. When I say so, give them a slap with the reins, and don't be gentle."

Jube eased himself down hip deep into the water and got behind the mule on the left. He waved at Douglas, and Douglas laid the reins down hard on the mules' backs. The team flinched and rocked the wagon, but they did not move.

"Ain't no use," Jube yelled. He worked his way back to the wagon seat. "Miz Erin, you slide over here and let me shoulder you to dry ground."

Erin started to protest, but Jube cut her off. "I ain't askin', I'm tellin'. Now slide over 'fore the gravel starts warshin' out from under these wheels."

"Are you sure you can carry her?" Douglas asked. "Perhaps I should do it."

Jube stared evenly at Douglas. "I've hauled things through these cricks since before you were in diapers, boy. You jist hold the reins till I git her on the ground, then I'll come back for you."

Jube balanced with one arm around Erin's back and the other beneath her legs. He lifted her from the wagon and they started their slow, halting walk to the bank. The sound of the water flooded Erin's ears. She clung to Jube's vest as he braced himself against the mule's flank. For a moment, Erin feared that they might be sucked between the animals' legs. Then the next thing she knew, she was sitting on the creek bank.

"Miz Erin, you all right?" Jube asked. "You look a might peaked."

"I'm fine. . .just a little shaky."

"You stay put. I'll go see about the preacher."

Just as Jube straightened up, Erin saw Douglas jump into the water by the side of the wagon. Douglas disappeared once, twice, and then the current pushed him downstream. The water threw him into the roots of an upturned tree.

"Grab on to those ruts!" Jube yelled. "I'll find something to pull you out!"

Jube ran to the edge of the creek and snapped a thick branch off a wind-thrown cottonwood. He stretched the limb across the water, and after three tries, Douglas finally grasped it. Jube pulled him in, and Erin ran to help as Douglas half climbed, half stumbled up the bank.

"Are you all right, Douglas?" Erin asked.

"Yes, I think so," he gasped. "I thought I could walk out alone."

Jube was standing over them. "You fool!" he said. "I ought to knock that smile right off your face. Didn't I say to wait? What kind of ninny jumps off a wagon on the downstream side in high water, that's what I'd like to know." Jube sent a scornful stream of tobacco into the creek. "I'll go git the wagon out. You two see if you can git yourselves back over to the road."

Two red spots burned on Douglas's cheeks. "Who does that old man think he is, talking to me like that?" He started to get up, but his shoes slipped in the mud and he fell flat. Erin reached out to grab his arm, but he jerked away and struggled to his feet.

Jube had managed to coax the mules out of the water, and he stood waiting by the wagon. They were a bedraggled lot. Douglas and Jube were soaked to the skin, and Erin's new traveling suit was wrinkled and streaked with sand. Jube helped Erin back in the wagon, then Douglas climbed up beside her. Nearly an hour had passed since they had started across the creek; the afternoon shadows were long.

"Preacher, I reckon I laid my mouth on you pretty heavy back there," Jube said. "But I jist didn't want nobody hurt is all. You gotta know that we have good reasons for doing things the way we do 'round here."

"I'll try to keep that in mind in the future," Douglas said tersely. "Thank you for helping me out of the water."

"I reckon you're welcome."

About a mile from the creek Jube suddenly pulled on the reins. "Whoa, mules."

"Why are we stopping?" Douglas asked.

"Well, Preacher, if you look up ahead, you might see. That hill there's a monster, and I figure with all this folderol in the back, the mules need a rest and a running start to make it up. Truth is, the road don't flatten out much till we git to the schoolhouse. The whole way is either up or down."

The mules seemed to sense what Jube wanted them to do. After a moment's rest, they took off at a trot and pulled the wagon several yards up the hill before the grade slowed them down. Erin's back was pressed hard into the seat as they climbed up the snakebacked trail. The mules huffed loudly with each step they took. Finally, they reached a spot that was not quite so steep, and Jube let them rest. He pointed to a clearing on their right.

"That's the Witbeck cabin," he said. "If you look close, you can see it through the trees." In the twilight, Erin could just make out a small gray cabin with a stone chimney. She yawned and tried to find a more comfortable position on the wagon seat.

"You're jist about tuckered out, ain't you, Miz Erin?"

"I admit, I'll be glad to get off of this wagon."

"Well, it won't be much longer, another mile or so."

The mules were tired, too. They had slowed considerably in the last few minutes despite Jube's repeated attempts to hurry them along. Erin's head pounded with every move the wagon made. She didn't care anymore what kind of home the Gillams had; all she wanted to see was a bed, any kind of bed, and the sooner the better. Douglas had given up the battle to stay awake some time ago, and his head nodded and bounced on his chest.

They came around a curve to a steep downhill stretch. Jube stopped the mules, stood up, and yelled with all his might, "Hey-hoo!"

Douglas jumped straight up in the air. "What is it?" he cried. "What's wrong?"

Jube laughed. "Nothing's wrong, Preacher. See that little portion of light there? Gillams' is right down the road. Git up, mules."

Douglas sat back in the seat. "I don't see why we had to make such a production of our arrival," he mumbled. "I feel as if we were leading a circus parade."

"Sorry if I scared you, Preacher, but it'd be smart for you to remember to give a yell before you set foot on a man's property, especially after dark. It ain't jist polite; it's a whole lot safer. Most folks here have dogs that don't like strangers."

The Gillams' house was at the bottom of the hill, where the road ended. The silhouettes of three people were in the open front door. They were a most welcome sight.

Chapter Three

Someone was knocking on the door. Erin sat up in her bed and tried to focus on the source of the sound. Then, she remembered. She was at the Gillams'. A woman was calling her name.

"Erin? Erin, you awake, honey? Breakfast is ready. You best git a move on."

Erin threw her feet over the side of the bed. The voice belonged to the woman named Mattie who had greeted her the night before. Erin blinked the sleep out of her eyes, remembering that there had also been a boy with blond hair, the younger brother, Ben, whom Jube had talked about. Vaguely, she also remembered her hand being lost between the huge fingers of a very large man who had introduced himself as Tucker Gillam.

The sun had not yet risen, and Erin lit the lamp and hurried to get dressed. She thought of locating the bathroom, but since the only thing to serve those needs was out somewhere behind the house, she decided to wait. She poured some water from the pitcher on the washstand and sponged her hands and face, while the smell of coffee and bacon hurried her along.

In the combination parlor and dining room, Mattie was hovering over Douglas, filling his coffee cup and nudging dishes toward him. When Mattie saw Erin, she set the coffeepot down.

"Good morning. Are you hungry, child? You jist come on over here and set down. The other men already et, but I reckon we got enough left to fill you up."

"Thank you, Mattie," said Erin. "It looks delicious."

Douglas stood up as she came to the table. "Good morning, Erin. Did you sleep well?"

"Yes, thank you. I can't remember ever sleeping so soundly."

Douglas sat back down on the bench, and Mattie poured Erin a cup of coffee.

"You must be near starved. Like as not that punkin-headed Jube didn't feed y'all enough yesterday to keep a bird alive. I got a fresh pan of biscuits in the oven. You jist help yourself, Erin."

Mattie disappeared into the kitchen. The table was crowded with dishes of eggs and ham, redeye gravy, thick sliced bacon, biscuits, coffee, and apple pie. *Imagine,* thought Erin, *apple pie for breakfast!*

Mattie brought out a fresh plate of biscuits and sat down. "Jube told us about your trouble crossing Lost Crick. I reckon that was one baptizin' that you wasn't counting on, huh, Preacher?"

Douglas nodded, but Erin noticed his smile was small and tight.

"If it hadn't been for Jube, I don't know what we would have done," Erin said. "Douglas was very lucky to come out of the creek unharmed."

Mattie smiled. " 'Pears to me it wasn't no luck a'tall. God had His hand on you children. It was Him who brought you through that troubled water."

"I guess I hadn't thought of it that way," Erin said.

"Well, study on it sometime. The Word says that our very hairs be numbered and that He causeth all things to work together for good to those who love Him. Ain't no need for luck when you're in the Father's hands." Mattie looked over at Douglas's plate. "Listen to me, a carryin' on while the preacher's dish goes empty."

"Thank you, Mattie, but I'm stuffed. I couldn't eat another bite."

"Land, Preacher, then we got to git you eating like a country boy. You could use a little meat on your bones. I expect you and Miz Erin will want some time to settle in this morning. There's still one more of your satchels here that needs to go over to the cabin."

Douglas had been assigned to a cabin? He glanced at Erin, a tiny frown between his brows, but he said nothing, only excused himself to go finish unpacking.

Erin turned back toward Mattie. The older woman was short and heavyset, an elfin butterball with a crown of white hair and twinkling blue eyes. The thing that Erin liked most, though, was the way Mattie looked when she had been talking about God.

"Now that we got rid of all the menfolks, I reckon we got jist a minute or two for us girls to git acquainted," Mattie said. "Now tell me, what made a pretty young thing like you come down here to the sticks to keep school?"

"Well. . .I don't know. It was just something I felt I needed to do. Would it seem childish to you if I said I felt that God had called me here?"

"Childish? Mercy, no! Was it childish when Moses got called up by God out of the wilderness? Surely it weren't childish for the Lord to call His disciples out of their fishin' boats. Being called is a special thing, to be took serious."

"Mattie, I have so many plans," Erin confided. "There are new ways of teaching, programs that I can hardly wait to start."

"It's a pleasure to see a young person so eager to work. You jist keep your eyes on the Master, child, and you'll do fine. And if ever you want someone to talk to, you come see old Mattie. It's a pure joy having another woman in the house."

"Thank you, Mattie, I'm sure I'll take you up on that." Erin folded her napkin and put it on the table. "Would you like some help with these dishes?" she asked.

"No, you take things easy today. If you can't find what you need, jist give me a holler." Mattie stacked the dishes and cups and went off into the kitchen.

It took several tries, but Erin finally arranged all her clothes into the wardrobe and dresser in her room. After she got her room in order, she wandered out on the front porch.

Yesterday's clouds had given way to a brilliant blue sky. It was quite some time until lunch, so Erin decided to go exploring. Erin had always loved horses, and Mattie had said she should feel free to roam, so she crossed the pasture and walked toward the barn. She turned into the open door, and suddenly, out of nowhere, a pile of filthy straw rained down over her head.

"Stop!" she cried. "Watch what you're doing!"

Tucker Gillam stepped out into the sunlight. "Well, excuse me, miss, but I'm not used to having young ladies sneak up behind me when I muck out a stall. Maybe you ought to let a person know next time you go poking your nose in someone's barn."

"I didn't know it was you, Mr. Gillam, I'm sorry. I meant no offense. Mattie told me it would be all right if I had a look around."

"No offense taken." He went on raking out the stall. "Sorry I missed you at breakfast, but farm folk have to git up early and work for a living. By the way, we ain't formal here—everybody calls me Tucker."

He pitched fresh straw into the clean stall. "You're welcome to look around here if you like," he said. "But until you figure out the difference between honey and horse manure, maybe I'd best have Ben to show you around."

"Fine, would this afternoon be convenient?"

Tucker leaned on the top of his pitchfork. "I wouldn't say it's convenient, but I believe we can spare Ben for one afternoon."

"Thank you, I'll look forward to it. Now, if you will excuse me, I think I had better go and change my clothes."

"Ma'am? You might want to wear something a little less fancy, if you have it, especially those shoes. Looks like all they'd be good for is a wrenched ankle."

Erin raised her chin a notch. "Thank you for your concern."

Tucker touched the brim of his hat and nodded his head. "See you at dinner, ma'am."

Erin turned and stepped into a pile of warm manure. Tucker's laugh was a deep rumble.

"Looks like you're gonna have to find those 'suitable' shoes a mite sooner than you thought," he said.

Erin did not reply. Instead, she walked briskly toward the house and slipped into her room. As she changed her soiled clothing, she could think of nothing but how aggravating Tucker Gillam was. He was big and arrogant, and he looked like the orphanage bulldog. He probably was admired around Lost Creek for his size, or perhaps for his money, but Erin was determined that she would not let him intimidate her.

As Erin sat by the window and let the breeze blow through her hair, she began to feel ashamed. She had been a missionary for less than one day, and already she had lost her temper. Mattie had said, "Just keep your eyes on the Master and you'll do fine," but keeping her eyes on God was not going to be as easy as she had thought. However, holding a grudge against Tucker was not only unchristian, she decided, it was also unwise. After all, his opinions held a lot of weight in this community.

Mattie rang the lunch bell and the men lined up at the washstand on the back porch. Erin peeked into the kitchen and saw Mattie beating a pot of mashed potatoes.

"There you are, Erin," she said. "Here, why don't you finish mashing these taters while I dish up the chicken. Men are plenty hungry by dinnertime; won't do to make them wait."

Erin picked up the spoon and tried to imitate what she had seen Mattie do. Though she tried her best, pieces of potato flew over the sides of the pot and the rest stuck together in gooey clumps at the bottom.

"Erin, those taters about done?" Mattie called.

"I'm afraid I'm making a mess. They look awfully lumpy."

Mattie inspected the pot and smiled. "Sometimes, you jist got to git mean with them." She added some cream and a big dollop of butter and whipped the spoon furiously until the potatoes turned light and fluffy. "There you be, jist took a little elbow grease. Now, git that bowl on the table while I dish up the rest."

The table was laden with bowls of green beans laced with bacon, creamed corn, fresh bread, gravy, radishes, sliced onions, a molasses cake, cold buttermilk, and something called "cracklin' " cornbread. It was a far cry from the skimpy soup and bread served for luncheon at the Manchester Orphanage.

"Y'all better git in here and eat your dinner before I give it to the hogs," Mattie called out the door.

Tucker came in, followed by Jube and a man Erin did not know; then came Ben and Douglas. Mattie made the introductions as the men sat down.

"Miz Erin, this here's Clay Reynolds. He's helping us during harvest. Clay lives down the road a piece. I reckon you know the rest. Now set down 'fore it gits cold. Preacher, would you favor us by sayin' grace?"

"Certainly," Douglas said. "Shall we bow for prayer? Our most gracious heavenly Father, we thank Thee for Thy very bountiful blessings, and for this great abundance of food. We thank Thee, oh God, for the hands that prepared it. Lead us now into Thy paths of loving-kindness this day. In Jesus' blessed name we pray, amen."

Everyone began to eat. Douglas and Erin watched in awe as the men stacked food high on their plates, then covered everything with gravy. Tucker poured coffee from his cup into his saucer, blew on it, and then drank directly from the saucer.

The headmistress would have much to say about country table manners, Erin thought. She searched for a topic of conversation to take her mind off their odd customs.

"Ben," she began, "Tucker said you might be willing to show Douglas and me around this afternoon."

Ben smiled broadly, and heedless of the food in his mouth, replied, "Yes'm. I'd be proud to, right after dinner."

"Jist remember to git yourself back here in time to clean that chicken house before supper," Tucker said. "And you'd best chew that food with your mouth closed, boy. We don't want our company thinking we ain't got no manners."

Tucker got up from the table and walked to the door. "Ben, you take good care of Miz Erin and the preacher," he said. "Remember they ain't used to hard walking."

"I'm sure we'll be fine," Douglas said.

"Well, watch out for them wampus kitties," Tucker warned.

Ben's eyes brightened. "Reckon I ought to take my rifle gun along, jist in case?"

"No, them wampus kitties don't usually come out before dark."

Douglas and Erin looked at each other. Could a "wampus kitty" be some kind of backwoods name for a bobcat? Or perhaps it was a name for a less than desirable member of their community. Erin made up her mind to keep a careful eye out when they went for their walk.

Ben showed them the chicken house and the pigpen, where a half dozen brown pigs were sleeping contentedly in a mud wallow. Douglas leaned on the fence and looked into the pen. "Are these all the pigs you keep?" he asked. "I thought Mr. Reynolds said something about a hog roundup."

"Oh, these hogs here is jist what we fatten up special for the family. The acorn mast they eat in the wild makes their meat bitter, so we feed 'em corn and slops for a month or two before we butcher. Tuck's got over a hundred fifty head of hogs ear-notched up in the hills."

"Ear-notched? What's that?" Erin asked.

"It's a lot like the branding they do out West, I guess. You jist cut the ear a special way when they's small—ours is under half crop, right ear—then, when we round 'em up for the market, we know whose pigs they are."

"Are the other livestock ear-notched?"

"No, ma'am, we only notch the hogs. Most folks 'round here notch cows, too, but the last few years Tucker's been favoring ear tags for them and the sheep."

They walked through a grove of fruit trees. The peaches had already been picked, but the apples hung thick and red on the branches, full of promise. Ben pointed towards another building. "That there's the smokehouse, and that little lean-to is jist for farm machinery." They were coming full circle to the front of the house. "The stone building that butts into the hill yonder is an icehouse, only one 'round here. We've kept ice right up to harvest some years."

"Ben, did your father build all this by himself?"

"Oh, no, ma'am. First was the homestead cabin that Grampa built, that's where Jube and the preacher sleep now. Grampa built the barn and most of the outbuildings, too. Then Pa and Grampa started on the big house. By the time I was borned, Pa and Tuck had added the second story. They built on the big kitchen and Mattie's room a couple years before Ma died."

"Your pa must have cared very much about this land to work so hard," Erin said.

Ben kicked at the gravel in the road with his toes. "I reckon nobody could farm as good as Pa did. Tuck, he takes real good care of things, though, and pretty soon I'll be able to work a full man's share around here. I'll be thirteen my next birthday."

"It'll be a pleasure to have some older pupils like you. Are you looking forward to starting school?"

"Being truthful, ma'am, I can't say as I am. But Tuck, he gave his word to Pa that I'd git schoolin' before I was growed, and both me and Tuck are set on keeping that promise, no matter how we feel about it ourselves."

"I see. Well, I think it's very good of you both to keep your word like that, don't you, Douglas?"

"Hmm? Oh, yes, of course."

"Tuck says a man ain't nothin' if he don't keep his word." Ben looked over into the yard. "That's about all there is to see around the house. Our land covers four sections along the river. Course, not all that's planted, most of it's woods pasture. Would you like to see the river, or are you all tuckered out?"

"We're not tired!" Erin cried. "Show us the way!"

Grapevines climbed from treetop to treetop creating a shadowy canopy of leaves across the road. Ben trotted on ahead, turning back from time to time to identify a plant or animal he thought might interest his guests. He stopped by an old walnut tree. "The main road runs straight on that way, but this way's shorter, if you don't mind it being a bit upturned."

Erin smiled at Douglas. "What do you think, Reverend, can a city boy like you climb a few hills?"

Douglas rested his arm up on a tree limb. "I guess the reverend can do anything the teacher can. Let's go, Ben."

Ben led the way to a hill so steep they had to hold on to tree roots to climb it. As Erin's skirts caught on weeds and branches, she envied the men their trousers. As Douglas and Erin gasped for breath behind him, Ben looked over his shoulder. "It ain't much farther, jist one more big hill. Do you need to rest a mite?"

"No, Ben, we're fine," Erin called.

Douglas wiped his forehead with his handkerchief. "I hope you're having a wonderful adventure, Miss Corbett."

A steep hill of river gravel stretched in front of them. Each step up they took sent pebbles tumbling down. Douglas took Erin's arm to try and help her get her footing in the shifting rocks, but he was so off balance himself he nearly knocked them both over. Ben scrambled to the top first and helped pull Erin up. She was laughing so hard by then that she could hardly stand.

From their vantage point, they could see a large stretch of the Courtois River. In some places it wound lazy and flat, and in others it suddenly narrowed and plunged downstream, rushing over fallen limbs and logs only to settle down around the next bend in deep, still pools. Ben started down the bank, sending out sprays of rocks in all directions. Douglas took a step after him.

"This is awfully steep, Erin. Do you want me to help you?"

"Not only can I get down by myself, sir, but I believe that I can get there before you."

"Really? Well, I'd like to see that."

Erin half ran and half slid down the bank, putting all her weight on her downhill leg, hoping she could slow herself down before she went over the edge. Instead, she tumbled over her skirts, arms and legs flailing.

"Erin, are you all right? Are you hurt?" cried Douglas.

"Miz Corbett, you jist went a flyin'! Have you broke anything?"

She shook her head. "Nothing is too damaged except my dignity."

Relief washed over Douglas's face. "Shame on you, acting like a schoolgirl and scaring me half to death."

Erin smiled naughtily. "I'm sorry, Douglas. But, you will have to admit, I did beat you down the hill."

"She's got you on that one, Preacher," Ben said.

Douglas sighed and shook his head. He looked at Erin for a moment and then he nodded his head as if he had decided something, though Erin could not imagine what conclusion he had reached.

For a time, they all sat on a smooth gray log and watched the river. The water was as clear as glass, each rock glistening in the riverbed like a facet in a huge, liquid diamond. Ben showed Erin the minnows, some tiny and brown, and the larger ones with red dots on their heads. They listened to the deep bass "garumph!" of the bullfrogs while blue dragonflies buzzed around their faces. Sitting there and listening, Erin discovered a calmness she had never known before.

Ben finally broke the spell. "I reckon maybe we better walk down and take the road. It's a tetch farther, but it's easier traveling."

They walked along the riverbank and soon came to the log bridge that was part of the back road to the farmhouse.

"Those black-eyed Susans are so pretty. May I stop and pick some?" Erin asked.

"Surely, ma'am, but if you and the preacher can find your own way back, I'd better be going on. It's gittin' late, and Tuck'll skin me for sure if I don't git that coop cleaned out. The house is jist a ways straight down the road."

"I'm sure we can find it," Douglas said. "You go on ahead."

Ben trotted on toward the house. Erin climbed off the roadbed to reach the flowers at the bottom of a little hill. Douglas started to follow, and Erin was suddenly aware that she and Douglas were quite alone, unchaperoned.

"Douglas," she said. "Would you mind picking some of those red flowers over there? They would look lovely with these yellow ones."

Douglas obligingly crossed to the other side of the road while Erin struggled with the bristly flower stems. She walked back into the shadows of a cedar grove to pick some particularly bright blooms, but just as she reached down, someone pushed by her and ran deeper into the woods.

Her scream brought Douglas running, but she was already climbing back up to the road when he found her.

"What's wrong? Was it an animal?"

"No. . .a man." She couldn't seem to catch her breath. "He ran right past me."

"What did he look like?"

"I don't know. I was so surprised, I guess I didn't really look at him."

"Well, it's all right now. It was probably some local boy prowling around in the trees. I imagine you scared him as much as he scared you." Douglas looked over his shoulder. "Let's get back to the house."

Tucker, Jube, and Clay were standing in a tight circle by the fireplace when they walked in. Jube's voice rose above the rest.

"That river weren't high enough to float two cows downstream," he said. "You know them heifers jist didn't lose theirselves without a trace."

Tucker looked up as Erin and Douglas came into the room. "Miz Erin," he said, "you look like you seen a haunt. Didn't Ben listen about not tiring you out?"

Douglas pulled out a chair for her. "Erin had a little scare," he said. "She was off to the side of the road picking flowers and some hooligan hiding in the trees jumped past her and ran into the woods."

Tucker looked at her sharply. "Did you git a look at him, Miz Erin?"

"No, he ran by too fast. You don't think it could be one of those 'wampus kitties' you mentioned earlier, do you?"

The men threw back their heads and laughed. "No, ma'am," Tucker said. "I can jist about guarantee that it weren't no wampus kitty."

"Miz Erin," Jube said, "wampus kitties is jist something that goes bump in the dark. Ain't no natural critter by that name."

Erin glared at Tucker. He grinned back at her, but then his smile faded. "I'd be obliged if you'd show me where you found your wampus kitty," he said. "I'm a mind to wonder if that kitty might know something about our missing cows."

Chapter Four

Erin slept fitfully during the night, awakened again and again by an intense itching that burned and spread. Finally, she got out of bed, lit the lamp, and pulled up her chemise to take a closer look. Ugly red bumps lined her hips, and on the back of her right thigh was a small black spot that wouldn't come off when she rubbed it. As she puzzled over it, she heard a noise in the hall and then a knock on the door.

"Erin? It's about time to git up." Mattie opened the door and saw Erin standing by the lamp. "Why, you're sure up early for a city gal."

"Mattie, would you look at this? I think I have some sort of rash. It itches terribly."

Mattie came over to the light and inspected her. "You got more of these—say where your drawers lie around your ankles and on your legs?"

"Yes. And on my arms, too. Do you know what it is?"

"You ain't got no rash, honey, you jist got chiggers."

"Chiggers? What is that?"

"They're a lot like skeeters, only they be tinier with no wings. They lay low in the brush and hop on when people go by. They itch like the devil, but they ain't nothing serious."

Erin pulled her wrapper back off her leg. "What about this? I can't get it off."

"Oh, now that there's a tick. A tick's a little blood suckin' bug. He's got his head good and buried in you, too."

"You mean it's alive?" Erin squirmed to get a better look.

Mattie chuckled. "Don't worry, child, we'll git him out. Hand me a match."

Mattie took the match and lit it, then blew it out and stuck the hot head on the tick; with her thumbnail and fingernail, she picked the insect off Erin's skin. "There. I'll git some salve for those chiggers and something to clean that tick bite. Next time you go out trampin' in the brush, you git some pennyroyal from the garden and crush it real good, then rub it on your arms and legs. That'll keep some of those critters off. Now, don't look so addlepated. Ticks and chiggers are jist a part of living in this country. You'll git used to it by and by."

Mattie's salve helped a little, but as Erin went into the dining room, she still felt as if little bugs were crawling on her, and she smelled vaguely of bacon grease. Mattie set the last platter on the breakfast table, and Tucker reached for a biscuit and slathered it with apple butter.

"Preacher, you about ready to see where you're gonna hold church?" he asked.

"The schoolhouse? Yes, I was going to ask if perhaps Erin and I could see it today."

"I got a little time this morning, so I thought I'd finish the railing on the steps over there. We been planning a pie supper for Saturday night. I was thinking you might want to fix up the place a bit for folks to see. It might git 'em fired up if they saw all them fancy books setting out and ready to go."

"That is an excellent idea," said Douglas. "Erin and I should be able to get things ready in a few days' time. Don't you think so, Erin?"

"Certainly. Are our supplies already at the school?"

Tucker poured his coffee in his saucer to cool. "Yes'm. We hauled in four fair-sized crates from the mission board last month, all full of books and maps and such."

"Wonderful," Douglas said. "Erin and I shall be ready to accompany you immediately after breakfast."

After Erin helped finish clearing the table, she went out on the porch and found Douglas scratching his back against a post.

"Chiggers?" she asked.

He turned around, surprised. "Oh, Erin, excuse me." He smiled ruefully. "Are you still enjoying your adventure?"

"Of course! A few little insects won't dampen my enthusiasm."

"Well, they've dampened mine, at least until I saw you at breakfast this morning. Your dress is most becoming."

"Be careful," Erin teased. "Or you will turn my head."

"Would that be such a bad idea?"

Tucker rounded the corner, lumber and toolbox in hand. "You two gonna lollygag all day, or you coming with me?"

"Aren't we taking a wagon?" Erin asked.

"It's only a mile or so, but if you don't think you can walk it. . ."

"Of course I can. I only wondered since you were carrying those boards and tools."

"Aw, they ain't nothing for a working man."

Erin handed Douglas the picnic basket Mattie had packed for them, and they started up the hill. Squirrels chattered angrily at them for disturbing their peace, and tan grasshoppers snapped away from their feet.

"Preacher, I hear you're all the way from Chicago," Tucker said.

"That is my home, but I have spent the past few years at seminary in Kentucky."

"Ain't that something, all the way from Kentuck. What in thunder brings a highfalutin man like yourself to these woods?"

"Well, my father is also a pastor and he thought perhaps this would be a good experience for a young minister like myself."

"Ma always said the first pancake of the morning was likely to be burnt around the edges. Is that what you're meaning, Preacher?"

"I suppose you could put it that way. We felt that this would be an appropriate place for me to smooth off the rough corners, so to speak."

Tucker shifted the load on his shoulder and looked over at Douglas. "You mean, it don't matter so much if you make a mistake here, it being a woodsy church, and you gitting paid by the mission board instead of by the people."

Douglas looked uncomfortable. "Of course it matters, but you are right, this particular position is of little risk to me. I would want you to know, however, that I will hardly get rich on the fifteen dollars a month the mission board pays. I certainly am not here for the money."

"I'm right proud to hear that, Preacher. But I'd have you to know that fifteen dollars cash money is more'n some folks around here see in a year, so if I were you, I'd keep the particulars of my earnings to myself."

"Thank you," Douglas said stiffly. "I'll keep that in mind."

Tucker turned his attention to Erin. "What about you, Miz Erin, you here for experience or—what did I hear the preacher call it?—you here for an adventure?"

So he had been listening to their conversation on the porch!

"I should hope to gain experience from any teaching position I accept," Erin replied. "And yes, I am quite excited about this assignment and about learning the ways of the people here. It is an adventure of sorts."

"Even when it comes with cow patties and chiggers?"

"Yes, even then, and I find it most indelicate of you to discuss such things."

"Yes'm, I reckoned you would." Tucker pointed up toward the top of the hill. "School's jist past that bend on the hilltop."

Erin hurried on ahead of the men, glad to have an excuse to get away from Tucker. "This is my school," she thought as she went inside the small, plain building. Her heart filled with joy. Soon, these desks would be filled with pupils eager to learn about everything in the world, and she would be their teacher.

Douglas had followed her inside, but Tucker remained in the doorway. "Reckon this'll do?" he asked.

"Yes, it will do just fine," Erin said. "I could use some water from the pump so I can start cleaning up."

"Bucket's in the corner," said Tucker.

Douglas hesitated, then he picked up the pail. "Of course," he said. "I will be right back."

Tucker watched as Douglas went out the back door. "He ain't exactly zealous about work, is he?"

Erin sat down in one of the pupils' desks. "You don't like us very much, do you, Tucker?"

Tucker reached one hand up and rested it on the top of the door frame. "That's matter of fact and to the point, ain't it? Truth is, it ain't a matter of liking or not liking you, Miz Erin. I got a little brother I promised to git schooled. If some religion comes along in the bargain, fine and dandy, that's the way Pa wanted it. But I want a teacher that's for certain sure gonna stay around more'n a couple weeks, and the last thing we need is a dude preacher who come to do his little thing until he can get a big church in the city."

"I think you are judging Douglas too harshly. He hasn't even had a chance to begin his ministry yet. He isn't afraid of hard work, either, he just isn't accustomed to rural life."

"No, I expect he's not, but if he wants folks to pay him any mind, he might should learn."

"Douglas and I will both learn, Tucker. I made a commitment to teach here, and I intend to do so."

"You're a pretty young lady, and I got nothing against you personal, but you ain't got a notion of what you're gitting into. Speakin' frankly, I think the first time this job gits hard or dirty, and it will, you'll be gone on the first wagon you can git out of here."

"Is that so! Well, I'm afraid you'll be sorely disappointed next spring when I lead our school in closing exercises."

"Not disappointed, jist surprised." Tucker picked up his toolbox. "I best git this railing finished. There's chores to do back at the house."

Tucker left shortly after dinner, having finished his work on the stairs. Douglas and Erin spent the rest of the day cleaning and unpacking. At the bottom of the first crate, Erin found a round-bodied spider with the longest, thinnest legs she had ever seen. She quickly pulled her hand out of its path as it scurried up the side of the packing box. "What sort of creature is that?"

Douglas turned the crate on its side and smashed the spider with his shoe. "I don't know," he said. "I'm afraid we didn't study much entomology in seminary."

"Speaking of seminary, did they teach you how to go about building a church?"

Douglas took a deep breath and let it out slowly. "Well, there are several programs I studied in school that could be implemented. My first priority will be to raise the quality of their church services. I am told that most backwoods churches have only a very rudimentary concept of formal worship. Then, I'll begin laying the organizational groundwork, setting up committees for Sunday school and special programs to increase attendance, and so forth."

"But, Douglas, I thought we were sent here to tell people about the Gospel. What if they don't want to change the way they worship?"

Douglas looked at Erin as if he were explaining something to a child. "I didn't mean to imply that the Gospel was not central to what we teach—but there is much more to mission work than that. I've had the privilege of a fine education and it is my duty to lift these people to a higher level of understanding."

"I hadn't thought of it like that," she said. "I'm afraid I don't know much about being a missionary."

"Don't worry, Erin, you will be fine."

The locusts were humming their afternoon song by the time the second crate was emptied. "I move we wait until tomorrow to open the next one," Douglas said.

"I'll second that motion. I need to borrow a broom and some rags from Mattie before I can clean this place properly anyway."

"Then I suggest we find our way home."

Douglas opened the door and the afternoon sunlight angled into the classroom. A gentle breeze whispered through the leaves and sent brownish-gray lizards skittering away from the warm sunlight where they had laid basking in the warm dust beside the school. Erin moved to stand beside Douglas in the doorway.

He turned his head toward her. "You're a lovely young woman, Erin Corbett."

"Thank you, Douglas, but I don't feel lovely. I'm covered with dust and cobwebs."

Douglas shut the door behind them, and together they walked to the road. He picked up a pinecone and threw it down the hill ahead of them. "Erin, we're going to be working closely together, so I think we should be honest with one another, shouldn't we?"

"Yes, of course."

"If we were still in society, I would send you little gifts and take you to dinners. But it's different here. I realize we've just recently met, but I am a man who knows what he wants, and I'm generally used to getting it. If you would agree, I would like permission to court you."

Erin looked down at the road, trying to slow her thoughts. "I believe I would like that, Douglas, but. . ."

"But what?"

"Well, for one thing, I don't think anyone else should know. There will be too many times like today when we'll be working together alone. People would misunderstand if they thought there was anything between us. It would damage the ministry."

"You're right, of course," he said. "Very well, we will keep it a secret for now, and I promise to be on my best behavior, even when we are alone."

Erin stopped to look down from the hilltop. The trees formed a lush green carpet, which covered ridge upon sculptured ridge of rugged land. "Look, Douglas, isn't that beautiful? 'I will lift up mine eyes unto the hills, from whence cometh my help. My help cometh from the Lord, which made heaven and earth.' "

Douglas stood quietly behind her. "Psalm 121."

"Yes. It's been my favorite since I was a little girl. God is going to bless this work, Douglas. It is going to be successful, you'll see."

"Well, if it isn't, it won't be from lack of trying on your part, Erin. Let's get back to the house before I am tempted to break my promise."

Chapter Five

"It's no use, Mattie. Your pie looks delicious, but mine looks as if the crust were made of cowhide."

Mattie chuckled. "Yours does look a little cattywampus, but it ain't bad for a first try."

"Maybe not, but I don't want to take this sad thing to the pie supper."

Mattie thought a moment. "Might be that I got a way to fix that. Suppose after we fancy up our boxes, you put your name in my box and I'll put my name in yours, then we'll carry our own pies into the schoolhouse."

"That wouldn't be honest, would it?"

"Oh, honey, you jist don't understand about pie suppers. Why, most of the fun is the gals trying t' fool the menfolks. Anything's fair! The young bucks git theirselves worked up in a terrible lather guessing which pie is their sweetie's, and then they try to bid everybody else out."

Erin looked down at her lopsided creation. "But you wouldn't want people to think you baked this mess."

"Child, I've lived 'round here these sixty years. Folks know I'm generally a good enough cook. It's no skin off my teeth if they hear I made up one bad pie. Anyhow, what I had in mind was to play a little foolery on Jube. That old coot's been aggravating me for nigh on to fifteen years now. He puts the high bid on my pies and then I'm obliged to spend the rest of the evening listening to his gabble. This way I can have the fun of pulling his leg a little—if you don't mind spending some time with the old buzzard."

"I don't mind."

"You best git changed then. I'll finish up these boxes."

Back in her room, Erin looked over her clothes in the wardrobe. She was tired of the plain work dresses she had been wearing for the past few days. She decided her white lawn would do nicely for a special occasion like a pie supper. They were to ride in the wagon, so she gladly put her low-heeled boots away and pulled out a pair of kid slippers. There was no reason, Erin decided, to look dowdy just because she was a missionary. She twisted her hair up high, inserted a horn comb, and pinned on a small straw hat, tilting it far forward. She looked in the mirror with satisfaction.

Erin was pleased when the men stopped talking as she entered the room. Douglas stood up and walked toward her.

"Erin, you are a refreshing sight," he said. "Won't you make an impression on the community tonight!"

Tucker cleared his throat. "Oh, she'll do that for sure, like a peacock in a chicken house. Where did a gal grown up in an orphanage get such folderol?"

"I earned it," said Erin. "I've worked afternoons and Saturdays in a millinery shop since I was fourteen."

Ben scowled at Tucker. "I think she's real pretty," he said. "I ain't never seen such fancy wearin' clothes."

"I never said she wasn't pretty," Tucker replied. "We'd best git on the wagon if you want to be there in time to vote for the beauty cake."

Mattie and Erin loaded their pies, then Tucker helped Mattie onto the wagon seat, while Douglas, Ben, and Erin found places on the fresh straw in the wagon bed. Tucker spoke to the horses and they trotted up the hill.

"Mattie," Erin asked, "what is a 'beauty cake'?"

"Oh, that's the money-makin'est part of a pie supper. Somebody bakes a cake, and the boys pay a penny a vote to pick the prettiest girl there. The girl with the most votes wins the beauty cake, and she shares it with them that voted for her. A good pie might bring a quarter or so, but the beauty cake can run as high as three or four dollars." Mattie rubbed her broad forehead. "Whilst I study on it, Preacher, I reckon you know that it wouldn't be fitting for you to make any bids tonight, especially on the beauty cake. Folks 'round here jist wouldn't confidence a courtin' preacher."

Douglas coughed nervously. "I had not thought of it like that," he said. "I'll try to see that I am nothing more than an interested spectator."

They rounded the corner and drove into the schoolyard, where Jube greeted them and made his way to Mattie's side of the wagon. "Need some help with them pies, do ya, Mattie?"

"You leave them pies be, old man, and mind your business. Erin and I can manage without your help. If you're jist burning to do a good deed, why don't you take the preacher around and let him meet the menfolks."

Jube spat on the ground. "All right, old woman, you don't have to be so tetchous. Some folks jist don't have no natural kindness in them."

Erin and Mattie picked up their pies and started toward the schoolhouse. Barefoot children scooted around the woods near the edge of the yard. Douglas and Jube joined a group of men assembled by the pump. From the coins they were exchanging, Erin assumed that they must be voting for the beauty cake.

There were a half dozen or so women clustered around the platform inside the school. Erin quickly realized, to her embarrassment, that most of the ladies were wearing the plainest of dresses, and only a few even wore shoes.

Mattie turned back toward Erin. "Well, c'mon, child," she said. "Don't jist stand and gawk, they ain't gonna bite you." She called to the other women, "Becky, Liza, all of you, come and meet the new teacher." Mattie motioned to a matronly lady standing next to a girl who looked to be about the same age as Erin. "Miz Erin Corbett, this here's the Widder Puckett and her daughter Bessie, and there's Carrie Witbeck, and this is Becky Keller, and Liza Reynolds. That's Lela Stiles and her daughter-in-law, Rose. Rose and Emmit jist got married last spring."

"Congratulations, Rose," Erin said. "It is so nice to meet you all. I hope to get to know you all better soon."

Obviously, the widow and her daughter were the fashion conscience for the community. While not elaborately dressed by city standards, their clothes were more stylish than the other women's, and their hats overflowed with feathers and ribbon. The widow eyed Erin's and Mattie's pastries.

"Why, Miz Corbett, did you make a pie, too?" she exclaimed. "Ain't it a wonder, a city gal who can cook."

"Well, actually," Erin stuttered, "I didn't. . ."

"City gals got to eat, too, don't they?" said Mattie. "Shouldn't be no wonder that Erin knows how to cook."

The widow pulled herself erect and peered down at Erin. "That's a beautiful dress you're wearing, Miz Corbett. Ain't nobody here seen such a fancy fine outfit. Looks like you came right off a *Bazaar* fashion plate."

"Why, thank you, Mrs. Puckett."

"Course," Mrs. Puckett continued, "some folks might say such truck ain't fittin' a gal who's given to be a missionary, but I'm more broad-minded than most. With a daughter like Bessie, here, I understand how much young gals like to dress in Sunday go-to-meetin' clothes. Bessie don't have no need of real fancy dresses, though, she being so naturally pretty. She's won the beauty cake two years in a row, you know."

"Really?" Erin said. "How nice. I wish you luck tonight, Bessie."

Bessie and her mother smiled identical toothy smiles and excused themselves. Mattie leaned close to Erin as they walked away. "Now, don't you pay her no mind," she whispered. "Naomi Puckett's been puttin' on airs 'round here for years. She's jist afraid you might outshine that daughter of hers."

There was a commotion in the yard as an odd little wagon pulled up in front of the door. The bottom half was a common farm rig, but a box house had been built over the bed with a door in back and a sloped roof on top. A man in a worn black suit and a wide-brimmed hat was driving. Next to him sat a rather unkempt-looking young man.

Mattie peered out of the window. "Looks like Brother Butler got hisself here," she said.

Mattie had told Erin a little about him. Since last winter he had been the circuit preacher. Each week he traveled to one of four different congregations in Washington County and held meetings on Saturdays and Sundays. Now that Douglas had arrived, the Reverend Butler's services were no longer required at Lost Creek Mission. To soften the loss of one of the reverend's more profitable churches, the community had planned this pie supper. All the money raised was to go to the Reverend Butler as a love offering.

The women made their way out of the schoolhouse to greet "Brother Silas" and gather their children together for the start of the pie auction. Erin found Douglas, and they watched the Reverend Butler work his way through the crowd, shaking hands and hugging children as he went.

"Evening, Brother Silas," called Mrs. Stiles. "Did Winifred come with you?"

"No, bless the Lord, that girl done twisted her ankle gitting water from the crick. I thought she best rest it."

"Well, tell your daughter we asked after her."

"I will, Miz Stiles, thank you kindly." The Reverend Butler stopped and looked in Douglas's direction. "How do, stranger. You must be the new college preacher they brought on, bless the Lord."

"Yes, sir, I'm Douglas Teterbaugh, and this is Erin Corbett."

Rev. Butler nodded to Erin and shook Douglas's hand. He removed his hat and wiped his oily forehead on his sleeve. "Well, bless the Lord, I'm an honest man, and I want you to know that they ain't no hard feelings about you coming in here and taking over my church. I jist praise the Lord that the folks will have regular preachin' every Sunday."

The Reverend Butler surveyed the group in the schoolyard. "You won't mind, though, if I go ahead with the protracted meetings. It's already been spread around that I'll be preaching God's Word twice a day for a whole week over on the riverbank, starting a week from next Monday."

"Well, no. . .of course not," said Douglas. "I wouldn't want to interfere with something that has already been planned."

"That's fine, jist fine. If you've a mind to, brother, I'd be proud for you to give the afternoon sermon at the meetings. Proper protracted meetings has at least two preachers, after all."

Erin could see that Douglas was struggling to be diplomatic. "Thank you, Reverend," he said. "But I think I'll do well to get started with the work here at the mission."

Rev. Butler looked off into the woods, then stared back at Douglas. "Well, do what you think best. I can understand a young preacher boy not being able yet to speak more'n once a week. It'll come, son, it'll come."

The Reverend Butler passed on by and went into the schoolhouse. Douglas said nothing, but Erin could tell by the flush in his cheeks that he was angry.

The boy who had ridden in with the reverend still leaned sullenly against the wagon. "Jube," Erin asked, "who is that young man who came with the Reverend Butler?"

"That'd be Butler's son, Enlo. The preacher's had a time with that one. Seems he's always into some kind of devilment."

"Douglas, maybe we should go introduce ourselves," Erin said. Douglas nodded and took her arm. As they got closer, Erin realized just how tall the boy was. Tucker Gillam was about the only man she had seen in Lost Creek who outsized him.

"How do you do, Enlo. I'm Douglas Teterbaugh. Jube tells me you are the Reverend Butler's son."

Enlo stayed slouched against the wagon, ignoring Douglas's outstretched hand.

"Well, ain't that nice," he said. "The new preacher coming over here special jist to meet me. And who is this pretty lady here? Ain't you gonna meet us up?"

"Certainly. Enlo, this is Miss Corbett."

"It's good to meet you, Enlo."

Enlo slowly looked Erin over from head to toe. "I ain't never confidenced schoolin' much, but seeing as you're the teacher, I reckon maybe I ought to study on it. I never seen such fancy geegaws, ear bobs and everything." Enlo scratched his head and turned to Douglas. "How about it, Preacher, do you git a little sugar on the side from Teacher now and then?"

Douglas's face turned scarlet. "Young man, unless you apologize to Miss Corbett immediately, I shall have to ask you to leave."

"You best be able to make me then, Preacher," said Enlo. He took a step toward Erin and smiled. "You think I should take up books, pretty teacher?"

Enlo's breath reeked of liquor. Douglas put his hand on the young man's shoulder and pulled him away from Erin. "I think you had better go, Enlo," he said.

Enlo's eyes narrowed; he pushed Douglas's hand away and shoved him violently to the ground. To Erin's horror, Enlo pulled a knife from his boot and held the tip to Douglas's chest. Douglas sat as if he were frozen to the ground.

The double click of a shotgun made everyone's head turn toward Tucker. The gun rested easily on his hip, but it was pointed directly at Enlo. "Drop it down, boy," he said quietly. Enlo reluctantly tossed the knife on the ground. Douglas scrambled to his feet.

"I will not have you talking to Miss Corbett like that," Douglas said.

"You make a big sound now that Tucker's gun is behind you, Preacher," Enlo replied.

Tucker set the gun down and walked toward Enlo. "You let your mouth run off in front of Miz Corbett, did you, boy?"

"I never meant nothing," Enlo said nervously. "I reckon I jist had me a little too much blue ruin."

"You know better than to come here drinking. But, drunk or sober, you best memorize this: If I hear you say one ugly word around Miz Corbett again, I'll show you a little frolic you won't soon forgit."

The Reverend Butler elbowed his way to the front of the crowd. He grabbed his son by the collar and pushed him up against the wagon. "You shamed me here in front of my people. You grieve me, boy. Now, you light a shuck out to the house, or I'll whup the devil out of you, here and now." Rev. Butler pushed his son in the direction of the road.

Enlo picked up his knife and put it back in his boot. "All right," he drawled. "But, don't you think this is done between us, Preacher, not by a long shot." Enlo stumbled down the hill and disappeared into the woods.

Rev. Butler faced the crowd. "He's a prodigal and a sorrow to my heart. I'm grieving for his meanness to you, Miz Corbett. I'd take it as a special kindness if you'd still let him come to your school. I reckon he's a mite older than most in your class, but we ain't never lived nowhere for him to git book learned."

Erin was none too anxious to have Enlo as a pupil, but under the circumstances she could hardly refuse. "There's no harm done," she said. "If Enlo wants to learn, of course he'll be welcome."

"Ain't it about time to git this pie supper started?" Tucker asked. "Where's Jube?"

"I'm right here! Ladies and gents, if you'll bring yourselves inside the schoolhouse, we'll git her going."

By the time Douglas and Erin went inside, the "married" pies had already been bought by their respective spouses and the main attraction of the evening was about to begin. Douglas and Erin found a place by Ben and Tucker near the front of the platform.

Jube held up an elaborately decorated basket with organdy bows. "Now, gents, you take a look at this fine piece of work. Looks like a good one to me. What's my bid for this pie?"

"Ten cents!" came a call from the back. Another young man bid fifteen, then the price went to twenty-five. Out of the blue, Douglas raised his hand and bid fifty cents.

"Douglas!" Erin whispered. "You aren't supposed to bid on any pies. What are you doing?"

"Don't worry, that's the Widow Puckett's pie. I heard one of the boys warn a friend not to bid on it. By purchasing her pie, I not only please the most prominent woman in my new church, but I also make a sizable gesture of good will toward the Reverend Butler by contributing to his love offering." Douglas seemed very pleased with himself.

The next pie must have belonged to the girl on Erin's right, because she blushed bright red when she saw who had won the bid. Soon, only Mattie's pie and Erin's were left. Jube picked up the pie that Mattie had carried in and held it up high. Erin wondered how he would manage to bid on the pie, when he was the auctioneer.

"All right, boys, right here we have a fine lookin' parcel, apple by the smell. . . what'll I hear for it?"

Tucker raised his hand. "Ten cents," he said.

Ben looked up at his brother in surprise. "You biddin' on a pie, Tucker? Since when?"

"Hush up. I'm jist doin' Mattie a favor. She asked me to bid on her pie so she wouldn't have to set with Jube all night."

Erin could feel herself flushing. What would Tucker do when he found out her name was on that pie? The price went up to thirty cents, but Tucker won the final bid. Erin would have to spend the evening with Tucker Gillam. She couldn't understand why Jube hadn't made a bid.

Jube held up the last pie. "Folks, this ain't exactly playing by the rules, but to tell you truthful, I took a little peek and I know who belongs to this pie. I'm willing to pay forty cents for it. Is there anybody of a mind to top my price? Going once, twice, sold! Now, Miz Mattie, you jist spread out the cloth, and I'll be there to set with you directly."

The crowd laughed and applauded. Ben poked a confused Tucker in the ribs. "Reckon you got mixed up on which one was Mattie's."

"Wipe that silly grin off your face, boy," said Tucker.

Jube held up the pie with Erin's name on it. "Tucker, looks like you git to share a pie with our new schoolteacher."

Tucker's face showed no particular emotion. He nodded to Jube and then looked down at Erin. "Miz Erin, soon as we git done here, I'll lay us a blanket out yonder by the wagon."

Erin turned back toward Jube to hear how everyone else had been paired off. Douglas took her arm and leaned toward her ear. "I didn't know you were entering a pie, Erin," he whispered.

"It seemed like the right idea at the time," replied Erin. "Besides, it is for a good cause."

"Of course. I was just surprised, that's all."

Jube finished reading off the pairs and then it was time to announce the winner of the beauty cake. "Everyone, listen up," he called. "We had us a close one tonight. Second place for the beauty cake goes to our new schoolteacher, Miz Corbett, with four dollars and sixty-two cents' worth of votes. Ain't she a pretty sight?" The crowd applauded, and Erin felt her face turning red again.

"Hold on now," Jube said. "One young gal got an even five dollars' worth of votes. Our winner for the third straight year is Bessie Puckett. We've had us a fine night. We raised thirteen dollars and forty-seven cents for Brother Butler's love offering."

Silas Butler stepped up onto the platform and took hold of the lapels of his suit coat. "Brother Jube, I jist want to say a glory be and thank you to everyone here tonight. Remember me in your prayers and don't forgit the brush arbor meetings coming up. There'll be a star in your crown for helping this poor old preacher. Lord keep you all until we meet again."

Tucker picked up Erin's basket and escorted her out into the schoolyard. He spread the blanket beneath an oak tree near the well. "Be careful where you set. I wouldn't want you to git that fancy go-to-meetin' dress all dirty."

"It is painfully obvious to me that I have overdressed for this occasion, Tucker. Please don't make it worse."

"Fair enough, why don't you cut us a slab of that pie?"

He watched while she got plates and a knife out of the basket and served him a generous slice. After a few bites he put down his plate and looked at her. "Miz

Erin, can you answer me a question?"

"I'll try."

"How is it your name got in the box with Mattie's pie?"

"How do you know this isn't my pie?"

"Well, for one thing, I've ate Mattie's pies since I was jist a boy, and I know Mattie didn't bake that sorry thing I saw sittin' next to this one on the table back home." Tucker grinned. "If you was wanting to eat pie with me so bad, why didn't you jist say so?"

"Mr. Gillam, it was certainly not my desire to dine with you!"

"Who was you wanting to 'dine' with then?"

"As a matter of fact, it was supposed to be Jube. Mattie said Jube always bid on her pies, and since my pie came out rather badly, she offered to switch, assuming Jube would bid on the one she carried in. She wanted to play a joke on Jube."

Tucker picked up his plate and laughed. "That Mattie. She asked me to bid on this pie to keep Jube from pestering her all night, knowing all along your name was in the basket. She's been at me for years to be more sociable. I reckon this was her way to make me do it."

"Then none of this really had anything to do with Jube?"

"Mattie still got her joke on Jube, all right."

"How is that? Jube's with Mattie. He got what he wanted."

"Yes'm, but he has to eat your pie."

Erin smiled. "I'll have to admit, it was a disaster. I do want you to know, though, that I had no intention of getting us paired together tonight."

"Don't fret about it. I reckon I know who you'd rather be paired up with." Tucker helped himself to a second piece of pie. "Your preacher friend ain't much of a hand at defending himself, is he?"

"Douglas stood up for me. Enlo was very rude."

"I don't doubt it; the boy was lickered up. If I hadn't stepped in, Enlo likely would've carved the preacher's ears off."

"We don't know that. Anyway, Douglas is a minister. Surely you don't expect him to brawl in the dirt."

"Don't matter what I think, but that's what some folks will expect of him, if it's called for. Fine words and a glad hand might work in the city, but this is rough country. It takes a firm way to git folks' respect."

"I'm sure Douglas can do whatever is necessary."

"Maybe. What about you? You reckon you can handle Enlo and his kind at the school?"

Erin looked straight into Tucker's eyes. "I'm quite capable of teaching a class full of children, Mr. Gillam. Just because I attended an orphanage school doesn't mean my education was second best. My teaching certificate is as good as anyone's."

"Never meant to say it wasn't. I only want you to think on what you're getting yourself into, is all."

In the twilight, people began loading up their wagons and preparing to leave. Douglas came walking toward the Gillam wagon, sandwiched tightly between Widow Puckett and her daughter.

"Tucker? Tucker Gillam?" the widow called.

Tucker stood up. "Evenin', Widder. Did you enjoy the supper?"

"My yes, the preacher's been fine company for us, telling us about all the big cities he's lived in and going to seminary and all. I think we got us a good one here. Tucker, I was wondering if you'd favor me by stopping at the house and bringing down a sack of chicken feed from the barn rafters. I must be gitting absentminded. I never noticed we was about out, and Emmit Stiles don't come by to do my heavy work until day after tomorrow."

"I'd sure like to oblige you," Tucker said. "But I was fixing to carry the Kellers home." A light twinkled in Tucker's eyes. "I expect the Kellers wouldn't mind waiting, but since the preacher's right here, maybe he could help you."

Douglas paused only long enough to give Tucker an irritated look. "I'd be happy to assist you, Mrs. Puckett."

"Ain't you kind," beamed Mrs. Puckett. "It won't take but a minute; we live jist up the road on Gobbler's Knob. Mayhaps you'd like to rest some in the parlor before you go. My Bessie's a fair hand at playing our pianny. It's the only one around these parts that I know of."

The widow's voice trailed off down the road as she and Bessie hustled Douglas off. Tucker started across the schoolyard.

"Where are you going?" Erin asked.

Tucker smiled sheepishly. "To tell Asa Keller that I'm fixing to drive him home."

Mrs. Keller insisted on riding in the back of the wagon, even though Erin urged her to ride on the seat. Noah and Walter quickly settled in by their mother, and Mr. Keller handed little Beth up and scrambled in behind her. Mattie had decided against riding home and was planning instead to walk with Ben and the Reynolds. Erin's first impulse was to walk along with Mattie, but the thought of even a mile on that rocky road in her high-heeled slippers made a wagon ride, even a wagon ride with Tucker, sound very nice.

With no mounting block to step up on, Erin was clumsy at getting into the seat of the buckboard. She was still fumbling with her skirts when Tucker grasped both her arms and whisked her up onto the wagon. He climbed across her, released the brake, and they were off.

Too soon, they arrived at the cutoff to the Keller farm. Asa insisted on walking his family in rather than taking Tucker's wagon over the rutted path in the dark.

Now that Tucker and Erin were alone, Erin wished she had walked home with Mattie, high heels or not. The wagon seat seemed too narrow with Tucker and her on it. No matter how she positioned herself, their shoulders kept brushing together.

As they continued, it dawned on her that they were going in the wrong direction. "Aren't we going to turn around?" she asked.

"No place to turn here in the dark, leastways not without chancing a wheel going down in the gully. Closest turnaround is still a half mile off. By then, it'll be quicker to take the back road across the bridge. You've never been this way, have you?"

"No. I've only seen the way Jube brought us in."

"It's a pretty road by day. There's persimmon trees and dogwood and redbud all through here. Pawpaws and sassafras, too." Tucker urged the horses to pick up the pace. "You still mad about me setting the Widder Puckett on the preacher?"

"It was on purpose, wasn't it? I thought any woman who runs her own farm could manage to get a little sack of feed down for her chickens."

"That shows how much you know, miss. We don't git to the store every little bit 'round here. No, the widder was tellin' the truth. That feed sack weighs upwards of a hundred pounds."

"I'm sorry. I didn't realize."

Tucker laughed. " 'Course, you're probably right. I'd bet my left foot that the widder has plenty of feed put back somewheres. She loves them old hens too much to let them go hungry. I reckon she's got the preacher in her parlor jist about now, and they're listening to Bessie bang out a piece on the pianny."

"It wasn't very nice to force Douglas into a situation like that."

"Maybe not, but it's better him than me, and if he's gonna be a preacher, he's got to git used to visiting. Besides, I kindly thought he had it coming, buying the widder's pie jist so he could git in good with her like he did."

Erin didn't want to admit it, but he was right on both counts. She supposed one evening with the Pucketts wouldn't do Douglas any harm.

The sweet night air eased down around their shoulders like a comfortable old quilt. The frogs and crickets and hoot owls each sang their part in serenade, and Erin looked up into the blue-blackness above her. My, but it was glorious! It looked as if God had swirled huge handfuls of fiery diamonds into the darkness, studding the sky with icy light.

"Aren't the stars beautiful tonight?"

Tucker looked up. "They are especially bright. . . 'The heavens declare the glory of God,' " he said quietly, " 'and the firmament sheweth His handiwork.' "

"That's from the Bible, isn't it?" Erin asked.

"I believe it's the Nineteenth Psalm. Don't look so surprised. You think you and the preacher are the only folks 'round here that ever read the Good Book?"

"No, of course not, I didn't mean it that way. I just had the impression that you didn't have much use for religion."

Tucker did not reply. He leaned forward and flicked the reins lightly on the horses' backs.

The air was cool, riding in the open wagon. Erin rubbed her hands over the gooseflesh on her arms. Tucker looked down at her.

"You catching a chill?"

"No. I'm fine."

He reached over and touched her hand. "You're cold as spring water." He stopped the horses and removed his suit coat. "Here, put this 'round you."

"I'm fine, really."

"Jist quit bein' stubborn and put it on." He draped the coat over her shoulders and she held it together in front of her.

"Thank you, that does feel better," she said. "It's kind of you to be concerned about me."

Tucker put his foot up on the wagon box and started the horses again. "Ain't nothing," he said. "Anyways, I dasn't have you coming down with the pneumonie; Mattie would skin me alive."

Chapter Six

Ben rushed through the kitchen, fishing pole in hand, just as Mattie was finishing the breakfast dishes. He grabbed a leftover biscuit from the pan on the stove and stuffed half of it into his mouth. Mattie slapped at his arm.

"Boy, don't you ever git filled up? I declare, it's all I can do to keep you fed these days." She scowled at Ben. "What's that pole in your hand for? You know how I feel about you fishing on Sunday."

Ben put an awkward arm around Mattie's shoulders. "Now, don't be like that, Mattie. Tuck said I could, and there ain't no church today anyway."

"Jist the same, it's the Lord's day," Mattie sniffed. "I reckoned maybe the preacher would give us a little Bible talk directly."

"Aw, Mattie, he didn't git home from the Pucketts' until after midnight. Like as not he won't even be up by the time I git back. And with the preacher starting church next week, and then school after that, this might be the last time I can go before winter." Ben grinned. "You know how much you like a sizzling pan of fresh goggle-eye."

Mattie appeared to be wavering. "All right, boy. You git along, but make certain you learn me a Scripture verse before dinnertime."

"Yes, ma'am!" Ben wasted no time heading out the door.

On impulse, Erin followed him onto the back porch. "Ben?"

"Yes'm?"

"Would you mind if I came along with you?"

"You like to fish, ma'am?"

"To tell the truth, I've never been before in my life, but I'd like to learn. Would you show me how?"

"Surely! I can learn you everything, how to feel when a bass is playing with your bait, how to hook the big ole bucketmouths, and how to head and gut 'em quicker than lightning. Oh—I reckon maybe you ain't quite ready for the guttin' part yet." Ben added quickly, "Don't you fret, I'll clean anything you catch, and maybe you could learn me a short Scripture verse I can say to Mattie when we get back."

"That's a deal. Let me get my bonnet and I'll be ready to go."

The morning air was still cool as they climbed along a bluff downstream of the bridge. Ben spoke quietly as he put their poles down. "See how greenish the water is before us? It don't look it, but that hole is deeper'n our heads. Shallow water's clear through, but the deep holes have color. Look close, there's a big ole granddaddy swimming down near the bottom right now."

At first, Erin couldn't see what Ben was talking about, but then a long gray shadow caught her eye as it slipped silently by in the emerald water.

"Ben, you didn't bring any bait. Don't you need worms or something to get them on the hook?"

"I was figuring to use crawdads. Crawdads and minners are about the best bait there is."

"Really? What are crawdads?"

Ben's eyes widened. "You ain't never seen a crawdad? C'mon down to that low bank over there and I'll show you."

They crunched across the shifting gravel to a place where the river was wide and shallow. Ben squatted down in ankle-deep water and carefully turned over a rock. A cloud of sand bubbled up where the rock had been, and when it cleared, a reddish-green miniature lobster appeared.

"That," Ben said, "is a crawdad." He reached down and snatched the creature up behind its claws, then he put it in a tin pail he had brought from the house.

"Are they hard to catch?"

"No, ma'am, not really. Do y'want to try?"

"Do you think I could?"

"Surely. Let me find a good'n for you." Ben waded over to the edge of a quiet pool of water. "Here's one you can reach from the bank," he said. "You want to grab him behind those pinchers. If you corner him head-on, he'll nip you. Once you start after him, don't stop, or he'll be gone before you git there."

Erin tried again and again, but all she managed to do was to get her shoes wet while the crawdad swam backwards into another hole among the rocks. Finally, she gave up taking aim and slapped her hand down on top of it. Its bony shell writhed between her fingers.

"Got him. . . Ouch!" she cried. She pulled her hand out of the water and saw that a small red welt was swelling on her ring finger. Mr. Crawdad swam back to his rocky home.

"Oh well. Let's hope I can catch fish better than I can catch the bait."

They walked back to the bluff, where Ben baited the hooks and dropped them into the water. He handed Erin a pole. "There," he said. "Now all we got to do is sit back and wait for the fish to bite."

The water sang cheerfully as it flowed over the rocks and wound its way downriver. Long-legged insects skated across the water's glossy surface, and in the distance, a cowbell softly clanged.

"You're very lucky to have grown up in a place like this," Erin said. "It's so peaceful and beautiful. Ben, did you ever think how great God must be to create such magnificent country as you have here?"

Ben leaned back on the log and turned his pole around in his hands. "I reckon I ain't thought much about God lately."

"Maybe you should. God loves us so much, Ben."

"If what you say is so, Miz Erin, I think God's got an awful queer way of showing it."

"Things have been hard for you, haven't they? I mean, with your pa and ma both gone. I know how much it hurts. I lost my parents when I was young, too."

For just a moment, Ben's eyes reflected pure pain. Then his pole suddenly arched and jerked back and forth until Erin was sure it would snap. Ben patiently worked the fish until it tired, then he lifted it out of the water. Ben said it was a small-mouthed bass, and a good-sized one, too. He pushed a thin rope through the gill of the fish and tied the ends to a limb near the river, then he threw the tethered fish back into the water.

"The next one'll be yours, Miz Erin." Ben balanced the end of his pole between his feet and pulled the hook down toward him to put on the fresh bait. He almost had it on when the pole slipped backward in the sand, pulling the hook deep into Ben's thumb.

"Ouch!"

Erin looked the other way while he pulled the hook out. The wound bled freely once it was gone.

"Let me see," she said. "That looks deep."

"Aw, it ain't so much. It is bleeding powerful, though, ain't it?"

"Yes, it is. You probably should wash it out."

Ben dipped his hand into the river, then Erin took a handkerchief from her pocket and bound it around the cut. Once the bandage was in place, the bleeding all but stopped.

"There," Erin said. "Does it still hurt?"

"Just a mite, but it ain't nothing to fret over." Ben looked at the bandage and smiled. "I reckon I'll have me a proud pucker of a scar from this one."

"Yes," Erin agreed. "With any luck, I believe you will. Should we go on back to the house so you can put something on that?"

"No, no need. Besides, I come here to teach you to fish."

For the next hour, they did just that. Erin had to admit that it was exciting to feel an angry fish lurching about on her line, but she was not sure she could ever bring herself to remove a fish from the hook.

"This is fun, Ben. I wish I had tried it years ago."

"You've caught a fine mess. Most women don't like fishin' and such, but you're different."

"Maybe I am, at that. The Reverend Teterbaugh will certainly be surprised when we show him what I caught, won't he?"

Ben swirled his feet in the water. "Can I ask you something, Miz Erin?"

"Certainly, Ben, ask away."

"Are you sweet on the preacher?"

"Sweet? What makes you think that?"

"Just wondering is all."

"I wouldn't exactly say I was 'sweet' on him."

"I don't think I like him much," Ben said. "He's a piddling sort, even for a city feller."

"That's no way to talk. I want you to promise me that you'll give the Reverend

Teterbaugh a fair chance. All right?"

"All right, Miz Erin, if you say so."

By midmorning, they had an assortment of bass, goggle-eye, and several pretty yellow-bellied fish that Ben called sun perch, all strung up on his rope.

"I expect we best head on back if we want to git these cleaned before dinnertime," Ben said. He slung the fish over his shoulder and they walked up toward the bridge. Little frogs bounced across the bank in front of them and plopped into the water.

Erin spotted a huge bullfrog peering up at them out of the plants at the water's edge. She walked right up to it, but the frog remained oddly still.

"Ben, isn't this strange? Why doesn't this big frog hop away like the little ones did?"

She reached down to touch it, but Ben called out, "Hold on, Miz Erin!" and trotted up behind her. He put the fish down on the ground and picked up a tree limb. Cautiously, he prodded at the frog. Then they saw. A large snake, hidden in the shadows of the bridge, was in the process of devouring the bullfrog. The snake thrashed angrily at the touch of Ben's stick.

"C'mon, let's git away from him," Ben said. "That's a moccasin, and I ain't going to disturb him while he's having dinner."

"But can't we do anything? That poor frog."

Ben put the fish back over his shoulder. "The frog's already dead, Miz Erin, but if I had me a rifle gun, I'd fix that old snake. I reckon I could rock it to death, but Tuck says they ain't no reason to take chances with snakes if they ain't bothering you. Moccasins is the meanest snakes around. Copperheads and rattlers, they'd jist as soon run, most times, than fool with a man, but moccasins jist natchurly love fighting."

Erin looked back at the snake, trying hard to settle the sick feeling that had settled in her stomach. "It seems so unfair."

Ben helped her up the embankment to the road. "That's jist how life is, Miz Erin. You do your best and hope nothing bigger comes along to swaller you up. Ain't no fairness to it a'tall."

Erin wanted to tell Ben that life was not always like that, that it wasn't all sorrow and cruelty, and God loved him—but how could she convince a boy who had known so much harshness?

At dinner, Erin had her first taste of fresh fish dipped in cornmeal and fried crispy brown. Tucker reached for another helping of buttery hominy and looked her way.

"Ben tells me you're quite a fisherman, Miz Erin," he said.

"Ben did all the hard work," she confessed. "I just held the pole in between times."

"Tucker," Ben said. "We saw us a big ole moccasin down under the bridge.

Reckon maybe we could git your rifle gun after dinner and see if we can git him?"

Tucker looked alarmed. "A moccasin? You didn't go messin' with him, did you?"

" 'Course not, Tucker. . . ."

"As a matter of fact," Erin said, "Ben kept me from practically putting my hand in that snake's mouth."

Tucker looked at Ben with approval. "It's a lucky thing he did. Moccasins have a powerful pizen in them. You best hear this, too, Preacher. You always got to keep an eye out for snakes here. They can be most anywhere, but they especially like holler logs and rocky ledges. Oft times, you'll find 'em sunning themselves in the middle of the road. Don't never put your hand in a place you can't see into, and watch real smart where you put your feet in the woods."

"Could a bite from one of these snakes actually kill someone?" Douglas asked.

"Depends on who got bit and how bad," Tucker said. "Younguns and old folks most often git mortal bites, but a big rattler could kill a grown man, too."

"Not all snakes are bad though," said Ben. "Black snakes eat rats and mice and such. It's a lucky thing to find one in your barn."

"There's also snakes," Jube said, "that do mystifyin' things, like hoop snakes that grab their own tails and roll down the road, or milksnakes that sneak into your barn at night and milk your cows."

Mattie pointedly picked up Jube's plate. "Old man, ain't you got nothing better to do than tell old wives' tales? Why don't you git back to work?"

"Pshaw! Them are facts, jist as sure as the world, and I'm hurt you suspicion me so." Jube's eyes twinkled as he grabbed another chunk of Mattie's gingerbread before he headed out the back door.

Douglas pushed his plate away and leaned back in his chair. "Tucker, with church services starting next Sunday, I'd like to take this week and visit as many families in the area as we can. I was hoping that you might let Ben show us around to the various homes."

Ben brightened. "Could I, Tuck?"

"Ain't you got some chores to do, boy?"

"Yes, sir."

"Then you best git to it, and have Mattie clean up that thumb before you git blood pizened."

Ben got up reluctantly and went in the kitchen in search of Mattie.

"Fact is, Preacher," said Tucker, "this ain't a good time for Ben to be gone."

"But I thought you had harvested your field crops."

"We have, for a fact, but that don't take account of gitting the grain to the mill, nor the orchard full of apples, nor butchering, not to mention putting up the vegetable garden."

Douglas held up his hand. "All right, you've made your point, but nonetheless, Erin and I must make those visits."

"Most folks live somewheres off the main road, Preacher. I expect you can find all but a few. I'll even set down and draw you up a little map. Then, 'round the end of the week, I reckon we could spare Ben long enough to show you to the back-off places."

"I guess that will have to do," Douglas said.

"I reckon it will. Now, if you want Ben to help you later on, I'd be obliged if you'd give us a hand cuttin' firewood. Takes a great pile of wood to see us through the winter. You can handle an ax, can't you?"

"I believe I can. I'll begin as soon as I change my clothes."

Chapter Seven

Erin picked up another stack of dishes and set them on the shelf. She seemed to spend half her day wiping dishes dry and putting them away; surely a missionary teacher should be doing more important things. Dirty dishes were so unpleasant, with the murky water and floating bits of food. But there was no use whining about it. Anyway, her school would be starting soon.

Mattie threw the dishwater out the back door, then she turned down the damper on the stove and set a pan of beans on the back burner to simmer. "Erin, I got the warshpot about ready t'boil out back. Why don't you gather up all your dirty clothes and we can keep each other company while we scrub."

Laundry! Erin had not even thought of that. At the orphanage, a laundress had been in charge of keeping the children's uniforms clean. Helping in the laundry room was a punishment chore that Erin had quickly learned to avoid. Well, of course she would be expected to do her own laundry here.

"I'll collect everything and be right there, Mattie."

"No need t'hurry, child. Mind, you wear something old."

Fire glowed under the big black kettle set by the creek downstream of the spring house. A raised wooden trough diverted water from the creek to fill the washtubs. A three-legged table made from half a log, flat side up, stood near the kettle. Erin looked around everywhere, but she saw nothing like the washing machines back at the orphanage, not even a washboard.

"Bring them things on down here," Mattie called. "I got everything ready to go. Here's the battling stick." She held out an oar-shaped paddle about a foot long. "Well, child, what ails you?"

"To tell the truth," Erin said, "I have had about as much experience doing laundry as I have had baking pies. I don't know the first thing about washing clothes like this."

Mattie set the battling stick down. "You sure have come to a foreign land, ain't you, child? Well, ain't no trick to warshing clothes. Bring them things over and dump 'em in."

Erin put her clothes in a water-filled tub at the end of the table.

"Git that shirtwaist there and put it on the battling block," Mattie said. "Then, take the stick and wail the tar out of it, like this." She took the battling stick and repeatedly slapped it down hard on the shirtwaist. "This here beats some of the dirt loose out of 'em, then you put it in the kettle to boil for a spell."

"How long will all this take, Mattie? I promised Douglas I would be ready to pay calls with him later this morning."

Mattie took her arm and pulled Erin in front of the battling block. "Won't take long a'tall if you ever git started. You beat these whilst I shave off some soap chips into the kettle."

In a short while, Erin's arms ached and her hands were blistered. By the time she finished the last of her clothes, the battling stick felt as if it weighed fifty pounds. She looked at Mattie with new respect, realizing now the strength required to complete household chores on a farm.

Mattie gave her a reprieve from battling and sent her to stir the clothes with a long wooden paddle. When they were finally clean enough to suit her, Mattie took the paddle, lifted some of the boiling clothes, and put them in the washtub that sat under the waterspout.

"Reckon you can git the rest of these out of the kettle, Erin?" she asked.

Erin scooped the clothes up with the paddle and balancing carefully, started over to the washtub. Unfortunately, she underestimated the weight of the wet clothes and just before she got to the tub, she lost her grip on the handle. The clothes fell on the sandy creek bank.

"Oh, no!" she cried. "Will we have to wash them all over again, Mattie?"

"No, I don't reckon so, that sand'll clean off, but you'll have to rinse 'em extra good."

By the time Erin picked up the clothes and rinsed them, her skirt was splotched with water and sand. She had stooped over to pick up one last stocking when Tucker's voice boomed above her head.

"Miz Erin, is that a new city way of warshin'? We generally don't put clean clothes in the dirt around here."

Erin angrily wheeled around, only to discover that Douglas was with him. Quickly, she tucked up the loose pins in her hair and tried to brush off the sandy dirt that clung to her clothes.

"Don't fancy up on my account, Miz Erin," Tucker said. "I jist come to see if you mind riding horseback on your visits today. The buckboard's needed for hauling grain to the mill. Preacher here says you can ride."

"Yes, I can, if you have a sidesaddle."

Tucker rubbed his chin. "A sidesaddle. I don't know as we have one. . . ."

"Tucker, don't you reckon your ma's old saddle is still up in the loft?" Mattie asked.

"It might be; I'd forgot all about it. I'll go see before I finish loading the wagon." Tucker readjusted his hat and strode off across the yard.

Erin bent over to pick up the washbasket, but it was heavier than she had anticipated. The best she could do was to lift one end and drag it toward the clothesline.

"Hold on," Douglas said. "Let me help you." Erin released the basket, forgetting about the ugly red blisters on her palms. Douglas grasped her wrists.

"Erin, what have you done to your hands?"

"It's from the laundry," she explained. "I'm afraid I'm not used to this kind of work."

"I should think not, and why should you be? You didn't come here to be a housemaid."

"I have to admit, I didn't think about laundry being part of my job, but it's nothing, really."

"I understand that we both have to pull our weight around here," Douglas said. "But I don't think being a missionary should require you to ruin your hands and complexion. After all, a lady is judged by such things in society, and you won't always be working in a backwoods church."

Neither of them realized that Mattie could hear their conversation. She walked over to Douglas, picked up the basket at his feet, and without a word, she went to the clothesline and began hanging up Erin's clothes.

"Douglas, I am afraid we've hurt her feelings."

"I suppose I'd better be more careful of what I say, but she'll be all right, Erin. After all, I only spoke the truth. Why don't we go ahead and start our visits? I'll meet you at the stable as soon as you can freshen up."

Erin didn't feel right about leaving, knowing Mattie had heard them. She walked over and reached into the clothes basket. Mattie pulled a clothespin from her mouth.

"Don't discomfort yourself, Erin," she said. "I can manage."

"Mattie, I'm sorry. I don't mind doing my share, really. Everything is just so new to me, that's all."

Mattie finished pinning the skirt to the line, then she turned toward Erin and smiled. "I know, child; it's all right." She took a pair of drawers from the basket and resumed her work. "Erin, the Lord has put you heavy on my heart," she said. "Your young head is so full of dreams and such. But you got to decide which dreams are from the Lord and which dreams are jist Erin's. I'll tell you a secret, child. You generally have to do some bone-tiring work to make the Lord's dreams come true, and even then your own strength ain't near enough. I jist want you to find God's best."

"I'm ready to work, Mattie, truly I am, and I won't complain again. I do want God to use me here at Lost Creek."

Mattie put her gnarled hand on Erin's. " 'Seek ye first the Kingdom,' child, and don't settle for nothin' less."

Erin quickly changed clothes and packed a lunch (or dinner, as they called it here) in a flour sack. She hoped she had not lost Mattie's respect with her hasty words. Somehow, what Mattie thought of her mattered very much.

Douglas was waiting for her in the pasture with a handsome buckskin gelding and a chestnut mare. He helped Erin onto the mare, and then he mounted. He reached down and patted his horse's neck.

"He's a beauty, isn't he?" Erin said.

They left the pasture and started down the road at a fast trot, then crossed the bridge and went on through the woods to where the road flattened out and followed a dry creek bed.

"I don't suppose you would be interested in a little race, would you?" Erin asked. "Say down to that fork in the road?"

Douglas pulled up his horse. "A race? Does the lady wish to make a wager?"

"I didn't think ministers were allowed to do that. All right, the loser washes the schoolhouse windows."

"Fair enough, ma'am. Anytime you are ready."

Erin kicked her horse into a full gallop. The horses' hooves pounded loudly on the gravel, and the rocking rhythm of the powerful horse beneath her made Erin want to go faster and faster as the dust and rocks flew up around them. They stayed neck and neck until the end, but just before the finish, Erin's horse pulled forward and beat Douglas's by a nose.

"I bow to the champion!" Douglas shouted, and he bent dramatically from the waist. They both were laughing so hard that they didn't notice the wagon until it was a few feet away.

"Well, how do, Preacher, Miz Erin," called Silas Butler. "I heard you all the way acrosst the crick. . . . From all the carrying on, I thought that there might be some trouble. Bless the Lord, you're all right."

"I'm sorry, Rev. Butler," Erin said. "I am afraid we were awfully noisy."

"Time was when people might take your cutting didoes like that the wrong way, you being out here alone and all, but I reckon most folks would make allowances."

"What brings you out on the road today?" Douglas asked.

"Oh, a widder woman from Grassy Holler's been poorly for some time now and she up and died night before last. The family sent for me to do the funeralizin'. We had us a fine shouting service to send her on. People come from miles around with enough food to feed Grant's army. You two jist out for a frolic?"

"No," Erin answered quickly. "We're on our way to the Kellers'. We intend to visit everyone we possibly can before we start church services next Sunday."

"Still head set on starting next week are you? Well, Preacher, I'd be obliged if you'd spread around about the protracted meetings as you visit."

"I will try to remember, Rev. Butler."

"Miz Corbett, I reckon I can save you a trip out to my place if you can tell me the particulars of when to start my younguns in your school."

"We are hoping to start in two weeks. I could let you know for certain at the brush arbor meetings."

"That'd be fine." The Reverend Butler wiped his face on a crumpled red handkerchief. "Well, the Lord bless you in your travels." He turned his horse and bounced the wagon up the hill.

"The old windbag."

"Hush, Douglas. He'll hear you."

"I'm sorry, but every time he sees me, he makes it a point to put me in my place."

"Think how he must feel with your taking over one of his churches," Erin said. "He probably doesn't mean to be rude. We're just not accustomed to these hill people's bluntness."

"Maybe so, Erin, but that man irritates me." Douglas pulled his horse's head up from the grass it had been eating. "If we want to make more than one visit today, we had better get going."

The Kellers were one family Erin was looking forward to visiting, since she had already met them on the night of the pie supper. Their house was much smaller than the Gillams' place. It looked like two little houses connected together by a covered passageway called a dog-run.

Erin and Douglas no more than got into the yard before little Beth and Walter and an assortment of hound dogs came running to meet them. Walter ushered them in the front door, while Beth went to the kitchen to fetch her mother. Mrs. Keller came out with a juicy blackberry pie and set it down on the table.

"Preacher, Miz Erin," she said. "It's so nice to see you again. We're proud to have you at our house. Come set and have a piece of pie. It's still warm." Mrs. Keller was already setting plates on the table.

"I'm jist silly about blackberries," she said. "Every year we dry all the children and me can pick."

"Mrs. Keller, this is about the best pie I've ever tasted in my life," Douglas said. "If you bring these along to the dinners on the ground each Sunday, I'm afraid I won't be able to concentrate on my sermons."

"Preacher, how you talk. Asa and me are happy as can be about having us an every-Sunday church and a school to boot. I been wishing for the children to take up books for quite a spell now. You jist let us know what can we do to help. Asa's a fine hand at making things, and I'd be proud to run up some curtains for the schoolhouse if you've a mind."

"Why, that would be lovely," Erin said. "Thank you."

The next home was the Witbecks'. The Witbeck cabin was made of hand-notched logs that had worn to a silvery gray, and the roof was covered with split wood shingles. A stone chimney stood on one end of the cabin, and Erin assumed the lean-to on the other end was the kitchen. The only light the cabin received was from one small window and the front door, which stood open. Douglas and Erin dismounted and walked to the edge of the yard.

"I don't see any dogs," Douglas said.

"Just the same, I think we should call out like Jube told us to."

Douglas shrugged and cupped his hands to his mouth. "Hello? Is anyone there?" Immediately, two skinny mongrels raced down the hill behind the cabin and came straight toward them. Douglas and Erin froze.

"Hello?" Erin called. "Mrs. Witbeck?"

The dogs were almost to the garden fence, when Mrs. Witbeck came out from behind a shed in the backyard. "Deke! Blackie! Git your worthless hides out of here. Go on, git!" The dogs slunk away to the other side of the cabin.

Douglas stepped forward and offered his hand. "Good morning, Mrs. Witbeck."

The woman's face brightened. "Preacher, how do! Don't mind them fool dogs, they got a lot of noise is all. What brings you and the teacher up here today? Come in and set."

The interior of the cabin was dark and cool and smelled of wood smoke.

"There's settin' chairs over yonder. Would you like some coffee?"

"No, thank you," Douglas said. "I'm afraid Mrs. Keller filled us up with pie and cider a little while ago. We just stopped by to invite your family to the first church service Sunday morning."

"And to see how many of your children will be coming to our school," Erin added.

"John and me's got three younguns, all tickled to death about the new school. Our oldest one's Will, he's ten, then there's Jackson, who's eight, and our leastun is Annie, she's six. They all went nut hunting with their daddy. I expect they'll be back right soon now. My twenty-sixth birthin' day is tomorrow and I been wishing for some black walnuts to make a cake, so John up and took off this morning to fetch me some."

"Many happy returns, Mrs. Witbeck," Douglas said. "I hope we will see you all at church Sunday."

"I reckon jist about everybody'll come to hear the new city preacher, don't you fret none about that."

John Witbeck and his children returned with a tow sack filled with greenish-black balls. Will took a ball from the sack and proudly cut it open, revealing the hard black walnut inside, while Annie sidled up to Erin and fingered the lace around her wrists.

"Are you stayin' for dinner?" Annie asked.

"We'd be proud to have you," said Mrs. Witbeck.

"That's very kind," Douglas said. "But we really should be going."

"You jist got here," Mrs. Witbeck said. " 'Sides, we got more'n enough, and you got to eat somewhere."

The Witbecks insisted despite their protests, and soon everyone was feasting on a combination of Erin's picnic food and Mrs. Witbeck's dinner. It was a pleasant meal, but Erin couldn't help feeling sorry that she and Douglas would not be having their quiet picnic together. Erin didn't want to admit it, even to herself, but keeping her mind off Douglas and on the mission work was becoming more and more difficult.

❧

Douglas and Erin rode out each morning for the next three days and made as many calls as they could before the sun set. As the week progressed, Erin began to understand why Jube had described the Gillam home as "a glory of a house." By Lost Creek standards, Tucker was wealthy indeed.

Most of their congregation lived in tiny log cabins with only one or two rooms. The homes were dark and crowded with no indoor plumbing. Brothers and sisters thought nothing of sleeping three or more to a bed. Many families walked a quarter of a mile to the nearest spring every time they needed fresh water.

Window glass was a luxury enjoyed by only three families. Most windows were covered with oiled paper or simply left open during the summer months and boarded up in the winter. In warm weather, all manner of flying "gallynippers" buzzed in the cabins at will. Leftover food had to be covered immediately with a cloth to keep away the flies.

Yet these people did not seem to consider themselves poor. The men they met were fiercely proud of their land and their families and in performing a good day's work. They were solid, practical people who seemed satisfied with their lot in life, much more satisfied, Erin realized, than most of the people she knew back home, who were incredibly rich by comparison.

Ben joined them on Saturday, as Tucker had promised. The last visits were in homes that were accessible only by footpath, and without Ben they would have been impossible to find. These deep woods cabins were the poorest of all.

The last visit they planned to make was to the Hinkles'. It took an hour of hard walking before Ben finally stopped and pointed to a cabin jutting out of the side of a hill.

"There it is," he said. "I best go first. Mr. Hinkle might take it in his mind to get ornery if he sees a stranger coming on his place."

The cabin leaned precariously on a piled rock foundation. Old rags had been stuffed here and there among the logs where the chinking had long since washed out. A spindly stand of corn grew in an uptilted field behind the cabin. Even the fragrant scent from the pine trees could not camouflage the smell of pigs and dogs and, apparently, people who used the yard for an outhouse.

"Mr. Hinkle? It's Ben Gillam. We come to see you."

A shadowy figure appeared in the doorway, then Mr. Hinkle stepped out into the yard. He was a thin man, dressed in a dirty union suit and ragged overalls.

"Howdy, Mr. Hinkle," Ben said. "I brung the new preacher and schoolteacher t'meet you."

Mr. Hinkle squinted at them through cold eyes. "What they want to come up here for?"

Douglas stepped forward and offered his hand. "How do you do, Mr. Hinkle. We've been visiting everyone to tell them that church services will begin tomorrow." After a moment, Douglas lowered his hand and put it in his pocket.

"We're also starting a school," Erin said. "I was wondering how many of your children might be old enough to attend."

"Well now, lady, jist what makes y'think I want my younguns going to any school of yours?"

There was a rustling sound from just inside the cabin door. "Seth, could I speak to you?" said a timid voice.

"Git in the house, Narcissy. You ain't fit to be seen."

Something in Mr. Hinkle's tone of voice irked Erin. She walked past him to the door of the cabin. "Mrs. Hinkle? I am Erin Corbett, the mission schoolteacher."

Mrs. Hinkle stepped into the doorway and nodded, then turned frightened eyes to her husband. "Seth, I'd be pleasured if the younguns could git some book learnin'," she said.

"I said to git in the house, woman."

Mrs. Hinkle stepped back from the door. She was obviously in a family way and due fairly soon from the look of it. A chubby little boy peeked shyly from around her skirts.

"Perhaps we could visit sometime when it is more convenient for you," Erin said. Mrs. Hinkle nodded again and disappeared into the darkness of the cabin. Erin turned back to Mr. Hinkle.

"I would very much like to have your children in our school. I hope you will consider sending them."

Mr. Hinkle did not look at her when he spoke. "Only got three younguns growed up to any size," he said. "The little'n, my boy Rabe, and Sariah. Got another three buried yonder on the hill. Took milksick when they was babies."

"I'm sorry," Erin said.

Mr. Hinkle looked blankly at her, then he continued. "Might let the girl go, she's too piddling to help much around here anyway. Might git her out from underfoot till the new one comes."

"That would be fine," Erin said. "I hope you'll think about sending your son, too."

"Don't know as I want no lady teacher telling my boy what to do. I'll study on it."

Mr. Hinkle picked up an ax that leaned against the cabin wall and walked abruptly off to a scattered woodpile down the hill.

They started back home, plodding down the steep path that led away from the cabin. Erin slapped at the tree branches in her way, forgetting that Douglas was behind her.

"Watch out!" Douglas cried. "Are you trying to decapitate me?"

"I'm sorry, Douglas, but when I think of Mr. Hinkle, I get angry all over again."

"If it is any consolation, I don't think Mr. Hinkle was too impressed with you, either."

"Mr. Hinkle don't like no woman standing up t'him like you did," Ben said.

"Perhaps I shouldn't have done it, but I felt so sorry for his poor wife. From the look of that filthy place, Mr. Hinkle doesn't waste much time taking care of his family."

"The Hinkles have always had a bad case of swamp measles, that's for certain," Ben said.

"Swamp measles? What is that?" Douglas asked.

"Oh, I reckon you'd jist call it being dirty. It ain't easy keeping a family clean what with the spring being off such a far piece from the house."

"Then why doesn't he build closer to water?" Erin asked. "It doesn't seem like that land he's on could possibly produce enough to support a family."

"Mr. Hinkle likes to keep to hisself," said Ben. "He ain't first off a farmer, anyway. Most cash money he makes is from selling nuts and sang root and wild honey and such to the Berryman store. And I reckon he does all right with his corn."

"He really grows enough from that sickly crop to make money?" Douglas asked.

"Not as it comes off of the stalk," Ben said. "But by the time he bottles it and packs it down the mountain, it's worth a considerable sum."

"You're talking about moonshining then," Douglas said.

"Liquor?" Erin said indignantly. "You know he makes corn liquor and no one does anything about it? Why not?"

Ben turned and held out his hand to help Erin over a large log that had fallen across the path. "Well, ma'am, most folks around here think that what a man does on his own property is his own business. People who say otherwise have been known to git theirselves hurt."

Chapter Eight

The next Sunday they pulled into a schoolyard filled with wagons. Even Tucker had consented to attend in honor of Douglas's first sermon. He helped Mattie and Erin out of the wagon while Jube tethered the horses.

People were packed inside the schoolroom. Children filled the small seats in the front, and the older girls and women sat in the larger desks toward the back. The men and boys stood along the walls or found places just outside, near an open window. The Reynoldses were there, and the Kellers, and the Witbecks. Bessie Puckett and her mother sat in prominent seats near the front. Mattie and Erin found seats just as Douglas strode up to the small pulpit that had been put on the platform in place of Erin's desk.

"Good morning," he said. "I am delighted to see such a grand crowd assembled to worship here today. Let us begin with prayer. Shall we bow our heads?"

Erin couldn't seem to keep her mind on what Douglas was saying. He was so handsome in his trim black suit, and his voice had a resonant quality when he was behind the pulpit. He seemed like an entirely different person. Erin could think of nothing she wanted more than to be a part of a ministry such as his. Perhaps their being assigned there together was more than just a coincidence.

Douglas had just begun to speak in earnest when Erin noticed some sort of disruption in the back corner of the room. Men looked at one another and shifted uncomfortably. The ladies near them fidgeted and began to fan themselves. Then Erin smelled it, too, the unmistakable odor of skunk. It seemed to be coming up from the floorboards. Douglas gamely continued preaching, not knowing why he had lost the congregation's attention, until finally the scent pervaded the entire room.

Isaac Reynolds wrinkled his nose. "Ooh-we!" he cried out loud. "Don't that polecat stink! He must be right under the floor."

A hasty evacuation followed. Douglas brought up the rear, holding his handkerchief over his nose. Several of the men began removing boards from around the foundation to provide the skunk a route of escape. The children laughed and ran about, while the adults stood in small groups commenting on what a shame it was that a varmint had spoiled church on the preacher's first day.

Erin was going to ask Douglas what she should do about Sunday school when she noticed that he was staring off toward the road. Amid the flurry of activity, Silas Butler stood quietly by his wagon, his arms crossed over his chest. Enlo sat on the wagon seat, holding the reins, with the same sarcastic smirk on his face that he had the night of the pie supper. Douglas made his way to them through the crowd.

"Having a little trouble, are you, Brother?" the Reverend Butler asked.

"Yes, it seems a skunk found his way under the building just as I began my sermon. Isn't that rather odd? I have read that skunks are mostly nocturnal animals, yet this one chooses to visit a noisy building full of people right in the middle of the day."

"Well, Brother, you jist never know about critters. I've seen them do some peculiar things in my time."

"I imagine you have," Douglas said. "What brings you here today? I thought you would be preaching somewhere."

"No, I ain't found a new church to take the place of this here one yet. Besides, with the protracted meetings starting tomorrow, I can't hardly travel too far off. Enlo and I been visiting some folks who don't go to church regular and givin' them an invite to the meetings. We were jist on our way now to set up the brush arbor." Butler looked across the yard. "It won't discomfort you none if I ask some of the men to help me, will it, being that you've kindly give up on the services and all. . . ?"

Douglas's cheeks burned. "By all means, go ahead," he said.

"Thank you, Brother, and you surely are welcome to come to the meetings, too. We're gonna have some real preaching there."

Douglas's eyes flashed fire. "Now look here. . ."

"Rev. Butler?" Erin said. "I just wanted to let you know that our school will start a week from tomorrow. Lessons begin at nine o'clock."

"Why thank you, Miz Corbett. My younguns'll be there for certain."

Families brought out their dinners and ate in the shade, and then many of the men went to help the Reverend Butler build the brush arbor. Before Jube left, he made a quick trip inside the schoolhouse to rescue Erin's *Kind Words* booklets so that they could at least have Sunday school for the children.

As soon as everyone finished dinner, Erin sat the children in a circle under the giant oak in the schoolyard and fumbled her way through her first lesson. The children squirmed, and Erin stammered, but somehow they got through it. By the time everyone began to leave, Erin was worn out.

Only four people rode back in the wagon to the farmhouse. Jube had left to help the Reverend Butler, and Ben was walking home with some of his friends. Tucker turned the wagon around and started the horses down the long hill home.

"Preacher," Tucker said, "I'll say one good thing for your sermon today—it was short."

Douglas was in no mood to joke about the day's service. "I suppose short sermons please you, Tucker," he said.

"They got their advantages. After that polecat came on out, we nailed the boards up again on the backside of the schoolhouse. I don't reckon you'll be troubled by any more varmints."

"I don't imagine we'd have quite that same problem ever again anyway," Douglas said. "Whoever did it would be too smart for that."

"You saying that skunk had some help gitting under the schoolhouse?" Tucker asked.

"Now who'd go and do such a thing?" Mattie said. "We ain't the kind of folks to do foolery on the Lord's day."

"The preacher might be right, Mattie. I found a gunnysack back of the schoolhouse that smelled something awful of skunk."

"If that is someone's idea of a joke," Erin said, "I don't think it's very funny."

The horses had just stopped in front of the house when Jube came loping toward them.

"What's wrong, Jube?" Tucker asked.

"We lost another cow, and this time they butchered her right spang on our land."

"Where?"

"Back in the woods between here and the river. I was looking for some saplings to cut for the brush arbor and I come acrosst it, not thirty feet from the road."

"Did you find any tracks?"

"No, you could see where the grass had been trampled, but there wasn't a trail anywhere off in the woods. They must have toted the meat to the road and carted it off in a buckboard. It was a fresh kill, last day or so."

"I better go take a look," Tucker said.

Mattie was as excited as a child at Christmas all day Monday. She hurried everyone through the morning chores, and as soon as dinner was done, she put all the leftovers in a stewpot and banked the fire in the stove.

"That ought to keep it for a spell," she said. "The water's hot in the reservoir, let's us have a bath before the meeting tonight."

The tin bathtub was dragged into Mattie's room, since it was closest to the kitchen, and Erin undressed and sat down. Mattie poured a bucket of warm water over her shoulders while Erin scrubbed.

"Are these meetings very different from regular church services?" Erin asked.

"Well, child, that depends on what you're used to. When I was a girl we had protracted meetings that'd last two weeks or more. People'd come from miles around and camp out right on the grounds. The men would make coverings of holiness, as they called them, to seat upwards of two hundred folks. The best meetings had at least three preachers. They'd start in at the morning and preach again in the afternoon, and then they'd have the big meeting with testimony times and prayer at night. Folks would sing and pray—and, Erin, sometimes you'd feel as if the hand of God jist reached down and touched that place. Those were precious days."

Erin stepped out of the tub and Mattie handed her a towel.

"This meeting won't be nearly as big," Mattie said. "Of course, size don't matter none to the Master. He's joyous to find jist one heart ready to let Him be Lord."

Mattie set out a quick supper that night, so that they could be on their way just as soon as the dishes were done. As Erin spread the dish towels to dry, Mattie picked up her bonnet and went to the stairwell. "Ben, you git a move on," she called.

Ben clomped downstairs looking uncomfortable and dejected in his Sunday suit. "It don't feel natural gitting dressed up on a Monday," he said. "This collar pinches my neck."

Mattie was not in a sympathetic mood. "You stop that whining and go fetch me an old quilt from the chest in the attic. I don't want to set on splinters all night. Mind you hurry, now."

"Yes'm."

"I best go see if that Jube has got hisself ready to go," Mattie said. "Like as not he's laying around that cabin gathering wool."

Tucker looked up from his book. "Mattie, why don't you stop flying 'round this room? Jube left for the meeting half an hour ago with some spare lanterns."

"Oh. . .well, I reckon we're ready then." Mattie pulled her shawl up around her shoulders. "Tucker, it wouldn't do you no harm if you were to come along."

"Not tonight, thank you. I'm gonna spend the evening with Mr. Dickens here."

Mattie sighed. "Well, do as you think best. Ben, you come on."

There was no need for a lantern as they walked to the meeting; a giant harvest moon lit their path with its warm light. Douglas took Erin's arm as they walked through the shadows.

"Mattie is certainly looking forward to these meetings," Erin said.

"Yes, but I'm not sure I share her enthusiasm. The moonlight is beautiful tonight, isn't it?"

"Yes, it is. I believe these meetings will be interesting. They'll give us a chance to meet people and to see what kind of worship services they're used to."

"I suppose," Douglas said. "Have I seen that hat before? It's very becoming."

"No, this is the first time I've worn it, thank you. I wonder why Tucker didn't come? Mattie said everyone comes to these protracted meetings. Sometimes I wonder why Tucker bothered to board us and help set up the mission. He doesn't seem to care much about the church. Have you noticed?"

"I've noticed he doesn't care much for me."

"I don't think he likes me much better. He can be so aggravating. But did you see what he was reading tonight? Imagine, a man like Tucker Gillam reading *David Copperfield*."

"Quite honestly," Douglas said, "I haven't given Tucker Gillam that much thought."

Up ahead, the arbor sat in a clearing on a wide gravel bank near the river. It reminded Erin of the jungle huts she had seen in picture books as a child. Young pine trees had been used for the support poles that held up a tree limb roof. Beneath the arbor, there were rows of split-log pews, and sawdust had been spread thickly on the ground. Lanterns hung on the posts and a special platform had been erected up front for the preacher to stand on. Mattie waved them over to where she had spread her quilt on a pew, and they took their seats.

The crowd hushed as the Reverend Butler stepped up on the platform. He raised his hand and smiled broadly. "Good evening, folks."

The crowd responded politely, but the Reverend Butler was not satisfied. "I said, good evening!"

This time the congregation gave a loud "good evening" back to the Reverend Butler. He seemed satisfied and continued, "Ain't God give us a glorious night? If you think so, say 'Amen!' "

Loud "amens" sounded from every corner of the arbor.

"Bless the Lord, I'm proud to see such a goodly crowd come out tonight." The Reverend Butler looked directly at Erin. "I thought to start off the testifying, maybe our new teacher would favor us with a word."

Pure panic overtook Erin. What could she possibly say in front of all these people? She dared not decline; after all, missionaries were supposed to be ready to speak "in season and out."

"Stand right on up, Miz Erin, so's we can all hear," said Rev. Butler.

She got to her feet, searching frantically for the right words to say. She was keenly aware of all the eyes that were now focused directly on her.

"Well, uh, I suppose. . .that is, I'm not sure where to begin. You see. . .I have, um, been a Christian most of my life. I asked Christ into my heart when I was a little girl." She wiped her sweaty palms on her skirt. "And when I heard a sermon about being a missionary to the poor people of Missouri—oh, not that I think the people here are poor—that's just what the evangelist said in his sermon." She was making a mess of this. "Anyway, here I am. Oh, and I hope, uh, that if you aren't a Christian, you will become one. Thank you."

When she sat down, Erin's heart was pounding in her throat. *That was perfectly dreadful,* she thought. *I practically called them all indigent bumpkins.* When they stood to sing a song before the offering, Erin slipped quietly away into the darkness.

Once she had made her escape, she stopped for a moment and watched through the trees. Rev. Butler was holding up a worn black Bible. "Bless the Lord," he said. "Tonight I'll tell you about the wheat and the tares. Hallelujah! I'm preaching out of the gospel of Matthew."

The Reverend Butler read haltingly from the Scripture, mispronouncing several of the words. His face glistened and his shirt clung to his back as he paced to and fro on the platform, pounding the podium and gesturing wildly.

"Are you wheat or a weed?" he shouted. "Wheat or a weed? Wheat or weed?"

Erin turned and walked down the road. In the distance, the whippoorwills were calling. "Wheat or weed?" they seemed to say. "Wheat or weed?" She had thought all the right words would be ready, but they had not come. It wasn't just nerves or being new at her job; something deep down wasn't right. "Wheat or weed?" She felt awfully weedlike tonight.

When she reached the edge of the yard, she did not go in the house for fear that Tucker would still be in the parlor. Instead, she walked around back and sat down on a stump by the little stream. In the distance, the hills stood out black against the night sky. The stream made soft gurgling sounds at her feet.

What was it that troubled her so? She sat in the quiet of the yard, trying to understand why she felt so incompetent. . .so powerless. Then, from the valley below, Erin heard the distant voices of the congregation singing the invitation hymn.

"Cast thy burden on the Lord," came the words, rising faintly through the trees. "Lean thou only on His Word; Ever will He be thy stay, Tho' the heav'ns shall melt away."

"Dear Lord," she prayed. "This is so much harder than I thought it would be. Please help me. Please do whatever it takes to make me the kind of missionary You want me to be."

She must have lost track of the time, for as she went back toward the house at last, Douglas and Tucker came out of the back door with lanterns.

"Erin, where have you been?" Douglas asked. "I looked everywhere for you after the service."

Tucker grinned. "I thought maybe you was et by a wampus kitty."

"I'm sorry. I went for a little walk. I didn't realize I had been gone so long."

They all went back into the kitchen, and Tucker blew out the lanterns. Douglas waited until Tucker had climbed the stairs.

"Erin, please don't ever run off like that again," he said. "I was terribly worried."

"I really am sorry, Douglas. I felt so stupid after giving my testimony tonight. I just had to get away."

"There was nothing wrong with what you said, and it was very unfair of Butler to embarrass you like that."

"No, I should have been able to speak. I am a missionary, after all."

"A very new missionary, who is allowed to make mistakes the first time she speaks publicly. You're just tired, Erin." Douglas slipped his hand over hers. "Get some rest." His lips brushed her forehead before he went out the door toward his cabin.

Chapter Nine

The sun had just begun to glisten through the trees when Erin started on her way to the schoolhouse. She had spent the entire week before school with her teaching books, preparing lesson plans. She planned to pattern her school after the great educator J. H. Pestalozzi. Erin had read Pestalozzi's philosophies in a book one of her teachers had loaned her, and his ideas fascinated her. Erin vowed her students would receive the most modern education possible, regardless of their modest facilities.

The school house was freshly scrubbed and ready for the children. *McGuffey Readers* were stacked neatly on Erin's desk next to the *Ray's Arithmetics* and the *Blue-backed Spellers*. Mattie had confided to Erin that Tucker had ordered the textbooks, enough for one set of books per family.

Erin checked the ink and quills and set out the Bible that the mission board had supplied. Finally, she walked down the hill to the well and drew a bucket of drinking water. That was a job, she decided, that would soon belong to one of the boys with stronger arms than hers.

A half dozen pupils were already clustered in the schoolyard though it was not yet eight-thirty. Beth Keller was there with her towheaded brothers, Walter and Noah. Erin recognized some of the Reynolds children, too, rolling in the dirt a few feet from the door of the schoolhouse. A broad-shouldered lad pulled them to their feet by the scruffs of their necks. *That must be the oldest Reynolds boy,* thought Erin.

Erin took the bell from her desk and went to the door. "Come in, children. . . come in quietly and put your dinner pails on the shelf, then we will go about getting your seats."

Erin asked everyone to line up by her desk. Beginning with the Reynolds children, she carefully printed their names in her roll book.

"All right, you are Isaac Reynolds. And how old are you, Isaac?"

Isaac gave her a toothless grin. "I'm seven, ma'am."

"Fine. And you are Joshua." Joshua nodded solemnly. Erin turned to the oldest boy. "I'm sorry, I don't know your name."

"My name's Ameriky Reynolds, and I was fourteen years old last fourth of July—that's why my daddy named me like he did—after our country."

"That is very patriotic," Erin said. "Ameriky, do you and your brothers know how to read?"

"Oh yes'm. Ma's been teaching us at home every bit she can. Even Isaac can pick out some words now and again, when he ain't being ornery." Isaac wrinkled a freckled nose and stuck his tongue out at his brother.

"That will do, Isaac," Erin said.

"My daddy said to tell you t'whup the fool out'n us if we give you any bother," Ameriky said.

"I don't think that will be necessary. You older boys sit near the back for now, and Isaac, you find yourself a seat on the boys' side near the front."

"Yes'm," said Isaac. "And Teacher?"

"What, Isaac?"

Isaac leaned toward Erin and whispered, "I think you're real pretty." He turned and trotted to his seat.

For the next hour, Erin interviewed a steady stream of children. At the end of the line, to Erin's surprise, were Rabe and Sariah Hinkle. Rabe seemed much like his father, with a bitter and hopeless air about him, though he was only eleven. Sariah was a pleasant surprise, though, for she crept up close to Erin's desk and smiled.

"Teacher, my name's Sariah and I brung ya these daisies from along the way to be a beauty on your desk."

"Thank you, Sariah," Erin said. "They're lovely."

She looked up then to see Enlo lumber in with a frail, dark-haired girl trailing behind him. He pushed the girl to the side and gave Erin a sullen look.

"Enlo, is this your sister?" Erin asked.

"Well, she sure ain't my sweetheart."

The children laughed at his joke, and Enlo smiled, obviously pleased to find an audience.

"Come here, Enlo," Erin said firmly. Enlo looked back at the children and sauntered over to her desk.

"Enlo, I think it would be nice if we spoke in respectful tones to one another. So, let's start again. I need to put your name and age in my roll book. How old are you?"

"Reckon I'm 'bout nineteen. Don't nobody know my birthin' date for certain."

"I see, and your sister. . ." Erin looked up and saw that the girl was still standing by the door. "Come here, dear, and tell me your name."

She crept up to the desk. "My name is Winifred, ma'am," she whispered. "I'm thirteen."

She was small for her age and rather homely, with an abnormality around her mouth—not a harelip exactly, perhaps a scar—that caused her to speak with a lisp.

"Enlo, you take a seat in the back row, and Winifred, perhaps you would like to sit next to Lela."

Enlo moved toward his desk, again shoving Winifred out of the way. "Move, snot nose," he snarled.

"Enlo! We will not tolerate name calling in this class," Erin said.

"I'm terrible sorry, Teacher," said Enlo, grinning. He slumped down into a back row seat.

They spent the rest of the morning passing out books, and then Erin had each child read from the *McGuffey's* and do some simple arithmetic. Of seventeen children, only eight could read, and a few more than that could "cipher." Erin decided it might be best to start most of them in the primer and allow them to progress at their own speed.

❧

As the first weeks went by, Erin encountered problems she had not anticipated.

The children's clothes were worn thin and yellowed from repeated washings in river water, and most of them wore no shoes. Though the children seemed to pay the weather no heed, Erin hesitated to send them outside to play with so little protection from the chilly autumn wind.

Her biggest problem, however, was classroom discipline. The titters and giggles at Enlo on the first day had been replaced by outright laughter, horseplay, and practical jokes. Twice, Erin had retrieved sweet gum burrs from her chair just before she'd sat down on them, and all manner of vermin and reptiles had been placed in her desk drawers. She was sure that Enlo was behind most of this foolery, but she could never catch him in the act. Pestalozzi's philosophies did not seem to be working very well in Erin's classroom.

"May I have your attention, class?" Erin said one day. "Remember that we will have our weekly spelling bee Friday afternoon using this week's lesson in your *Blue-back*."

Out of the corner of her eye, Erin saw Enlo poke Rabe Hinkle in the ribs. Enlo said something and they both went into convulsions of laughter.

"Enlo, do you want to share your joke with the class?" Erin asked.

"Naw, I reckon this bunch of clod-kickers jist wouldn't understand what we was talking about."

"Then please be quiet."

Enlo shifted in his chair. "No city woman teacher is gonna tell me when to shut my mouth. If I want to talk, I'll talk."

The silence was uncomfortable as teacher and pupil glared at each other, neither backing down. Erin did not know what to do next, but Ben made the decision for her. He stood up by his desk.

"Teacher said to hush your mouth, Enlo."

Enlo heaved himself to his feet and turned toward Ben.

"Class," Erin said nervously. "I think we're all a little tired. We'll dismiss a few minutes early today."

Enlo gave Ben a withering look and skulked out of the door with Rabe close at his heels. The rest of the children filed out while Erin gathered up her papers. She sat down in her chair and closed her eyes, but her rest was short-lived. Angry voices sounded out in the schoolyard.

"Teacher's pet!" Enlo taunted. "Ain't you jist the sweetest thing."

Erin hurried to the door. Ben had set his books on the ground and stood square in front of Enlo.

"You best move out of my way, Butler," Ben said.

"You think you're such a much, telling me to shut up, Mr. High-and-Mighty Gillam. Maybe I ought to thump you on the head a little, then you might think twice before you try to take up for the teacher."

"Enlo," Ben said, "unless you want to git your ears pinned back beside your head, you best turn your shiftless self towards home."

"You ain't near big enough for that kind of talk, little Ben. Must be real nice having the teacher at your place. She tuck you in at night and kiss you on the ear?"

Ben flew into Enlo with both fists flailing. Erin ran out into the yard and shouted for them to stop, but the boys ignored her. They were both stronger than she, so there was nothing Erin could do to make them quit.

To Erin's relief, Jube came running across the yard and wedged himself between the boys. The rest of the children scattered as Jube struggled to keep them apart. Enlo lunged at Ben, but Jube caught him with an open-handed cuff that sent him reeling backward.

"That's enough!" Jube shouted.

Enlo sat up and put his hand to his face. "Old man, you like to broke my jaw."

"When I like to, boy, I will. Now, git yourself on home."

"Enlo," Erin said, "I think your father and I should have a talk before you return to school."

Enlo straightened himself slowly and took a few steps. Before he continued on, he turned and spat on the ground at Ben's feet. Ben tried to pull away from Jube, but Jube had a firm grip on his arm.

"Hold on now," Jube said. "Jist settle down. Are you all right, boy?"

"Yes, sir, I reckon so." Ben wiped away the blood that trickled from his nose.

"Well, you better have a purty stout reason for fighting at school by the time you git to the house, or Tucker may jist finish off what Enlo started. You git on down the road and have Mattie fix you up."

Ben picked up his books and turned to go.

"Ben?"

"Yes, ma'am?"

"Thank you for standing up for me in class. I'm sorry it got you into a fight with Enlo. I'll explain things to Tucker, if it will help."

"No'm. I reckon if you can't take Enlo on, you sure ain't no match for Tucker."

Ben disappeared around the curve in the road, but his words still pricked at Erin's heart.

"You been having trouble at the school, Miz Erin?" Jube asked.

"Oh, a few students have been somewhat difficult, but I think in time we can all be friends."

"Well, what in the world, if those ya-hoos don't straighten up, you jist tell ole Jube. I'll come clean their plows for you."

"Thank you, Jube, but I'm afraid this is one problem I have to solve on my own. I just wish I knew where to start."

The next morning brought a cold wind and low, gray clouds. The children arrived and formed a circle around the stove, warming icy fingers and toes. Already the cold had brought on sniffling noses. As they warmed themselves, the room began to buzz with their voices.

"Have y'heard, Teacher?" Ameriky asked. "There's gonna be a barn raising next Saturday for Emmit and Rose Stiles."

"A barn raising?" Erin asked. "What's that?"

The children stared at her in disbelief. "Ain't you never been to a raising?" asked Noah Keller.

"I'm afraid not. Perhaps you could explain it to me."

"Well," Noah said, "it's the way folks help a family put up a new barn. In betwixt chores, Emmit's been felling trees out in the land below his cabin. He's notched the logs and piled them all together. Now that he's got enough logs for a cow barn, the men'll come and help him build it and put on a roof. And if it ain't too dry, they'll burn the brush from off the trees and there'll be a grand big bonfire."

"Then comes the fun part," interrupted Walter Keller. "After they're all done, we'll have us a play party with a big bate of food and singing games nigh on to midnight."

"That sounds very nice," Erin said. "I'll look forward to it."

There was a noise by the door. Will Witbeck and Rabe Hinkle had snatched Sariah's lunch pail and were throwing it back and forth between them. Erin forced herself to speak in a pleasant tone.

"Boys, please stop that and take your seats. Everyone, sit down so I can take roll."

The children went reluctantly to their desks. Everyone was present except Enlo and Winifred. Erin was going to have to make a visit to the Reverend Butler's to resolve the problem with Enlo, but she was not sorry to get a reprieve from him.

Rabe Hinkle raised a grimy hand.

"Yes, Rabe?"

"Would it discomfort you if I put another log on the fire, Teacher? It's a mite cold back here by the window."

"Go ahead, Rabe."

Perhaps Erin was making some progress, after all. Rabe had never raised his hand before for anything, and he had spoken politely.

Rabe took some wood from the box and carefully put it in the stove. He seemed to take quite a while to situate the log.

"That's fine," Erin said. "Please take your seat, Rabe."

Erin had turned to write on the blackboard and didn't see that Rabe had smuggled a glowing piece of kindling back to his desk. As she reached up to print a spelling word, five loud explosions popped in the back of the room. Erin jumped around in time to see Ameriky Reynolds dancing in the aisle, slapping sparks out of his back pocket.

Erin heard a few uneasy snickers from the back of the room. The rest of the children waited anxiously to see what their teacher would do next. Ameriky wasn't hurt, but the sparks had burned several holes in the back of his overalls.

"Rabe Hinkle, you come up here this instant," Erin said, so angry she could barely speak.

Rabe's eyes opened wide and he walked forward.

"What did you put in Ameriky's pocket?" Erin demanded. Rabe shifted his feet and stared at the floor. "Rabe, you will tell me this instant what made all that noise!"

"Firecrackers," he murmured. "But they wasn't mine. I didn't bring 'em."

"Ameriky could have been badly burned by that prank, Rabe, to say nothing of the lack of respect you showed for your school. Now, you just march yourself home for the rest of the day, and don't come back unless you can abide by my rules. If you ever try such nonsense again, I'll take a switch to your behind."

Rabe hesitated a moment, then he walked out the door. Erin wasn't finished yet. "I want to know who brought those firecrackers to school. Whoever did it might as well confess. There'll be no recess or dinner until you do. We'll just sit here and wait."

After a few minutes, a hand went up on the boys' side of the room. "Yes, Ludie?"

"They was mine, Teacher. I never thought about them hurting nobody, though, honest."

"I see. Well, I think you'd better go on home, too, and tell your parents what you've done."

Ludie picked up his books and walked out the door like a whipped puppy.

"What is wrong with you children?" Erin cried. "I came here wanting to teach you, wanting to share all the wonderful things in these books, and what do you do? You play pranks and giggle and whisper. Don't you think I have any feelings? Don't you want to learn?"

Erin looked at the children's faces. "It's time for recess," she said. "Class is dismissed."

She sat down at her desk, vaguely aware of the children's raucous play outside the window, blinking back tears. She didn't hear the light footsteps behind her. Grubby fingers touched her hand, and then Sariah Hinkle put her arms around Erin's neck.

"I'm sorry for our orneriness, Teacher," she said.

Erin felt her anger begin to melt away. "That's all right, Sariah. We're all ornery sometimes."

"Even you, Teacher?"

"Especially me. But do you know what, Sariah?"

"What, Teacher?"

"There's Someone who always loves us no matter how ornery we are."

"You mean God."

"That's right. God loves us very much, and He'll always be there to forgive us and take care of us."

"My mama says that, too. Last spring Mama and me prayed and I asked Jesus to come into my heart. Mama says that God loves my daddy and Rabe and everybody."

"She's right, Sariah, and He wants us to love each other, too."

Sariah's small face was thoughtful. "Teacher? Don't it jist make you feel warm all over?" She jumped down and scampered out the door.

Chapter Ten

The day of the barn raising began with a sunny sky. Tucker hitched up the horses and helped Mattie and Erin into the wagon. Mattie balanced her "Scripture cake" in her lap on the wagon seat, while Douglas and Erin held on to a big pan of beans in the back. Jube and Ben had left earlier on foot. Tucker turned the horses off the road onto a rough wagon trail that led uphill through a pine grove, then plunged down among dense stands of hickory and walnut.

The Stiles's home was the smallest that Erin had seen yet, with huge old oak trees surrounding it on every side. Tucker pulled the horses up in the yard and set the brake.

"Well, Preacher," he said. "You ready to do a man's day of work?"

"As ready as you are, Tucker. Just show me where to start."

"You can take the toolbox over to where the men are working. I'll be there directly."

The women were already busy in Rose's cabin. It would be dinnertime soon, and the men would be hungry. Plank tables had been set up in the yard to accommodate the crowd.

Widow Puckett was waiting for them on the porch. "Mattie Cotter, did you go and bring that Scripture cake of yours? You know I've been wanting to learn the secret of that recipe for ages."

"Ain't no secret, Widder, jist a little of this 'n' that." Mattie nodded towards Erin. "Erin helped me bake this one."

Rose was busy in her tiny kitchen. Erin hadn't seen Rose for several weeks, since she had reached her period of confinement and had been staying home from church. All this extra work must be hard on her in her condition; she still looked like a child herself.

"Good morning, Rose," Erin said. "How can I help?"

"I appreciate the offer, Miz Erin, but everything's nearly done. I was jist fussing over the pots. We're gitting ready to go out and look at the working. Asa Keller says he can raise a barn wall faster than anybody, and he's taking on all comers."

They went out to the field where the men were working. Some men worked in teams, lifting the notched logs into place. Others worked to one side, cutting wood shingles for the roof. Douglas had been teamed with Clay Reynolds and John Witbeck. Erin couldn't help but notice the strained look on Douglas's face as he attacked yet another log.

The women returned to the cabin, and after checking the pots on the stove, they picked up the piecework they had brought with them and found seats on the few chairs in the room or on Emmit and Rose's bed. Mattie had told Erin to bring some sort of stitchery to do, so she pulled out a hook and some thread from her bag and began to crochet a doily.

"How pretty, Miz Erin," exclaimed Becky Keller. "I always admired crocheting, but I never did learn."

"Of course that kind of work is fine," sniffed Widow Puckett. "But a farm wife don't have much use for such fancies. I taught my Bessie here to quilt and sew and do such work as a country woman needs to know about." The Widow Puckett peered up at Erin from her work. "I heared you had some trouble at the school this week, Miz Corbett."

"Oh, well, it was just a schoolboy prank," Erin said. "Nothing to be alarmed about."

"Ludie told me about them firecrackers," said Mrs. Stiles. "We're right sorry for what happened. He ought to have knowed better."

"I hear the younguns is getting a little out of hand, cutting didoes right in the middle of their lessons," said the widow.

"We've had a few discipline problems," admitted Erin. "But I am sure as we come to know one another better, things will settle down."

"If 'twas up to me," the widow snapped, "I'd settle it with a little peach tree tea and some old-fashioned schooling instead of all these newfangled ideas."

"Widder, let Erin alone," Mattie said. "She ain't hardly had time to git started yet." Erin gave Mattie a grateful glance. Mattie put her sewing back in her basket and got up. "We best be gitting dinner," she said. "The menfolks will be ready to eat soon."

The women followed Mattie to the stove and began to dish up the meal and carry it outside to the table. The table was crowded with dishes: ham, chicken, fried rabbit, squirrel stew, beans, hominy, cornbread, biscuits and jelly, sweet potatoes, loaves of fresh bread, pickles, sauerkraut, and applesauce. For dessert, there was Mattie's Scripture cake and a dozen dried-apple pies.

The men sat at the table while the women poured coffee and refilled their dishes. Never had Erin seen so much food consumed so quickly. When she reached over Douglas's shoulder to fill his cup, she noticed how pale his face was.

"You tired?" she asked quietly.

"A little. Don't say anything. They're watching to see if I can keep up with them."

The men filled their plates and filled them again. Then, one by one, they began to make their way back toward the field.

"You about ready, Preacher?" Jube asked.

Douglas stood up stiffly and stretched his arms. "I suppose so, Jube. Let's get it done."

The afternoon progressed much as the morning. After the women and children ate at the second table, they cleaned up and set the leftovers back for the meal to follow. The women sat down to more handwork and conversation.

Erin learned that the Reverend Butler was expected back sometime today from a revival in Palmer, and he was anxious to get Enlo back in school. The ladies also let it slip that Mr. Hinkle was angry with Erin for sending Rabe home. The Hinkles were not at the working today, Erin supposed, because of Narcissy's advanced pregnancy.

Since the barn was not very large, the men finished early in the afternoon. The children made their way in from playing in the woods, and families soon were enjoying a relaxed supper in the yard. Douglas looked drawn and tired as he sat down on the quilt beside Erin.

"Are you all right?" she asked.

"Yes, but I don't think I'll be moving very fast in the morning."

Jube and Tucker looked none the worse for their day's work. Tucker took a hefty bite of ginger cake and washed it down with spring water. "Preacher, I 'spect you're about wore out," he said. "You done a fair job of work today."

"I take that as a high compliment coming from you, Tucker." Douglas leaned closer to Erin and said softly in her ear, "Would you walk out back with me? I would like to talk to you alone."

Erin glanced around at the others. She found Tucker's knowing eyes resting on her face, and her chin raised. "All right, Douglas. If you're sure you wouldn't rather rest."

Douglas shook his head and got to his feet. They strolled through the trees, then leaned against an outcropping of rocks behind Emmit's new barn. "I'm very proud of you," Erin said. "You didn't give up, even though they deliberately gave you the hardest jobs."

"Well, it's over now. How was your day?"

"Oh, as Mattie would say, it was 'tolerable.' Why did you want to talk to me?"

Douglas leaned toward her and placed his hands on hers. "This isn't the way I planned it, but with your school and the church work, I've hardly had a moment alone with you." He fidgeted with his shirt collar and cleared his throat.

"What is it, Douglas? Is something wrong?"

"No, no, it isn't that. I just envisioned this happening in a more appropriate setting, certainly not in a barnyard."

"What do you mean, Douglas?"

"That first day, when we met at the depot, I thought you were the most beautiful creature I'd ever seen. In the time we've been here, I've found that you're not only lovely, but also a most gracious young woman, someone well suited to the ministry, and someone deserving of a lifestyle fitting a fine lady. I can offer you that sort of life, Erin. When I complete my assignment here, my father has promised to arrange for me to pastor one of the largest churches in Chicago. I'd like for you to be my helpmate in that work, Erin. . .I am asking you to marry me."

Erin sat quietly, not knowing what to do or say.

"Erin, do you have an answer?"

"You've caught me by surprise, Douglas. Perhaps the Lord did bring us together here. Your proposal is very flattering. . . ."

"Then accept it!"

"Would you give me some time to pray about it?" asked Erin. "I want to be absolutely sure."

Douglas smiled broadly. "Of course. Erin, I know this is right. We could be married next summer, just as soon as our assignment ends here."

"Well, I suppose I hadn't necessarily intended to stay here more than one term, and we would be serving in another church. But first, they'd have to find another teacher to take my place."

"I'm sure they can find someone. Erin, we will have a wonderful life. The church I will pastor has a beautiful parsonage, and I'll show you such a time in Chicago. With you at my side, I'll be the envy of every man in town."

"Imagine, our own beautiful home. It is what I've always wanted."

Douglas pulled Erin toward him and kissed her. Then his arms encircled her and he kissed her again, more insistently. So many emotions tumbled inside of her, but one thing Erin knew, she liked being in Douglas's arms. Reluctantly, though, she pulled herself away.

"Douglas, someone might see. We must continue to be discreet in public," she said.

"That will prove difficult, I assure you."

Douglas reached for Erin again, but bare feet rustled in the leaves behind them. Erin whirled around to find Ben staring at her. His face showed a mixture of disbelief and betrayal.

"Mattie sent me to come fetch you," he said. "The singing games is about to start." He spun around and ran off to the front of the house.

"Do you suppose he saw us?" Douglas asked.

"I'm afraid so," said Erin. "I'll talk to him. I hope I can make him understand."

The men had built the brush from the logs into a huge pile, and now, as the sun sank behind the trees, they lit the bonfire. The children danced around the flickering light, and the grown-ups soon joined them in a circle. Someone began to sing, and then the others joined in, the sad, sweet ballads rising into the growing darkness.

Erin stood between Tucker and Mattie at the edge of the circle. The singers' voices changed now, became faster and happier, and someone began to clap. Erin discovered that she was patting her foot to the rhythms, and soon she, too, was singing.

"Miz Erin," Tucker said softly in her ear, "I'm jist beginning to think we might make a country girl out of you yet, jist maybe, mind you." She looked up into his firelit face and saw the warmth in his eyes. "I been thinking on it," he said. "Maybe it's time you and me come to an understanding."

Erin smiled. "You mean a truce?"

"You might say that, I reckon. I expect I've been a little hard on you now and again."

"I'd like it very much if we could be friends, Tucker."

Tucker's deep bass voice joined the others on the chorus of a new song called "Weevily Wheat":

> "Oh, don't you think she's a pretty little miss?,
> and don't you think she's clever,
> and don't you think that she and I
> would make a match forever?"

The song ended, and Tucker led Erin back to the wagon where Mattie had left a crock full of apple cider. Tucker handed her a cup and she drank down the golden liquid.

"This is good," Erin said. "So much singing dries your throat." She looked over her shoulder at the lively circle around the fire, and she laughed. "I can't imagine what the headmistress at the orphanage would think. She was very strict when it came to social gatherings. I'm sure she'd find this one much too boisterous for her taste."

"Well, regardless, I'd allow as she did a fair to middling job of raising you up right."

"Thank you, Tucker." Erin looked around the yard. "I wonder what has happened to Douglas."

"I expect the preacher can take care of hisself, least for a few minutes, anyway."

"Just the same, I shouldn't have abandoned him."

"Like as not he's over buttering up the widder and her man-hungry daughter."

"Tucker, couldn't you and Douglas try to get along? Really, if you would give him a chance, Douglas is very nice. You saw how hard he worked today. And he is a man of God, after all."

Tucker stared down at Erin. "Appears to me you got more than a passing interest in the preacher."

"Well, I. . .it isn't that," she stammered. "I would defend Douglas even if we weren't. . ."

"Weren't what?" Tucker's gray eyes pierced through Erin's. "You're fixing to marry that hoon yock, aren't you?"

Erin looked away from him. "I haven't given him a definite answer."

"You're jist enough of a ninny to say yes."

"As a matter of fact, I might. But, even if I did, we don't intend to announce it for some time, and I'll finish the school year regardless, so I'd appreciate it if you would keep this to yourself."

"You got no more business to marry that city boy than the man in the moon. You can do better, Miz Erin."

"My personal life is none of your concern, Mr. Gillam, and I'll thank you to keep your nose out of my affairs."

Tucker shook his head. "I might a knowed you ain't no different from the rest. There ain't no city woman alive that wants anything but fancy geegaws and an easy life. You figure one year here with us poor crackers pays all your dues? Don't you fret 'bout my keeping your secret. That ain't the kind of news I would care to pass on."

Chapter Eleven

The mood was decidedly unpleasant at breakfast on Monday morning. Ben ate silently, casting angry glances toward Douglas and Erin between bites. Tucker sat at the head of the table, grumpily mixing molasses and grits together on his plate. Jube kept to himself, still groggy from the late hours he had kept over the weekend. Mattie and Douglas were the only cheerful souls in the room, and they tried their best to encourage a polite conversation.

"Good attendance yesterday, don't you think, Mattie?" Douglas asked.

"Right smart, and after a party night, too."

Jube sipped loudly from his saucer, and then set it down to cool. "Tucker, you reckon I ought to check on the widder this morning?"

"You might, she was real upset about losing them chickens."

"I don't blame her," Mattie said. "It's shameful to think a body can't leave her place for an evening without some outlaw sneaking in and stealing the livestock right smack out of the yard."

"I have some time this morning," Douglas offered. "If you like, I can ride out and see if I can find any signs of the intruder."

Tucker hardly looked up from his plate. "Naw, Preacher, I expect you best leave that to Jube and me. But if it's work you're looking for, Mattie's real busy in the kitchen this time of year."

Erin set her milk glass down loudly on the table and glared at Tucker, but Mattie jumped in before she could say anything.

"Tucker, you're as tetchous as an old sow this morning. You know I wouldn't let the preacher, nor any other man, in that kitchen long as I run this house."

"If you haven't any plans for this morning, Douglas, I could use your help at the school. This might be the last day of nice weather, and I thought I would take the children on a little picnic in the woods. It would help to have another adult along to keep them all together."

"It would be my pleasure, Erin."

Erin smiled a pointedly charming smile at Douglas. "Thank you," she said. "Maybe some of the boys who have been causing trouble will think twice about misbehaving with a man present."

Tucker looked up from his meal. "You been having more troubles at the school besides that ruckus between Ben and Enlo?"

Erin hesitated. "Well, yes, some. Mostly just talking out and playing pranks. Nothing serious."

"What pranks?" Douglas asked. "You haven't said anything about pranks before."

"It's nothing, really, toads in my desk drawers, burrs on my chair, things like that."

"Did you whup the boys that played these pranks?" asked Tucker.

"No, I didn't. I don't believe in whipping children."

"You see, Tucker, the finest schools of education no longer condone corporal punishment," Douglas explained.

"Huh," Tucker scoffed. "Your finer schools might change their minds if they knowed some of the younguns around here."

"J. H. Pestalozzi says that learning must first be based in mutual friendship between student and teacher," Erin said. "When that relationship is established, education can begin. A good teacher does not have discipline problems."

"Horse apples!" cried Tucker. "That J. H. Pester feller ain't never taught at Lost Crick. Like as not he's some old goober out of a book that's been dead for fifty years or more."

"Now, wait a moment," said Douglas. "I hardly think you are qualified to second-guess Erin's methods. She has a teaching certificate, after all."

Tucker ignored Douglas. "What about this here picnic? Are you so far ahead with your lessons that you can afford to take the day off to play in the woods?"

"We are not taking the day off. J. H. Pestalozzi says. . ."

"Oh, corn, here she goes again with that Pester feller," Tucker moaned.

"J. H. Pestalozzi says that children can learn many things from nature. They need more than just schoolwork and chores, you know."

Tucker grunted, unconvinced, and went back to eating his breakfast.

"My methods may seem strange to you, but I just want these children to have as progressive an education as any child in St. Louis," Erin said.

"Jist as long as you ain't having a play day," Tucker conceded. "But, I still think more could be learned in the schoolhouse."

"I think Erin knows what she is doing," Douglas said.

"I don't recollect asking for your opinion, Preacher," said Tucker. "Miz Erin, I don't care if you stand on your head and spit buckshot, if you think that will make you a better teacher, but I expect you to put a stop to any tomfoolery going on and learn them children what they come there for."

"I will handle the children, Mr. Gillam."

"See that you do, Miz Corbett."

Erin stood up and pushed her chair in firmly under the table. "I need to start for school or I'll be late," she said. "Ben, would you please walk along with me this morning and carry that box of slates that came from the mission board? It's too heavy for me."

Ben looked up at Erin, clearly annoyed. "I reckon I'd ruther not."

Tucker threw down the napkin from under his chin. "Benjamin Daniel Gillam, either you haul yourself out of that chair right now and help Miz Erin, or I'll guarantee you won't be setting down for your supper."

Ben sat still.

"You hear me, boy?" Tucker bellowed.

After a moment's consideration, Ben gave up the struggle. "Yes, sir," he said. "I'll git my books."

"Thank you, Ben. Douglas, if you'd come to the school around nine-thirty, I believe we'll be ready to go."

No matter how fast Erin walked on the way to school, Ben managed to keep a good amount of road between them. "Ben, please wait," Erin called. "Please. . .I want to talk to you."

Ben stopped and looked down at the road while Erin hurried to catch up with him. "I want to git on to the schoolhouse," he said. "Got some tradin' to do with Ameriky."

"I see. Well, maybe you could spare me just a minute. Ben, I know you're upset with me. I don't blame you. It must seem as if I've told you a boldface lie."

"You did! You said you weren't sweet on the preacher, then I come and see you two kissing right spang in the broad daylight."

"I'm sorry about that, Ben. It was impulsive of us. But I wasn't 'sweet' on the Reverend Teterbaugh at first. At least, he and I had no understanding between each other at that time."

"Meanin' you got this 'understanding' now?"

"Yes, Ben, I suppose we do."

Ben clenched his fists and turned away. "It ain't fair! You gonna up and marry that preacher and he'll take you out of here jist as quick as he can go. You said you was staying; you told us you had plans for our school."

"Ben, I won't leave before the school term is up, I promise. Nothing is settled yet, anyway. I'm sorry. I didn't mean to lie to you, but sometimes you can't anticipate where life will take you. Perhaps God brought Douglas into my life because He intends for us to serve Him together."

"Maybe God works that way for you. All I know is, He ain't never brought nobody into my life; He jist takes them out."

Ben got a firm grip on his bundle and ran up the road to the school. The sunshine seemed dimmer, somehow, as Erin followed him up the hill.

Inside the schoolhouse, Erin took roll, noting that Enlo and Winifred were absent again. Erin was relieved that she would not have to contend with Enlo on their hike.

Douglas appeared in the doorway. "Rev. Teterbaugh, come right in," Erin said. "Class, I have a surprise for you. We're fortunate to have the reverend as our guest today. I'm sure you will want to show him what a well-behaved class you can be." Douglas smiled at the children.

"All right, I believe we're ready. You older boys will take the lead. Keep your eyes and ears open. I want you to look at these woods as if you were seeing them for the very first time."

The children streamed out of the schoolhouse door and scrambled up the hill, with Douglas and Erin following close behind. As they walked along the winding trail, the children pointed out tracks of opossum, raccoons, deer, and even a bear, who obviously did not know he was supposed to be hibernating.

As they crested a hill, the children jumped from log to log and ducked between the trees. The boys swung from grapevines like young monkeys. Dry leaves crunched beneath their feet as they darted in and out, calling as they ran. Sariah

Hinkle and Annie Witbeck skipped along hand in hand, wrapped up in the sweet joy of childhood friendship.

"They're having such a good time. I almost hate to spoil it by making them start their lessons."

"If you don't, Tucker will never let you hear the end of it," Douglas said. He touched Erin's hand. "Teacher, you look beautiful this morning."

Erin pulled her hand away and smiled. "Stop your flattery and come along before we lose the children."

Just then, a scream echoed through the trees. Erin looked ahead and saw a cluster of terrified children frozen around Sariah Hinkle. Ben ran up with a tree branch in his hand, raised it above his head, and sent it crashing down just a few inches from where Sariah lay. Erin ran toward the children as Ben repeatedly thrashed the ground with his stick.

"Ben, what is it?" Erin cried.

Ben bent over Sariah, who was now sobbing loudly. The bludgeoned carcass of a large copper-colored snake lay next to her in the fallen leaves. Ben had both hands on the child, trying to keep her still. Erin sat down and pulled Sariah into her lap. Blood trickled down from two red fang marks just below her right knee. Erin had never felt so helpless in her life.

"Ben, run and find Tucker," she ordered. "He'll know what to do. Tell him to hurry."

"Yes'm. It'd save time if the preacher could tote her back to the road. We could meet you with the team."

"Fine, Ben; we'll meet you. Now go!"

"Don't let her thrash about none," Ben called over his shoulder. "It makes the pizen work faster."

Douglas bent over to inspect Sariah's leg. "Should we try to cleanse the wound or cover it with something?"

"I don't know, Douglas. I've never seen a snakebite before."

Sariah moved restlessly in Erin's lap. "Teacher, it hurts."

"I know, honey. Ben went to get help. You try and be still."

Douglas carefully lifted Sariah in his arms. Erin looked around for Sariah's brother. "Rabe, run and tell your father that Sariah's been hurt. Tell him we'll take her to the Gillam place."

Rabe turned without a word and ran in the direction of his cabin.

What had been a pleasant walk a minute ago seemed like an endless trek now as Douglas hurried back over the trail with Sariah. Erin moved along with the rest of the children, praying silently all the way.

Tucker and Ben were already driving the buckboard toward them as they came down off the hill. Tucker jerked the horses to a stop and jumped down. He took Sariah and carried her to the back of the wagon; she looked like a rag doll in his arms. Tucker gently laid her down, then he reached into his pocket and pulled out his knife.

"This'll hurt a mite, punkin', but we got to git it done."

Sariah nodded. Erin watched in horror as Tucker took a firm hold on the child's leg and cut an X shape over each fang mark with his knife. Sariah blanched and bit her lip, but she remained quiet. Tucker leaned over, put his mouth to the wound and sucked, then he turned and spat the blood on the ground.

"Preacher, you got a clean kerchief?" Tucker asked.

Douglas fumbled in his pockets and handed his handkerchief to Tucker. Tucker smiled at Sariah. "You're a brave little gal. We'll git you back to my place and Mattie'll have something to make you feel better. You jist hang on a little while longer."

Tucker tied the handkerchief on tightly, just above the swelling on Sariah's leg.

"Miz Erin, you ride back here with her," he said. "Keep her still and prop up her leg so it won't throb as much."

Erin climbed up over the back of the wagon and turned to see the rest of the children waiting by the side of the road. "School is dismissed, children," she said. "You may go home."

Sariah and Erin settled down on some horse blankets in the wagon bed. Tucker was already back on the seat with Ben.

Mattie was waiting in the yard when they pulled up. Sariah seemed quieter now; she didn't cry out as much as when she had first been bitten.

"How bad is it?" Mattie asked. Tucker looked at her, but he did not answer aloud.

"You bring that child into my room," Mattie ordered. "I got the bed all ready."

Tucker carried Sariah in and laid her down. Sariah's forehead felt cold and clammy, and her leg was swelling at an alarming rate. She began to shiver, and Mattie covered her with a blanket. Then Mattie took charge.

"Tucker, we'll need the medicine jug and turpentine and some clean rags. You better bring me an extry cover, too. Ben, you haul me in some water and set it on the stove, then git to your chores. Ain't nothin' more you can do."

They both left to do as Mattie asked. Mattie stayed next to the child, stroking her and speaking softly. There was a love in Mattie like Erin had never seen in anyone before.

Tucker returned with a jug and a small drinking glass. Mattie removed the cork and poured out a few swallows of clear liquid.

"Drink this down," she said. "It don't taste good, but it'll ease the hurt."

Sariah drank it, but it made her cough. "It burns, Miz Mattie."

"I know, angel, it'll pass. You try and sleep."

Mattie put the child's leg up on a pillow and cleaned the wound with the turpentine Tucker brought. "Erin, I'd appreciate it if you'd make up a fresh pot of coffee and see to dinner. We got a long day ahead of us and likely some extry mouths to feed."

"I'll do my best, Mattie, but I'm not much of a cook. You will call me if I can help with Sariah, won't you?"

"Yes, child. Now, don't you fret, I've doctored more than one snakebite in my time."

Tucker followed Erin into the kitchen and began building up the fire in the cookstove. There was a strained silence until Erin finally got up the courage to ask what was on her mind.

"Tucker, you said before that snakebites usually weren't fatal unless the victims were very young or very old. Is Sariah old enough. . .I mean. . .Sariah's not going to die, is she?"

Tucker put in one more piece of kindling and replaced the lid. He was choosing his words carefully. "It ain't easy to say. Copperheads don't commonly give a mortal bite, but Ben said it was a big snake. From the swelling, I'd say she got a goodly dose of pizen. Snakes don't oft times strike this time of year. I guess she must have stepped right on top of him. I reckon we'll jist have to wait this one out."

"But surely the doctor can give her something."

"Mattie done give her about all there is to give."

"There's got to be more we can do! We're so isolated here. Perhaps I could send a wire to St. Louis for a specialist."

"By the time anyone could git here, it'd be all over, one way or the other. Jube went to get Doc Stone. Doc'll pull her through if anybody can. If you're so direct minded to do something, why don't you find that preacher and see if you can't git him to go out to the Hinkle place. Narcissy's gonna need some help to git her through this, what with her time nigh due."

It took Jube several hours to locate Dr. Stone, who had been out on a call near Picayune Ridge. The doctor arrived at sundown on a tired-looking sorrel mare. He dismounted and took a leather satchel from the saddle horn. The doctor's shoulders drooped as he walked, and his black suit coat was shiny at the elbows. Mattie said he had been riding these isolated trails for nearly twenty-five years. He looked accustomed to little sleep and long rides through dark woods.

Dr. Stone came into the bedroom, set his hat on Mattie's dressing table, and went to work. Sariah's leg was doubled in size from thigh to toe. The bite area had turned blue-black, like a bad bruise, and had swollen hard to the touch. The doctor felt Sariah's head and looked into her eyes. The child seemed only half conscious, staring passively as the doctor examined her.

"Any nausea, Mattie?"

"Not yet. She started to chill, but I give her some medicine whiskey and it seemed to help."

"She's been awfully thirsty," Erin said. The doctor looked up, aware for the first time that there was a stranger in the room.

"Adam Stone," Mattie said, "this here's Miz Erin Corbett, the new missionary teacher. Sariah got bit whilst they was out on a school picnic."

"How do you do, Doctor."

The doctor nodded. "Pleased t'meet you." He turned his attention back to Sariah. He opened his bag and handed Mattie a small paper envelope. "Give her one of these powders in some water. We'll try to keep her fever down, if we can."

Mattie took the medicine from the doctor. "You got to git to another call, or you planning to stay on awhile?"

Dr. Stone looked at the pale child who slept fitfully next to him on the bed. He rubbed his chin with his fingers and pulled at his ear. "I reckon I'll stay on awhile. I don't like the sound of her breathing. We won't be out of the woods on this one for a while yet, Mattie."

"I reckoned not, Adam," Mattie said softly.

There were footsteps on the porch and the front door slammed. "Where's my Sariah?" a voice demanded.

Erin stepped out into the parlor and saw Seth Hinkle. By his swagger, it looked as if he had more than his share of liquor in him.

"Rabe says you got my Sariah here. I come to git her."

"She is in here, Mr. Hinkle, but she is in no condition. . ."

"Don't tell me about no condition." He pushed past Erin and stopped inside the door. "Who told you to call for the doc? I ain't paying for no doctor. You ain't got no right to call for him without my say-so."

"You needn't worry 'bout the money," Mattie said. "Tucker'll take care of the doc. Do you want t'know about your little'n, or are you too drunk to care?"

A faint light of awareness gleamed in Mr. Hinkle's piggish eyes. "Is she ailin' that bad, Doc?"

The doctor rubbed his chin thoughtfully. "Seth, it's a bad bite. I'd be hard put to say how it'll come out. I'll do my best for her, I give you my word on that."

Mr. Hinkle staggered toward Erin. "It's your fault," he said. "You with your highfalutin city teaching ways. You're the one what said I should send my younguns to your school. Well, I sent 'em and look what come of it."

Dr. Stone turned around to look at Mr. Hinkle. "Seth, there are snakes all over these hills. Sariah could have gotten bit going to the outhouse."

"No, it's all the teacher's fault. . .her and that dandy of a preacher they got."

Mr. Hinkle's words burned like hot coals. He had spoken aloud what Erin had dared not think since the moment Sariah had been bitten.

"And I'll tell you another thing," Mr. Hinkle said. "You let her git bit, you can jist take care of her. A man's only meant to bear so much. My woman's about to birth again and she won't hardly git up out of bed herself. You can jist keep Sariah here."

"Seth Hinkle, you're drunk," said Dr. Stone. "Now you git on out of here, or I'll throw you out myself." The doctor took a deep breath. "Go sober up and take care of Narcissy. We'll send word when there's a change."

Mr. Hinkle put on his torn felt hat and staggered out of the bedroom. He stopped unsteadily at the parlor door and pointed his finger in Erin's face. "If my girl dies, it's on your head, missy."

Erin looked at Sariah lying motionless underneath the covers, and then she ran blindly through the back door, past the springhouse to the apple grove. She flung herself on the ground and cried until no more tears would come, but she was no more at peace than before. Getting to her feet, she brushed at the stains on her skirt from the wind-thrown apples that lay rotting on the ground beneath her. "If my girl dies. . ." The words tumbled over and over in Erin's mind.

She couldn't think of it anymore. She wouldn't. She would think of something else. The least she could do was to make good on her promise to Mattie and get dinner. She walked stiffly back to the house.

Tucker was standing at the stove with the coffeepot in his hand.

"How is Sariah?" Erin asked.

"Holding on. Doc's with her. Mattie went over to check on Narcissy. I was fixing to take the doc some supper."

"I'll do it; I promised Mattie. Hand me the coffeepot, would you, please?"

Tucker handed Erin the pot, and she poured the dark liquid into Mattie's china cup.

"You all right?" Tucker asked.

"Yes, I'm fine." Erin knew her red eyes and disheveled appearance were evidence to the contrary, but she had no energy to discuss it with Tucker now.

"I reckon I'll git some chores done. I'll be in the barn if you need anything."

"All right, Tucker, thank you."

"Miz Erin?"

"Yes?"

"Doc told me what Seth Hinkle said to you. Don't pay him no mind. He talks through a jug most of the time. I know I come down on you about taking them children on the picnic, but that snake could have been anywheres. There's no reason to blame yourself."

"Thank you, Tucker."

Erin took the tray to the sickroom. Dr. Stone was sitting in a straight chair next to the bed, watching Sariah. Erin put the tray down and sat on the side of the bed. Sariah's forehead was hot. Her leg was swollen and red, and the wound area was now covered with open blisters.

"Is she doing all right, Doctor?"

The doctor looked at Erin and rubbed his hand over his chin. "I'd hoped we'd not have such a rough time. Copperheads generally are the lesser of evils with snakes around here, but she's having a bad reaction. I just don't know."

"Surely you'll be able to tell something soon. By morning we should know, shouldn't we?"

Dr. Stone put his calloused hand over Erin's. "I'm afraid the effects of the venom don't reach their peak until the third or fourth day."

"Four days? She can't stand this for four days."

Dr. Stone took a wet cloth from the basin and wiped Sariah's face. "It will get worse," he said. "The venom affects the blood, makes it so it won't clot. Along with the fever, there'll be tissue damage, her gums may bleed, might be blood in the urine and stools, and breathing trouble. There's also the chance of infection in the wound itself."

"Can't you do anything, give her something? There must be a medicine. If it's a matter of money. . ."

The doctor got up from his chair and walked to the window. "It isn't about money. There simply isn't anything to give. I read where some New York doctors are working on a serum. . .maybe in a few years. . .but not now. All we can do is try and keep her comfortable."

Sariah stirred, and Dr. Stone took advantage of the opportunity to put a teaspoon of water into her mouth.

"Do you believe in prayer, Doctor?"

The doctor placed the spoon back in the glass. "As long as I've been tending folks, I'd be a fool not to. I've seen the impossible too many times."

For the first time since the accident, Erin felt a surge of hope. She needed to pray. God wouldn't let this beautiful child die if she could just pray hard enough. She determined to spend every spare minute lifting Sariah up to God in prayer.

The doctor came by as often as he could between calls, but after the first night, Mattie and Erin took over caring for Sariah. Douglas volunteered to fill in for Erin at the school until Sariah was better, and she agreed. Erin could think of nothing else but Sariah. She made a constant effort to pray for the child.

The nights were the hardest, when time seemed to crawl, an endless cycle of cold compresses, drinks, and changing of night clothes and bed linens. On the third night, Sariah seemed to improve a little, and Mattie agreed to leave Erin with the child while she got some sleep in Ben's room. It had turned cold, so Erin wrapped up in a quilt and settled into Mattie's rocking chair.

The next thing Erin knew, someone was sitting on the edge of Sariah's bed. Startled, she leaned forward in the chair and tried to get up, but her feet were caught in the coverlet.

"Set still," Tucker said. "She's all right. I jist put a fresh poultice on her leg." He looked over at Erin. "Why don't you go on to bed. You're tuckered out."

"No, I'm all right. Besides, I don't want Mattie to miss another night's sleep."

"Mattie's taught me a trick or two about nursing sick folks. I'll set up with her. You ain't had no more sleep than Mattie. You go on."

Erin knew she would not be able to stay awake all night. "All right," she said. "But only for a few hours. Wake me around two o'clock and I'll spell you."

"Fair enough. Now you go get some rest."

Tucker bent over Sariah and carefully sponged her face. For such a rough looking man, he had a gentle touch. Erin decided that Sariah would be in good hands. She stumbled to her room and fell asleep at once.

Erin opened bleary eyes to a room full of light. The hands of the little brass clock showed it was after nine o'clock. Why hadn't anyone awakened her? She put on her wrapper and hurried out of her room. Tucker and Dr. Stone were drinking coffee at the dining room table, but they both stopped short and stood up when they saw her. The door to Mattie's room was shut tight.

"Why is the door closed?" Erin asked. "Where's Mattie?"

The doctor offered Erin a chair. "Sit down," he said. "There's something we need to tell you."

"Where is Mattie?" Erin insisted.

"I'm afraid we got a sorrow for you," Tucker said.

"Mattie?"

"She's not here," said Tucker. "She and the preacher went to make a call at the Hinkles'."

Erin ran to Mattie's door and flung it open. There on the bed lay Sariah's still, small body, the lines of pain now erased from her face.

"No! She wasn't supposed to die. . . . I prayed! Oh dear Lord, it's my fault. . . it's my fault!"

Through a fog of grief, Erin felt the doctor firmly leading her to the sofa. Tucker was kneeling down in front of her, so she had to look him in the eyes.

"You listen here," he said. "There wasn't nothing anyone could do. The pizen was jist too much for her. It wasn't nobody's fault."

Tucker's words meant nothing to Erin. If God was just and merciful, why would He let a child like Sariah die? She had prayed for her. Why hadn't God answered? A wave of rage swelled up within her and demanded release.

She pounded her fists into her lap, and when she felt Tucker's hands grip her wrists, she twisted free and began to flail at him. Tucker encircled her in his arms, rocking her back and forth as one would calm a small child. Dr. Stone brought a cup with some bitter-tasting liquid and held it to Erin's lips. Gradually, the storm subsided, as the doctor's medicine blunted her pain. She heard Dr. Stone say, "She'll sleep now."

The funeral took place at two o'clock the next day. Mr. Hinkle had grudgingly agreed to use the schoolhouse for the service since his cabin was so small, but he was adamant about Silas Butler performing both the service at the school and the graveside ceremony in the family plot behind the Hinkles' cabin.

The schoolhouse was packed full as the Reverend Butler stepped up on the platform. Sariah lay behind him in an open pine casket lined with white muslin. Just before the service began, Tucker and Dr. Stone helped Narcissy Hinkle to a seat up front by her husband.

Bessie Puckett began the service with a song, but the words held no comfort for Erin, and nothing the Reverend Butler said as he continued with Scripture and his sermon helped ease the pain. Emotions were running to a high pitch by the time the mourners lined up to view the body. Erin was glad that Douglas took her arm and hurried her outside.

The congregation waited while the family took their final viewing, then the casket was nailed shut, and everyone began the long walk to the Hinkle cabin. Someone brought out a chair for Narcissy by the graveside. Seth and Rabe stood next to her, but neither father nor son showed the slightest hint of emotion. Mattie held the littlest Hinkle boy in her arms as the Reverend Butler moved through the graveside service.

"We send her soul to God and commit her body to the ground." Butler threw a handful of dirt into the open grave. "Earth t'earth, dust t'dust, looking forward to the last day and life in the world to come." Rev. Butler stepped away and several of the men began shoveling the dirt into the grave. The congregation sang softly until it was completely filled; then, family by family, they started on their way home.

Douglas and Erin walked back slowly. Neither of them said anything until they reached the house. Douglas stopped outside of the door. "I'm not hungry. I believe I'll go on to bed. You'll be all right?"

"Yes, Douglas. Good night."

Erin went inside, feeling burdened and heavy beyond anything she had ever felt before. The house was quiet. She supposed the men were catching up on chores in the barn. Yellow lamplight flickered out of Mattie's doorway.

"That you, Erin?"

"Yes, Mattie."

"Come here, child."

Erin walked to the door. Mattie was sitting in her rocker with her Bible open in her lap. "Come and set, Erin. I want to talk to you."

"I'm awfully tired, Mattie."

"It's been a day to make a body tuckered, ain't it? Rest yourself there on the side of the bed for a minute."

Erin walked over reluctantly and sat down. Mattie searched her face in a way that made Erin feel as if she could see to the bottom of her soul. "You're hurtin', ain't you, child?"

Tears welled up in Erin's eyes. If only Mattie knew how badly she hurt.

"What is it, Erin? You can tell ole Mattie."

Erin dropped to her knees in front of Mattie's chair. Mattie reached out and gently patted her shoulder while tears rolled down Erin's cheeks.

"Mattie, everything's gone wrong. Tucker was right; this job is too hard for me. I want to go home."

"You got no call to blame yourself about Sariah. It was an accident."

"Maybe. But it wouldn't have happened had I kept the children at the school. Anyway, it's more than that. I've failed as a teacher. I can't even keep discipline in my own classroom. Mattie. . .I'm not sure I want to be a missionary. I prayed harder for Sariah than I have ever prayed before in my life. Why didn't God answer me?"

Mattie stroked Erin's hair. "He answered you, child. He always does. Sometimes He says yes, sometimes no, and sometimes wait, but He always answers. I reckon this time He jist didn't give you the answer you wanted."

"But it's so unfair. She was just a child."

"I know, honey, I don't understand it either, but I been on this old earth long enough to learn that the Lord's ways ain't our own. We got to learn to leave it to the Master and trust Him for His reasons."

"It wasn't supposed to be like this, Mattie. I had wonderful plans. I thought I could reach those children. But it's no use. I can't go on with it. I just don't have the strength."

Mattie let Erin cry for a moment, then put her hands beneath Erin's chin and lifted her head. "You know, Erin, you're right," she said quietly.

"What?"

"You're right. You can't do this job. You jist ain't got what it takes."

Erin sat up, freshly hurt that Mattie had agreed with her.

"Erin, there ain't nothing good you can do in your own power. None of us can. The sorrowful thing is that most folks live their whole lives and never find that out." Mattie's eyes were full of love as she continued, "You come here with your big city schooling, ready to change us poor country folk every which way."

Erin started to protest, but Mattie held up her hand. "Now, let me finish. There ain't nothing wrong with dreams or edgycation, and heaven knows there's things here that need changed. . .but real changes, they have to come from the inside out."

In her heart, Erin knew Mattie was right. Erin realized, to her embarrassment, that she had almost felt as if she had done God a favor by becoming a missionary. "What do I do now, Mattie?"

"Jist talk to the Lord, child, and tell Him how you feel."

Erin took a deep breath and bowed her head. "Father, I came here thinking I would show these people what being a Christian is all about. Instead, I've made a mess of everything I've done. I can't handle this job; I'm not strong enough. But if You still want to use me. . .if You want to work through me. . .here I am."

Erin felt wrapped up in the heavenly Father's own strong arms. She raised her head and smiled tremulously. "Mattie, do you think the people here would let me have another chance?"

"I reckon they would, but I'll tell you truthful, there's some folks that think you and the preacher are all store-bought clothes and book learning and no gumption."

"Well, I can't really blame them for that." Erin thought for a moment. "Would it help if I tried to learn the ways of the people here? What if I were to dress more sensibly and learned how to cook and do chores? Would that help earn their respect?"

"I reckon it'd be a good way to begin, and I'd be proud to teach you anything you want to know. Listen, Tucker said he was gonna go on with the butchering tomorrow while the moon is full. He'd been putting it off with the funeral and all. I can't think of a better way for you to start learning."

Chapter Twelve

"Well, look at you, Preacher!" cried Jube. "We might make a farm boy outta you yet."

"Glory," said Tucker. "You givin' up the ministry for the farm? I never thought I'd see you in overalls."

"Have your fun, Tucker, I expected it. Erin talked me into this. She seems to think that we need a better understanding of your customs if we are to have an effective ministry here. So, I am ready to learn all there is to know about butchering swine."

Tucker chuckled. "This really your idea, Miz Erin?"

"Yes, mine and Mattie's. With all that has happened, well. . .I realized I've been rather arrogant, thinking that people would be impressed with me just because I have a big city education. I know now that I'm going to have to earn their respect. So, I intend to start by learning how to do the work of a farm wife, and Mattie's promised to teach me."

Tucker took all this in with great interest. "That'll bear watching," he said. He pushed himself away from the table. "If you want to learn, let's git at it. We're burning daylight."

Tucker and Ben went to the hogpen and cornered their first victim. Douglas and Erin watched while Tucker crept close and felled the animal by delivering a sharp blow to the back of its head with the blunt side of his ax. Ben helped Tucker hang the pig up by its back legs, then Tucker took out his knife and cut deep into its throat. Erin took a deep breath and swallowed hard as she watched the blood run down on the ground.

Jube's voice came from behind her shoulder. "Don't let it worry you," he said. "That ole pig never felt a thing. Tucker's not one to let no animal suffer."

"Jube, you and the preacher gonna give us a hand scalding this hog, or you gonna stand and jaw all day?" Tucker asked.

"I'm coming. Don't git your chickens in a flutter."

Jube and Douglas helped carry the hog to a cast-iron pot in the yard that was filled with boiling water. The men lifted the animal up and dipped the front half in.

"Careful now," Jube said. "Don't leave it in there too long or the hair will set."

The men laid the carcass out on some clean boards. Jube gave Douglas a knife and showed him how to scrape against the grain of the hair to pull it off.

"Now we're ready to hang this porker up," Jube said. "Ole piggy will hang by his heels jist as nice as you please."

Jube removed the head, and Ben took it into the kitchen, then Tucker pointed to a large tin tub. "Preacher, fetch me that gut basin, if you would."

Douglas dragged the tub over and pushed it under the pig. Tucker cut through the belly skin from one end to the other.

"Miz Erin, if you'd go ask Mattie to git us some pans, we'll be needing them directly," Tucker said. "All right, Preacher, you make sure all the innards go in there, while I make this last cut." Douglas bent down to grip the tub.

When Erin returned, Tucker and Jube were busy cleaning out the carcass and Ben was standing nearby, but Douglas was nowhere in sight.

"Here are the pans, Tucker," she said. "Where's Douglas?"

The men looked at one another. Erin thought she detected a gleam of amusement in their eyes.

"Well," Tucker said, "I ain't for certain, but I suspect that he's out back of the barn losing his breakfast."

"If he is ill, don't you think you ought to go find him?"

"Now don't git your feathers ruffled," Tucker said. "I'll go after him by and by, if he don't show up on his own. He'll be all right. He ain't the first man to have his stomach turned by butchering."

Erin wanted to tell them how mean they were being, how much she resented them putting Douglas through this, but she held her tongue. They weren't asking him to do anything they weren't doing themselves.

The kitchen was filled with every available pot and basin. There was a pot on the stove for rendering lard, another for boiling the hogs' heads, and a pan sat on the table for scraps that would be chopped into sausage. The entrails were set to soak in salt water and were cooked as time allowed. The men cut up the larger pieces, the hams, shoulders, and roasts, and salted them down for storage in the smokehouse. The smaller cuts were sent into the kitchen. Then the whole process would begin again on another hog until finally all four had been butchered. Everything had to be done quickly while the meat was still warm so that it would not spoil. Erin understood now what Mattie meant when she said that they used everything the pig had but the grunt.

Douglas had returned to work, but Erin noticed he stayed well clear of the actual butchering area, concentrating his efforts on salting the meat and setting it in the smokehouse. Meanwhile, all afternoon Tucker brought in tub loads of meat and set them in front of her on the table. Perhaps it was her imagination, but when he brought in the last basin, she thought she saw a small measure of admiration in his eyes.

The men finished their work in the twilight and cleaned up the yard. Mattie put some boiled tongue and liver pudding out with sliced bread for supper so that the men could serve themselves while she finished her work in the kitchen.

Erin couldn't ever remember being so tired. Stray strands of hair clung to her face. Her hands were swollen and nicked from her clumsy work with the knife, and there was a sharp pain between her shoulder blades.

"Only thing left now is to pour off the lard," Mattie said. "You go rest yourself at the table and have some coffee. I'll finish up."

"Mattie, how do you do it? I'm exhausted."

Mattie smiled. "Well, child, first thing you learn about being a country girl is, you always got strength to do what you have to. The Lord won't put no more on your shoulders than you're able to carry."

"Wagon's pullin' in the yard. Looks like Brother Butler," called Ben.

"I wonder what he wants," Erin said.

"Pigs' feet. That man's plumb foolish about pigs' feet. I told him we was butchering and he asked me would I save him some feet," said Mattie.

Tucker walked to the back door. "Shame he couldn't show up for some of the work."

Mattie gave Tucker a slap on the arm. "You hush that talk and let him in, Tucker Gillam, or I'll take a switch to you."

Tucker did as he was told and the Reverend Butler blustered through the door.

"How do, Tucker, Miz Erin. Miz Mattie! Bless God, it's good to see you! I'm sorry to trouble you on your butchering day, you being so busy and all."

"Not so busy that I forgot your pigs' feet," Mattie said, and she handed him a box packed full.

"Well, bless your heart for thinking of me like that. You'll surely have a crown of glory in heaven, Miz Mattie."

Butler tucked his prize underneath his arm and turned to Erin. "The main reason I come by was to see you, Miz Erin. I've been meaning to come talk to you about Enlo."

"Yes, I apologize for not visiting your home before now to talk to you, but with the funeral and all. . ."

"Ain't no need to apologize. I jist wanted you to know how sorry I was for the ruckus he caused. Enlo's always been hardheaded. But a glorious thing done happened. I was preaching at the Courtois church last week and Enlo got religion! He's sorry for his meanness, and he wants to come back to school, if you'd have him."

"If Enlo is ready to abide by the class rules, he is welcome to return."

"Oh, he'll mind, Miz Erin. I promise you that."

"We will see him Monday then."

Rev. Butler spoke his good-byes and set his hat back on his head. Douglas came into the kitchen just as he drove away. "So, Enlo has reformed, has he?"

"You heard?" Erin asked. "What do you think?"

"I suppose time will tell, but in the meanwhile, I wouldn't turn your back on him."

"Ain't that kindly a cynical attitude for a preacher?" Tucker asked.

"I guess maybe it is, Tucker."

Chapter Thirteen

"Carry your books to school, Miss Corbett?"

"Well, sir, I don't know; folks might talk."

"Let them," Douglas replied. "These people aren't happy unless they have a story about the preacher to tell over their Sunday chicken."

"Come get these books, and don't be so cross," Erin said. "I need to get an early start so I can see what you've done to my school while I was gone."

"Don't worry, everyone survived. Though why you would actually look forward to returning to that crude, chaotic group of children is beyond me."

"I'm afraid the chaos is mostly my fault, but it's a beautiful morning for a new start."

Douglas laughed. "Erin, have you even looked at the sky? It's cold and dull and gray."

Erin stopped in the middle of the road and looked at Douglas. "I'm serious about this," she said. "I intend, by God's grace, to make this school a success."

"All right, Erin, I just don't want you to be hurt if things don't work out."

"I mean to make it work."

Douglas seemed surprised by her determination. "I'm sure you do," he said. "But it would hardly be the end of the world if the school folds. In all the time we've been here, I have yet to persuade these people to listen to a word I say. They haven't budged an inch. I'm not sure they can be reached."

"Of course they can be reached, Douglas. Perhaps you should make some effort to adapt to their ways. . . ."

"Don't start that again, Erin. I don't think I'll ever look at another slice of bacon without feeling ill."

They walked up the schoolhouse stairs and went inside. "Let's not quarrel," Erin said. "I didn't mean to upset you."

Douglas put his arm around her waist and pulled her close to him. "I couldn't be upset with you for very long." He kissed her gently and then cupped his hand beneath her chin. "Very well. Do whatever you like. But please try to remember that our term is only for one year. There's no point in getting too attached to these children." He took his watch from his vest pocket. "I must go. I promised to visit Narcissy Hinkle and her new baby this morning. Good luck today, Erin."

The children arrived and scuffled noisily to their seats. Sariah's desk was painfully empty, as was her brother's. Erin wondered if Rabe would ever be allowed to return to school. Just as she closed her roll book, Enlo and Winifred appeared in the doorway.

"Enlo, you and your sister are tardy," Erin said. "We begin school at nine o'clock. Please be sure that you are on time tomorrow."

Enlo took off his hat and stepped forward. "Yes'm. We would've been here, except a big stick of firewood flew up and hit Winifred whilst she was chopping this morning. It took some time for Pa to doctor it up." Enlo stepped aside to reveal the bandage on his sister's arm.

"I see. Are you all right, Winifred, or would you like me to send someone for Dr. Stone?"

Winifred dropped her head and spoke softly. "No'm, Pa done tended it already."

"Please take your seats then."

To her surprise, Enlo obeyed without a word.

"Good morning, class," Erin began. "It is good to be back with you. I hope you were helpful to the Reverend Teterbaugh in my absence." Erin stepped in front of her desk. "The past week has been difficult for us all. Sariah was a very special little girl and we'll miss her. We can take comfort in the fact that she is in heaven now, and we can trust that God is taking good care of her."

Erin leaned back on her desk and looked into the children's faces. "I'm afraid that our school has gotten off to a rather bad start. That is mostly my fault. You see, this is my very first school, and I have much to learn about being a teacher. But, starting today, things are going to be different. I would like us all to be friends, but you must understand that from now on, I will not tolerate any nonsense. No more pranks, no more talking out, nor any more horseplay. Anyone who chooses not to follow the rules will be punished. Do you all understand?"

There was a quiet chorus of "yes, ma'ams."

"Good."

❧

The next few weeks brought a virtual transformation in the children. A consistent routine and firm discipline solved most of the behavior problems, and in the process, the children began to show real academic promise. For the first time, Erin felt the pure joy of helping young minds learn.

Several of the children were very bright indeed. Ameriky Reynolds was completing arithmetic assignments almost as fast as Erin could hand them out, and he had a remarkable ability to recall dates. Jackson Witbeck, though only eight, was nearly ready for the fifth reader, and Beulah Stiles could draw beautifully detailed pictures of the animals she saw in the woods.

Of course, not all of the children were as gifted, and Erin wasn't sure what to think about Enlo. He was polite and compliant enough, but there was still something about him that made her uneasy. Erin felt guilty doubting the boy's sincerity, but something about him just didn't ring true.

Winifred was a problem of a different sort. She was a shadow, slipping silently in and out of place. When she spoke, her eyes never left the floor. Her rounded shoulders seemed to carry a burden far too heavy for one so young. Surely there was a way to ease the sadness that enveloped her. Erin determined to pray daily that God would somehow use her to touch the child's life.

One afternoon, snow began to fall a few minutes before the end of the school day. Winter had come to Lost Creek at last. Even the older children couldn't resist peering out the windows as the first flakes floated to the ground.

"The first snow is always special," Erin said. "You may go, but remember to do your homework."

The children grabbed their books and ran out with their faces toward the sky. They danced between the snowflakes, their mouths open wide to catch them on their tongues. Everyone left quickly, except Ben.

"Did you forget something?" Erin asked.

Ben shifted nervously. "No'm. I was jist wondering if you'd have need of someone to rub the board clean."

"All right, Ben. Thank you."

Erin turned in her chair and watched him while he worked. Ben had generally done his best to ignore her and Douglas ever since the barn raising. His willingness to help now puzzled her.

"Thank you for erasing the boards, Ben."

"Ain't nothing, jist thought it needed doing." Ben stopped and stroked at the wool on the eraser. "What changed you, Miz Erin?"

"Changed me? What do you mean?"

"You're different than you was. . .not jist at the school, makin' us mind and all, but other times. You're sort of peaceful-like now. You kindly remind me a little of Mattie."

"That is about the nicest thing you could say to me, Ben." Erin sensed a door was opening in Ben that might never open again. She walked over to the recitation bench. "Come here," she said. He sat down on the bench beside her. "I don't know how else to put it except that God changed me. I got to a point where I couldn't go one step farther on my own. I wanted to give up and go home. Then Mattie showed me that I had to admit how weak I was before God could make me strong. Anything good you see in me is God's doing."

Ben seemed to be considering what Erin had said. "You reckon God would do the same thing for me?"

"Of course He would, Ben, if you asked Him."

"I don't know. I always thought God was mostly out ready to stomp on folks for their meanness. I reckon I been mad at Him for a long while now."

"That's all right. God's big enough to handle your anger. Just be honest with Him. He loves you more than anything, Ben."

"Would y'show me what to do?"

"It's not difficult. First, you need to tell God you've sinned—you know—done bad things."

"I done plenty of sins, I know that. I feel right bad about it sometimes."

"God gave us a way to get rid of those bad feelings," Erin said. "Imagine if you went home and deliberately broke out the kitchen window. . . ."

"Tucker'd have my hide for that."

"I guess he would, and you would deserve it, too. But what if Jube stood between you and Tucker and said, 'I'm taking Ben's licking for him because I love him.' That's sort of what Jesus did for us when He died on the cross."

"I reckon Jesus must love us a lot."

"He does, Ben, and if we'll ask Him into our hearts, He'll give us that love inside to stay."

Ben frowned. "I don't know as I understand that part about asking Jesus into your heart."

"That's just a figure of speech. It means to be a Christian you have to ask Jesus to be your Savior and Lord. He'll save you from your sins and give you eternal life—and then you have to let Him be in control of your life. Do you want that?"

"Yes'm. I reckon I do."

"You can ask Him right here and now, if you'd like."

Ben bowed his head. He was silent for a long moment, but when he lifted his head, his eyes sparkled. "It really works, don't it, Miz Erin!"

Erin put her arm around him and hugged him tight. "It surely does, Ben."

"I reckon my ma and pa would be real happy about this, don't you?"

"From what Mattie has told me of your parents, I think they would be very pleased."

"I wisht I knew how Tuck will take to it. Won't Mattie be happy, though?" Ben thought a moment. "Miz Erin, could we keep this our secret, jist until Sunday? I'll git Tucker to come along to church somehow and I'll go forward at the altar call. It'll be my surprise, and it'll let everyone know all at once."

"All right, Ben, it'll be our secret until Sunday."

There was hardly a dry eye in the church that next Sunday when Ben walked down the aisle. Douglas was so surprised that someone had responded to his message, he nearly forgot to give the benediction. Mattie shouted "Glory!" with tears of joy streaming down her face. Even Jube was making use of his handkerchief. Only Tucker stood stoically among the group surrounding Ben, as the entire congregation came by after the service to give him the right hand of fellowship. When they were done, Douglas shook Ben's hand, too.

"We will have to set up a baptism service when the weather warms up, won't we, Ben?"

Mattie looked at Douglas indignantly. "Foot, Preacher! What's wrong with right now? Ben ain't no warm weather Christian, are you, boy?"

"But it's so cold. There's ice on the creek."

"Ice can be broken, Preacher," Jube said. "I'll be glad to do it for you."

Douglas scanned the room for a possible ally. "Tucker, you're Ben's guardian. I'll not go against your wishes. What do you think?"

Tucker looked at Ben thoughtfully. "I reckon if the boy's decided to git religion, he'd better start out standing up for what he believes."

So Ben was baptized in Lost Creek that very afternoon in the presence of most of the members of the mission church. Jube broke away the ice with an ax while the congregation sang "Amazing Grace." Douglas and Ben waded out waist deep into the creek, then Douglas quickly prayed a blessing and plunged Ben under the icy water. Douglas and Ben wrapped themselves in the blankets Mattie had waiting for them, and Mattie grabbed Ben by the shoulders and kissed him roughly on the cheek.

"I been praying for you since you was birthed," she said. "I know without a shadder of a doubt that God has His hand on your life, boy. He's got something special for you. You heed His call when it comes."

Ben blushed and mumbled something, but Erin could tell he was pleased by Mattie's words. Tucker walked away without comment. He untied the horses and climbed up on the wagon seat. Erin wasn't sure whether Tucker had gone along with this winter baptism out of respect for Ben's decision or because he wanted to see Douglas waist deep in freezing water, but at least he had not tried to squelch his brother's newfound faith.

Tucker drove the horses faster than usual as they headed back to the house so Douglas and Ben would have to spend no more time than was necessary in their wet clothes. The icy dip seemed to have no ill effect on Ben, but Douglas was sniffling before they even got home. Mattie sent him to bed in the cabin and began boiling beef broth on the stove.

"When that's ready, Mattie, I'll take it over to Douglas, if you'd like," Erin said.

Mattie gave her a wry smile. "All right, child." She put the hot broth in a large bowl and covered it with a dish. "Mind you don't burn yourself, and tell the preacher if the broth don't work, I'll bring him some of my special tonic."

Erin balanced the bowl in her hands and made her way out the back door, being careful not to slip on the steps. A fine, powdery snow sifted down on her hair and caught in her eyelashes, and the air was clean and cold.

Erin was so intent on getting to the cabin without spilling Douglas's soup, that she nearly walked head-on into Tucker as he came from the barn. His arm steadied her on the slippery path.

"Easy there, or you'll be wearin' what's in that bowl."

"It's broth for Douglas," Erin said. "I was just taking it to him."

"Ben's baptizin' give him a chill, did it?"

"I'm sure he'll be fine. By the way, I wanted to thank you for supporting Ben in his decision."

"I ain't one to stand in another person's way when it comes to religion. Besides, I promised Pa I'd let Ben decide for himself."

"But you think Ben is wrong, don't you?"

"Not wrong exactly, jist green as grass. Takes a few years on a man to make him think clear about such things."

"Meaning you don't believe in what Ben did or in what we teach at the mission?"

"Meaning I got considerable doubts about it. People who really live by what you all preach are few and far between, Miz Erin."

"That may be true, but it is a poor excuse to disbelieve the Gospel."

Tucker gave an exasperated sigh. "Miz Erin, why don't you save such talk for boys of Ben's age and git that broth into your little preacher friend."

He turned around and stomped back into the barn. Erin walked on to the cabin, puzzled by Tucker's reaction.

Lamplight glowed in the cabin window, but there was no sound of footsteps when Erin knocked on the door. She knocked again, and this time she heard a hushed, "Come in."

Erin cracked the door open and peered inside. "Douglas?"

Across the room, Jube lay on his bunk, snoring so loudly it seemed to vibrate the window glass. Douglas sat up on his bed by the door. "Come in, Erin."

"Are you sure it's all right?"

"I can guarantee you won't bother Jube, and I don't feel up to doing anything improper."

Erin walked in and pulled a chair next to Douglas's bed. "Mattie made you this broth. How do you feel?"

"Like I have been frozen alive. I'll probably catch my death."

Erin felt Douglas's forehead. "You have no fever. You'll feel better after you drink this."

"If I get this kind of attention, I may linger on for several days."

"Thank you, sir, but I'll warn you that I'm not at all patient with invalids. Drink this while it's hot. Mattie said to tell you that she has some tonic ready if the broth doesn't work."

"I hate to think about that." Douglas began spooning up the broth.

"Wasn't it exciting to see our first profession of faith today?"

Douglas put his spoon back in the bowl. "Ben tells me you had more to do with his decision than I."

Erin smiled. "He asked me to keep it a secret until today. He wanted to surprise everyone."

"Ben likes you. He says you're doing a good job with the school, Erin. I'm sorry if I haven't been as interested in your work as I should."

"Douglas, the children are finally learning. They're like little sponges, soaking up everything I say. I never dreamed being a teacher would be this exciting."

Douglas looked at Erin uncertainly. "I hope you will find other roles in life as fulfilling, such as being a minister's wife. You never have given me a final answer to my proposal, you know."

"No, I suppose I haven't."

"I need you, Erin. I need your spirit and your simple faith. Can't you see, we are a perfect complement to one another. Don't you want to share in my ministry?"

Jube grunted and rolled over on his side.

"It isn't that," Erin said quietly. "I've barely gotten started with the school. The children are just beginning to show promise."

Douglas took her hand. "I give you my word, we'll find the school a new teacher. Say yes, Erin. I can't bear waiting for an answer any longer." He pulled away. "Or perhaps I'm a fool to think such a beautiful young lady would care that much for me."

Erin put her hand back into his. "Don't talk so, Douglas. I'm sorry. I know it isn't fair for me to put you off."

"Does that mean you have an answer now?"

"All right, Douglas, my answer is yes. I'll marry you."

The soup bowl slid to the side of the bed as Douglas leaned over to give Erin a kiss. "My dear, you've made me the happiest man on earth."

He reached into the dresser by his bunk. "I was saving this for Christmas, but since it's just two weeks away, I think you should have it now." He opened a small box. "This was my mother's. I'd like you to have it as an engagement ring." He slid the garnet ring on her finger.

"Thank you," was all Erin could say.

"Let's go tell everyone right away," Douglas said.

Erin thought a moment. "Well, yes, I suppose we could, but perhaps it would be better to wait for just a little while. Why don't we tell everyone on Christmas Day?"

"Very well, we'll put the ring back in its box until Christmas, but you keep it in your room. As long as you have it, I feel as if our engagement is official."

The sky was nearly dark by the time Erin left the cabin. The snow had stopped, but it seemed much colder. For some odd reason, the twilight made Erin feel afraid. As she hurried along the path, the snowy yard that had earlier been so calm and clean now seemed eerie and empty.

Chapter Fourteen

The children's enthusiasm about the school Christmas party made the last few days of the winter term pass quickly. Erin had promised the children a Christmas tree, the first for most of them, with tinsel and candles. This would be a party the children would remember all of their lives. Erin could hardly wait for it to begin.

That morning Mattie was up early cooking a breakfast of fried pork chops and hot applesauce. Douglas ate before everyone else and, as a special favor to Erin, went to the schoolhouse to start the fire and put the finishing touches on the tree. Mattie was setting the platters on the table when Tucker and Jube stomped up on the back porch. They were covered with white from head to toe.

"Mercy!" Mattie cried. "Shake that off outside. I ain't got time to follow you around with a rag."

"Sorry, Mattie," Tucker said. "It's coming down something fierce."

All during the meal, Jube was keeping a watchful eye on the window. "Miz Erin, I best hitch up the mules," he said. "It'll be a slippery walk to school this morning."

"Oh no, Jube, thank you. I love to walk in the snow, and there's only a few inches right now. Besides, Douglas has the cutter at the school already. I can ride home with him."

Tucker frowned and wiped his mouth on his napkin. "If this keeps up, there'll be a foot or more by the time school lets out. That road can git tricky in the drifts, especially with a city boy driving. I'll bring the sleigh for both of you this evening and carry you in."

"I appreciate your concern. But I think Douglas is more than capable of getting us home in the cutter. After all, he grew up driving through the streets of Chicago."

"Well now, that makes all the difference in the world. City driving will come in handy when the snow gits so high you can't see the sides of the road. Like as not you'll be in a ditch or a drift before you git out of the schoolyard."

Erin folded her napkin and put it on the table. "I assure you that we can manage to find our way home without damage to your cutter or your livestock," she said. "Now, if you will excuse me, it's time I left for school."

"Miz Erin, you are the stubbornest woman I ever laid eyes on," exclaimed Tucker. "When you and that preacher boy bury the cutter, you cut that horse loose. At least he's got sense enough to find his way home."

Erin put on her coat and slammed the door behind her. As she walked down the hill, the snow fell in fluffy clumps so heavy they made soft plopping sounds as they landed. Blankets of white capped even the smallest tree branches with a layer of icing. The muffled calm of the winter forest began nudging away at her angry thoughts.

The program began with fast-paced games called "Snap" and "Winkem," and then, when the children were ready to settle down, Erin taught them how to play "Authors" using the essays they had studied so far in their *McGuffey's*. Next, each child "spoke a piece" that they had written about Christmas. Erin was reminded again how much she had taken for granted, as she repeatedly heard children wishing for a pair of shoes or a few hair ribbons for their Christmas present.

The younger children entertained them by acting out the nativity story as Douglas narrated. Despite the fact that Joseph tripped on the platform and Mary's "donkey" repeatedly threw her from his back, the play was quite a success. After the actors removed their costumes and were given a round of applause, Erin brought out the baskets laden with special holiday treats. Mattie's sweet cider had been heating on the stove with some cinnamon and cloves, and the children drank it as if it were nectar.

It was then that Erin noticed something peculiar about Enlo. He was seated in the back of the room, and for the past hour he had not joined in the class activities. Fearing he might be ill, she went back to see what was wrong. She had only to come within a few feet of him to detect the source of the problem. *Corn liquor!* Apparently he had kept it hidden on his person in some sort of flask.

"Enlo, I am disappointed in you," Erin said. "You were doing so well lately."

"Aw, Teacher, don't be tetchous. I's jist celebratin' a little early is all."

"That kind of celebration isn't allowed here, Enlo. I'm afraid you'll have to go home."

Enlo didn't move. Douglas stood up from his seat by the stove. "Miss Corbett asked you to leave."

Enlo leaned forward in his desk. "You reckon you can make me go, do you, Preacher?"

Over to her left, Erin saw Ben, Ludie Stiles, and Ameriky Reynolds move silently across the room until they stood shoulder to shoulder behind Douglas. By the crestfallen look on Enlo's face, he had seen them, too, and realized that he was outnumbered. Enlo got to his feet.

"I don't want to stay at no babies' play party anyhow." He picked up his hat and walked unsteadily out of the door.

"What a shame," said Erin. "I thought perhaps we were reaching him."

"You can't help everyone," said Douglas. "There's no reason to let Enlo spoil the party for everyone else."

"You're right. Class, let's take our seats and we'll begin singing the Christmas carols."

As Erin listened to the children's clear, sweet voices, her heart filled to the brim with the happy spirit of Christmas. She never imagined so much joy could come from such a simple celebration. When the children finished singing their final song, Douglas went to the front of the room and ceremoniously removed the muslin that had been draped over the Christmas tree. Erin lit the candles, being careful that none of the upper branches would be touched by the flames. The children sat silently, their eyes dancing in the candlelight.

"Oh my, Teacher!" exclaimed Noah Keller. "Ain't it the prettiest thing you ever did see?"

Douglas and Erin began passing out the cookies and candy. Then Erin pulled a box out from under her desk and gave each child their pair of mittens.

"It's jist too much to behold," said Mary Stiles. "Thank you, Teacher." She handed Erin a box wrapped in a red handkerchief and tied with string. "It's from all of us," she said. "We wanted you to know it pleasures us that you're our teacher."

The package contained a carefully embroidered sampler with all the students' names on it. "Thank you. This gift will always be special to me. I'm proud to be your teacher, and I'm proud of everyone in this class, too. Now, since the snow is getting so deep, I think perhaps we should all be on our way. Some of you have a long walk home. Have a happy Christmas, and I'll see you in three weeks."

The children left, carrying their booty and shouting "Happy Christmas" over and over. Erin had just begun to clean up, when the door came open and Winifred Butler slipped back inside. She fumbled in her dress pocket, then she rushed toward Erin and pressed a small bundle in her hand. In the next instant, she bolted for the door.

Wrapped inside an old piece of newsprint was a tiny cross carved of wood and a note that said, "Teacher, I think yore real nice. Winifred."

Douglas read the note over Erin's shoulder. "Looks like you've made a friend."

"I hope so. I have a feeling that child needs one."

"We'd better go, too," Douglas said. "The snow is still coming down hard. Can you get things ready in here while I hitch up the horse? I'll bring the cutter around to the front so you won't have to walk so far in the snow."

Erin blew out all the candles on the Christmas tree and closed the damper on the stove. She had just picked up her coat when she heard footsteps on the back stairs. She wondered what Douglas had forgotten. She put down her coat and opened the door. It was Enlo.

"What is it, Enlo? I thought I made myself clear. You're to go home."

Enlo lurched into the schoolhouse. Wherever he had been, it was obvious that he had not stopped drinking. He leaned toward Erin until he was just a few inches from her face.

"Now, Teacher," he said. "It's Christmas, and I didn't even git no presents."

Erin gathered his gifts from her desk and held them up to him. "All right, here is the candy and mittens we gave to the rest of the students. Have a happy Christmas, Enlo. Now, I really think you should go on your way."

Enlo smiled. "Thank you, Teacher, but I come to git my real present. I ain't had my Christmas kiss."

The look in Enlo's eyes frightened her. Erin stepped back, trying to put her desk between them, but he grabbed her arm.

"Enlo, you'd better let go of me. Douglas will be back in here any minute."

Enlo pulled her over toward him. "Let the preacher come," he said. "I'll show him how to treat a lady."

Enlo lunged toward her, and without thinking, Erin slapped him across the face as hard as she could. Anger flashed in his eyes. "Feelin' feisty, are you? I can take care of that, too!"

Enlo pressed Erin's shoulders hard against the blackboard. She heard Douglas at the front door.

"Enlo, let go of her immediately."

Enlo smiled and released his hold on Erin. He turned to Douglas. "I been waiting a long time for this, Preacher. Ain't nobody here to help you now."

The poker from the stove was leaning against the wall in the corner. Erin backed away to try and retrieve it. If only Enlo wouldn't notice her!

"Think about what you're doing, Enlo," Douglas said nervously. "You're only going to get yourself into more trouble. Why don't you go on home like Miss Corbett told you to?"

"You know what, Preacher? I think you're afraid of me, and I'm gonna show Teacher here jist how yeller you are."

Enlo reached into his boot and drew his knife. "Here's how it is, Preacher. You light out of here and I won't put a mark on your pretty face, but you go and try to fight me, and I'm gonna skin your hide jist like a rabbit for Saturday stew. Now, how d'you want it?"

Douglas looked over at Erin. He wavered a moment more and then stepped towards the door. "It seems you leave me no choice."

"Douglas?" Erin watched in disbelief as he opened the door.

"We both know I'm no match for him, Erin. I'll go get help. I'll be back, I promise you."

Enlo laughed. "You do that, Preacher. She might kindly need someone to see her home when I'm through."

"You'd better not harm her, Enlo."

"Or what, Preacher? What you gonna do?" Enlo moved the tip of his knife toward Douglas, and Douglas edged out the door. Enlo laughed and dropped his knife to the floor. He grabbed Douglas by the collar. "Shoot fire, Preacher, I don't even need the knife."

Enlo doubled his fist and hit Douglas square on the jaw, sending him headlong into the door frame. Douglas's body crumpled and he fell to the floor unconscious.

Enlo smiled and walked toward Erin. With her hands behind her back, Erin took a firm hold on the poker and waited until he was within striking distance. Just as he came at her, she swung the poker at him. It hit him hard enough to cause a stream of blood to run down his cheek, but not hard enough to stop him. He wiped his face with the back of his hand.

"Oh, you'll pay for that, Teacher." He tried to pull Erin down to the floor, but she fought to stay upright. He pulled again and she fell sideways onto the stove. The flesh on her left hand seared on the hot metal, but she pushed free, only to have him catch her and throw her down on a desk. He pinned her shoulders, and then his lips were on hers. She tried to turn away, but he pressed his weight on top of her, tearing at the buttons on her shirtwaist.

"Now, don't carry on so, Teacher," he whispered. "I won't hurt you. You're not so high and mighty now, are you, Teacher?"

Erin frantically felt below the desk for anything that she might use as a weapon. Then, for an instant, it was quiet, and in the distance she thought she heard. . .yes, it was. . .sleigh bells! She reached beneath the desk again, grabbed a book, and flung it hard toward the windows. It found its mark and went crashing through the glass.

"Help!" she screamed. "Help me!"

Enlo clamped his hand tightly over her mouth, but Erin heard Tucker's booming voice call to the team and then the sleigh bells jingled furiously. Enlo lost no time making a retreat through the back door.

"Erin?" Tucker was calling to her as he ran up the stairs. "Erin! Where are you?"

She tried to stand, but she couldn't stop shaking long enough to get her balance. Tucker lifted her and helped her into one of the desk seats. "What happened? Are you all right?"

"Yes, I think so. . .it was Enlo." Then, she remembered. "Douglas. . .he's over there. Enlo hurt him."

Tucker looked over to where Douglas lay. He took Erin's coat off the chair where she had left it and wrapped it around her, covering her badly torn shirtwaist, and then he went to Douglas and carefully rolled him over on his back. "He's got a fair-sized knot on his head, but I expect he'll be all right. I best git you two back to the house."

Tucker reached for Erin's hand, but she pulled back in pain.

"What's wrong?"

"I burned my hand when I fell against the stove."

Tucker gently took her hand in his and pulled away the scorched sleeve. "That's a bad burn," he said. "It's already blistered up."

"Funny, it doesn't hurt very much."

"It will. You set here with the preacher while I unhitch the horse from the cutter."

Tucker tied the horse to the rear of the big sleigh, then he came back into the school. He carried Douglas out and covered him with a lap robe. Finally, he came in for Erin.

"Would you be more comfortable in the back with the preacher, or would you ruther ride on the seat?"

"If you don't mind, I think I would rather ride up front with you."

Tucker put his arm around her waist. "You jist hang on to me," he said. "I'll have you home in no time."

There was a flurry of activity when they arrived at the house. Tucker carried Douglas into Erin's bedroom, since Mattie's bed was not long enough for a full-grown man. Jube went for Dr. Stone, and Mattie guided Erin to a chair by the fireplace. At first, Erin felt as if she were a spectator to everything that happened around her, but a cup of strong tea and the warm quilt Mattie wrapped around her shoulders brought her to her wits. Mattie sat down next to Erin with a plate of salted butter and began doctoring her hand. Tucker was right; it had begun to hurt.

"How is Douglas?" Erin asked.

"He don't seem too bad hurt to me. Tucker'll stay with him till Doc gits here." Mattie pushed the hair back that had fallen around Erin's shoulders. "You hurt anywhere else, child? You know you can tell ole Mattie if that boy. . ."

"No, Mattie, nothing except a few blisters and bruises."

The back door opened, and Jube hustled Dr. Stone in.

"Glory, Doc, how'd you git here so fast?" Mattie asked.

"Jube found me at Widder Puckett's. Her bursitis is acting up again."

As the doctor went in to examine Douglas, Tucker came out and unlocked the gun cabinet in the front hall. He and Jube each took a shotgun and a handful of cartridges. Tucker wore a grim look that Erin had never seen before.

"You'll be going right out, I reckon," Mattie said.

Tucker nodded. "Ain't no telling if the snow might start up again and wipe out the tracks by morning."

There was concern in Tucker's eyes when he looked at Erin. "Mattie, you have the Doc check on Miz Erin when he gits done with the preacher," he said. "From the looks of the schoolhouse, Enlo got pretty rough."

The shotguns frightened Erin. "Enlo wouldn't have done it if he had been sober," she said. "He's only a boy, really."

"Being young and drunk don't excuse it," Tucker said firmly.

"Don't fret, Miz Erin," Jube said. "We don't aim to use these 'lest Enlo don't give us no choice."

"That old couch ain't fit to sleep on," said Tucker. "You bed Miz Erin down in my room tonight, Mattie. If we git back before morning, I'll bunk out with Jube. Tell Ben to look after things while we're gone."

"Wait a minute," Mattie said. She took a woolen scarf off the peg by the door and wrapped it around Jube's neck. "There, you old fool. I reckon I got enough to do 'round here without you coming down with the grippe."

"Don't wait up," said Tucker, and then they were gone.

After Dr. Stone checked Erin over, Mattie got a nightgown and wrapper from her room and they went upstairs. Erin had seldom been on the upper floor of the house, and it felt strange now to be in Tucker's room.

The day and Dr. Stone's pain medicine were taking their toll. By the time Erin changed into her nightclothes, she dropped gratefully into the soft feather bed and went to sleep.

When Erin awoke the next morning, it was already light enough for her to see Tucker's room. There was a sense of order here, like one might expect in a banker's room, but certainly not a farmer's. A massive secretary desk dominated the south wall. Its shelves were filled with books.

Erin slipped out of bed and walked over for a closer look. A title caught her eye, *The Harmony of the Gospels*. She had seen some of the same texts on Douglas's shelves in the cabin. Erin opened the cabinet and took out a Bible commentary from the bottom shelf. There was an inscription on the inside of the cover: "Always put God first. Love, Pa and Ma, May 1877."

This was a pastor's library. Why would Tucker have these books in his room? They didn't look as if they had been touched for quite some time. She saw something sticking out of a concordance on the top shelf, and she took the book down and carefully pulled the paper out. It was a Certificate of Ordination, dated July of 1878, and it had Tucker's name on it. Tucker was an ordained minister!

While Erin was considering her discovery, she heard the clank of milk pails outside in the yard. Breakfast must be almost ready. She quickly returned the book and put on her wrapper.

Mattie was busy at the stove frying eggs when Erin came down. Ben had the milk on the porch and was filling the milk cans. The empty pails dropped with a loud bang, and he raced through the door.

"Mattie! Tucker and Jube are back. They're coming up the road right now!"

"Fine, boy, ain't no need to git so flustered. They know their way in. Go take your coat off and set down to the table."

Tucker and Jube came in the house and went straight for the coffeepot. Tucker rubbed his hands together over the stove. Erin couldn't stand not knowing. "Tucker, did you find Enlo?"

Tucker sighed. "No, Miz Erin. We tracked him back to his pa's cabin, but he'd already lit out of there, too."

Tucker and Jube exchanged looks.

"What's wrong, Tuck?" Mattie asked.

"We found Silas Butler in his cabin. He's dead."

Chapter Fifteen

"What about Winifred? Where is she?"

"I don't know, Miz Erin. Wasn't no sign of the girl nor Enlo. We found Butler on the floor, shot in the chest. These tags were laying to the side." Tucker scattered half a dozen ear tags on the table.

"Those are from our cattle!" Mattie exclaimed. "Land sakes, I knew Enlo was a dilatory sort of boy, but I never thought him to be a murderer and a rustler to boot!"

"We have to find Winifred," Erin said. "If Enlo would kill his own father, there's no telling what he would do to her."

"I know. Soon as Jube and I can get a bite to eat, we'll go round up some men to hunt for them." Tucker looked toward the dining room. "Ben, you might as well come around from that door. I know you're there."

Ben stepped sheepishly into the kitchen.

"You reckon you can ride over to Berryman and have Mr. Doss send word to the sheriff at Potosi what's happened?" Tucker asked.

Ben stood up straight. "Yes, sir, Tucker, I'll go right now."

"You won't either," Mattie said. "Not before you eat some breakfast."

"I ain't hungry, Mattie, honest."

"Mattie's right," Tucker said. "Another half hour more or less won't matter now. It's too cold a ride for an empty belly."

Fatigue showed around the men's eyes, but they filled their plates quickly, eager to get back out and search for Winifred.

"How's the preacher?" Tucker asked.

"Good enough to set up and take a meal," Mattie said. "I believe he can move back to the cabin tonight."

Jube and Tucker set out again to find Winifred, and Ben left on horseback for Berryman. Mattie and Erin were left in the quiet of the morning with the breakfast dishes.

"Do you think Winifred is all right?" Erin asked.

"I don't know, child, but there's a bigger Hand that's workin' in this. Let Him simmer on it awhile."

"Mattie, you really believe God has a plan for everything that happens in our lives, don't you?"

"Well, surely the Good Book says so."

Erin realized she was still wiping a dish that was long past dry, and she reached for another.

"What troubles you, child?" Mattie asked.

"Do you think God has one special person picked out for us to marry?"

"Well, I reckon God always has His best planned out for us, if we're willin' to see it. You believe you found that person, do you?"

Erin put the dish up on the shelf. "I thought perhaps I had, but now I'm not so certain."

Mattie spread a fresh cloth over the kitchen table. "It's been a tiresome day or two—ain't no time to be deciding for sure on such things. But you mind this, don't never marry a man who ain't a friend first, and don't settle for someone who has less a heart for God than you do. No matter how pretty the package, you won't be happy."

Erin spent the rest of the day thinking about what Mattie had said. She couldn't deny she was deeply hurt by Douglas's attempted desertion at the schoolhouse, but to give up on the plans they had made seemed awfully harsh.

I'm being silly, she thought. *Douglas loves me. This will all work out in time.*

Tucker and Jube finally came home late that night. Tucker pulled a chair up close to the hearth and struggled to take off his boots. He looked exhausted.

"I think the coffee is still hot," Erin said quietly. "Mattie banked the fire in the stove before she went to bed."

"You're a little old to wait up for Santy Claus, ain't you?"

Erin had forgotten this was Christmas Eve. She watched Tucker hold his stiff fingers in front of the fire.

"There's a beef roast in there, too, if you're hungry."

"We had a bite at the Kellers', but some hot coffee would go real nice."

Erin went to the kitchen and poured him a steaming cup. "I'm afraid it's very strong."

"Long as it's hot. I'm about frozen." Tucker took the cup and sipped loudly. "That is stout, but it hits the spot."

"Did you find anything?"

Tucker shook his head. "We walked the better part of twenty miles, but there was no sign of Enlo or Winifred. The wind had blown over most all the tracks."

"I guess there isn't anything more we can do, is there, except to pray. Winifred was just beginning to open up to me at school."

"She is a quiet little thing." Tucker looked at the bandage on Erin's hand. "Is that hurting you?"

"Oh, no, not really. It just throbs a bit if I don't keep it propped up."

They watched the orange and yellow flames dance among the logs. The warm firelight illuminated Tucker's face as he poked at a piece of wood that had fallen on the hearth. Erin thought it odd that she had found him so unattractive when they'd first met. In his own rugged way, she decided, he was almost handsome.

"Tucker, why did you come after Douglas and me yesterday after I told you not to?"

Tucker grinned. "Could be I'm the only one around here who can out-stubborn you."

"You might be right. Anyway, I am glad you came when you did. I don't think I thanked you."

"No thanks needed," he said. "But you're welcome. While I think on it, there's something I want you to have, kindly a little Christmas present. I best give it to you now, because I jist might sleep through part of Christmas."

Tucker reached up and took a small green box down from the mantle. He handed it to Erin. She opened the box and found a delicate cameo pin.

"It's beautiful."

"I know it ain't much for a city gal like you, but you're doing a good job at the school, and you took the grieving out of Ben. I wanted you t'know I'm grateful."

"I'll treasure it, Tucker, thank you."

"You're welcome." He yawned. "I'm bone tired. I believe I'll go on up to bed. Merry Christmas, Miz Erin."

"Merry Christmas, Tucker."

Christmas morning dawned cold and bright. Delicious smells penetrated Erin's room, so she dressed quickly in the cold and went to the kitchen.

Mattie had outdone herself for Christmas breakfast. Chicken was frying on the stove, ham and eggs were in the warmer, and the oven was full of yeasty sweet rolls. Presents sat stacked on each chair, ready for opening. Erin hurriedly added her gifts to the piles. Ben passed by her at the kitchen door with silverware in his hands.

"Good morning, Ben."

"Happy Christmas, Miz Erin."

"I see I've been replaced," Erin said to Mattie in the kitchen.

Mattie laughed. "I thought the boy might be too growed up for Christmas this year, but he was up before the chickens, trying to hurry things along so's he could open his presents."

At Mattie's summons, everyone assembled for breakfast. Tucker was there despite his prediction that he might sleep in. Douglas came in looking pale but otherwise recovered.

"May I talk with you later?" he whispered to Erin. "Perhaps in the barn after breakfast?"

"All right."

Douglas slipped by her to his seat. Ben wolfed down every bite of his breakfast and sat waiting impatiently while everyone else finished. Tucker laughed aloud at him.

"Boy, I ain't never seen such a case of allover fidgets," he said. "Go on, git to your presents before you bust."

Ben grabbed for his packages. There was a new shirt from Mattie, a copy of *Pilgrim's Progress* from Douglas and Erin, and a prized slingshot from Jube. The last present was from Tucker. It was a Bible. Ben carefully turned the pages.

"It's Ma's, ain't it, Tucker?"

"I reckon she'd want you t'have it now. Mind, you take care of it."

"I will, Tucker, thanks."

Brown paper piled up high on the table as the presents were opened. Erin came to Douglas's gift and lifted the lid of a velvet jewel case. Inside, on a red lining, were a pair of stunning gold earrings with diamond centers and a brooch to match. Douglas looked at her expectantly.

"They are beautiful, Douglas, but it's too much."

"Nonsense. I had my father send them from Chicago. A beautiful lady deserves beautiful things. Here, put them on so I can see how lovely you look."

Douglas's voice seemed just a trifle too loud as he removed Tucker's cameo from Erin's collar and pinned on his brooch. Erin's cheeks flushed. She glanced up and saw that Tucker was watching her carefully. He frowned and Erin looked away. She picked up Tucker's brooch and put it in her pocket.

She took a load of dishes into the kitchen and put them in a pan full of hot soapy water. What was she going to do about Douglas? His gift was lovely, but she could not get the scene at the schoolhouse out of her mind. Still, she had no reason to care if Tucker Gillam was disappointed in her. She owed him no explanations.

Mattie looked over her shoulder. "Erin Corbett, I told you not to git that hand wet. Now git out of that dishwater."

"I'm sorry, I forgot. There's so much to do for dinner, I was just trying to help."

Mattie sighed, but her eyes smiled. "Won't help none if you git the sickness from blood pizen. Go set at the table and I'll put on a dry bandage."

Erin sat down obediently while Mattie removed the wet dressing. "Mattie, would you answer a question for me?"

"If I can, child."

"Well, that night I slept in Tucker's room, I noticed all the books he has. . .and I saw his ordination certificate."

"You must'a done some powerful hard noticing."

"I suppose I was being nosy, but I can't help wondering. . .why did Tucker leave the ministry?"

Mattie thought for a moment. "I reckon he wouldn't have sent you up there if he cared that you saw them things."

"You think he wanted me to see them?"

Mattie nodded. "I don't expect he'd own up to it, though, even to hisself."

"Why did he quit the ministry, Mattie?"

"Oh, 'twas more than one thing, really. Mostly, it was a little gal named Laurie, prettiest thing you ever seen, but that's kindly jumpin' ahead of the story."

She sighed. "See, Tucker got his start in the ministry from a preacher who settled in here jist after the war. Brother Roberts was a big man with friendly ways. I reckon that's why Tucker took to him so. They'd oft times burn lamplight together and Brother Roberts would teach Tucker what he learned when he was at Bible college. Tucker's Ma and Pa had one of their proudest days when Tucker got ordained to preach.

"Tucker took a church a half day's ride north of here and was doing right well. That's when Laurie and her parents moved into the valley and joined his congregation. Tucker fell plumb foolish in love with her, and they was fixing to take the world by its ears."

"They were going to marry?" asked Erin.

"Oh yes, jist as soon as all the particulars could git arranged. Laurie's family hailed from Kansas City, and her granddaddy helped Tucker git called to a city church up there somewheres. Laurie was tickled pink that she was going to get out of these sticks and go back to where she was raised."

"So she and Tucker moved to Kansas City?"

"No. It didn't work out that way. Before they could git hitched, Brother Roberts was killed sudden-like from a fall off his horse, and Tucker felt the call to come back here and pastor where he growed up.

"At first, Laurie went along with the idea, but after she took a hard look at the kind of life she was bound to have here, she told Tucker he'd have to choose between her and his country church. Tucker stood his ground, and as far as I know, he never heard from her again. Word had it that she run off with a dry goods drummer not six weeks later."

Mattie shook her head. "Long about then, Tucker's ma took bad sick. She had the consumption and she suffered something terrible at the end. Seems like Tucker took his hurt about Laurie and Brother Roberts and his ma out on the Lord. He allowed as he jist couldn't confidence a God who'd let his sweet mama suffer so. Didn't help that the woman who'd promised to work shoulder to shoulder with him turned her back at the first sight of plain living. He locked his preachin' books up and buried hisself with farm work, helping his daddy. It bittered him and now it's like he's got a hard spot on his heart when it comes to religion."

"I think I understand how he felt. . .I mean, well, it's hard when people don't live up to our expectations, especially those given to the ministry."

"We're all walking the same path, child, even those called to preach," Mattie said. "Some jist ain't as far on their journey as others. That's why we got to keep looking to the Master as our guide, instead of the folks on the road around us."

"At least I understand why Tucker was so skeptical when we first came to Lost Creek," Erin said. "He told me I would turn and run home when I saw what kind of job this was going to be."

"Ain't no finer man in these hills than Tucker Gillam. It's jist that he and his Creator got things that ain't settled atwixt each other."

Erin went to collect the men's coffee cups from the parlor. Through the dining room window, she saw Douglas going into the barn. She had forgotten about her promise to meet him after breakfast. She took the cups into the kitchen and got her coat.

The wind in the yard was bitter cold. Erin was glad to reach the relative warmth of the barn, but just as she got to the door, she heard loud, angry voices from inside.

"You mean to tell me you was leaving her alone with Enlo?" Tucker asked.

"If you will put me down, my good man, I will try to explain," Douglas replied angrily.

"Don't tempt me, Preacher. If I put you down right now, I'll do the job proper."

Erin rushed in the door. Tucker had Douglas pinned up against the wall, his feet dangling above the dirt floor.

"Tucker, stop it this instant!" Erin demanded. "Let him go!"

Tucker set Douglas down on his feet and stepped back. "I thought the preacher got hurt trying to look after you. Why didn't you tell me this namby was leaving you to fight off Enlo by yourself?"

"Perhaps I thought it was none of your business. Douglas and I haven't even had a chance to discuss it yet. Besides, brute force isn't the answer to everything, you know."

Tucker picked up his hat from the floor and brushed it clean, then he shook his head. "Well, aren't you two a pair." He gave Douglas a disgusted look and walked out the barn door.

"Thank you for standing up for me, darling," Douglas said. "I wasn't sure you understood."

"I'm not sure I do."

"Erin, you don't think I intended to leave you with Enlo, do you? I would have come back. . .you do believe that, don't you?"

Tucker's big chestnut mare whinnied from her stall. Erin went over to her and stroked the horse's neck. "I'm not sure what to believe, Douglas. Perhaps I have judged you too harshly."

Douglas took her hand. "Don't make this a stumbling block between us," he pleaded. "I'm sorry you're upset, but when we get back to the city, this dreadful incident won't matter anymore. I'll make it up to you, I promise I will. Now, give me your pretty smile and say it's all right."

"It isn't that simple, Douglas. . . ."

Douglas drew Erin close and pressed her head on his shoulder. "We're not in the same class as these people, Erin. We weren't bred to deal with their violence and their base way of life. Our assignment is nearly halfway through, and then I promise I'm going to see to it that you have everything you've ever done without."

"You sound as if you simply intend to mark time here until our term is finished," Erin said. "There is so much to be done here, Douglas. Don't you think God called us here for a reason?"

Douglas leaned back against a post and inspected his fingernails. "I'm not sure what you mean by 'God calling us here,' Erin. I'm here because my father insisted I get practical experience in the ministry before he would help me get a position in a good church."

Douglas saw the disappointment in Erin's eyes. "Erin, you're overwrought, and who could blame you after the ordeal you've endured. This isn't the time to discuss theology. Kiss me, and then let's go in and have a cup of tea. We can talk about this later. I'm nearly frozen."

Erin turned away. "No, Douglas, you go on ahead."

"Very well, I'll be in the cabin should you change your mind." He buttoned his coat over his chest and stormed out across the yard. Erin leaned her face against the mare. Douglas seemed to be slipping farther and farther away.

The day after Christmas, Erin sat at the breakfast table feeling grumpy and out of sorts.

"What ails you, child? You hardly touched your food."

"It's nothing, Mattie. I'm just not particularly hungry this morning."

Mattie sniffed and carried the last dish into the kitchen. She always took it personally when someone didn't eat one of her meals.

After they finished the dishes, Mattie began to pack a small wooden crate full of medical supplies. Tucker stopped short on a trip to the barn when he saw what she was doing.

"Is Rose Stiles fixing to have her baby, Mattie?"

"Could be anytime now. I thought I'd take these things on over to the house today. Leastways, they'll have what they need if her time comes before I can git there. It'll be that much less I have to tote along when I'm in a hurry."

As Tucker started toward the door, they heard a soft tapping sound at the front of the house.

"I believe that's someone knocking on the front door," Mattie said.

Tucker opened the door, and there on the porch stood Winifred Butler! Mattie hurried to the forlorn little figure. "Are you all right, child? Come set by the fire and git warm." She led Winifred over to Tucker's big armchair and wrapped her in a quilt.

"Did your brother hurt you, honey?" Tucker asked. "Do you know where Enlo is?"

Winifred shook her head. "No sir, I ain't seen him. I come here for something else. I come to turn myself in to the sheriff and git arrested."

"You?" Erin said. "What could you have done that the sheriff would want to arrest you?"

Winifred's eyes filled with tears and she looked down at the floor. "It was me who kilt Pa."

Tucker bent down in front of her. "Now you look at me, Winifred, and you tell me the truth. Did Enlo make you come here and say that?"

"No, sir. I'm tellin' the honest truth. I ain't seen Enlo since the night. . .the night Pa died. I'm ready to go to jail for what I done, Mr. Gillam. It don't matter what happens to me anyway."

"Of course it matters," Erin said.

Tucker pulled the quilt over Winifred's trembling arms. "Winifred, supposin' you start at the beginning and tell us how all this come about."

"First off," Winifred began, "there's some things about my pa that folks around here don't know. Preachin' wasn't his only way to make a living."

"Many ministers have other jobs besides preaching," Erin said. "What else did your father do?"

"I'm real sorry, Mr. Gillam, but pa was the one who butchered your cattle. It started out that Pa'd only take a chicken or two when we was hungry, but then he got to where he would sell the meat at the places he preached. Nobody seemed to mind him selling meat on the side. They figured he raised it his own self."

"Our tags were by your pa when we found him," Tucker said.

Winifred nodded. "Pa was real perturbed about them. He'd told Enlo to bury all that truck, but I reckon Enlo kept 'em for play pretties. Pa was fixing to strap Enlo for it."

"Then Enlo was involved in the stealing," Erin said.

"Yes'm. Pa's had Enlo working with him for five or six years now. I used to have a sorry feeling for Enlo, especially when Pa whupped him, until I figured out Enlo liked his job of work. Pa sent Enlo to school so's he could keep an eye on things and know 'bout folks' comings and goings. When Enlo got sent home for fighting with Ben, Pa beat the whey outta him. That's why Enlo come back and behaved hisself, least until he found that Christmas whiskey."

Erin could scarcely believe that this was the child who had barely spoken ten words at school. A dam seemed to have broken, and the pent-up words kept tumbling out.

"What happened the night of the school party?" Tucker asked.

"Pa was fit to be tied when he found them ear tags. Said he was gonna teach Enlo to do such a stupid thing. Then Enlo come in gabblin' on about how he'd kilt the preacher and that you had caught him fooling with Miz Corbett. Pa took out his razor strap and layed into Enlo, calling him shiftless and low-down and such, till finally he wore hisself out. Pa thought on it awhile and said he reckoned we'd better move on. We've never stayed nowhere more'n a few months. Pa told Enlo to light out for his brother's place down in Reynolds County, and he put Enlo out the door right then and there. After that, I started packing things up, while Pa got to drinking. The more he drank, the madder he got at Enlo for making us move in the dead of winter. Enlo wasn't there no more, so Pa come after me."

Tears were pouring down Winifred's cheeks. "I couldn't take no more, Mr. Gillam. I didn't want no more beatings. He done other things, too. . .things pas ought not to do. Whenever he got drunk like that, he'd come after me."

Erin thought of the cuts and bruises Winifred had come to school with and wished now that she had paid them more heed.

"What happened when your pa came after you with his strap?" Tucker asked.

"I told him if he touched me again, I was gonna run off and tell what he done, but he jist got madder and come at me anyway. I ran out the door and I reckon when I slammed it shut, Pa's shotgun fell off the pegs. I heared it fire, and when I looked back inside. . .Pa was laying on the floor, and he weren't breathing."

Winifred wiped the tears from her face with her palms. "I'm ready to take whatever's due me for what I done."

"Winifred, listen, honey," Tucker said. "Ain't nobody gonna do nothing to you, don't you worry 'bout that. I promise that I'm gonna see to it that you git taken care of proper from now on."

Chapter Sixteen

Erin opened the oven and held her hand inside as she had seen Mattie do. The oven felt hot enough for the cornbread, she supposed, so she set the pan in and shut the door.

Tucker came in from his morning chores and looked around the kitchen. "Where's Mattie?"

"Gone to the Stileses'. Emmit came by for her just after breakfast. Mattie said she thought it would be awhile yet, since it's Rose's first baby, but she went on anyway. Poor Emmit was beside himself with worry."

Tucker poured a cup of coffee and looked in the pot of beans bubbling on the stove. "You fixing dinner?"

"Yes, I am. It may not be as good as Mattie's, but there's plenty of it. Sit down and I'll fill your plate."

"Ain't that something. I never thought I'd see the day you could turn out a respectable meal on your own."

"I had a good teacher. It looks like you may have to live off my cooking for a while. Since Rose's mother still has children at home, Mattie thought it would be easier if she stayed and took care of Rose herself during Rose's lying-in time, especially since school is out and I can take over here."

Tucker sat down at the kitchen table. "I expect we'll manage. Did the preacher and Jube get off to Berryman all right?"

Erin hesitated. Tucker was not going to like this piece of news. "Well, Jube left about an hour ago, but Douglas didn't go with him."

"Why not?"

"He had another one of those headaches. It came on all of a sudden. I think he ought to see a doctor. Sometimes head injuries can cause problems for years afterwards."

"The only problem the preacher had was when he figured out how many drifts they'd have to break to git to Berryman." Tucker got up and reached for his coat. "I best go see if I can catch up with Jube. That old man's got no business shoveling out snowdrifts by himself."

"Oh, he didn't go alone. Ben went with him. He promised to shovel all the snow."

Tucker looked uncertain, but he draped his coat over the chair and sat back down. "I reckon Ben is big enough to do a man's job of work. When I was his age, Pa and me was splittin' the chores pretty much down the middle. I forgit the boy is 'most nearly grown." Tucker picked up his fork and began to eat. "Maybe I should've had Jube wait for some of this snow to melt, but I wanted to git word to the sheriff about what happened with Winifred and the Reverend Butler. Still, it ain't that far to Berryman, and the cutter is light enough to skim over most of the drifts. Sure was a storm we had. I ain't never seen the like of it."

Erin looked out the kitchen window. The ice that had come with the storm two nights before still covered every tree branch. Sunlight sparkled off the crystal casements with blinding beauty. Nearly two feet of new-fallen snow blanketed the yard.

Her attention was diverted by the smell of something burning. Her cornbread! Erin hurried over to the oven. Fortunately, the cornbread was only brown around the edges. She reached in to retrieve it, but her bandaged hand wouldn't bear the weight of the pan, and it was too heavy to lift out one-handed. Tucker saw her predicament and jumped up to help her.

"Your hand still hurting you?"

"It seemed to be healing," Erin said. "But this morning some of the blisters broke open, and it's a little sore."

Tucker gingerly touched the bandage. "I can feel heat. You best let me have a look."

"Don't be a goose. I've spent the last two hours over the stove. Both of my hands are hot. Now, go finish your dinner." She poured Tucker another cup of coffee. "Do you think Winifred is happy at Widow Puckett's?" she asked.

"Two days is a little too soon to tell, ain't it? She seemed happy enough when I walked over to check on them yesterday. The widder and Winifred was busy cutting down some of Bessie's old dresses to size. Winifred looked like she'd struck gold. I doubt she's ever had more'n two dresses at one time."

"I'm glad. I hope the widow will be kind to her."

"Don't fret about that. The widder has a tongue sharp enough to cut whetstone, but she's got a good heart. She wouldn't let on, but she's twice as happy to have a youngun in the house again as Winifred is to be there."

Erin lifted the butter out of the window box and set it on the table. "Tucker, does it bother you that the Reverend Butler was, well, a charlatan? I mean, I know you have your reasons, but you seem to have a skeptical attitude toward the church. I hope you don't think we're all in the Lord's work for selfish gain."

Tucker sipped his coffee and chuckled. "I was wondering when you'd git around to this. Mattie told me you asked her about the books up in my room. Miz Erin, I reckon that's a subject best left closed between us." His tone of voice was pleasant, but it was clear by the firm set of his jaw that he meant what he said.

"I'm sorry if it seemed I was prying," said Erin. "I'm going to take a plate over to Douglas. There's more food on the stove, if you want it."

Tucker smiled mischievously. "I'd forgotten all about the preacher. Now, he's one of them unselfish reasons you come to Lost Crick for, ain't he?"

Erin put her shawl around her shoulders and went outside, shutting the door firmly behind her.

❧

Tucker was splitting wood in the side yard when Erin started back to the kitchen. "How's your preacher?" he asked.

"Asleep. Now, if you'll excuse me, I have work to do."

Tucker took off his hat and bowed in her direction. She had just reached the house when she thought she heard someone calling.

"Did you hear that?" Erin asked. "It sounded like Ben."

She was right. Ben trotted over the rise and down the hill toward the house. Tucker and Erin ran to meet him.

"What's wrong, boy?" Tucker asked. "Where's Jube? Is he all right?"

"Jube's all right," Ben said breathlessly. "He sent me here for you and Mattie. It's the Kellers. Their cabin roof is caving in with the weight of all this snow. Mr. Keller waved us down when we went by his place. He's trying to shore up the rafters before the whole thing falls, but it's heavy work. Miz Keller already hurt her back trying to help. Mr. Keller didn't want Jube to try it, so they said I should come git you. They want Mattie to come, too, if she can, to help look after the younguns. Miz Keller's abed, and those two boys of hers are giving her fits."

"Mattie's not here, Ben," said Erin. "She went to deliver Rose Stiles's baby."

"You want me to go after someone else, Tucker?"

"No, you git in the house and warm up. I'll hitch up the sled and go see what I can do."

"I'll get my coat," said Erin. "I'm going with you."

"No, you ain't. I'll have to take the back road over the river to git the big sled through to the Kellers' in all this snow. It's a long, cold ride. You stay here and look after Ben."

"Ben can look after himself," Erin said. "Besides, Douglas is in the cabin."

"You ain't used to this kind of weather. You'd be frostbit before we left the yard. Once we git the roof fixed, I'll take those younguns over to the Witbecks' if Becky's that bad off."

"There's no reason to take those children out in this weather and crowd the Witbecks' little cabin when I can go with you. If Becky's hurt, she'll need a woman to look after her. Now, either you let me ride with you, or I'll walk the hill road through Gobbler's Knob like Ben did."

Tucker took off his hat and ran his hand through his hair. "All right. Go inside and git that medicine bag Mattie keeps in the kitchen, jist in case Becky's in need of some doctorin'. And you git a scarf for your own self and some mittens. Be back here in five minutes or I'll sure leave you standing."

Erin hurried into the kitchen and looked underneath the table for Mattie's bag. The room tilted dizzily when she stood up. Thankfully, when she took a few deep breaths, her vision gradually cleared. Tucker would never let her hear the end of it if he knew she was lightheaded from a few hours' work in the kitchen. Well, there was no need to let on and give him the satisfaction.

Tucker already had the horses hitched and was waiting in the yard. He took the carpet bag and set it in the back of the sleigh, then he helped Erin up on the seat. Tucker spoke to the horses and the sled began to glide smoothly across the snow.

The bells on the horses' harnesses jingled merrily, as if there were no urgency to the trip at all. But thick gray clouds were moving in over the sun, and the wind began to blow in cold bursts. The icy branches rattled and bumped against one another, and pieces of ice broke off and fell into the snow with muffled thuds. The temperature was dropping, and Erin guiltily realized she had forgotten both the mittens and scarf Tucker had ordered her to bring along. She pulled her hood further down on her head and shoved her hands deep into her coat pockets.

The road was completely obliterated by the heavy snow. Though she had traveled through here many times, Erin had no idea where the side of the road ended and the woods began. A few inches either way meant the difference between traveling on and plunging into a snowy ditch. Twice the horses floundered and Tucker had to go in after them, unhitch, pack the snow with his boots, and lead the team out of the drift. Finally, he would rehitch them, and they would be on their way again.

They seemed to be crawling at a snail's pace as the horses struggled in snow up to their withers. The wet cold seeped deeper through Erin's woolen coat, and she began to shiver, even though she tried hard to sit still. Tucker reached in back of the seat and pulled up an old horse blanket.

"Drape this over your shoulders," he said. "Maybe next time you'll listen."

Erin gratefully took the blanket and pulled it around her. "How much longer until we get to the bridge?" she asked.

"Not long, if we don't git stuck in any more drifts."

Tucker tried to turn his coat collar up around his ears, but he couldn't do it with one hand on the reins. Erin reached over and pulled it up for him. Tucker looked at her for a moment and then went back to driving the team.

"I'm sorry I make you so angry," Erin said. "I'd like you to understand why I insisted on coming along, but I'm not sure how to explain it to you. It's just that I want the people here to be my people now, too. I care about them very much."

For an instant, Tucker looked as if he wanted to believe her, then just as quickly, his eyes grew cold. "So, we're your people now, are we? Maybe till come spring, when the preacher gives you a better offer. You don't let people into your heart for a time, then jist set 'em aside when something fancier comes along. You been here five months. You ain't even begun to know what really caring for these people is."

"Couldn't I care about the people here and about Douglas, too? And did it ever occur to you that city people need churches and ministers?"

"Of course they do, but that ain't what the preacher is about, and you'd know that were you jist honest with yourself. That preacher won't never be anywhere but at some high-toned church where he can have fine clothes and eat supper with society folks. That's why the preacher wants you. He needs a pretty wife who can entertain his guests and charm the deacons and look grand on his arm by the church door on Sunday morning. You'll git a square deal though—fancy dresses, a big ole house, maybe even a servant or two. If that's what you want, fine and dandy, but don't go talking to me about your calling to the people here at Lost Crick."

"How dare you! By what right do you think you can talk to me like that? You're in no position to evaluate anyone's ministry. You abandoned the ministry!"

Tucker stared at the road up ahead. The bridge was just a few yards away. "You're right," he said. "I did leave the ministry. So, I reckon you and me'll have something in common when you go to marry that preacher."

"Tucker Gillam, you are the most infuriating man I have ever met, if I. . ." Suddenly, the countryside spun dizzily out of control. Erin grabbed for the side of the sled and held on. Tucker stopped the horses.

"Miz Erin? What's wrong?"

The trees and ground were returning to their rightful places, but the dizzy spell left Erin weak. Her hand was throbbing.

"It's nothing. Haven't you seen a woman swoon before? We spoiled city girls are taught how to do it at an early age. Let's get going."

Tucker put his hand under Erin's chin and turned her face toward him. "Look at you. You're pale as milk, shivering and sweating at the same time. I'm gonna take you back to the house." He picked up the reins and started to back the horses away from the bridge.

"No, you won't! We're halfway there, and the Kellers need our help. Now, you drive those horses across that bridge and no nonsense!"

"That ain't for you to decide."

Erin realized that once they crossed the bridge, it would be nearly impossible to turn the horses on the narrow road until they were almost to the Keller farm. On impulse, she grabbed at the reins and urged the team on. The horses pranced nervously, but Tucker regained control.

"What in thunder do you think you're doing? Are you trying to git us killed?" He grabbed her wrists and forcibly removed her hands from the reins. A hot pain shot through Erin's bandaged hand and up into her arm. She bent over and breathed deeply, determined not to cry out.

"I'm real sorry," Tucker said. "I forgot about your hand. I sure didn't mean to hurt you none. Here, let me see."

Her hand did hurt, but not badly enough to let Tucker Gillam have his way. She would make him take her to the Kellers'. This was her chance.

"The blisters must have all broken," she said. "The bandage is soaked through. It might frostbite, mighten it, by the time we drive back to the house?"

"It would in this cold for sure," Tucker said. "Mattie usually has clean rags in her medicine bag to use for bandages. You might could wrap one over it to keep warm till we git home."

"Would you mind getting the bag? I don't think I feel up to crawling over the wagon seat."

"You set still, I'll fetch it."

Tucker put the reins down and stepped out of the sleigh so that he could reach into the back. Quickly, Erin picked up the lines and slapped them down hard on the horses' backs. The startled animals took off with a jerk, leaving poor Tucker in a snowdrift by the side of the road.

The homemade sleigh was harder to handle than Erin had anticipated. She tried to drive it straight, but it slipped to the right just as it started over the bridge, leaving one runner hanging precariously over the edge. Erin could hear the water rushing beneath the ice.

The horses balked and reared as the weight of the sled pulled them backward toward the river. There was a sickening sound of splintering wood as the team twisted in their harnesses and broke away from the sled. For a brief instant, the sled teetered on the edge of the bridge. Somewhere behind her, Erin heard Tucker call her name. Then the sled plunged down, breaking the ice and throwing her into the middle of the river.

Erin grabbed on to a log that lay partially submerged in the water and struggled to keep her head above the surface, but the weight of the sleigh pushed up against her with the full power of the river's current. "Dear God, help me!" she prayed. The sled shifted and sent her beneath the surface. She forced her head up, coughing and sputtering. She heard Tucker calling her, but she could not speak. The weight of the sleigh crushed against her chest. The sled pushed her under again, and she felt the frigid water go down her throat. Then everything went black.

The nothingness was quiet, warm, almost pleasant. But something was pressing on her back. Perhaps it was the sled. No, it was someone's hands, pushing. The hands let go, and Erin's lungs made an involuntary gasp for breath. The numbness disappeared, and she was caught up in a paroxysm of coughing that brought up quantities of water.

"Easy, Erin," the voice said. "Don't fight it, let it out. Now, try and breathe slow-like."

Tucker's hands pushed firmly on her back again. Erin struggled to sit up, but his hands were on her shoulders, forcing her to keep still. "Don't move around jist yet. Is there feeling in your arms and legs?"

Erin carefully moved each limb. "That's good," Tucker said. "Do you have especial bad pain anywhere?"

"My side hurts," she said hoarsely. "Where the sleigh had me pinned."

"All right now, roll over easy. Let me do all the work. Let's see can you sit up."

Tucker carefully lifted under her shoulders, and she managed to get in an upright position. She tried to focus her eyes, but it seemed as if she were looking through a red fog. She touched her hand to her forehead. There was blood on her fingers. Tucker already had his handkerchief out.

"Don't fret, Erin. The cuts ain't that bad. Head wounds always bleed like a stuck pig. It's nearly stopped."

Cold began to set in like Erin never could have imagined. It made the chill she'd felt earlier in the sleigh seem like a summer picnic. Her fingers and toes were numb and swollen, and her teeth chattered together so hard she was sure that they would break.

"We got to git you warm. There's nothing dry enough around here to build a quick fire. I reckon we'll have to walk on out."

Erin saw that Tucker's clothes were no dryer than hers and realized that he must have gone into the river after her.

"Tucker. . .I, I'm so sorry. Such a. . .foolish thing to do."

"Hush. Ain't no time for that."

"It will be dark soon, won't it?"

"We got no time to waste, that's a fact."

"The horses?"

"They're probably in the next county by now. Here, see if you can stand up."

Tucker lifted her to her feet. Immediately, her head began to swim. Her wool skirt hung in heavy, frozen folds; even her shoes were stiff.

"Can you put your arm 'round my neck?" Tucker asked.

Each step felt as if someone was sticking a knife into her ribs. They hobbled along for perhaps fifty feet until Erin's legs gave out. Tucker eased her down to the ground.

"I'm sorry," she gasped. "I can't do it. Leave me here and go get help, Tucker. I just want to go to sleep."

Tucker took a handful of snow and rubbed it roughly on Erin's cheeks.

"Stop!" she cried and tried to turn away.

"You can't go to sleep, you understand? You got to stay awake. We're going on." Tucker slipped his arm under Erin's legs and picked her up.

"You can't carry me all that way. . .it's too far."

"Never you mind. We'll make it."

The pain in Erin's side was no better with Tucker carrying her. Even though he tried to be careful, he couldn't avoid jolting and sliding in the snow. She could hear his heart pounding as he strained to get them back to the farmhouse.

The numbness was coming again, and Erin welcomed it. She wanted to be away from all the cold and pain. Through the mist in her mind she kept hearing Tucker's voice. He was trying to talk to her. He sounded so tired. Poor man. She wondered what he was saying. Then it was dark and warm, and she couldn't hear Tucker's voice anymore.

Chapter Seventeen

Erin smelled coal oil. She opened her eyes and saw a lamp burning on the nightstand. Next to it sat the little brass clock. With so many quilts on her, how could she still be so cold? A violent shudder overtook her body, and she felt a horrible pain in her side. She looked at the sleeve of her flannel nightgown. At least she was dry. The wet wool skirt was gone.

Someone was coming in the room. "Tucker?"

Footsteps quickened across the floor. "You're awake. I heated up these flatirons and wrapped them in flannel. They'll help git you warm." He put the irons under the covers and sat down on the bed.

"Thank you." Erin touched the sleeve of his shirt. "You'd better change your clothes, too, or you'll be sick."

"Don't you fret about me. I worked up a good bit of sweat gitting us back here."

"I really am sorry. It was such a foolish, willful thing to do."

"Hush up." Tucker felt her cheek with the back of his hand. "Are you hurting?"

"Some. My side hurts when I breathe."

"Preacher's making a pot of tea. Think you can take some?"

"I'll try."

"How's your hand feel?"

Erin smiled weakly. "It's the only thing on me that's warm. It's infected, isn't it? That's why I have a fever."

"No, it's jist a little tender is all." Tucker did not meet her eyes. "I'll fix you up a bread and water poultice directly. It'll take the fire out. I sent Ben over to the Reynolds's place. Clay'll git the doc here quick as he can."

Douglas came to the door with a cup in his hand, but when he saw Erin, he stopped. "Erin," he said. "My goodness. . ."

"Well, bring it on in," said Tucker. "She can't sip it from the doorway."

Douglas carried the cup to the foot of the bed, but he seemed reluctant to get any nearer. Erin's hair was matted with blood from the cuts on her forehead. She could feel scrapes and bruises all over her body.

"Give me that, Preacher."

Tucker's hand supported Erin's head while he held the cup to her lips. The warm tea tasted good, but after a few swallows, she was too tired to want any more. She turned her head away and closed her eyes.

Tucker's weight left the bed. Erin heard him put the cup on the nightstand and walk to the doorway. She could hear him and Douglas talking, but she was just too tired to keep her eyes open.

"Is she asleep?" Douglas asked.

"Maybe. It's hard to say with that fever. I wish the doc would git here."

"Yes, so do I," said Douglas. "Tucker, this may not be the most appropriate time to ask, but you don't suppose there'll be any permanent disfigurement, do you? The hand is not so important, her sleeve could cover that, but what about the cuts on her face?"

"I'm not sure I understand your meanin', Preacher."

"You know, in my line of work. . .appearances can be important."

The conversation grew more intense, but they spoke quietly, and Erin could no longer make out what they were saying. She had the most peculiar feeling she had lost something that once had been very important to her, but it didn't seem to matter now.

There was a scuffling sound at the foot of the bed and then a crash. When Erin opened her eyes, she saw Douglas sprawled against the dresser. His lower lip was bleeding. Tucker stood in front of him with his fists doubled.

"I've seen some snakes in my time," Tucker said. "But you take the blue ribbon hands down. For two cents, I'd take you outside and fix your wagon."

"Tucker?"

Tucker turned away from Douglas and went to Erin."Lay back down," he said, pulling the quilt back across her chest. "You got to keep still until the doc gits here and can bandage those ribs proper. I'm sorry, Erin. I won't hurt him no more. He jist made me so mad."

"It's all right, Tucker. I heard what he said." Erin looked wearily at Douglas.

"I thought you were asleep," said Douglas. "You misunderstood me. Certainly, my first concern is for your welfare."

"Your ring is in the box on the dresser," said Erin. "Please take it and go."

Douglas picked up the ring and turned it between his fingers. "Perhaps that would be best, for now," he said. "We'll talk when you are feeling better."

"Git out, Preacher," said Tucker.

"I didn't mean it like it sounded," said Douglas.

"Git out, now."

Douglas put the ring in his vest pocket and left without another word.

Erin was vaguely aware of sounds and movements around her. At first, it was Tucker who seemed to be constantly fussing over her. His hands pressed a cloth on her forehead, and if she opened her eyes, he would try to make her drink. He kept putting something hot and wet on her hand. It made her hand hurt, but he put it on anyway. All Erin wanted to do was sleep. Why wouldn't he leave her alone?

After a while, there were other voices and other hands. Ben was there with ice cold spring water. He had such a frightened look in his eyes that Erin wanted to tell him not to be afraid, but she was too tired.

Then Jube came in, his loud voice filling the room, followed by a kind-looking man with gray hair. The man looked at Erin and tugged on his ear.

I must be really sick, Erin thought. *Lost Creek people only send for the doctor if you are very sick.*

Tucker and the doctor were talking. Erin thought they both looked sad. After awhile, Dr. Stone sat down on the bed. "Can you understand me, Erin?"

Erin nodded her head.

"I'll be truthful with you," the doctor said. "That dunk in the river forced water into your lungs. You have the pneumonia. It ain't too bad yet, but it'll probably get worse before it gits better. The real problem is that infection from the burn on your hand. I don't know if your body can fight both things at once." Dr. Stone rubbed his chin thoughtfully. "Truth is, honey, if it gits much worse, I might need to amputate the hand to save your life."

Erin shook her head back and forth across her pillow. "No! I won't let you!" She pulled at the quilts, straining to get out of the bed.

"You lay back down, young lady," Dr. Stone said. "Those ribs aren't fully broken yet, but they will be if you start thrashing about."

Tucker reached across with a cool cloth to wipe the perspiration that beaded on her face. "Erin, listen to the doc," he pleaded. "We're talkin' about your life."

Erin frantically searched for Tucker's hand. "You've got to promise me. Promise me you won't let him."

Tucker looked in agony. "I can't promise something like that, Erin."

"Please, Tucker. It's my choice. . .my life."

"Doc? Ain't there anything else you can do?" Tucker asked.

"Well," Dr. Stone said slowly. "We could try a drain. I've seen it work before, but it's chancy."

"Please, you've got to try it," Erin begged.

Dr. Stone thought for a moment. "All right, but I won't make any promises. Now, you settle back and rest."

Erin laid back, exhausted, and fell into a fitful sleep, but the smell of vinegar and mustard soon awakened her and made her cough. Dr. Stone was putting a vile-smelling poultice on her chest. Then came the smell of sulfa powder as the doctor tended her hand. The hours passed by in a succession of evil-tasting medicines, compresses, and plasters.

There were softer hands on Erin's body now, changing her into a fresh nightgown. "Jist rest, child," Mattie said. "You're in the Lord's hands."

Erin tried to do as Mattie said, but one moment she was burning up and the next she was so very cold, and then it seemed as if her body was possessed by fits of coughing.

Everyone looked so concerned. Erin wanted to tell them not to worry, but it was too hard. It didn't matter anymore; she just wanted to sleep. She wanted to feel that warm numbness she had felt before.

Sleep finally came, and Erin gratefully began to slip further and further away. It seemed that all she needed to do was let herself go, and all the pain would be gone. If only something deep inside would allow her to give up so that she could find the rest her body craved.

The heaviness was gone. There was no more burning heat in Erin's hand, and the weight had been lifted from her chest. She turned her head on the sweat-soaked pillow, and in the early morning light she saw Mattie sitting in a chair next to her bed. A Bible lay open in Mattie's lap, and her head rested on the chair back.

"Mattie?" Erin's voice had barely whispered, but the sound was enough to awaken one so accustomed to sleeping lightly by another's sickbed.

"Erin? Oh, Erin, praise God! I thought we'd lost you." Mattie's hand went instinctively to Erin's forehead. "Your fever must have broke during the night."

Erin lay still for a moment and tried to piece everything together. "You were at the Stileses' place, weren't you?" she asked. "Did Rose have her baby?"

"Rose had a strapping baby boy. I was beside myself with worry about you until I could find someone to tend Rose."

"How long has it been?" Erin asked.

"Four days since the accident."

"That long? The last I remember, Dr. Stone was here. He was talking to me about my hand." A terrible thought seized her, and she pulled her arm out from under the covers. She sighed with relief.

"The drains worked," said Mattie. "It was nip and tuck, but Doc's a good man."

"Are the Kellers all right?"

"Got their roof fixed and Becky's back is on the mend. Clay Reynolds went over and helped them after he got Doc for you."

"And Douglas, where is he? I don't remember seeing him since that first day."

Mattie didn't answer. Erin could tell by the look on her face that she was trying to decide what she should say.

"It's all right," said Erin. "Douglas is gone, isn't he?"

"Two days ago. Jube drove him out to Berryman. He figured to catch a ride to Steeleville and take the train from there. He said to tell you he 'regrets the situation.' I'm sorry."

"You were right, Mattie. You told me to seek the Kingdom first, but that's not what I did. I was more in love with the idea of having a family and a home of my own than I was with what God wanted to do in my life. Douglas and I are on two different paths."

"Don't fret about it, child. You know the saying, 'God never closes a door without He opens a window.' "

Winter sunlight streamed in the room. The snow glittered and sparkled in the yard. "It's so bright outside," Erin said.

"Does it bother you, child? I'll pull the curtain."

"No, don't. I think it's beautiful. It's good to see the light again. These past few days have been nothing but a dark blur."

"If you think you can handle it, I'll go warm you a cup of broth. I best wake Tucker on my way and tell him you're back among the living."

"But it must be hours past sunrise," said Erin. "Why is Tucker asleep in the middle of the day?"

Mattie smiled. "You don't recollect anything, do you, child? Why, Tucker's been by your side day and night since the accident. Doc Stone finally came by last evening and threatened to beat him with an ax handle if he didn't get some sleep. He's been stretched out on the couch ever since. I'll go get him."

Erin could hear Mattie's voice, then Tucker's, and then the sound of heavy footsteps hurrying to her door. Tucker rushed into the bedroom, then stopped up short when he saw Erin. Tears welled up in the big man's eyes and ran down his cheeks. He moved the chair closer to Erin's bed and sat down. "You sure you're feelin' all right?" he asked softly.

"I'm not ready for another sleigh ride yet," said Erin. "But I'll be fine."

"Has Mattie told you everything that's happened?"

"She told me about Douglas. She also told me you've been wearing yourself out these past few days. I'm sorry I caused you so much worry."

"Erin, I've had a parcel of time to think whilst you was so sick. . . . I've done considerable prayin', too. It come to me that I been mule stubborn with the Lord these last few years. Ain't no excuse for it. I knowed better. I jist turned away from His call. I'm so rock-brained it took almost losin' the most important thing in my life to git my attention."

"I'm not sure I understand."

"I reckon I am talkin' clear as mud." Tucker leaned over and took Erin's hand. "What I'm tryin' to say, Erin, is that I love you. I have since that first day you come bustin' in the barn door, but I jist wouldn't admit it. I know you're used to fancy courting, but the fact of the matter is that I'm rough as a cob about such things. I can't offer you much but a plain and simple life, but I give you my word, if you'd see fit to marry me, there'd always be a roof over our heads and food on the table. I'd do everything I could to make you happy." Tucker's eyes searched Erin's, waiting for a response.

Erin couldn't help thinking how different Tucker's proposal had been from Douglas's. There was no flattery, no promise of great status or wealth, just a pledge of love and loyalty.

She realized then she had found the real treasure. The home she had always craved could not be found with a handsome young man who had assurance of money and social position—but it was here with Tucker in a simple house where love was based on friendship and trust and their mutual faith in God.

"Tucker," she said, "I'd be proud to be your wife."

Tucker took her in his bearlike arms and held her close. When he touched her, she felt something deeper than she ever had with Douglas: a deep and abiding assurance that God had brought them together to this place, that He had a special plan for their lives, and that their love would continue to nurture and grow. The people of Lost Creek truly had become her people.

Erin was finally home.